MW01092176

THE KEEPER ORIGINS BOOK 1

DRAGON'S REACH

J.A. ANDREWS

Dragon's Reach, The Keeper Origins Book 1

Copyright © 2020 by JA Andrews

Website: www.jaandrews.com

Cover art © 2020 by Deranged Doctor Designs

Illustrations © 2020 by Dominique Wesson

For Jason

MARSHAM CLIFF

NIDEL WOODS

Black River

Innsruk □

Torren

Marshwell □

Colbreth Castle □

Stonehaven □

THE BLACK HILLS

Polbrook □

EASTERN REACHES

Ebenmoor □

Lingua River

Folhaven □

TREMMEN HILLS

Molas □

Cliffson □

Immusmala

SOUTHERN SEA

Map of
TALLUS

THE
CITY
OF
IMMUSMALA

DOCKSIDE

PRIORY OF
THE HORN

VEIL GATE

VEIL WALL

DRAGON
PRIORY

GRAND
STADIA

PHOENIX
PROIORY

The Sanctuary

SMOKE

Sable breathed in the wild, fresh scent of the leaves, leaning close to peer between the low branches. The shadows were deeper than she'd expected, and she couldn't make out any more wine-red berries tucked between the darkening leaves.

A raven cawed out a grating cry above her, and she glanced up, pausing at the sight of a red-tinged cloud. The walls of the ravine around her were ruddy with evening light, too.

"The sun's setting," she called over the burbling of the brook. "Let's go."

"Wait!" Ryah's little voice came from the far side of the bush. "My basket's still low."

Sable peered through the branches, catching a glimpse of her sisters. "How many have you eaten?"

There was a moment of silence.

"None," Ryah said in a small voice.

The word brushed against Sable with pinpricks of cold, not on her skin exactly, but cold all the same. She laughed. "Liar."

A pair of giggles came from behind the leaves.

Sable picked up the empty basket from lunch and her own

mounded basket of berries, catching one before it rolled over the side. "Talia, how many do you have?"

"A good amount," her other sister answered evasively.

Sable rounded the bush to find the two small girls squatting next to their half empty baskets, their guilty smiles dyed a deep red.

"Aren't they delicious?" Talia asked brightly.

Ryah peered at Sable's basket. "Didn't you eat any?"

"None," she said, imitating Ryah's little voice.

The girls squinted up at her.

"I wish we could tell if she was lying," Ryah whispered.

"Her lips look red," Talia answered.

Sable took Ryah's hand and helped her stand. "It doesn't matter how many I've eaten, because I also filled my basket. You two together don't have a full one."

"You're fifteen," Talia pointed out. "That's older than both of us put together, so you should have more berries than both of us put together."

Sable raised an eyebrow.

Talia smiled innocently. "There just weren't many on this side of the bush."

Another brush of coldness touched Sable, and she gave Talia a pointed look.

Her sister giggled. "I mean, I thought we'd have more time. The sunset came too fast!"

A tendril of warmth curled around Sable at these words. Not the humid warmth of the ravine, but something more comfortable, and more elusive. "That, at least, is the truth," she said with a grin.

She waited while the girls gathered their baskets before shooing them toward the narrow trail. "See if you two can refrain from eating the rest before we get home."

Ryah skipped out onto the path with her half-full basket, and Talia followed. Sable glanced up again as she fell in behind them. It did feel like the sun was setting early. Between the narrow walls of the ravine and the tall bushes along the path, only a thin strip of the sky was visible, but it had a rosy hue.

The two girls traipsed ahead of her, their voices bubbling along with the noisy stream.

"I climbed to the third branch in the apple tree yesterday," Ryah said, the words warm.

Talia's mouth dropped open. "By yourself?"

Ryah nodded and Talia looked back questioningly.

Sable smiled. "She's telling the truth."

"Well," Talia said in a confidential voice, "I climbed up on the stool, and touched mama's elvish bow."

Ryah let out a little gasp.

Sable glanced down with a raised eyebrow. "That's true, too," she said. "Even I've never touched that."

"What did it feel like?" Ryah asked, her voice breathy with wonder.

"Just like wood," Talia said, her voice slightly disappointed as they climbed past the bushes at the top of the ravine. "But the red fletching on the arrows is very soft."

"How did you reach the..." Ryah's question broke off as they pulled to a stop.

Over the hills in front of them, the western sky was stained with a rusty, brown haze. The sun hadn't set, but hung low in the smoke, glowing like a seething red coal.

Sable broke into a run.

The hills around them were tinted red from the dark sun. Sable heard shouting as she neared the last turn, and caught her first whiff of smoke. The trail curved around a rock outcropping and wound into the village between the bakery and the smithy.

Sable stumbled to a stop along the bakery wall, staring into the village square.

Ahead of her, nearly every building burned.

She pulled her sisters behind her. Two buildings across the square were already collapsed. Fire raged on another roof, spinning up in a tower of flame. Bodies lay on the ground and black-clad raiders plowed through the chaos, swords red with blood.

Sable stared at the scene for a terrible, breathless moment.

A hooded raider tossed a lit torch onto the thatch above the smithy. A flicker of flame grew, then raced up the roof with a savage roar.

The raider caught sight of the girls and turned his masked face toward them. His eyes dug into Sable, glittering black in his shadowed face. He took a step toward them, sliding a long, curved sword from his scabbard. "Draconek nadra!"

Ryah screamed. Sable dragged the girls behind the bakery, darting through the herb garden. She leapt over plants and shoved through a gap in Old Lady Hennder's bushes.

Sable twisted to look over her shoulder. The man crashed behind them, trampling vegetables with black leather boots, and shouting strange guttural words that echoed off the house.

The girls tore through Old Lady Hennder's beans.

"Mama!" Talia screamed as they scrambled over the low wall into their own yard.

Sable yanked the girls to a stop. Their own house was a blackened heap, charred and smoldering. Smoke billowed up into the sky shrouding the yard in shadows.

"Mama?" Ryah whimpered.

But the yard, from what was left of the house to the steep hill that rose behind it, was empty.

Curses from the raider behind them, snapped Sable into motion and she pulled the girls toward the only shelter she could see—the bushes along the back of the yard.

"Draconek nadra!" the raider bellowed again, bounding over the wall, closing the distance.

Sable shoved the girls into the bushes and turned to face him, throwing her hands up as though she could stop his blade.

Only steps away from her, he choked out a scream, and fell. His black body sprawled across the ground at Sable's feet, a red-fletched arrow sunk deep in the back of his neck.

Behind him, her mother nocked another arrow into her elvish bow.

"Mama!" The word ripped out of Sable's throat more a gasp than a word. Sable took a step forward, but the viciously curved bow in her mother's hand stopped her.

Her mother hurried over, pulling the younger girls out of the bushes and looking them over. Ryah burst into tears and Talia stood shaking, clutching the basket of berries to her chest.

Screams and shouts rang through the smoke from the village.

"More are coming!" Sable's father called, running into the yard, holding a sword she'd never seen before. He grabbed her shoulder. "Are you hurt?"

She shook her head, the action twitchy and fast. "Why are they here?" she asked. It was a childish question. She knew it was, even as the words tumbled out of her mouth.

They were raiders. There was no reason.

Her father turned to stare at the smoldering remains of their home. "I don't know," he said quietly.

The words cut across Sable's chest, cold and sharp as a knife. She flinched and spun to look at him. He'd lied? He never lied. Not to her.

He glanced down at her, realizing what he'd done. Instead of explaining, he merely shook his head. "Take your sisters and hide in the root cellar." He pushed her toward the small door set in the hill.

Sable planted her feet. "Why are they here?"

He grabbed her shoulders. "I love you, Issable." The warmth of that truth enveloped her. But the truth was so strong the ruddy light filtering through the smoke coalesced around him. Strands of auburn in his dark beard caught the light, tracing waves in the curls.

He pressed a kiss to Sable's forehead, the feel of his lips and the tickle of his beard so real compared to the elusive sensations of his words. "I need you to keep your sisters safe."

It was the pleading in his voice that made her nod, and she pulled her sisters to the cellar. They scrambled in, clinging to each other.

Shouts came closer, and Sable pulled the door shut behind her.

Two raiders strode into the yard.

Sable's mother turned and readied her bow. Her father positioned himself between the men and the cellar. Sable pressed her face against a crack in the door, staring at her father, terrified not only by the sight of him with the unfamiliar sword, but also by how easily he held it.

The yard sat in deep, red gloom. The two men, dressed all in black, were like shadows. The taller of the two snapped out a command, and three more men stepped into view, staying back, each holding a bow aimed at Sable's parents.

Sable's father watched them warily. Her mother stood beside him, keeping her bow trained on the commander.

"Derchtu perrot." The commander's voice was steely, but there was satisfaction in it.

The incomprehensible words contained enough truth that Sable felt the warmth of them, even from this distance.

The commander motioned to the raider next to him, and they walked forward until they stood in front of her parents. He looked at them with cold eyes. "Draconek retchhet yedenwelz."

Her father let out a short, scornful laugh. "You don't control nearly as much as you think."

Sable's gaze snapped to her father. He looked like a stranger, holding that sword and understanding these monsters.

The commander shrugged. "We control enough," he answered in a heavy accent. "Surrender, and you will live."

Sable's mother planted her feet more firmly.

The tip of her father's sword rose, ever so slightly. "Never."

The commander studied them for a moment, then nodded to the raider beside him.

The raider's blade flicked out in a blur of movement.

Her father tried to block the attack, but it was too fast. The sword sliced into his chest.

Sable slapped her hand over her mouth to muffle her scream as he fell.

A cry ripped out of her mother, feral and savage. She swung her bow up toward the raider's chest.

But he was already lunging, cutting into her arm. The elvish bow dropped, and the raider's sword bit deep into her stomach.

She toppled to her knees and curled forward.

The commander grabbed her hair, twisting her head up to face him. "You could have just surrendered."

"Never to you," her mother said, the words ragged. "Free people will always fight you."

The man shrugged. "Then they will lose. Wasting everything they could have been. Wasting their regretful little lives."

Sable's mother looked down at her husband's body, then at the ruined house and the yard. "There was nothing regretful or little about our life here." Her gaze brushed past Sable behind the cellar door. "It was more than I deserved." She turned back to the raider. "I regret nothing." The warmth of the words wrapped tightly around Sable.

The commander let go of her hair like dropping a rotten berry. She crumpled to the ground, and he brushed off his hands. "What a waste."

His warrior drew back his sword for a killing blow.

An inarticulate scream tore out of Sable and she shoved the door open, rushing across the yard at the man.

"No!" her mother screamed.

Sable flung herself at the raider. He caught her arm with his free hand, jerking her to a stop. She pounded her other fist against the unyielding leather armor on his chest.

The commander barked out a laugh. "You have a daughter?"

"Stop!" her mother struggled to rise.

Sable yanked at her arm, but it was held in an iron grip. The commander leaned close, his glittering dark eyes boring into her over his mask. "She looks just like you."

"She's just a child!" her mother spat at the commander. "You coward!"

He stiffened at the word, then flicked his hand carelessly at Sable and her mother.

The other raider lifted his sword and Sable tried to fling herself away from him. But his grip was hard as stone.

A red-fletched arrow sank deep into the raider's eye.

Sable screamed and tore out of his grasp as he spun and fell, landing lifelessly across her mother. The commander turned to face the bushes along the back of the yard. Arrows shot out of the shadows. The man bellowed out a command before three arrows took him.

The raider archers fired into the bushes.

Sable dropped to her knees and crawled to her mother. The fallen raider's black boot lay flung across her mother's neck, and Sable scrambled over him. Strips of leather crisscrossed up his boots, and she grabbed a strap with bloody fingers, and yanked it off, pleading with her to move. Her mother's head merely lolled to the side, her eyes unseeing and lifeless.

More raiders poured into the yard, met by arrows raining from the shadows.

Ryah and Talia clung to each other at the door of the root cellar, staring into the yard in horror. Sable shoved herself up and ran to them.

Pushing the girls back into the darkness, Sable turned to see her parents' bodies.

Dark shadows moved out from the bushes on the hill. Tall, foreign looking men stepped into the yard, their elven bows loosing arrow after arrow. The closest turned slowly, his eyes meeting Sable's. His long face was full of terrible, cold resolve, but a hint of sympathy crossed his face at the sight of her.

He flicked his fingers toward her, and the door of the cellar slammed closed, plunging her into darkness.

Sable sank down, clinging to her sisters. Through the slats in the door, the battle wore on. Her sisters curled up against her, their bodies shaking. She pulled them close while the flames outside slowly burned themselves out and the cries dwindled down to silence.

Sable stared at the door until there was nothing but darkness, choking smoke, and the haunting call of ravens.

PART I

"The origin of the Keepers is intrinsically connected to the creation of
Queensland, and her very first queen.
Back in the days when the land was peppered with loosely connected
cities, a looming threat grew in the east. And those destined to shape
nations came together, almost by chance."

-from *The History of the Keepers*, by Alaric, Court Keeper, in the 391st
year of Queensland.

CHAPTER ONE

Ten years later

THE UPSTAIRS HALL of the Broken Mast Tavern crowded around Sable like guards drawn up too close. She forced her breathing to stay slow, partly to take the edge off the stench of old fish, partly to keep the edge of loathing off her face.

The huge form of Boone stood guard outside Kiva's office, arms crossed over his massive chest, eyes devoid of emotion. Even though Sable was taller than the first time she'd been shoved down this hall ten years ago, her nose still barely came up to Boone's elbow.

"Lovely day," she murmured. Knowing better than to expect an answer, she ducked around him and into the room.

"It is a lovely day, Sable," Kiva drawled, his voice smooth and almost charming.

"I'm sure it is somewhere," Sable answered.

The gang boss of the Vayas leaned back comfortably behind a large desk, which filled most of his office. The two small windows were open, but the breeze did nothing more than stir the midday heat. Despite the warmth, he wore a brocade vest in such a rich blue it almost gave the impression she was speaking to a proper merchant. He motioned for her to sit in the cramped space across from him.

Pete, Kiva's second bodyguard, stood in his usual corner, crowding the room even more. The thick dwarf scowled behind his black beard and wooly brow.

Sable pulled the chair out until it hit the wall. She sat and leaned back, straightening her legs in the small space between herself and the desk, as though spreading out might stretch the entire building and allow a little more freedom.

Kiva looked the way Sable always imagined a goblin might. He was barely taller than she was. His hair, an unremarkable walnut color, hung down to his shoulders, curling wildly. His narrow face was sharpened by the pointed beard that ran along his jawline and jutted out from his chin. His thin-lipped mouth was wide enough to look like it was continually spread in a humorless smile.

Sliding around his fingers were the bright green loops of his pet vayakadyn snake. The creature was no thicker than his thumb, but its bite held enough venom to kill a man Boone's size in a few agonizing minutes.

But it wasn't Kiva's goblin-like qualities or the horrid little snake that made these meetings so unpleasant. It was the sharp coldness Sable knew was coming.

"Lord Renwen," Kiva began in his placid drawl, "slimy little scab that he is, has increased the number of ships he's docking in port and has not paid the additional fee."

Instead of the icy chill of lies, Kiva's truthful words added an uncomfortable warmth to the summer afternoon. Sable hid her surprise behind a look of faint interest.

"He's increased the guards on his merchandise," he continued, "so it's too costly to confront him outright." The words remained true. "He should know better than to cheat the Vayas."

Sable studied him. He was telling the truth? Kiva never told the truth.

Pete stood next to her, oblivious to everything she felt.

Sable focused on what Kiva had said, instead of how it had felt. "Renwen?" That was a bigger fish than he usually sent her after.

Kiva nodded. "He's wiggled his way into the graces of Lord Trelles himself."

Sable didn't bother to hide her surprise at that. If Renwen was close to the head of the Merchant Guild, he'd become a very big fish indeed.

"As well as into the graces of Trelles' daughter," Pete said, the smirk visible through his beard.

Kiva's face remained unamused. "A rumor I cannot use unless it is confirmed." He focused on Sable. "I sent Pete and Boone to locate Renwen's business ledger. But they couldn't find it."

Pete's smile faded. "It's not in his office," he said, a churlish edge to his voice.

Kiva ignored him. "I need that ledger if I'm to prove what he owes me."

The change was stark. Kiva's words slashed across the room, cold and sharp.

Sable tried to keep her face bland. There were the lies she'd been expecting, although it made her wonder why he really wanted the ledger.

"I should have sent you from the beginning, Sable." Kiva fell back into his customary, mildly pleasant expression, and the room settled into the ordinary air of a conversation that carried neither deeply held truth, nor purposeful lies. "But you have a tendency to bend my rules. I need things done as I say this time."

She stayed leaned back in her chair, and laced her fingers together across her stomach. "I always do what you say."

"No. You always get what I want, so I overlook how often you don't do what I say."

She smiled at him. "I only alter your plans when they need improving."

Pete gave an irritated grunt.

Kiva fixed the dwarf with a quelling look. "I sent you to find a simple ledger, Pete, yet you brought me nothing. I sent Sable to find me a silver horseshoe, and what did she bring me?"

Pete's beard shifted as he clenched his jaw in irritation. "A horse," he quipped.

"Yes. A silver horse. She's earned some leeway over the years." Kiva leaned toward Sable, his gaze intense. "But this time, I want nothing touched." His words pushed against her again, warm with truth. He felt so strongly about the words that he grew slightly brighter. The afternoon light caught on the curls of his hair, bringing out amber strands.

It had been a long time since she'd seen someone who cared this deeply about something, and Sable tried not to react. Whatever Kiva wanted that ledger for, it was more important to him than any job he'd ever given her.

She held up her hand. "I vow to not even touch my feet to the floor."

Pete snorted in annoyance, but Kiva let out a huff of amusement. "I can't have this theft lead back to me. Your job is to merely find where the ledger is kept. I will do the rest." The little green snake stretched its neck out toward Sable and fixed her with dead eyes. "Regardless of how many pretty things the man has, Sable, leave them be."

She pulled her eyes away from the reptilian gaze. "Even small things?"

"You know Renwen's brother is head constable, don't you?" Pete grumbled.

She glanced at the dwarf. The head constable? That would complicate whatever plan Kiva made for the actual theft. "Of course. Everyone knows that." Her own lie felt as cold as Kiva's, but neither man noticed.

No one ever noticed.

Kiva spread his fingers. The green snake curled around his wrist. "So you see why it's such a delicate situation."

"Then why did you send these two?" Sable gestured to Pete in the corner and Boone outside the door.

Kiva shrugged. "Everyone makes mistakes." He fixed her with a piercing look. "Except you, Sable."

She forced a smile.

Every step of her life for the past ten years had been a mistake.

"Find me the ledger by tonight," Kiva said. "I have an important meeting in the Sanctuary." The seemingly innocuous words wrapped warmly around her with so much truth Sable clenched her hands together, and Kiva smiled at what must look to him like shock. "But I'll be back by dusk. I expect your report when I return."

Everything about him looked as rich and bright as if he stood in full sunlight. The deep blue fabric of his vest revealed threads of rich sapphire. The scales of his snake glittered a brilliant emerald green as it stretched toward her.

Sable stared at him. "The Sanctuary?" Whatever was going on there, it was as important to him as the ledger. Maybe more important. "I thought the priories had magical defenses to keep thieves out," she said, hoping a wry smile covered her surprise.

Kiva shrugged. "Hopefully not for thieves invited by Prioress Eugessa herself."

Sable's eyebrows rose. "Congratulations."

The Sanctuary was the seat of the three Grand Priories that governed the city. An invitation was unheard of for a man as disreputable as Kiva. His efforts to portray himself as a legitimate businessman must be gaining ground.

Kiva gave her his easy smile. "Thank you." He leaned forward, and his charm cracked ever so slightly. An almost palpable threat shone through. "Go. Find me the ledger by tonight."

Sable stood. "Tonight," she agreed, keeping her tone easy.

He gave her his smooth, slippery smile. "Always a pleasure working with you, Sable."

She gave him a slight nod and left before the disgust showed on her face. No one worked with Kiva. They worked for him, under him, or were crushed beneath him, but they never worked with him.

Sable pushed through the thin, crooked door to her room, the slimy feeling from Kiva clinging to her more than usual. She sank down onto her bed, aiming for the soft spot where the mattress stretched between the wooden slats.

"How'd it go?" Talia asked, not turning away from the wall where she was focused on a set of thin, charcoal lines.

Sable closed her eyes and lay back. "As fun as a meeting with Kiva can be."

"All lies again?"

"No. Actually, he told the truth a couple times, which was almost worse."

"If you were boring like the rest of us," Talia said, leaning closer to her drawing, "talking to him would only be mildly unpleasant."

"No one thinks Kiva is only mildly unpleasant."

The small room felt lighter than the grim streets of Dockside. Charcoal sketches of rolling grasslands and smooth oceans covered every inch of the walls. They were captioned in swirling letters with snippets of songs or poems, and the fact that barely anyone besides herself and Talia could read them made them all the more precious.

Two beds sat against opposite walls, on either side of one small table holding a hairbrush, a needle, and a ball of thread. The bits of color scattered around the room, the bright blue curtains and the yellow blooms of sandweed on the table, were all Talia. Sable had left everything bare until her sister had brought bits of life in.

Sable breathed deeply. Even the dank smell of Dockside was held at bay by the scent of dough and woodsmoke hovering around her sister.

Talia looked nothing like a goblin. She was light and effortless. Her dress was dingy and her cheeks eternally smudged with charcoal or flour, but her eyes were bright and she hummed softly while she drew.

The gloom of Dockside never rubbed off on Talia.

Sable pushed herself up. "Will you paint my face?"

"For the festival?" Talia glanced over her shoulder. "Can I make you glamorous and daring? Beautiful and winsome?" Her face lit. "Can I make you into a monster?"

Sable smiled, and the last of the unpleasantness that lingered from Kiva faded.

A wide, eager smile spread across Talia's face. "There will be so many monsters at the Red Shield Festival you'll fit right in."

"I need washed-out and unmemorable." Sable stood, picking up a black tunic. "A shop courier."

Talia frowned. "You have to work?"

8

Sable pulled off her tunic and replaced it with the courier's. Her pants were reasonably clean and dark grey enough that they'd work. "If we want Kiva to keep providing room and board," *And allow you to work somewhere as honest as the bakery,* "I'm at his beck and call, even on festival days."

Talia set down her charcoal stick and wiped her hands on her dress. "Someday I'm going to paint you as a terrifying monster, or make you so stunning the entire world will fall over at your beauty."

Sable moved to the bed closer to the window. "The whole world falling over sounds like it would cause problems."

"What's a problem is me having to constantly make you less interesting than you are." Talia set her brushes and powder boxes next to her. "Stop smiling or the powder is going to stick in the crinkles around your eyes and you'll get haggard and old instead of washed-out and unmemorable."

"That could work, too." Sable bit her lip to chase away the smile and focused on the wall. The section Talia had been working on was wiped clean of its old drawing and marked with new, light lines of a building with tall spires. "The Dragon Priory?"

Talia gave a little disgruntled hum. "I can't make the spires weightless enough. They keep looking like pointy ears."

"It could be the lesser-known Bunny Priory."

Talia laughed. The hairs of the wide brush flitted across Sable's forehead, dusting her with an earthy smell.

"Are you a scurvy courier from the docks tonight?" Talia asked. "Or a proper courier from up the slope?"

"Proper enough that I can walk on the slope without arousing suspicion." She needed to be able to walk among the huge houses at the very top of the slope, but there was no point in worrying Talia with that.

Talia held Sable's chin with steady fingers, but a frown creased her face. "There was a trial today. Six thieves, all sentenced to the prison ship galleys." Her brush paused for a moment. "The darker parts of the city always sounded worse coming from Talia. "You'll be careful, right?"

9

"I'm just scouting," Sable assured her. "I'll be done by dark, then we can go to the festival."

Talia's brush started moving again. The drawings on the walls drew Sable's gaze, past the stormy sunrise over the ocean and the jagged lines of cliffs, coming to rest, as always, on the coastal hills of the Eastern Reaches.

Her gaze traced the hillsides, looking for the one valley that should be speckled with snug, wooden homes. As many times as Talia drew the hills by the sea, she never added the town, and Sable couldn't bear to ask her to.

Although maybe Talia didn't draw it because all she had was a charcoal stick. The homes would only look like burned husks of wood. The way the three sisters had last seen them.

Talia began talking about the bakery, and Sable focused on her voice, trying not to remember Ryah's little face. So many things had gone wrong over the last ten years. Sable had done so many things wrong. But at least one sister was still here, protected from the worst of it.

Talia's voice skipped along, telling Sable the latest in the battle of the head baker and a persistent cellar rat. The slight weight of the powder covered Sable like a second skin. Making her cheeks appear fuller, softening the sharp lines that years of too little food and too much worry had worked into her face. Shaping her face into someone's whose life had gone how it should have.

For the thousandth time, she turned herself into the person Kiva needed her to be, and locked all her worries and regrets inside, trying to somehow keep them from tainting her sister.

Because the only thing that would make Dockside worse would be if it changed Talia.

CHAPTER TWO

LORD RENWEN LOOKED like a dead fish. One of those pale, sickly ones that flopped around, trapped in a puddle at low tide.

From Sable's perch in the tree outside his window, she watched the District Manager of Ink Production and Delivery hunch over his desk. His skin was more pallid than his pale yellow shirt, and his sand-colored hair hung limp in the heat. His cheeks were clean shaven in the fashion of the wealthiest merchants, and he continually sucked them in as he smoked his pipe, pulling his face into a decidedly fishy shape.

From the rumors of Renwen's rise in the Merchant Guild, she'd expected someone more...engaging.

Sable twirled a twig between her fingers, letting it dance across her knuckles. If Renwen were to glance out the window into the hot afternoon—which he hadn't since opening his ledger book hours ago—the leaves should cover her, her dull clothes and dark hair blending with the shadows.

She had the urge to jiggle the branch, just to see if there was anything that would break the monotony and make him look up.

But thieving and scouting were never exciting. Not if done well.

The new recruits came up with plans full of action and deception, and a week later were in the stocks.

No. Proper thieving should always begin with proper scouting, which was exclusively made up of patient watching. Watching to find out where the prize was kept, how closely it was guarded, and most importantly, why it was treasured. Was it valuable? Rare? Sentimental?

The first two were easy, but stealing something sentimental was always messy. People would spend their whole lives trying to get something like that back.

Thankfully, Renwen's ledger fell firmly into the "valuable" category.

Although, in this case, the value was so high, Kiva was going to be hard-pressed to steal it cleanly.

She leaned her head back against the trunk. The early summer air blustered past her in fits, smelling wild and clean, as though it came from a different part of the world. A part with more interesting things. Like gnomes or elves or green fields dotted with fairies.

The breeze was edged with the soot of the city, with sharp veins of dredgeweed smoke from Renwen's window cutting through it, but the body of the wind was different. Unrestrained. Free.

It called to her the way the hills in Talia's drawings did, with ideas of escape and freedom.

But no one escaped Dockside. She'd once imagined working her way up the ranks of Kiva's thieves could do it, but getting close to Kiva just tightened the noose. Her dreams of freedom had been traded for an agreement to hand over every cent she stole in exchange for lodging, communal food halls, and the assurance that Talia could stay working somewhere as sheltered as the bakery.

And there was the fact that handing over every cent she stole kept Kiva's Fangs from chasing her down and killing her.

Kiva kept a running ledger tracking each expense. No one ever brought in enough from their work to outweigh the growth of their debt.

Except Rabbit.

Rabbit had reached legendary status in Dockside by setting up a business trade that made Kiva the legitimate owner of two woodworking shops. The opportunity for him to enjoy the perks of a respectable business owner up on the slope had freed Rabbit and set him up for life outside the city.

Or that was the rumor. No one Sable knew had ever met Rabbit.

The sound of coins clinking caught her attention.

Right. Renwen.

Lord Renwen's motions were stiff and precise as he dropped another stack of coins into a carved wooden box.

Too stiff, really. A dead fish should be limp.

He swept the last pile of bronze nummi into the box, followed by five neat stacks of silver mons. The last coin on the table was a rich yellow, and Sable leaned forward.

Renwen had a gold solidus?

He picked up the coin and ran his thumb over it before dropping it into the box.

She'd only seen two gold coins before, both of which had been on highly guarded display outside the Merchant Guild, proof that the new gold mines in the Tremmen Hills were more than just rumor.

The sun dropped closer to the horizon and Sable shifted on the branch. What exactly was Kiva's interest in this tedious man? The sooner the man put away his ledger and left for the festival, the better.

She took in his emotionless face with a sinking feeling. What if Renwen didn't plan on attending the festival tonight? If she was stuck watching this dead fish of a man instead of enjoying the start of the festivities, she'd be hard-pressed not to steal something from him to pay for it.

A silver dish sat on a table near the window looking smug. As though it knew that was an empty threat.

Renwen snapped his box closed.

Finally.

He set down his pipe and stood, carrying the box across the room with a straight back. The wall Renwen approached was full of dark wood shelves, and Sable stretched to see where he put it. Kiva's order not to steal from Renwen was clear, but it never hurt to know where a man kept his coins. Instead of setting it down on a shelf, he grabbed a small statue of Amah, goddess of light, and pulled.

The entire shelf swung out like a door. Sable shimmied farther forward to see behind it. The thinning branch bent and rustled, dropping the leaves outside his window.

"Amah hide me," she breathed. But Lord Renwen didn't turn before stepping around the shelf. Past him, Sable caught a glimpse of a small closet. She pushed a thin sprig of leaves out of her way. The closet shelves held boxes and pouches. He set down the coins and picked up a black ledger the same size as the one he'd been writing in for hours. It was even tied with an identical black cord.

He had two ledgers?

Which one did Kiva want?

She glanced back at Renwen's desk and froze.

A woman stood in the open office door, peering into the room.

Sable barely breathed. If the woman looked out the window, she'd see Sable's face clear as day. And it would take longer to climb out of this tree than for someone to rush out into the yard and catch her. Sable pulled back slowly, letting the leaves inch back in front of her face, berating herself for being so careless.

The woman was tall and slender and wore a silk dress that was probably worth more than anything in Renwen's room, except his gold solidus. The lavender bodice deepened to a dark, rich purple as it flowed down the skirt. And if the silk itself wasn't expensive enough, the dragons embroidered near the bottom of the skirt, winding around each other and reaching up amidst swirls and flowers, made it clear the dress was Kalesh.

Her face was painted to a smooth, flawless finish. Spikes of glittering hairpins held her honey-colored hair in an elaborate pile on her head. Between the Kalesh dress and the sparkles in her hair, everything about her declared "merchant's daughter" in a haughty, vapid voice.

She stepped into the office, one delicate hand pressed to her lips to keep from laughing. The open bookshelf hid Renwen from her sight, so she glided closer.

"Hiding in a secret room?" she teased.

Renwen started at her voice, then quickly slid the second ledger behind a box.

He rolled his shoulders quickly, then settled them down into a more casual position and stepped out to face her. "Secret rooms are among my favorite places, my dear Ingred." He flashed her a smile that, aside from being in his pale, dead-fish face, was almost charming. His entire posture was relaxed, and without a trace of his former stiffness, Renwen grabbed her waist and swung her into the closet with him, planting a kiss on her lips.

Sable stared at him for a moment, shocked by the change, before taking advantage of their distraction to scoot farther back into the tree. She paused when she could just make them out through the leaves.

So, Lady Ingred and Lord Renwen were more than a rumor. Kiva would be interested in that information.

Ingred's wealth made Renwen look like a pauper putting on airs. Her father, Lord Trelles, was the leader of the Merchant Guild, and possibly the wealthiest man in the city. Ingred was known for two things: spending obscene amounts of money in the shops, and being utterly spoiled.

She was a completely useless person.

Ingred pushed away from Renwen, a smile playing on her lips. "Don't muss me. I just stopped by for a quick visit." Her voice wafted out the open window. "This is such a small secret room. You can't tell me you're scared of someone stealing things from such a little stash."

"This little stash holds more wealth than whole districts in the city," he said mildly.

She waved her hand at him. "Those districts should be leveled and used for something better. Like new abbeys or shops. I'm just saying that your secret room is smaller than I'd expected."

Renwen stood in the closet doorway with his back to Sable, a bit of his former stiffness returning. "Had you grown up in any house but your father's, you might see it differently."

"I wasn't insulting you, Renny. I think it's quaint." She stepped farther into the closet. "They sentenced the thief who stole from my aunt to the slave galleys this morning," she said in an off-handed way.

"They caught him this quickly?"

Ingred waved a hand. "They sentenced someone who matched his description. Someone dirty. It's so hard to tell them all apart. I don't see why they don't just hang them all and get it over with."

She opened a wide, ornate chest. Renwen took the chance to roll his shoulders again and clasp his hands behind his back before leaning on the closet doorframe. Sable raised an eyebrow at the effort he was expending to appear casual.

"Look at all the pretty things!" Lady Ingred said. "How delicate." She turned and held up a tiny, silver star pendant hanging from the thin chain. "This is lovely."

His hands clenched. "That was my wife's." His voice stayed relaxed, but the words grabbed Sable's attention. For the first time, there was a warm pressure to them. The substantial feel of truth.

Ingred paused. "Did she wear it often?"

"Before she fell ill, she wore it almost continually."

Ingred considered the necklace. "Would you like to see it on me?"

He reached out and took it from her hand. "You deserve something better than this." His voice sounded the same, but Sable felt the cold slice of a lie.

A flicker of irritation crossed Ingred's brow.

"I do have something else for you," he said smoothly. "Something more fitting to your station."

He dropped the necklace into his pocket and stepped past her, reaching into the chest. She fixed him with a pout, but he ignored her and pulled out a chain with a large, green emerald.

The lady's eyebrows rose as she touched the stone with a gloved hand. "You could give me both."

Renwen opened the necklace and waited for her to turn around. "I wouldn't insult you with another woman's jewelry." His words had fallen back into the feelingless half-truths of common conversation.

Ingred turned her back to him. "And a common woman at that."

Renwen's hands twitched, but he fastened the chain around her neck.

She spun and flashed him a smile. "How does it look?"

"It's almost as beautiful as you." He took her hand and led her across the room. "Shall we call for wine?" Dropping into a chair with an ease Sable wouldn't have imagined him capable of, he pulled Ingred down onto his lap.

"I wish I could, Renny." She giggled. "It's been such a trying day. Piddy, my secretary, is pregnant! I thought she was just getting fat, but now I find she's become completely useless! I had to let her go, of course. The nerve of her destroying her life without a thought to my inconvenience."

"Didn't she get married last winter?" Renwen asked.

"Yes, but she swore to me it wouldn't affect her work. And now this!" Ingred crossed her arms. "It's dreadful trying to find good help. Just dreadful."

"You could hire a male secretary. No risk of him becoming pregnant."

"A man?" Ingred asked, shocked. "In my dressing room? Planning my days? Renny, you say the most scandalous things!"

He raised an eyebrow. "I didn't realize you were so close to your secretary. I only see mine once in the morning."

"Piddy has been by my side for two years."

Renwen gave a faint smile. "Surprising she found a way to get with child then."

She swatted his arm. "She stopped living at our house when she got married. I should have known it would end in disaster."

"Let's call for wine," Renwen suggested again.

Ingred shook her head. "I've already stayed too long. I only came to tell you that my father wants to check the Guild ledger. He'll be coming by tomorrow."

Sable straightened. Renwen kept the ledger for the Merchant Guild? She glanced back at the book he'd been so painstakingly writing in. That explained Kiva's interest.

The three Grand Priories were the real power in the region. But the Merchant Guild grew more powerful every year. Over the last decade they'd gone from merely organizing trade in this city to operating trade routes through all the surrounding towns, and gaining a foothold even among the cities of the Northern Lords.

In the two years since Kiva'd obtained his woodworking businesses, he'd been trying, unsuccessfully, to wriggle his way into the

Merchant Guild. Having intimate knowledge of each member's account would give him a lot of leverage to wriggle with.

"I'm perfectly happy to show your father the numbers," Renwen said. "I have no secrets from him." The lie sliced into Sable with a cold slash. Renwen pulled Ingred close again. "The only thing I have to hide is that his daughter has access to my house." He held up a key. "What's mine is yours, my dear."

She gave him a coy smile. "Unless it once belonged to your wife."

His smile broadened, but he didn't answer the accusation. "Once my loan is approved, it'll be enough to impress even your father, and we can stop sneaking around."

She leaned into him. "But the sneaking is fun."

Sable toyed with the fraying edge of her sleeve as she studied the woman. Maybe it was the sneaking around that was the draw for Ingred. Renwen's fake charm might be enough to help him rise in the ranks of the Guild, but Lady Ingred couldn't possibly be attracted to him. Surely she could have her pick of men.

Ingred looked thoughtfully up at him. "Do you really think the new mine will produce gold?"

Sable's finger paused. Ah. There was the draw. She focused back on Renwen. The man kept the ledger for the Merchant Guild, and had a new gold mine? Maybe she'd underestimated him.

Renwen shrugged casually. "The other two are. No one knows how much gold is in those mountains, but I aim to be among the first to find out." He squeezed his arms around her waist. "Stay a bit longer."

"I can't keep my father waiting." She stood and twirled away from him, pausing at the door to touch the emerald at her neck. Her eyes lingered on his pocket with the silver necklace. "Thank you."

Lord Renwen stood and offered her a deep bow. She slipped out of the room, closing the door behind her. He fished the necklace out of his pocket, and rubbed his thumb over the silver pendent. A pained expression seeped onto his face, as though it had been waiting just below the surface. For the first time, his expression looked honest. He closed his eyes, and Sable almost felt a twinge of pity.

When he opened his eyes, though, the expression was gone. He straightened his back and strode to the closet. Putting the necklace away, he picked up the second ledger and locked his office door before sitting stiffly back at his desk. He opened both books, carefully copying numbers into the second book and adding more.

Sable watched him work with more interest than before, considering the second ledger. He'd hid it from Ingred, so it must contain something valuable. Something he was hiding from the Merchant Guild's leader.

Sable tapped her fingers on her leg. If she could deliver that kind of leverage over the Guild to Kiva, it was the sort of thing that might earn her...

Her fingers stilled.

That was Rabbit-level treasure.

An idea took shape, and she sank back against the trunk.

Maybe Lady Ingred wasn't so useless after all.

The plan was almost too simple. Sable turned it over in her mind, but couldn't find a flaw. That silver necklace was the key, and the fact Renwen felt sentimental about it would work to her advantage for once.

She needed to see what was on that second ledger.

It was directly against Kiva's orders, but if this book was as valuable as it seemed, he'd thank her in the end. Yes, this was well worth risking Kiva's fury.

Sable took a breath, trying to find the wild air from before, but all she smelled was the sour dredgeweed from Renwen's pipe. Renwen wouldn't leave for the festival until close to dark, and she should wait an hour past that before she came back. Maybe two.

But a restless hope had formed inside her, and the Red Shield Festival beckoned to her like some glittering, magical creature. She'd get Talia and enjoy the festival for a bit, then come back when Renwen was gone.

Sable's report to Kiva would be expected long before that, but the idea of earning her way out of Dockside echoed the wild freedom she'd smelled on the wind.

Kiva could wait.

CHAPTER THREE

Sable found her sister mending a tear in her grey dress.

"You're back early." Talia tilted her head. "Were you attacked by a tree?"

Sable ran her hand over her head. Two small twigs tumbled to the floor. "Yes. I barely survived."

"Your braid didn't." Talia put aside her sewing and picking up their thinly bristled brush. "Sit."

Sable sat sideways on the bed and let Talia pull out her braid and begin brushing.

"How did things go?" Talia asked.

The hope Sable had been alternately nurturing and stifling tied her tongue for a moment. "It went well," she managed.

She folded her hands in her lap and mulled over her plan for the night. What if the ledger wasn't anything important? But then why would Renwen hide it? How much would Kiva think it was worth? Her mind spun through the same questions over and over as she rubbed one thumb over the other.

"You're nervous," Talia said.

Sable stilled her fingers. "I need to finish that job tonight."

"You're not done?"

"Just a little more to do," Sable said absently.

Talia fell silent, her irritation at the vague answer evident by the sharp tug of the brush through Sable's knots.

Sable winced and looked for a change of subject. "Renwen looks like a dead fish."

Talia gave a snort of laughter.

"Everything about him is pasty and pale. Yet for some reason, Lady Ingred sneaks into his house to dally with him."

The brush paused. "You saw her? Is she beautiful?"

Sable shrugged. "In a horrible sort of way. Of course, anyone looks good next to a dead fish. She is currently deeply frustrated by the fact that her personal secretary had the audacity to get pregnant by her new husband."

"How dare she," Talia murmured.

"Ingred had to let the woman go, of course, now that she was useless."

"She fired her for getting pregnant?"

"Ingred sounded disappointed that poor Piddy wasn't just getting fat."

"Charming." Talia was quiet for a moment before brightening. "Of course this means the position is open. Kiva could get you a job there as a jay. He's supposed to have contacts everywhere in the merchants' families."

Sable snorted. "I don't think I'm spy material."

"It could be fun, though. Pretending to be rich and living in a house like that."

Sable shook her head at Talia's eternal naiveté. "Not fun. Being a jay is the most dangerous job Kiva has."

"But I bet Ingred's secretary wears nice dresses."

Sable pulled her head away from Talia's hands, ignoring her protest, and looked at her sister. "Did you know three of Kiva's jays have been hanged since spring?"

Talia paused. "Three?"

"Kiva likes to keep that sort of thing quiet. The Merchant Guild found out they were not who they said they were and hanged them the next morning. No trial. No chance to run and tell more secrets. Just hanged immediately."

"That's...terrifying." Talia tapped the brush against her lips, troubled.

"Of course, even without the threat of hanging, I'm not sure being her secretary would be worth it. You'd have to be around Lady Ingred all day."

Her sister gave her a quick smile. "That depends on how nice the dresses are." She began on the braid again. "Will the scouting take long tonight?"

Sable almost brushed off the question, but her sister's hands felt so competent and grown up in her hair. Maybe Talia was too naive, but she wasn't the little girl who Sable needed to shelter from the harsh realities of Dockside. She was eighteen. And if this ledger was as valuable as Sable thought, it was time to start sharing more.

"I'm not going back to Renwen's to scout," Sable said.

Talia paused.

Sable lowered her voice. "I'm going to get the ledger myself."

"Sable," Talia hissed. "You can't."

"I can. Better than anyone else in fact."

Talia began braiding again, not quite as gently as before. "If it's something you can do, it's something you could explain to someone else."

"Do you know any other thief who can read?"

Talia was quiet for a moment. "This is a bad idea, Sable. Why risk disobeying Kiva this blatantly?"

"Because he won't be mad. When he sees what I've found, he'll be pleased. I promise."

Talia didn't answer. Sable didn't need to see her to know she had that little wrinkle of disapproval between her brows.

"Did he ask you for another silver horseshoe?"

Sable smiled. "Why is that what everyone remembers?"

"Because he asked for a horseshoe, and you brought him a horse."

"Not a real horse. Just a stamp."

It had been one of the earliest jobs Kiva had given her. She'd been sent to steal a silver horseshoe from a silversmith. But when she'd scouted and seen how much the man loved it, she knew it would never work. He hung it on a peg over his desk and polished it every night. It was far too sentimental to steal.

But she'd seen the stamp of a horse he used for all his official business. He'd spent an hour filling out purchase orders, sealing each with the stamp.

That night, she'd snuck into his office and positioned the horseshoe to look like it had fallen from its peg and knocked papers off his desk into the coals of his fire. Then she'd pried the metal horse stamp off its wooden handle, which was by far the most challenging part of the night. Finally, she lit the wooden handle where the stamp had been, letting it char, then tucking what was left into the edge of the coals.

Kiva had used that stamp to purchase all sorts of things, and as far as Sable knew, it hadn't crossed the smith's mind that the stamp was stolen instead of melted until a month later, when he began receiving all the bills.

"That was mostly luck." Sable could feel Talia's hands on her back, finishing the braid. "It's some luck this time, too, but he's still going to be pleased."

"How pleased?"

The words Sable hadn't intended to say pushed their way up. "More than ever before. Pleased enough it might actually give us freedom from..." She waved her hand at the city around them.

"Kiva would move us closer to the docks? Into a better room?"

Sable turned to see her sister's face alight with excitement. "That's not what I—"

"Oh, Sable..." Talia's voice was breathless. "Finally! We could move somewhere..." She glanced at the peeling ceiling and the dark blotch of mold below the window. "Better!"

Sable shook her head at the hope in Talia's voice. "The only place we'd be moving is further under Kiva's thumb. We don't need his version of better. We need freedom. Real freedom. Freedom from him."

"Don't tell me anything else. I'll just worry if I know." Talia breathed out a sigh. "A better room!"

Sable didn't answer. Kiva had offered Sable a better room a dozen times. Every time, she'd refused. Living on the fringe of Dockside meant worse accommodations, but it allowed her to believe a path out might exist. And it kept Talia from Kiva's grasp.

Talia picked up a small piece of fabric to tie at the end of the braid, and Sable turned away from her. When Talia spoke again, her voice was softer. "I'm sure whatever you're planning will go well, because today is a lucky day. Right?"

Sable stiffened.

Talia's voice turned wistful. "She'd be sixteen."

It had been Sable's first thought this morning. Ryah's absence had been a tangible thing all day.

"I know you don't like to talk about her," Talia said quietly, "but sometimes I do. I miss her. I wish we could have brought her to this place. Where we have food and shelter."

Sable's shoulders tightened.

"I don't mean you didn't give her those things," Talia said quickly. "You kept us alive. As long as you could."

The past ten years stretched out darkly, and for the thousandth time, the pang of guilt and loss pushed words toward the surface that should have been said long ago. This was another thing Talia was old enough to handle, and today was as good a day as any. Maybe better.

Not only was it Ryah's birthday, it was also a full moon. The nights Sable snuck away to make restitutions at the small priory always felt a little more…sacred than other days.

Talia turned away and set the brush on the table. Sable looked at her sister's back for a long moment, then opened her mouth, searching for the words to start.

"I want to go to the Choosing tomorrow," Talia said.

Sable's words squeezed to a stop. They hadn't been to a Choosing in ten years. Why go without Ryah?

Talia tucked her powders into their bag, not looking at Sable. "If Britta likes her powdering tonight, I'm going to ask her if I can borrow a dress."

Sable grabbed Talia's arm. "Britta?"

"Yes." Her sister pulled away. "You never show anyone your face when I paint you, but Callie did, and Britta was impressed."

Sable stared at her. Britta was Kiva's woman, as cold and vicious as he was. "You're painting Britta?"

"She wants to look good for the festival tonight," Talia continued, her expression partly eager, partly defiant, "and she specifically requested me."

"No," Sable said flatly. "You cannot get involved with her, Talia. I have been trying to keep you safe from Kiva ever since—"

"He treated Ryah and me for the fever. I know," Talia cut in, her voice hard.

Sable closed her mouth. If only it were that easy. The medicine had been cheap. It had been that cursed scarf...

Talia raised her chin. "You're trying to better our position. So am I. Getting the attention of Britta and Kiva will only help. I'm tired of working in that bakery. I'm tired of having no money. I don't want anything fancy, Sable." She looked down at their feet. "Just shoes without holes and clothes that fit."

"You know we don't have money for those things." The words left a sour taste in Sable's mouth.

Talia shook her head. "I can make you look like gutter filth or the handmaiden of a prioress. You know I'm as good as anyone Kiva has." She lifted her chin. "Better maybe."

Sable reached for Talia's hand. "Don't go near Britta. Please. Not tonight."

Her sister pulled away. "Britta is not that bad." She didn't raise her eyes to meet Sable's. "Neither is Kiva."

"Talia, you don't know what they're like—"

"Ryah would have been supportive," Talia snapped.

Their baby sister's name hit Sable like a punch. "This has nothing to do with Ryah." Her voice echoed off the walls. "Kiva is dangerous. Gaining his notice is dangerous. Why do you think I've worked so hard to stay away from him?"

"Stay away from him? You steal for him all the time!"

Sable pushed herself to her feet. "I steal because I have no choice, Talia! When you're under him, he takes everything, even your choices. I do it all to keep you out from under him."

Talia looked at Sable coldly. "I know you want to keep me separate from everyone else." She stepped closer, and Sable had to look up slightly to meet her eyes. The warmth of the truth filled Talia's voice. "But I'm tired of living here. Tired of working all day baking in a hot kitchen."

After all these years, she still couldn't see. "Talia—"

"You've taken care of me for years, Issable."

Sable drew back at her full name.

"But I don't need you to take care of me anymore. You are always trying to control everything." Talia straightened her shoulders. "There are things outside your control, and I'm one of them." Talia pushed past her and stopped at the door. The glance she gave Sable was more hurt than angry. "Be careful tonight," she said roughly. Without waiting for an answer, she left, the door banging shut behind her.

Sable stayed in the empty room, dropping her head into her hand as Talia's footsteps echoed down the wooden stairs outside their building.

If Talia was getting closer to Kiva, it was time to get out of Dockside.

Any lingering doubt about the ledger disappeared. She'd get it and convince Kiva it was worth their freedom.

When the sounds of her sister were gone, Sable checked the stairs to make sure no one was near. She turned back and knelt by her bed, lifting one of the floorboards. Pulling out a small pouch, she poured its contents on the bed. It was only a handful of tarnished coins, but they were *hers*. This wasn't money she'd stolen. It was the wages from small jobs she'd snuck in over the past ten years. Weeding a woman's garden while scouting out her neighbor's home. Occasionally being hired to deliver real packages when dressed as a courier.

The coins glinted dully. Eight silver mons and twelve bronze nummi.

The pang of guilt at hiding this from Talia was stronger than usual. But it was better if she didn't know. If Kiva found out Sable had her own stash… That wasn't the sort of danger she'd expose her sister to.

Sable squeezed the coins in her palm. There were so few, but they were enough to start a life somewhere new. They would have to be.

CHAPTER FOUR

SABLE TUCKED the pouch into its hole, like a little seed of hope buried under the drab floor.

She glanced out the small window. Dusk was settling, but she had at least an hour before she could risk sneaking into Renwen's room. But the hope of the ledger and the idea of Talia working close to Kiva tonight made her antsy.

The festival was starting, and Atticus's acting troupe would be there. She could almost hear his rich, deep voice weaving stories for the crowd. She stood. That was the exact distraction she needed.

The wooden stairs creaked under her weight as she headed down to the street. Kiva's Vayas, named for the aggressive, green vayakadyn snake that killed dozens of people along the water's edge every year, controlled Dockside up to the wall separating the harbor from the rest of Immusmala. The leaders of the gang lived closer to the center, in crumbling, old mansions.

When she reached the street, Talia was nowhere to be seen. Sable considered going after her, but if Talia was working with Britta, she'd be near Kiva. And Sable couldn't go near him until she had the ledger.

The city of Immusmala sat on a peninsula jutting out into the sea like a long, skinny hill. The wealthier someone was, the higher up they lived. Dockside, situated along the water in the southeast corner, was as far from those heights as any place in the city could be. And as far from the festival.

Sable started uphill.

The stench of old fish pressed down between the buildings under the evening heat until she could taste it. She wound up past gaming houses, taverns, and brothels, toward respectable parts of the city. Eventually, the buildings straightened and brushed themselves off. The stench of fish blew away, replaced with the cleaner smell of the sea, and the cobblestones knit themselves into smooth streets.

Sable smoothed her tunic, making sure it didn't look too dirty before she reached the enormous houses that lined the Spine, the wide avenue on the top of the hill, running straight through the heart of the city. It wasn't fully dark yet, but in honor of the Red Shield Festival, torches wrapped in Sailor's Hope, a seaweed that burned red, had already been lit, giving the street an eerie, ruddy glow.

Sable walked along the edge, avoiding the more crowded center of the street, until a carriage approached, crowding everyone to the side. An eager cluster of admirers hurried along with it, dropping coins and jewelry into offering baskets that hung from the side.

Through the window, she caught sight of the immense form of Eugessa, Grand Prioress of the Priory of the Horn. The second most powerful person in Immusmala, and the woman Kiva had met with today. Her hair was dyed a burnished copper, her face powdered a puffy white. The bored flicks of her hands as she cast blessings over the crowd were undercut by a sharp gaze. She wore the white robe of a prioress, and her neck, arms, and fingers were crusted with jewelry.

If Prioress Eugessa was here, Kiva would be done meeting with her, and back in Dockside, probably waiting for Sable's report.

She paused in a doorway to let the carriage and the crowd pass, when two men caught her eye. Pete and Boone stood at the next corner, looking directly at her. The dwarf looking grim, the ever-silent Boone glowering at her.

She hesitated a moment before walking toward them.

Maybe Kiva was more anxious for this report than she'd thought.

"You were supposed to report to Kiva by dusk," Pete said, glancing at the darkening sky. "This is not a good day to keep him waiting."

Sable gave them what she hoped was a reassuring smile. "I need to go back again."

"You were there for hours already," Pete said.

She crossed her arms. "You've been following me?"

"We checked up on you," Pete corrected her.

Boone nodded, his expression bleak. "Kiva is livid."

The huge man spoke so rarely that Sable paused. Kiva was never livid. He was unflappably cold and calm. "About what?"

Pete shrugged and his eyes shifted warily. "You ask him."

Sable frowned. "I've never seen Kiva livid."

"You don't want to," Boone said. "It's like he's turned into his little green snake and wants to bite people."

That was definitely the most words she'd ever heard him say. He looked serious. Almost nervous.

Maybe going back for the ledger was a bad idea. She should just go tell Kiva what she'd found, like he'd asked.

Except the hope of freedom overshadowed that idea. She shook her head. "I need more time. I'll be at Kiva's office tonight. Before midnight."

"Are you headed to scout now?" Pete asked.

Sable fixed him with an irritated look. She couldn't tell them she was planning to kill time at the festival until she could steal the ledger she wasn't supposed to touch. "Kiva gave me the job. Let me do it."

Pete shrugged. "It's your neck. But even you won't be safe if you cross him today."

"I won't cross him then." Ignoring Pete's disapproving look, she turned away and headed up the avenue.

Kiva had sent them to check on her? That was unsettling. She resisted the urge to look back, but instead of continuing toward the festival, she turned onto a side street and ducked into a shop, watching to see if anyone followed.

When no one appeared for several minutes, she started again, winding through side streets, checking over her shoulder often.

When she rejoined the Spine closer to the Sanctuary, it was decidedly darker, but the wide avenue burst with noise and people pushing toward the festival. Flashes of vividly colored clothes and wild, monstrous masks jostled past. The red torchlight flickered across it all, flinging shadows wildly through the crowd.

On the far side of the street, a towering black-hooded form stalked silently toward the Sanctuary, his face covered by a red veil. His cloak was so dark the torchlight merely sank into it, and he moved like a shadow himself.

The baledin. A creature of legend, said to drain the life out of a person with merely a touch.

Sable kept her eye on him. It was just a man, walking on stilts, but she was glad that monster walked down the far side of the street. The Sanctuary would be full of more baledin, along with every other monster imaginable, creeping through the ruddy torchlight of the Red Shield Festival.

Until midnight tomorrow, when the High Prioress would call out into the night for the god Isah to save them. Monster costumes would be cast off and burned in a huge fire. The priories would light braziers, and the Sanctuary would glow like a candle at the tip of the city.

Hundreds of lanterns topped with circles of red paper would be released, floating up into the sky like a blazing shield, while the people thanked Isah for his protection from the darkness.

Above the heads in front of Sable, the Veil Wall came into view, its gate flung open to the city. The public was only allowed into the Sanctuary during festivals, and she hurried forward with the rest of the crowd. Passing through the gate was like stepping through a portal into another world.

Instead of the closely crammed buildings of the city, the Sanctuary was a wide-open plaza. Small mounds of grass and trees dotted the vast, stone courtyard. At the end of the Sanctuary, at the very tip of the city, rose the three Grand Priories. Situated in a u-shape, each stretched their twin spires up toward Amah, the goddess of light, and Isah, the great defender.

Sable headed toward the booths along the edge of the plaza, looking for one specific stage, and one specific old man.

She passed artisans selling rugs, paintings, and sculptures. Several guards stood at a booth displaying a thick bracelet made of gold. A red ribbon hung at the corner, signifying the artist was invited back to the Midsommer Festival in a month to compete in the grand competition of the arts.

Glittering, green light caught her eye at the very end of the booths. Sable smiled and headed toward the familiar stage. The light came from a potted tree in the back corner, sitting on a table. The tree itself was only half Sable's height, but it looked like an aged maple. The trunk was thick, the branches gnarled and crooked, and the leaves, while perfectly shaped, were tiny.

But the most remarkable part about the tree wasn't its size. The amazing part was that nestled in its leaves were tiny, green points of light.

The Duke's Figment of Wits Traveling Troupe was known for this tree and the classic plays they performed. There were none of the modern, crude comedies here, mocking whichever wealthy family was currently out of favor with the Merchant Guild. The stage was farther away from the priories than usual, but it was a testament to the troupe's popularity that there was still a crowd.

On stage, the same tall, dark-haired man as always played the part of Epophus. He was clean-shaven, like the wealthy merchants who paid barbers to shave their chins every morning. But unlike the usual merchant solemnity, his face was warm and quick to smile. Every year on opening night, they performed the same plays, and Sable smiled at the familiar words.

When Demonda came out, Sable's smile faltered.

This was not the same woman as last year. This woman's black wig was too tall, her face painted brightly enough that Talia would have clucked disapprovingly. The actress moved with an authoritative air, directing Epophus around with so much severity that Sable almost left. But her scene soon ended, and Epophus was back in the battle with the evil dwarven tyrant.

Sable tried to weave her way through the crowd, toward the stage. A large man, jockeying for a view, shouldered her out of his way, then another, until she was pushed to the side of the audience. A dark curtain stretched out in front of her from the corner of the stage, and she caught a glimpse of light behind it.

Creeping around the end, she found a small, sheltered area between the front and back curtains. Crates lined the space, which lay in deep shadow. Sable stepped into it. The whole stage lay before her, looking oddly stretched from the side, and she sat, leaning against one of the crates. The dwarf appeared on stage alarmingly close to her from a slit in the backdrop, looking taller than she'd ever seen him. His face paint was bright, and everything from his leather warrior costume to his short-trimmed russet beard stood out in sharp detail. When he called out his battle cry, Sable knew it was the same dwarf from other years.

He wasn't much like Pete, or any of the few dwarves she'd seen in Immusmala. There was a gruffness about the actor, but none of the menace.

Sable sank back against the crate, hugging her knees to her chest. Hidden in the shadows, she let herself be carried away by the story.

Epophus declared his farewell to Demonda, but instead of ducking backstage as usual, he jumped down into the space where Sable sat.

She sucked in a breath and pulled her legs in tighter.

After the brightness of the stage, the man felt blindly along the tops of the crates across from Sable and cursed quietly.

"The wine bottle is to your left," she whispered.

The man's hand stopped, and he turned toward her, peering into the shadows. This close, she could see wrinkles around his mouth and creases around his eyes. He was considerably older than she'd expected, easily old enough to be her father.

"Unless you're looking for the hammer to fight off Demonda," Sable continued, keeping her voice low. "That is farther to your right."

The man let out a short, quiet laugh and reached for the wine. "Tempting," he murmured. He took a long drink, then rubbed the back of his neck. "You didn't sneak a nicer actress into these shadows, did you?"

"Sorry."

He emptied the bottle. "How about more leeswine?"

Sable gave a little laugh. "No."

"What good is sneaking into places you're not supposed to be if you don't bring useful things?"

"I was sneaking more for myself than for you. I wanted to see the greatest Epophus in history defend his love and vanquish the evil dwarf."

The man gave a small smile. "Flattery is nearly as good as wine."

Demonda strode across the stage, fiercely declaring her love for Epophus. The man sighed.

"You could use the hammer on yourself," Sable offered.

"That is getting more appealing by the moment." He set the empty bottle back on the crates and rolled his neck again.

"Good luck," Sable whispered.

"Thanks, sneaky woman in the shadows."

He climbed back on stage, looking young and heroic again, and swept his lady love up in an embrace, promising her rides on his flying horse if she'd run away with him. The rest of the play, despite Demonda's imperious acting, was entertaining.

Finally, the story reached its bittersweet end. The flying horse was lost, Epophus had sacrificed himself, and Demonda lay weeping on his still body. Into the silence, an older man entered the stage to address the crowd.

Sable leaned forward.

"Bells of truth ring like cries in the night," he called out. "If only the world would listen."

It was Atticus, his hair rolling around his head in white waves, beard hanging down his chest, trimmed but not tamed. Silver threads edged his black doublet, glittering in the torchlight.

As always, he looked like a man who'd stepped out of a different part of history. Someone who'd seen more of the world than Sable could imagine.

"How can what lies firmly in the past still be fixed so deeply in us?" Atticus's lines rolled over the crowd, the speech familiar and warm. "How can we still hear the cries of the bell that has long since faded? How, when our eyes should be able to see clearly, are we still blinded by yesteryear's fog?"

Sable closed her eyes to feel his voice, rich and warm, not pressing so much as wrapping around her. Whenever Atticus spoke, there was truth in his words, and after Renwen, Kiva, and the rest of this day, she craved the feel of heartfelt truth. The actors of the Figment of Wits troupe were always entertaining, but Atticus was the one who drew her back year after year.

"Hardships and trouble will find us, but the real tragedy..." Atticus paused.

She opened her eyes to see how he'd brightened. Every detail stood out in perfect relief, as though the lanterns had focused all their light directly on him.

"Lies in a life imprisoned by itself," Sable whispered.

Atticus's voice lowered to a somber note. "...lies in a life imprisoned by itself. The darkest parts of the human soul crave the shadows, wrapping around itself to hide, grinding itself to pieces."

He turned to look at Epophus and Demonda lying still on the stage. "Human hope is found in its great fear, breaking down the wall and letting in another soul. The light from a kindred spirit can't heal the brokenness, but it pours into the weakened soul the strength to stand again."

"And that is where the deep goodness lies," Sable whispered.

"And that is where the deep goodness lies." Atticus knelt and placed his hand on Epophus's head. "Not in life or in death, but in love that redeems the broken, transforming the common, human soul into a stunning being of light and wonder."

He bowed his head, and Sable stared at him, a stunning being of light and wonder himself. If other people could only see and feel truth the way she could, Atticus would be the most famous man in the world.

The audience waited in silence.

"Bells of truth ring like cries in the night..." His soft words spread through the quiet. "If only the world would listen."

The words hung in the air for a breath before the crowd broke into applause. Sable closed her eyes, feeling the last of Atticus's words fade into the night.

When she looked again, he had faded into a regular man, illuminated by a few torches on the stage. The other actors joined Atticus, bowing in turn, while people tossed coins into the tall, ceramic jug at the front of the stage.

"The Duke's Figment of Wits troupe," Atticus called over the noise of the plaza, "will take a short break, but the story of *Terrelus* will begin as soon as it is fully dark. Go only far enough to find your friends and bring them back!"

With a final set of bows, the actors left the stage.

Sable glanced up at the sky. Only the western edge was still light. She couldn't see the full moon past the Grand Priories yet, but it must be rising.

She should head to Renwen's, but she lingered. The dwarf and the dark-haired actor came back, hanging a different curtain across the back of the stage. Flashes of blue and silver flickered in the lantern light, and even though she knew they were just bits of painted metal, it took her back to that first morning she'd seen Atticus.

She and her sisters had barely arrived in the city, and she'd hidden in a warehouse to escape a brewing gang fight in the alley. But she'd caught sight of a glitter of fairy light. Glints of red, gold, and blue. She'd stayed in the shadows, enthralled, listening to Atticus and his troupe practice *Terrelus*.

The dark-haired man played a ridiculous constable in the play, and his performance was funny enough it almost made her like constables.

But as much as she wanted to see the play again, it was getting late. Renwen would surely have left for the festival by now.

She started to stand, but Atticus stepped back on stage, tearing a chunk of bread off a small loaf, his face illuminated in the torchlight. The bread reminded her she hadn't eaten in hours.

She waited for him to walk away, but he stood still, looking toward the Dragon Priory with an unreadable expression on his face. He let out a sigh that sounded partly mournful, partly resigned.

Without looking at her, he asked, "Did you enjoy the show, little shadow?"

CHAPTER FIVE

SABLE FROZE, leaning against the crate.

When she didn't answer, Atticus walked over and set a lantern down on the side of the stage. She blinked at the bright light while he sat on the edge.

"We hang these curtains," Atticus continued, running his fingers along the fabric, keeping his voice mild, "so the audience stays in front of them. A good amount of planning goes into what the crowd will see. When you creep into the side, you throw all of that off."

Sable gave him what she hoped was a disarming smile. "I thought it was perfect."

When he spoke again, he sounded pleased. "Are you hungry?"

Sable glanced at the bread. "How did you know I was here?"

"Nothing happens around my stage that I don't know about." He ripped the bread in half and tossed one piece to Sable.

It was so soft her fingers sank into it. "Thank you." She took a bite. It was spongy and rich, with a hint of honey.

She'd never been this close to Atticus. His wavy, white hair curled around his head like a mane, and his equally white beard lay in neat waves down his chest. Even close up, he looked as though he'd stepped out of a story.

"So you enjoyed the show?" he asked. "Even from over here?"

Sable nodded. "Epophus was excellent. He doesn't usually settle into his roles until the second day of shows."

Atticus straightened at her words. "You are a fan, aren't you?"

"But tonight he was wonderful...Despite Demonda."

He laughed, a rich, deep sound. "How many times have you seen us perform?"

"This is the ninth summer." Sable pulled off another piece of bread. "Why do you always open with the same plays?"

"It gets me comfortable."

"You're not already comfortable on stage?"

"It's not being on the stage. It's the fact the stage is in this plaza." His voice, as it so often did, held the warm richness of truth. "This city is a complex place. Sometimes I need time to settle."

Sable took a bite and glanced at the glimmering tree on the far side of the stage. "How does the tree glow?"

He leaned toward her. "Magic."

She almost laughed, until she realized he had spoken the truth.

"What was your favorite part of the performance?" he asked, not giving her time to question him more.

The answer was out of her mouth before she'd even thought about it. "When Epophus says, *There is no longer a pathway home.*"

"Ahh..." Atticus nodded. "A lover of the tragic."

"I don't think it's tragic. It's hopeful." Sable closed her eyes. "*So I take my feet and turn them toward the newly risen sun, for what use is there in dwelling in the shadows when light beckons? Though the darkness covers all I once loved, and though I love it still, my feet shall lead me on, and my heart shall one day follow. And one morn, I shall see the light for what it is.*" She paused. It was hard to stop the words once they'd started rolling.

Atticus was silent for a moment, his eyes narrowed. "Where did you learn that?" His voice was sharper than before.

Sable laughed. "From Epophus."

"That is the newest version. Tonight is the first time we've performed it."

"It was the first time I'd heard it with those words. I like it better than the old version. It has a smoother flow."

His brows drew together. "Is it always this easy for you to memorize words?"

Sable took another bite of the bread and shrugged. "If they have a rhythm. I can never remember the words to some plays, like *Ceren's Lament*. Those are just words, and while they sound familiar, they're more like talking than...whatever Epophus does."

"I agree. Ceren's lines are difficult to memorize." He paused. "How much of Epophus could you recite?"

Sable shrugged. "I've never tried."

"But if you did?"

"I doubt I could do it perfectly. But I could get most of the lines right."

He considered her for a long moment. "My name is Atticus."

She laughed. "I know. I'm Sable."

"Nice to meet you, Sable." He glanced at her tunic. "What do you do when you aren't hiding where the shadows fall at the side of my stage? Work as a courier?"

"No." It was surprisingly easy to talk to Atticus. How long had it been since someone asked her anything about her life? She had the fleeting urge to tell him everything—Kiva, Talia, Renwen. Everything.

Instead, she settled with, "I do a lot of different things."

He considered her words. "Do you like the things you do?"

"No." The answer came quickly enough that he raised an eyebrow. "But it pays for my food and room."

Atticus put the last piece of bread into his mouth and chewed slowly. "Have you ever thought of being something more?"

The question caught her off guard. "Like what?"

"An actress."

She snorted. "I can't say that I have."

"With a memory like yours, you'd have no problem learning lines. And that's the hardest part."

"No, thanks." She glanced up at the darkening sky. "Thank you for the bread. It was delicious. And thank you for letting me watch. It was nice to step into a different world than my own for a time." She stood.

He held out a hand to stop her. "I need a second lady."

She paused at the odd phrase. He looked so earnest she couldn't hold back a smile. "Most men are content with one. At least one at a time."

He gave a huff of laughter. "My acting troupe needs a second lady —the actress who plays the supporting roles to the first lady."

"What happened to your last one? Did you lose her?"

Atticus gave a small sigh. "No. I promoted her. I lost my first lady to a guard with…" He got a dreamy look on his face and pitched his voice higher. "*An exquisite chin.*" His face fell back into an expression of annoyance.

Sable smiled. "Not much you can do against a chin. Especially an exquisite one."

"So I've learned. I had to promote Lady Merilee to first lady." His voice was carefully neutral. "Now I'm short one actress. There are only a few plays Merilee knows the first lady's lines for, and almost every one of them needs a second actress."

"I'd venture to say what you really need is a new first lady. I'm sure your Lady Merilee is a lovely person, but she almost destroyed your show." Sable brushed off her pants. "If I run across any second ladies, I'll send them your way."

"I only need you to act for a week." His voice held a pleading tone. "I didn't think I could find anyone who could learn the lines quickly enough for such a short time." He leaned forward. "But you could."

Sable started to shake her head, but he hurried to continue. "We're leaving Immusmala and visiting towns along the coast."

His words made her pause.

"We'll perform in Folhaven and Molas. Most of the other towns on this trip are so small that you won't have heard of them, and most people from Immusmala wouldn't care about them if they had. They'll be easy shows with minimal lines on your part. I will pay you three silver for the six shows."

Sable raised an eyebrow. Three silver for a week's work?

"And you'll get to travel all the way to the Eastern Reaches."

The idea caught at her. The Reaches…

Seeing her interest, he continued. "After the first week, we'll pick up my real first lady, then Merilee can go back to second lady, and your job will be done. We'll spend two weeks practicing in a town near the Nidel Woods, where we will perfect our masterpiece for the Midsommer tourney. After that, we'll travel back here to compete. We'll be gone a month."

A whole month. She shook her head again, but Atticus charged forward.

"If you decide you like acting, you can audition against Merilee to be second lady in the tourney play. I'll pay you three more silvers if you perform with us on the way back." His voice held a tinge of desperation. "And if we win the tourney, the second lady's portion of the winnings is thirty silver."

Her eyes widened. *Thirty silver*? The words were warm with the truth, and Atticus's face was earnest, but the whole conversation raised more objections than she could voice. She settled for the most obvious.

"You don't know if I can act."

"Acting can be taught."

"Then someone could teach Merilee," Sable pointed out.

Atticus laughed. "Acting can only be taught if the student is willing." He leaned forward. "Maybe it wasn't coincidence that led you to hide where the shadows fall at the side of my stage. Come back tomorrow during the day. We can try out a few scenes. Someone with your memory..." He looked at her with so much intensity she almost backed away. "I have a place for you. And, trust me, you want it." His voice dropped to a conspiratorial whisper and pointed to the front of the stage where the red ribbon hung. "We've already won our spot as one of the three troupes competing in the Midsommer tourney. And this year, we're going to win."

She raised an eyebrow. "Like you've done the last nine years?"

He grinned. "This time, I have the perfect play, and in a week, I'll have the perfect actress. Come be a part of it."

Sable shook her head. "You know nothing about me."

"I am good at reading people." He smiled. "Have you ever traveled along the Tremmen Hills?"

The words tugged at something deep inside Sable.

Her refusal stuck in her throat. Atticus was leaving the city. A longing for the freedom it offered surged through her, but she shook her head. "I can't leave for a month. I have…responsibilities."

Atticus's lips tightened, but he nodded. "If you change your mind, Sable, you know where to find us."

She looked across the dark stage, her gaze lingering on the glowing tree. How far would it travel? What sort of people and places would the fairy lights see? What would it feel like to be outside Immusmala? To have a life not tied down to one dingy room under the thumb of a gang boss?

She shook her head. She couldn't leave the city. Not without Talia.

"Thank you for the bread," she said quietly.

Before he could say anything else, she ducked around the corner of the stage, heading across the plaza to the city. It was time to go to Lord Renwen's house for a more realistic chance at freedom.

CHAPTER SIX

SABLE LEFT her worn boots in the cool grass alongside Renwen's house, along with her socks that had been darned so often they were barely foot-shaped. The stones of his house were perfectly regular with deep, clean seams, and her fingers and toes found holds almost effortlessly. She sat in his open office window, brushing off her fingers and toes. Leaving chalky footprints from the window to his secret closet would ruin everything.

A bright streak of moonlight shone through the branches of the tree outside, filling the room with patches of silvery light. She slipped in, carefully crawling over a small table at the window, trying to ignore the silver dish sitting on it that she couldn't take. She focused on the bookshelf across the room and her plan. But her bare feet sank into the thick rug on the floor, and she stopped, wiggling her toes deeper into the softness. Forget stealing silver dishes, she should steal this rug.

She crossed the room and pulled on the statue of Amah. The shelf swung open soundlessly. It took a moment in the dark closet to find one ledger on a shelf to her left. After a few moments of feeling behind boxes, she found the second. She carried them both to the table by the window and unrolled them.

The first book held entry after entry of merchant payments to the

Guild, charges for services, and account balances. The second, though, was better.

Next to entries identical to the first ledger, there was a second line of numbers showing slightly different values. These were added up and labeled in code.

From just the first page, it looked like Renwen and someone named Lord Panto had taken nearly a hundred silver from the Guild, whether from shorting their payments or exaggerating their expenses.

This was better than she'd hoped. There were records for at least two dozen of the city's most prominent merchants listed here.

This was worth a fortune.

She closed the books, her hands shaking slightly, and put the official ledger back where it belonged.

Time to cover her tracks. She opened the jewelry box.

"Sweet Amah," she whispered. Neat line of gems and silver glittered in the moonlight. A thin ring, shining with a warm, golden hue, lay off to one side. Sable ran her fingers over the rare metal.

The necklace she was looking for lay in a tray by itself, and she picked it up. The pendant wasn't a star, but a small flower. Very small. And too light to be real silver.

Lord Renwen must have been a different sort of man when he gave his late wife a necklace like this. She hesitated, until a glance at the rest of the treasure crushed the growing sympathy for him.

Sable tucked the necklace into her pocket and smiled grimly. Let Renwen think Lady Ingred had taken the necklace and his secret ledger.

Sable paused before closing the jewelry box, tempted by the neat piles of coins along one edge. But they were neatly stacked, so Renwen would notice those missing. Besides, Ingred would never bother stealing a handful of coins.

Out of curiosity, Sable slid open a drawer in the front of the box. In the dim moonlight, she could see a glitter of rings and gems, tangled together and disorganized. Sable stared at the riches for a moment. It was so jumbled, maybe Renwen didn't know what was in here. She rummaged around until she found three average-sized rings that looked alike. The absence of one would be easy to overlook, right?

She tucked one into her pocket. It was a full moon tonight, after all. And it would be nice to have something for the small abbey. She ran her hands over the gems. A handful would buy her and Talia a life beyond anything they'd ever imagined.

She pushed the drawer closed before she could take anything else. One indistinguishable ring she might get away with. A handful was too much.

The climb down from his window was as easy as descending a ladder, even with the ledger tucked beneath her arm. She pulled back on her boots and worn socks, which felt rougher than ever after Renwen's rug, and walked quickly back to Dockside, holding the book gently and trying to rein in the hope that kept rising in her. The theft had been the easy part. There was still an uncertain, fairly dangerous conversation with Kiva to navigate.

When she reached the upstairs hall in the Broken Mast tavern, she stopped at the frowning form of Boone.

Kiva's outraged voice cut through the air from the next room.

"See?" Boone whispered. "He's livid."

There was a crash, and Boone tensed.

Sable's hand tightened around the ledger she'd been ordered not to touch. "I'll come back," she whispered, taking a step backwards.

"Sable's here," Boone announced over his shoulder.

She glared at the huge man.

"You had better have an explanation for being so late, Sable," Kiva's voice snapped into the hall. "Or, by Amah's horns, I will have you flayed and your body hung from the docks."

Sable winced, then smoothed it into a smile before stepping up to the door. "Amah doesn't have horns."

Kiva stood behind his desk, hands braced against it, his face thunderous. Pete leaned back in his corner, his stocky frame drawn in as though he'd like to disappear through the wall. A broken tankard lay on the floor, ale dripping down the wall. Sable stepped in warily.

Kiva's glare caught on the ledger. "That cannot be what I think it is." Sable froze at the dangerous tone of his voice. "Not when I specifically told you to take nothing from Renwen's office." There was a lethal bite to every word.

"It's not what you think," she assured him. She almost didn't say the next words. But if she gave up control of the conversation now, she'd never get it back.

"I want my debt cleared." She held up the ledger. "I want out."

She waited for him to laugh at her audacity, but Kiva merely stared at her, his expression growing colder.

"You blatantly disobey me," he began in a soft voice, "then expect a reward?" He reached into a wide basket on his desk and pulled out his thin, green snake, letting it slither between his fingers. "Give me a reason why I shouldn't let Vaya bite you right now."

The green scales of Kiva's snake glinted in the lantern light. Emotionless, reptilian eyes fixed on her, and Sable forced herself not to shift. "You know I always get you what you want."

"Which is the reason you're still alive." He lowered himself into his chair.

"According to your records," she began, sitting on the front edge of the chair, "I owe you sixty-eight mons, three nummi,"

"Renwen's ledger—even if it were obtained in a way I approved— isn't worth more than twenty."

That was a blatant lie, but she let it go. "I learned three things tonight that you want to know. First, the rumors of Renwen and Lady Ingred are true." She waited for a sign of interest, but Kiva's expression didn't change. "Second, Lord Trelles is coming tomorrow to evaluate Renwen's ledger because he's keeping books for the entire Merchant Guild."

Kiva's didn't react to that either, confirming he had known what the ledger was supposed to hold.

She leaned forward and opened the book. "But most importantly, Renwen has a second, secret ledger showing how over a dozen merchants are skimming money off their payments to the Guild."

Kiva stared at her for a moment before leaning forward and running his finger down the line of numbers.

Sable left her fingers on the corner of the book while he studied it, unwilling to release it yet. Her palms felt damp, but at least her hands weren't trembling. When he looked up, his face held a greedy edge, but he fixed Sable with a calculating look. "So you stole the one thing he values more than his official ledger." He shook his head. "He's not going to let this go without a very big fight."

"Luckily for us, that fight is going to be directed at Lady Ingred."

Kiva's eyes narrowed. "How can you be sure?"

Sable smiled. "Because I disobeyed you enough to take two things from Renwen's office."

A dangerous glint flashed in his eyes as she reached into her pocket for the silver necklace. Her finger bumped something else and she froze—the ring.

Sweet Amah, she'd taken three things.

Pushing the ring to the side, she pulled out the necklace. "Lady Ingred came to visit Renwen today and wanted this. He refused her. She was...put out."

Kiva took the necklace and studied it. "What would Lady Ingred want with something this worthless?"

"It belonged to Renwen's late wife. I think Ingred only wanted it because he wasn't interested in giving it up. He did give her a key to his house, though." Kiva raised an eyebrow. "And they discussed two things. How much she wants that necklace, and how much her father wants to see his ledger." Sable gave him a tight smile. "So when Renwen discovers the necklace gone, along with his secret ledger..."

Kiva set the necklace down and leaned back in his chair, a hint of a smile curling up the corner of his mouth. The expression was predatory. "He'll blame the one person he can't accuse of stealing from him. Lord Trelles' spoiled daughter."

"And he'll be convinced Trelles has his ledger."

"This might ruin Renwen," Kiva mused. His smile widened. "You are a treasure, Sable."

She left her own smile on her face, hoping it hid her lack of enthusiasm for the sentiment. "I want my debt cleared."

His smile faded as he considered her.

Sable forced herself to hold his gaze. "I want out of the gang, free and clear."

His eyes grew cold, colder maybe than she'd ever seen them. He didn't move for a long moment, and the seat of the chair felt hard beneath her.

She'd overstepped. She could feel the conversation slipping away. She'd played this wrong. Or maybe whatever had angered Kiva earlier had doomed her from the beginning. She should have asked for something different. Something smaller.

Slowly, Kiva nodded. "This is worth sixty-eight mons."

His words had the warmth of truth.

"And three nummi," she pressed, barely believing him.

He shrugged and nodded, as though it was a little thing. Pulling his own ledger out of his desk, he opened it. "You can even keep the necklace. It's not worth the effort to sell."

Sable picked it up and clenched it in her hand, watching him flip to the page with her long column of numbers and zero it out. She let out a frayed breath.

It was done.

Paid.

She sank back, searching his face for some trick. Kiva always wanted something. Always had some sort of leverage.

But the ledger was clear.

She was free.

Sable stuffed the necklace into her pocket. "Goodbye, Kiva." She stood, feeling oddly light.

The displeasure she'd expected didn't come. Kiva leaned back in his chair and tapped his quill on the desk, an amused smile twisting his features. "Where will you go?"

She stepped toward the door. "Away."

His expression didn't change. "I'm surprised you'd leave your sister."

"Talia's coming with me." Sable stabbed her finger toward the ledger. "That balance was for both of us. Everything from that scarf at the beginning, to food, to paying you for the sad excuse of a room. I have more than paid you back."

"For this, yes."

She stopped at the words.

"As tonight proved, your ability to read is invaluable. I have so few people who can." Kiva watched her closely, and Sable searched for some point to his words. "Like your sister."

A new coldness gripped her.

"That's the reason I granted her request, you know." Kiva turned to a page further back in his ledger, and turned the book toward her.

Sable stared at Talia's name at the top of a new stack of numbers. "One hundred and fourteen silver?" she whispered.

Kiva left the book open with the impossible sum. "There's something you forgot to tell me about Lady Ingred. She's in need of a secretary."

Sable stared at him. "What does that matter?"

"I happen to have influence over who would be hired, and Talia has asked for the job."

The enormous sum on the ledger rooted Sable's feet to the floor. "What job?"

"Lady Ingred's secretary." Kiva cocked his head to the side. "You're usually quicker than this, Sable." He gave her a lazy smile. "Talia is the newest member of my jays."

CHAPTER SEVEN

"The chance to have someone that high in the Trelles household…"
Kiva shook his head. "I've been waiting for this for a long time. It's
brilliant. And it was all Talia's idea."

"A jay?" Sable's hand clenched into fists. "Talia has no skills to spy
on anyone!"

"She can read, is a pretty little thing, is good at painting faces, and
helped Britta with some fashion choices tonight. She'll work wonderfully with Lady Ingred."

Sable stared at him. Three jays had been hanged this spring. And
those were the ones she'd heard about.

She leaned her hands on the desk, fixing him with a furious look.
The snake snapped its attention to her, but she ignored it. "We had an
agreement." The words were low and ragged. "I give you everything,
and you leave Talia alone."

"Which I have always abided by," Kiva answered calmly. "But
when she came to me, asking for a job, how could I refuse? Surely you
wouldn't want your sister to stay unhappy in the bakery. Did you
know she was under the impression she had to stay at that job? And in
that tiny room?"

"Talia will not be part of this." Sable flung her arm out at the tavern. The snake coiled back and hissed. "Any of this."

"She began earlier tonight, Sable. A new room in the Nest, new clothes. She has a certain level of fashion to maintain if she's going to be seen with Lady Ingred."

The Nest? He expected Talia to live with the most powerful members of the Vayas? A wave of fury rolled over her.

Sable crossed her arms. "No."

Kiva shrugged and closed the book. "It's already done."

He pulled another paper out of the drawer of his desk, but his voice had felt warm this entire time. She didn't need to see the contract containing Talia's wide, flowing signature at the bottom to believe him.

"She's already begun the training process. It'll take a couple days to get things sorted and get her placed in the household, then she'll live with Lady Ingred in order to be available to her constantly."

Everything in Sable railed against the idea. "You won't get someone as untrained as Talia hired into a position like that!"

Kiva leaned forward. "I could get her placed in any merchant's house in the city."

Sable shook her head. "Talia is leaving with me."

"If she leaves, she'll breach her contract. And if she breaks her contract, I'll have to send out the Fangs." Kiva tilted his head. "Do you think Talia could get away?"

Sable's jaw clenched. Talia wouldn't escape Kiva's well-paid, well-connected, well-trained band of killers. Nowhere in the city would be safe. The few times anyone tried to leave Kiva without paying their debt, the Fangs made a messy example out of them.

But Talia wouldn't be any safer working as a jay.

Sable pointed at the ledger. "She'll never last long enough to be able to pay that off."

"If she's smart, she can work it off in ten years."

Sable clenched her jaw before she called him a liar.

"Or…" The smug smile he'd been fixing her with faltered, and she caught a glimpse of a hungry look. "I have a job for you."

She drew back. "You think I'm going to work for you? After this?"

"To free your sister, yes."

"Then what? You'll have another job, and another?"

He leaned forward, his face fierce, feral. "No. One job only."

His look cut through the fury clouding everything in her mind, and she cut off her sharp response. The conversation had just shifted slightly, Kiva's control showing the slightest crack.

She forced herself to study him. This job was what Kiva wanted.

This entire conversation had been leading here. It wasn't just greed in his eyes, it was something more jagged.

Whatever Kiva wanted, he wanted it desperately.

"It was enlightening meeting Prioress Eugessa today." The warmth of the truth in his words squeezed around Sable. "She has a ring."

She watched him warily. "Eugessa has a lot of rings."

"But only one is shaped like a butterfly with blue stones." His face brightened, standing out sharply against the rest of the room. "I want it."

Sable tried to remember Prioress Eugessa's chubby fingers waving from the litter. She'd worn a dozen rings. "Why?"

Kiva gave her a flat smile. "I like blue butterflies." That was a cold lie. Until he spoke again. "You bring me that ring, you *and* your sister are free to leave."

That was the truth. Warm, bright, vibrant truth.

She had more questions than she could sort through, so she settled for the most obvious. "Why me?"

"The same reason you're always so valuable to me. You're resourceful and you can read. The good prioress has very distinct ideas of what Amah's blessing looks like. Did you know she will not allow anyone in her priory—not even couriers—unless they can read? She says an education is a sign of Amah's pleasure."

Sable stared at him for a moment. "You're planning to get me into the Priory of the Horn as a courier?"

He leaned back. "I don't have a plan."

"So you want me to figure out a way into the priory, which is guarded with not just more Sanctus guards than anywhere else in the city, but also with magic? Then locate and steal a piece of jewelry from the second most powerful woman in Immusmala?"

"Unless you think you can pull it off her fat fingers in broad daylight."

"She's surrounded by Sanctus guards at all times."

"As you've proven time and again…" He gestured to Renwen's ledger, "you're a capable woman."

"You can't be serious."

"You have two days."

She sank down into the chair. "Impossible."

Kiva smiled grimly. "After the festival is over, the Veil Gate will be closed to the public and the prioress will leave the city to tend her beloved sheep to the north. So you have until the day after tomorrow; otherwise, you'll have to wait until the Midsommer Festival in a month."

Sable stared at him. "You can't possibly expect me to do this."

"Under the circumstances…" The smile fell from his face. "You should fall at my feet, thanking me for another chance."

The truth in his words was so strong that everything about him grew more vivid. She searched his face for a clue as to what he was talking about.

He nodded toward Pete. The dwarf stumped forward and dropped a pouch onto Kiva's desk. The coins inside it clinked.

Sweet Amah. The coins from under her floorboard.

Her hand twitched toward it.

"You've been keeping things from me, Sable." Kiva's voice was low and dangerous.

A cold fear gripped her. Her denial died on her lips. "You searched my room?"

"*My* room," Kiva reminded her. "I allow you to live there. Pete and Boone had their suspicions you had stolen something from Lord Renwen that you weren't supposed to." He looked at Renwen's ledger again. "Apparently with good reason."

Pete and Boone had been in her room—had Talia been there? "The money's mine. Talia knew nothing about it."

"Oh, I know." Kiva smiled. "I'm not sure whether she's more upset about the horrible room you've kept her in for ten years or the money you hid from her." He ran his finger over the snake's scales. "But little sister is furious."

Sable dropped her gaze to the pouch. Talia would be furious. But Kiva had fallen silent, and any thoughts about Talia were overshadowed by the dread of what he would say next.

No one hid things from Kiva.

"I thought our agreement was clear," he continued coldly. "You bring me everything you get, and I generously take care of you and your sister."

Her mind raced. There was no way out of this.

She'd have to run.

The fastest way out of Dockside was straight up the avenue, but she'd never outrun the Fangs. They'd be waiting downstairs in the tavern. Maybe right outside the door. Her hands clenched into fists on her lap.

Kiva's hand closed over the pouch and he dropped it into a drawer with a small clink.

The sound tore out the small hope those coins had held for so long. Ten years of sneaking scraps, gone. And now he would… What? Kill her? Her eyes stayed fixed on the spot on the desk where the money had been.

"I'll take this as the first payment against Talia's loan."

She looked up sharply.

"You thought I'd have you killed?" He studied her. "I considered it." The smallest smile curled up the edges of his mouth. "I'm still considering it. But you've been profitable for me over the years, Sable, so I'm giving you one chance to redeem yourself."

She knew the words were a lie without having to feel them. Kiva never gave second chances.

But the edge of hunger was back in his face. This had nothing to do with redeeming herself.

She studied him, her fear tempered slightly by the truth of the situation. "You really want that ring."

His face grew bleak. "I do." He leaned forward. "So use that cleverness of yours to get it for me in the next two days, or figure out a way to outrun my Fangs."

CHAPTER EIGHT

SABLE WOVE through the buildings of Dockside, which crowded around her like filthy, towering walls. Above her, she could only see a slice of the dark sky and a handful of stars.

Her money was gone and Kiva had set her on an impossible task. But now that she was out of his office, those felt like slaps compared to the real blow.

Talia had joined the jays.

She started toward her room. There had to be a way to stop this.

When she reached her own building, the window was dark.

She rushed up the stairs and pushed open the thin door. "Talia?"

Moonlight spilled into the room, and she froze. It wasn't the empty bed or Talia's missing clothes that stopped her.

It was the walls.

The drawings were destroyed, wiped off with long, wet strokes. The charcoal scenes reduced to streaks of grey that bled out in long, black drips.

Sable gripped the doorframe. Her clothes were tossed in a corner, the blanket yanked off her bed, the gaping hole in the floor was black and empty.

She sank to her knees. The hope she'd had earlier was gone,

leaving her empty. Talia couldn't be a jay. Sable would find her and explain everything. Then Talia would come back.

The plan sounded ridiculous, even in her own mind. Talia had a contract and a debt. She'd already moved into the Nest.

Sable shoved herself up and hurried down to the alley. She ran back through the dark streets until she reached the Nest. The three-story building was lined with windows, each topped with a wide block of stone like heavy, disapproving brows. All the jays had rooms there, even those who spent most of the time in powerful houses. But the Nest was dark.

She stared at the building for a moment, catching her breath. Of course no one was here. The festival had started and Talia would be there. Everyone would be there.

Breathing heavily, she started uphill. She gripped the ring in her pocket. She'd taken it for the small abbey, but maybe she should keep it. Use it to start a new life with Talia. Except there was nowhere in the city Kiva wouldn't find them. And without the ring, she'd have nothing to give the small abbey.

The full moon hug unruffled in the sky. Sable tried to pull some of its tranquility into herself. This was the one night each month she could atone for what she'd done. She couldn't neglect that, couldn't add that to the misery of the day.

When she joined the Spine, it was crowded with people. A monstrous mask leaned out of the crowd and leered at her, and she shied away from it.

The Veil Wall came into view above the heads in front of her, and she lengthened her stride, desperate for the wide, clean air of the Sanctuary. But when she squeezed through the gate, shoulder to shoulder with the rest of the city, the air was just as close and warm in the plaza as it had been on the street.

Sable weaved through the crowd, looking for long hair and the right face. But there were too many people moving in too many directions. Music mixed with laughter and voices in a dizzying din.

Shrieks from behind made her spin.

A black-hooded figure, his face shrouded in a red veil, stood a head above the rest of the crowd. The baledin reached out in her direction, looming toward her. She shoved through the crowd to get away, her heart pounding, finding herself facing the long, yellow shape of a Kalesh dragon.

There was no way she was going to find Talia in the constantly shifting crowd, but she kept searching numbly until a familiar voice caught her attention.

"The old stories are always timely," Atticus called.

He stood on the stage with the glowing green tree, his voice like honey, always flowing with a warmth that wrapped around her. The broken feeling inside her craved the feel of it, and she walked closer.

"The old stories remind us," he continued, "that our enemies may be less evil than we pretend."

Sable snorted at the idea.

"And those we love, more complex."

The truth of that part hurt deeply.

"When we consider—"

The long, low toll of a bell rolled over the crowd, and Atticus paused. A ripple went through the plaza as every face turned toward the Veil Gate.

"Behold!" Atticus said with a devout voice. "Our Holy Mothers!" The words sounded like a proclamation, but unlike his lines from moments ago, his voice had a complexity to it that Sable couldn't quite sort out.

White horses pulled a wagon into the plaza, carrying a dozen bells of different sizes and four white-robed women. The shimmering silver that edged their gowns marked them as Mira.

The wagon was encircled by Sanctus guards, the Sanctuary's private security force, holding red torches, their dark uniforms making them seem more like bits of the night rather than part of the luminous wagon.

One Mira lifted her hand. The silver at her cuff caught the torch-light, and the air hummed with anticipation. She flicked her fingers in the direction of a large bell, without touching it. A long, low note rolled across the plaza, thrumming in Sable's chest. The other Mira danced their fingers in the air, and the smaller bells sang out lilting notes, flitting over the deeper tones like fairies across a dark pond.

The crowd parted as they crossed the plaza toward the three Grand Priories. Behind them, another wagon rolled through the gate, a tall, throne-like chair perched on it. Eugessa, Grand Prioress of the Horn, waved rounded, heavy arms at the crowd, and a surge of frustration rose in Sable. Eugessa's red curls glowed in the torchlight, and her hands glittered with more rings than Sable could count. One of them might very well be a blue butterfly, but Sable would never reach it past her line of guards. If her freedom depended on that ring, it was never going to happen.

Eugessa's black unicorn walked alongside the wagon, its neck and sides muscled, feet feathered with black hair that swung with each step like black capes. From the center of its head, a thick, black horn grew, glinting darkly in the torchlight.

Long ago, before the city, Kiva, and all the ugliness, Sable's mother had told her stories of unicorns.

But they'd been nothing like this one.

Everyone gave the unicorn a wide birth as it moved through the crowd.

As the next wagon rolled through the gate, Sable gladly turned away from Eugessa.

Moving smoothly into the square, this wagon held no throne. The Grand Prioress of the Phoenix stood in the center of an empty platform. Under a sheer veil, long, white hair hung down her back over her white robe. She looked thin, frail even, and her shoulders hunched forward. But the arm she held out was a steady perch for her own creature—a stunning, flame-colored phoenix. Feathers in hues of red, orange, and yellow cascaded down and swayed slightly with the movement of the wagon.

The prioress murmured something to the bird, and the phoenix stretched its wings and shot high into the air. Tongues of fire lit the edges of its wings and tail. A wake of sparks trailed behind it as it arched over the crowd, gliding in a wide circle around the plaza.

A longing filled Sable at the sight of it. A longing for something she couldn't name. Something she always forgot she was missing until she saw the bird fly.

The Grand Prioress of the Phoenix rolled on, and the people turned back toward the gate.

The peal of the bells stopped, and everyone held their breath. One deep tone rang out from the largest bell, thrumming with hope and wonder.

Through the richness of the sound, something glittered at the gate. The crowd let out an awed murmur as the final wagon glided into the square. The High Prioress stood in the center, wearing the same white robe as the others. Except there was nothing the same about her.

Vivaine had been High Prioress for decades. Through her sheer veil, her skin was smooth, brows set in gentle lines of pity and mercy. Her hair was as white as everything else, her face serene.

Despite her age, she stood tall and straight, raising her hands toward the crowd in gentle blessings. Thick bands of gold glittered around her wrists in warm, rich contrast to all the white. It had been rumored the Merchant Guild had gifted the prioress gold from the new mines, but Sable hadn't imagined so much of it.

The torchlight didn't stain the prioress's robes to a ruddy hue like it did the horses. Instead, she almost glowed with a pure, white light, as though the moon, long lost behind clouds, had draped its light over her. Or, as so many in the city claimed, Amah herself blessed the woman with holy light. Throughout the crowd, heads bowed and hands reached out toward the woman who communed with the goddess on their behalf.

Something shifted around the prioress's feet. Flashes of silver rippled along a sinuous shape.

The dragon.

The creature's face was tucked away on the other side of the wagon, and Sable could only see a long, smooth section of his back. Stretched out, he might be longer than the wagon, but curled around the High Prioress, he seemed small, almost tame. The scales of the creature caught the torchlight and the glimmers of white light that seemed to emanate from the prioress herself, causing shimmers of gold and silver to roll across his body.

The ache of the past years stole Sable's breath. The first time Ryah had seen the High Prioress, she'd wanted to run to her. Sable and Talia had held their little sister back, grasping her chubby hands, trying to explain that no one approached the High Prioress.

When the wagon had reached them, though, the prioress had looked down at Ryah and graced the child with a smile of pure goodness.

"She's a star from heaven," Ryah had whispered.

That had been the start of a dream for Ryah. She'd created her own white robes from discarded fabric, and a little white veil to wear over her face. She'd memorized the prayers of the abbess at the tiny abbey near their hovel and would pray them over Talia and Sable every night.

Over those hard months, Ryah's cheeks had thinned, her hands losing their thickness and shrinking to skin and bones. They'd all thinned, and still Sable had thought she could fix things.

Until Ryah had started coughing.

Until Talia had come home with the cursed orange scarf.

Sable's eyes filled with tears. How had it all gone so wrong? Ten years ago, she had promised her sisters she'd find them a home. A safe one. How had she failed so completely?

The High Prioress moved on through the plaza, and Sable caught sight of the full moon high in the sky. It was past midnight. She glanced toward the crowd again, but there was no way she was going to find Talia here.

And it was a full moon.

Sable headed for the gate, feeling in her pocket. The ring was still there.

The avenue outside the Sanctuary was dotted with people heading home. She glanced behind her, almost expecting Pete and Boone to be trailing her again, and a tendril of fear curled up her neck. She walked quickly down the Spine, nearing the streets that headed down into Dockside, her fear shifting to anger. Kiva did not get to follow her tonight. Not where she was going. He didn't get to taint yet another place.

At a street leading down toward Dockside, she turned and broke into a run, ducking into the first alley. Unlike the well-lit Spine, there were few torches on this road, and she crouched in the shadows, trying to slow her breathing. She gripped the side of a crate next to her, watching.

No one followed.

She rubbed her hands over her face. This day had been too much. She was turning into a paranoid mess.

She started to stand when a man turned off the Spine, pausing for a moment before walking down the hill. With the brightness of the avenue behind him, she couldn't make out his face, but he peered into the dark alleys as he hurried toward Dockside. Sable shrank back into the shadows until he passed.

Maybe she wasn't a paranoid mess.

She waited a few more minutes before heading along an alley that didn't go into Dockside, but paralleled the brightly lit Spine. She made a few more sharp turns, but saw no more signs of being followed.

When the Spine curved to the left and began to weave downhill toward the southern edge of the city, Sable reached the shop with the turtles statues by the door. Why someone had originally put them there, she didn't know, but the building now belonged to a dress-maker, and during the day, the turtles were dressed in the latest hats and shawls.

She turned onto a smaller street that passed quickly out of the wealth of the Spine, and into the dilapidated buildings of the Bend.

Set inside a wide curve in the city's outer wall, the Bend was built into a depression that grew soggy every spring and summer, staying damp all fall and winter. The wood of the buildings rotted at their base, and cobblestones dipped into and out of the mud. Her left boot was permanently darker than the other, thanks to an unfortunate slip into a puddle one night.

The Bend was home to the Muddogs, a gang just as ruthless and vicious as Kiva's Vayas. If she kept to her usual path, hopefully they'd let her be.

She ducked down small, winding alleys, picking her way around the deepest mud puddles until she reached the street that ran along the base of the city wall itself. The wall stood easily five times her height, hiding the moon behind it, leaving the sky above it a smudgy mess of moonlit clouds and darkness. The wall itself was a sheet of black.

In the middle of a block of crumbling buildings, a small abbey sat in a yard of mud. The gate was closed, so Sable climbed over the fence and followed a rough stone path around the side of the abbey, moving to the third window.

It was open to the summer night, the room inside dark. She could barely see the four beds lining the walls. Sable leaned her head into the window. In the gloom, she couldn't make out any details, but she stayed for a long moment, opening her eyes wide, hoping they'd adjust enough for her to see.

She almost never felt the urge to pray. Amah and Isah, if they cared about anyone, seemed to have left Sable to her own devices. But each full moon, at this small abbey that no one of importance ever noticed, the shortest, most heartfelt prayers breathed out of her. There weren't even words. Just a longing, a plea for mercy.

Pushing herself away from the window with a weary sigh, she continued down to the last window. This one was open, as well. Sable pulled the ring out of her pocket and rubbed her finger over the gemstone. She listened at the window and heard quiet breathing.

The abbess here was a far cry from Prioress Eugessa. There were no Mira in tiny abbeys like this one to fill the air with wonder and magic. No Sanctus to guard them from danger. Only one aged woman who cared for the poor, housed the homeless, and fed anyone who showed up at her door. If there was any justice in the world, places like this would have enough money to do all their good works, and Kiva and Eugessa would be begging on the street.

A flicker of defiance rose up in Sable, directed at something she couldn't name. She gently set the ring on the windowsill.

A papery whisper came out of the room. "That didn't sound like coins."

Sable peered in, seeing nothing in the darkness. "Something a bit different tonight, Holy Mother," she whispered. "Take it to someone you trust, and they should pay you well for it."

The abbess was silent for a moment. "Is it ill-gotten?"

Sable let out a small laugh. "Probably many times over." There was a deep rightness in leaving this ring here. As though it were being washed and made new again. "Now you can redeem it for some better purpose."

"You are an angel straight from Amah," the old woman said.

Sable shifted at the words. "I've dealt with too many ill-gotten things to be an angel."

The abbess made a thoughtful sort of hum. "Perhaps you, too, are being redeemed for a better purpose."

In the strange feel of this place, the words sounded as though they might actually be true, and Sable leaned into them. "It's too late for all that, Holy Mother."

"Every full moon, you are generous."

"Every full moon, I make poor amends for all the things I've done, and left undone."

The woman made a noise, although in agreement or dissent, Sable couldn't tell.

"I will pray for you, child. And thank Amah that you live."

Sable's hand tightened on the windowsill, and for the briefest moment she wanted to say…something.

But there was nothing to say. She pushed away from the window.

There was no where to go, except back to her horrible little room in Dockside. Talia wouldn't be there, and Kiva would start a new tally for her rent, but there was no where else to go.

In a place like this, maybe the abbess's words meant something. But in the rest of the world, they were just sounds fading away in the night.

CHAPTER NINE

SABLE'S SLEEP was the same as always, dreams interlaced with shadows and fire, ravens diving through the air, guttural shouts echoing around her, black boots pounding closer.

She jolted awake, the dry taste of smoke lingering on her tongue, her heart pounding hard enough to shake her entire body.

She sat up, shaking off the dream. The room was still dim enough that it took her a moment to make out the ruined pictures on the wall and remember everything from last night. She dropped her head into her hands, running over her options again.

She'd never pay off Talia's debt working for Kiva, but stealing from Prioress Eugessa was impossible. She was too guarded to steal from during the day, and at night her priory was an impenetrable compound.

A third option kept demanding her attention.

Sable could leave the city with Atticus. Head to the Eastern Reaches and see if she could find a place that felt like home.

Except Talia was trapped in the jays.

Sable pushed herself out of bed. She needed to at least talk to her sister. In all the years they'd lived in this horrible little room, Talia had complained about working in the bakery and longed for better things, but she'd never blamed Sable.

The smeared, grey lines on the wall mutely pointed out that this time was different.

She dressed quickly and went to the table to comb her hair, but the comb was gone. As was the brush. All that was left was one small leather hair tie. Sable ran her fingers through the tangles and wove it into something resembling a braid.

Outside, dock workers shambled toward the harbor for the dawn shift. She jogged deep into Dockside and the buildings grew marginally less dilapidated. She reached the Nest, the crumbling ornamentation that used to cover the building visible enough that she could almost imagine what it had been like back when people wanted to live in Dockside.

Above the door, carved into the stone, were the words "Stockford Inn." A dozen windows faced out over the street. Along the sides, more looked up the hill and down toward the sea. Talia would love a room overlooking the water.

She paused. Talia would love everything about living here, and everything about living in Lady Ingred's home.

There was a guard at the front door who looked vaguely familiar. Sable greeted him, and he didn't stop her from walking in. What stopped her was what lay inside.

The walls were bright white plaster, catching the early morning light and giving the room a warm glow. To the left sat a huge, ornate fireplace, a painting of green, rolling hills and the wide, sparkling ocean above it. Velvet chairs in rich colors formed little sitting areas. The furniture was a little worn, but clean. Even the floor beneath Sable's feet was spotless.

At the far side, an opulent staircase rose to a landing, then split and continued up in both directions. The room was empty, except for an older woman sitting at a table near the stairs, doing some needlework and drinking from a delicate cup. Sable smoothed her hands over the front of her tunic, feeling more out of place here than she had in Lord Renwen's room. The woman looked up, and if she noticed anything distasteful about Sable, she hid it behind a proper smile.

"I'm looking for my sister, Talia," Sable began, the words feeling awkward. Did she need a better reason to be here? "She just moved in yesterday. I know it's early, but I was hoping I could see her."

"My name is Beatrice," the older woman said with a formal tone. "I'm the head matron of the Stockford." She gave Sable an expectant look.

Sable stared at her for a moment. "Oh, the Stockford. I've never heard the Nest called that." The woman kept the mild smile fixed on her face, and Sable realized she was waiting for an introduction. "I'm Sable, matron of a very small room at the edge of Dockside..." She paused. "Although if Kiva owns the room, am I still the matron?"

The woman raised one sculpted eyebrow.

"Of course I am. Because Kiva owns this place, and you're the matron. So yes, I'll stick with Sable, matron of a very small room."

Beatrice considered her. "You and Talia resemble each other."

Sable paused, wondering if that reflected poorly on her sister. "We do? She's tall and so..." Sable cast about for the right word, looking around her. "Well, she's like this place. I'm a lot more like 'very small room'."

Beatrice tilted her head toward the wide staircase. "Talia is in room 211." She gave Sable a polite nod and turned back to her needlework.

"Thank you." Sable started up the stairs, trailing her hand on the smooth railing. On the second level, she stepped into a wide hallway, lined with doors, running the length of the building. The floor was smooth under her boots, wood darkened with age and polished with use. The hall was perfectly still, and Sable moved quietly until she found room labeled 211. It must face the back of the Nest, so it was unlikely Talia had a good view. Sable glanced back down the hallway. Talia wouldn't care about the view outside when she had the rest of this place.

The building around her had the same sort of feel her courier disguise always did. Like it was meant for a different sort of person. That no matter how long she wore it, it would never fit.

She stepped up to the door and heard muted voices. Talia was already awake? Sable paused, then knocked quietly.

Talia opened the door and stared at her in surprise for a moment before grabbing her arm and pulling her inside.

"Sable!" Talia's arms wrapped around Sable tightly. "I was going to come find you today! I'm sorry I didn't talk to you last night. It all happened so fast. And..." She pulled back. "I'm sorry about the drawings. I was mad about the money, and Kiva said it had been your choice to stay in that room, but I regretted the pictures as soon as I did it."

"You have every right to be mad." Sable kept her hands on her sister's arms. "I should have told you about all of it. There's so much I should have told you."

The room was long and thin. The walls were white, the window curtains a thick red fabric, and the floor the same polished dark wood as the hall. A bed covered in smooth linens butted up against the wall beside the window, a small desk nestled in the far corner, and a wooden wardrobe stood beside the door. Talia's overly talkative, overly cheerful friend Callie sat on the bed, giving them a wide smile Sable couldn't bring herself to return.

Sable focused back on her sister. "I'm sorry for..." The list was so long she didn't know where to start. And the things she'd planned to say were crowded out by Callie's presence and how different Talia looked. She was clean, her simple nightgown new, her auburn hair combed so smooth it shone. "I should have told you the truth about everything," Sable continued, "but I was trying to protect you and—"

"I don't need to be protected." Talia stepped back.

"I know. But for years, you did. I guess I just never stopped."

Talia sighed in annoyance. "That's what Callie said."

Sable tried not to show her irritation that Callie was involved in this conversation in the first place. "If I could go back and change things, I would."

Her sister's look softened into something more like resignation. "I've always half expected you to have a stash of money somewhere, and it's better that I didn't know about it. I didn't have to pretend to be shocked. Or angry."

Sable winced.

"I know you don't think being Lady Ingred's secretary is a good idea," Talia continued before Sable could answer. She glanced around the room with a look that was half-apologetic, half-hopeful. "But I think I can do it." Talia gave her a familiar smile and the uncomfortable feel of the Nest smoothed a little.

"Are you going to come live here, too?" Callie asked. "You could get out of that horrible little room Kiva gave you."

"And be a jay?" The words came out sharper than Sable expected, and Talia's smile grew more strained. Callie's chatter was irritating on the best of days, but this early in the morning, when Sable had hoped to find Talia alone, it was unbearable. "I have no desire to join in something as dangerous as the jays."

"No jay who's good at their job gets caught," Callie said confidently.

Sable stared at her. "You can't believe something that stupid."

"Sable," Talia said sharply, "be civil."

Sable clamped her mouth shut. This wasn't how she wanted this visit to go. She looked for something positive to say. "This building is amazing." Her tone wasn't exactly warm, but she tried to pull the edge of irritation out of it.

"Isn't it?" Talia's voice was higher than normal. She crossed the room. "Come look out the window."

To the left, the steep slope of Dockside fell away down to the harbor. The nearest buildings were low, so there was an unobstructed view past the city wall to the hills that stretched away along the ocean. The water glittered in the morning sunlight.

"It's beautiful," Sable said. "If you don't look too closely at Dockside."

Talia smiled. "I never do."

Sable couldn't join in Talia's obvious happiness. All she felt was a dull ache.

"I can still go to the Choosing tonight," Talia said brightly.

"I never thought you two cared about the priories," Callie said.

Sable glanced at Talia. "We find it fascinating," Sable said, trying to move the conversation along.

"No, we don't." Talia's face sobered. "Our little sister used to dream of being a prioress."

Callie straightened. "You have a sister? Why have I never met her?"

Sable turned back to the window, not wanting to hear the rest of the story.

Talia let out a ragged breath. "We don't have a sister anymore."

CHAPTER TEN

CALLIE MADE A SYMPATHETIC NOISE, but Sable stayed facing the window.

"Ten years ago, she died of the red fever," Talia said quietly. "Ryah was angelic. She thought the white dresses of the prioresses were the most beautiful things ever. She would listen outside the windows of the little abbey near where we lived and memorize the prayers."

Sable pressed her eyes shut, not wanting to revisit these memories.

"She even built a little altar in the corner of our tiny room and draped this old scrap of fabric over it so she could lead prayer times for us."

"She sounds sweet," Callie said quietly.

Sable heard rustling and turned to see Callie wrap Talia in a hug. She tried to keep her unreasonable irritation off her face.

"She was," Talia told her, dashing her hand across her eyes. She glanced outside. "You'd better get to the bakery."

Callie sighed, and with one last hug, left.

Sable sank down onto Talia's bed, dropping her head into her hands. Her sister was quiet for a moment, before sitting next to her and leaning her head against Sable's shoulder.

"I know you don't want me to do this," Talia said quietly, "but I want me to."

Sable pressed her hands against her head. "This isn't safe, Talia. If anyone finds out you're spying for—"

"And staying in Dockside would be safe?"

Sable looked up. Talia's face was so firm, so assured, that Sable barely recognized it. She reached up to brush a lock of hair back from her sister's face. "That's why we should leave."

Talia pushed Sable's hand away and stood, irritated. "There is no leaving, Sable. That's been your dream for years. Are we any closer?"

"We were—" Sable clamped her mouth shut. *Until you came here.*

"There is nothing better outside of Dockside." Talia paced the room. "If we go to the Bend or to the north side, there's just more of the same. You just need to…" She ran a hand through her hair in frustration.

"I just need to what?" Sable demanded.

"Learn to be happy in the world we live in." Talia crossed her arms. "You've spent so long hating it, so long trying to get away from it, that you haven't bothered to see anything good in it."

"Good?" Sable demanded, standing. "What is good about living in a world where someone else owns us? Kiva regulates our food, tells us where to live, gives us work. And you've moved further under his control! There was a time we were free, Talia."

She drew back, her expression curling into incredulity. "That life is gone, Sable. It burned to the ground with everything else." Talia leaned forward, tears in her eyes, her expression furious. "And nothing you can do will ever get that back. It is *gone.*"

Talia stabbed her finger at the floor. "This is what we have now. This world with these people and these rules. The only thing we can count on is each other. But the longer you hold onto this impossible dream of yours, the less I can count on you. And the less you and I actually get to be together."

Sable stared at her. "I can't stay in this life," she whispered.

Talia clenched her jaw. "But you can't leave." Sable shook her head, but Talia grabbed her hand before she could say anything. "Can we not fight about this today? We can go to the Choosing tonight, and tomorrow, once the festival is over, we can figure out all of this."

There would be nothing to figure out, but Sable nodded. "I'll meet you at the Veil Gate." She walked to the door. Even the festival felt dull.

"Thank you," Talia said quietly.

Sable nodded without turning and left.

Sable stood on one of the stone walls that encircled the trees in the Sanctuary plaza. Prioress Eugessa had been in front of the Priory of the Horn most of the morning, overseeing the long line of tables full of food. Sable watched her, even though she was too far away to see what her individual rings looked like.

On festival days, each priory laid out an enormous spread of breads, cheeses, nuts, and fruits. Behind Sable, the Prioress of the Phoenix walked through the crowd of people at her tables, placing her hand on their heads in blessing, handing out small rolls from a basket on her arm. The phoenix watched from a tall perch against the building. It sat in the shadows, but the reds and oranges of its feathers glowed like coals.

Neither of the other prioresses mingled with the crowd. The High Prioress stood at the top of the wide stairs leading to the Dragon Priory. The platform lay in the shadows, but the prioress was bright, as though a ray of sunlight wrapped around the building just for her. The silver dragon curled around her feet, looking more like a mound of glimmering scales than a live creature.

The only slight Sable had ever heard against the Dragon Prioress was an outlandish tale from her youth when one of the mythical baledin had caught her and killed her handmaiden. An ugly rumor had spread that she'd sacrificed her handmaiden to save herself. While no one really treated the rumor as truth, the story was well-known.

Prioress Eugessa spent the morning sitting on a chair, ornate enough to be a throne. She draped her hand on the unicorn's dark withers, talking quietly to it. Her white robe cascaded over her wide girth, pooling on the ground around her like the frothy edge of a wave.

Occasionally, she descended to offer a prayer for the people at her tables, pausing to bless the wealthy, casting calls of repentance over the poor. Mostly, though, she sat in her throne, occasionally waving her hand at the crowd in something vaguely resembling a benediction. Every time she moved her hand, her rings glinted in the sunlight.

The next time Eugessa started down the steps toward the feasting table, Sable wove her way to the table.

The prioress's copper hair curled in shining rings. Her face, powdered to a pale, chalky white, was fixed in a look of bored benevolence. Her eyelids glittered with a green paint that reminded Sable of the scales of Kiva's snake. Eugessa walked down the far side of the table, reaching her hand toward the people crowded around it, muttering about blessings and unicorns.

"Festive day, Holy Mother," Sable said, giving Eugessa a quick bow when she approached. "Your rings sparkle with the goddess's favor!"

Eugessa let her gaze run over Sable, taking in the plainness of her clothes. A hint of disdain crossed the prioress's face as she held out her hand, the rings glinting on her thick fingers. "Each of these represents a blessing from Amah," Eugessa said, her voice sugary sweet.

On her smallest finger sat a glittering, blue butterfly.

Sable stared at it.

Eugessa's fingers were fat enough that her rings nestled in rolls of skin. There was no way that ring could be slipped off.

"The butterfly is especially lovely," Sable said, trying to see it better.

The wings were silver, set with a handful of blue gems. But they didn't glitter as brightly as the ones in the other rings. They were small and different sizes. A few were cloudy. Sable had to guess, it wasn't worth a tenth of what the other rings were.

"That ring was one of the first gifts I received from Amah," Eugessa said. "A blessing for my hard work and dedication. Back then, I guided the lost in a tiny abbey near the river, but I was dedicated to the goddess's work, and when two poor, dying souls found me, the care and comfort I offered led them to give me all their worldly possessions."

The woman's words had the warmth of truth in them, but there was an oddness there, too. A sharpness. Not a lie exactly. But…something.

The feel of people's words didn't depend on whether something was really true. It only mattered whether they believed it. Prioress Eugessa seemed to believe it and know it was a lie at the same time.

Sable scanned the rest of the rings on the prioress's hand. Every one of them was higher quality than the blue stones on the butterfly.

"You may not be able to tell, but it is not as valuable as these other gifts I've received," Eugessa continued. "However, I wear it as a reminder to myself that the goddess blesses those who please her. When we first begin, our gifts are humble." Her mouth pinched slightly in disapproval as she glanced at Sable's empty hands. "If you work harder to please Amah, perhaps she may bless you one day, as well."

Sable bowed her head, partly to appear thankful, partly to hide the disgust she knew was written on her face.

"The blessings of Amah and Isah be upon you," Eugessa intoned. "Festive day." She moved down the line without glancing back.

With Eugessa disappearing down the line, Sable picked up a sweet roll and walked away from the table, two warring thoughts swirling in her mind.

First, in order to get close enough to Eugessa to get that ring, Sable would probably have to be her personal handmaiden.

But second, and possibly more important—that ring wasn't worth stealing.

CHAPTER ELEVEN

WHAT WAS KIVA PLAYING AT?

He'd set her on an impossible task. Fine. That was to be expected if it would bring both her and Talia freedom. But why have her steal the least valuable thing Eugessa possessed?

And what about that ring made him so angry?

Sable went back to her tree to watch the prioress finish her rounds at the table and climb back up the stairs. Maybe she'd read him wrong. Maybe Kiva wasn't angry about the ring at all. Maybe he was just furious at Sable for disobeying and hiding money.

She let her head sink back against the tree. It was a miserable truth, but if she were being honest, she'd known it all along.

The ledger and the ring were just distractions. The idea of paying off Talia's debt was a dream. Her sister was trapped, and if Talia was here, then Sable would stay. She'd spend the next couple days helping Talia get ready for her new job and preparing her for the dangers, and then Sable would go back to work.

She gazed around at the crowd. The festivals were the best pickpocketing days of the entire year, and she was wasting it on Kiva's little ruse. Tomorrow, when the festival was done and the Veil Gate closed, she wouldn't only lose access to Prioress Eugessa, she'd lose access to this big, profitable crowd. With a sigh, she turned away from the prioress and looked at the crowd, picking out the easy marks.

Ignoring the familiar trapped feeling settling on her again, she headed toward an ostentatious looking young man with a silver cuff button hanging loosely from his sleeve. As she approached, he turned, and she caught a glimpse of his face. He looked around, his eyes wide as he stared at the phoenix and talked with the woman on his arm.

Breathing a silent apology, Sable pulled out her tiny knife and brushed past him, cutting off the button and dropping it into her own pocket.

When the setting sun cast long shadows across the square, Sable made her way toward the Veil Gate. People already drifted toward the Grand Stadia for the Choosing.

There were others standing on the short wall around a tree near the gate, but she jostled her way up onto it and found a spot where she could watch for Talia.

The day had gone well. Excellent, really. She never quite understood why the wealthiest people came to the square during the feasting hours. They certainly didn't need the food. Still, they showed up in their finery, wearing festive hats and silver-buttoned shirts.

The best thing about festival finery was that it wasn't everyday finery. The rings people wore every day were well-fitted and molded into their fingers. Sliding off a ring someone wore every day was nearly impossible. But a ring that was only worn for festivals, the ones that shifted loosely on fingers, was just a matter of a well-timed jostle.

The second best thing was how many coins everyone carried. The plaza was full of women with small purses of coins.

Sable had found enough marks that she'd filled the small pocket sewn inside her tunic with coins, the one inside the waist of her pants with the cuff button and two thin, silver rings. She'd even tucked a pair of copper hairpins up under her own braid where they wouldn't be visible. She should have been pleased. The coins alone were worth two silver mons. But Talia's debt—one hundred and fourteen mons...

The number sat like the Veil Wall in front of her. There was no way past such a number.

You need to learn to be happy here.

Talia's words kept nagging at her. There was a logic to them, and it was how her sister would survive this. She'd be happy about the clothes, the food, and the opulent rooms with Lady Ingred. She'd find a way to not think about the debt or the fact she had no freedom. She'd enjoy what she could. How was it that Talia always focused on the good parts and didn't let the rest chafe at her?

Sable watched the crowd for Talia's auburn hair. As the sun sank lower, Sable checked the growing crowd near the Grand Stadia.

"Festive day, Sable," Talia said from below her.

Sable glanced down to see her nearly unrecognizable sister.

The most obvious change was the new dress. Her formless, grey shift had been replaced with a dark blue dress nice enough that Sable would have considered her a mark if she saw her in the crowd.

Talia held a light grey bag, and Sable saw with approval she had the strap wrapped around her wrist and her hand closed over the top. The front of her hair was pulled back and braided into an intricate knot, the rest hung down her back in smooth, clean locks. Her face was bright, painted with just enough color to make her hazel eyes stand out.

"I've never been able to sneak up on you." Talia grinned. "Are you distracted, or did you just not recognize me?"

Sable climbed down, still staring at her sister. "Both."

"Kiva's not as bad as you think," Talia said, linking her arm through Sable's and starting toward the Grand Stadia. Sable started to object, but her sister continued. "He gave me money to go shopping. I bought this dress and was measured for more. I'm supposed to have a whole closet full in the next two days. Then there are hairpins, sashes, and shoes." She pointed her foot, showing off narrow, black boots.

As Talia prattled on, Sable kept stealing glances at her while they maneuvered through the crowd. Talia looked...happy. Her voice skipped along with a carefree sort of enthusiasm that Sable hadn't heard in...long enough that she'd forgotten that this was how Talia used to sound. Always prattling on about something with an airy merriment. Aside from the "Kiva's not as bad as you think", which Sable wanted to burn out of her memory, the rest of the chatter was achingly familiar.

Sable gripped Talia's arm tightly, not sure if her sister's change left her more happy or more terrified.

"Oh!" Talia reached into her bag. "I bought something for you." She pulled out a thin bundle of undyed wool and handed it to Sable.

She unrolled it and stared at a pair of socks.

"I wanted to buy you prettier ones, but I figured you'd like plain more."

Sable ran her fingers over the socks. The weave was smooth and the seam at the toe so small she could barely feel it.

New socks.

"Talia," she breathed. "I…"

Talia grinned. "You're welcome. I thought it was time someone helped you for once."

Sable closed her fist around the socks. "I love them," she whispered.

Talia steered them to the nearest tree and pointed to the short wall around it. "Sit and put them on. You can't tell me you don't want to get rid of those horrible things you're wearing."

Grinning, Sable sat down on the wall and unlaced her boots, pulling them off, then stripping off the dingy, stained, lumpy socks she'd had for longer than she cared to think about. "I've never wanted to get rid of anything more."

Talia picked up the old socks with a grimace, then shoved them into a small gap between the soil and the wall. She pushed a little dirt on top of them and brushed off her hands.

"Those might kill the tree," Sable pointed out.

Talia wrinkled her nose. "I doubt the tree will notice. They were more dirt than sock."

Sable pulled on her new ones.

They felt like blankets wrapped around her feet. And not like the blankets she'd used in the past ten years. A proper blanket. She slipped her boots back on and wiggled her toes. The boots were still worn, the left still darker than the right, but the socks were glorious. No wrinkles, no holes, no seams to dig into her skin.

She looked up to see Talia beaming. "This is the best gift I've ever gotten."

Talia offered her hand, and Sable took it, standing and pulling her sister into a hug.

"I'm sorry, Talia," Sable whispered into her hair. "I'm sorry I haven't been able to give us things like this, and that—"

"Stop." Talia squeezed her tightly. "You've done everything for me." She pulled back and looked Sable in the eye. "Even if I bought you socks every day for the rest of your life, I couldn't pay you back."

"You should try, anyway," Sable said, rolling up onto her toes. "My feet have never been this happy."

Talia linked her arm through Sable's again, and they walked toward the Grand Stadia, leaving the old, dirty socks behind.

They moved with the crowd through an arch in the looming wall of the theater. A long staircase rose toward the center of the building. When they emerged into the sunlight at the other end, they stood half way up the arc of benches in the outdoor amphitheater. The wide stage was below them at the far side.

"Let's get close to the stage," Talia said.

Sable wiggled between two groups of people, pulling Talia behind her, managing to move down two rows before she was blocked again.

"This is the sort of place that needs smiles, not sneaking," Talia whispered. She moved along their row until she came up behind two young men. "Excuse me," she said, slipping her arm in between them. "Festive day to you."

When the young men glanced at her bright smile, their irritation shifted to smiles. They moved aside to let her pass. "Festive day," they both returned. Their smiles faltered slightly when Sable squeezed through too, but by then, Talia had climbed down a row to an older gentlemen she greeted just as warmly.

In a surprisingly short time, Talia had found them space on a bench no more than a dozen rows from the stage, which was as close as they could possibly get. Immediately in front of them was a low, stone wall separating the wealthy lower section from the rest. Below the wall was a wide aisle with a line of guards facing up at the crowd, ensuring the commoners in the population stayed back. Past them, merchants and nobles filled the rows. White dresses and veils of abbesses from around the city filled an entire section at the far side.

Sable gave Talia an appraising look. "The dress is already paying off."

The sun was low in the west, painting the light stones of the theater with a soft, amber light. An old abbess dressed and veiled in white stood in the center of the stage and held a small scroll aloft, reading a long, droning prayer over the crowd, who paid her no heed. Two Mira walked along the stage, igniting torches merely by touching them.

Sable leaned against the low wall in front of her, watching the few, favored wealthy climb up to the balconies on the side walls.

"Can you imagine how much that red dress costs?" Talia asked, watching one woman settle herself in a balcony seat.

"I could live for a year by selling anything any of them are wearing," Sable said.

"Not what those two are wearing." Talia nodded toward a second balcony where a couple in plain, grey robes seated themselves. Both looked to be in their thirties. He looked around the Grand Stadia with a curious, pleased expression, his hair curled in an unruly sort of way, while the woman next to him kept her attention firmly, and sternly, on the praying abbess. "They'd fit better in Dockside than up there."

"I was going to say maybe they were two commoners who'd somehow won a seat of honor," Sable said, "but that woman doesn't look happy enough to have won anything."

On the other hand, the two men entering the first balcony did look like they belonged there. The first was an older man in the stiff military garb of a Northern Lord. Everything from his uniform, to his hair, to his close-cropped beard was tightly contained. Countless details on his clothes were edged with red or silver. He ignored the crowd and sat, facing the stage like a statue.

The Northern Lords were in charge of a handful of independent, militaristic city-states that warred or allied with each other, depending on the season and the lords' moods.

Next to the Northern Lord, a white-haired man in a bright orange robe sat down. The embroidered white dragon curling down his sleeve marked him as the Kalesh Ambassador. The Kalesh Empire was a vast power far to the east, past the plains and the desert. A few Kalesh merchants traveled from the Empire with goods to trade, but the trip was long, and most wares were too fine for any but the wealthiest merchants in Immusmala to afford. Only the most affluent, like Lady Ingred, had dragons on their dresses, plates, or wall hangings.

The two men, emissaries from the lands to the north and distant east, were supposed to show the peace Immusmala shared with the peoples around her. In truth, the Northern Lords were too divided and small to pose the city of Immusmala any threat, and the Kalesh Empire lay so far to the east only the most adventurous Kalesh merchants ventured as far as Immusmala.

More people filed into the theater behind Talia and Sable. For something as short as a Choosing, some didn't bother to sit. They just shuffled as close to the stage as they could, pushing the sisters up against the short wall.

Talia linked her arm with Sable's again, her eyes fixed on the stage, drawing Sable's attention back to the old woman still praying. Most of the abbesses earned their way into the Grand Priories after years of service in the smaller abbeys spread through the city and across the countryside. But each year, at the Choosing, the silver dragon decided whether one hopeful would step directly into the most influential priory in the city. Of the hundreds of hopefuls, only three were selected for the Choosing, and many years, the dragon chose none of the three.

Of course, people didn't come for the hopefuls. On the few years one was actually chosen, the abbesses celebrated by flinging coins into the crowd, thanking the people for the gift of a new novice.

Talia looked at the people around them, who were busy talking amongst themselves. "Ryah would be listening to the abbess."

"Ryah would know the prayer by heart," Sable said.

"Remember how that grumpy old abbess from down the street doted on her? I don't think that woman liked anyone else in the world." Talia smiled sadly. "The whole world loved Ryah."

Sable nodded, repeating the truth every memory of Ryah ended on.

"The whole world loved Ryah."

Talia shifted. "I'm sorry I brought her up last night. I don't know if Ryah would have been pleased I've joined the jays. I know..." She paused. "I know it's not honest work like the bakery. But I'm tired of being hungry and dirty."

Sable held Talia's arm tightly. "She'd probably want both of us to be better than we are."

A hand landed on Talia's shoulder.

"Festive evening, ladies," Kiva's voice was low, right in Sable's ear.

She spun to face him. His goblin smile was pressed up close. Too close. She tried to back away, but she was penned in by the low wall. A flicker of amusement crossed his face at her discomfort.

"Festive evening, Kiva," Talia said brightly.

He turned to take in Talia's hair and dress, then nodded approvingly. "It's nice to see you dressed as you should be." Reaching out, he took Talia's hand and kissed it.

Sable clenched her fists to keep from knocking his hand away, but Talia gave him a wide smile.

"I confess, I didn't recognize you at first," Kiva continued, holding her hand close to his lips. "I was merely coming to greet Sable when I realized the angelic creature on her arm was you."

Kiva dropped Talia's hand. In contrast to last night, his face was cheerful today. The enthusiasm was as out of place as the anger had been, and Sable missed his habitual, unreadable calm. Still, this eagerness was better than the dangerous look from last night.

With a smirk, Kiva reached for Sable's hand. She crossed her arms and he paused.

Talia gave Sable an alarmed look. "I apologize for my sister..."

Kiva waved her words away. "Sable's defiance amuses me." He fixed her with a slow, lazy smile, but his eyes were still bright with interest. "I'd let everyone defy me if they made it as worth my while as she does."

Sable kept her arms crossed. He'd never approached her in public before, and he was being entirely too pleasant. "I assume the ledger has proven useful?"

He grinned widely, but she still tensed as he leaned toward her.

81

Something about him reminded her of his pet snake, coiled to strike.

"Not only that," he said quietly, "but Lord Renwen himself apparently fled the city early this morning in a great hurry, looking terrified." His eyes were fixed on her with an uncomfortable intensity, and Sable had the distinct impression he didn't care about Renwen.

She couldn't think of anything to say to him, so she left her arms crossed and waited for him to get to whatever topic he did care about. Except he did nothing but watch her, his eagerness growing slightly feral.

"Have you been enjoying the festival?" Talia asked him, breaking the awkwardness with a cheerful voice.

"I have." Kiva turned away from Sable and let out a slow breath. "I've especially enjoyed seeing Prioress Eugessa up close."

She tensed again.

"I was at the prioress's table earlier," he continued easily, "and—as she will tell you herself—she's a fine example of someone who has been blessed by the goddess. Did you know she came from poverty?"

Talia shook her head, and Kiva nodded. "She was born in the Bend and lived there until a local abbess found her and trained her. And now look at her, dripping with wealth. I believe she had at least one ring on every finger." Kiva looked back at Sable. "You were near her table, as well."

His words were casual, but Sable watched him warily. He'd had her watched? Again?

"Being so close to the prioress," he said, eagerness bleeding back into his face, "you must have taken away a valuable blessing yourself."

Sable stared at him, speechless. He thought she'd already stolen the ring? The impossible-to-steal ring?

At her hesitation, Kiva's expression grew darker.

"I saw all her rings." Sable's voice betrayed her tension. "I was surprised that some look so much less valuable than others."

"To her maybe." His eyes narrowed. "Even her least valuable jewel would be priceless to someone else."

Talia glanced between the two of them warily.

Sable studied him. The blue butterfly wouldn't be priceless to anyone. Except, apparently, Kiva. "It was hard to tell past all her guards."

"I wonder why she has so many guards?" Talia broke in with a nervous laugh. "No one would steal from a prioress."

Kiva didn't look at her.

"I agree," Sable said, trying to keep her voice firm. "It would be a death sentence. The thief would be caught and hanged before they even got close."

He crossed his arms. "Surely someone with your skills could manage it."

Sable shook her head. "It would be impossible."

A muscle in Kiva's jaw twitched. "Desperate people find ways to do the impossible." He lifted his gaze to the woman on stage, who still droned out her prayer.

Sable glanced at the stage, too. Even though she'd already made the decision to go back to work for him, and already spent the day stealing for him, she still had to force the next words out. "Those sorts of people, after really considering stealing from a prioress, would realize they're better off working at the job they already have." Her voice sounded far more resentful than she'd intended.

Kiva turned back to her, and she could almost feel the fury rolling off him. "And what of someone with no job to go back to?"

Sable snapped her gaze to his face.

"What of someone whose life depended on it?" His voice was deadly serious, and a cold fear crawled along Sable's back. "Along with the lives of those they loved? Because they'd lied to—and stolen from—dangerous men?" He bit off each word.

Talia stiffened.

Kiva's deep, seething anger from the night before was back. "For that person's sake, and their family's, we'd better hope the impossible can be achieved. And quickly."

Sable stared at him, a hollow fear growing feeling trapped by the wall behind her and the crowd pressed in on all sides. When he leaned closer, she flinched.

"Or when the Veil Gate closes tomorrow, that person will lose everything."

CHAPTER TWELVE

WITHOUT GLANCING AT TALIA, Kiva turned and pushed through the crowd, climbing up several rows to stand next to Britta.

Sable turned back to the stage, her mouth dry.

"What was that?" Talia demanded quietly.

"Nothing."

She grabbed Sable's hand. "It wasn't nothing!"

Across the theater, Prioress Eugessa and Prioress Narine sat in the first balcony, attentively listening to the abbess pray. Eugessa's ring-encrusted hand lay nonchalantly on the balcony rail.

"You're going after one of her rings?" Talia hissed, still facing Sable.

She let out a long breath. "Like I said, it's an impossible job. I thought he was just trying to make a point." She glanced back to where Kiva stood. He watched the prayer, his face schooled in a cold calm. "No one could get to it."

"Then what will you do?"

Sable shook her head. "I have no idea."

A single, low bell rang out across the theater, and a door at the back of the stage opened. The prioress closed her scroll and backed away from the center of the platform. Vivaine, the High Prioress of the

Dragon Priory, walked out to the center of the stage and raised her hands toward the crowd.

The Grand Stadia quieted.

Against the warm, golden glow of the stage in the evening light, the pristine dress and white veil of the prioress glowed pure white. Sable wanted to dismiss her and her useless blessings, but the High Prioress's brightness felt hopeful and refreshing. The opposite of everything Kiva stood for, and something in Sable longed to believe it was real.

The silver dragon stood by her side, evening light rippling across his scales. His wings were tucked back sleekly along his body, and his serpentine face, held aloft on a muscular neck, came up to the prioress's waist. She rested her hand on his head.

Sable had never seen the dragon this close. He was no more than a dozen paces away, and Sable could make out his intelligent grey eyes, slit with long, reptilian pupils. Everything about the scaled creature was fierce and vicious.

In a smooth motion, Prioress Vivaine lifted her veil and gave the crowd a warm, gentle smile.

"On this first festival of the summer, we thank Amah," she called out, and the crowd spoke the next words with her. "Mother of all, giver of light, giver of all that is good."

Talia spoke the words quietly, but Sable couldn't bring herself to join in.

"And we thank Isah," Prioress Vivaine continued, prompting the crowd to join her. "Father of all, protector of light, keeper of all that is good."

Sable curled her hands in to fists. Isah clearly wasn't protecting either herself or Talia.

The High Prioress let the crowd quiet. "Today, we have the honor of meeting the hopefuls. These novices have trained and prayed for years to prepare themselves for unwavering service to Amah. They come from all parts of our land, from different homes and different ways of life."

Three women, dressed and veiled in white, filed onto the stage.

"Three hopefuls will stand before the dragon this day, and we shall see if Amah is pleased to select one."

Prioress Vivaine's voice rolled over the crowd as she repeated the duties of an initiate. Should one of these women be chosen, she would enter the priory and reside there for the rest of her life. She would begin a year of isolation from the world where she would not see a single person outside the priory.

"I wonder what life these hopefuls are giving up?" Talia said quietly.

"I'd give up Dockside in a heartbeat," Sable said.

"You could be a hopeful," Talia whispered. "If the dragon chose you, you'd be out of Kiva's grip."

Sable snorted. "There would have to be a lot wrong with that dragon for him to pick me as a novice."

"How do you think he picks?" The cheerfulness in Talia's voice felt a little forced. "By smell? You could eat something and dribble it down your dress so you smelled good."

Sable raised an eyebrow. "I'd prefer not to smell tasty if I'm meeting a dragon."

The High Prioress turned to the veiled hopefuls who stood like white pillars

The dragon slid forward, and the crowd grew quiet.

The first hopeful stood straight, hands held stiffly by her side, as the dragon moved closer. He circled her. Stretching his head up, he sniffed, his breath fluttering the edges of her long veil.

He moved to the second. Sable could see a slight tremble in this one's veil. The dragon fixed his gaze on her for so long even the High Prioress leaned forward. The dragon shifted his focus to her hand, and the crowd stood perfectly still.

The High Prioress took a small step forward, but the dragon pulled back, turning his attention to the third hopeful. The High Prioress relaxed back into her former position as the dragon considered the last young woman. He circled her twice before stopping between her and the second hopeful.

The dragon tilted his head just slightly toward the second. Sable caught a twitch of excitement in the High Prioress's hand, but her face stayed calm.

With a snort, the dragon turned away from the second hopeful and touched his snout to the hand of the third.

After a breath of shocked silence, the crowd erupted in cheers. The chosen jerked her hand away before looking down at the dragon and tentatively lowering her hand again. The dragon allowed her fingers to brush the top of his head, then slid back to the High Prioress's side.

Prioress Vivaine smiled broadly at the young woman. She gestured for her to come to the center of the stage, then lifted her veil to reveal the stunned face of a girl who couldn't be older than fifteen.

"I think that's Lord Wrenwith's daughter," Talia whispered.

Sable glanced at her. "The cotton merchant?"

With a troubled expression, Talia studied the new novice. "Her name is Jayne, and if what Callie says is true, she's...not what I would consider novice material."

Sable waited for her to continue, but the High Prioress raised her hands for silence. The crowd quieted, and Jayne knelt to receive a blessing.

Talia leaned closer and whispered, "Callie says Jayne Wrenwith is the girl to watch if you want to learn how to flirt."

The girl on the stage bowed her head beneath the prioress's hand. Prioress Vivaine's voice rose and fell in melodic swells as she prayed the traditional prayer of thanksgiving over the new novice.

"She doesn't look like a flirt," Sable whispered.

"Maybe I'm wrong," Talia said, not sounding convinced.

The High Prioress finished praying, then grasped the initiate's hand and raised her to her feet. She turned the young girl toward the crowd and stepped to the side of the stage, a pleased smile on her face. Shouts and cheers renewed, and the new initiate lifted her hand in blessing toward them all.

A line of veiled abbesses streamed out of the back of the stage and greeted their newest sister.

Sable glanced at the High Prioress, who stood a little to the side, considering the second hopeful with a thoughtful expression. The two unchosen girls backed up, moving out of the way of the celebration surrounding the new initiate.

Something about the second girl caught Sable's attention.

"She must be devastated," Talia said quietly. "I thought the dragon was going to pick her."

"So did I."

The long, white dress and veil covered the girl from head to toe, but something about her sent a shiver of uneasiness through Sable.

A line of musicians filed out and began a rousing song. The abbesses stationed themselves along the front of the stage, holding bulging pouches of coins, and the crowd roared to life. Just past Talia, a man tried to climb over the wall to where the wealthy sat, but the guards pushed him back.

While the abbesses prepared to throw their coins into the crowd, the High Prioress crossed the stage to where the two unchosen waited. She raised her hand in blessing to each of them, then lifted the veil of the first hopeful, kissing the forehead of a young, dark-haired girl who looked more overwhelmed than sad.

The second hopeful clasped her hands together tightly, and shifted. Every movement she made had a terrifying familiarity, and Sable's uneasiness turned to cold fear.

"No..." she whispered. She twisted to look back at Kiva, but couldn't see him through the crowd. The woman behind her shoved up against her back, pushing her against the wall. The audience surged forward, stretching their hands toward the abbesses.

Only Talia still watched the High Prioress curiously.

Sable stared at her sister for a sickening moment, but before she could say anything, the abbesses reached in their pouches and flung coins out into the crowd.

Chaos erupted.

Sable's fingers clenched on the top of the wall as she turned back toward the High Prioress, who gently lifted the second hopeful's veil.

The girl's face, set stubbornly in a smile against the tears in her eyes, was achingly familiar.

Sable's breath tore out of her.

"Ryah?" Talia's fingers dug into Sable's arm. "It's Ryah!"

CHAPTER THIRTEEN

RYAH'S SMILE was a perfect copy of Talia's. She stood there in front of the entire Grand Stadia, blinking back tears of disappointment, and Sable wanted to claw her way to the stage and pull her veil back over her face.

"Ryah!" Talia screamed, stretching over the wall. The noise of the crowd drowned out her voice and the nearest guard stepped forward, pushing her back. She spun to Sable, her face stunned. "It's Ryah! It's her!"

Sable grabbed Talia's hand. "Stop!"

"She's alive!" Talia looked wildly at Ryah, then back at Sable, her face desperate. "She's not dead! She's—"

"Stop!" Sable hissed, shooting another glance back toward Kiva, but there were still too many people in the way to see him. There was wild motion everywhere as people reached up for the flying coins or scrambled on the ground for ones that had fallen.

Sable looked over to see Ryah kneeling to receive a prayer from the High Prioress, far away from all the other commotion.

When she looked back, Talia stood perfectly still, staring at Sable with dreadful, accusing eyes. "You knew." It wasn't a question.

· · ·

"She had to be safe." Sable grabbed Talia's shoulders. "I couldn't let her be caught, too. I had to keep her away from Kiva."

Talia yanked away, shoving against the person behind her.

"Kiva didn't know she existed." Sable reached for her again. "I couldn't let her—"

"You told me she was *dead*." Talia's voice was furious. "She's been alive this whole time? And you lied to me?"

"Talia…" Sable reached for her sister's hand, but Talia pulled away. "I couldn't tell anyone. I couldn't risk Kiva finding out. Can you imagine Ryah trapped in the gang? Forced to steal or…or something worse?"

Talia leaned back over the railing. "*Ryah!*" she screamed, but the din of the crowd smothered her voice.

The High Prioress finished with the unchosen, and the two girls filed out the back of the stage and out of sight.

"Where does she live?" Talia demanded.

Sable shook her head. "We have to leave her there. Talia, she's the only one of us who's free."

Talia turned with a snarl, and Sable stepped back from the fury pouring off her sister. "She is my *sister*! Where is she?"

When Sable didn't answer, Talia drew herself up. "You don't have to tell me. It's public record where the hopefuls come from. I'll find her myself." She turned and shoved her way up into the row behind them.

"Talia!" Sable yelled. "Wait! I'll take you. I—" But Talia pushed her way through, and others surged forward to take her place at the wall, shoving Sable back.

The abbesses continued to throw coins into the crowd, and Sable stared after Talia, her stomach in a knot.

A man pressed up against Sable's shoulder and she turned to shove him away, but came face to face with Kiva.

"Is that true? That sweet hopeful who almost joined the priory is your sister?"

She opened her mouth, but the denial died on her lips.

"Very interesting. Now that her hopes of joining the priory are dashed, we'll have to offer her a home with us."

She tried to shove him back, but he grabbed her wrist and clenched it so tightly she couldn't hold back a cry of pain.

He leaned even closer. "Can you imagine the things a face that innocent could do? I do believe I'd hand her all my money if she just asked." He glared at her. "First money under your floorboards, now this. What else have you been hiding?"

Sable wanted to smash her forehead into his smug, horrible face, but he twisted her wrist and slicing pain shot up her arm.

He glanced in the direction Talia had gone. "I think I'll send dear Talia back to the Nest for her own safety today, then find her sister. Families should be together, don't you think?" He let go of Sable's arm, but leaned forward until his face was so close she could smell his dank breath.

Sable hugged her aching wrist to her chest, but raised her chin to glare at him. "Leave my sisters alone."

"You don't seem to understand the situation." His voice curled with fury. "I want that ring from Eugessa."

"Why?" Sable demanded. "It's worthless."

"If you don't get it for me," he said, eyes burning with a wild, raw rage, "I will kill you, and your sisters will be mine with no one to protect them."

Sable stared at Kiva, fury and fear warring inside her. His voice didn't just wrap around her with warm truth, it pressed hard against her like the writhing crowd.

"I am watching your every move," he hissed. "Eugessa leaves the city tomorrow. Get me my ring by then, or start running." He turned and shoved his way through the crowd.

The abbesses had finished throwing coins to the people and were filing off the stage. The crowd around her began to relax, spreading out slowly. Sable took a step after Kiva.

He was going to find Ryah.

The elderly abbess who had raised Ryah wouldn't stand a chance against Kiva. Before the night was done, he'd have both Ryah and Talia.

She pushed her way out of the theater and into the plaza. The crowd clustered around her like waves in the ocean, every face looking familiar and threatening. She started toward the Veil Gate and the tiny abbey in the Bend that felt terribly far away.

But by the nearest tree, she caught sight of Pete and Boone watching her.

She couldn't lead them straight to Ryah. After a moment, she turned and started toward the Priory of the Horn instead, pretending she was heading toward Eugessa.

Sable found a tree and leaned against it, the bark against her back feeling safer than the open threat of the plaza. She forced herself to take a moment and assess the situation.

There was no way to get the butterfly ring. Even if Sable could use the chaos of the plaza to get into the priory, Eugessa was still wearing the ring. If the woman took it off to sleep, that might not be for hours.

What Sable needed to do, was get to Ryah. She could probably lose Pete and Boone in the city, but what if Kiva had more people following her?

A constable strode past, a boy in tow pleading his innocence, heading for a cluster of wagons sitting next to the Veil Gate. There was already a small crowd of pickpockets and belligerent drunks there, waiting to be transported to the city jail.

Sable let out a long breath. Kiva would stop following her if she got arrested.

The thought made her pause. Getting away from a handful of over-worked constables and out the gate had to be easier than getting rid of Kiva's men.

If only she could find a constable who would arrest her, then let her go.

She pushed off the tree. She did know a constable. Of sorts.

She headed down the long line of stages and booths lining the side of the square. Pete and Boone followed at a distance. A small, light-colored bottle caught her eye, and she stopped at a wagon selling a remarkable number of useless things.

"Is that leeswine?" she asked the short, wiry merchant standing in front of his wares.

He grinned at her through a curly blond beard. "It is, my lady. The finest you'll find in the plaza."

"How much?"

"How much do you have?" he asked curiously.

She raised an eyebrow. "Barely any. But hopefully enough for a bottle of leeswine. I need it for a very important purpose."

The merchant glanced at her, taking in her worn clothes, gaze lingering on her one darkened boot. "Six copper nummi."

"Leeswine is barely wine. No one would pay that."

"If they needed it for a very important purpose they would."

She gave him a flat look. "I have these." She pulled the two copper hairpins out from under her braid. They weren't worth six nummi. Maybe two.

The merchant examined them. "Do they have a good story?"

"What?"

"They're not worth much as they are, but a good story makes everything more valuable." In contrast to the stuffy heat of the crowded plaza, the truth in his words wrapped around her with a comforting warmth.

She let the feeling soothe her just a bit, offering him some truth in return. "I stole them from a woman who was pretending to be richer than she really is, while pickpocketing people in an effort to get my hands on one hundred and fourteen silver mons so I can buy my sister's way out from under the grasp of an evil gang boss."

The merchant's eyebrows rose, then he let out a long, rolling laugh, then handed her the leeswine.

She took the cool, smooth glass in her hand, staring at him. "That wasn't a funny story."

"Maybe not now, but in the future, you may find it so. 'Tis the way with most things."

"Right," she said, turning away.

"May the leeswine serve your very important purpose, m'lady!" he said with a bow.

"Thanks," she muttered.

With her offering, she continued until she could see Atticus's stage. She paused at the booth just before it, pretending to examine some hats. Pete and Boone stopped a little way back.

She moved around to the to the side of the booth, until she could see between it and the stage. The man who'd played Epophus sat with his legs dangling off the side of the stage, leaning back against the table that held the glowing tree. Green light filtered down on him where he rested, his head tilted back, eyes closed.

The actor looked more worn than he had the night before.

Sable picked up a hat with a wide rim and feathers spraying out from the side. She tried it on, tilting her head to see her reflection in a small, polished silver plate, and shielding her face from Pete and Boone.

"Epophus," she called quietly.

The man didn't move.

"Epophus," she said with more urgency.

He opened his eyes and blinked sleepily, glancing around.

"Here," she said, without turning more than her face toward him.

He raised an eyebrow, taking in her worn clothes and eyeing the hat. "Yes to the hat. It brings out the shabbiness of your shirt."

Sable gave him a smile. "I have a job for you."

"I already have a job."

"This one will be quick." She held up the bottle of leeswine.

He considered her for a moment, his eyes lingering on the bottle. "Do I know you?"

"I watched your show last night from the shadows at the side of the stage."

He smiled. "Ahh, Sneaks. Here I thought you were made of shadows and darkness." He glanced toward the back of the stage. "How long will this job take?"

The sun had fallen behind the hills to the west, but the eastern sky was still blue, devoid of stars. "We'll be done before the moon rises. It'll be the fastest bottle you've ever earned."

He rubbed his hands over his face, then returned his gaze to the bottle and nodded reluctantly. "Leonis."

She paused. "What?"

"My name. I just want to make sure you know I'm not really Epophus."

Sable grinned. "I don't want you to be Leonis or Epophus. I need a less famous, less heroic you."

CHAPTER FOURTEEN

SABLE WAITED in front of the Priory of the Horn. In the twilight, torches flickered along the front of buildings and the Sanctuary walls, creating a warm glow along the outer edge of the square, but leaving the alleys between the building full of shadows.

Pete and Boone were not far away. The dwarf stood on a small rise next to a tree, and Boone stood on the flagstones beneath it, still a head taller than the crowd around him. Her skin prickled at the thought of how many other eyes might be watching. Moving casually through the crowd, she headed toward the alley between the Priory of the Horn and the low building next to it. There was no way into the priory from there, but hopefully it would look like she was trying.

The sky above had darkened to a deep blue, the only light lingering over the western hills in a smudge of pale violet. Time was moving too fast, but Sable forced herself to move calmly.

Even when Kiva found the name of Ryah's abbey, the building itself would take time to locate, and the Bend was deep in the Muddogs' territory, so Kiva would have to approach the situation with some delicacy.

She slipped into the shadows of the alley. As soon as she was in the gloom, she ran toward the back of the building. A chimney stuck out of the wall halfway down the building, and she ducked behind it, peering back toward the plaza. Above the heads of people milling near the front of the building, she saw Boone looking down the alley. Before he or anyone else could follow, she ran to the back corner of the priory.

Behind the building was another deeply shadowed alley between the priory and the tall city wall. She paused. There were no doors, and the windows were placed high up on smooth walls. But thankfully, the lack of entrances meant a lack of guards.

"Sneaking around here," a voice right next to her said, "could get you arrested, young lady."

She spun, and let out a breath that was half laugh, half gasp. She hadn't heard Leonis approach. "That's what I'm hoping, good constable."

In the darkness, she could just make out a constable's round hat and a thick, bushy beard. "You grow facial hair quickly, Epophus."

"That's Constable Epophus to you, Sneaks," he said sternly. "And I believe we're on a tight schedule here. The moon will be up before you know it, and I do have another engagement tonight."

Sable glanced down the alley. Boone had moved closer and was nearly to the shadowed edge. "We're in luck. That dull looking mountain of a man is part of our audience. He has a dwarvish friend, too. As long as they're paying attention, let the show begin."

"Stop!" Leonis bellowed with a commanding enough tone that Sable flinched.

Boone jerked to a halt, too, backing up next to the nearest bystanders, who looked curiously into the alleyway.

"You think you can sneak around here?" Leonis shouted, grabbing her arm and pushing her roughly back toward the square. Her shoulder hit the wall, and she grunted.

"Sorry," he muttered.

"You're doing great." Sable rolled her shoulder against the pain. "Very authoritative."

"Always happy to play the under-appreciated constable." She caught the quick flash of teeth before he started a grumbling, chastising tirade against her trespassing behind the priory.

When they reached the end of the alley, she caught Boone's eye and forced herself to give him a look of desperation and wild supplication. He did nothing more than watch and cross his arms.

Leonis half pushed, half steered her out into the square. Sable watched Boone disappear into the crowd as Leonis tugged her forward. The people slowed their progress until they broke out into a surprisingly open space. Leonis pulled her to a stop. Right in front of them towered the black form of a baledin.

The red-veiled face slowly turned toward her. The hand stretching out of its cloak was a dead, greyish black, the fingers clawed.

Sable tried to pull back, but the crowd behind her was too close. The people shouted and jeered at the baledin as he reached out and wrapped his hand around her arm. His fingers were terrifyingly bone-cold. She yanked away, but couldn't break his grip.

"No killing this one," Leonis said easily. "At least not before she's served her time in a cell."

The red veil turned to Leonis and gazed at him for a long moment, then released her and swung toward someone else in the crowd, making the people scatter like skittish birds.

Leonis looked at her with a grin. "You know he wasn't a real baledin, right?"

"His hand was so cold," Sable said, crowding close to Leonis as he pushed through the other side of the crowd.

"They soak their hands in cold water, then color them with soot for effect."

She took a deep breath. "Have you ever played one?"

Leonis glanced over at the big, black shape moving away through the crowd. "Atticus doesn't like baledin, and he pays my wages, so no." He led her toward the cluster of constable wagons at the far end. "The baledin did give you the appropriately fearful expression of a woman being arrested, though."

They moved on, and Sable caught sight of one face she recognized, watching her from a tree. She let the fear she felt at seeing him fill her face, and he returned her wide-eyed look with a smirk.

"Who exactly are we fooling?" Leonis asked quietly. "Not that it matters too much, but it's nice to know if I'm fooling heroes or villains."

"They're all definitely villains." She glanced around. "Honestly, I'm not sure who the heroes are."

"Constables. It's we constables who are the unsung heroes." He glanced down at her worn, dingy clothes. "What noble cause am I assisting you in?"

Sable blew out a breath. "I need to get to my sister before the villains do."

Leonis was quiet a moment. "That sounds like a worthy cause. What's your sister like?"

"I have no idea." Sable stretched her neck to see the Veil Gate past the crowd. "I haven't spoken to her in ten years."

"You are a strange young woman, Sneaks," Leonis murmured.

They moved through the crowd toward the constable's wagons, and Sable was suddenly aware of how many real constables they were approaching.

"What do we do when we get there?" Sable asked.

"Just follow my lead."

They passed near a torch. In the light, his beard looked tatty and constable hat was black instead of dark blue. His coat was stuffed, giving the normally lean man a pudgy gut. As they approached the milling constables, he called out, "A rogue to lock up for the night."

The eyebrows of several real constables rose as Leonis led Sable around the back of the wagons.

"What's this about?" a constable demanded. "Who are you?"

Leonis pulled her out of view of the plaza before yanking his beard down and grinning at the constable. "Just giving the lady a taste of adventure! We run Night of Danger Adventures. Luella here paid to experience a true-to-life arrest by one of you fine constables." He pulled off his hat and bowed to the man. "Or as good an impression as I can do."

"Well, move along." He fixed Leonis with a stern look. "No more games. We're trying to work."

"Yes, sir." Leonis snapped off a bow.

Sable glanced toward the Veil Gate, and paused. It was so close, but the area was now brightly lit with torches and anyone still watching would see her cross, plain as day.

Leonis nudged her, and she turned to see him unbuttoning his constable's cloak. He pulled out a long green shawl and a matching green hat. "Your affects, my dear. Can't have you walking away looking like a criminal."

The shawl was thin with tattered edges, the hat a little lumpy. "You're brilliant." She shot him a grateful look and swung the shawl around her shoulders and tucked her hair up into the cap.

"How do I look?"

"Just like you did when you hired me, Luella," he assured her. "Do you need anything else?"

Sable sighed. "I need a way out of an impossible situation."

She paused and a flicker of hope sprang up inside her. She could take Ryah and Talia and leave.

She grabbed Leonis's arm. "Is Atticus at the stage?"

"Atticus is always at the stage." Leonis glanced across the square to The Duke's Figment of Wit's stage, lit with torches. "Which is where I should be right now."

"I need to talk to him before I go."

Leonis raised an eyebrow. "This way then, Lady Luella."

The two of them, a young woman in a green shawl and cap and a man in nondescript trousers carrying a bundle that, to the close observer, might look like a constable's jacket tucked into a hat, crossed the plaza.

Leonis led her back to the torchlit area between the back of the stage where they found two tall caravans. Both wagons had tall sides and low-arched roofs made of wood. The nearest was painted a deep blue with lighter, swirling patterns climbing up the sides, the other was a rich scarlet with golden yellow trim.

A wide door was open at the end of the blue wagon, and the woman who'd played Demonda stepped out. "Finally!" She hissed at Leonis. "Where have you been?" Her gaze fell on Sable, and a sharp disdain curled her lips. "Who is this?"

"Lady Merilee," Leonis said with a short bow, ignoring her questions and her tone. Moving past her, he led Sable to the red wagon. Atticus sat just inside the open door on a long bench that ran along the wall. He took in his actor's face with a look of relief, but only gave a short, "Good," before turning away.

Two people in long robes sat in the wagon with him—a man with unruly curls and a pinched-faced woman who squinted toward Sable.

It took her a moment to place them. It was the grey-robed couple who had sat in the balcony at the Choosing. They didn't look any more impressive up close than they had from far away.

"This young lady needs a word with you," Leonis said.

Atticus glanced at Sable as she pulled off the green hat, and his eyes widened in recognition. "Tell me you're here to accept my offer."

Leonis raised an eyebrow, and the couple leaned over for a better look.

"I am," Sable answered. "If I can bring my two sisters."

Leonis raised an eyebrow. "You have two? Do you know either of them?"

She shot him an annoyed look.

Atticus shook his head. "I don't have the room, or the funds, to take on two passengers."

She stepped forward. "I'll work for free." The desperation bled into her voice.

Atticus considered her for a long moment.

Funneling all her need into her voice, she pleaded, "I have two mons..." She dug into her pocket for the things she'd pickpocketed earlier. "And this silver button and two rings. You can have it all to pay for our passage." She clung to the hope that was slowly slipping away. "Please."

She couldn't read Atticus's expression, but the man behind him gave her a sympathetic look.

"That's barely enough payment for one, Sneaks—" Leonis began.

"I accept," Atticus cut him off.

Leonis stared at Atticus. "We don't have room to—"

Atticus gave him a pointed look. "You have a lot to do before the play."

Leonis shook his head and walked toward the other wagon, muttering under his breath.

Atticus faced Sable and crossed his arms. "You are agreeing to join our troupe as second lady for the next week without pay. The two mons, button, and two rings buys you and your sisters passage for up to the next month, when we will return here. But once your week of acting is over, you are free to leave at any time."

A wave of relief rolled over her at his words. "We'll definitely be leaving before you get back here."

"We need to roll out at dawn," he said. "Be here with your sisters and payment. We will not wait."

Sable nodded quickly. "Thank you." Sable glanced up at the sky, which was black now, and her relief soured a little at how late it was.

Leonis walked by with an armful of props, and she held out the green hat.

He gave her a bemused look. "Sounds like I'll see you again, and you might need it to get out of the Sanctuary."

She shot him a quick smile and tucked her hair back into the cap. "Thanks for your help."

Pulling her hat down tighter, she started for the gate.

"Thanks for the wine," Leonis called after her.

"What wine?" she heard Atticus ask, his voice thick with disapproval.

On the far side of the street, a towering black-hooded form stalked silently toward the Sanctuary, his face covered by a red veil. His cloak was so dark the torchlight merely sank into it, and he moved like a shadow himself.

The baledin. A creature of legend, said to drain the life out of a person with merely a touch.

CHAPTER FIFTEEN

SABLE MOVED AS QUICKLY as she could along the Spine without drawing undue attention. She needed to get to Ryah, but Dockside was closer, and she could grab Talia on the way.

When she reached the small, winding alleys that led toward Dockside, she broke into a run, pulling the hat down low over her head. She worked her way to the alley behind the Nest, expecting to see at least one guard. But the alley was empty. There were no doors or windows on the first floor, but the stone would be easy to climb. She counted windows. Talia's flickered with candlelight.

Ignoring the thought of how angry Talia would be, she felt the stone wall for a good handhold. Shimmying up the rough rocks, Sable climbed until her head was even with the window. She looked in, her breath coming in short gasps that had nothing to do with the climb.

Talia sat at her desk leaning over a piece of paper, sketching something with a charcoal stick. A handful of drawings lay around her on the floor and the bed. The candlelight flickered off the light walls, giving the whole room a welcoming glow. Talia had changed out of the dress from the Choosing, wearing old pants and tunic. Her hair hung in front of her face, and Sable couldn't tell her mood.

The rest of the room was empty. Sable took a bracing breath and tapped on the window. Talia glanced up and a cold anger spread across her features as she strode to the window.

Sable ducked while she swung it open. "Can I come in?"

"No." Talia crossed her arms and positioned herself in front of the window, fixing Sable with a furious gaze.

Sable shifted her hands on the window frame. "Talia," she started. "I'm sorry I didn't—"

"You lied to me," Talia hissed. "For years! I thought she was *dead*!" The last word flew through the night, and Sable flinched. Everything about Talia brightened. The drab brown of her shirt shifted to a rich, honey color. The dim candlelight caught on long strands of her hair, tracing them like lines of embers. Flecks of gold shone out of her eyes, narrowed with fury.

"I know," Sable whispered. "I'm so sorry. I didn't know the best way to keep her safe. When I first hid her, you were still so little, I thought if you knew, you'd let the secret slip."

"And now?" Talia demanded. "I'm eighteen. Do you still think I can't keep secrets?"

"It's not that simple—"

"It is! You could have told me at any time. Just like you could have told me about the stash of money you had hidden under the floorboards where I slept every night! What else have you lied about?"

Sable gripped the window ledge. "Nothing! Come with me, Talia. I have a way for us to get away from Dockside. You, me, and Ryah. All of us."

"Kiva is going to get Ryah," Talia whispered matter-of-factly. "He'll have her by morning."

Anger flared inside Sable. "Not if I get her first."

Talia shook her head, looking at Sable as though she'd gone crazy. "Kiva will find her. If we try to run to a different part of the city, he'll find us and kill us all." She lifted her chin. "I can take care of her here, Sable. Kiva says he'll find her good, wholesome work—"

"Where? Are you going to give her your old bakery job? Or are you going to dress her up like Kiva wants and use her sweetness and innocence to rob people? Because he wants her stealing for him. He wants to own her the way he owns the rest of us. And I am not going to let him get her. That's the whole reason I put her into hiding in the first place!"

Talia looked at her, fury warring with something else on her face. "You were perfectly willing to put me under Kiva's control." Her words felt almost hot, and Sable could see every line and shadow on her face in perfect clarity.

Sable stared at her. "You think I saved Ryah, but not you? I didn't put you under his control. *You* put us both here."

"By being sick?" she demanded. "Ryah's sickness got her a home in some safe abbey somewhere, but when it came to me, you went to Kiva for help?"

"It had nothing to do with being sick." Sable almost stopped there, but this was something else Talia was old enough to hear. "Remember the orange scarf?"

"Of course I remember it. It was the most beautiful thing I'd ever seen. I took it from that horrible old woman, but by the time I got better, you'd sold it." She stepped forward. "It was the first beautiful thing I'd had, but you took it."

"I would have," Sable admitted, "if I'd had the chance. But that night, after you fell sick, two of Kiva's Fangs came."

Talia's eyes widened. "Why?"

"Because that horrible old woman you'd stolen from was a Fang's mother."

Talia's mouth dropped open, and she took a small step back. "No, it wasn't." All the warmth evaporated from her words, and she'd faded to match the muted colors in her candlelit room.

"The Fangs wanted to kill you. It took everything I had to convince Kiva to take us in exchange. They took the scarf, and the next morning, we moved into our horrible little room."

Talia stared at her. "And Ryah?"

"She was sleeping in that back closet. She was so sick, I'd laid her as far from us as I could so we wouldn't wake her. They never saw her. You were feverish and sleeping, so I took Ryah to an abbey across the city."

Talia sank down onto her bed, the anger draining from her face.

"You should have told me," she whispered softly. "Of everyone, I thought you were the one I could trust."

A slice of guilt dug into Sable. "I know." She shifted her toes in their holds on the wall. "I'm sorry, and I'll do whatever I can to make it up to you, but to have time to do that, Talia, we need to leave now."

"We'll never make it out," she said dully. "Kiva's men are everywhere. He has so many more than I thought he did."

"We'll be gone by dawn. He doesn't know we're running. Come out the window with me."

"I can't. Britta is coming to discuss my clothing. If I'm not here, she'll be suspicious."

Sable paused. "Can you sneak out once she's gone?"

Talia frowned. "Possibly."

"Good." Sable glanced down at the alley behind her. It was dark and quiet. "Meet me at the Veil Gate before dawn. Bring everything you want, because we're not coming back."

"This will never work."

"It will. Trust me. I'll get Ryah and bring her." Sable watched her for a moment. Talia's face was a tangle of confusion and pain.

"Promise me you'll come," Sable said. "The Veil Gate, before dawn."

Talia shook her head. "I'm not ready to promise you anything."

"Please—"

"But I want Ryah." Talia looked down at her hands, the words deeply true.

Sable let out a ragged breath. That would have to be enough for now.

A dog barked somewhere near the docks, and Sable glanced up at the stars that moved too quickly across the sky.

"I'm sorry, Talia," she whispered, then shimmied down and dropped quietly into the alley.

She looked back up at the window, but it was closed and empty. Sable stared at it for just a moment, hoping Talia would look out, but when she didn't appear, Sable broke into a quiet jog and ran uphill, out of the alleys of Dockside.

She moved swiftly along the Spine, glancing behind herself often.

As far as she could tell, no one followed. Discarding any attempts at secrecy in favor of speed, she ran through the dark streets. Past the middle-class merchant homes, down into the Bend. The thought crossed her mind that the Muddogs would be suspicious of someone running through their territory, so she slowed to a fast walk. Hurrying too much to avoid all the puddles in the muddy streets, her feet were soaked before she reached the street that ran along the wall. She paused again in a dark corner, but the night was still.

She slipped down the street and over the fence, working her way to the window along the side. As she neared it, a new fear grew.

Ryah had fallen ill in the small hovel the three girls had shared, then woke up here, surrounded by strangers. She wouldn't have even known whether Sable and Talia were still alive. After ten years, what could Sable possible say now to convince Ryah to come away?

Sable set a trembling hand on the windowsill and peered into the darkness, trying to make out the shapes of the four sleeping girls. But she could see nothing. She started to reach in to find Ryah's sleeping body, hoping she was in her bed below the window, when something moved.

"Hello, Sable," a quiet voice said.

CHAPTER SIXTEEN

SABLE FROZE, her hand clenching the sill.

"I thought you might come tonight." The voice was low, but the familiarity of it tore into Sable.

"Ryah?" she whispered.

"Who else would you expect to find in my bed?"

Sable let out a long breath. "How did you…" Questions swarmed in Sable's mind. Ryah knew she would come? "How long…" She stopped, the sheer number of things she wanted to know crowding out her questions.

She heard Ryah give a short huff, whether in amusement or anger, she couldn't tell.

"For years, I've known you come every month. I've tried to stay awake more times than I can count, but even if I managed it, I never heard you." She was quiet for a long moment. The shadows shifted, and a barely perceptible shape sat up in the bed below the window. "Sometimes I'd convince myself you were just a ghost."

The words dug under Sable's skin. Ryah had known all this time that she'd been deserted here? Knew Sable could get her, but didn't?

Sable gripped the windowsill. She wanted to reach out to her sister, but she couldn't bring herself to move. "I'm sorry, I..." All the reasons she'd ever had suddenly felt thin.

"Why are you here?" There was a catch in Ryah's voice, and it took a moment for Sable to place it. She'd been crying.

The Choosing...

Sable closed her eyes. Amid everything else, she'd forgotten what a devastating day this must have been for Ryah. She took a deep breath, tamping down all the things she wanted to tell her. There was too much to say, but not enough time.

"We have to leave."

Ryah was silent, and Sable waited for her objection.

"And go where?" Her voice sounded steadier.

"Out of the city."

Another pause. "Now?"

Sable nodded. "I'm sorry. It's my fault. There's this man who saw you at the Choosing and—"

"He's not the sort of man I want to find me?" she asked.

Sable didn't answer.

"But I'm safe here."

Sable let out a bitter laugh. "Not from a man like Kiva." She glanced toward the street along the front of the abbey.

"The boss of the Vayas?" Ryah asked in surprise.

Sable's attention snapped back to her sister. "You know Kiva?"

"Only by name."

Sable stared at her sister's dark form. How did a girl in an abbey this far from Dockside know Kiva's name? She bit back the new questions. "Well, I know him, and we need to go...quickly. If we can get away before he finds you, we'll be safe."

"And..." Ryah paused. When she spoke again, her voice trembled. "And Talia? Is she..."

"She'll meet us in the morning."

"She's alive?" Ryah's bed creaked as she knelt and came up close to the window. "I was never sure. I remembered her getting sick when I did. Then when she wasn't here with me..."

"She's alive," Sable whispered with a wave of guilt. Both sisters had spent ten years thinking the other was dead. "I'm sorry. I'll explain everything, I promise, but I have to get you safe."

Ryah was quiet. Her sister's long hair was up, and she was dressed in a light-colored nightgown.

"You haven't spoken to me in ten years." There was no accusation in her voice, but Sable flinched. "Why should I come with you now, in the middle of the night?"

"Because I love you." The words were out before Sable could even think through them. "Even if everything I've done has been wrong, I did it trying to protect you and Talia—but tonight is the first night I really can. By sunrise tomorrow, we can all be safe, away from this entire city and the people who want to use us."

"The goddess has always kept me safe," Ryah argued.

The goddess was too choosy about whom she kept safe.

"Please, Ryah?"

Her sister was quiet for a long moment. She was going to refuse. The wood under Sable's hands was rough. Splinters dug into her palms, but she squeezed it harder. What was she going to do if Ryah refused?

Her sister let out a quick breath. "I've been waiting for you to come get me for years. I have to tell the abbess goodbye."

Relief rolled over Sable. "Hurry."

Ryah slipped away from the window and Sable crept over to the abbess's window. She heard the door creak open.

"Holy Mother?" Ryah whispered. Sable climbed up on the rock below the window until she could see inside.

The dark shape of the abbess stirred on the bed. "Yes, child?"

"My sister is here."

There was a long silence, then a barely audible sigh. "Good evening, angel," the abbess whispered.

"Good evening, Holy Mother," Sable said quietly, checking toward the street again.

"My dearest Ryah, you're leaving." The abbess's words weren't a question.

"Leaving the city," Ryah said. With every word, Sable felt a tangle of emotions. It was Ryah's voice, but richer and older. And so much more serious. "Will you tell the others goodbye for me?"

"Of course." In the dim light, Sable saw the abbess open her arms, and Ryah rushed into them. "I will miss you dearly, child," she said in a muffled voice.

Sable watched the two, the ache in her heart growing. At every turn, at every desperate moment, she had chosen wrong. She wanted to climb through the window and drop at the feet of the abbess and Ryah, to plead with them to understand that she'd only been trying to keep everyone safe. That there had been no other choice. That there still was no other choice.

But her hands stayed gripped on the windowsill. There was no time. Kiva was coming, and if he got his hands on Ryah...

Beyond all the things Sable needed to tell her sister, there were a thousand things to say to this abbess who had taken in a sick child and given her a home. Who cared for these children the way someone should care for them. This woman who'd somehow offered hope in this muddy, desperate corner of a wider, desperate city.

But all Sable could say was, "Ryah, we need to go."

A sharp hitch in Ryah's breathing answered.

"Gather your things quickly, child," the old woman said. "If you're called away in the middle of the night, it seems best to hurry."

Ryah left the room, but Sable lingered at the window. She didn't know the abbess's name. It had been conscious choice not to learn it. Somehow, not knowing the details about Ryah's life had kept her more separate, and thus safer.

"Thank you, Holy Mother," she whispered, looking for the words to convey everything she owed this woman. "Thank you for keeping her safe for so long."

"Protecting the helpless is the work Amah and Isah most desire." She stayed on the bed, but Sable could make out her frail form sitting up. "Perhaps it is the only thing they truly desire."

Sable let out a huff. "Someone should tell that to the rest of their followers."

"Their true followers know," she said simply. "You know it."

Sable stiffened. "No one should use me as an example of what the gods want."

"Ten years ago, you gave up your sister to keep her safe. She tells me there was another sister, as well. I can only imagine you sacrificed as much for her. You gave of the little you had every full moon to help Ryah." The abbess's words flowed across the room and wrapped around Sable with warmth. They pressed up against her, pushing against the hardness filling her.

"That sounds better than it actually was," Sable whispered.

In the darkness, she saw the abbess raise a hand in blessing. "May Amah keep you and guide you." The familiar benediction felt different here. The strength of the prayer filled the small room and poured into the warm night. "May she wrap you in her gentle arms and soften all the world has hardened."

Sable pressed her eyes shut. She'd never heard those final words, and they sank into her, deep into a place that had been closed off long ago. A place that still echoed with her mother's prayers.

Sable dropped her head forward until it rested on the windowsill. Every muscle stayed coiled, poised to flee, yet she paused, surrounded and held by the words.

"May Isah protect you and keep you," the Holy Mother intoned the common blessing, then continued in her own words. "May he give you strength to do the things that must be done, to care for those you can, and to choose the paths that are best, even when they seem too hard."

A gentle hand touched Sable's head, and she flinched.

"You are a child of the gods, Issable," the abbess whispered.

The use of her full name caught Sable's breath.

"Let their blessing fall on you," the abbess continued. "There is strength in the goodness of it, despite everything you see around you."

Sable took a quivering breath. She raised her head to find the abbess's ancient, wrinkled face just inside the window. The abbess believed in the words so deeply she was slightly lighter in the dark room. Like a bit of thin moonlight had found her.

The warmth of the blessing surrounded Sable, standing in contrast to all her thoughts. "Every choice I've made has been wrong," she whispered.

The abbess gave her a wrinkled smile. "That is the curse of life. Judging your past actions in the light of what you know now." She tilted her head. "Give your past self grace, my child. She did the best she could."

A slight breeze stirred the night, but the tendrils of the prayer still lingered. Again, Sable wanted to climb through the window, kneel at this woman's feet, and pour out everything – all the fear, the guilt, the wrongness of everything she'd done, her anger toward Kiva. Everything.

But the night was passing quickly. "I'm sorry to take Ryah from you," she whispered, "and I'm sorry if trouble will come because of it."

The old woman shrugged. "There is always trouble coming from somewhere."

Sable let out a long breath. "This trouble might be more than you can handle."

"No trouble is too much for the gods."

Sable bit her lip at the sentiment. "Then I hope the gods are paying attention."

She climbed down from the stone and started back toward Ryah's window.

The abbess's wavering voice followed behind her. "They are always paying attention, Issable."

Sable paused, not sure if that was reassuring or frightening. She looked in Ryah's window and found her leaning over one of the other beds, whispering something. She'd changed out of her nightgown and into dark clothes. Her hair, which had hung free during the Choosing, was braided up into a sort of crown around her head. Sable glanced toward the road again and bit her lip, trying to give Ryah time.

Her sister slowly moved to the next bed.

"Ryah," she said, trying to convey her urgency and her apology into that one word.

Ryah stopped and straightened. She stood with her head bowed for just a moment before crossing to the window and handing Sable a small bag. Sable made way for her sister, and Ryah swung her feet over the ledge and scooted out.

Sable reached out to help her, but drew back before touching her.

Ryah dropped down, and Sable could make out her face. Nervous, uncertain, questioning.

Sable stepped closer. She wanted to wrap her arms around her little sister, like she'd done years ago. She wanted to beg for forgiveness, but Ryah wasn't little anymore. She was sixteen, and met Sable's gaze from an even height. Her baby sister's face was older but sweet and almost innocent with her wide eyes, still holding a bit of the roundness from years ago. But she was so much more serious.

Sable hesitated, the distance between them was too much to cross. She opened her mouth to say something, anything, but a rustle near the road caught her attention.

Two shadows climbed over the front fence.

"They're here," Sable whispered, her heart pounding. If Kiva had sent his Fangs…

She slung Ryah's bag over her own shoulder and grabbed her sister's hand, pulling her toward the back of the abbey. The yard was hemmed in with fences too tall to climb easily, but they'd need to try. Sable ran toward the back of the yard, her feet sinking into the damp earth, but Ryah pulled her to the right.

"There's a gap over here," she whispered.

Sable followed her to the side of the yard. A scraggly bush sat in front of the fence. Ryah knelt and crawled past it. With a final look back at the abbey, Sable followed, her hands squishing into mud. On the other side of the hole was another muddy yard.

Sable stood and shook the mud off her hand while Ryah turned left, heading straight for a tree against the back of this property. She scrambled up the trunk with enough familiarity that Sable paused at the bottom to watch. In seconds, Ryah climbed out onto a thick branch that hung over the fence and dropped down out of view. Sable followed her sister, who was already pushing her way through bushes at the side of the next yard.

Sable caught up and took Ryah's arm. "That's the house behind the abbey. It's too close. We need to get away from here."

Ryah pulled her arm away. "The abbey needs some guard dogs."

She was so serious. When had her laughing, happy sister grown so solemn?

With a rustle that was deafeningly loud in the still night, Ryah shoved through a gap between two bushes and disappeared.

Sable swore and followed. As she stepped out into yet another muddy yard, she heard her sister let out a low whistle. Three short notes and a longer trill. The yard was wide and open, and Sable stepped into it feeling exposed.

She stepped up next to Ryah, facing the house. "We don't have time—"

A shape moved on the back porch. A man with a shaved head walked down the stairs and stepped into the yard. Dark lines of tattoos swirled over his scalp and down his neck. His arms and chest were bare, except for more tattoos, and a dark, leather collar wrapped around his neck.

Sable grabbed Ryah's arm. A Muddog.

Ryah pulled away and hurried up to him, whispering and pointing toward the abbey. She glanced back at Sable, and with an irritated look, waved her closer. Sable stepped toward them, watching the man warily. He fixed her with a flat, suspicious look

"This is my guardian angel," Ryah said. The man looked unimpressed. Ryah turned to Sable. "How many are here? And from which gang?"

"I saw two," Sable whispered. "Vayas."

His eyes narrowed. "Why are the Vayas in the Bend?"

"They want Ryah," Sable answered. "But when they don't find her..."

He nodded. "The snakes will pay for coming to the doghouse." He turned toward the house and let out another whistle. Four quick, low blasts. Three more shapes moved in the shadows, and Sable took a half-step back. The tattooed man whispered to them, then they ran toward the abbey, scrambling over the tall fence with practiced ease.

Ryah reached forward and set her hand on the man's tattooed chest. "Amah bless you, Tomm," she breathed. "Thank you."

He gave her a quick grin and put his hand over hers. "Any time, little sister. I'm not sure Amah wants to be a part of what's coming next, but the abbey will be safe." He glanced at Sable. "Where are you two going?"

"Away," Sable answered shortly.

He narrowed his eyes. "You need more than a guardian angel, Ryah. I'll call you an escort."

Sable glanced at Ryah. An escort? Of Muddogs?

"No," Sable said, and the man's face hardened. "That won't be necessary. But thank you."

A shout came from over the fence, and Ryah spun toward it.

Sable put a hand on her arm. "We need to go."

The man gave Ryah a wicked grin. "I don't want to miss the fun. Off with you, little sister." He fixed Sable with a hard glance. "Keep her safe, snake."

Sable forced herself not to step back from him. "I'm not a snake," she whispered.

He took her in with an unimpressed gaze. "Well, you'd better have fangs or claws or something, because if Ryah gets hurt, the Dogs will find you." His voice was thick with the threat. He gave Ryah a quick nod, then ran across the yard and over the fence.

"You've made some interesting friends," Sable whispered.

More shouts came from the abbey, echoed by children's shrieks. Ryah took a step toward it.

"Your Dogs look capable," Sable said, pulling her away. "We need to go."

Reluctantly, Ryah followed.

The two of them ran past the side of the Muddogs' house and up through the streets of the Bend, keeping to the alleys that lay in shadows, crossing the moonlit ones only when absolutely necessary. The sounds of the fight at the abbey quickly faded. Kiva probably only sent two Fangs this deep into the Bend. They were only after one girl, and he invited enough trouble just sending his men into the Dogs' territory. But still, Sable kept them moving as quickly as Ryah could handle as they climbed back into the better parts of Immusmala.

When they reached the Spine, Ryah's breath came in gasps, and Sable slowed to let her rest. The avenue headed east, almost straight toward the rising moon. Moonlight spilled along the street, leaving only the right side in shadows. Sable moved quickly across the avenue to comparative safety.

"Where are we going?" Ryah asked, coming up next to her.

Sable glanced at her sister, struck again with how she looked familiar and unfamiliar at the same time. But Ryah was right here beside her. The hope she'd tried to hold in check all night flared up. "Thank you for coming with me. I know it was abrupt and..." Unexpected? Chaotic? Rude?

"There was obviously a good reason for it," Ryah answered, glancing back toward the long-gone abbey with a worried frown.

"Your friends will keep them safe," Sable assured her. "There's no way the Vayas were expecting resistance. They thought they'd only find children and an elderly abbess."

Ryah nodded, but her mouth was tight with worry. Sable took in her face again, feeling like she needed to get to know it all over again. Ryah was sixteen now, not a child of six who'd been left feverish and dying at the door of the abbey.

"I've been dreaming about the day I could come get you for years," Sable said quietly. "And I always pictured it more...calm. And happy."

Ryah didn't meet Sable's gaze. "Why did you wait so long?"

Her sister's tone wasn't accusing, but that didn't make it less painful. "Because it hasn't been safe. It's never been safe."

Ryah huffed out a breath. "And it's safe tonight?"

"No. It's more dangerous than it's ever been."

Ryah was quiet for a long moment, and Sable searched for something more to say.

Finally, her sister sighed. "You didn't tell me where we're going."

"We're meeting an acting troupe that is leaving the city at dawn. They're willing to take us with them."

Ryah raised an eyebrow. "Why?"

"Because I'm working for them," Sable said. The idea of acting was a bit ridiculous, but she'd face that difficulty when it came. As long as they were out of the city, everything else would take care of itself.

Sable glanced behind them. "How loyal are your Dogs?"

"They watch over the abbey," Ryah said vaguely.

"That's..." Sable paused. The Muddogs were at least as violent as Kiva's Vayas. "Why? Does the abbey do something for them?"

Ryah shrugged. "Mother Perrin prays for them."

Sable laughed. "You can't tell me it matters to them. What's the real reason? Do they stash things in the abbey? Do the kids work for them?"

"No!" Ryah answered indignantly. "They just like—" She glanced at Sable, then looked forward again. "Us."

It was impossible to tell for sure in the darkness, but it looked like Ryah might be blushing.

"It's you they like!" Sable let out a long laugh. "All this time, I've thought you were unprotected in a hidden abbey, but you've been..." She grinned at Ryah, who kept her eyes fixed ahead, "making friends with the Muddogs."

The corner of Ryah's mouth quirked up. "It's not like that."

Sable laughed again for the first time in what felt like ages.

"Not long after I came to the abbey," Ryah said, "and recovered from the fever, more cases of it sprang up in the Bend. Since I'd already had it, I visited the sick and tried to help. When I heard the men in the house behind us were sick, the abbess sent me to them with some bread. I had no idea who they were." She gave a weak smile. "I was wearing my whites, because we'd just finished morning prayers, and I think they didn't know what to do with the little girl at their door, so they let me in to see the two men. One was Tomm, the house boss you just met, and the other was his younger brother, who was much sicker. They both recovered. Since then, the Muddogs have offered to help the abbey whenever Mother Perrin needed it."

"Or whenever you needed it." Sable grinned. "Well, I'm done worrying the group of frightening Muddogs will let anyone follow us."

Ryah let the smile spread across her face. "We're probably safe."

Sable let out another laugh, shaking her head. "The whole world loves Ryah."

CHAPTER SEVENTEEN

THE VEIL GATE stood open and the far end of the plaza was still packed with people. Atticus's wagons sat at the end of the line of vendors and entertainers. The stage had been dismantled and the pieces stowed away.

As Sable and Ryah drew near, the dwarf from the plays stepped out to meet them.

"You must be Sable." His voice was gruff and body thick. The top of his head was no taller than Sable, but he was wider than her. He stood with his arms crossed and legs planted, as solid as a rock. "Where's the other sister?"

"She's meeting me at the Veil Gate before dawn." Sable turned to Ryah. "Stay here. I'll be back with Talia soon."

Ryah nodded, and gave the dwarf a small smile. "I'm Ryah."

"Thulan," he grunted. "There's a pile of curtains in that wagon if you need a place to sleep."

Ryah headed toward the wagon, and Thulan watched her with a frown. "We're takin' on a lot of strays," he muttered turning away. "This many people is going to make sleeping arrangements snug."

The abbesses spoke to the crowd from the priories at the far end, and all the people had moved near to watch, leaving this end of the plaza empty. Moonlight lit the Sanctuary, but a tree not far from the guardhouse provided a bit of shadow. From there, she should be able to see out the gate and have a view of most of the avenue. Two constables guarded the gate on the city side, and two Sanctus on the inside. A few thick clouds scuttled across the sky, and Sable waited for one to cover the moon.

Moving quickly, hopefully casually, Sable strode to the tree and sank down next to its trunk. When the moonlight reappeared, she shifted into the shadow. She grabbed the lowest branch and pulled herself up into a fork in the trunk where she could sit and wait.

The night was warm, but a cool breeze smelling of saltwater worked its way through the branches occasionally. The guards milled around, a few people hurried through the gate toward the priories, but mostly, this end of the plaza was still.

Worry simmered in Sable, just under the surface. Could Talia get out of the Nest undetected?

As the moon neared its peak in the sky, Sable rubbed her hands across her face. The tree trunk dug into her back, but she was too tired to care. Between Renwen's ledger and dropping the ring off at Ryah's abbey, she'd gotten little sleep last night, and tonight looked like it might be worse.

A single, low bell began tolling from the priories, and Sable shifted until she could see around the trunk, watching for the lights to appear.

As the deep sound echoed through the plaza, she could make out the shapes of four Mira standing along the front of the Dragon Priory. They lifted their arms, and a red spark of light appeared above each.

Slowly, the newly lit lanterns were released, the four lights rising slowly into the air. The papery top of the lanterns, shaped like shields, glowed a deep red.

The crowd held more lanterns aloft, and the Mira stretched their hands out toward them.

Pinpricks of light appeared above the crowd.

One rose, then another, then a dozen more.

In a breath, the air between the priories was filled with red lanterns floating up into the dark sky.

The silent shields ascending into the sky pulled at Sable, drawing out an old longing for the protection of Isah. A shield around Talia. Protection around Ryah. Something powerful that could shelter them from the world.

The years when she and Talia had stood under the rising lanterns, the canopy of red had stretched above them like an actual shield. It was the only time of year Sable could almost believe the god Isah was real.

But here, so far from the lights, the shields looked fragile. As they reached the top of the priories, the breeze caught them and pushed them out over the sea in a long, thin cloud of light.

She lay her head against the trunk, while the lanterns floated away in the vast darkness of the night.

She closed her eyes against the dark night, her body sinking more heavily against the tree.

A rustle sounded beneath the tree. Sable jerked her attention down to find Leonis leaning casually against the trunk, holding the bottle of leeswine.

"Anything exciting happening, Sneaks?" he asked quietly.

Sable rubbed her face. The lanterns were gone, the plaza nearly empty of people. The moon had moved toward the west. She must have dozed off. She let her head fall back onto the trunk.

"Nothing at all."

"I thought you could use a second pair of eyes." He took a long drink from the bottle.

Sable considered him for a moment. His face was more somber and a little more haggard than it had been. He looked exhausted. Had Atticus sent him to keep tabs on her?

"Thank you, but you don't have to lose sleep for this."

"I don't sleep much when we're in the city," he said, sitting down and leaning against the trunk. "I'll sleep once we're not surrounded by stone and people. Once we can see forests."

"You know you're leaning against a tree, right?"

He turned his face up toward the branches. "This isn't a tree. It's just a decoration for people to try to convince themselves they're not really living away from the true world."

Sable laughed. "I thought I was the one anxious to leave the city."

"The first day is always tolerable, but tomorrow will be the third, and that is entirely too long. It's time to get back to living things. Where the night is noisy with the sounds of the wind and animals, not crowds and constables."

From past the gate, she could hear a constable's whistle and some distant shouting. "I don't know what that feels like."

"It feels like you're alive."

He shot an annoyed look toward the wagons. "Besides, Lady Merilee is still awake, and I can't bear to listen to her any longer. If you're her replacement, I'm here to offer you any help I possibly can."

"I'm not her replacement. I'm supposed to play second lady." There was a small bit of lantern light coming from the wagons. "But Atticus is crazy to hire me."

"I heard he's not hiring you. You're volunteering."

Leonis peered toward the gate. "Who am I looking for? Does sister number two look like sister number one?"

Sable considered the question. "More than I'd realized. Her hair is longer and straighter, more auburn. She's eighteen and will look nervous. And maybe angry."

He laughed. "Take a few hours to rest. I'll keep my eye out for any young women at all and wake you if I see one."

Sable glanced down at him, the comforting warmth of the truth in Leonis's words wrapped around her.

"Thank you." She settled back against the trunk again, focusing on the gate.

She had no memory of closing her eyes, but she was soon racing through alleys, trying to outrun the fires blazing behind her. A huge, black raven dove at her…

She jerked awake at the feel of someone grabbing her foot, guttural shouts fading away with the dream. The eastern sky was deep blue instead of black.

Leonis stood, his hand tight on her foot, looking toward the gate. "Stay hidden."

Sable peered into the avenue, looking for Talia's form. She saw nothing but a few shapes lingering near the mouth of an alley.

"Do you see her?" she whispered to Leonis.

He glanced up at her, but in the darkness, she couldn't read his expression. "No, but aren't those the two men we did that constable show for?"

Sable froze. Pete and Boone.

Boone leaned against one of the buildings, while Pete slowly stomped in and out of the alley.

"How did they find me?" she asked, not meaning to say it out loud.

"Maybe your sister let your secret slip." Leonis said.

Sable shook her head. "She wouldn't do that."

"Well then, she'll be walking directly past them."

Sable clenched her hands into fists. The sun would be up soon. Over near Atticus's wagon, she could see movement as they prepared to leave.

"Perhaps it's time you told me who those two upstanding gentlemen are," Leonis said mildly.

Sable sighed. "They might as well be Fangs." At Leonis's blank expression, she continued. "They're two thugs who work closely with the gang boss in Dockside. Not Fangs, though. Those would just kill us and leave us in an alley. These two report directly to Kiva. He uses them for surveillance on his more personal jobs."

He raised an eyebrow and looked back at the gate. "If I'd known I was performing for such an alarming audience yesterday, I'd have asked for two bottles of wine." He pushed off the tree. "I'll go check it out."

"Wait," Sable hissed, but the tall man was gone, walking casually toward the gate.

He gave the guards a friendly nod and walked down the avenue so he'd pass right in front of Pete and Boone. When he reached them, he paused and said something. Pete pointed down the avenue, and Leonis continued. He disappeared from Sable's sight for so long that she was ready to climb down after him. But then he reappeared, holding a small bundle. Stopping by Pete and Boone again, he handed them something, then walked back through the gate. He strolled to the tree and sat, opening his bundle to reveal two sweet rolls.

"They're not alone," he said quietly, taking a bite. "There's someone in the alley behind them."

"Who?"

He paused. "A young woman with long, straight hair."

Sable drew in a sharp breath. "They have Talia? Is she hurt?"

Leonis paused. "I don't think she's there against her will. When I first stopped, she said hello to me, then when I came back, I heard her teasing the big fellow."

Sable stared at the two in the alley. Talia was with them? By choice?

"When I gave her a sweet roll," he continued, "she said thank you as though she were just out for a cheerful morning lurk in an alley."

Leonis took the final bite of his roll, rewrapped the other, and brushed his hands on his pants. He stood and glanced toward the gate, sighing. The eastern sky was growing brighter by the moment, and Sable could clearly see the resigned look on Leonis's face.

"I'm sorry, Sneaks, but dawn is almost here. If you're coming with us, now's the time."

Sable looked at the gate, her mind searching for a different answer.

The plaza was already starting to brighten. If she was going to cross to the wagons without giving Pete and Boone a perfect view of her, it had to be now. But still, she lingered. Talia couldn't be working with Kiva. If she could just talk to her…

But Ryah was waiting with Atticus.

"You coming?" Leonis asked.

A breath that was almost a sob tore out of Sable, but she shifted on the branch so she could climb down.

When she reached the ground, Leonis handed her the last sweet roll. "Maybe the thugs will get tired of waiting and she'll be alone when we roll through the gate."

The hope in his voice was too thin to deserve an answer.

CHAPTER EIGHTEEN

SABLE'S WALK back through the shadowy plaza to Atticus's wagons felt exposed. Pete and Boone...and, worse, Talia...would be able to see her if they looked in the right direction. While the two men probably wouldn't recognize her in the darkness, Talia might.

"I can't leave Talia," Sable said finally.

"This isn't you leaving her. This is her deciding not to come," Leonis pointed out.

"They'll think she knew. That she covered for me."

"For her to be with them, she had to tell them you weren't arrested and told them your plans. She's obviously working with them now. There's no reason for them to blame her."

"Just because someone is working for Kiva doesn't mean he'll treat them well."

"She's obviously valuable to him."

Sable paused, but nodded. Talia was worth a lot more to Kiva healthy and working than tortured and broken. Even more if she trusted him and worked with him willingly.

Leonis set his hand on Sable's shoulder. "We'll be back in Immusmala in a month. That's enough time for things to settle down. You can get to her then. I'll even help you. If she's valuable to him, she'll be safe in the meantime."

"You don't know that."

"I know that men protect the things that will give them power or money. If your sister offers him that, she'll be safe."

Sable glanced back toward the gate and blew out a long breath. "I wasn't planning on coming back."

Leonis snorted. "The places that hold those we love have a way of pulling us back, whether we want to be there or not."

Atticus's wagons were hitched to plodding looking horses. Ryah talked quietly to Atticus and the dwarf. She glanced over and a wave of relief rolled across her face when she saw Sable.

Sable paused when she saw the two grey-robed people from the balcony at the Choosing standing there, as well.

Atticus stepped forward to meet them. "Do you have the money?"

Sable pulled her payment from her pocket and handed it all to him.

Thulan leaned forward. "That's it?" he grumbled. "We might as well be picking up stray dogs."

"It's what Atticus agreed on," Leonis said. "And there's only one sister now, so it's actually more per passenger."

Atticus looked at Sable questioningly.

She opened her mouth, but couldn't answer.

"The second wasn't able to make it," Leonis said.

"Where's Talia?" Ryah asked.

Sable shook her head. "She's...decided she'd rather stay." The words sat heavy in her mouth.

Ryah looked toward the gate. "We can't leave her."

"We can, though," Thulan said. "We can leave all of you."

Merilee came around the corner of a wagon dressed in a tight black tunic, several silver necklaces, and a flamboyant red skirt. Without a wig, her hair was smooth and blonde. Without her makeup, her face was thin and chiseled into a tight, disapproving look.

"What are we waiting for?" She gestured at Sable, thin, silver bangles clinking together on her wrist. "Drive away the riffraff. The faster we're through this dull day of travel and back to civilization, the better."

Leonis made an exasperated noise, and the grey-robed couple exchanged looks.

"Because no one wants to spend the day traveling along the most beautiful stretch of coastline in the world," Thulan muttered.

"Pure torture," Leonis added dryly.

Atticus ignored them. "There's no one to drive away," he said to Merilee. "Sable is our new second lady."

The woman's gaze swung over and landed on Sable so quickly Sable almost felt it. Merilee took in her hair, which was probably disheveled enough to warrant the disgusted look it got, to her feet. Her gaze lingered on the one dark boot.

"She can't be second lady. She's nobody."

Whatever Sable had expected, it wasn't that, and she let out a short laugh.

Ryah stiffened. "Nobody is a nobody."

Merilee frowned, sliding a sparkling pendant along the silver chain at her neck. "Says the other nobody." She lifted her chin. "I'm Lady Merilee of Colbreth Castle." The words were more a judgment on Sable and Ryah than an introduction of herself. "You're not titled, are you?"

Sable crossed her arms. "I don't think we're rude enough to be titled."

Thulan snorted, and Leonis laughed. Even the severe woman dressed in grey smiled.

Merilee turned on Atticus. "You cannot be serious about hiring her."

"I'm always serious about my troupe," the old man said.

"What acting has she done?" Merilee turned back to Sable. "Where have you performed?" It was a fair question, but the tone irritated her.

"All over the city," Sable answered. "Smaller roles mostly. Couriers, shop workers, things like that."

"Just yesterday," Leonis added, "she played a convincing criminal being arrested right here in the festival. And I've seen her do a very good impersonation of a shadow."

Sable nodded, grinning. "Those are just some recent performances."

"Sable will be joining us," Atticus said firmly, "as well as her sister, Ryah."

Merilee barely spared Ryah a glance. "And what does she bring?"

"Ryah," Atticus answered, "has met the High Prioress."

Sable glanced at her sister. She'd already told Atticus about the Choosing?

"Maybe it will come in handy." Atticus's voice sounded light, but the warm truth of his words caught Sable's attention.

Merilee frowned at Ryah. "How does that help us?"

"It may not." Atticus shrugged. "But it is interesting."

What was more interesting to Sable was that the warm truth in his voice wrapped around her snuggly. What did he find so important about Ryah?

"And she will be traveling with us," Atticus continued, "whether or not you see the value in it, Lady Merilee." He smiled at Ryah. "It's been a while since we've had anyone holy along for the ride."

"I'm not holy," Ryah objected. "I'm just—"

"That's where I've seen you!" Leonis interrupted. "You were at the Choosing."

Thulan snapped his thick fingers. "You're the sad girl."

"I thought you were going to be chosen," the man in grey said.

Thulan turned to Atticus. "We don't need a prioress."

"I am not a prior—" Ryah started, irritated.

"Thulan," Atticus said mildly, "the whole point of these festivals is to gain the attention of the High Prioress."

Thulan looked unimpressed. "You're the only one who wants the attention of a High Prioress, Atticus," he grumbled. "The rest of us just want to get away from this city."

Sable glanced at Atticus, but he didn't object. The man did have high hopes if he thought he'd get the High Prioress's attention. Ryah couldn't help with that, but Sable didn't want to point that out now.

Thulan pointed at Ryah. "Keep your prayers inside your own head, Prioress. The rest of us don't want to hear them."

Ryah's mouth dropped open slightly in shock.

"She's not a prioress." Sable didn't bother to hide her irritation.

"Atticus," Merilee said, "I had expected you would have spent your time here finding a real actress for the second lady."

"We're not trying to replace a real actress for second lady," Thulan said. "We're trying to replace you."

Leonis laughed, but quickly turned it into a cough at Merilee's glare.

Atticus shot the dwarf another quelling look, but he didn't completely hide his amusement. "Regardless, I've hired Sable, so I hope your judgment is off, Lady Merilee. At least this once."

The Sanctuary grew lighter by the moment. Atticus glanced east and motioned everyone toward the wagons. "It's time to leave. The sun waits for no man." He gave Lady Merilee a bow. "Or lady."

Atticus walked to the driver's bench of the first wagon. Amused, the couple in grey robes followed him.

Merilee sniffed in irritation and moved to the back of the red wagon. When she opened the door, the gentle, green glow of the fairy light tree filled the wagon like the entrance to some different type of realm. Sable watched the glowing lights until Merilee pulled the door shut.

Thulan grinned as Merilee disappeared. "Welcome to the group, girls," he said. "If you're going to annoy Merilee, maybe it won't be so bad dragging you two along."

Before they could answer, he climbed up into the driver's bench of the blue wagon and gathered up the reins. Leonis went to the side of the red wagon and pulled open a window. Inside, the branches of the glowing green tree were visible. Stepping up on a small ledge, he flipped open a portion of the roof as well, leaving the top of the tree open to the sky.

Leonis climbed down and motioned the girls to the back of the blue wagon, holding open the door. "You two might want to make yourselves scarce until we get away from the lurkers. The most comfortable seats are in the curtain piles."

A bench ran along one wall inside the wagon, holding crates and baskets. If the other side held a bench, it was completely covered by piles of folded black curtains. Ryah climbed in and Sable turned back toward the gate.

Atticus's wagon started moving.

"If you don't come, Atticus won't take Ryah, either," Leonis said quietly, "The deal was for you, Sneaks, not your sister."

Sable glanced up at Ryah, sitting on the pile of curtains and clutching her bag to her chest. Talia could at least take care of herself, but Sable needed to get Ryah away from Kiva. With a nod, Sable climbed up and settled on the pile next to her sister.

"I'll see if she happens to be alone as we pass." Leonis pushed the door closed, leaving them in murky darkness. He didn't sound hopeful.

The wagon lurched into motion, and Sable braced herself against the side as it turned, bumping over the stones in the plaza. Thin cracks around the door and two different windows let in a little of the dim morning light, but Ryah was merely a lighter shape sitting on the dark curtains.

"She's really not coming with us?" Ryah asked quietly.

Sable took a deep breath. "She's with some of Kiva's men outside the gate. She's obviously told them where we are and they're waiting. If they see us, they'll take us to Kiva. I don't know what they'll do to me, but they'll force you to work for them. At best, you'll be stealing."

Her brow furrowed. "I never would."

"Then they'd hurt you." Sable sighed. "Or kill you."

"Is Talia stealing for them?" There was a hint of something hard in Ryah's voice.

The question cut into Sable. Talia and Ryah hadn't even had a chance to see each other, so any explanation of Talia's actions right now was bound to sound bad to Ryah. "No. Until recently, she had a job working in one of Kiva's bakeries." She bit her lip. Keeping secrets had alienated Talia. Sable might as well try the truth with Ryah. "But a short time ago, she agreed to join his jays."

"What's a jay?"

"Spies Kiva has positioned around the city."

Ryah frowned.

"She's not the sort of person who would be a spy. She's just tired of living in poverty. She got a job working for the daughter of a wealthy merchant."

Ryah looked down at her hands, and Sable wished she'd explained it differently.

When Ryah spoke, it was quiet. "Comfort and safety are hard things to turn down."

"If you go to Talia, it's what you could have, too," Sable answered honestly. "Well, not real safety, but the gang's version of it. Kiva provides housing and food in exchange for work. He was excited when he learned about you. His comment was that with your face, you could convince anyone of anything."

Ryah straightened. "I couldn't do it. I couldn't steal things."

Sable let out a short huff. "It's easier than you think."

Her sister looked at her for a long moment, considering her words. "But you aren't a jay, are you?"

"It was bad enough to be a thief for him. Being a jay puts you more deeply under Kiva's control. All I've ever wanted is freedom from him." Sable stared dully at the closed door. "I knew Talia wanted the comforts more money would bring, but I never imagined she'd pick that over freedom."

Sable rubbed her face. Her eyes were gritty with exhaustion.

Through the thin gap next to the door, she could see the pale stones of the plaza as they passed. Once they reached the Veil Gate, she moved closer and pressed her face against the gap. The stocky form of Pete and the enormous shape of Boone came into view. Sable twitched back.

But a shape moved in the alley behind Boone. A woman, leaning casually against the wall. Sable caught the flash of a smile.

Even in the shadows, Talia was unmistakable.

CHAPTER NINETEEN

SABLE LEANED CLOSER to the gap next to the door, holding her breath.

Pete watched the wagons roll by with a lazy boredom. Sable stared at Talia, looking for any sign of distress, but her sister just leaned against the wall, looking tired. Pete said something, and Talia gave him a small smile.

Sable sank back onto the pile of curtains. The worry for Talia that had filled her fizzled into numbness.

How could she?

The wagons continued down the cobblestones of the Spine. Elaborate buildings and extravagant homes were visible through the thin gaps in the wood, then the wide avenue heading down to Dockside. Occasionally, bits of the glittering sea sparkled past everything else.

The wagon slowed and turned, heading toward the River Gate and away from Dockside. Sable dropped her head into her hands.

How had she not known Talia was lying about coming?

I'm not ready to promise you anything, but I want Ryah.

The memory left a sour taste.

Talia hadn't lied. She never agreed to come at all. She'd only said she wanted Ryah.

"I hope she's safe," Ryah whispered.

For so long, her fear had been that getting to Ryah would be the problem. And here sat her baby sister—older, steadier than Sable could have ever imagined, close enough to touch.

Sable dug her fingers into her scalp.

But Kiva—of all the things he controlled in her life, of all the things he'd taken from her, she'd never once imagined he'd take Talia.

Ryah lay down on the pile of fabric, her face drawn with worry. She closed her eyes, her lips moving. Sable let out a breath.

Good. Maybe if Ryah asked Amah to watch over Talia, the goddess would actually listen.

With Dockside lost over the hill, Sable pushed open the shutters covering a small window in the wall across from them, letting in a little morning light. Thin clouds blanketed the eastern sky, and the sunlight hit the tallest buildings with a harsh light.

The door swung open, and Leonis peered in at them. "Assuming we're a safe distance from Dockside, walking is more pleasant than bumping along in the wagon."

Sable glanced at Ryah, who nodded. They climbed down and walked with Leonis alongside the blue caravan. Thulan slumped down on the driver's bench of the wagon, holding the reins loosely, looking half-asleep. Lady Merilee and the two grey-robed people were out of view, but voices drifted back from the front of Atticus's wagon.

The buildings lining the avenue were extravagant. The River Gate ahead of them was the most traveled entrance to the city, and shops along this portion were second only to the grander ones along the Spine. The stores were just opening, and most of the people they saw were shop workers or delivery boys with armloads of packages.

Sable walked next to Ryah. In the morning light, her sister looked older and more tired. Less like Sable remembered her.

Leonis asked Ryah about herself, and Sable chimed in to fill in any gaps Ryah didn't know about herself and Talia.

"So, Sneaks," Leonis said, turning to Sable, "one sister feels at home in an abbey, the other in a gang. That's an odd combination."

Sable shook her head. "Don't expect an explanation from me. The abbey makes sense. But choosing the Vayas?"

"Maybe the security the gang offered outweighed the risk of leaving," Ryah offered. "In her own way, maybe she was trying to keep us all safe."

"There's nothing safe there," Sable answered.

"That depends on what she's trying to protect herself from," Ryah pointed out. "You want freedom and are willing to risk everything for it. But Talia wants a place to live and food to eat, and to her, it's worth sacrificing her freedom to get it."

Sable shook her head, but Ryah was right. That was exactly what Talia wanted. Except she'd actually chosen it over her sisters. "She doesn't realize how much danger she's in."

They reached the bottom of the long hill, and the avenue turned, revealing the city wall with the River Gate thrown open.

They walked in silence for several minutes, before Ryah asked, "How are we going to get Talia out from under Kiva?"

Sable kept her eyes fixed on the gate. "I have no idea. Unless one of you knows a way to earn more than a hundred silver over the next month."

"You can become a famous actress," Leonis suggested.

"Even if Atticus were paying me, he only offered three silver."

"For second lady on a trip away from Immusmala, three silver is generous. It's the trip back, when we'll perform our tourney play, that we'll actually earn money."

"What are you performing this year?" Sable asked.

"Don't know yet." Leonis glanced up at the red wagon. "The old man's been working on something for ages but won't tell us what. Judging from his excitement, it'll be something good. And the better the show, the more money we'll make."

Ryah looked at him curiously. "Who pays you?"

"The audience. The more we impress them, the more they give. And winning the tourney itself pays."

"How much?" Ryah asked.

"Three hundred silver to the winning troupe."

Ryah's eyebrows rose. "Three hundred?"

Leonis nodded. "Atticus gets a third, then the rest is split up among the actors, depending on the roles we played."

"So, in addition to my winnings as second lady," Sable said dryly,

"I'd have to rob several of you to get my one hundred fourteen silver."

Leonis grinned. "Probably."

A long, warbling note came from inside Atticus's wagon. Leonis shot a glare toward it. The note turned into a scale, rising up into the morning air. It wasn't exactly unpleasant, the notes were clear, but there was a nasal tightness to it.

"No," Thulan groaned. "Too early!"

"If she could act," Leonis said, "all the singing might be forgivable."

"If she doesn't act well, why does Atticus keep her?" Ryah asked.

"She hasn't been with us long," Thulan answered. "But she's useful because her family is noble and wealthy. The fact she joined an acting troupe verges on scandalous, so the nobility always want to see her." Looking back toward Atticus's wagon, he yelled, "No singing!"

Merilee ignored him and began a long, slow ballad. Thulan growled and sank lower on his bench.

Leonis rolled his eyes and looked back at Sable. "Now that Merilee's not here to be condescending about it, what roles have you played?"

Sable paused. "None."

Leonis stared at her for a moment, then exchanged glances with Thulan.

She gave them a weak smile. "Don't worry. I don't expect it to go well, either. At this point, I'm keeping 'rob the troupe' as my top plan for getting money."

"Judging by your associates in Immusmala," Thulan said, "I'm guessing that might be in your skill set."

"Why did Atticus hire you?" Leonis asked.

Sable shrugged. "I can memorize lines when I hear them."

"How many lines?"

"All of them."

Leonis raised an eyebrow. "That's a useful skill. Maybe you'll work out after all. If you unseat Lady Merilee and take first lady, you might not make a hundred silver, but you'd have to rob less of us to get there."

Sable shook her head. "Atticus has another actress he wants as first lady."

Leonis's eyebrows rose. "Who?"

"Someone on the Eastern Reaches."

Thulan made an approving grunt. "That's a good sign."

"Who's he looking for?" Ryah asked.

"A real first lady," the dwarf grumbled.

Merilee began a new song, and Leonis winced. "It must be Zephony. If Atticus is trying to get her out of retirement, his play must be a good one."

They drew closer to the River Gate. High above them, city constables moved along the top of the wall. Sable looked through the open gate, hoping to see the Tremmen Hills.

But there was no green. Just more stone buildings and the same avenue stretching on.

Voices floated back from Atticus's wagon.

"Who are the two in the grey robes?" Sable asked.

"Scholars. The cheerful one is Jae, and the serious one is his wife, Serene," Leonis answered. "At this time of year, they travel with us to the southern edge of the Marsham Cliffs, then they'll go north to wherever they spend the rest of summer. In the fall, we'll pick them up again and bring them back here."

"They sat in a balcony at the Choosing."

Leonis nodded. "They live at the priories during the winter and spring. You wouldn't know it by looking at them, but they're part of the highest circles in the city."

"Then why do they travel with Atticus?" Sable asked.

Leonis laughed. "Because Atticus has connections everywhere."

They topped a small rise, and Sable's breath caught. Buildings continued down the road, but past them rolled stunning green slopes. The Tremmen Hills rose like soft piles of green wool, dotted with rocky outcroppings. Thin trails wound up the slopes and disappeared into the valleys between them.

The air felt different. Sable breathed it in, and past the dusty smell of the wagons and the horses, she caught the smell she'd found in the tree outside Lord Renwen's window. Wild and fresh.

Behind her, the city surged up the hill with Talia still somewhere in it. And she would be for the next month, Sable thought uneasily. Ryah glanced back at the city, and Sable's worry for Talia tangled up with the relief that Ryah was safe.

And, if Sable were being honest, she was relieved for herself, as well.

She looked at the wagons rolling down the road. It wasn't worth a hundred and fourteen silver, but a job as Atticus's second lady would earn her more than anything else she could think of. So if Atticus wanted her to fill some small roles, she'd give him the best second lady he'd ever had. And when it came time to pick his second lady for the Midsommer Festival, she'd just have to beat out Merilee for the role.

The woman's voice still floated out of the wagon ahead of her. It couldn't be that hard to be a better actress than Lady Merilee, could it?

All she needed was an actress's equivalent of looking for a horseshoe and finding a horse.

PART II

"It was always about her sisters, you understand. Yes, the entire world ended up at stake, but even then, it was still about her sisters."

-from Keeper Sini's letters to Queen Madeleine, in the 410th year of Queensland.

CHAPTER TWENTY

THE WORLD ahead of the wagons was incomprehensibly green. Farmhouses replaced the city building, stretches of grass between them. A low, rolling hill pushed the road up against the edge of the Lingua River to a wide, low bridge. Not far beyond it, the cobblestones ended, and the wagon bumped onto hard-packed dirt.

Jae and Serene appeared from the far side of Atticus's red wagon. Serene opened the door and climbed inside.

Jae introduced himself and his wife, and fell in beside them. "I'm sorry your sister didn't come." There was the slight warmth of truth to his words.

"So are we," Ryah answered.

"I'm very interested in chatting with you," he continued.

"That's not a compliment," Serene called from the wagon. "He's interested in chatting with anyone, at any time,"

Jae grinned. "That's true. And for now I'll have to settle for chatting with only one of you, because Atticus would like to talk to you about tonight, Sable."

"Tonight?" she asked.

"You did come with us to perform, Sneaks," Leonis said. "And

Folhaven is the biggest town outside of Immusmala. We're definitely performing tonight."

The idea snaked uneasily into her, but she nodded and headed toward Atticus's wagon. She found him sitting on the scarlet red driver's bench, the reins held loosely in his hands. He looked different sitting on a wagon than he did striding around stage. His beard was a bit disheveled, and the tunic he wore was a common, undyed linen.

He motioned her up, and she climbed over the painted line of golden yellow flowers along the edge of the bench, taking a seat next to him. The smell of horses mingled with the damp smell of grass.

"I wasn't sure you'd come without your other sister," he said.

She sighed. "Talia chose to stay. I don't think I could have changed her mind. At least not before you left."

He considered the words. She thought he'd ask more, but he just nodded. "How familiar are you with Lady Argent, Terrelus's cousin?"

"Fairly."

He handed her a small, loosely bound bundle of papers. "Here is the script. Can you have the lines memorized by tonight? She's only in scenes three, five, and eleven, but her words are pivotal to the story, so they must be right."

Sable looked at the thin script on the front page. "I can't..."

Atticus's eyes widened in realization. "You can't read."

"I can read," Sable objected. "But reading won't help me remember. I need to hear them said by someone who says them well. Could you recite them to me? It shouldn't take long. I've heard them before, but it's been a long time."

Atticus frowned slightly.

"Or I could ask Leonis," Sable offered quickly.

"No. He'll take liberties. Have Thulan read them."

The dwarf? "Leonis seems more..." Sable searched for the word. "Able to act like Lady Argent."

Atticus laughed a deep, rich laugh. "I wouldn't mention that to either of them. If you want a good feel for the lines, get Thulan to read them." He chuckled again. "We'll run through them when we stop for lunch to see how you're doing. By midafternoon, we'll be in Folhaven and busy until the show, so I hope you can learn lines as fast as you claim you can."

It wasn't remembering the lines that had her worried. "How big of a crowd will we draw?"

"The size of the crowd doesn't matter."

She paused. "How can it not?"

He ran his fingers through his beard. "What is Lady Argent trying to convince her cousin of?"

"To let go of his jealousy before it destroys everyone he loves."

"Do you think she's right?"

Sable nodded, looking at the green hills slowly passing next to them. Flashes of colored birds flitted among the trees. "Every single time I hear her, I find myself hoping that this time, Terrelus will listen."

Atticus grinned. "Every time I play him, I hope the same. And that is the important part. When you say Argent's lines, don't think of people listening to you. Immerse yourself in the need to make Terrelus hear you. The audience isn't there to see you think about them. They want to see you heartbroken over the choices of a man who could be great, if only he could overcome his own demons."

"How do you do Terrelus's lines then? You can't really want him to say them."

Atticus looked ahead of them, down the road. "In most characters, including Terrelus, there are things I agree with. Truths I feel."

Sable nodded. There was the one section where the truth of Atticus's words always warmed her. "When he claims..." She closed her eyes to remember the words. "*I cannot but love her. I would face the gods themselves, could they be found. I would change everything on earth—save her.*"

She opened her eyes to find Atticus looking at her sharply. "Why did you pick those words?"

Sable paused, suddenly realizing she'd misstepped. She shook her head. "I'm not sure." Her own words felt cool with the lie.

Atticus's expression didn't waver. "I think you are." He considered her for a long moment, before the sharpness in his face shifted to interest. "Do you know which words Leonis agrees with when he's Epophus?"

Of course she did. She waited for it every time she saw the play. But she wasn't about to tell Atticus that. He turned his attention back to the road, waiting for her answer with a tension in his hands. She cast around for something evasive to say.

And then it struck her: She was sitting on a wagon with Atticus.

Atticus, the leader of The Duke's Figment of Wits Traveling Troupe. Who, without any real compensation, was helping her and Ryah escape a city she'd never even hoped to leave.

He deserved some honesty.

"His final speech," she answered, "where Epophus declares that he never had any other choice. That the world had set him on his path, and to have picked any other life, he would have betrayed himself."

Atticus didn't move. "And Thulan?"

The dwarf was harder. "There's a moment as the warrior in Epophus's tale." She tried to remember the lines, but that section of the play was a bit chaotic. "When he talks about the arrows not shot."

Atticus let out a small laugh. *"The only bolts of mine that did as I wished were the arrows not shot."* He turned back to Sable. "How do you know that?"

It felt odd to put it into words, but there wasn't any way to pretend she didn't have an unusual skill now. "I can feel when someone tells the truth, when they really believe what they're saying."

"Feel it?"

She thought for a moment. "Feeling is the best explanation. There's a warmth to the truth. Like a thick blanket wrapping around you. It's not the same as the warmth from the sun, or a fire, but if someone really believes what they're saying, I feel a...sense of warmth around me."

"Does it actually have to be true? Or just something they believe to be true?"

"It's all about how much they believe it. The more strongly they believe it, the more I can feel it. If they're lying, it feels sharp and cold instead." She expected some sort of disbelief, but the man merely looked ahead. A slight frustration at the incompleteness of the description nagged at her. "It's not really a feeling, though. It's..." She sighed. "I don't know how to explain it. Occasionally, when someone is really passionate about what they're saying, they even look different. Brighter, clearer."

Atticus was silent for a moment. "That's..." He ran his fingers through his beard, and looked back at her with great interest. "Do people tell the truth often?"

She let out a laugh. "Barely ever." He raised an eyebrow. "That sounded worse than it is. Most conversations are about things people don't care about one way or the other. But occasionally, someone says something that is utterly true, that they mean with everything they are. And that feels different."

"Do other people notice?"

Sable shook her head. "Usually the most truthful statement is tucked in the middle of the rest of it."

Atticus looked down the road. "That is one of the most unique talents I've ever heard of. How many people know about it?"

"Only my sisters."

He glanced at her. "The one who stayed in Dockside knows?"

A chill rolled over her at the thought of Talia telling Kiva. It took no imagination at all to see how he would view such a talent.

She drew back a little from Atticus, realizing how much she was sharing with a stranger.

"Thank you for telling me," he said, meeting her eye. "I won't use it against you, Sable." The warmth reassured her more than the actual words.

"I owe you more than you can know for taking Ryah out of the city." She tried to make the words convey how deeply she felt them.

He gave a slight smile. "Then pay me back by being the best Lady Argent any audience has ever seen."

Sable glanced at the play. "I intend to."

"I have no doubt you'll do fine," he said, his voice thin and cool.

"Liar," she said with a smile before climbing down from the wagon and walking back toward the others.

Leonis and Ryah looked at her curiously when she returned. Thulan gave her the briefest glance.

"Lady Argent," she told Leonis, holding up the papers.

"Excellent. I'll run through your lines with you."

She gave him an apologetic look and started toward the wagon. "I'm supposed to work with Thulan."

The dwarf scowled. "Why?"

She paused. "Atticus said if I wanted a feel for how the lines were said, I should come to you."

"I can play Lady Argent," Leonis objected.

Thulan snorted. "You make her sound like a spineless noblewoman."

Leonis frowned. "She is. She's useless. Wastes time arguing with Terrelus when she'd be better off locking him in her wine cellar to keep him from doing anything stupid."

Thulan let out an annoyed huff. "Lady Argent is the only one in the entire play with any sense. If Terrelus would listen to her, he'd actually accomplish what he set out to do."

Sable nodded. "I agree with Thulan."

"They never would have let him live there in peace," Leonis objected, sounding irritated.

"He ran away before he bothered to try!" Thulan threw out.

Leonis jabbed a finger at the dwarf. "You're going to fault the man for leaving a place he didn't want to be anymore?" His voice rose. "You?"

Thulan growled.

"Are we still talking about Terrelus?" Sable asked, glancing between the two. "Because I don't remember him running from anything."

"Doesn't he start a battle?" Ryah asked timidly. "I thought everyone died at the end of the play."

"If Terrelus had left," Leonis snapped, ignoring her, "at least he'd have had reason to. He wouldn't just be running away from ghosts."

Thulan's gaze flattened and Leonis, after a withering look at the dwarf, lengthened his stride and stalked to Atticus's wagon. Thulan glared after him, exhaling with a rough, rumbling anger.

CHAPTER TWENTY-ONE

SABLE CAUGHT RYAH'S EYE. She'd shrunk back from the argument and met Sable's look with wide eyes.

Thulan stared forward, angrily muttering something under his breath.

After a moment's hesitation, Sable climbed up onto the blue driver's bench and sat at the edge, as far from the dwarf as she could. The wagon rocked irregularly back and forth. But despite the awkwardness of the motion and the fact she sat by an angry dwarf, it was almost soothing. The last two nights' exhaustion caught up with her. Her head spun and her body felt numb as it melted into the bench. She rubbed her face, trying to clear away the tiredness.

This was the closest she'd ever been to Thulan, at least during the day. Everything about him was built on different proportions than she was. His legs, clad in dark wool trousers, were burly, his worn boots, hanging well above the floor of the wagon, were wide and heavy. Resting on his lap, he held the reins loosely between fingers that were not only twice as thick as Sable's, but covered with leathery skin. In fact, a lot about Thulan was leathery. He wore a leather vest over his broad chest and scuffed, leather bracers on his arms.

The bit of skin visible around his beard and bushy eyebrows was leathery, as well. His russet hair, pulled into several wide braids, hung down his back.

Unlike most of the other dwarves she'd seen, Thulan's beard didn't hang long and wild to his waist. It was neat and trimmed, only a few fingers' width past his chin. With no neck to speak of, the beard still touched his barrel chest, but for a moment, Sable was struck by how he wasn't as brawny as she'd expected, despite being far more burly than any human she'd ever met. The urge to ask him about caves and tunnels, whether he'd lived in them and why he'd left, almost outweighed the severe, closed-off expression on his face. Almost.

Instead, she cleared her throat. "I see why Atticus wanted me to talk to you about Lady Argent instead of Leonis."

Thulan glanced over at her, then turned his attention forward again. "Why are you talking to anyone?"

"I need someone to recite Argent's lines." She held out the papers. "Probably only once."

The dwarf gave an annoyed huff and reached for them, handing Sable the reins in return. She took the thin straps of leather and held them at arms' length.

"What do I do with these?"

Thulan gave her an incredulous look.

"I've never driven a wagon. Actually, it's been ten years since I've even ridden in a wagon."

He looked at the horses plodding mindlessly behind the caravan in front of them. "I think you can handle it."

Flipping open the papers, he set his finger on the top of a page and frowned at her. "You open scene three by yourself."

"Is that bad?"

"It's harder to get your bearings when you have no one to play off of." The dwarf shrugged. "No way around it. You'll start after Leonis finishes the constable's speech declaring his intention to hound Terrelus to the end of the world."

"*Come wind or storms or hoary frost.*" Sable nodded.

"That's the one. He'll clear the stage, and your lines begin as follows..."

Thulan glanced at the lines before closing his eyes. He breathed deeply, erasing the scowl and replacing it with an air of worry. "An ill-bred wind disturbs the night." His voice was still deep, but smoother and somehow feminine. "There's a foreboding echo to the owls' mournful songs."

Sable was caught off guard for just a moment by the change in the dwarf, but she focused on the words. Thulan's voice rose, pleading, and Sable felt the longing as Lady Argent pleaded with the stars and moon and "deep musing shadows of the night" to impart their wisdom to Terrelus, to soothe his mind.

Thulan's words rolled on, and Sable drew them in, letting them line up neatly in her mind. The more the wagon rocked, the more sleepy she felt, but she forced herself to keep listening. When the dwarf finished going through them, Sable thanked him and handed him back the reins.

Thulan frowned at her. "That's all you needed?"

Sable nodded. "I knew most of it already."

"Then go find Leonis to coach you through some movements. Because you can't just stand on the stage like a stone."

For the next hour, she walked next to Leonis as he coached her through different ways to stand, pointed out which gestures were awkward on stage, and gave her general pointers.

Jae and Serene walked in front of them. Serene kept her nose buried in a book, holding it closer to her face. Jae chatted cheerfully with her in a mostly one-sided conversation.

Ryah had gone to the back of the wagon to rest, and Leonis had gone through Sable's scenes twice before she let out an especially long yawn.

"When was the last time you slept?" he asked.

Sable rubbed her face. "It's been a while."

"Go lie down in the back. When we stop for lunch, Atticus will walk you through more of it. You'll want your wits about you and we don't need Lady Argent falling asleep on stage tonight."

She almost objected, but it was barely midmorning and the idea of lying down was almost irresistible. Ryah was already asleep on the pile of curtains, so Sable climbed up next to her and settled in.

The curtains were rough, the air in the back warm and dusty, but the moment Sable curled up against the pile of curtains, her eyes closed. Even the jostle of the caravan wasn't enough to keep her awake.

Her dreams began with green hills. She walked through them— flew through them. Tasted freedom and spread new, feathered wings so wide they brushed the neighboring hilltops.

A black raven dove out of the sky, streaking toward a ravine. It shot through Sable's wing, ripping it apart. Feathers scattered on the wind and she crashed down into ferns and mossy rocks. She stood, surrounded by a warm, damp gully, the walls blanketed with vibrant green leaves.

And then, deep in a crevice, it began.

The green darkened to black. Shadows grew, covering stone and leaf. Flames laced the edges and flickered in the depths. Pounding boots echoed off the rocks.

Not here, she pleaded. *Not these hills.*

She turned to run, but the world in every direction was nothing but darkness and flames. Ravens circled above her in the purpling sky. She sank down on the grass and found it to be nothing but ash. Sable grasped a handful and let it trickle through her fingers, just as she had a thousand nights before.

She curled forward onto the scorched ground. *Not here. Not again.* The ground beneath her shook at the approaching boots. The fire drew closer, and she pressed her eyes shut against it.

Heat crawled up her legs.

She jolted awake.

The sun streamed in through the wagon window, landing hot on her calves.

She rubbed her face, trying to banish the dream. When her heart slowed, she sat up. The back door of the wagon was split into two parts, the top half flung open. Outside, the Tremmen Hills rose unscorched and vibrantly green.

The wagon rolled off the road onto the grass. They must be stopping for lunch. An unexpected twinge of nerves thrummed through her.

Atticus would want to run through the play. Lady Argent's lines weren't hard, but saying them in front of the troupe sounded…uncomfortable.

The wagons pulled to a stop, and Ryah woke, stretching and peering out the back. The sisters climbed out to find Thulan and Jae unhitching the horses. Atticus called for Leonis, Merilee, and Sable.

"To save time," he said, "we'll just go through the scenes Sable's in." He glanced at her. "Do you know the rest of the play enough to know where those are?"

She nodded, the motion feeling a bit wooden. Her whole body felt wooden, actually. Her legs felt oddly sized, her arms too heavy to hang but too awkward to cross. Merilee's bracelets jingled as she crossed her arms with perfectly natural ease and gave Sable a critical look.

"Leonis." Atticus motioned to some empty space near the red wagon. "Please finish up the scene before Lady Argent appears."

The tall man strode across the grass, his gait and expression matching what she'd come to think of Terrelus over the years. He began the speech at the end of his scene, ending with, "Come wind or storms or hoary frost."

He came off the imaginary stage and gave Sable a little bow, waving her on.

She stepped onto the exposed piece of grass, feeling the eyes of the others on her.

She opened her mouth, but realized she had no idea how to start Lady Argent's lines. The words were gone.

Atticus's brow knit together, and Merilee let out an annoyed sigh. Leonis's expression shifted from pleasant expectation to a grimace.

"An ill-bred wind," Atticus prompted.

The words came rushing back, and Sable grabbed onto them. "An ill-bred wind disturbs the night." Her voice sounded as wooden as everything else. "There's a foreboding echo to the owls' mournful songs." The words were there now, all lined up. She focused on them, trying to block out everyone's eyes. She knew she should be moving, but every movement felt more awkward than standing still. So she shuffled a few steps to the side, hurried off the rest of the speech, and breathed a sigh of relief when she'd said the last words.

Silence greeted the ending.

"That was terrible," Merilee said.

Atticus shot the woman an annoyed look. "It was a fine first try. The words were right."

"There's a bit more to it than saying the right words," Merilee said with a sniff.

"You don't have any scenes with Sable," Atticus pointed out. "Why don't you go get lunch?"

"I'd rather see what sort of mess you've hired."

Atticus clenched his jaw and turned to Sable. "You're focusing on the wrong thing, Sable. You should be thinking about what Argent is saying. Not about us."

"I realize that," Sable said, trying to keep her voice calm. "But it's impossible not to focus on all of you staring at me."

"We're staring at you right now and you're talking like a normal person," Merilee let her gaze run over Sable's stiff body. "Almost."

Sable glared at her. "That's because these are my words."

Atticus scrubbed his fingers through his beard. "Let's try the next scene. Maybe it'll go better with Leonis there."

Leonis retook the grassy stage and began the next scene.

It was easier saying her lines to Leonis, who played Lady Argent's husband. She had him to focus on, at least partly, and he was not stiff at all.

"Better," Atticus said when they finished. "Let's try the scene with Terrelus."

He strode onto the grass himself and began the lines before Lady Argent would appear and try to draw him back from the tragedy he raced toward.

Atticus was even easier to play across from than Leonis, and Sable finally began to feel Lady Argent's words, at least a little.

"It's getting better each time," Leonis said with a little too much encouragement for it to feel genuine.

Lady Merilee toyed with one of her necklaces. "If she only had a hundred more times to practice before she saw a stage," she said with a sweet smile, "she'd be ready."

Sable glared at her.

"Go get lunch," Atticus ordered Merilee. "You, too, Leonis."

When they walked away, he ran through her scenes two more times, helping her stand, move, and gesture in ways that started to feel almost comfortable. Without the others watching, it was easier to say her lines with meaning. Until she saw Merilee watching her with a contemptuous frown. Suddenly, everything about her felt wooden and awkward again.

She shot the woman a glare, and Atticus sighed. He gave Sable a serious look. "At the next full moon, the biggest opportunity of the year will be presented to the troupe. Winning the Midsommer tourney isn't just about a large prize. It puts the troupe in front of the prioresses, the heads of the Merchant Guild, the Northern Lords visiting Immusmala, and enough wealthy people that the winners always receive at least one offer of patronage."

"For the first time," he continued, his voice low, "I have a play that could win. In a week, I'll have the only actress who can pull it off. But until then, I need this show to go well, so people are eagerly awaiting us when we come back through in a few weeks."

He ran his hand over his beard. "You said every line right. I've never met anyone who can memorize like that. And if you can work out the rest of it, you'll do great. But if everything you do on stage is awkward and stiff, I can't put you in front of people. I can't ruin the troupe's reputation."

Sable nodded, even that motion feeling wooden.

He gave her an apologetic look. "And if you're not acting for us, I can't afford to have you and Ryah traveling with us, either." He set his hand on her shoulder. "But, I know plenty of fine actors who started out as horrible as you."

She pulled her gaze back to him. "Horrible?"

He smiled. "Parts were horrible, yes. When you focused on becoming the character, though, you did fine." He squeezed her shoulder. "I think you can do it."

The truth of his words wrapped around her, and she leaned into them.

"Let's get some lunch."

She followed him over to the others, feeling less sure of the upcoming play than she had before.

Serene handed her some cheese and cold chicken. The woman leaned toward Sable. "You need to be Lady Argent."

"I know," Sable told her, trying to keep the irritation out of her voice. "But I don't know how to be a rich lady."

Serene was quiet for a moment. "The reason we love stories is because we find things in them we can relate to. An emotion, a hope, a fear. Lady Argent isn't a rich lady. She's a person. No one cares about how much money she has. We care because she's afraid for Terrelus.

"I record a lot of stories that Jae and I hear," she continued, "and until I find a way to relate to at least one of the characters, the story is always flat." She glanced at where Jae talked and laughed with Thulan. "Jae has never had any trouble relating to any character. But for me, it's harder. It may be difficult for you, too, but you can find a way." She glanced back at Atticus. "He'd normally give you time to settle in, but he's set on winning the Midsommer tourney." She looked back at Sable. "If tonight goes badly, I wouldn't expect another chance."

CHAPTER TWENTY-TWO

It took until mid-afternoon to reach the town of Folhaven. Sable practiced her scene with Leonis several times, said her monologue to Ryah, and even tried rehearsing with Thulan. But after three unsuccessful tries at relaxing, the dwarf threw up his hands and shooed her off his wagon.

By the time small buildings began to line the road and the wheels rolled onto cobblestones again, Sable had lost any hope of the night going well. The green smell of the hills was tainted with woodsmoke and dust again, and the same trapped feeling she'd always had in Immusmala crept through her.

She walked quietly next to Ryah and Leonis alongside Thulan's wagon. Despite the morning's nap, Sable's head felt heavy, her eyes dry. Leonis, on the other hand, looked perfectly fresh.

"You didn't sleep any more than I did last night," she said. "Why are you so awake?"

"You think I could sleep during the first hours outside the city in days?" Leonis looked insulted. "The Tremmen Hills!" He pointed to the green slopes. "They're more beautiful than anything else you'll see at this useless end of the world. Who needs sleep when you have this view?"

Sable yawned again. "Me."

Atticus called for Leonis, and the man headed toward the red wagon. Sable tried to ignore the growing knot of worry inside her.

"It's not hard once you get used to it," Ryah said.

Sable glanced at her. "What isn't?"

"Performing. I've done services and read the death rites. I even did the naming rites once for a baby." Her face sobered. "And the death rites for it on the next full moon."

Sable tried to imagine Ryah standing at the head of the abbey, reading the prayers of the day or dabbing the head of a new baby with linoil at a naming rite. All she could see was Ryah, six years old, dressed in the stained, wrinkled white linen they'd found behind an inn, her little face serious as she said prayers in her tiny voice.

"I was nervous at first. But then I saw their faces." She glanced at Sable. "The people at funerals are the hardest. They all want something I can't give them. Their loved one back. All I can do is say the prayers and offer Amah's peace." She shook her head slightly. "It's never enough, but it's all I have. It's all anyone has, really. So I try to focus on what I'm there to offer."

"A play isn't as important as funeral rites, though," Sable said.

The buildings around them grew larger and more numerous, the street more busy.

"I don't know," Ryah said. "I think we become better people when we spend time imagining what other people are living through. Maybe it's your job to make Lady Argent believable to these people. Give them the chance to be her, even from the distance of the audience."

Sable nodded. That was why she sought out Atticus at the festival every year. That feeling of living the story, of being someone else, even for a short time.

Folhaven stretched away from the road, and the streets they crossed were busy with people going about their day.

She glanced over at Ryah. "When did you become so wise?"

"They fed us wisdom at the abbey." She smiled. "Because there usually wasn't enough food to go around."

Sable sobered at the thought.

"It worked out," Ryah assured her. "Amah always provided enough. Often, I believe, thanks to you and your offerings."

"It was so much less than I wanted to give. And the abbey needed so much more."

Ryah set her hand on Sable's arm. "It was like goodness straight from heaven."

Sable snorted. "Believe me, that money did not come from heaven. Most of it was stolen from the wealthy on market days. And I suppose stolen from Kiva, too, since I was supposed to turn it all over to him."

Ryah thought for a moment. "I think Mother Perrin knew that. She always prayed an extra blessing on that money when it came. Maybe to cleanse it from its dubious past."

Sable laughed. "It needed it."

"She prayed for you, too, you know."

Sable pulled to a stop. "What?"

"She prayed for your safety and that your heart wouldn't be broken by the world. That it would stay generous and kind."

Sable started walking again. "It wasn't generous or kind to begin with."

"Yes it was. And it still is. Even the Muddogs knew we had a guardian angel that came."

The wagons rolled into a wide square.

Late afternoon light filled the space. Folhaven was smaller and cozier than Immusmala. None of the buildings were particularly tall. The shopfronts were made of wood, colorful awnings hanging above them, piles of goods spilling out into the square. A boxy building with a half-dozen uniformed men standing in front of it sat at the far corner. The town's militia looked almost as crisp and clean as the constables from the big city.

Atticus pulled the wagons up to the largest building on the square. The stately Millstone Inn.

Merilee climbed out of the back of the wagon. She'd donned a brown wig and wore a rich, blue dress. Still wearing her silver necklaces and bangles, she nodded and waved to the nearby crowd, looking very much like Lady Merilee of Colbreth Castle. The crowd gawked at her like she was an empress. She announced she'd be singing in the common room of the Millstone and needed someone to carry her wardrobe. A young man eagerly volunteered and, after being loaded down with a large crate, followed her to the inn, a good number of the crowd trailing behind him.

Sable followed Leonis to the back of the red wagon, trying to not think about the coming performance. The fairy tree lit the interior of the wagon with a soft, green glow, even in the afternoon light. It was carefully packed between crates and piles of supplies against the front wall, sunlight landing on the leaves through the open ceiling and window.

"How does it glow?" Ryah breathed, leaning toward the tree. "Is it…magic?"

"It's my sede tree." Leonis's face was soft in the green light. "And yes, it's magic…of a sort."

"It's amazing," she uttered. "I've never seen anything like it."

"There isn't anything like it. Not in this part of the world."

Leonis's gaze lingered on the tree for a moment before he pulled out a bundle of wooden poles for each of them. Sable took one, and with a lingering look at the tree, followed him. For the next hour, they worked with Thulan and Leonis until the beams resembled the skeleton of a stage. The platform itself was made up of twelve flat wooden pallets, each wide enough Sable could just stretch her arms across them, pinned together to make a wide floor.

Despite the two actors' continual bickering, the stage went together with well-practiced ease. In a short time, they hung curtains behind the stage and stretched them out from the front corners. Leonis and Thulan together picked up the planter holding the glowing green tree, Leonis straining slightly under the weight, while Thulan carried it with more ease. They placed it on the small table at the back left corner of the stage.

When everything was set, Leonis and Sable ran through her scenes again in the open space behind the stage. The motions slowly became more natural. When Thulan paused to watch, though, her body suddenly felt ill-sized and twitchy again.

Finally, Leonis called for a stop. "The stage will be so bright tonight you'll barely see the crowd. Maybe that will work in our favor." He motioned for her to follow him to the red wagon. "You're considerably smaller than our last Lady Argent. We'll need to find a different dress." He opened a crate of costumes and rummaged deep into it until he found a rust-red gown. "Try this."

The fabric was thin, shiny, and would fit a woman twice her width.

Sable raised her eyebrows. "How many of me are you planning to fit in here?"

Leonis dug a thin, red cord out of the box. "Width we can fix. How's the length?" At her hesitation, he added, "Just try it on, Sneaks, so I can see if it works."

She climbed into the wagon and closed the door, quickly changing in the dim, fragile privacy. When she climbed out, the fabric hung around her like a deflated tent, but Leonis gave a grunt of approval. He wrapped the red cord around her ribs like a corset, gathering extra material in the back and forming it into a shape that looked remarkably dress-like.

Sable smoothed her hands over the front of the dress. The fabric was dark, with highlights of rich red where the sunlight hit it.

Leonis nodded. "As soon as we wash your face and Thulan does something about the mess of hair on your head, you'll look like a proper Lady Argent."

Thulan came around the side of the wagon and stopped, frowning. "The red dress?"

"Of course," Leonis said.

"You should have picked the sapphire one."

"The sapphire is too stuffy."

"It's refined."

"This one is refined without being boring." Leonis set his hand on Sable's shoulder. "She looks perfect in red."

Thulan grunted his disagreement and pulled a small box from the wagon. Brushes and combs of all sizes lay next to hairpins and leather hair ties. The hairpins weren't particularly pretty. She picked one up that had a green bit of glass set in the end and flakes of copper paint chipping off.

"It doesn't matter how it looks up close," Thulan said. "It only matters if it looks good from the audience." The dwarf looked at her hair critically. "When's the last time you bathed?"

Sable shrugged. "I swam in the ocean last week."

Thulan let out a huff. "Humans." He led Sable to a bucket of water behind the wagons. "Get your hair wet."

For the next few minutes, Thulan rubbed soap into Sable's hair that smelled of pine and lemon, rinsed it out and started the process over. Then he grabbed a small stool off the back of the wagon. "Sit. This could take some time."

Sable dropped down onto the stool and braced herself for the yank of the brush through the tangled mess of hair. When Thulan started, though, it was with surprisingly gentle persistence, working the knots out from the ends, just the way Talia always had.

The thought curdled into loneliness. Talia should be here, prattling away happily about this new town, this new life. It shouldn't be a dwarf smoothing out Sable's hair.

How could she? The question swam to the surface again. How could Talia possibly have sided with Kiva? How could she not see the truth?

The answer was obvious. Talia didn't see the truth because Sable had worked so hard to hide it from her. All those nights downplaying Kiva's control, brushing off the frustration of having to work for him, trying to give Talia a sense of security that didn't exist. Lying about being safe in Dockside.

Talia trusted Kiva because Sable had worked so hard to keep her from fearing him.

Thulan pulled the brush along Sable's scalp, dragging out the last of the knots. She took a deep breath, trying to calm her fears. In a month, she'd find a way to talk to Talia and convince her of the truth.

Thulan's fingers dragged gently along Sable's scalp, drawing up small sections of hair and weaving them together.

"That looks pretty." Ryah's voice came from behind Thulan.

"Her hair isn't terrible once it's brushed," the dwarf said. "Thin and limp, but not horrible."

"Could I use one of the brushes?" Ryah asked.

Thulan gave a grunt of assent, and Ryah came into view, pulling out her own braid and letting her hair fall around her shoulders. She brushed through it, and with her auburn hair hanging around her face, she looked young and carefree.

"Lady Merilee doesn't help with costumes and hair?" Ryah asked.

"Lady Merilee only helps herself," Leonis said, coming up and rummaging through some crates. "Where's the hair chalk?"

"The other crate," Thulan said.

"What's hair chalk?" Ryah asked.

"Powder that will darken Atticus's hair." Leonis pulled out a small clay pot with a cork. "He doesn't exactly look like a young man with his white hair and beard."

Ryah's attention caught on something over Sable's shoulder. Her brush paused. "What are those people doing?"

Sable tried to turn her head to look, but Thulan gave an annoyed grunt and tugged her head forward again.

"You've never seen a funeral?" the dwarf asked.

"Where's the abbess?"

"Those folks can't afford an abbess fee."

Ryah's mouth dropped open. "Fee?"

"Funeral fee, naming fee, binding fee." Thulan tugged more hair into whatever he was doing on Sable's head. "You holy women charge for everything. The common folk are better off on their own."

Ryah's face darkened in indignation. "A fee? For doing the goddess's work?" She took a step, then paused, looking down at her clothes. "Do you have an abbess's robe?"

"What for?" Thulan snorted. "Are you going to go perform the rites?" His voice rolled with scorn.

Ryah straightened her shoulders and raised her chin. "Yes, I am. And I'm not going to charge a fee to offer prayers for their loved one's soul and their own peace."

Thulan's fingers kept gathering Sable's hair. "Don't bother. The world doesn't need more holy women."

"We have a white dress," Leonis said, pulling a different crate closer. "But it's for an angel costume and is probably more elaborate than you'll want."

"That's fine," Ryah answered firmly. "As long as it's white."

The sharp end of a hairpin jabbed along Sable's scalp and she let out a little yelp.

"Atticus won't want the dress used so the holy girl can play abbess," Thulan grumbled.

"When did we use it last?" Leonis asked. "At the harvest festival?"

"I want no part of this," Thulan muttered, but he stopped fiddling with Sable's hair for a moment. "The basket along the wall, I think."

Sable took his moment of distraction to turn her head as much as she could. Between two of the buildings across the square she caught a glimpse of an open hill dotted with gravestones, and a cluster of people.

"Here it is." Leonis pulled out a white gown covered with ruffles and lace.

Ryah's eyebrows rose. "Nothing less…fluffy?"

Leonis gave her an amused look. "You wanted white. This is it."

Ryah took a bracing breath. "It's perfect. Thank you." She took it out of his hand and pulled it on over her clothes. The dress was so large it sagged off one shoulder and the hem lay in the dirt. She shifted it around, trying to make it settle well.

"That might not work." Leonis gave Ryah an apologetic look.

"It's fine," she said with determination.

Leonis laughed. "Not the word I would use." Atticus called him from around the wagon, and he started toward the old man. "Sorry we don't have anything else," he said over his shoulder.

"Doesn't the Phoenix Prioress wear a silver necklace? Something like a flower?" Sable asked.

Ryah nodded. "It's a firebloom. Shaped like a flower, but the petals are flames."

"Well, I don't have a firebloom," Sable said, reaching into her pocket. "But I have this." She pulled out the silver, flower necklace Lady Ingred had wanted.

"It's beautiful!" Ryah breathed out.

"Put it on." Sable glanced down at the ill-fitting dress. "It can only help."

"You're getting the hem dirty," Thulan grumbled while Ryah fastened the necklace. "Clean the dress before you put it back."

"I will," Ryah said stiffly. She tried to smooth down one of the ruffles, but it sprang right back out.

Thulan's fingers paused in Sable's hair. "You look ridiculous, Your Holiness."

Ryah tried again to shift the dress to fit better on her shoulders and shot him an annoyed look. "It doesn't matter how I look. It's the blessings and prayers that matter." Glancing over at the funeral, she straightened her shoulders.

"Then why even bother with the white?"

"Because," Ryah said with an unenthused look at the dress, "the white represents the purity of Amah. It has nothing to do with me." She hoisted the dress up higher onto her shoulder and started toward the funeral.

"Stop," Thulan said in exasperation.

Ryah spun toward him. "I understand you see no point in these prayers, but those people will. They deserve to hear the prayers and ask the blessing of the goddess. Amah does not require fees for her blessings to be poured out, and I will not stand by and let those people miss out just because some abbess has ignored her duties."

"You can go prattle off your prayers, Holy Mother," he grumbled, "just not like that." Pulling a wide, white sash out of the same crate, he wrapped it around Ryah's waist, flattening the front of the dress, pleating the sides and back until the gown almost fit. Taking a hairpin out of the brush box, he pinned the back of the gown over on itself, tightening up the neckline.

"That's a little better," he muttered, looking critically at the fluffs of white lace around the skirt. "I never did like this lace, though." With a sharp tug, he ripped a ruffle away from the dress.

Ryah gasped. He scowled at her, and she bit her lip.

In moments, the three layers of lace had been torn off and Ryah stood in a more simple gown. It wasn't pretty, but it was white and might be mistaken for an abbess's robe. From far away. By someone who had never seen one.

The resemblance to the way Ryah used to dress up was astonishing. She had the same determined look she'd had when she'd sat Talia and Sable down to hear prayers before bed every night.

"You still look ridiculous." Thulan ripped off a section of one of the discarded layers of lace and found a white hair comb. Placing the lace against her head, he pushed the comb into the crown of Ryah's hair, letting the lace hang down like a veil. "But at least you look more like an abbess than anything those folks have ever seen up close."

Ryah touched the veil gently, smiling at him. "Thank you."

The dwarf scowled. "Go do whatever useless thing you want to do and get out of my way. I still have the impossible task of making your sister look like a respectable lady."

Ryah smoothed the dress and straightened her shoulders before heading toward the funeral. Sable shifted on her stool so she could watch, expecting Thulan to object, but he just moved behind her and started working on her hair again. Ryah crossed the square, walked between the buildings, and up onto the hill. She was near the group before they noticed her. She stopped a little ways back. There was a bit of hesitation in her motions as she gestured to the open grave.

Whatever was said, the people parted, and Ryah took her place at the head of the grave. From this far away, Sable couldn't see her sister's face clearly, but when the small figure raised her hands, the mourners all knelt. In that moment, there was nothing young or unsure about Ryah. She lifted her face toward the sky and said words Sable couldn't hear, but could almost feel.

Thulan's hands stilled in her hair.

"Thank you," Sable said quietly. "That was kind of you to fix the dress for her."

The dwarf's hands started moving again with brusque tugs. "If it keeps the girl's prayers away from me, it's worth it. And I've always hated that dress."

The sun started dropping toward the hills to the west before Thulan was done tinkering with Sable's face and hair. The dwarf painted her face faster than Talia ever had. And with almost no chatter, which felt odd.

Ryah spent time with the mourners, moving from standing before them to sitting with them around the now covered grave. Sable found herself wishing she could hear their conversations, hear what her little sister was capable of.

Thulan was standing in front of Sable, adjusting bits of her hair, when Ryah left the mourners and walked back through the square. As she got closer, she took in Sable's appearance with wide eyes. "You look beautiful! And rich!"

Thulan handed Sable a silver plate to see her reflection, and she didn't recognize herself. Her hair was pulled up elaborately into a set of braids that wound around each other, pinned together with silver hairpins. And her face looked older. Different powders had created shadows on her skin and gave it an aged look, dark pencil lined her eyes into a more sophisticated shape, and her lips were deep red. She stared at herself, speechless.

"You're welcome," Thulan grumbled. The dwarf leaned around the edge of the wagon and called for Atticus.

"Thank you," Sable said slowly. "It doesn't even look like me."

"That's the point," Thulan said. "If Leonis had dressed you in the sapphire dress, you'd be perfect."

Atticus and Leonis came around the end of the wagon. Atticus's white hair had been darkened to brown, giving him a strangely young appearance. He was dressed in a splendid, dark grey doublet.

Leonis grinned and bowed. "Lady Argent, you are stunning! Who knew washing the streets of Immusmala off you would make such a difference?"

"It's the hair," Thulan said.

"It's the dress," Leonis said. "But the hair doesn't hurt."

Atticus studied her with an air of one gauging the value of a piece of art. "Cleaned up you're quite striking. You make an excellent Argent." He caught sight of Ryah and frowned. "What are you wearing?"

Ryah glanced at Leonis. "There were mourners without an abbess. " She shifted under Atticus's gaze. "I couldn't do the rites without a white dress, so..."

He turned to Leonis. "That's the angel dress."

"It was," Leonis agreed. "But admit it, Atticus. It was ugly. And it made an ugly angel. If you want someone to play one again, get a better dress."

Atticus let out a low laugh. "It was ugly. I'm not sure it's much better now, but you can keep it."

Ryah's eyes widened. "Really? Thank you!"

Atticus waved off her enthusiasm. "It's no good for anything else now." He turned to Sable. "Are you ready?"

Sable forced herself to nod. Thulan and Leonis exchanged glances, but didn't say anything.

"Show me," Atticus said.

Sable tried to ignore the people around her and focus on the frustration she always felt at Terrelus's fears, the tragic ending he dragged them all toward, as Lady Argent's first line came into her mind. She closed her eyes and pictured a dark night, blocking out the image of the four people watching her. Argent's lines had always rung so true.

"An ill-bred wind disturbs the night. There's a foreboding echo to the owls' mournful songs." She continued, wondering where Terrelus had gone, worrying at his anger.

She paused at the end of Argent's first speech and opened her eyes. Ryah broke into applause, and Leonis smiled widely. Even Thulan nodded in approval.

"Well done." Atticus said. "Are you confident with all your lines?"

"Yes. Thulan said them perfectly earlier," Sable said. "They're easy to repeat."

"Thulan was amazing!" Ryah agreed. "I could hear from inside the wagon. It was the best Lady Argent I've ever heard!"

The hint of pleasure touched Thulan's eyes.

Ryah grinned at the dwarf. "I was almost convinced you were a woman!"

"Yes!" Sable agreed.

The pleasure evaporated from Thulan's face.

Leonis let out a snort of laughter that he tried to convert into a cough, and Atticus grimaced.

Thulan fixed Ryah with a glare. "Atticus, keep your stray humans away from me."

Atticus opened his mouth, but Thulan shoved between Sable and Ryah and stormed away.

Ryah's mouth hung open in shock and she rubbed her shoulder where the dwarf had pushed past her. She met Sable's gaze with an utterly confused expression. Thulan disappeared from view and Leonis let out a long, rolling laugh. Atticus shot him a glare.

"I..." Ryah paused. "What did I say?"

"I should have clarified," Atticus began. "But I thought you knew."

"What is going on?" Sable demanded. "Ryah didn't say Thulan *was* a woman. There's no reason to be insulted."

Leonis dropped his head into his hands, his shoulders shaking with laughter. "Please, stop talking," he gasped.

Atticus shot Leonis a quelling look. "Ryah's words were insulting, I don't really blame her."

Sable stared at him. "Blame who?"

"Thulan," Leonis said, still chortling, "is a female dwarf."

CHAPTER TWENTY-THREE

RYAH CLAPPED her hand over her mouth, her eyes wide.

Sable glanced at Atticus, who nodded with a rueful expression. "Thulan is a…a woman?"

"I'd stick with 'female dwarf.'" Leonis let out another laugh. "There's a movement among dwarf women to call themselves dwarvesses, but that doesn't roll off the tongue, and Thulan doesn't like it." Leonis paused. "She doesn't really like talking about herself at all. You're better off just avoiding any topics related to her. Or dwarfs. Or beards. Or caves."

"It's hard, at first, to tell male dwarves from females," Atticus continued. "The males are thicker with longer beards. But if you haven't seen many dwarves, as I'm sure you two haven't, it's tricky. We probably should have mentioned it." He looked in the direction Thulan had gone and sighed. "She'll be back before the show. Leonis, it's time to start gathering a crowd."

Atticus headed toward the square, and Leonis, still chuckling, ducked around the curtains and onto the stage. Sable heard him call out across the square.

Ryah slid her hand the tiniest bit away from her mouth. "She already hated me so much," she whispered.

"Now that we know,"Sable said, keeping her voice low and trying not to laugh, "it seems obvious, doesn't it?"

Ryah nodded, grinning. "The beard is somehow feminine. I was just caught up in how...dwarvish it was." She shook her head. "I thought the white dress was a bit of a breakthrough between us, but now..."

Sable blew out a long breath that still ended in a chuckle. "You'll win her back. The whole world loves Ryah."

The gathering crowd in front of the curtains cheered at something Leonis said, and the awkwardness Sable felt about Thulan was instantly replaced by the awkwardness of having to actually climb on stage.

Ryah took in Sable's face and sobered. "You said your lines magnificently."

She steered Sable toward some food set out on top of a large crate. A loaf of dark bread, some bright orange cheese, and chunks of white fish wrapped in lettuce. A wineskin sat on the table, and Sable poured herself a small glass and took a swallow of the dry, crisp wine.

"This is a terrible idea," Sable said, gesturing toward the stage. "I'm too nervous for this to go well." She glanced at her little sister. "Were you nervous at the funeral today?"

Ryah picked up a piece of fish. "On the way over, I was terrified. If Thulan hadn't been frowning at me, I might have turned back. But then I heard one of the mourners crying, and..." She stared at the fish without taking a bite. "The funeral was for a father of five children. His wife was thin, and the children looked hungry. There were aunts, uncles, and one grandmother. When I walked up, they actually looked afraid. They thought I was there to make them pay or tell them to find another gravesite. Can you imagine?" Ryah's mouth tightened into a thin line. "When I offered to pray with them, the mother broke down in tears. They'd never had an abbess pray over their family. Never once. No naming rites for the babies, no funerals. Their handfasting was performed by the grandfather." She blew out an angry breath. "Unconscionable."

"Aren't the abbeys in Folhaven governed by the Grand Priories in Immusmala?" Sable asked.

Ryah nodded. "Each town has an abbey in charge that reports to Immusmala, but they largely run their own town." She frowned at the buildings around them. "So far, I'm not impressed with Folhaven."

Sable finished the wine. Her fingertips tingled and the sharp edge of her nerves had softened when Thulan came stomping toward the food.

"Thulan," Ryah began. "We're sorry... We..."

"We didn't..." Sable paused.

Without looking at either of them, Thulan took the rest of the bread, the cheese, and the wineskin, then walked away.

Ryah bit her lip. "I don't know how to apologize. I almost said, 'We couldn't tell you were a woman.'"

Sable laughed. "It has never occurred to me before tonight that female dwarves existed."

A few minutes later, Leonis climbed off the back of the stage. Thulan's voice came back through the curtains now, her voice rolling over the gathering crowd in words Sable couldn't quite understand.

"Almost time to begin." Leonis said enthusiastically. "Let's make sure your dress is still in good shape."

A few minutes of fiddling and tightening later, he deemed Sable ready. The sun had just dropped below the horizon, but the square was still lit with evening light.

"You look amazing," Ryah said.

"Can't even see the dirty street rat who was with us a few hours ago," Leonis said with a grin.

Atticus and Thulan appeared off to the side of the stage, along with Jae and Serene.

"Do Jae or Serene act?" Ryah asked Leonis.

"No. Jae is a great storyteller, but he never shares our stage. The two of them generally find a tavern nearby to spend the evening. Jae tells stories, and Serene records tales other people tell."

There was a small commotion at the door of the Millstone Inn, and Lady Merilee emerged, dressed for the show. Her silver jewelry shone brightly over the elegant green dress of Terrelus's doomed love as she came to stand backstage.

"The crowd from inside the Millstone will be here shortly." She gave Sable a critical look. "You should have put her in the sapphire dress," she said to Thulan. "It's more elegant."

The dwarf gave Merilee a long look, then shook her head. "The sapphire is too stuffy. The red is perfect."

Atticus walked over with a bounce in his step, his eyes bright. "Almost time. Merilee, you gathered an excellent crowd." He smiled at Sable. "You make a magnificent Argent." He looked at the actors. "Bells of truth."

Sable waited for him to say more, but Leonis, Thulan, and Merilee answered, "Cries in the night."

With one last nod at everyone, Atticus pushed past the curtain on the side of the stage.

Sable raised an eyebrow at Leonis. "Was that the line from Epophus?"

He nodded. "Atticus says it before every performance. I think he's trying to invoke the next part."

The line from Epophus had always been one she'd felt especially strongly from Atticus. *Bells of truth ring like cries in the night. If only the world would listen.* She turned the phrase over in her mind. Like cries in the night. Truth wasn't really like that at all. It was more like warm light from the sun.

She caught a glimpse of torchlight from the stage and a wave of nerves rolled over her, all thoughts of bells and truth chased away. Sable let out a long, shaky breath. "I'm not sure I want the world listening tonight."

"It's going to be fine," Leonis said, patting her shoulder and moving closer to the curtain.

Atticus's voice was clear as he welcomed the crowd and introduced the story of Terrelus.

"Tell me the opening lines," Ryah whispered from beside her.

Sable focused on her sister's face. The crowd applauded something Atticus said, and she realized she had no idea how to start.

"*An ill-bred wind disturbs the night,*" Ryah prompted. "Just remember, it's ill-bred to stand on a stage and not say any words." Sable focused back on her sister's smiling face. "You aren't ill-bred, are you?"

Sable let out a short laugh. "I'm probably the most ill-bred actress to ever play Lady Argent."

Ryah took Sable's hand. "Poorest maybe, but not ill-bred. Ill-bred people don't give up everything to save their sisters."

Sable squeezed her hand.

"How many times do I say ill-bred before it starts to feel like I'm ill-bred?" Ryah asked with a grin.

"About that many."

"Before I performed my first naming rites, Mother Perrin repeated the opening lines a hundred times. It's the starting that's hard. Once you're going, you just keep going."

Leonis and Thulan stood at the side of the stage behind the curtain. Atticus raised his voice, and the dwarf slipped through into the torch-light. Behind the curtains, shadows grew. When Atticus and Thulan exited the stage on the other side, Leonis pulled on his constable's hat and strode through the curtain, calling out for the missing Terrelus, demanding justice, declaring his intention to track down the man.

Atticus lit a small lantern and hung it from the side of the wagon. "You're up, my lady," he said to Sable with a grin.

Taking a deep breath, she walked to the stage. The front of her dress caught on the edge of the short crate that served as a step, and she almost tumbled through the curtain. She heard Ryah's sharp intake of breath behind her as she caught herself on the edge of the stage.

Ill-bred indeed. She straightened and smoothed out her dress.

Through the slit in the curtain, she could see the stage brightly lit. Lanterns sat along the front of the stage, filling the platform with light. They were shuttered on the side toward the audience, though, leaving the crowd past them obscured in gloom. A bit of a breeze ruffled the curtains and set the lights of Leonis's tree quivering, as though they might burst into a dance. Sable focused on the lights, trying to ignore the tumultuous thoughts and emotions roiling inside of her. This was a terrible idea. The number of lines she had to say suddenly seemed overwhelming.

"Come wind or storms or hoary frost!" Leonis declared, turning with a flourish and heading toward her. She moved to the side to let him through. He gave her an encouraging smile as he passed.

She took a bracing breath. "Ill-bred," she muttered, then pushed the curtain aside.

The stage spread out before her like a wooden wasteland, except for the gentle glow of the tree. She tried to focus on it, but after the dimness backstage, the torches were blindingly bright, and she could barely make out the green fairy lights. The faces filling the square in front of the stage were dark and ghostly, all staring expectantly at her. She stepped forward and raised her eyes to the sky. Past the torches, she couldn't see any of the stars, if they were even out yet, but she looked anyway.

Ill-bred...

"An ill-bred wind disturbs the night." Her voice was thin and weak. The inflection was all wrong. She thought of Thulan this afternoon and tried to imitate her. "There's a foreboding echo to the owls' mournful songs." That was better. A little.

The words continued to flow out of her mouth, in a strangely detached way. They were stiffer than she wanted, and her body felt wooden. But she paced across the stage, trying to ignore the faces watching her.

Despite the curtains hanging around the stage, she felt utterly exposed. There was nowhere to hide, no shadows to sink into. Even the glitter of Leonis's tree felt as though it was only there to make her more visible.

Her speech was half done, but she was still strained and stiff. There was no way Atticus was going to keep her on as an actress after this. Everything was wrong. The dress was too fine, her hair too sculpted. Her hands shook, and she clasped them together, trying to get her words to loosen. To make them sound like the prayer they were.

But it was no use. The lines were lifeless. Even Merilee had done better than this.

Argent's big ending, her heartfelt plea to the stars and angels, fell limply out of Sable's mouth. When the last words were said, she found herself at the far corner of the stage, the exit terribly far away. She froze, hearing a titter of laughter from the audience. With nothing else to do, she started toward the exit and repeated the last line. It fell as flat as the first time. She pushed through the curtain and into the relief of the darkness.

CHAPTER TWENTY-FOUR

SABLE STEPPED off the stage to find Atticus and Leonis waiting. Atticus's brow was creased, and Leonis, now dressed as Lady Argent's husband, winced.

"I—" she began.

"This is what you get, Atticus," Lady Merilee said, whisking past them with a tinkle of bracelets, "for hiring from the slums." The curtains parted and closed behind her, and Sable stared after her, her hands clammy.

Serene stepped up and set her hand on Sable's arm. "Leonis, drag out your next scene. I need some time with her." Leonis raised an eyebrow, but nodded. He gave Sable a smile that looked more like a grimace and climbed on stage.

Serene pulled Sable away from Atticus. "You aren't being Lady Argent," she said quietly.

"Because I'm not Lady Argent," Sable hissed at her. "I'm not any kind of lady."

"You have to feel it," she said, unperturbed by Sable's anger.

"I can't."

"You have to try to convince Terrelus that he's making the wrong decision."

"What's the point?" Sable flung at her in a whisper. "Terrelus isn't going to change his mind."

"But Argent doesn't know that yet."

Sable shook her head. "Lady Argent is impotent in the story. Maybe she's the one with the truth, but he doesn't listen to her." An irrational fury at Terrelus rose in her. "He refuses to listen. No matter what she says, he's going to make the same stupid mistake he always does and ruin everything for everyone."

Serene's eyebrow rose, and a slow smile spread across her face. "There it is."

"There what is?" Sable demanded.

Serene leaned forward. "You," she whispered, "have a Terrelus in your life."

"I do not." Sable turned and paced toward the wagon. "The man is just irritating."

"You," Serene continued, "have someone in your life who's making the wrong choices and won't listen to you. Otherwise, Terrelus wouldn't make you so angry."

Sable stopped short.

Talia.

All the anger that had just been tangled up around Terrelus smoothed out and focused on Talia. Sable turned slowly back toward Serene who was watching her closely.

The woman nodded. "Good. When you're on stage, don't think about our Terrelus. Think of *your* Terrelus. The man in this play is lost. We all know it. But yours may not be. Your words could change the course of your own Terrelus's life. Maybe bring him back from the brink."

"Her," Sable said quietly. "Bring her back from the brink."

"That passion, that anger you have… It's what Argent feels, too. You are Lady Argent more than you know." She glanced at the stage. "And you're on."

Sable nodded and climbed up on the side of the stage, fixing her mind on Talia. Taking a deep breath, she pushed the curtain aside and stepped back into the torchlight.

The stage was more manageable with Leonis standing near the

glowing tree. He turned and greeted her. Instead of focusing on him or her own fears, Sable pictured Talia, back in Immusmala, willingly placing herself under Kiva's control.

The words spilled out of her. "I dread, dear husband," she recited the lines to Leonis, "that Terrelus is poisoned by words I cannot hear." The truth of it tore at her. "He counts his friends as his enemies, and his enemies as friends. The ones who seek to help him are the ones he pushes farthest away."

Leonis continued his lines, and Sable caught sight of the vague forms of the audience, but pushed the idea of them away and thought of Talia again. The sick feeling she'd had since leaving Immusmala was still there, and she focused on it.

Her next lines, desperate wishes that Terrelus would see the truth, spilled out easily. The rest of their conversation wound through worry, frustration, and resolve.

"If any voice can reach him," Leonis finished, taking Sable's hand. "it is yours."

She didn't need to manufacture the doubt in her next lines. "I fear he thinks of me as his enemy." She took a deep breath. "But I will try. I will do everything in my power to open his eyes to the truth."

Leonis looked up at the sky. "Then you must hurry. The night is growing late and there is a fateful wind."

She walked off stage with Leonis. As soon as the curtains closed behind them, he grinned at her. "That was excellently done!"

She leaned against a wagon, listening to Merilee's stern voice speaking to Thulan on stage. The tangle of emotions from the scene started to calm, and she looked up into the night sky. The play rolled on, the others taking their turns on stage.

Finally, Atticus walked past her toward the stage. "Now, try to convince me." He stepped through the curtains and began Terrelus's lines, bemoaning the way his friends had forsaken him.

"Whatever you did before," Leonis whispered, "do it again."

Sable nodded. Everything inside her felt complicated and tight. She closed her eyes and focused on Talia. What would she say to her sister? What would convince her to listen?

Leonis nudged her, and Sable heard Terrelus speak the lines that should bring her onstage.

The fears Lady Argent had for Terrelus, the inevitability of his actions, the danger he was putting himself—and others— in, filled her again. They weren't exactly the words Sable wanted to say to Talia, but they were close.

She took a deep breath and stepped back into the torchlight.

Atticus stood across the stage, looking moodily over the crowd. Everything about him was decided.

"Terrelus," she began, and Terrelus's face turned hopeful at the appearance of his favorite cousin, "things with us are not the way they were before." The truth of it took her breath away for a moment.

At her words, his face grew grim. "I thought I could trust you, cousin." A thread of bitterness wound through his words.

The conversation continued, but Terrelus only grew more distant. Sable watched the change in him, her heart sinking. This was his final chance to turn from his path, and he still refused to see the truth.

"Please," she whispered her line. "Please hear my words. My heart breaks for the path you're choosing."

Atticus turned to her. For a moment, his resolve wavered. She saw it in his eyes, the longing to believe her. Almost. He stepped toward her.

Sable started to reach for him, everything inside her stretching toward him, throbbing with the hope that his mind would clear. Tangled with the hope that somewhere, Talia was reconsidering, seeing the truth.

The world around her stood perfectly still. The audience frozen, waiting.

"Please," she whispered again.

But Terrelus's jaw firmed, and the hope that had filled the theater cracked. His shoulders straightened and the softness dissolved off his face. "I thought, of all people, you would understand."

The words cut into her. Talia's words rang in her head. *I thought, of everyone, you were the one I could trust.*

Argent's last line burned in Sable's throat. "I do understand. But you are wrong to do this, love." The tears in her eyes were real. "I would give everything I have to save you from it."

"The night moves on," Terrelus said coldly. "Go find your bed, cousin. We have nothing left to say."

Sable stared at him for a moment, the truth of his refusal, of Talia's betrayal, freezing her. With no lines left for Lady Argent, and nothing left inside herself to offer, Sable turned and stepped off the stage.

Sable climbed down from the stage and collapsed onto a crate alongside the wagon.

"That was wonderful!" Ryah said, hurrying up to her.

Sable leaned her head back and closed her eyes. Her arms felt heavy in her lap. "That was exhausting."

"You mean exhilarating," Leonis said.

"No, I don't."

Merilee and Thulan disappeared onto the stage for the final tragic scene, and from Atticus's yelling and Thulan's battle cries, the play ended as it always did—with poor Terrelus's death.

The audience burst into applause, and Leonis motioned for Sable to come stand near the curtain. Through a gap, the fairy lights flickered. Leonis waited until the fallen Terrelus rose and bowed to the crowd, before stepping on stage himself. Sable followed while the city square echoed with applause.

For the first time, Sable looked at the crowd. There must have been a hundred people crowded near the stage, their faces just visible in the torchlight. Leonis stood next to Thulan, Merilee, and Atticus. First the dwarf, then Merilee, then Leonis stepped forward and bowed. Leonis motioned toward Sable with a flourish, and she stepped to the front of the stage. Awkwardly, she bowed her head toward the crowd. An eruption of cheers greeted her. She glanced up in surprise before backing up between Leonis and Atticus.

"See?" Atticus said quietly. "Everyone loves a passionate Lady Argent."

He stepped forward to thunderous applause, bowing more than once to the crowd. People at the front of the crowd pushed forward and dropped coins into the ceramic jar sitting on the front of the stage.

Atticus finally held up a hand and they quieted.

"Thank you," he began. "It is always a pleasure to join the good people of Folhaven on a beautiful evening such as this. Regretfully, we must be on our way tomorrow." A spattering of boos rang out, and Atticus acknowledged them with another bow. "But we will return to your fine town in less than a month." He stepped forward to the edge of the stage and lowered his voice. "And you will not want to miss that performance.

"For the Midsommer tourney in Immusmala, we have an original, never-before-seen play to share with you." He paused, and a conspiratorial smile peeked through his beard. "This particular play involves a future prioress, a baledin…and a loyal handmaiden."

A ripple went through the crowd. Leonis stiffened. Thulan let out a short, low growl.

"A month!" Atticus called out. "Right here in Folhaven's square. Bring your families and your friends for a night to remember!"

With a final bow, he led the way off the stage.

Behind the curtain, Atticus walked over to the back of the wagon and pulled the wineskin off the hook. He leaned against the wagon and turned toward the others, an amused expression on his face.

Thulan pushed past Sable and stomped up to him. "Explain yourself, old man."

Leonis stopped a little behind Thulan, his arms crossed, a hard expression on his face. "I didn't realize you developed a death wish."

"Atticus!" Jae's sharp voice came from the side of the stage. He and Serene strode toward them, both looking enraged. "What are you doing?"

Even Ryah looked at Atticus with a concerned expression. "I'm sure he didn't mean the High Prioress and her handmaiden."

"Oh, I think he did," Leonis answered. "I just don't understand why he'd do such an idiotic thing."

Sable moved over beside Ryah. Thulan's and Leonis's anger was palpable.

"I did indeed mean our holy lady, the High Prioress of the Dragon Priory," Atticus answered.

"That ugly rumor about how she sacrificed her handmaiden to save herself?" Sable asked.

"It's a story that has never been told correctly," Atticus said. "And I think that is a shame."

"I think it's an exciting idea," Merilee said, brushing off a stool to perch on.

Leonis shot her a glare. "It's never been told correctly because anyone who's tried to make the rumor into a play has mysteriously disappeared."

Ryah shook her head. "Those are more lies. The High Prioress wouldn't hurt people."

Thulan snorted. Jae and Serene exchanged looks.

"Maybe it was a divine act of the goddess then," Thulan said dryly, "because the two troupes I know of who tried to tell the story both definitely disappeared."

Ryah glared at the dwarf.

"What game are you playing, Atticus?" Jae asked.

"No game." Atticus spread his hands. "I agree that the other troupes have rarely been seen since those performances—"

"Have never been seen," Thulan corrected.

"But," Atticus continued firmly, "that is because they told it wrong."

Ryah shook her head. "It's not because of anything. The High Prioress wouldn't make someone disappear just because she didn't like their play!"

Thulan ignored her. "And you're going to tell the legendary, slanderous rumor the right way?"

"It's time someone did."

"Yes!" Merilee said, clapping and setting her silver bracelets jingling. "And it should be us. Everyone will want to see this. Atticus, this is a brilliant move. No more stuffy old plays. The people want something fresh and tantalizing."

"And when the High Prioress…" Leonis glanced at Ryah. "Or the goddess comes for us, what then?"

Atticus smiled faintly. "The only thing the High Prioress will do is thank us."

There was silence for a heartbeat.

Thulan crossed her arms and considered Atticus with narrowed eyes. "The story of the handmaiden isn't just a rumor, is it?"

Jae and Serene snapped their attention back to Atticus, and Leonis groaned.

Atticus took a drink of wine. "No."

Leonis let out a humorless laugh. "Let me guess. You know this intimately."

Atticus met Leonis's gaze and nodded.

"Intimately?" Thulan asked. "As in first-hand?"

Atticus gave the dwarf a long look before nodding again.

Thulan let out a long breath and ran her hands through her hair.

Leonis made an exasperated noise. "Well, that explains a lot."

"A whole lot," Jae agreed.

"You know the High Prioress?" Ryah asked in awe.

Merilee's mouth fell open. "Atticus, dear! How have you never introduced us? My family would love to have the prioress visit Colbreth Castle!"

"I knew her a long time ago," Atticus answered.

"And you were there?" Thulan asked. "The day her handmaiden was killed by a baledin?"

Atticus dropped his gaze to the ground. "Not until after it was done."

"Then you don't have first-hand knowledge," the dwarf pointed out.

"I found them both—the High Prioress and her handmaiden. I saw the scene, heard the prioress's explanation."

"This is a brilliant idea," Merilee gushed.

Thulan shook her head. "This is a terrible idea."

"News of this will reach Immusmala by midday tomorrow," Jae agreed. "This is a horrible idea."

"We have tried to win the Midsommer tourney for years," Atticus said. "This is the way to do it."

"No," the dwarf said. "This is the way to end up in a prison cell. Or wherever High Prioresses throw their enemies."

"You haven't even read the play yet," Atticus said mildly.

"I don't want to."

"And yet you will." Atticus glanced at Jae and Serene. "As will you. The story needs to be known."

"This is why we're going to find Zephony," Leonis said with a sigh. "You want her to play the High Prioress."

Merilee stiffened. "Zephony?"

Atticus nodded. "She's the most talented first lady I've ever worked with."

Merilee's smile grew strained.

"Doesn't she argue with you a lot?" Jae asked.

"She'll never do it," Thulan said.

Atticus shrugged. "She'll join us when she hears what we're doing."

The group continued to argue, but Atticus was adamant it would work. "When we reach Zephony," he told them, "I'll give you copies to read. And when we're done, if you still think it's a bad idea, you can walk away from it. I won't hold it against you."

"If we walk away," Thulan demanded, "who will you get to act?"

Atticus shrugged and glanced at Sable. "Apparently you can just find actors wandering the streets of Immusmala." He ignored Merilee's snort of derision. "So I'll be fine."

Thulan rolled her eyes, then she and Leonis walked toward the stage, muttering to each other. Climbing up on a tall crate, Leonis started pulling down the curtains.

Jae sighed and leaned against the wagon, while Serene fixed Atticus with her normal stern look. Merilee had fallen silent.

Atticus glanced at Ryah and Sable. "You two don't want to heap on your own words of disapproval?"

"If the story sets all the ugly rumors about the High Prioress to rest," Ryah said softly, "I think it's a good thing."

Atticus gave her a small smile. "Thank you, Ryah. That is exactly what it will do." He turned expectantly toward Sable.

"If Zephony is first lady," Sable asked, glancing at Merilee, "is the role of second lady open?"

"If you're interested," he answered with a smile, "you and Lady Merilee can audition for the role."

"You can't be serious," Merilee interrupted, her voice harsh. "I'm not auditioning for a role I already have."

"No one has any roles yet," Atticus said. "No one has even read the play."

"She's a street urchin!" Merilee flung her hand at Sable so violently her bracelets almost flew off. "It's embarrassing enough to have to work with her in a town like this. In the festival it will be humiliating. She can't even act!"

"She did spectacularly," Ryah objected.

"If Sable can't act," Atticus said mildly, "than you should have nothing to worry about."

Merilee shot Sable a scathing look, then spun and strode toward the inn.

Atticus watched her go, an unreadable expression on his face. When she was out of sight, he turned to Sable. "If you are so inclined, I would love to have you audition for the second lady role. But regardless of who plays, I hope you will both stay around to watch the performance. I promise you, everyone will be talking about it."

Sable watched Merilee disappear into the Millstone. Tonight hadn't gone as terribly as she'd expected. Maybe she could beat Merilee in that audition.

"Speaking of things that are bound to kill us," Jae said, "everyone in the tavern says if we head east, we'll be walking into a fiery death."

CHAPTER TWENTY-FIVE

ATTICUS RAISED AN EYEBROW. "What kind of fiery death?"

"There are rumors of burned towns," Jae said. "Lots of rumors. Far out on the Eastern Reaches."

Sable straightened. Beside her, Ryah's shoulders tightened.

"Nothing concrete," he continued, "and the stories were all about attacks during the night by an unseen enemy. Towns burned to the ground."

Ryah grabbed Sable's hand and squeezed it tightly.

"But no one knows which ones," he continued. "They mentioned the plains and the far eastern stretches of the Black Hills. It's probably just raiders." Jae paused. "Still, there was something troubling about the rumors."

"Serene," Atticus asked, "do you think they were troubling?"

She measured her words. "They sounded like they will cause trouble, even if they're based on nothing. For being just stories about raiders, there were a lot of them."

Voices floated back from in front of the stage, and Sable felt a moment's shock that people were still there. All the worry from the play was gone, replaced with the sickening memories of death and bodies turned to ash.

Atticus glanced toward the stage and straightened his doublet. "I'm neglecting the crowd." He looked back at Jae and Serene. "I'd appreciate if you two would keep your ears open for news. It would be good to know what we're walking into. Especially if one of those towns is a scheduled stop."

The three headed toward the front of the stage. Sable wrapped her arms around herself and watched them go.

"Towns burned? That sounds like…" Ryah began.

Sable nodded, glancing around the square of the unfamiliar town. "Dockside and the Bend suddenly sound sort of safe."

Early the next morning, sunlight squeezed through a gap by the wagon door, falling warm and bright across Sable's legs. Next to her, Ryah still slept, her face peaceful against the pile of curtains. Sable watched her for a moment, the worry from last night's news of burned towns still lingering. Ryah had been safer in the Bend than Sable had known, protected by the Muddogs. Now she was sleeping in a wagon, headed toward the Eastern Reaches, and possibly vicious raiders.

Sounds trickled into the wagon as Folhaven stirred, sounding much like the early mornings in Immusmala. Dockside suddenly felt uncomfortably close still, and Sable sent a little prayer up to Amah that Kiva hadn't discovered that she'd left the city. Talia hadn't known Sable intended to, so with any luck he was scouring Immusmala for them. And with every day they traveled away from the city, it was less likely they'd be found.

A shadow fell across the gap and Leonis called in, "Good morning, ladies. Still a bit of packing up before we can leave, and I certainly don't intend to do all the work myself."

"Shocking," Thulan muttered, rolling over and sitting up from where she slept up near the front of the wagon.

Loading the last of the troupe's belongings didn't take long. Sable was tucking in newly filled water skins when Lady Merilee came out of the Millstone in a dress too nice for a day of travel. A young man trailed her, carrying her crate, heaving it into the wagon for her.

"Thank you, dear," she said, patting his cheek dismissively before climbing up into the wagon herself. "Atticus," she called, "I'm ready to leave."

Leonis glanced at her. "You'd be better off walking."

"I am not walking through the wilds," Merilee said primly.

Leonis laughed. "We are headed into the wilds. Which is the exact reason you'll want to walk."

Merilee raised her chin. "I'm fine here."

"She'll be out by lunch," Leonis said to Thulan.

"She'll be out before the Black River," the dwarf answered.

Sable and Ryah fell in beside Leonis, walking by the wagon that Thulan drove. Outside Folhaven, the road became decidedly rougher. They hadn't yet crossed a river when Atticus's wagon hit a deep rut and Merilee let out a shriek. Her head appeared at the back. She'd removed her wig, and her blonde hair stuck out, disheveled. She clambered out, almost falling onto the road when the wagon hit another rut. Dusting off her dress and straightening her necklaces, she glared at Leonis, who grinned at her, before stalking to the far side of Atticus's wagon.

"Before the river," Thulan said with a smug smile.

"How long until she starts complaining?" Leonis asked.

"Why is everything so dirty?" Merilee called out, her voice annoyed.

"Not long," Thulan answered.

They crossed the wide delta of the Black River around mid morning, and the road ran back into a forest of heavy trees.

Leonis came up next to Sable walking with a spring in his step. "Do you think your memory would work at a card table? Could you remember which cards have been played?"

"Not unless you told me them as they were played, preferably with a memorable cadence," she said.

Leonis sighed. "A shame. We'll stop in Molas tonight, and the gambling tables there are always busy."

"Sable can tell when someone is telling the truth, though," Ryah said.

Sable looked at her sharply, and her sister gave her a sheepish grin.

"You have no idea how often I've wished I could do that. So many people came to the abbey with stories of hardship, and I wanted to help them all, but it was so hard to determine whose stories were real and who was lying." She frowned. "Mother Perrin always erred on the side of generosity, but there were plenty of times I wished we could tell."

Leonis studied Sable. "You can read it in their faces? Or their body language?"

Sable almost lied, but Atticus already knew. It probably was inevitable that the rest of the troupe would find out. "It's just the way the words...feel," she answered reluctantly. "Sometimes they feel true. It's not something I can really explain." She glanced at Ryah with a frown. "Which is why I don't bring it up."

Ryah shrugged apologetically. "But I want to know how it works."

Sable sighed and turned back to Leonis. "Tell me about yourself. Make some of it a lie and some of it the truth."

Looking intrigued, he began, "I am an only child." Those words were true. "My mother died when I was very young." The lie was so thin it almost cut the air. "My favorite flower is the purple moth's wing." More truth. "And my name is not Leonis," he ended with a cold lie.

"You are an only child," Sable began,"but the thing about your mother was a lie. Your favorite flower was true." She smiled. "And your name is definitely Leonis."

A slow grin spread across his face. "I've known Thulan for six years."

"Lie."

"Eight years."

"Truth."

"I think Atticus has too many friends in too many places."

Sable laughed. "True."

He raised his voice slightly. "I think Thulan needs to lighten up about the no-one-knows-I'm-a-female thing."

The dwarf looked over from the seat of the wagon and scowled at him.

"True," Sable said.

Leonis grinned at her. "This is the best thing to happen to me in a long time."

"True." She eyed him. "But nothing is happening to you."

"Come with me to the gaming tables tonight," he said eagerly. "We'll split the winnings. All you have to do is let me know when someone's lying."

Ryah frowned at him. "You're going to cheat?"

"It's not cheating," he objected. "Reading your opponents is the basis for all card games. That's all I'm doing."

Sable glanced at Ryah, who still frowned. Sable had gone to the gambling tables in Dockside only once, determined to read her opponents and win money, but Kiva's men had been watching the table closely, and she hadn't wanted to make him curious about her card skills.

More than that, though, she hadn't been able to shake the fact that cheating at cards would be how Kiva would use her gift if he knew it existed. The thought had been enough to stop her from ever going back.

But back then, Talia hadn't been in danger like she was now, and Leonis had a point, reading opponents was the goal of the game. Reluctantly, she nodded, and Leonis grinned wider.

"This'll be fun." He glanced at the front wagon rolling down the road. "Does Atticus know of your little skill?"

She nodded.

"Of course he does," Leonis said. "Still, let's leave this little plan between us. Atticus isn't all that fond of my gambling—"

"Or your drinking," Thulan said from the wagon.

Leonis waved her words away. "Tonight is the last real tavern we'll visit until we get back here. We'll use it as a practice run."

It was barely mid-afternoon when they stopped at a small town on the coast.

They stopped the wagons at the top of the sea cliffs along the edge of town. Far across a wide bay, the city-topped cliffs of Immusmala were visible as a bit of jaggedness on the horizon.

With the sea behind them, they fell to setting up the stage. Thankfully, this was not the huge stage they used in Immusmala and Folhaven. That one had taken over an hour to assemble. This one was a simpler version that Atticus used in smaller towns. The wide backdrop of black curtains was considerably smaller, and the platform only used six of the of wooden pallets.

Townsfolk began to gather in the square, many of them calling greetings to Leonis, who headed off to chat with them. Thulan called him to come back, but he just waved and disappeared into the crowd.

"Figures," Thulan muttered to Sable and Ryah. "You two showing up is helping him get out of even more work than usual." She handed them each a curtain.

The sun was low in the west by the time they hung the last one. Leonis showed up when all that was left was for him and Thulan to carry his tree onto the corner of the stage.

Sable stepped up close to it and peered at the lights, which twinkled like tiny stars.

They were...lights.

She wasn't sure what she'd been expecting, but something more fantastical than tiny glowing heads on short stalks nestled in a clump of leaves.

"Beautiful, isn't it?" Leonis's expression, bathed in the soft light, looked pleased.

"It is." Sable tried not to sound disappointed. "The first time I saw it, I imagined each light was a tiny fairy dancing."

"Me, too," Ryah said.

Leonis smiled. "Maybe you two don't know what fairies look like." He rubbed his hands together and looked at Sable eagerly. "Ready to win some money?"

Ryah still looked disapproving, but Sable nodded.

He led the way toward the tavern. "You stand next to me, with your hand on my shoulder. If they tell the truth, push down."

When they walked into the common room, it was almost full. Merilee's voice floated down the stairs as she ordered a bath. Thulan sat up at the bar, looking stouter than usual on a tall stool. Jae, Atticus, and Serene chatted with townsfolk.

A few voices from the card tables called for Leonis to join them, and he picked the one with the best dressed men.

"Sable, meet Lord Hollan, the wealthiest man in..." Leonis gestured around the inn. "Whatever backwoods town this is. Sable's new to our troupe and to cards. I thought I'd educate her a little."

"All she'll learn from you is how to lose," Hollan said with a grin.

Once they sat, Sable set her hand on Leonis's shoulder. There was little talking during the first round by anyone but Leonis, who explained the rules.

When the second round started, Sable asked, "How do you know how good your hand is?"

"My hand is excellent," Lord Hollan said. At the warm truth of his words, she pressed into Leonis's shoulder. "But my hand is always good."

"Mine is excellent, as well," the man to his left agreed with a cool lie. She lightened her hand. "Of course, every hand played against Leonis is a good one." More truth to that statement.

With a laugh, she pressed down, and Leonis shot the man an annoyed look.

The hand played out and Leonis lost to Lord Hollan, who did have an excellent hand.

The game continued. Sable pressed into Leonis's shoulder when appropriate, judging both words and sounds of satisfaction or annoyance that they made. As Leonis won a few hands, the others began to talk less and focus on their cards more.

Behind Sable, Thulan and Serene ate at a table with an older couple.

"Ya probably won't take my advice," an older man said, "but I'd rethink heading too far east. Ain't nothing but trouble on the Eastern Reaches these days."

The woman nodded. "Towns burned and people killed, all at night."

Memories of fire and darkness moved just under the surface of the conversation. Sable tried to ignore the echoes of unintelligible words shouted in the shadows.

"It's been years since we've heard so much about raiders, but they occasionally come up from the sea, murdering and stealing. That's the sort of trouble folks out there invite. They live too far away from the rest of the world."

"Sneaks," Leonis said with an irritated voice, dragging her attention back to the game.

She glanced back at the table, realizing she was gripping his shoulder tightly. They were partially through the next hand, Leonis's cards decidedly mediocre.

"Sorry," she muttered, relaxing. "But there are interesting things going on in other places."

He grabbed her hand. "The only interesting thing is right here."

"Fine," she told him, refocusing on the table. "But you'd better win spectacularly."

He won five more hands before the others at the table decided they'd had enough. Leonis bade them goodbye and stood, tucking the coins into his pocket.

"Almost seven silver," he whispered as they walked away from the table. "That's quite a talent you have there."

Sable nodded, less enthusiastic than he was. Her share of the winnings was nice, but between cheating at the game and the overhearing the rumors she felt unsettled.

Atticus called to them from the door, and motioned them outside. The world had grown dark. Past the stage, across the water, the dim light of Immusmala was visible, like ruddy, fallen stars.

Sable stood with the others behind the stage as the crowd gathered up front, looking at the city. Somewhere over there, Talia was surrounded by Kiva and his world. Their lies sinking deeper into her. By the time she got back, would Talia even listen to her?

Even rumors of burned towns in the east were nothing compared to that fear, and Sable clung to it as she waited for her turn on stage.

The play went reasonably well. When they finished and Atticus announced to the crowd that they'd be back to tell the story of the

High Prioress and the handmaiden, the crowd reacted with enthusiasm.

Over the next two days, as the troupe moved farther east, Jae entertained them with stories. He'd sit on the blue driver's bench next to Thulan and spin enthralling tales of trolls, sea monsters, or strange hermits in the woods. When he did, Serene would put down her ever-present book and walk next to Sable, keeping up a wry commentary on Jae's storytelling. Jae cheerfully put extra emphasis on the parts Serene criticized.

Even Merilee took a break from her incessant singing to walk close enough to hear, while never quite joining the group.

The towns they stopped in each night became steadily smaller. The crowds shrank, too, but their enthusiasm stayed high. Each night, Sable grew more comfortable with Lady Argent. She never stumbled in her lines, and each time, it became easier to connect her feelings for Talia with Terrelus. Sable began to think she could get used to a life of regular meals, beautiful scenery, and mostly enjoyable companions.

But the better Sable performed, the more hostile Merilee grew. She found countless things to correct about Sable's acting and treated her with outright contempt away from the stage. Thankfully, Merilee preferred solitude to the company of the rest of the troupe, so she spent most days walking by herself on the far side of the wagons. It seemed her wardrobe did not include any clothes appropriate for walking on dusty roads all day, because she constantly wore uncomfortable looking dresses and all her jewelry. As soon as they reached any town, she'd secure the best room she could find. She'd hide there or, if she could find a crowd large enough, sing for them.

Ryah fell into a pattern in each town also. She'd don her white dress and wander through the crowd. Within an hour, news would spread and people would bring babies and young children for blessings, the ill came to her for prayers, and the elderly asked her to recite from the holy scrolls.

Atticus, after watching her with a bemused expression, let her continue, as long as she didn't try to do anything from his stage.

The High Prioress and her dragon, Sable thought for the hundredth time, *made a terrible mistake at the Choosing.*

The fifth day out from Immusmala dawned grey and Sable stepped out of the the wagon into a cool, misty drizzle. Thulan pulled up her hood and climbed up onto her wagon. Lady Merilee, giving the sky an affronted look, lifted the hem of her dress and climbed into the back of Atticus's wagon, adjusting her jewelry with a huff.

"There aren't many towns past here," Leonis said, walking beside Ryah and Sable. Unlike everyone else, his head was bare and he didn't seem to mind the wetness of the day. "By lunch, we'll be out of the forest. Unfortunately, the plains are ahead of us, which are boring. It's probably why there are no towns to speak of. We'll sleep along the road tonight, hopefully reaching Ebenmoor by midday tomorrow."

By nightfall, they were surrounded by short, bristly brush. The plains stretched as far as Sable could see, the road cutting through them nothing more than a scratch in the landscape. They pulled the wagons just off the road. Thulan built a fire and began puttering over a pot. Leonis came up behind her and peered into it.

"No," he said firmly. "Not barley soup."

"I like barley soup," Ryah said.

"Thulan's tastes like dirt," Leonis groaned.

"That's because I put dirt in it," the dwarf answered, stirring the pot. "If you don't like how it tastes, have the holy girl bless it."

"It needs so much more than a blessing," Leonis muttered.

"You could cook for once," Thulan pointed out.

"I'll just starve." Leonis stalked away.

The soup turned out to be warm, filling, and tasted nothing like dirt. Leonis did return, stealing the bowl Thulan had filled for herself, and grumbling his way through the meal.

As the first night without an inn, Merilee demanded to have Atticus's wagon all to herself, and was duly outraged that no one was swayed to give it to her. Scandalized by the idea of sleeping in the same wagon as the men, she joined Sable, Ryah, and Thulan. She tried to steal most of Ryah's curtains, until Thulan threatened to make her sleep on the road.

The sky was still overcast, but when the moon rose over the horizon, Sable caught a glimpse of it between the clouds, and was shocked to see that it was only half full. How had there only been a handful of days since the full moon? Such a short time since she'd sat in the tree outside Lord Renwen's window and thought herself trapped in Immusmala.

That seemed like a life she'd been a part of long ago. She fell asleep to dreams of open spaces and star-filled skies, but when the fires and boots and darkness came, they destroyed even that.

The next morning, she awoke to damp, grey mist surrounding the wagons. The world faded into obscurity a stone's throw in every direction, and the fog dampened any attempts at conversation. Even the continual crunch of the wagon wheels sounded muffled. Her damp feet were the only part of the morning that didn't feel like a dream.

It was hours before the sunlight shouldered its way through the mist, landing warm on her skin. The fog thinned, but the grass of the plains was barely more interesting.

"Finally." Leonis pointed to a dark smudge far ahead and to their left. "The Nidel Woods."

"Is there anything out here?" Ryah asked.

"No big cities," Leonis answered.

"No human cities," Thulan corrected him. "The dwarven city of Torren is enormous."

"True. And there are a good number of elves in the forest," Leonis agreed.

"Don't you live out here somewhere?" Sable asked Jae.

"Serene and I summer with some others in the Nidel Woods."

"What do you do all the way out here?" Ryah asked.

"Mostly enjoy books."

Ryah glanced up ahead to where Serene walked next to Atticus's wagon, her usual book pressed up close to her face. "Serene has been enjoying her books this whole time."

"Reading, yes, but not writing much. We have a library of books and scrolls we've written that record the history of the land. Things we've witnessed or heard of while staying in the Sanctuary. Interactions between the High Prioress and the lords to the north. Reports from the Kalesh Ambassador."

"Burned towns?" Ryah asked.

He nodded. "If we see evidence of raiders out here, we'll record what we find. They've caused trouble in the past."

Above the distant forest, a dark grey clump of clouds caught Sable's attention.

"Tell us about something happier than burned towns," Sable said. "Because my eyes keep looking for smoke."

"If there are murderous raiders ahead of us," Thulan said from the wagon, "at least we won't live long enough for the High Prioress to make us disappear."

"There is something over there," Leonis said, shading his eyes against the sun. He paused and glanced at Jae. "It does look a bit like smoke, honestly."

Jae peered ahead.

"Maybe it's just heavy clouds," Ryah said.

Thulan grunted in disagreement. "It's smoke."

"Which direction is Ebenmoor?" Sable asked.

Jae glanced at her with a tight look, then looked back toward the dark spot in the sky.

"Oh," she said softly.

CHAPTER TWENTY-SIX

OVER THE NEXT HOUR, the haze continued to lift. The edge of the Nidel Woods shifted from a blur to spiky pines, and the dark cloud on the horizon grew to be distinctly smoke. They topped a rise and, across a small valley, Ebenmoor came into view.

Or the remains of it.

Charred beams jutted up like the scorched bones of a massive creature. Piles of smoldering, black debris gave off trails of smoke, twisting up into the sky.

The entire town was gone.

The first stinging scent of smoke reached them, and the only sounds were the creak of the wagons and Serene closing her book with a sharp snap.

"Raiders never hit towns this large," Jae said, staring at the destruction.

"Leonis," Thulan called, but Leonis was already climbing up onto her wagon to take the reins. Without stopping the horses, the dwarf swung down and went to the back.

"Sable," Ryah whispered, gripping Sable's hand tightly. Her face was pale, eyes wide. "It's just like—"

"I know." Sable squeezed her hand. "I know."

Movement in the sky caught Sable's eye. In the midst of the smoke, black specks circled.

Ravens.

Atticus pulled his wagon to a stop next to a long line of bushes. "Serene!"

She strode up to the front of the wagon, Ryah and Sable following.

Merilee came to stand beside them, frowning at the town. The woman was more disheveled than Sable had ever seen her. Dark circles under her eyes proved that sleeping in the wagon had gone as poorly as she'd expected.

"This is exactly why I'd never live out here," Merilee said.

The road ahead rolled down a hill before crossing a river and swooping up toward the smoldering ruins of Ebenmoor.

"Is there anyone in the town?" Atticus asked Serene.

She shook her head. "It's still too far away."

Atticus fixed her with a hard look, which she returned.

Finally, she gave a huff and turned to face the town. "You're annoying, Atticus."

Serene studied the burned town for a handful of breaths. "No one."

There was no motion, aside from the ravens.

"Of course there's no one there," Merilee said. "We've come all this way for nothing."

"Shut up, Merilee," Thulan muttered.

"Don't tell me what to do, dwarf! I—"

"Quiet." Atticus's voice cut across hers. "There's no one nearby?" he asked Serene.

"That's not what you asked," Serene said, irritated. She scanned the plains around the town.

Sable looked over the grass. There were relatively few bushes around. The ones next to the wagon blocked the view to the south, and she took a few steps to see around them, but in every direction, the plains looked empty.

Serene's eyes narrowed and she turned her attention to the bridge over the river. "There's someone down there."

Sable pulled her eyes away from the burned buildings and circling birds to look at the bridge. There was no one visible.

"Not moving," Serene added.

Sable looked at her. The woman had to hold books at the end of her nose to read them. How could she see into the reeds beneath the bridge?

"Injured," Serene said, sounding more decisive.

"Probably dead," muttered Merilee. "We should turn around right now and get out of here before we're dead next."

"Can you be more specific than 'down there'?" Thulan slid a thick leather bracer over her forearm.

"Far side of the bridge, a little to the left," Serene said.

Thulan looked skeptically toward the tall reeds along the bridge, hiding everything near the water. "Can't find anybody who's easier to see?"

Leonis opened a small door under the driver's bench of the blue wagon and pulled out a thin, scuffed bow and a quiver of arrows. "Why don't we have a good bow?" he muttered.

"Because you're the one who wants one," Thulan answered, reaching past him to draw out a heavy, thick-shafted war hammer. "And you waste your money on wine and gambling."

"You could buy me one," Leonis pointed out, stringing it quickly and slinging the quiver across his back.

"I'm not even sure you know how to use it." Thulan answered. Despite the ease of their words, their voices were both low. The dwarf started down the hill.

"I can use it better than you can use that hammer." Leonis followed her. "What are you going to do, repair the city?"

"At least then it would be made right," Sable heard Thulan say quietly. Whatever Leonis answered, she couldn't make out.

Jae came up out the back of the red wagon with a short sword sheathed at his waist and started after the other two. Serene took a step to follow, but Atticus placed his hand on her arm. "If someone's injured, we should get ready to help them."

She kept her eyes on Jae, but nodded reluctantly.

Ryah crowded up against Sable. Atticus's face was tight as his gaze scanned the land around them, coming back to the smoking remains of Ebenmoor.

"Maybe your friend is safe," Ryah said to him. "Maybe she got away before the fire. The woods aren't far."

Atticus was quiet for a moment. "Zephony wasn't the type to run into the woods without a fully stocked carriage and a half-dozen servants."

"Sounds like she had too much sense to live out here," Merilee muttered.

Sable watched the three figures moving down the road. Aside from the dark smoke stirring over the town, and the occasional sharp call of a raven, the plains were still. Just before the bridge, Leonis positioned himself next to the road, his bow ready, while Thulan and Jae moved cautiously across. When they reached the far side, Thulan climbed down next to the river and knelt, motioning for Leonis.

Next to Sable, Serene blew out a long breath, scanning the hills again.

"They found someone," Ryah said, pointing at the bridge.

Serene let out an irritated growl. "I found someone. They merely followed directions. So, unless you know how to find more people out here, be quiet and let me listen." She stalked away from them a few paces and closed her eyes again. "You're loud enough just being alive."

Ryah stared at her, open-mouthed, and Sable started to object.

Atticus raised his hand to stop her. "Let her work."

"Work how?" Sable whispered to Ryah. Her sister frowned and shook her head.

At the bridge, Jae and Leonis lifted a man, supporting him between them. His head hung forward, and he leaned heavily on their shoulders. With Thulan bringing up the rear, still holding her hammer, they started up the hill.

"I still can't see anyone else," Serene said.

"Our new friend looks like he'll need some help." Atticus said.

"I can help," Ryah offered. "We've cared for a lot of wounded people at the abbey."

"Good." He went to the red wagon and pulled a blanket out, directing Ryah where to find a basket with some bandages and herbs.

Sable went to get a waterskin from the blue wagon. When she

climbed back out, the others were nearly back up the hill. Merilee stood backed against the red wagon, her face pale, clutching her necklaces and watching the hurt man. His dusty brown hair fell over his face, one side matted with blood that ran down into his beard like a dried, black river. His shirt was ripped open at the shoulder, mud and blood staining his sleeve and his side. His feet barely shuffled along the ground.

Leonis and Jae laid him on the blanket near the bushes, and his eyes rolled back in his head. Aside from the deep gash on his shoulder and a cut on his temple, Sable couldn't see any other injuries.

Ryah knelt beside him, wetting a cloth and cleaning the cut on his head. She placed her hand on his forehead. "He's feverish."

Atticus stood near his feet. "Can you hear me?"

The man let out a low groan and his eyelids fluttered open. His eyes were unfocused.

"Are you alone?"

The man groaned again.

Serene knelt across from Ryah and placed her hand on his forehead.

"There was no sign of a struggle at the bridge," Thulan said. "It looks like he tumbled down the slope on his own."

"Could you see anything more in Ebenmoor?" Atticus asked.

"Bodies," Thulan answered, her voice grim. "All close to the buildings."

"This head injury is shallow." Serene said. "His shoulder and some bruised ribs are the worst of it. I don't think anything is broken."

Ryah glanced at her. "His ribs?"

Serene pointed to the area under his wounded shoulder. "Three ribs are damaged."

"How can you tell?" Ryah asked.

Serene waved the question away and leaned closer to his shoulder. "Clean this up a bit more so I can see it better." She stood, turning to Atticus. "You won't get anything out of him for a while."

Sable's gaze went to the town. Broken walls and collapsed roofs rose up like pieces of her nightmares come to life. Unrecognizable piles of blackened things lay strewn on the ground. Smoke rose in lazy columns. A handful of ravens spiraled in the sky or perched on the ruins.

A hand on her shoulder made her jump. Jae stood next to her, his expression concerned. "Why does this terrify you?"

"It doesn't terrify you?"

Jae searched her face for a moment. "With you and your sister it's more."

Ryah kept her eyes fixed on the young man, cleaning grime off his shoulder. Her hands moved with practiced ease, almost absently, but everything about her posture was tense.

"Our town was burned like this." Sable's words were barely a whisper, and Jae leaned forward to hear her better.

"When?"

"Ten years ago."

"What town?" His voice was tense. "How big was it?"

"Pelrock. It was small." She glanced at the smoking ruins. "Much smaller than Ebenmoor. Down near the coast." The next day, a few survivors from another town had found Sable, Ryah, and Talia, and taken them all the way to Immusmala.

Jae squeezed her shoulder. "I'm sorry. I remember that summer. It was the worst raids in a long time. At least a half dozen towns were destroyed." He looked back at the town with a troubled look. "But even that summer they didn't hit anything as big as Ebenmoor. I've never heard of them hitting something this big."

"Never?" Atticus asked.

Jae shook his head. "The raiders come in small bands, usually from ships, so they attack towns and homesteads near the coast, not all the way up here."

"Where do they come from?" Ryah asked.

"No one knows." Jae stood. "Thulan, Leonis, let's go make sure it's safe for the wagons to pass."

Leonis cast a reluctant glance at the burned buildings, but retrieved his bow. Thulan was already striding down the rutted road toward the town.

Serene set one hand back on the man, and the other on the ground next to her. Sable thought she saw something shift in the bushes next to her, but when she looked again, they were still.

Atticus called for Sable, and she went to help clear a spot near the door in the red wagon. Serene stood, brushing her hands off and motioned for them to put him in. He was heavy, but between them all, they managed to lay him inside.

"That's where I sleep!" Merilee protested, finally coming closer.

"You can snuggle with him tonight then," Sable told her. "I'm sure he'll need help keeping warm."

Merilee looked at her, appalled. "He's getting blood everywhere! Leave him on the ground!"

The man's head lolled to the side, but despite Merilee's cries, the gash on his shoulder had mostly stopped bleeding.

"Atticus!" Merilee turned to the old man, her bracelets tinkling as she placed her hands onto her hips. "Make them stop!"

"Help make him comfortable," Atticus told her sternly, "or get out of the way."

Merilee gave him an indignant look. "I am the first lady of this troupe, and that affords me a level of respect I am not receiving. This is what you get for dragging us all out into the wilderness and picking up stray—"

"Give me your scarf," Serene interrupted her, holding out a hand. "I need a bandage."

Merilee gasped, placing her hand on the light green fabric around her neck. "This is silk! And that man is not my responsibility. I didn't want to come out here in the first place." She stalked away to stand near the front of the wagon.

Sable glanced around the wagon. "I'll find you something else for a bandage."

The edge of Serene's mouth curled up. "Ryah already has one. I just figured asking Merilee for hers was the quickest way to get some quiet." She opened a small, ceramic jar. The sharp scent of garlic and onion filled the wagon. She rubbed some of the brownish, lumpy paste into the wound before Ryah tied a bandage around his shoulder.

At a distant whistle, Atticus looked toward the town. "They're waving for us to come. Serene, would you drive Thulan's wagon?"

"Atticus!" Merilee gasped from around the corner of the wagon. "We are not going closer!"

"We're going past and into the forest so we can find a safe place to stop." He looked around the plains. "Somewhere less exposed."

Her face paled. "What if whoever killed them is still there?"

"Thulan wouldn't be telling us to come if they were," Atticus answered firmly. "Let's go."

Serene glanced at the wounded man. "Call me if he wakes," she said to Ryah, before heading to the driver's bench of the other wagon.

The smell of garlic was strong enough that Sable hooked the door so it would stay open. Ryah sat on the floor by the man's head, continuing to clean dirt and blood off his face. The wagon was crowded with crates and stage poles, but Sable found a seat on the bench that ran along the wall.

The man wasn't particularly old. Maybe a little older than Sable, but he couldn't be much older than thirty. The wagon bumped down the hill, then jolted over the bridge. Merilee didn't climb into the wagon, but walked close to the back door, her arms wrapped around herself.

As they turned toward the town, Ryah's hands stopped and she stared out the door. Sable crawled down next to her and put her arm around her sister's shoulders.

"It's just like home," Ryah whispered.

"I know." The town was coming steadily closer with its smoke and death. The call of ravens cut across the plains. Trying to keep her voice calm, Sable added, "The raiders are gone, though, and we'll be past it all soon."

Ryah nodded a little too quickly. The wagon slowed to a stop, and Sable tightened her arm around Ryah, but all she heard was Thulan's voice. The dwarf climbed up on the blue wagon, and Serene came back to the wounded man.

"Did they find anyone alive?" Sable asked quietly as they shifted to make room for her.

Serene shook her head.

The wagon started moving again, and Ryah leaned against Sable. A raven called out loudly, and Ryah flinched. Sable's eyes were fixed on the grass they could see out the back of the wagon.

Serene glanced up at the two sisters, then dug into her bag and handed Ryah a long, grey shawl. "I need more bandages. Rip that into strips." She pulled a small bowl and pestle, out as well, and dropped some tiny, dried, black berries into it. "Grind these up as fine as you can," she told Sable.

The note of command in her voice made Sable press the pestle into the berries without thinking. They were tougher than she'd expected, and she focused on them, having to push hard to get one to crack. A sharp scent stung her nose.

Not berries. Peppercorns.

"Why am I grinding pepper?" She glanced at the unconscious man. "Are we going to cook him? You've already made him smell like garlic."

A smile curled the corner of Serene's mouth. "We obviously won't get to restock our food in Ebenmoor, so…"

An entirely inappropriate laugh bubbled up inside Sable.

Ryah looked up, appalled. "That's not funny."

Sable pressed the back of her hand to her lips to hide her smile.

"If you're not a healer," Serene continued, still smiling, "you don't get a say in what we're doing. Just grind." She glanced at Ryah. "And rip."

Sable turned back to the bowl, trying to grind the hard corns that kept shooting out from under her pestle. Something outside caught her attention, and she glanced up.

The first burned building moved slowly past, broken and burned. The corner still stood, but the roof had collapsed, crushing everything else. Flapping wings moved along the ground.

Sable's hand gripped the bowl, her fingers squeezing the pestle so tightly it pressed against the bones of her fingers.

Serene looked somberly at the raven, then reached out and pulled the door closed, blocking their view. "Grind," she said gently.

Sable stared at the closed door, an old, deep rage stirring at all this death and destruction. The horror of this town mingled with the memories of all the death long ago, and the aching loneliness that night had left. The hole the raiders had torn in her life was still there, and still fresh.

A hand touched her arm and she looked up to find the ferocity inside her mirrored in Serene's face.

The woman squeezed her arm. "Don't let it fill you."

Sable tried to look away, but Serene held her gaze. From Serene's hand, a soothing warmth seeped into Sable's skin, almost seeming to wind its way up her arm and fill her chest. It didn't dispel the cold emptiness, but it thawed the edges.

Sable let out a long, unsteady breath, pushing away the cutting edge of terror and rage.

Serene's face settled back in its usual expression, but for the first time, Sable thought it looked less stern, and more like tightly controlled anger.

"Don't let it fill you." Serene released Sable's arm, but the warmth didn't disappear. It hummed quietly through her, not driving back the emptiness, but fighting to balance it out.

CHAPTER TWENTY-SEVEN

IT DIDN'T TAKE LONG to reach the forest. When Serene finally opened the back of the wagon, there was nothing to see but tall trees. Instead of smoke, the smell of pine needles swirled in, cutting through the smell of garlic and onions.

Serene looked out the back, her brow creased in concentration. She glanced at Ryah. "Could you find out if Atticus has any marjor leaves for a poultice?"

Ryah glanced outside uncertainly, but nodded and climbed out of the wagon.

"Be careful," Sable called after her.

"She'll be fine." Serene leaned over the injured man, probing his ribs. "There's nobody near."

Sable stared at the woman for a long moment, uneasiness warring with curiosity. "How do you know?"

Serene's hand paused. She looked at Sable, gauging her. Then she dropped her gaze back to the man. Sable expected a sharp answer, but Serene merely said, "I can sense living things."

The words were warm with truth. "You can...see them?"

Serene looked out at the trees. "It's nearly impossible to explain. I can't see it or feel it, but the energy in living things is bright." At

Sable's confused look, Serene sighed. "The grass outside has tiny little bits of energy in each blade, like tiny sparks of light. The trees have more, but are like pillars of coals. Whereas you and I are like bonfires."

Sable glanced at the man. "And him?"

Serene frowned down at him. "He's dim, but given rest, I think he'll brighten." She glanced outside. "I can sense reasonably far, and there aren't any people near us."

The man's shoulder looked considerably better than before. Sable stared at the wound for a long moment. "Did you…heal him?"

"Yes. I can move energy, too. When we first found him, I took some and put it in him, helping the wound heal." There was a touch of defiance in her shoulders.

"You took energy from…the grass?" Sable asked.

Serene laughed. "The grass doesn't have enough energy to do anything. Certainly not healing. I drew energy from the bushes that were next to us. Trees would have been better, but on the plains, there aren't a lot of options."

"That's…" Sable turned the idea over in her head. Part of her wanted to back away, but another part found it remarkable. "That's…amazing."

Serene's eyebrows rose. "Most people call it terrifying."

"It's got a little of that, too," Sable answered with a faint smile. "But it's mostly amazing."

Serene's shoulders loosened. "Not a lot of people agree." The man groaned, and Serene placed her hand on his forehead, frowning. "I need to ask Atticus about what herbs he has." She stood paused at the door. "If he wakes, try to keep him still."

A dozen questions swirled in Sable's head, but the woman climbed down and disappeared around the corner of the wagon.

Serene could do magic.

Sable turned the idea over in her mind as the wagon bumped along the forest road.

That seemed like it should feel more alarming than it did.

Sable looked out at the trees. How must the world look to Serene? The trees towering like pillars of life, grass carpeting the ground with little snippets of energy, bugs gleaming in the air like summer glowflies.

The wagon wheel slammed into a rut, almost sending Sable toppling onto the man. She caught herself, but he let out a groan and his eyes fluttered open.

"Where am I?" he whispered. His lips were dry and his voice sounded parched.

"In a wagon," Sable answered, reaching for the waterskin.

He blinked at her. "I figured that much out."

She let out a small laugh and offered him the water. "Right. We've just entered the Nidel Woods and are looking for a safe place to camp."

He took a long drink. "Are we far from Ebenmoor?"

Sable shook her head. He looked at her for a moment, then his eyes slid shut.

"I'm Sable," she said.

"Andreese." He opened one eye. "Everyone calls me Reese. How did I get in here?"

"We found you by the bridge." She paused. "Do you remember... what happened?"

He nodded and turned his gaze out the back of the wagon to the trees. "I remember." He tried to sit up, but let out a gasp of pain and sank back.

"Don't." Sable placed a hand on his chest. "Your ribs are bruised."

Andreese gritted his teeth. "I figured that out, too." With a bracing breath, he shoved himself up, groaning.

"You're supposed to stay still," she objected, but he was so determined, she leaned forward to help him sit up, getting a strong whiff of garlic.

He let out a hiss of pain, and sat for a moment with his eyes closed. "Thank you."

Sable shifted a crate behind him, and he leaned back on it gingerly.

"Thank you again." He motioned for the water, and using his uninjured arm, took a long drink.

She started to stand. "I should let Serene know you're awake."

"Don't go!" He grabbed her arm, his fingers feverishly hot, and she sank back down at the pleading in his voice.

"Sorry," he mumbled, pulling his hand off her arm. "Who's Serene?"

"She's…" Sable paused. "A healer, I guess. She's to blame for the foul-smelling concoction on your shoulder."

He leaned his head back. Ryah had wiped some of the blood off his face near the gash, but there was still a matted, dark line in his beard. The death and destruction of Ebenmoor hung almost palpable in the air between them, but it felt intrusive to bring it up.

When he spoke, it was so quiet she almost didn't hear.

"Everyone in town?" He kept his eyes fixed out the window, his mouth a tight line.

"I'm sorry," she whispered. The flash of pain that crossed his face almost undid her. "Did you…have a family there?"

"An aunt. She ran the butcher shop, and I hunted for her."

Sable opened her mouth to say something, but what was there to say? She glanced out through the open wagon door. "The attackers didn't come into the woods, did they?"

Andreese rubbed his good hand across his face. "No. They headed east down the river."

She paused before asking the next question. "It was raiders, wasn't it?"

"I suppose." He frowned. "But well-dressed for raiders. Dozens of them, all in black leather, faces covered in masks."

Sable pulled her knees up to her chest. "How did you get away?"

"I didn't. I chased them to the bridge, but there were too many." He tried to sit forward again and let out a grunt of pain. "I need to follow them."

She set her hand on his arm. "Lie back. You're going to make it worse. You can't go after them."

He pushed her hand away. "Yes, I can."

"A single man against dozens of raiders? Even if you were the greatest fighter in the world, even if you weren't injured, it'd be idiotic."

His face turned pale with fury. "They killed *everyone*."

The words tore into her. "So you're going to chase them down and die yourself?" The thought of his death—of yet another death—lit a fuse inside her. She pulled her hand off him, all her fury at the raiders directed at him. "If you're so eager to die, we should have just left you at the bridge and saved ourselves the effort."

"I didn't ask for your help," he snapped, shoving himself up and falling heavily to the side, hissing in pain.

She crossed her arms to stop herself from reaching out to help him. "You were dying!"

"I might as well be dead!" He fixed her with a glare. "You have no idea what I lived through. You have no idea what it's like to see monsters destroy everything you know. Everything you love."

A matching fury rose in her, and even though she knew, somewhere in the back of her mind, that it wasn't directed at him, she leaned closer and glared at him. He smelled of blood and smoke and the sharp tang of garlic. "I know *exactly* what you went through. Loved ones burning around you, everything you know turned to ash."

His eyes shot daggers at her.

"And I know all you want to do is kill them. But you can't. If they find you—" She stopped. It was stupid to argue about this. She sank back, blowing out a breath. "If they find you, they'll just slaughter you like they slaughtered everyone else."

Serene stalked around the end of the wagon and looked inside, glaring at Sable. "When I left you to care for him, I didn't mean you should work him into a frenzy so he re-injures himself."

"I'm trying to keep him safe," Sable retorted. "He wants to chase down the raiders."

The wagon slowed to a stop, and Serene crossed her arms, fixing Sable with an annoyed look. "From now on, Ryah and I will care for our guest. You can help by finding firewood so I can boil some herbs."

"Gladly." Sable climbed out of the wagon.

Serene stopped her before she could walk away, closing her eyes.

"No one nearby." Serene opened her eyes. "But stay close." She turned back to Andreese. "Lie back down," she said sternly. He began to protest, but she made an irritated huff. "You're not going anywhere. I need to look at your shoulder. And stop moving so much.

I didn't go to the trouble of healing you just to have you injure your ribs more."

"They're *my* ribs," he said, his tone more sulky than angry.

"Not for long, if you're set on chasing down raiders," Sable muttered.

Andreese shot her a glare, but the edges of Serene's mouth curled into a smile. "Firewood," she said. "Please."

Sable turned and headed into the quiet forest, walking quickly to get away from the annoying man. She didn't need to go far, though, before the quiet of the forest dulled the edge of her irritation. Moisture from the morning fog dripped down from the branches, pattering down on the forest floor. The air was warm, birds and squirrels chittered at each other, and the voices around the wagons grew faint.

She stopped before she went too far, just standing and letting the peace soak into her. Something about the forest caught at her memory —it was that wildness she'd smelled in Lord Renwen's tree, the freedom and vastness of the world around her.

Walking slowly and quietly, unwilling to disturb the silence, she gathered a few sticks. There were plenty scattered along the forest floor, but most were damp.

She was ready to turn around when she saw a long, low thicket ahead with a good number of dead branches. She reached it and set down the wood she'd been carrying.

The caw of a raven cut in the woods.

Her hand froze and she looked up, searching for the bird.

A sharp crack sounded from past the thicket. Then another. Her breath caught and she squatted down, peering through a gap in the branches. Her heart thundered in her ears until she was afraid she wouldn't hear anything else.

But another snap came, and she saw a shape moving deep in the trees.

A man, dressed in black.

His hood was pulled up, his face covered with a mask. His black boots were crisscrossed with strips of black leather, wrapping up his calves.

CHAPTER TWENTY-EIGHT

SABLE'S HEART pounded and she crouched down.

The man was heading toward the thicket, and there was nowhere else to hide, so she slipped in through a gap between two bushes. Inside, the bottom of the thicket was like a long, low tunnel. Stems rose out of the ground and branches arched out, leaving a low open area with enough room for her to crawl through. She moved deeper in, the ground beneath her hands hard and dry.

Through the tangle of bushes, she caught glimpses of the man walking slowly, looking at the ground as though tracking something.

Keeping her head low, she could see his boots as he moved, slowly and with a pronounced limp, disappearing behind trees for seconds at a time. She tried to slow her breath, but it trembled slightly and sounded loud in her ears.

The movement of something closer—and smaller—caught her eye.

A young child.

Dressed in a green, hooded cloak, her steps dragging, a little girl moved away from the man tracking her.

The child darted from tree to tree, her path leading her toward the end of the thicket. Sable crawled in that direction until she reached the edge of the bushes. The branches here were more heavily leafed, but there was a gap, almost too small for Sable to crawl through, leading out. She scooted forward on her stomach until she was at the edge of the leaves. She could hear the child drawing closer.

When the green cloak moved into view, Sable waved her hand and caught a flash of wide eyes from under the hood. Sable motioned for her to come. The girl paused, glancing behind her. Sable tried to see the warrior through the bushes, but saw nothing but leaves.

The girl scurried to the edge of the thicket and knelt. Sable shimmied backwards to give her room. The little cloaked figure turned and backed in on her hands and knees, pausing once she was under the leaves.

"Come farther," Sable whispered. "We can go deeper."

But the girl stayed where she was, reaching up to touch a branch with a blue-gloved hand. There was a shushing noise so low Sable could barely hear it, and the tunnel past the girl began to close.

Sable pressed her hand to her mouth to muffle her gasp.

Branches extended. Twigs swelled and stretched across the opening from all sides, forming a thick lattice.

When the tunnel was closed off, the little girl toppled to the side and lay still.

Sable stared at her collapsed form. The end of the thicket was substantially denser than before, and she couldn't see through it. She reached for the girl's foot, but heard the crunch of a footstep, sounding much closer than before. Then another. Sable stayed still, straining to hear each step, praying the girl wouldn't make a sound.

The steps paused near the end of the thicket. The girl didn't move, and Sable barely dared to breathe. Her heart pounded too fast in her ears, measuring out the endless moment with frantic beats.

The man moved again, limping past the end of the thicket.

When she couldn't hear him anymore, Sable grabbed the girl's small legs and pulled her into the center of the bushes, cursing as several low hanging branches caught on the cloak and snapped loudly. The girl's body was limp, and dirty. Spots on her cloak were wet with something dark. Sable gently rolled her over, hoping she wasn't hurting her.

The hood slipped off her face, and Sable yanked her hands back. This was not a little girl.

CHAPTER TWENTY-NINE

THE CREATURE before Sable was roughly the size and shape of a very small child. But that was where the resemblance ended.

She—at least Sable was reasonably sure it was a girl—had pasty skin with a bluish tinge that looked more like hide than flesh. Her nose was long and thin. Long ears thrust out past wild black curls of hair. Her body was wiry and thin, her huge eyes closed, her mouth a wide, lipless gash.

She wore a dark green dress under the cloak. Beneath the grime, the material looked rich. The sleeves were lined with a buttery yellow fabric. She wore thin boots that tied almost up to her knees, and were still barely longer than Sable's hands.

Sable drew back, staring at the creature. She didn't look vicious. But her fingers were like blue-tinged tree roots that looked as if once they gripped something, they would never let go.

There were no more noises in the forest. For a moment, she toyed with the idea of leaving the creature here, but if this was an enemy of the raiders, that should put her on Sable's side.

Sable crawled close to the creature and examined her. The blood on her clothes must have belonged to someone else. Besides some scratches on her arms and face, Sable could see no injuries. She shook her gently, but the creature's head lolled to the side, and she didn't wake.

Sable rolled the creature onto her back. Grabbing her cloak by the shoulders, Sable began to back out of the thicket, pulling her along. The creature was light, but each pull was irritatingly short, with sharp branches jabbing into Sable as she worked her way backwards. Finally, she reached the gap she'd first entered through, and peered out into the quiet forest. Seeing nobody, she crawled through and with a final pull, brought the little creature out.

Leaving behind the meager pile of wood she'd collected earlier, Sable wrapped the creature carefully in her cloak, and lifted her up. She weighed less than a child, and Sable could feel her bony arms and legs through the material. Walking as quickly as she could, she hurried back toward the wagons.

She glanced down at the bundle in her arms. What was she carrying? A goblin? The thought almost made her put the thing down. But goblins were supposed to be green, weren't they? And this thing had made the branches grow over the tunnel. Goblins didn't do anything with plants, did they? Maybe she was a tree sprite? Sable had always assumed magical creatures like that were beautiful. Whatever she held wasn't exactly ugly, but no one would call her beautiful.

Sable breathed a sigh of relief when she saw Thulan gathering her own stack of wood.

The dwarf looked pointedly at the bundle in her arms, raising an eyebrow. "That's not firewood."

"There's a raider here," Sable whispered to the dwarf.

Thulan's gaze swung through the woods.

"He was tracking this…" Sable paused, unsure what to call her.

"Where?"

She nodded back over her shoulder. "Back that way, heading south."

"Only one?"

"That's all I saw. He was limping."

Thulan turned and hurried back to the wagons, calling quietly for everyone's attention. "Sable saw a raider," she said when they'd gathered.

Merilee gasped. Her face was still pale and she stood closer to the group than usual, casting worried looks into the forest.

Serene asked which way he'd gone, then faced into the woods for a long moment. "He's not nearby." She frowned. "Blasted trees make it hard to see any distance, though."

Sable gently set down the creature and explained what happened.

Serene knelt next to her, unwrapping the cloak. "A kobold!"

Sable stared at the creature. A kobold. That made perfect sense. The magical little creatures that could fix things. She'd "fixed" the end of the thicket.

Leonis came over with a wide smile. "I love kobolds!"

"Is it supposed to be blue?" Ryah asked.

"They come in lots of colors." Jae looked curiously at the creature.

Thulan motioned to Leonis as she picked up her hammer from the seat of the wagon. Leonis grabbed his bow and followed her to the edge of their camp to keep watch.

"Blue?" Atticus drew closer. "That's Zephony's kobold."

"Of course she's Lady Zephony's," Merilee said. "Who else would have a kobold out here in the wild except a lady?" Her gaze fell on Andreese, who leaned against the wagon, holding his ribs. "I'm Lady Merilee of Colbreth Castle," she said with her normal air of disdain.

Andreese scowled slightly at her tone. "Right. And I'm...Lord Andreese of Ravenwick." His voice dripped with sarcasm, but Merilee's face brightened.

She stepped closer. "I've heard Ravenwick is lovely. It's nice to finally meet someone of quality."

He raised an eyebrow. "I..."

"My lord," Merilee simpered.

Sable stared at her for a moment. She really believed he was a lord? Andreese met Sable's glance, looking just as surprised, but when Merilee dropped into a curtsey, he gave Sable an amused shrug. When Lady Merilee looked back up, he managed to dip his head in a bow before wincing and holding his side again.

Sable snorted and looked back at the the kobold.

"How badly is she hurt?" Atticus asked, kneeling down.

"I don't think the blood is hers," Sable said. "She looked tired, but she didn't collapse until after she made the branches grow."

Serene leaned over the creature. "She may just be exhausted."

The kobold moaned and her eyes fluttered open, her irises huge circles of deep purple. Her skin was still light, but the blue was richer. At the sight of all the people around her, she shrank back.

"Hello, Purnicious," Atticus said gently. "Don't worry. You're safe."

The kobold blinked up at him before her eyes widened in recognition and she sat up. "Atticus, sir?"

"Where is Zephony?"

Purnicious caved in on herself. She wrung her hands together. The tips of her long, blue ears bent down and she pressed her eyes closed. "Gone, sir." Her voice broke. "My mistress is gone." She looked up at Atticus with teary eyes. "I tried to get her out. Tried to stop the flames. But they were everywhere. And the black men crawled over the town like roaches in a larder."

"How dreadful!" Merilee stepped closer to Andreese and clutched his arm. He let out a grunt of pain, but she ignored him, looking fearfully into the forest.

"Lord Andreese might not be the one to look to for protection," Sable pointed out. "He's got broken ribs."

"They're not broken," he said through clenched teeth.

"My apologies, my lord," Sable said dryly. "You're in prime fighting shape."

"We saw Ebenmoor," Atticus said softly to Purnicious, ignoring the others. The kobold covered her face with her hands.

Sable caught a flicker of movement from Andreese as he fixed his gaze on the treetops. The ragged sense of loss that had been lurking around his face was suddenly obvious, and she regretted the sharpness of her last comment.

Atticus set his hand on Purnicious's shoulder. "There was nothing you could have done."

Sable leaned toward the kobold. "How did you escape?"

Purnicious cracked apart her blue fingers to look at Sable. She drew in a sharp breath and dropped her hands to her lap. Tears streaked through the dirt on her cheeks, but a look of adoration filled her face.

"My lady!"

Merilee snorted.

For once, Sable was inclined to agree with her. "I'm not a lady. I'm just…Sable."

Purnicious wiped her face with the corner of her filthy cloak, which only smeared the dirt. She scrambled onto her knees, facing Sable. "You saved me!" Purnicious crawled forward and grasped one of Sable's hands in her own. Sable tried not to pull away from the gnarled fingers. The little kobold sniffed, but fixed Sable with a look so ardent she didn't dare move.

"Lady Sable," Purnicious breathed, devotion in her voice. "I am yours. For as long as I draw breath." The sadness in her face was tempered with joy, and the effect was transformational. She smiled, showing little white teeth behind her thin mouth. Her blue ears curled up at the ends, and her fingers, though oddly shaped and colored, gripped Sable's hand with warmth and gentleness. "My skills, my strength, my devotion… All is yours."

Sable glanced around uncomfortably. "That's not necessary. We were just trying to escape from that man."

"And if you're looking for a lady," Merilee said, watching the creature with a shrewd look, "you've got the wrong woman. My name is Lady Merilee, and I live in Colbreth Castle."

"You saved me," Purnicious said warmly to Sable, ignoring Merilee. "I am yours."

Merilee let out an exasperated breath.

Sable shifted. "But you also saved me. So does that mean I'm yours, too?"

Purnicious laughed, a long, rippling sound, like a bubbling brook.

Sable looked up to find everyone watching the exchange with differing levels of amusement. "What's happening?"

"How are you so uneducated?" Merilee asked. "Purnicious, dear, come over here. I'll get everything set straight for you. You can ride in the wagon next to me."

Serene shot Merilee an annoyed look before looking back at Sable. "You don't know much about kobolds, do you?"

Sable paused. "They fix things."

"Fix things?" Purnicious's eyebrows rose in indignation. "A farm-hand fixes things. Kobolds are artists. We take the mundane and craft it into glory. We raise palaces from sawdust. Castles from broken stone. A royal gown from a scrap of fabric."

"Sorry," Sable said, pulling on her hand gently. The kobold did not release it. "I didn't mean to be insulting. That sounds...amazing."

"It is," Purnicious said with a wide smile.

"And if you save a kobold, Sable," Jae said with a grin, "you and your family earn its loyalty and service for its lifetime."

Sable looked down at the kobold. "Then aren't you still loyal to Zephony's family?"

"Mistress Zephony had none," Purnicious said sadly.

Merilee smiled sweetly at the little creature. "I can save you from a life of obscurity and poverty."

Purnicious paid her no heed, and looked up into Sable's face with eagerness and devotion.

"That's very generous, Purnicious," Sable said, "but I don't... I can't..." She glanced down at her faded clothes and worn boots, the left one still darker than the right. "I don't have anything." She shook her head. "I can't take care of you."

Purnicious smiled at her. "You have it backwards. *I* will take care of *you*."

"If you're foolish enough to not want a kobold," Andreese said, "I'll take her."

"I didn't say I didn't want her," Sable objected.

Purnicious finally fixed Andreese and Merilee with a glare. "I'm not available for taking. If Lady Sable releases me, I will honor her wish. But I am not beholden to you, Lady Merilee, or you, wastrel."

Andreese's eyebrows rose.

"I think you mean Lord Wastrel," Sable said, grinning.

"There is nothing lordly about him," Purnicious sniffed.

"I'll take that as a compliment," Andreese said, "if being lordly means being anything like your mistress. Zephony was a conceited, noble, pain in my—"

"Enough," Atticus interrupted, looking at Andreese. "Zephony was our friend." He looked at Purnicious. "And Andreese is our guest, as are you. Now, we have more serious matters to discuss."

"Like how do we know there aren't more warriors in the woods?" Ryah asked.

"They left," Andreese said. "I saw them. They all went east."

"Obviously not all of them," Sable muttered.

"I believe the wastrel is mostly right," Purnicious said, addressing Atticus and ignoring Andreese's scowl. "The one following me was alone. I first saw him in a ditch along the edge of my mistress's..." She swallowed, "my former mistress's house. I thought he was dead. I tried to bury him." She looked slightly abashed. "But instead of burying him under the dirt he lay on, which would have been simple, I decided I'd rather crush him under rocks. Since the only rocks I had were pebbles, growing them took more energy than was probably wise." She gazed back at Sable, a pleading look in her eyes. "But I just wanted to crush him."

"Understandable," Sable assured her. "I would have, too."

"Before I could finish, he woke and tried to grab me, so I ran. He chased me." She beamed up at Sable. "Until you saved me." She reached out and took Sable's hand in her ropey blue fingers. "Please, Lady Sable, may I have the honor of serving you?"

Sable shifted. "Can we not call it serving? I'm happy to have you work with me." She glanced at the others. "I think."

Purnicious's face lit up. "Then I'm happy too!"

"Now that we've settled that," Serene said dryly, looking up at Jae. "We should capture the warrior."

"We should kill him," Andreese corrected her.

"No." Jae said firmly. "The rumors have been spreading for a fortnight, and Ebenmoor was just attacked last night. We need to talk to the man. Find out who he is and where he's from. If towns as big as Ebenmoor are being hit, these raiders are far stronger than any we've seen in the past."

"We need to get away from here as fast as these miserable wagons will carry us!" Merilee said. "We need to get back to civilized lands immediately."

Jae glanced at Atticus. "We need to talk to him."

Atticus nodded. "I agree."

He called Leonis and Thulan back. When they arrived, Leonis squatted down next to Purnicious. "Do you know Haps? Old fellow? Long, green hair?"

Purnicious thought for a moment. "There was a Haps who used to tell tales about the elves when I was small."

"You're still small," Andreese said.

Purnicious scowled at him and flicked a finger at his boot. The laces shrank, pulling together tightly. Andreese grunted and bent over, hissing in pain as he yanked out the knot. He stood and grasped his ribs, glaring at Purnicious, who smirked at him.

"That's Haps!" Leonis said. "I haven't seen him in years. He made me the best bow I've ever used. Easily as good as elven made."

"Leonis," Atticus interrupted, "we need to track the raider."

Leonis glanced at Sable. "Can you show me where he went?"

A sinking feeling ran through her at the thought of going back into the woods, but she nodded.

"I'll stay here with Andreese," Ryah offered, her voice calm, but her face pale.

"As will I," Merilee declared, gripping Andreese's arm again.

"I'm not staying behind," Andreese said, extricating himself and pushing away from the wagon with a grimace of pain.

"We shouldn't split up," Atticus said. "Leonis and Thulan can track him. The rest of us will follow at a distance." He frowned at them. "Quietly. Otherwise, we might scare him into hiding."

"I can track a wounded man," Leonis said stiffly, "even if he tries to hide."

Purnicious stood and fell in next to Sable as she started back toward the thicket, sticking close to her leg. Sable stayed in between Thulan and Leonis, watching the woods warily. At the thicket, Sable pointed in the direction the warrior had gone. Leonis leaned against a large tree, peering at the ground and scanning the forest.

He stood there for so long that Thulan let out an impatient sigh.

Leonis grumbled, "Between Sneaks, Purnicious, and the warrior, there was a bit of activity around here. Give me a minute."

"We've already given you plenty." Thulan started forward, passing Leonis and studying the ground. She pointed at a dark spot. "Looks like blood."

Leonis glared at her. "Of course he went that way. I was trying to figure out how fast."

Thulan snorted and started down the trail, her normally heavy footsteps remarkably soft. "He traveled on the ground, not up in the leaves."

"When someone moves through the trees, the whole forest changes," Leonis said, irritated. "If you want to know more than the size of their foot, you look up." Thulan didn't answer. Leonis glanced back at the others. "Everyone stay back."

"Of course," Andreese said, following closely behind them. "Wouldn't want to be there when you found the devil."

The others did hang back, though, waiting until Thulan, Leonis, and Andreese had moved a little way through the trees.

When they were nearly out of view, Atticus started forward. "Please, stay close."

Purnicious crowded up close to Sable's legs. Merilee squeezed in between Sable and Ryah, gripping their arms. Her face was pale, and her hands shook slightly. She pushed the two of them a little ahead and peered over their shoulders, as though they were her protection.

"This is a mistake," she muttered. "I shouldn't be here. I should be home." She looked around the woods with wide eyes. "Nothing at home was as bad as this."

"I thought your family lived in a castle," Ryah whispered.

"We do." If Merilee hadn't been using Ryah as a shield, the fear in her voice might have made Sable feel sympathy for the woman. "I cannot afford to die before I've played a famous role."

Sable looked pointedly forward in an effort not to roll her eyes. Ryah managed to keep her face more sympathetic, patting Merilee's hand.

Far ahead, Thulan and Leonis walked side by side, occasionally pausing, Thulan studying the ground while Leonis peered up into the trees. At each stop, Sable found herself holding her breath.

Despite their quiet grumbles at each other, Thulan and Leonis moved quickly, each stopping at small signals from the other. Andreese spoke quietly to them, pointing out things on the ground.

Finally, the dwarf held up her hand and everyone stopped.

Merilee's grip on Sable's arm tightened painfully and she crowded closer. Sable let her, finding her presence slightly reassuring. Thulan motioned for the group to stay where they were and crept forward. Leonis nocked an arrow, his attention fixed on the base of a huge tree. Andreese held a short knife in his hand and crept along behind Thulan.

When they stopped, Sable caught sight of something long and dark at their feet.

Thulan straightened and crossed her arms and looked back at the group. "Don't think we're going to get much information out of this one," she called.

CHAPTER THIRTY

THE RAIDER SLUMPED in the hollow of the wide tree trunk. He was clad entirely in black. His pants and shirt were made of a thin linen, covered with a hard, dark leather armor. His black hood was pulled up, despite the warmth of the day. A mask hid his face, except for his eyes, which were closed. One arm hung awkwardly to the side, his hand covered in blood. His chest rose in shallow breaths.

Leonis planted himself in front of the man, an arrow nocked, and nodded to Thulan, who stepped close enough to pull the sword out of the man's belt. He handed it to Andreese, who swung it slowly in the air, testing its weight while hunching awkwardly over his sore ribs. The man on the ground didn't move.

Serene stepped forward and knelt next to him, pushing his hood back to show dark, cropped hair. She set her hand on his forehead and closed her eyes.

The group stood like some sort of mismatched guard. Only Leonis and Thulan—and maybe the injured Andreese—could be called fighters, yet there was something in the way the rest stood together, willing to protect each other, that Sable clung to.

Hiding in the cellar years ago, Sable had felt helpless. In the thicket with Purnicious was the same. But here, among the others, was different. She was no more powerful than she'd ever been, yet she was surrounded by people she had begun to trust. Sable could feel them around her, connected to her by newly forming, thin threads.

Sable straightened her shoulders.

No more cowering.

No more letting fear keep her shoved back in a hole, praying the danger would pass. Anger at everything this man had done replaced the fear. She pried Merilee's hand off her arm and stepped forward.

Serene kept her eyes closed. "He doesn't have long."

"A shame," Andreese said darkly.

"Can you heal him?" Atticus asked Serene.

"Heal him?" Andreese demanded.

Serene kept her eyes shut, but shook her head. "He is bleeding inside his chest, his head, and somewhere in his stomach."

"Can you wake him?" Atticus asked.

Serene frowned. "He'll be in terrible pain."

"Good," Andreese said, and Sable nodded.

Atticus waited patiently until Serene opened her eyes. She glanced at him and let out an annoyed huff. "You won't have long, and he may be in too much pain to answer you."

"Thank you." Atticus squatted down at the man's feet.

Serene pushed the man's mask down. His face was long, jaw thin, nose sharp. His mouth hung open slightly. Serene shook out her hands and glanced at the others. "Hold him still."

Leonis set down his bow and knelt on one side of the man, holding down his wounded arm. Thulan did the same to the other.

No more cowering.

Sable pushed herself forward and dropped down by the man's feet. She forced herself to set her hands on the leather straps of his boots, pinning him down.

Serene put her palms on the side of the warrior's face and closed her eyes again.

For a heartbeat, nothing happened.

Then the man's eyes flew open and he let out a cry of pain, his face twisting in agony.

He thrashed his legs, and Sable threw her weight on them. Thulan and Leonis leaned down on his arms and chest to keep him still.

Serene gave an irritated growl, her hands gripping his face.

Beneath Sable, his movements weakened. Slowly, the man calmed, although his eyes flickered wildly at the people around him.

Serene made a shushing noise. His fierceness faded until the man looked up at Atticus with a dull expression.

"Hurry," Serene said between clenched teeth.

"Where are you from?" Atticus asked.

The man's gaze unfocused, he muttered something unintelligible but defiant.

"Where are you from?" Atticus repeated, fixing him with a hard look.

His legs were still, and Sable relaxed her grip on them slightly. The man returned Atticus's cold gaze for a long moment, then began to speak.

The words were foreign and guttural, the sounds coming from back in his throat.

Andreese flinched, and Serene's eyes widened. A chill ran across Sable's neck. The language that filled her nightmares.

"That's Kalesh," Jae said, stepping up next to Atticus.

Sable looked up at him in shock. The raider spoke Kalesh?

"*Tel mordu es?*" Jae asked.

The man's gaze flickered to Jae and he answered.

"He's from the Golden Land," Jae translated. "It's what the Kalesh Empire calls itself."

Atticus considered the man for a moment. "Are you alone?"

In answer to Jae's translation, the man let out a rasping, gurgling laugh and answered with words that surrounded Sable with a faint sensation of warmth.

Jae raised a sharp gaze to the woods around them. "There are countless more. They cover the land like..." He paused, searching for a word.

"Water engulfing the land and never drawing back," Serene finished.

Wings flapped at the top of a nearby tree. A huge raven settled and fixed the group with black eyes. Ryah's face paled.

The words squeezed around Sable like warm, thick mud.

Sable's hands tightened on his leather boots. "He's telling the truth."

Several people glanced at her, but Atticus just nodded.

"Why are you here?" he asked.

Jae translated. A slow, cold smile spread across the man's face. A string of words rolled out of him, rhythmic and chanting. They wrapped around Sable with an almost feverish heat.

The man's eyes closed and his voice rose with a fanatical passion, cutting through the woods like a call to arms.

Jae's face grew harder the longer the man spoke. "Cleanse the land. Burn the filth. Raze the chafe. Clear the way. Prepare the ground for the..." He paused, "the touch of the holy. Cleanse the land..." He shook his head. "It repeats."

The man just chanted on. His head lolled back and his voice grew weaker.

"Serene?" Atticus asked.

She shook her head. "He's almost gone."

"A little more," Atticus said.

Her lips tightened into a thin line, but she nodded.

The man groaned and his eyes opened again. Sable felt a new tendril of fear watching Serene grip the man's face. This whole situation felt unreal. A monster come to life from her nightmares, and Serene...

Sable watched the hardness in Serene's face. Whatever she was doing was much more on the terrifying side than the amazing one.

"How many of you are here?" Atticus asked.

The man clenched his jaw, not answering.

Atticus crossed his arms and waited. After a moment, a humorless smile spread across the warrior's face as he spoke.

"We are everywhere," Jae translated. "Already among you. Right next to you." He glanced at Atticus. "Living in your temples."

Atticus fixed the man with a hard gaze. "In our priories? Do you mean your ambassador?"

Jae translated. The man let out a wet, coughing laugh before he spoke.

"Soon, we will crawl through your harvests," Jae said, "and raze your fields."

The man began to chant again, slower.

"A prayer." Jae's face filled with disgust. "Remember my deeds, the blood spilled, the land cleansed. Remember my deeds and curse those who ended my service."

"Who do you pray to?" Atticus asked.

Jae translated the question, but the man paid them no heed, his words rolling on and on.

"What's that?" Jae asked, pointing to the arm Leonis was gripping.

The warrior's sleeve was pushed back to reveal a long line of black tattoos.

Leonis shoved the sleeve up. Sharp, angular lines and symbols ran up his forearm.

"Definitely Kalesh," Serene said, leaning forward.

The warrior's voice droned on and he opened his eyes again. He stared at the group around him with contempt. He met Sable's gaze. She gripped his legs tighter, refusing to look away. No more hiding.

A smug smile twisted his lips, and Sable's heart lurched. The man still spoke, but his words suddenly lost their fervor.

No longer a prayer, he just repeated them mindlessly.

His eyes sharpened.

Sable gripped him tighter, her palms slick against his boots.

The warrior's gaze moved to Serene, who still knelt by his head, peering at the tattoos on his bloody arm.

A flash of silver near his other hand caught Sable's eye.

The still chanting warrior wrenched his arm out of Thulan's grasp and flung it toward Serene's chest

"Serene!" Sable lunged forward, grabbing for the warrior's arm. She got her fingers around it, but he tore out of her grasp. Jae cried out behind her.

Serene flung herself back, twisting away, but not far enough or quickly enough.

The blade slammed deep into her thigh.

She screamed and rolled away.

"Serene!" Jae's voice was filled with terror and rage.

Sable scrambled up onto the warrior to hold him down. A cry of pain ripped out of him when she pushed down on his ribs. Thulan and Leonis threw their weight onto his arms again, Thulan wrenching the knife out of his grasp.

Sable leaned toward his face, years of fear turning into fury. "No more," she hissed. The words directed at both him, and herself.

Jae dropped and clutched the warrior's neck with one hand, the other hand slamming down onto the ground beside his head. The man's eyes widened in fear, and the color drained from his face.

"Jae..." Serene gasped.

He ignored her and leaned toward the man, his face so close Sable leaned back. Jae's body quivered with fury as he crushed the warrior's neck. Sable caught sight of a wisp of smoke rising from Jae's other hand, planted on the ground.

Leonis let out a sharp hiss and yanked his hands away from the warrior's arm. Under the angular tattoos, the warrior's skin blanched. The man's eyes bulged and face twisted in panic, but Jae only leaned closer, snarling.

Thulan shoved off the man's other arm with a curse.

"Jae!" Atticus snapped.

Beneath Sable, cold seeped through the thick armor, leeching the heat from her hands with a burning pain. Icy shards stabbed up her through her arms and her fingers whitened.

She shoved herself off the man, rubbing her freezing hands together.

The warrior, even freed from everyone's hold except Jae's, barely moved. His feet twitched weakly, his fingers feebly scrabbling at Jae's hand.

A steady stream of smoke rose from the earth beneath Jae's other hand. A tongue of flame slipped between his fingers.

Sable scrambled back.

"Jae," Serene said louder. She reached her hand toward him, but stopped before touching him.

Jae ignored her. He leaned close to the man's white face and hissed, "*Ak sadetu smuret, kossetu smuret.*"

The swirl of warmth from those words was so strong that Sable drew away.

The man's eyes widened one last time. Then his face went slack.

Serene let out a long breath and Jae, after staring at the dead man for a moment longer, shoved himself back.

Thulan slipped a knife from her belt. Leonis had an arrow pointed at Jae's chest. Andreese pointed the Kalesh man's sword in the same direction.

Jae sat with his head down, chest heaving, hands curled into claws.

Sable stared at the hands that had just sucked the life out of the Kalesh warrior. She raised her gaze to Jae's unruly hair.

His robe was grey, not black, and there was no red veil over his face, but the word rose to the surface anyway.

"Baledin," she whispered.

CHAPTER THIRTY-ONE

SERENE REACHED out slowly to touch Jae's arm.

He shuddered and looked up at her. His gaze fell on the knife in her thigh and he turned toward her. "Bandages!"

No one moved.

"What just happened?" Leonis asked in a low voice, his arrow still aimed at Jae.

"I need bandages before I can remove the knife," Jae snapped.

Serene reached over and touched Jae's cheek, turning his head to look at her. Her face was tight with pain. "Answer their questions before they kill you."

Jae turned to look at the group. Ryah and Merilee clung to each other, hiding behind Atticus, who merely looked resigned. Purnicious stood with her arms wrapped around Atticus's leg, quivering. But Jae's gaze paused on Leonis, Thulan, and Andreese pointing weapons at him.

Jae slowly raised his hands. His palms were bright red. The grass where he'd touched the ground was black and smoldering.

"You're a baledin," Sable whispered again.

"There are no baledin," Jae said, annoyed.

"Really?" Thulan asked. "Because it sure looked like you just sucked the life out of that man."

"That man..." Jae's voice curled around the words, "just tried to kill Serene. Would have killed us all given the chance."

"We're not arguing that fact," Thulan said.

"We are not baledin," Serene said through clenched teeth, holding her thigh.

"We?" Leonis shifted his attention to her.

"We are..." Jae paused, shrugging, "just people. You have nothing to fear."

"Sucking the life out of someone sounds like something to fear," Thulan pointed out.

"We can move energy," Jae said. "It's called *vitalle*. We can draw it out of things or move it into things. But we don't walk around draining people of life."

Leonis glanced at the body on the ground. "Our Kalesh friend tells a different story."

"You all know Jae and Serene," Atticus said, his voice tired. "They are not monsters."

"We're not sure what they are," Thulan said.

"They're baledin," Sable repeated.

Atticus shook his head. "You don't even know what that word means."

"If it means they kill Kalesh," Andreese said, lowering his sword, "it sounds all right to me."

Thulan fixed an accusing look on Atticus. "You knew?"

"I know many things about all of you. And I trust Jae and Serene completely. As you always have." Atticus set his hand on Leonis's arm. "Put down your weapons."

Neither Leonis nor Thulan relaxed.

"Serene's leg needs attention," Atticus said, "and we're wasting time when we should be looking for shelter."

He stepped in front of the weapons aimed at Jae, and both Leonis and Thulan stepped back.

"I still have this shawl," Ryah said quietly, holding out a bundle of cloth to Jae. "You can use that for a bandage."

Jae glanced up at her. "Will you help me?"

Ryah hesitated, but nodded. Sable stepped forward to stop her. Atticus put his hand on her shoulder.

"She's not in danger," he said.

Sable could feel the truth of his words, but she didn't relax until the knife was out, the bandage wrapped around the wound, and Ryah had stepped away.

"We need to get back to the wagons and clean the wound," Jae said, helping Serene stand.

"We also need to find a better place than the wagons to spend the night." Atticus glanced up through the pines at the sun, which had started heading to the west. The raven still sat high in the nearby tree. "There isn't an army of these men near us, is there?"

Serene shifted and grimaced, leaning into Jae. "There's no one close."

"This man believed there was," Sable pointed out.

"We need to talk to someone who knows what's going on," Atticus said, looking at Thulan.

The dwarf's face hardened. "No."

"They'll know if there's an army in the east and how many towns on the plains have been burned."

"They won't care enough to find out why," Thulan replied.

"But they'll know more than we do."

"Who are we talking about?" Andreese asked.

Thulan didn't answer. She merely scowled at Atticus.

Leonis slung his bow over his shoulder. "The dwarves live in the Marsham Cliffs and have a clear view of the plains."

"The dwarves won't help," Andreese said. At Thulan's glare, he shrugged. "They won't. Surly, unfriendly folk."

Sable shot him an annoyed look. "That's rich, coming from you."

Thulan ignored them both and turned back to Atticus. "It's out of our way."

Atticus snorted. "I think it's safe to say our plans have changed."

The dwarf shook her head. "It's a stupid idea."

"Do you have a better one?"

"Of course not. The humans around here are useless, and while there are elves farther north, they're even worse." She crossed her arms. "I'll take you, but I want double pay for the summer. And I'm not ever playing that fishman role again."

Atticus gave her a small smile. "Your regular pay for the summer, plus the knowledge you helped countless people." At Thulan's deepening frown, he added, "But no more fishman."

"Fine," Thulan grumbled.

Atticus nodded. "Let's get moving then."

Jae and Serene started back through the woods, her arm over his shoulders. Atticus and Merilee followed.

"What do we do with him?" Ryah asked, her eyes still fixed on the dead man. "We can't just leave him."

"Yes, we can. We can leave him to rot, like he did to Ebenmoor." Andreese said coldly. "Like he'd have done to us if he could."

"Let's go," Thulan said.

Sable stayed next to Ryah, neither moving as they stared down at the body. "I hate this man," she whispered.

"So do I." Ryah's voice had never sounded so ragged. "And yet..."

Sable fixed her eyes on the horrible black boots.

A fierce rebellion rose against everything this man stood for, and a rebellion against the heartlessness of leaving him here to rot, picked apart by the raven.

"And yet..." Sable agreed quietly. She knelt and pushed some of the leaves and pine needles over the man's feet.

Thulan crossed her arms and fixed them with a disapproving look.

"We need to go," Andreese said firmly.

Sable picked up a handful of needles. "You don't have to wait."

"You can't be out here alone," Andreese leaned heavily against the tree, holding the Kalesh sword limply at his side. "Let's go."

Sable ignored him.

"Just hurry," Thulan said.

Purnicious stood several feet back, her hands clenched into fists, her face drawn with hatred.

"Will you help us cover him?" Sable asked her.

"He would not do the same for you," Purnicious whispered.

"We know," she said quietly. "People like him destroyed our entire town and killed our parents."

Thulan looked up sharply, and Andreese glanced at her.

Purnicious looked at the sisters for a long moment, then nodded. "I'm doing this for you, Lady Sable. Not for him."

Sable stared at the boots. "I'm doing it for me, too."

Purnicious knelt down and set her blue hands on the ground. Without looking at the dead man, she stilled. A mound of earth rose, covering his legs, stomach, and finally piling up against the trunk, hiding his face.

Sable gave her a small smile. "Thank you," she whispered.

Purnicious tried to stand, but her legs gave out.

"Let me help," Sable said, picking her up. The kobold rested her head on Sable's shoulder.

"Amah keep your soul," Ryah said over the grave. "May she heal it and bring it to the light." She looked at the pile of dirt for one more moment before turning toward the wagons. Andreese followed her.

The raven in the tree shifted, and Sable glanced up at it. "And may Amah keep the rest of your people away."

Sable followed her sister, and Thulan fell in beside her. Ryah talked quietly to Andreese. Sable heard snippets about raiders and parents. Purnicious's dark head rested on Sable's shoulder, her eyes closed.

Sable glanced at Thulan, her hammer slung up on her shoulder. Her forearms were thick and muscled, but as she walked, Sable wondered how she had ever missed the fact she was a woman.

"Thank you for waiting," Sable said.

Thulan gave a grunt in acknowledgment.

"The place you're taking us... Is that where you're from?"

Thulan nodded stiffly.

"How long ago did you leave?"

"Nine years."

"Why?"

A twitch of pain—maybe anger—crossed Thulan's face.

"Sorry," Sable said quickly. "It's not my business. There are a million reasons to leave home. If I can ever get both sisters out of Immusmala, we're never going back."

Thulan glanced over, her rich, brown eyes guarded under her bushy eyebrows. "Raiders killed your parents?"

Sable swallowed, but she nodded. "Ryah was only six," she answered quietly. "It was just like Ebenmoor."

"Were they Kalesh?"

She thought back to the boots and the strange language. "I think so. Although I didn't know that until today."

They walked in silence for several minutes before Thulan spoke. "I lived in the caves with my husband, Brunn, and our two boys." Her voice was warm with truth, her eyes distant.

"Brunn was a guard at the southern entrance, where we're headed." She gestured in the direction of the Marsham Cliffs. "I worked nights at the silversmith. One night, there was a cave-in."

Sable glanced over at the dwarf. Thulan kept her eyes straight ahead.

"Three caves were destroyed, including my home." She fell quiet for a moment. "Brunn and the boys were crushed. They probably didn't even wake before..."

Purnicious made a sad little noise, and Sable debated asking the question that rose in her mind. It would be easier to leave the story there, horrible but distant. Except Thulan's sons deserved to be remembered.

"What were your boys' names?" Sable asked quietly.

Thulan's breath hitched. "Neron and Thon." She stared into the trees. "They were six and four."

Sable searched for something to say, but she had nothing to offer in the face of loss like that.

"The next morning," Thulan continued, "I left. Out of the cliffs and into the forest."

"Have you been back?"

Thulan shook her head. "There's nothing for me there."

They fell into silence for a few minutes. The only sounds the crunch of pine needles under their feet.

It was Thulan who spoke first. "What were your parents' names?"

Sable's throat tightened. "Stephan and Amelia." The names felt unused and rough, but the sound of them was heart-achingly wholesome.

Thulan nodded slowly, and they continued walking in silence.

When they reached the wagons, Jae and Serene sat apart from the others. Serene leaned on a wagon wheel, and Jae bent over her leg, cleaning the wound.

"They're not going to bite you," Atticus said in an annoyed voice, coming around the wagon.

"It's not biting we're worried about," Leonis muttered.

Jae turned to look at them, his face ragged. "I'm sorry about before. I shouldn't have…" He rubbed his palms. "I've never done anything like that before. I just saw him attack Serene, and I…"

Andreese leaned against the other wagon wheel, his arm wrapped around his ribs. "If it makes you feel better, Jae, you almost paid for it dearly. I was a breath away from throwing the sword when you lunged. You almost got it in your back."

Atticus ran his hands through his white hair. "Jae and Serene are no more a danger to you than they've been this entire trip."

"That's what we're all coming to grips with," Thulan said. The dwarf rocked back on her heels, her eyes fixed on Atticus. "Between announcing we'll do a forbidden play and bringing two baledin into the group, it feels a bit like you're trying to kill us all."

"There was only ever one baledin," Jae said, exasperated. "Two generations ago, there was a man who did kill some people. But we aren't like him."

Serene sank back against the wheel. "We could be. We just choose not to."

"That's not helping," Atticus said to her. He turned back to the group. "Serene and Jae are no more dangerous than Thulan is with her hammer, or Leonis with his bow."

"I'm certainly more dangerous than that," Serene said under her breath.

"Serene!" Atticus said, exasperated.

"I am." She leveled a look at the old man. "Even Jae is more dangerous than either of them. And, frankly, he's not that dangerous."

"It's true," Jae agreed. "I can't do a quarter of what Serene can."

"So the weak one can kill a man by touching him," Thulan said to Leonis. "I'm not sleeping for the rest of this trip."

"Jae can kill an almost dead man by touching him," Serene corrected. "I don't think he could kill you."

"Don't think?"

"Honestly, I probably couldn't," Jae agreed. "But Serene could, just by touching you."

Atticus groaned. "You two are making this worse."

"It's the truth." Serene shifted and let out a hiss of pain. A spot of red seeped through the bandage on her leg. "And I see no need to hide it." She looked at the others. "If you think we're a threat to you, you're wrong. Yes, we have powers you don't understand, but they come at a high price."

The glade was quiet for a moment.

"We're wasting time," Atticus said. "Anyone who doesn't want to be near Jae and Serene is free to leave. But I'm taking them and the wagons to the dwarves. We've lost Zephony, and there may be a grave threat to the entire land. We need to find out all we can, and figure out what to do next."

Several people shifted uncomfortably, but no one spoke.

"Then let's get moving," Atticus said.

It was past midday when Thulan led them to a road along the edge of the forest that led east toward the dwarves. The dark remains of Ebenmoor smoked on the plains to the south, but Sable kept her eyes on the forest and the occasional glimpses of the towering Marsham Cliffs beyond it.

Ebenmoor fell out of sight, but the pall of the destruction hung over them. Sable gazed over the dreary grass of the plains. There were no signs of anyone, Kalesh or otherwise, and they moved as quickly as the wagons would allow.

The group traveled mostly in silence. Serene rode up on the wagon with Atticus, and Jae walked next to her with none of his usual stories. The rest of the troupe gave them a wide berth.

The Marsham Cliffs ran along the eastern edge of the Nidel Woods, a sheer rock wall jutting up ten times taller than the forest. To the south they dwindled down quickly into a pack of ragged hills.

They reached the base of the cliff in the late afternoon. Thulan took the lead, heading north along its base, her face set in a dark expression. The bottom of the cliff was riddled with huge boulders and smaller rocks that had tumbled down from high above, and their path occasionally dipped into the edge of the forest to get around larger piles.

The sun fell low in the west until the treetops caught the last of the sunlight, leaving the space between the forest and the cliffs purple with shadows. Above them, the dusty rock face still glowed orange.

Thulan finally stopped at a large rock outcropping, studying the ground. "We'll leave the wagons here." She looked up the cliff with a troubled expression.

"What's wrong?" Leonis asked.

She waved her hand to the ground around them. "Do you see any tracks?"

Leonis glanced at the earth. "No."

"There should be tracks." Thulan glanced back up at the cliff and made an annoyed noise. "We'll go up here. Bring some food and a skin of that plum wine. They're always more welcoming when fed."

"The only food we have left is potatoes," Leonis said. "And not many of those."

"Dwarves like potatoes," Thulan said.

They unhitched the horses and Thulan waited impatiently near the rocks, muttering to herself. When they were done, she disappeared behind a large rock, appearing moments later a dozen paces up the cliff face.

"Aren't dwarf doorways supposed to be secret?" Ryah asked. "Are they going to be pleased when a whole group shows up on their front steps?"

"They don't need to be secret," Thulan called back. "If they seal it, there's no way even an army could get in."

"Good," Leonis said, "because there might be an army out here."

Sable slung a waterskin over her shoulder and moved around a huge boulder and found a thin path. Thulan's footsteps were clearly visible in the dust, but the dwarf had ducked out of sight behind another rock.

"We're climbing up that?" Merilee asked.

"You're welcome to stay here with the horses," Leonis said.

"And be murdered in my sleep? I'll risk the filthy dwarf hole," she muttered.

The climb was steep, and in a short time, Sable was higher than the forest. To the west, the trees rolled out like a soft rug, the land beyond it nothing more than a hazy brown. To the south, the forest dwindled at the edge of the dusty green plains, which continued as far as she could see.

Merilee's complaints grew quieter the farther they climbed. When Sable glanced back at her, the woman was looking down the cliff, a terrified expression on her face. The trail switched back a few times, and Sable's legs were burning before Thulan stopped at a jagged outcropping. She stood for a moment, before stepping forward and yelling directly at a rock.

Sable came up next to her and saw a thin crevice between a large boulder and the rock face. Thulan pressed her face into the gap and shouted. She waited for a moment, then yelled again, trying to shove one stocky shoulder into the crack.

Sable looked into the crevice. "Is there anyone in there?"

"Of course there's someone in there. The southern door is one of the main ways into the forest. The next closest is a day's walk north. They leave it cracked for fresh air. They just don't like to open it to strangers." She turned back to the door. "But I'm not a stranger, you miserable cowards," she yelled. "Open the door and talk to me or I'll get Brunn's ghost to come haunt this door for the rest of time!"

No answer came from the gap. Sable glanced down at the dusty ground. Thulan's footprints were the only ones visible.

Serene came up behind them, one hand pressed into her thigh, her face set in a look of annoyance. "Thulan, who are you yelling at? There's no one past that rock."

Thulan waved her off. "Of course there's someone in there." She raised her voice again. "A whole unit of useless guards who are too stupid to recognize one of their own."

The rest of the group gathered behind Serene on the thin path, craning to see past each other.

"Thulan," Serene said, leaning heavily against the cliff face. "There is no one in there."

The dwarf shook her head. "They wouldn't leave the southern door unguarded." She turned to Sable. "You're skinny. Shimmy in there and open the door."

"Me?"

"When you get in, there's a wheel on the wall to your right. Turn it. The door will swing out."

Sable looked into the dark crevice, then glanced at Serene. "You're sure there are no angry dwarves in there?"

"I'm sure," Serene said. "Hurry. My leg is killing me."

Sable stepped up to the crack and slid her shoulder in. It was snug, but she pushed forward. Ahead of her lay a shadowed room that smelled dusty and stale. After a few steps, the gap widened. There was enough light to see that the room she stepped into was small and round.

It was empty, aside from a table, some shelves, and an enormous pile of clutter against the far wall.

Thulan called from outside, and Sable found a broad wheel mounted on the wall next to the door. She turned it. The door shifted out of the way effortlessly. Thulan came storming in.

With the dwarf came a stream of sunlight showing a room covered with a thick layer of dust.

Thulan came to a stop.

It wasn't clutter against the far wall.

The wide doorway leading deeper into the cliff was filled with rubble from the collapsed tunnel beyond it.

CHAPTER THIRTY-TWO

THULAN STARED at the rubble as Serene limped in behind her and sank onto a bench by the table with a sigh of relief. Jae sat next to her and everyone else filed into the cave.

Thulan walked over to the pile and pressed her ear to it, shushing the rest of the group. She stood unmoving for a few moments. "They're not even trying to clear it." She stepped back. "Why aren't they trying to clear it?"

"A better question might be why haven't they already cleared it." Leonis blew dust off a loaf of bread on one of the shelves, revealing circles of blue-green mold. "No one's been here for a while."

Thulan came over to the shelves, picking up a dried-out pitcher. "Even if there was a collapse, they wouldn't leave all this unattended. They'd come around and gather up everything useful." She looked again at the collapsed hall, and when she spoke, it was almost to herself. "Why haven't they cleared it?"

Andreese sank down gingerly on the bench near Serene. "I'm not walking back down that path. Not in the dark."

"I'm not going back into the woods," Merilee said. "Not with those warriors on the loose."

"Yes," Atticus said. "Unless Thulan has a compelling reason not to, we'll stay here tonight."

Thulan's gaze ran over the dusty room and she gave a single nod, her face unreadable. Without a word, she strode to the door and disappeared outside. Everyone stood still for a moment, until Jae went and knelt down next to a small fireplace sunk into the wall, arranging wood in it from a nearby pile.

There was a wide emptiness around Serene and Jae. Leonis set out the food they'd brought on a counter along one wall, Atticus rummaged through the dwarven shelves, Ryah sat on a bench across the room, and Merilee, after a worried glance at the table joined her, apparently deciding sitting by a commoner was preferable to sitting near Serene. Sable stayed awkwardly near the shelves, holding the waterskin.

Serene unwrapped Andreese's bandage. He didn't look exactly comfortable next to her, but he sat still while she examined the wound. She glanced up at the room, a question on her lips. But seeing how far away everyone was, she paused.

Her gaze fell on Sable and the waterskin. "Could you boil some water?" She asked quietly.

Jae still knelt by the fire arranging wood, but Sable nodded, taking her time finding a pot and cleaning the dust out of it. She ran out of things to do before he'd lit the fire, and approached him cautiously. His fingers were stretched out next to a small pile of kindling, and with just a touch, a small flame appeared. She drew in a breath, and Jae winced.

The flames caught, and Jae fed another stick onto the fire. The wood crackled loudly in the quiet room, and Sable realized how often Jae was the one who talked, telling stories or just chatting.

The isolation wrapped around him struck her as familiar. A distance between him and those who didn't understand his powers. Even with Talia knowing Sable could feel truth, there'd always been something isolating about the fact her sister couldn't really understand, a very faint separation between them because of it.

Sable knelt next to Jae and picked up a sliver of wood. "Can you burn this?"

His palms were still bright red, and he moved his hands gingerly, but he reached out one finger. Flame curled up the wood, and she dropped it into the fire.

She hung the pot on a hook above the growing flames, and picked up a twig, holding it out toward him.

He lit it, a small smile pulling up the edge of his mouth.

Sable picked up a pebble, holding it out with a raised eyebrow. Jae let out a snort of laughter and shook his head.

"Disappointing," she murmured.

She picked up pieces of bark, chips of wood, even a scrap of fabric, holding each one out. Jae didn't speak, but he lit each item and when the water started boiling, he pulled it off the hook and handed it to her with something almost resembling his normal ease.

Sable brought the water to Serene, who glanced back at Jae. "Thank you," she said quietly.

Sable sat down next to Andreese as Serene pulled her hand off his shoulder.

"That's all I can do for now," Serene said, sinking back and closing her eyes. "Sable, could you wrap it?"

Andreese shifted so Sable could reach his shoulder. His wound had shrunk to a thin cut. Sable touched it, astonished at how much it had healed. She picked up a new bandage as Andreese held his arm out toward her.

He looked at the door where Thulan had disappeared. "I knew the dwarves would be no help," he said quietly.

Sable snorted. "Because you knew this would be deserted?"

"No. It just never pays to trust them."

Sable stopped and stared at him. "You ingrate," she whispered. "Thulan helped find you and save you."

"Thulan's obviously not a normal dwarf or she'd have known the others left this area long ago."

"Are you always this horrible to people?" Sable asked, tugging the bandage roughly around his arm.

"Sorry. I..." He rubbed his hands over his face. "Everything hurts. Especially breathing."

246

"Maybe you shouldn't speak until you're better," Sable suggested, dryly.

Serene gave a small smile, not bothering to open her eyes. "That could take weeks."

Sable tied the ends of the bandage together, not bothering to be particularly gentle. "Sounds perfect."

Andreese shot her a flat look, then turned to Serene, touching his ribs gently. "Do you have anything to help with the pain?"

"Or the attitude?" Sable asked.

Serene laughed. "I'll look for some wartroot in the forest tomorrow. It'll make your mind a bit foggy, but it should dull the pain."

He glanced toward the door again. "I wouldn't object to dulling my mind either."

Thulan came back in and dropped onto the bench across the table. "I climbed up to the lookout at the top of the cliff. From there you can see south to the ocean, and quite a ways east as well. There's no army on the plains," she announced. "An army large enough to be a 'drowning wave' would be clearly visible from up here."

Merilee let out a sigh of relief. "Then we have time to get away."

"It does give us some time," Atticus agreed, taking a seat on the edge of the bench near Serene. "But we need to discuss what we should do with it. Ebenmoor changes things."

The cave quieted.

Atticus looked around the room. "If there is a Kalesh army coming, we need to warn people."

"But there is no army," Thulan pointed out. "If there's an army out there, it's weeks away."

Atticus scratched his beard. "He said the army would raze the fields while we reaped. If they're coming near harvest, they would still be weeks away."

"Then we have about two months to raise our own army big enough to stop the Kalesh," Jae said. "And I don't think there are that many warriors in this whole part of the world."

Sable wrapped her arms around herself, chilled by the idea of a tide of black-clad warriors flowing across the plains.

"We need to tell the Northern Lords," Andreese said. "They're the only ones who have any sort of military strength."

"And Immusmala," Jae added. "There are enough city guards and merchant guards to put together a decent force. The city can't be left unprepared."

"First, we need to warn Merrick," Serene said.

"Who's Merrick?" Merilee asked. "Does he have an army?"

"No. He's the man who runs Stonehaven, where Jae and I spend the summer."

Merilee frowned. "Is he...like you?"

Serene shot her an annoyed look. "Yes. And if the Kalesh are in these woods, we need to warn him so he's not left unprotected."

"You people don't seem unprotected," Thulan pointed out.

"You have nothing to fear from Jae or Serene." Atticus sighed. "You never have."

"Unless we knife Serene," Thulan said under her breath. But there was a slight smile behind her beard.

Jae scowled at her, but Serene laughed.

"You two can't go to Merrick's," Atticus said to them. "We'll need you in Immusmala if we have any hope of getting the High Prioress, or any of the Northern Lords, to listen to us. I don't want to spend days and weeks waiting before I get an audience."

Serene's smile twisted into a grimace

"We won't be much help with that," Jae said. "We didn't leave the High Prioress on the best of terms."

Atticus raised an eyebrow, waiting.

"She wants to control us," Serene said bluntly.

"She doesn't want—" Jae stopped. "She knows about the library we have, and the history we've been keeping, and she thought the books would be safer, and of more use, in her priory. So scholars from everywhere could read them."

"And she'd have control over what was read and what was written," Serene added.

"The High Prioress is always trying to further education in the city," Ryah said. "She'd use the writings for good things."

Andreese snorted. "Prioresses never do anything that selfless."

Ryah frowned at him. "I've seen the work she does."

"The High Prioress may want the books for a good reason," Jae said in an unconvinced tone. "But she won't be prioress forever. And the next one might not be as inclined to protect them. We told her we wouldn't mind making copies of some of them for her, but that the main library needed to stay with Merrick." He glanced at Serene. "She didn't take it well."

"And we can't go back to her and bring up anything against the Kalesh," Serene said. "The ambassador was there for the discussion and firmly agreed with the prioress."

"So?" Atticus asked.

Jae waited for Serene to continue. When she didn't, he gave her a resigned look. "So… Serene might have insinuated he was a little too anxious to gain the prioress's favor. And may have reminded him that prioresses didn't marry and would never dally with any man, never mind a foreigner."

Atticus let out an exasperated breath.

"Everyone was thinking it," Serene said. "He fell over himself to be next to her and fawned over her every decision. It was annoying."

"She didn't take that well, either, as you can imagine," Jae continued. "She said the only reason we'd keep the scrolls and books from her was because we were hiding something, then demanded we bring her the entire library. When we refused, she told us we were no friends of Amah and should leave the priory until we were ready to reconsider."

Atticus looked at the two for a long moment. "That's why you showed up at my wagons a day early."

Jae shrugged. "It seemed best to move out of the priory and let her calm down."

Atticus blew out a breath and looked around the room. "That's going to make things harder. I gather she knew you would be traveling with us?"

"We never kept it a secret."

"Speaking of the Dragon Prioress," Leonis said to Atticus, "if it's true that you know the story of her and the baledin first hand, then at some point in time you and the good prioress were…close." He grinned at the old man. "Which is impressive, even for you. But I assume by the fact we've never been invited to the Dragon Priory, the situation between you two has changed."

Atticus gave him a faint smile. "You would be right in that assumption." He looked slowly around the room. "But we don't need just the High Prioress's ear. We need the Northern Lords and the merchants, as well. And, unless we plan on spending the next year trying to get audiences with all these people, there's only one way to speak to all of them at once."

Thulan groaned. "You're not still thinking about that, are you?"

Atticus ignored her. "The winner of the Midsommer tourney will get to perform in the Grand Stadia. Every prioress, merchant, foreign diplomat, even the Kalesh Ambassador will be there. With that platform, when everyone is still gathered after the play, we can tell them about the Kalesh all at once."

The room stared at him in silence.

"It'll be far more effective to tell them all at once," he said. "No one is going to want to hear this news, but belief is contagious. If we can convince a few, more will follow."

"If we want to win the tourney," Leonis pointed out, "we're missing one very important element."

Atticus nodded and glanced at Purnicious. "We traveled to Ebenmoor to ask your former mistress to join us for the play."

The kobold's eyes widened slightly.

"I'd be honored to play the High Prioress!" Merilee beamed at Atticus.

Sable straightened. Without Lady Zephony, there'd be an open role. Sable could be second lady in a play that might actually earn some money. What had Leonis said? The second lady earned thirty silver?

"Actually," Atticus said, "I had hoped both you and Sable would audition for the role of High Prioress."

Sable stared at him. "What?"

"Audition?" Merilee demanded. "But the role of High Prioress is the first lady, right?"

"It is," Atticus said. "But we need to be sure we have the right actress for it."

"The right actress?" Merilee's voice rose, stabbing a finger at Sable. "She's played a half-decent Lady Argent a half-dozen times. She's not even a real actress, never mind the right one."

"Nevertheless," Atticus said mildly, "we will have auditions. I'd like to see Sable's take on the character."

"You would?" Sable asked. The additional money the first lady would win was tempting, but... "You think I could play first lady in a play that is bound to be..." She looked around the room for some support.

"Complicated," Thulan offered. "And nuanced."

"At the very least," Sable agreed.

"You played an excellent Argent," Serene said.

Sable frowned. "That hardly qualifies me for the tourney."

Serene shrugged. "Seems like acting well is the only qualification there is."

Thulan nodded. "I think you could do it."

"Me, too," Ryah said.

Merilee looked at them, mouth open. "You're all crazy."

"This might be the first time she and I agree," Sable said. Still, the money was tempting. She glanced at Atticus. "How much would a first lady win?"

"Sixty-five silver," Atticus answered.

Sable stared at him, momentarily stunned. "I'll audition."

The old man smiled. "Wonderful."

"Ridiculous," Merilee huffed.

Atticus looked around the group. "We have three weeks until the tourney. I had planned to spend a couple weeks in Ebenmoor practicing before we headed back to the city." He shook his head. "Part of me thinks we should rush back to Immusmala to tell them what's happened here, but I doubt anyone would listen to us."

"The prioresses aren't even in Immusmala during these weeks," Jae said "They'll be visiting the smaller abbeys to the north. There's never anything going on in the city during this time. If we wait until the festival, the prioresses will be back, and the Northern Lords will be there as well. Even the Merchant Guild will be attending things in the Sanctuary. That's the time to reach everyone."

Atticus thought for a moment. "If there's no immediate threat from an army, we need time to practice anyway. Would Merrick let us stay with him for a little while?"

Jae nodded. "There's plenty of room, and Stonehaven has a good-sized wall, so it's safer than the woods."

"How long will it take to get there?"

"We can be there by nightfall tomorrow."

"Perfect." Atticus turned to Andreese. "You are free to come with us, as far as you like. We'll be stopping in several places before Immusmala, or you can come all the way to the city. If there's a war brewing, any number of places will be glad for another young man to help with protection."

"There's also a skilled healer in Stonehaven," Serene added. "She might be able to help your ribs more than I can."

"I don't have anywhere else to go at the moment," he said, the words sounding a bit hollow. "If you're going to the Midsommer Festival, I may be able to help. My uncle serves under one of the Northern Lords. If you don't win the tourney, I might still be able to get us an audience with him."

"I thought *you* were a lord," Merilee said, frowning at him.

Andreese shot her a weak smile. "Well, I'm lordly."

"You're grouchy enough to be a lord," Sable pointed out, but she tried to pair it with a small smile.

Andreese let out a very small huff of amusement.

"Even if we do win the tourney, Andreese," Atticus said, "we might need to speak with the Northern Lords individually." He glanced outside. "Since we have nothing to do tonight beyond sit in a cave, I believe it's time I told you the story of the high prioress and her handmaiden."

"Finally," Thulan said under her breath. "Then we can decide how quickly to leave you alone with your insane idea."

"Or whether it's insane enough that it's brilliant," Leonis added, "and we want to stay."

"You'll want to stay," Atticus assured them.

"If you don't tell us soon," Thulan said, "I'm leaving just because you've made me wait too long."

Atticus stood and walked over to the fire, stoking it before turning back to them. "What do you know of the story?"

"In her youth, the High Prioress was set upon by a baledin," Leonis said, "and either sacrificed her handmaiden to save herself or the handmaiden sacrificed herself."

Heads in the room nodded.

"*The* baledin," Jae corrected. "There was only ever one. And I'm inclined to think the handmaiden sacrificed herself,"

"She sacrificed her handmaiden," Andreese said. "One way or the other."

"What's that supposed to mean?" Ryah asked.

"Prioresses are hardly known for their selfless generosity," he answered. "If the handmaiden had survived and the prioress hadn't, the handmaiden would have been blamed no matter how it'd happened, and probably imprisoned or killed."

"Have you ever actually met a prioress?" Ryah demanded.

Atticus held up his hand to stop the bickering. "Good. This room covers most of the opinions people will have when they come to the play. It does no good to argue about it when you're all ignorant of the truth." He smiled. "So let me enlighten you."

CHAPTER THIRTY-THREE

ATTICUS RUBBED HIS HANDS TOGETHER. "Our story begins fifty years ago with nineteen-year-old Vivaine, before she'd joined a priory. Before she ever intended to." There was a general rustling around the room as everyone exchanged looks. He stopped, taking in all the raised eyebrows. "You all know the High Prioress's name is Vivaine, right?"

There were a few nods.

"We know," Ryah said.

"We just don't hear it tossed around causally," Sable added.

"Then you'll need to get used to it," Atticus said with a smile.

Vivaine stood in the smithy, tilting the sword to catch the firelight. The weight of it tugged at her wrist, and the unasked question hung in the air just as heavily. Flickers of light danced along the blade as she moved the metal slowly, watching them skitter like wildfire sprites.

"It's beautiful."

It was, but the words fell flat and the forge was quiet for a moment. The blade was everything Balin had hoped it would be, everything he'd worked so hard for. Medium length, wide blade, the hilt carved from a rich brown wood and wrapped with leather.

She shifted her grip on it. "The handle feels warm."

Balin nodded. "It's terren wood. The elves say it has magical powers. It warms quickly under your hand and holds the heat longer than any wood I've ever seen."

Along the center of the blade, near the guard, the smooth iron was etched to a rough surface and glowed with a copper color.

"A different kind of metal?" she asked.

"Just a solution that colors the iron," Balin answered with a smile. "A horrible smelling concoction. Too much combat and it will scratch off."

Vivaine moved it through the pattern of the most recent strokes he had taught her. The blade sparked with firelight.

She set down the sword on the table beside her. "It's a little heavy for me."

"Because you have child-sized hands," he said, but the teasing tone didn't quite work.

His attempt at humor made her smile, though. "You mean perfect hands."

"Yes," He stepped closer, taking her hands in his strong, callused ones.

She focused on their intertwined fingers, but the smile slid off her face. This hadn't been how she'd imagined this night would feel. So many things had changed since Balin had received the sword's commission. "Do you think you can sell it for the price you'd hoped?"

"I'm not selling it."

The words felt heavy.

"I want you to keep it for now," he said quietly.

"What will I do with it?" She stepped back, but he kept hold of her hands.

"Keep it safe until I return."

Vivaine shook her head.

"The master says he'll teach me." Balin's voice was tense with excitement. "He says I'm older than usual to show the aptitude for it, but that my powers are stronger than most beginners."

Vivaine looked up at his expression, which was as conflicted as his voice had been. "I'm glad."

Balin raised an eyebrow. "You don't look glad."

"Neither do you."

He sighed. "Part of me is. But part of me wishes I'd never done that mess with the fire and we could just continue as we were."

More than a part of her felt the same, but she forced herself to sound happier than she felt. "Did he say you'd be able to control the fire?"

"Vivaine, there's so much more than that." Balin dropped her hands and stepped away, his voice growing more eager. "Controlling fire is just a tiny piece. Master Horen says that once I learn to control my power, I can use it to do almost anything. I can even use it to heal. Can you imagine? Being able to heal someone with…" He waved his fingers through the air.

"Magic?" Vivaine offered.

Balin laughed. "He says it's not magic. It's energy. But it seems like magic to me."

His laugh finally brought a smile to Vivaine's face.

"When I'm done, we'll sell the sword and use the money to travel." He stepped closer again, his face bright. "Healing in the different towns we find. You with the herbs, and me with magic."

"You'd give up the forge?"

He looked around the small smithy. "I don't know. Maybe we could do both. Maybe we could spend the winter here, traveling during the summer. There are so many possibilities."

Balin stretched his hand toward the fire. "I can't control it, Viv. I can feel the fire, just past my fingers. I could draw it in, but I can't control it. That first night I pulled it out of the forge, I could have burned down the smithy. I could have killed us both. I could have burned down half the village." He lowered his voice. "I'm afraid I'll do something terrible. I need to learn how to control it."

"Of course you do," she answered, and she meant it. "It's just the selfish part of me that wants you to stay." She turned back to the sword and trailed her finger along the etching on the blade. "How long will you be gone?"

Balin paused. "Two winters."

Her finger froze. "Two?"

"I know it's a long time," he said quickly. "Longer than I'd expected. But Master Horen says there is so much to learn."

The time stretched out ahead of her like a dark shadow. Two winters. All that time before they could build a home, build a family, start the orchard and the garden.

"Come with me," Balin said, his voice hopeful. "There's a small town right outside Confin Keep. With the knowledge you have of herbs, the local healer would surely hire you to help."

Vivaine shook her head. "I don't know enough. Not yet. You need to train, and so do I. In two winters, I should know everything Mistress Yavik does about herbs."

"I know." Balin stepped close and wrapped his arms around her. "I'm just looking for ways we can be together."

Vivaine leaned against him.

"When I return," he said, "we'll travel. We'll visit towns and help the sick. Between my skills and yours, we'll want for nothing."

Vivaine rested her head on his chest. *Until tonight, I already wanted for nothing.*

Thulan shifted and crossed her arms. "How much dramatic license have you taken with this story, old man?"

A smile broke through Atticus's beard. Outside the door the sunlight had faded and his face near the fire was the brightest part of the cave. "More here than in the rest. I pieced this section together from what Vivaine told me over several years. But the part everyone is actually interested in, the part with the baledin, I heard from her mouth the day it happened. I wrote it down that night. Other than writing it down as she spoke, it's the closest I can get to her words."

The cave was quiet for a moment.

"Just how close were you and Vivaine?" Leonis asked, eyebrow raised.

Atticus shrugged. "I've never had to be particularly close to someone for them to tell me things."

Leonis crossed his arms. "That's not an answer, old man."

"We were close enough that I know the truth. May we continue?"

"No," Sable said. "How do you know she told you the truth?"

"No one lies to Atticus," Leonis said.

"I doubt that," Sable answered.

Leonis raised an eyebrow. "Have you?"

"No," Sable answered, with a spark of indignation at the idea. She thought for a moment. "Actually, I have. The first night I met him, I told him I was a courier..." She trailed off. She hadn't told him that. Atticus had asked her if she was a courier, and she'd answered evasively.

"You didn't really lie, did you?" Leonis asked. "And have you told him more than you meant to?"

A wave of uneasiness washed over Sable. That very first night they'd talked, she'd told Atticus she could memorize things she heard. And the first day on the road, barely out of sight of Immusmala, she'd told Atticus how she could feel the truth.

Thulan nodded. "We all have."

Sable turned back to Atticus. "Why?"

"When people talk to me, they tell the truth." The old man shrugged. "I don't make them, if that's what you're wondering."

"He doesn't convince them to." Leonis agreed. "They convince themselves."

Sable stared at Atticus. He had never pushed her to tell him anything. Each time they'd talked, she'd chosen to explain herself.

"So we didn't need your special talent to tell us the Kalesh man was telling the truth earlier," Jae said. "He was talking to Atticus, so he was telling the truth."

Sable straightened at the words. "Atticus!" she snapped. "You told everyone about me?"

He started to shake his head.

"Told them what?" Merilee demanded.

"Sable can feel when someone is telling the truth," Leonis said.

Merilee frowned. "That's not so special. I can tell when someone's lying to me."

"Probably not the same way she can," Leonis said with a grin.

Andreese looked over at Sable curiously.

"Atticus didn't tell anyone," Thulan reassured Sable. "He never does. Leonis, on the other hand..." She nodded toward him with a long-suffering expression. "Can't keep a secret to save his life."

Sable fixed the man with an annoyed look.

"It's an interesting skill, Sneaks," Leonis said unapologetically.

"Regardless," Atticus said, "the story I heard from Vivaine is true.

"Now, at this point, Vivaine and Balin said goodbye under a wide oak." He glanced at Leonis. "We'll need your tree. It comes into the story several times." He turned to Thulan. "And we'll need a sword that can, at the very least, glitter, but hopefully produce actual sparks."

Thulan looked at him for a long moment. "That won't be easy."

"Doesn't matter. It's essential."

Thulan nodded, and Atticus threw himself back into the story.

Over the next two years, Vivaine learned from the local healer. The people of the nearby towns began to come to her with their illnesses and injuries.

And then one day, on a trip deep into the forest looking for herbs, she met some elves.

While most of their healing involved magic, they had tremendous knowledge of plants. In exchange for herbs that didn't grow in their forest, they taught Vivaine some of their healing lore.

And with the knowledge from the elves, Vivaine's reputations for healing spread.

But the world grew darker. As they did every generation, raiders attacked and the next season a crippling sickness ran through town, killing many, including the healer. Vivaine heard rumors about Master Horen's students performing amazing magic and traveling across the land, but none ever came to her town.

She had several suitors who offered her the safety of their home, but she waited for Balin, counting the days until he returned, trying to keep the hope alive that he would.

She considered selling his sword several times, but it didn't feel like a thing that belonged to her. Instead, she used it to practice the way Balin had taught her. It was heavy, but the extra effort it took to wield burned off her frustrations.

Vivaine hurried home one evening, anxious to reach her parents' before darkness fell. She avoided the forest paths, as everyone did those days, keeping to the torchlit village roads. She was almost home when a black-cloaked shape stepped out of the shadows toward her.

She backed away slowly, her heart pounding.

"Vivaine?" it asked quietly.

The nearest torchlight cast red light on an almost familiar face.

She hesitated. "Balin?"

He walked forward, and she drew in a breath. His once kind features had grown hard, and his eyes peered at her with an unnerving intensity. "Of course it's me."

"You've got to be joking," Jae interrupted.

"Balin was a baledin?" Merilee asked, shocked.

"*The* baledin," Jae said tiredly. He looked thoughtfully at Atticus. "We never knew much about him, though."

Leonis shook his head. "So, not only did Vivaine know the baledin, she loved him."

Atticus nodded.

Everyone was silent for a moment.

Merilee clapped her hands together, her bracelets jingling. "This is the sort of scandalous play people want!"

"You think this is *not* going to get us killed?" Thulan asked Atticus.

"We're dead." Leonis agreed.

"May I continue?" Atticus asked.

"Sure," Thulan muttered. "Can't see how it could get worse."

The closer Balin came to Vivaine, the more she wanted to back away. "You've changed," she said softly.

"You haven't," Balin answered.

She kept herself still, trying to match his face to her memories. "What has happened to you?"

"I've learned so much." The intensity in his voice was almost frightening. "I can do things you'd never believe, Vivaine." He reached for her hand, but she pulled back. He pressed his lips into an irritated line, but kept his voice soft. "Come with me. I have so much more training to do, but I told the master I needed you with me to continue. We've waited too long already."

"More training? Does learning to heal take so long?"

"Heal?" Balin frowned. "Healing is simple. I've learned so much more than that. It's not only fire I can move, Vivaine. I can move energy. Come with me. You don't even need to pack. I can buy anything you need."

"I can't leave. There's no other healer here." She searched his face for something she couldn't quite name. "I thought when you came back, you'd stay."

Balin shook his head. "I can't. There is too much to learn." He leaned forward and smiled. For a moment, his face softened. "I am the most skilled student my master has ever trained." He held out his hand and a bit of flame from the nearest torch flew over and sat in his palm. "I can move fire through the air, Vivaine. I can pull it from anything. From the tree…" He stretched his hand toward the nearest tree, and the flame in his palm grew. "From the grass. From any living creature." He reached toward her. "I could pull it from you."

Vivaine stepped back, and he laughed. "Don't worry. I won't. I don't need to. There is energy everywhere. Do you realize how much of life uses fire? I can warm a house with a thought. I can heat a forge to the perfect temperature and maintain it with almost no effort. I can make tiny pinpricks of fire that can etch wood. I can warm ovens or kilns. Harden clay and soften metal. Melt stone to liquid and reform it. I can turn sand into glass. Vivaine, there is nothing fire can't do."

She searched his face. "It can't heal."

"Vivaine…" Balin's voice was gentle, and she heard the man she used to know. "You use fire to boil water, to clean knives. You know there are many uses for it. And I can do so much more than fire. I can help plants grow. Sense where living things are. I can... Just come with me and see."

"Where?"

"To Confin Keep. You'll love it. There are beds made from the softest down, a cook prepares three hot meals every day. There's even magic in the privies that blows the smell away."

Vivaine smiled at the idea, then glanced at the scattered buildings around her. "I don't know if I can leave."

"Just for a time. Come for a season and see what you think. If you don't love it, we'll come back here."

"Do you promise?"

"I do. I know I said we'd settle here when I was done, but I knew nothing of the world when I left. I want to show it all to you. The possibilities are endless, Vivaine. Master Horen's students travel widely. We counsel leaders and prioresses. We defend towns from monsters. Staying here would be giving up more than you can ever imagine."

"She doesn't go with him, though," Ryah broke in. "You're not going to tell us that the High Prioress actually went to live with the baledin."

"Eventually," Atticus said, "Vivaine agreed, and the two spent several seasons at Confin Keep. But she did not grow to love it. Balin grew more focused on his magic, more driven by it."

Sable glanced at Jae and Serene. "Is Confin Keep the sort of place you two live with Merrick?"

"It was an old military outpost that's since been abandoned," Jae answered. "The man who ran it, Master Horen, was like Serene and I, but a bit...militant. We wouldn't have agreed with a good number of his teachings." He frowned. "Merrick is probably old enough to have visited Confin Keep back when it was in use." He paused. "He's old enough he might have met Balin. He definitely met Vivaine when she was young."

"That's something I'd like to talk to him about," Atticus said. "When Vivaine and Balin lived at Confin Keep, she convinced him to come with her to nearby towns every few weeks so she could tend to the sick. There was a constant struggle within Balin. When he studied magic, he became obsessed, staying up through the night studying, forgetting to eat. When he left with Vivaine, he'd relax and they could talk, laugh. But after a few days, his temper would shorten and he would grow anxious to return to his studies.

"The two had gained a reputation for healing, and requests soon came from the surrounding area, asking for their help.

"It was on a summer day in the small town of Ennsruk when things finally fell apart."

"Folks are calling it the 'white death'," the aged Abbess Bett said when they reached the town. "There've been two deaths already and three more are sick. It begins with a wet cough, proceeds rapidly to weakness, then they grow pale. I've never seen anything like it. Folk who are normally nut-brown fade to the color of an eggshell. Their faces wither and wrinkle, like they've aged thirty years, and they grow weaker until…"

Vivaine and Balin followed her toward the abbey.

"Who's been affected?" Vivaine asked.

"I can't see a pattern. The two who died were an elderly man, who was already weak, and a healthy, twenty-three-year-old farmer. The three sick now are two women in their thirties and a boy of twelve. They live in separate parts of town. I can't see that they all ate anything in common, or even were in the same place at any time. Each has family who are perfectly healthy."

"So no one has recovered? Someone could have gotten the cough, but if it didn't progress past that, you might not have heard about it."

"I thought the same, so I've been asking. As far as I can tell, there have been no cases but these five."

She led them into a stone abbey along the edge of the village. Lying on three low beds, were the sick. If the abbess had not said the first were two middle-aged women, Vivaine would have guessed they were grandmothers. Their skin was white and dry, like wrinkled paper. The young boy next to them slept restlessly, but his face was pale, as well.

Vivaine set out her herbs and began mixing some tea. Balin knelt by the feet of one woman. He bowed his head and set his hand on her leg.

"She's incredibly weak." He glanced up at Abbess Bett. "How long has she been ill?"

"Two days." The abbess's face was drawn with worry.

He furrowed his brow. "I'd say she has hours left, at most."

"She's visibly worse than this morning." Bett looked helplessly at the others. "They're all worse."

Vivaine spent the afternoon examining the ill, but found no remedy they responded to.

Balin tried to pour energy into the young boy, tried to help his body regain strength, but it only slightly delayed the sickness.

By nightfall, the first woman died.

By midnight, the second.

By noon the next day, another man was brought in with a deep, wet cough.

Balin made him comfortable, while Vivaine spent the afternoon questioning the village about possible connections between the sick.

She learned nothing of value. Her ministrations that day were useless, and the young boy died as the sun set. She tried an elven tea on the last sick man, with low hopes. The next morning, though, the cough that woke her sounded better, less deep.

She hurried to the sick room and stopped in her tracks. It was not the villager coughing. That man lay senseless, his skin terribly pale.

The rough cough came from Balin.

Vivaine tried everything, but Balin's illness progressed exactly like the others. Around midday, yet another man was brought in.

Vivaine sat next to Balin, his face slowly draining of color like the two men past him. If only she could find something that would strengthen them. She put her ear to Balin's chest. Even through his shirt he felt warm, his heartbeat slow and weak. If only she had something to speed up his heart.

She straightened quickly, looking at the abbess. "Do you have blood thistle nearby?"

"We try to uproot it when we find it," Bett said. "It kills the animals if they eat it."

"Where would I find some?"

"There's been a troublesome patch west of the village near the old bridge."

Vivaine knelt next to Balin and set her hand on his hot forehead. His skin beneath her hand was bone white. "I'll be back soon."

His eyes focused on her momentarily before closing. Taking a basket, she hurried out. She found a few thin blood thistle plants where the old woman had said.

When she returned, Bett stood outside. "Get him and get out," the abbess cried. "Get out of our town and let us die naturally!"

Vivaine hurried inside.

Balin was out of his own bed, kneeling between the other sick men, one hand on each of their chests.

But they weren't sick men any longer. They were dead.

Not white and withered from the disease. Just dead.

Balin took a deep breath, then looked up, meeting her gaze from a perfectly healthy face.

"What did you do?" Vivaine whispered.

CHAPTER THIRTY-FOUR

VIVAINE STEPPED CLOSER to the men, who looked just as she'd left them. No more withered, no more pale, but clearly dead.

"What did you do?" she repeated.

"Ended their suffering."

"You killed them," she whispered.

"The disease had already killed them." Balin stood. "It was a waste to let the last of their energy fritter away. I had to act or it would have been gone."

She stared at him. "But how are you stronger? You tried putting energy into the boy, but it didn't help."

"It helped some. I just couldn't give him enough." Balin looked down at the two men. "I was able to get more for myself."

The dead eyes of the men stared up toward the ceiling. Balin's face appeared as healthy as it had the day before.

"It cured you?"

Balin stretched out his hands and looked at his red palms. "I don't know."

"Get out," the abbess hissed from the doorway. "You were supposed to be healers!"

Vivaine opened her mouth, but could find no words. She set the basket of blood thistle on the floor. "In a healthy person, this makes their heart beat too fast, but in someone weak, it might strengthen them a little."

The woman looked at her coldly. "I want nothing from you. I'll tell everyone what you have done. You two won't be welcome anywhere."

"Vivaine had nothing to do with this," Balin said. "And don't pretend those two were going to see another sunrise, no matter what we did."

"Leave." The abbess pointed out the door. "Now."

Vivaine gathered up her herbs. She paused at the abbess. "I'm sorry…"

The old woman leveled a furious look at her, and Vivaine stepped outside.

"When you tell people what happened," Balin said, stopping close to the old woman, "you will tell them it was me. That Vivaine had nothing to do with it."

"Or what?" Bett looked defiantly up into his face. "You'll suck the life out of me, too?"

"Maybe," Balin said in a low growl.

"Balin," Vivaine whispered. "Let's go."

His jaw clenched, but he turned and walked out of the abbey.

"Baledin are more terrifying," Leonis said, "now that I know the rumor started with people actually getting the life sucked out of them."

Atticus nodded. The fire burned low, leaving the side of his face lit, but the rest of the cave in ruddy shadows. "The abbess stayed true to her word," he said, "and the story spread quickly of a black-robed creature they called the baledin who killed with a touch."

A few faces turned toward Jae, but he kept his eyes fixed on the fire.

"Did they find a cure for the disease?" Ryah asked.

Atticus shook his head. "The 'white death' claimed a few more victims from the town of Ennsruk, then stopped as suddenly as it had started. Within a season, the sickness itself was blamed on the baledin. Not long after, he was to blame for any unexpected death. The connection between Balin and the baledin was tenuous, but enough rumors hovered around Vivaine that people began to shun her.

"Except for a few more bouts of weakness, Balin remained healthy. But he was also distant and threw himself back into his studies with renewed vigor. Summer turned to fall while Vivaine stayed at Confin Keep and waited. For what, she did not know.

"Until one day she found the sword Balin had forged so long ago, tucked in the back of a closet."

Vivaine stepped to the middle of the room, trying to remember the old movements Balin had taught her. Each swing and twist brought back the hopes from long ago, when she'd waited for him to return. Dreams of traveling and healing. Dreams that had dried out like the brittle leaves outside the window.

Balin walked through the door, his eyes filled with their normal exhaustion and restlessness, the black robe he always wore hanging on his thin body. He stopped at the sight of the sword.

Vivaine kept her eyes on the blade. "This is not the life we wanted."

He shrugged. "We didn't know what we wanted. We didn't know what was possible."

She looked up at him. "We planned to do good."

"Gaining knowledge is good, Vivaine. It leads us to be more capable, more influential."

There were glimpses of the Balin she'd once known in his face, but they were darkening more and more into shadows.

"I'm not doing anything good," she whispered. "So I'm leaving."

His face grew incredulous. "No, you're not. If you're bored, I can find you some useful work. You could copy scrolls for Master Horen, or help with his herb storage."

Vivaine shook her head. "I want to be a healer, but no one here trusts me anymore."

Balin let out a growl. "I told that worthless abbess not to bring you into it."

"We can hardly blame her," Vivaine said. "You love your studies here. I need to find a place to do what I love."

He stepped closer. "I need you here, Viv." His voice was serious, urgent.

She looked away and rubbed her thumb over the leather wrapped hilt. "You don't need me. I'm not sure what you do need these days, but it's not me."

He was silent for a long moment, and when she looked up, he was glaring at the sword. "Fine," he said coldly. "Take that with you. It's a worthless reminder of all the foolishness we left behind. Don't bother to bring it back when you come home."

He turned and stalked out the door.

Vivaine watched him until he was out of sight, but he never looked back.

She gathered some traveling clothes, her bag of herbs, and the sword. She hesitated before stepping out the door, afraid it would break something inside her to actually go. But the dry leaves tumbled across the ground in front of her, headed off in their own direction, and she stepped out after them.

If anything broke as she left, it was a very small thing compared to all that had broken before.

She traveled far enough west that no one knew of Ennsruk or the baledin, and started working as a healer for the priory in Polbrook. By the time she'd been there a year, she heard tales of Balin and his power. With his magic, he'd protected several villages from vicious beasts, and she smiled as she heard him spoken of as a hero.

It took another year before new stories of the baledin reached her.

The baledin, they said, were red-veiled men, dressed in black who traveled widely. Their skin withered and paled until they stole life from another and were revived.

"It was Balin?" Sable asked. "Still killing people?"

Ryah glanced around at the others. "Why?"

"He hadn't been healed," Thulan said. "Had he?"

Atticus shook his head. "That first day, he'd given himself strength, but the sickness continued and he weakened, until he found more energy. I've traced the stories, and I believe at first he only took life from those who were already dying. But in time, that wasn't enough, and he had to use healthy people."

"Where did the red veils come from?" Merilee asked.

"Those began showing up in the later stories. Maybe it was just some exaggeration. Maybe Balin was getting too well-known and covered his face. I'm not sure."

"Vivaine realized it was him when she heard the tales," Sable said. "She wasn't 'set upon' by the baledin, was she? She sought Balin out."

Atticus sighed. "When she realized what was happening, she couldn't ignore it. She went for help to the only other magic users she knew—the elves she'd worked with long ago. She brought Balin's sword. It was the most valuable thing she owned, and she needed something to barter with. They'd have little use for the blade, but the terren wood hilt would be of some value.

"Her visit with the elves deserves a story in its own right, but for our purposes, it is enough to know that her elven friends did not take the sword. Instead, they imbued the hilt with the ability to absorb heat from the sun.

"For a normal person, it would be merely a sword. But if someone had the ability to control energy, it could act like a vessel, holding energy until it was released.

"But it was dangerous—the power would have to be well-controlled and released slowly, or it would flow out all at once, destroying any who tried to use it.

"Vivaine returned to her priory and sent word to Balin, asking to meet her in a small grove along the Black River."

The night before they were to meet, Vivaine's handmaiden, Lavelle, rushed into her room. "There's been a killing, mistress! Some poor soul by the river. There's no mark on him, but he's dead as can be. Like someone pulled the life out of him!" She wrung her hands. "They say it's a baledin!"

Vivaine sank into a chair. "Poor soul," she whispered. Whether she meant it for the victim, or Balin, she wasn't sure.

"You can't go out tomorrow, mistress. It's not safe."

"I'll be fine," Vivaine said absently.

"But, mistress—"

"I'll be fine," Vivaine said more firmly.

The next morning, Vivaine dressed not in the pale, healer's robe, but in her old traveling clothes. The soft, linen shirt and worn, leather vest felt comforting. At Lavelle's raised eyebrows, Vivaine said, "What I need to do now is from my old life, not my life here. I'll be back by nightfall." She picked up the wrapped sword and left the priory.

When she reached the glade, it was empty. She paced near the trees, swinging the sword in her hand. Her palm was damp on the hilt as she wondered whether he would come. Wondered whether she wanted him to.

A noise in the trees made her spin. Lavelle stood in the shadows, looking curiously at the blade.

Vivaine hurried toward her handmaiden. "You have to leave. You're not safe here."

Lavelle's shook her head. "I'm not leaving you out here alone."

"Lavelle—" Vivaine began.

"Baledin!" Lavelle whispered, clutching Vivaine's arm and looking past her.

Vivaine turned to see Balin, cloaked in black with his hood pulled up, standing at the far side of the glade.

"Stay here," Vivaine commanded Lavelle, extricating her arm from the woman's grip. She gripped the sword and crossed the grass to Balin, stopping several steps away from him.

His cheeks were thin, but his familiar smile played across his lips.

"Vivaine," he said quietly. "I've missed you."

The sound of his voice broke into the loneliness of the past few years and she almost stepped forward. "I can help you," she said quietly.

Balin's eyes dropped to the sword, and his smile spread. "My sword. I'm glad you still have it." His studied it for a moment. "It holds a great deal of power. What have you done to it?"

"Promise me you won't kill anymore, and I'll show you."

His smile faded.

"I know it's been you," Vivaine continued, pitching her voice low so Lavelle couldn't hear.

He turned a cold look on Lavelle. "She knows, as well?"

"No," Vivaine said quickly. "No one knows. Balin..." She reached for his hand. His furious gaze snapped back to her, and she drew her hand back. "Promise me you'll stop killing, and I'll tell you how it works."

Balin fixed her with a look so dark she stepped back. Anger, bitterness, and pain warred across his face. "You have no idea what I've gone through. What I've suffered. Your blood thistle does slow the disease, but even then, it would only take eight days for it to kill me. *Eight days,*" he hissed. "I have five days of strength. By the sixth I'm dangerously weak."

Vivaine's hand tightened on the sword. "You kill someone every six days?"

Balin's hands clenched into fists at his side and he let out a bitter laugh. "You shouldn't have tried to find me."

She held up the sword. "I have the solution for you here. The elves made it."

He shrugged. "Their magic doesn't interest me."

"This should. It can give you the energy you need, Balin. But they warned me it must be used carefully—"

"Balin?" Lavelle's awed voice came from behind Vivaine. "Mistress, why all the secrecy to meet with such a great man? It's an honor to meet you, good sir." She curtseyed deeply and flashed him a smile. "When I first saw you, I thought you were the baledin come to kill us."

"Return to the priory, Lavelle," Vivaine said curtly. "Balin and I are almost done."

"No," he said, his voice emotionless. "Stay a moment, Lavelle."

"Please, Balin," Vivaine pleaded. "She knows nothing."

Lavelle's smile faltered.

Balin turned haunted eyes to Vivaine. "I had no choice. If you'd stayed with me, Viv, we could have tried to find a cure together. But you left me." His jaw clenched. "I've tried to only kill those who deserved it."

Lavelle stepped back at the words.

"Let all that be in the past," Vivaine pleaded.

A flicker of anger, and regret, crossed his face. "I'm sorry, Viv. No one can know who I am." He stepped forward and took Lavelle's hand.

The handmaiden let out a small gasp and Vivaine reached out to separate them.

"Don't touch me, Viv," he commanded her.

Vivaine paused one hand outstretched, the other gripping the sword with white knuckles. "Let go of her."

Lavelle whimpered and tried to pull away.

"Balin!" Viviane grabbed his hand, trying to separate them. A terrible coldness seeped into her palm. It slid up her arm, draining all the warmth and life out of it.

He met her gaze with a broken look. "I didn't want to do this, Vivaine. Not to you."

She tried to pull away, but her fingers were locked on his hand. The icy cold stabbed into her chest. Lavelle fell to her knees, Balin still gripping her hand. The handmaiden's arm was bone white, her face fixed in a look of terror.

"Balin, stop!" Vivaine pleaded.

She didn't recognize the ruthless expression on his face as he turned away from her.

Vivaine gripped the sword. The handle felt warm compared to the frigid cold slowly filling her body.

"Please," she whispered, but Balin didn't look at her.

Her knees buckled. Next to her, Lavelle crumpled to the ground.

Mustering the little strength she had left, Vivaine swung the sword at his arm, trying to break his hold. The blade skipped off something hard beneath his robe and skittered along his forearm, sinking effortlessly into his stomach.

Balin gasped and Vivaine let go of the hilt in horror. He dropped Lavelle's hand, and the handmaiden's arm fell limply to the ground.

A searing, yellow light burst out from where the sword pierced Balin's body. His eyes widened as he grabbed at the blade and fell to his knees.

"Slow it down!" Vivaine cried. "It's giving you energy but you have to slow it down!"

Balin looked at her, his expression shifting from stunned to an accusing betrayal.

"Why did you leave me?" he whispered. "I never wanted to do this."

The light from the sword grew brighter. and Vivaine shielded her eyes from it. A feral, animal scream tore out of Balin.

In a flash, his robe caught fire. He cried out one more time before a burst of flame consumed him.

CHAPTER THIRTY-FIVE

THE ONLY NOISE in the dim cave was the crackle of the fire.

"She...killed him?" Ryah finally asked in a soft voice.

"Inadvertently," Atticus answered, "but yes. Balin was drawing energy out of the two women, so when the sword touched him, he drew the energy from that, as well. And it was just too much."

Sable glanced around at the others. Their faces, dim and red in the firelight, looked equally stunned.

"But..." Ryah started, then closed her mouth.

"Why didn't she tell anyone?" Merilee asked. "Killing a baledin..." She glanced at Jae, seeing his frown. "Killing *the* baledin would have made her a hero."

"Because she couldn't bring herself to tell the whole story." Atticus turned to the fire and stoked it brighter. "To tell any of it, she'd have to reveal what Balin had done for so many years. As it was, he simply disappeared, and no one in his order knew why. He'd fought off enough trouble that it was easy to believe he'd finally met something that had bested him."

"In a way, he had," Leonis pointed out.

Atticus nodded. "Vivaine was devastated. Lavelle was dead, Balin was gone..."

"How do you come into this story?" Thulan asked.

"When Vivaine arrived in Polbrook, I was a low-ranking grunt in the town guard. As such, I often pulled what they called holy duty and had to patrol the streets around the priory. It was set in a corner of the city where nothing ever happened, so the job was avoided whenever possible. But not long after she came, I met Vivaine, and she and I formed a friendship of sorts.

"The morning Vivaine met Balin, I was on duty. Lavelle told me Vivaine was in danger. I went to my superior and asked for the day off. But by the time I followed them, I was too late. When I reached the glade, I saw Lavelle dead and Vivaine kneeling by what looked like the remains of a fire. There was nothing left of Balin."

"If Vivaine didn't want the story told back then," Jae asked, "what makes you think she will want it told now?"

"No one remembers Balin now. He was well known only in one small part of the land, and his name and reputation have fallen into obscurity."

Sable glanced at the old man. "Did she swear you to secrecy?"

Atticus shook his head. "She only asked me to keep it to myself while people remembered Balin."

"If you're still alive and she's still alive, there have to be others who knew him," Serene pointed out.

Atticus nodded. "There may be a few, but when we traveled near Confin Keep last year, I checked the records and asked the bards in town. No one tells stories of Balin any longer. He's all but forgotten."

The cave was quiet.

"What happened to Vivaine afterward?" Merilee asked.

Atticus toyed with a small stick, his gaze distant. "Balin's and Lavelle's deaths struck her hard. I was the only one who knew the truth. She told the Prioress the baledin had attacked them, but was too upset to finish the story. The rumors started there. Most people thought she'd been the victim of a terrible attack. But even back then, there were those who blamed her for Lavelle's death.

"She continued her work as a healer, but drew even more apart from everyone around her. For a time, I saw her often. She would never speak of Balin, but I think it was comforting for her to be around someone who knew what had happened."

Atticus tossed the stick into the fire and looked around the room. "It was almost a year before she decided to join the priory. I would guess she gave the full story to the Prioress at that time.

"That was near the time I met a traveling theater troupe who wanted an inexpensive guard. The lure of seeing more of the world was enough for me to accept."

He combed his fingers through his beard. "I didn't see Vivaine for ten years. The next time I encountered her, she was moving quickly up the ranks in the Dragon Priory in Immusmala. Her reputation was much as it had been in Polbrook, and even among the abbesses, she was well-thought-of and highly respected as a healer. Since then, I have spoken to her on occasion."

The room was quiet.

"Well, if nothing else, it'll certainly get us attention at the festival," Leonis said.

"It will win us the festival." Atticus leaned forward. "We'll perform it four times before we reach Immusmala. Our first two will be in small towns along the coast. Enough people should be headed to Immusmala for the festival that if we take our time, word should travel ahead of us. By the time we perform in Molas again, we should have a good crowd. And by Immusmala, people should be lining up to hear."

The cave dissolved into questions about the play, all of which Atticus answered easily. The questions about his relationship with Vivaine received less satisfaction.

They tossed around theories about whether any Kalesh were coming or if they were already here. Whether the man they'd questioned had any real knowledge or was just a brainwashed soldier.

Eventually, the conversation dwindled.

"With the Kalesh nearby," Jae said, rising, "we should keep an eye on things. I'll take first watch."

"Wake me at midnight," Leonis said, then glanced at Thulan. "I'll wake you up as soon as I get tired. Or bored."

"So, midnight?" the dwarf asked with a smirk, rolling onto her side.

Sable settled down on an empty section of the floor. The area was well stocked with blankets, and she folded one up as a pillow. Purnicious sat along the wall, looking sad. The poor little creature had spent a good deal of the day in tears. Sable made a small bed for the kobold in the space next to her own and motioned her over.

Purnicious stared at the little bed, her brow creased in a frown. "For me?"

Sable paused, realizing she had no idea where kobolds slept. Or if they slept. "Only if you want it."

"This is perfect!" Purnicious sat down hurriedly.

Sable stared at her for a moment. "Didn't Lady Zephony give you a bed?"

"Oh, yes. I had my own room in the attic, and it was lovely. She let me decorate it however I wanted. But at first, I slept in the kitchen with the hunting dogs."

Sable frowned. "With the dogs?"

"They were nice dogs," Purnicious said quickly. "Many kobolds live their whole lives in the kitchens."

"Well, I don't have a kitchen." Sable sighed. "I don't have any home at all." She gestured to the floor. "I have blankets that belong to missing dwarves. But you're as welcome to them as the rest of us are."

Purnicious pulled the blanket over her legs, looking a little awkward.

Sable bit her lip. "Did I say something insulting? You don't have to sleep here. You're welcome to do whatever you want."

Purnicious gave her a nervous laugh. "You're my mistress. You decide where I sleep."

"No. That is not how this is going to work." She looked at the little creature. "How do I release you from this obligation you feel? You should be free. Able to do things like decide where you're going to sleep."

Purnicious's purple eyes widened. "Not yet," she pleaded. "Give me a little time. This bed is wonderful!"

Sable stared at her. "Don't you want to be free?"

Purnicious curled in slightly. "I'd rather be part of a family."

The words caught Sable off guard.

"Give me a month," Purnicious said desperately. "Then if you still don't want me, you can release me."

"It's not a question of wanting you. I'm just not comfortable feeling like I own you. I've felt owned before, and it's..." Sable shook her head. "I wouldn't wish it on anyone."

Serene limped over and laid out a blanket on the other side of Sable. "That's not how she sees it. Among all the fascinating magic kobolds have, the bond they create with their masters and mistresses is particularly strong and gives them a deep sense of belonging. If they lose it, like when Zephony passed away, it's difficult for them."

"What do you do if you don't have a mistress?" Sable asked Purnicious.

The little kobold shrugged. "There are kobold who live deep in the forest. I could go back there, but being with a mistress is so much better." She looked pleadingly at Sable. "Give me a month."

Sable felt a twinge of guilt at the creature's wide, frightened look. "Of course. A month. Let's do this for a month, then we'll see."

Purnicious let out a long sigh of relief and smiled. "Thank you, mistress."

"But we will have some rules," Sable said. "You will sleep where you want, eat what you want, and generally do what you want."

The kobold looked at Sable eagerly. "I want to sleep here." She settled back and pulled the blanket up over herself with a wide smile. "This is wonderful."

Sable smiled and lay down next to her. The blanket underneath her did little to soften the hard floor. She shifted, trying to get comfortable. Purnicious set her hand on the edge of the blanket, and it swelled until it was soft and springy. The one folded under her head thickened, and the one on top of her grew comfortingly heavy.

"Thank you!" Sable shifted in the cozy blankets.

The kobold beamed at her and tugged Sable's blanket up, tucking it under her chin, like her mother had done long ago.

"That's wonderful, Purnicious. I can't remember ever being this comfortable."

"Good," she whispered sleepily. "Everyone calls me Purn."

Sable smiled. "Thank you, Purn."

"You're welcome, mistress."

Sable let out a short laugh. "Everyone calls me Sable."

Purn yawned. "But I will call you mistress." In moments, the kobold's breathing slowed.

Sable pulled the blanket up to her cheek. It was soft and warm. The socks Talia had given her were no longer clean, but when Sable rubbed her feet together, they were still soft.

In the darkness of the small cave, the blanket and the socks felt like a sort of armor. No. They felt like something more comforting.

Home.

Somehow, they felt like home.

The next morning, when Sable leaned over to grab her boots, she stopped.

The leather was smooth and dark, the toes no longer worn. The old stain on her left boot was gone, leaving them both the same rich, brown color. She slipped her foot in, and it wrapped around her as comfortable as always. But they looked...respectable.

She found Purnicious seated at the table, running her hand along a strip of fabric. Each time she reached the end, new strands of fabric appeared, and the bandage grew longer. Her hair was tamer this morning. The black waves that had stuck out in all directions yesterday were a bit more orderly. Next to her, Serene folded bandages into a small basket.

"Did you fix my boots?" Sable asked the little kobold.

Purnicious flashed her a quick grin. "I'm too tired to do everything I wanted, but I could help a little. They were very worn."

"Thank you! They're better than when I got them."

Sable watched the bandage grow a little longer. "Does it tire you out to do all this?"

She shrugged. "The boot was just a thin layer of leather. And this fabric is thin, too. Now, if you wanted a whole dress made, that would take a lot of time and bellishing. But fixing little things is easy."

"Bellishing?" Serene asked.

"That's what I call it," Purnicious said. "It's really called *augmea*, but that word gets stuck on my tongue. I bellish."

Serene nodded. "If I were to make more of something, I would say *augmentus*."

Purnicious gave her a sympathetic look. "You should think of better words. Try bellish next time."

Sable considered the little kobold. "Can you bellish food?"

"Yes, but some isn't worth it. Bread is easy, but things like meat and fish are harder." She frowned down at her own hands. "It's very hard to bellish animals or people. Very hard. The bits are all different from each other. Even just the meat of an animal..." She shrugged. "It is very hard."

"Can you make more silver?"

Purnicious grinned. "I can make *less* silver. Shrinking anything is easy."

She set her finger on a thin string from the bandage that had fallen to the table. Almost faster than Sable could see, the thread shrank down to a tiny speck.

Purnicious looked pleased at Sable's surprise. "I could make more silver if I try very hard, but so slowly it's not worth it. The bits of metal hold on to each other very tightly and must be lined up just so. It costs more in food to keep up my energy than I'd be able to make with the silver."

"Well, thank you for fixing my boots." Sable looked down at her feet. "It's been a long time since I've worn a pair this nice."

Sable looked at the little creature's wide, blue face and bright purple eyes. "I've heard that kobolds can...disappear. That they instantly travel somewhere else."

Purnicious nodded. "We call that blinking. Although disappearing and blinking are two different things," Purn said. "Disappearing happens whenever I want."

She faded from sight, taking the bandage with her.

Sable reached forward slowly and felt the kobold's arm, even though she couldn't see her. Purnicious came back into view, smiling wide enough to show little white teeth. "I don't go anywhere. I just make the world hide me."

Sable paused. "I have no idea what that means."

"I stretch the world around me," the kobold said, as though it were the most obvious thing in the world, "and sit in a pocket."

Sable looked at Serene. "Does that make sense to you?"

The woman tapped her lip and considered the kobold. "Maybe."

"But when I blink…" Purnicious took the piece of bandage in her hand and brought the two ends together. "I just fold the world up and step to the other side."

Sable stared at her for a moment. "You fold the world up."

The kobold nodded enthusiastically. "Just fold it!"

"How do you know where you'll step to?"

"I can see it. I could blink to the path just outside, because I can see through the rock and know where it is. If we were outside, I could blink down to the base of the cliff." She grimaced. "I could try to do that from in here, but it's too far away for me to see well. There's a chance I'd blink into a tree or into the ground. No one can survive that sort of thing."

The sheer number of questions raised by the little speech silenced Sable for a moment. She glanced at Serene, who listened with interest. Sable finally settled on the simplest question.

"You can see through rock?"

"For a little distance." Purnicious cast a sad look toward the rock-slide at the back of the cave. "There's a lot of rock there. I can't see past it."

She looked back at Sable shyly. "The only thing I can always see, no matter how far away, is where my mistress is." Her smile faded. "That's how I knew Mistress Zephony was gone. I couldn't see her any longer." She set her hand on Sable's. "And it's how I knew you were my new mistress. I can see where you are and what's around you."

Sable's hand twitched, but she forced herself not to pull away from Purnicious. "You can always see me?"

"She can," Serene said, "but she's completely loyal to you."

"Is that supposed to make it more comfortable?" Sable asked.

Purn fixed her with an earnest look. "People always feel strange about it at first, but no matter where you are in the world, if you call me, I will come."

Sable opened her mouth, but any words that could express the unwelcomeness of this information felt too insulting to say to Purnicious's face.

"Can you hear what's going on around me?"

She shook her head. "Not really. I can tell if there are people around you, but I don't hear talking. Unless you call my name. And I don't hear that as much as feel it."

Sable considered the little creature, trying to come up with a non-insulting reply.

"I don't think you understand her level of loyalty," Serene said. "Purnicious is utterly devoted to you. She is made happy by what makes you happy. It's led to horrible misuse of kobolds, as you can imagine, but they stay devoted. Both to you and your family."

"Oh, yes!" Purnicious nodded. "I am happy to help Ryah, as well."

"Can you always see her?"

Her brow puckered. "Not like I can see you. I think if she were far away, I would lose track of her. But when she's close, yes."

Sable considered the little creature. "How many mistresses have you had, Purn?"

"Four, and three masters."

Sable raised an eyebrow. "How old are you?"

Purnicious looked at her blankly.

"Kobolds don't keep track of things like that," Serene said. "They're so steeped in magic, they don't age like you or I do. Kobolds don't grow old. If they die, it's either because of an accident or because they misused the energy inside them."

Purnicious nodded somberly. "Sometimes masters and mistresses need things that are too much."

She rolled up the bandage she'd been working on and tucked it into the little basket on the table. "I'll take these down to the wagons." She gave Sable an earnest look. "You'll get used to me. I promise." With a *pop*, she disappeared.

Serene met Sable's eyes. "It's a significant thing to have a kobold."

Sable looked at the empty spot on the bench between them. "I was just trying to help her get away from the Kalesh man."

"Give it some time," Serene said.

The rest of the group started cleaning up from the night, so Sable folded the blankets she'd used and carried them over to the shelves where Ryah was organizing them. Thulan stood with her arms crossed, studying the collapsed hallway that should lead deeper into the cliffs. Sable paused for a moment, feeling like she should say something, but Ryah, with a bracing breath, moved first.

She stepped up next to the dwarf. "I'm sorry," she said quietly.

"For what?" Thulan's voice was harsh.

"For..." Ryah motioned to the rubble. "For all of this."

"Why? Did you cause it."

"No." Ryah's voice remained gentle. "But I know what it's like to not know what happened to those you love."

Sable felt a wave of guilt at the words.

"There's no one left here that I love." Thulan stayed facing the door.

"How long did Brunn work in this room?"

It took several moments for Thulan to answer. "Eighteen years."

"Then these walls hold more grief for you than just the missing guards." Ryah considered the dwarf for a moment. "We have a prayer for those who have been gone a long time. I can pray it, if you'd like."

The dwarf faced the cave-in, her body tense. Sable braced for whatever harsh thing Thulan would say. But instead, the dwarf gave a small shrug.

Ryah stepped forward and laid a hand on the rubble.

"For those who no longer walk with us, but still move within our hearts,

For those whose hands are out of reach, but whose touch we still feel,

For those who can never be untangled from our past, or our hopes, or our souls,

May their names be spoken by our lips and heard in our ears.

Bless us with the strength to carry the loss, and may we remember them well."

Ryah's voice trailed off, and the cave was utterly silent. Thulan stood still, her attention fixed on the rubble. Andreese looked down at the floor. Leonis and Atticus were both quiet. Sable blinked away the memory of her parents' faces.

Ryah glanced at the dwarf. "I'm sorry you didn't find something more encouraging here."

Thulan didn't move.

Ryah set her hand on the dwarf's shoulder. Sable expected Thulan to pull away, but she stayed still. "I'm sorry you didn't find something that still felt like home."

Thulan didn't answer or turn. Ryah squeezed her shoulder, then dropped her hand and walked away.

"I stretch the world around me," the kobold said, as though it were the most obvious thing in the world, "and sit in a pocket."

CHAPTER THIRTY-SIX

SABLE STEPPED OUTSIDE with the others not long after, into the cool morning shadows. They'd eaten the last of the potatoes the night before, and her stomach was empty for the first time since she'd left Immusmala.

Thulan had climbed up to the lookout again, but there was still no sign of an invading army, so they headed back down the cliff.

At the bottom, Andreese led Jae, Ryah, and Sable into the woods.

"If we can find a leafy pine, we should be able to find green pine nuts," Andreese said, peering up into the trees. "There are tons of them near the southern edge of the forest. Hopefully there'll be some this far in."

They searched for a few minutes, rewarded not only with a leafy pine that had discarded enough nuts to fill the small bag Andreese had brought, but also a low row of scarletberry bushes that were bursting with red fruit.

"I love scarletberries," Jae said, gathering the small fruit. "And Serene is going to die of happiness."

Back at the wagon he found Serene holding a handful of spiky leaves. "I found wartroot," she said to Andreese. "Let me make you some tea." Her face lit up when she saw the fruit in Jae's hands. "Are all those for me?"

Jae paused and looked down at the berries. "Of course, my love."

"Thank you!" She leaned over and kissed him on the cheek. "I'll be right back with tea, Andreese."

"That was a stunning display of affection," Leonis said, watching her leave and taking some berries out of Sable's hand.

"I know." Jae grinned, popping a couple berries into his mouth. "I'm almost too shocked to eat a few before she gets back."

They put the berries, except those Jae was reserving for Serene, next to a pile of nuts on the driver's bench of one of the wagons. Sable took a handful of each and ate them slowly. They were far tastier than they had any right to be.

"You didn't find a cooked pig out there?" Merilee asked, looking at the dwindling pile of food unenthusiastically.

"No, but there is always good food at Merrick's. If we hurry," Jae said, "we can get there before dinner."

Ryah took a handful of nuts and berries to Thulan, who was hitching the horses. The dwarf straightened and took them, meeting Ryah's gaze with a complicated expression. "Thanks, Ryah," she said before turning back to the horses.

Ryah hurried back over to Sable. "She's never used my name before," she whispered.

"The whole world loves Ryah," Sable whispered back, and her sister smiled self-consciously. "Eventually."

Serene came back around the wagon with a small cup for Andreese. "Here's the wartroot tea. If you drink this, it should numb the pain." The edge of her mouth curled up slightly. "It will numb your entire body actually, so you'll be clumsy, but more comfortable."

"Worth it." He took a sip. "How did you get it hot so quick?"

Serene gave him a tight smile and wiggled her fingers toward the cup. Andreese's froze with his lips on the cup. He glanced into the cup, then shrugged. "If it dulls the pain, I don't care how you did it." He took a long drink.

Thulan climbed up on the first wagon and started off, following Jae and Serene further north along the cliffs. The dwarf's hammer sat on the bench beside her, and Leonis walked alongside her, his bow slung over his back. Sable and Ryah fell in behind Thulan's blue wagon, and Andreese came behind them, with Atticus's red wagon bringing up the rear. Merilee, looking as irritated as she had since she learned about the auditions, walked by herself near Atticus's wagon.

They hadn't gone far when Purnicious appeared at Sable's side out of nowhere, her dark curls splayed out wildly, greeting them with a cheery smile.

"Why did your old mistress live so far out on the Eastern Reaches?" Sable asked her. "If she was a famous actress, she could have lived anywhere."

"Because," Andreese answered from behind them, "she wanted to be the wealthiest, most arrogant person within a day's ride."

Ryah gave him a reproachful look. "Andreese!"

"My mistress," Purnicious said, with a glare at Andreese, "liked the quiet of the Reaches. She kept a home there for years, but spent most of her time in Immusmala and the cities in the north. Until five years ago, when she had earned enough money from her acting to live comfortably and was tired of the intrigue and politics of the city." She glanced back toward Atticus and lowered her voice. "And after a falling out with Atticus, she moved out here permanently."

"What sort of falling out?" Andreese asked.

Purnicious looked up at him with a disapproving look. "That's hardly any of your business, wastrel."

"Very true." Ryah nodded. "It's none of our business."

"Why do you call him wastrel?" Sable asked.

"Because even though he hunts for his aunt's butchery shop..." Purn paused, "or did," she said more slowly, "he always did the least work he could. You could never get him to put extra effort into anything."

"Extra effort?" Andreese said, incredulous. "Your mistress wanted me to climb the cliffs to find green finch eggs. Do you have any idea how hard it is to reach green finch nests? Or how few eggs they lay? Not only was I not going to waste days on a ridiculous job, if I did it too often, we'd kill all the green finches in the area. Just so the great and noble Lady Zephony could have a delicacy."

"She only asked you for those once," Purnicious said, setting her small, blue fists on her hips.

"You're right. The other times, it was three young fawns for a stew that required only their tongues. Or eighteen pygmy boars for, well... I have no idea what she'd use eighteen boars for. I spent my days hunting game for my aunt so people could eat. Not so some pompous actress could recreate the delicacies of her glory days."

Sable, finding herself more sympathetic with Andreese, changed the subject. "Purnicious, how did you come to work for Zephony?"

Purnicious's purple eyes shot one last irritated look at Andreese before turning back to Sable. "It all started because I tend to...overdo things. It had been a long time since I had a master, and I lived with a colony of kobolds farther up the forest. I was walking along the Marsham Cliffs one day when I saw an outcropping that vaguely resembled a kobold."

"Gnome rock?" Andreese asked.

Purn gave an indignant huff. "It does not look like a gnome!"

"It looks exactly like a gnome." He looked at Sable. "It's carved perfectly like a gnome."

The kobold shot him a venomous look and turned back to Sable. "This stone, which vaguely resembled a kobold, caught my eye. And..." She shrugged, and her expression turned a bit sheepish, "it seemed like a fun thing to do to make it look more like a kobold."

Andreese's mouth fell open. "You carved gnome rock?"

Purnicious's long, thin fingers curled into fists. "It's not a gnome!"

"Will you let her talk?" Sable said to Andreese.

He waved her off. "Why didn't you finish? The head is great, but the body is barely carved at all. Was it supposed to be holding something?"

"Do you realize how difficult it is to reshape stone?" Purnicious demanded. "Each individual grain is held together with enough strength to withstand almost anything. To shape it, you must isolate and copy those individual grains. Then the new one has to be shifted into position." She glared at him. "Do you have any idea how hard it is to shift grains of stone against each other?"

Andreese blinked at her. When he answered, his voice was thoughtful. "No. I don't think I do."

Ryah raised an eyebrow at the answer.

"Please continue with your story, Purnicious," Sable said. "And ignore Andreese. I think it's amazing that you can shape rock."

"Thank you." Purnicious sniffed. "I got involved in my work and worked too long, as I have a tendency to do. Night fell, but there was a full moon, so I kept working." She grimaced. "By midnight, I was only done with the head, but I had exhausted myself to the point that I couldn't walk home. I was too tired to even build any sort of shelter or concealment. I just fell asleep against the rock."

The little kobold sighed. "When I woke, I was being carried by this man—" She shot a glare at Andreese "—who was also too stupid to know the difference between a kobold and a gnome. He thought he'd found a gnome and that I would lead him to treasure in my burrow."

"Do gnomes have treasures in burrows?" Sable asked.

"Maybe." She pursed her thin lips into a look of disgust. "Dirty little creatures that spend too much time underground. But this man carried me back to a campfire with two of his companions, and they tied me up. The night was still young. I must have barely slept at all before he found me."

"Couldn't you have blinked away?" Ryah asked.

She shook her head. "Blinking takes as much energy as walking, and at that point, I wasn't sure I could walk yet. So I lay there and slept until near dawn. They had camped at the edge of the forest, and one of them saw a carriage on the plains. They waited until it got close, then ambushed it."

The kobold grinned. "But it was Lady Zephony's carriage. She'd been in a hurry to get home and had taken advantage of the full moon to travel through the night. What they didn't know was that she felt bad keeping her guards up all night, so she'd let two rest inside the carriage while the third drove. The brigands waylaid the carriage to find three well-armed guards protecting it."

Andreese let out a short laugh. "I bet that surprised them."

Purnicious raised an eyebrow at him, but nodded. "Lady Zephony's guards made quick work of them, and when two of them investigated to make sure there were no more brigands nearby, they found me, trussed up. Lady Zephony untied me and brought me to her carriage. She gave me breakfast." Purnicious smiled sadly. "So I've served her gladly for the last twelve years." The tips of her long ears bowed down. "Until yesterday."

Andreese had fallen silent, and Ryah looked at the kobold sympathetically. Sable squeezed Purnicious's shoulder.

"If you don't need anything mistress," Purnicious said quietly, "Atticus asked if I'd fix some of his curtains."

Sable nodded, and Purn disappeared with a little *pop*.

"You two are very different ages for being sisters," Andreese finally said from behind them. "You're only sixteen, right, Ryah? And Sable, you must be in your twenties."

Sable glanced back at him. His voice was amiable, and he had a mildly pleased look on his face.

"Sable's twenty-five," Ryah answered. "Our other sister, Talia, is eighteen. There were two brothers between her and Sable, but they died as babies," she finished quietly.

"I have no brothers or sisters," he said thoughtfully. "Never did. No living ones or dead ones."

Ryah raised an eyebrow at his casual tone.

"I also have no parents, either," he continued blithely. He turned his face up toward the sky with a slightly vacant look in his eyes. "They died from a sickness when I was ten."

"I'm sorry to hear that, Andreese," Ryah said.

"Call me Reese. The only people who ever called me Andreese were my parents and the officers I reported to. The name makes me feel like I'm in trouble."

Sable turned to look at him. "Are you all right?"

"I feel great." He smiled at her, and she realized she hadn't actually seen him smile before. "It's been a long time since I've been this deep in the woods."

His toe caught on a root and he stumbled forward, grabbing Sable's and Ryah's shoulders to keep from falling.

"Thanks!" he said cheerfully and stepped up between them.

Sable moved to the side to make room, and glanced at Ryah. Her sister met her gaze with raised eyebrows.

"I never have a reason to come this far north. There's plenty of game along the southern edges, and all the good nut trees grow there. More along the western edge, but there's still plenty near Ebenmoor and I never saw much use in traveling this far, plus I never wanted to have to carry whatever I killed back that far." He took a breath. "Although I do think the woods get...brighter up here. Don't know how to explain it." He frowned at the surrounding trees. "Same trees, same bushes, but it gets brighter."

The words tumbled out of his mouth so quickly Sable had to focus to follow them.

He turned to Sable and gave her an intensely questioning look. "Do you think it's getting brighter?"

She laughed. "I think the sun is getting higher in the sky."

"No." He frowned again. "That's not it. It's something else."

"So even when you're in a good mood, you still disagree with me?" Sable asked.

Serene came from around the wagon in front of them, smirking. "Sometimes wartroot makes people chatty."

"This is great!" Andreese said enthusiastically. "My ribs don't hurt at all. They've been hurting. A lot. And I'm afraid I've been a bit on edge because of it."

Serene raised an eyebrow. "You think so?"

"I do." He ran his hands through his hair, leaving it more unruly than before. "And I'm sorry. You've all been very generous. But every time I breathe, it hurts. Not that I should apologize to you," he said, turning to Sable. "You haven't been particularly nice."

"How long will this last?" Sable asked Serene. "I'm undecided about whether I like the quiet, grumpy version or the chatty, argumentative one better."

Serene grinned. "A few hours. By midday, he'll be back to normal."

"I'm not normally grumpy," he objected. "I'm friendly. People like me."

Sable laughed, but he looked so offended she tried to press her lips together into a more serious look.

"They do. I'm usually very nice— Oooooh!" He stumbled again and grabbed Ryah's arm to steady himself. "My feet don't feel quite right. Like they've grown very, very large." He peered down. "But they look the same, don't they?"

"They do," Ryah said, steadying him, trying to stifle her laughter.

"I just hope we don't run into any trouble this morning," he told her seriously, "because I don't think I'd be very good in a fight."

Not able to hold it in anymore, Ryah let out a peal of laughter, and after a minute, Andreese joined her.

"I won't be," he said, still laughing and pointing to his sore ribs. "This is the side I hold my sword with. I'm not nearly as good with my left hand." He looked earnestly at Ryah. "Usually I'm very helpful in a fight. Had lots of training. Used to lead a company of soldiers— Ow!" He grabbed Ryah's shoulder as he tripped again, this time he just left it there.

"I'm sure you are." She patted his hand encouragingly.

"You're the nicest one of this whole group," Andreese told her.

"Um... Thanks, Andreese," she said.

"Call me Reese." He leaned closer and, in a loud whisper, added, "You're much nicer than your sister."

Ryah glanced at Sable and pressed her lips together to hide a smile.

"You shouldn't get involved with the priories, though," he continued. "They're not as good as you think. I know you won't believe me, because you're very young..." He stopped walking and looked at Ryah sharply. "How old are you again?"

"Sixteen," Ryah reminded him, pulling on his arm to get him walking again before Atticus's horses caught up to them.

He nodded sagely. "See? Very young. I'm thirty. Or thirty-one, maybe. Yes, thirty-one. When I was sixteen, I was already training. You don't look like you've experienced many interesting things in life. You've been shut up in an abbey too long. But you're still nice."

Ryah raised an eyebrow, but Andreese didn't notice. He turned his gaze back up to the treetops and his toe caught yet again.

Sable briefly considered giving him a shove so he could have a proper fall. Instead, she took his arm to steady him. "You should keep your eyes on the ground, Andreese. Help you keep track of those giant feet."

He gave her a serious look. "That's a good idea."

"I'm very smart," Sable said dryly. "To be honest, thirty seems young to have led a company of soldiers."

"Thirty-one," he corrected her, looking at his feet. "Started in the ranks when I was eighteen. Had my own company by twenty-five."

Ryah looked at him skeptically.

"Company of what?" Sable asked. "I didn't realize the Eastern Reaches had a military."

"Wasn't here." He poked himself in the side. "This wartroot really is amazing. I can't feel my ribs at all."

Sable glanced at the wagon Thulan drove ahead of them. "As fascinating as this conversation is," she told Ryah, "Thulan said she'd work with me on the script for the play this morning. You have fun chatting with the general here."

Ryah's eyes widened in alarm. "No! Stay! Everything Reese says is so…interesting, you wouldn't want to miss anything."

"I'll have to manage," Sable smiled. "He only wants to talk to the nice sister anyway."

"Bye," Andreese said a bit vacantly before turning back to Ryah. "Have you ever hunted? It's not the hunting that's hard, really. Anyone can learn to shoot a bow. The hard part is the tracking…"

Sable gave Ryah a wave, which her sister returned with a desperate look. Without waiting to hear more about tracking, Sable walked up to find Thulan.

The small trail was so ill-suited for wagons that the dwarf was leading the horses instead of jolting around on the seat.

"Ready to practice?" The dwarf handed Sable the reins and pulled out a neat stack of bound papers. "Which part? Vivaine or the handmaiden?"

Sable glanced back to see Merilee still walking next to Atticus's wagon, reading her own copy. The play felt more complex now that Atticus wanted to use it to get them a platform in Immusmala to talk about the Kalesh, but one part of it was still perfectly simple. The first lady made more than twice as much as the second. Sixty-five might be only half what Sable needed to get Talia free, but it was more than she'd find anywhere else. "Vivaine."

Thulan gave an approving nod and began to read. The lines were so well-written they were almost effortless to learn, and Thulan only had to repeat a few sections more than once. There was a lilting feel to the words. Not happy, exactly, but almost poetic. The scenes with Balin were gripping, the encounter with him at the end, terrifying.

Vivaine was an easy character to slip into. Her feelings toward Balin reminded Sable of Talia again, and the regret and guilt Vivaine felt were familiar enough that the lines flowed easily.

They paused to rest the horses around midmorning.

"We need to discuss props," Atticus said to Thulan. "We need the sword to put off sparks." Atticus held up a dull, short sword he'd pulled out of a crate. "This will be painted, the hilt decorated, and we'll need it to spark three different times. At the beginning, with the elves, and in the final scene."

"Sparks or glitter?" Thulan asked.

"I'd prefer sparks. Actually, I'd like flames to run along it, but I'm guessing that is too much to ask."

Thulan took the sword and examined it. "A fire would work if there were small channels along the blade."

Purnicious popped into view next to Sable. "I can put channels in it."

Thulan glanced at the kobold with a dubious expression, but Purnicious drew her finger along the flat of the blade, leaving two sharp groves running along the center. Everyone stared at her in silence for a moment.

Thulan grinned at Atticus. "You can have a flaming sword. We'll need to paint the grooves with oil, or maybe liquor, between scenes, but with a little work, it could be very dramatic."

Atticus considered the kobold. "It has just occurred to me how Zephony always had so many amazing costumes."

Purn gave him a sad smile. "The story you told last night would have brought Zephony out of retirement. Even if it meant working with you again."

"Why was she mad at you?" Sable asked him.

"Because he wouldn't write roles like Vivaine for her," Leonis said. "She only wanted plays with a spectacular first lady."

"It's true," Thulan agreed. "Zephony wanted Atticus to write plays just for her to perform."

"She regretted leaving," Purnicious said, a little sadly. "She always spoke fondly of this troupe."

Atticus patted her little shoulder. "I've never worked with a more talented actress."

Around midday, they paused again to rest the horses.

Ryah hurried up to Sable. "Reese needs help foraging. I told him you'd be happy to."

Sable cringed. "Is he still chatty?"

"No. The wartroot wore off and he's back to grumpy."

"Is that better or worse?"

Ryah thought a minute. "Well, it's quieter."

"Sable!" Andreese called, coming out from behind the wagon. He held the sword they'd taken from the Kalesh warrior and two bags. "Come help. Bending down kills me, and the nuts will all be on the ground."

"This should be fun," she muttered.

Andreese was quiet as she followed him into the woods. He cradled his ribs tightly with his right arm, holding the Kalesh sword in his left hand.

"Do you need to hold the sword?" she asked.

"Do you have a Kalesh scabbard?" he snapped

A jab of irritation went through her at his voice. But every breath he took was shallow, and her annoyance came with a touch of guilt. His steps were slow, and he watched the ground and the trees closely.

"Stop walking so close to me," he grumbled.

"I've decided," she said. "I prefer you on wartroot."

"Let's bruise your ribs and see how much you like walking around."

298

Sable blew out a long breath, trying to dredge up some patience. He stumbled over a root and gasped in pain, his face pale.

"Is it worse today?"

"Yes, it's worse," he snapped. "Did I act like this yesterday?"

Sable raised an eyebrow. "Maybe you should have Serene look at it."

"Maybe if you'd help me look for food instead of yammering, we'd get back to her sooner."

Sable clenched her jaw against a sharp retort. "Right. Green pine nuts and berries." She turned and started walking again, realizing she didn't remember what a leafy pine looked like.

They walked in silence for a few minutes. "Ahead to the right," he said between gritted teeth.

Now that he'd pointed it out, she recognized the wide, flat needles of the leafy pine, and hurried toward it. Andreese leaned against the tree trunk, breathing shallowly and gripping the bag, while Sable gathered handfuls of the nuts off the ground.

She turned, holding a small pile of the soft, green nuts to find him pushing himself off the trunk, his eyes scanning the trees. "Do you smell that?" he asked in a low voice.

Sable sniffed the air. "Smoke? Maybe Thulan started a fire."

"To cook what? We have no food."

Sable paused. "A homestead nearby?" She caught a sharper scent mixed with the smoke. "What are they burning?"

Andreese held the bag open for the nuts in her hand. "We need to get back. Now."

She glanced down at the dozens of nuts still lying on the ground. "What about all these?"

"Leave them. I think there are more Kalesh—"

Merilee's scream cut through the woods.

CHAPTER THIRTY-SEVEN

ANDREESE THRUST the bag of nuts into Sable's hand and broke into a run back the way they'd come. She gripped the bag and ran with him.

He made it a handful of steps before curling his arm around his sore ribs. With a low growl, he kept running, the sword gripped in his hand.

"The Kalesh?" she whispered.

He nodded and paused, leaning against a tree, his breath coming in short gasps.

She peered ahead, but could see nothing but trees. "How do you know?"

"The scent in the smoke. It's a spice they use in their fires. Supposed to please their dragon emperor."

"Their emperor is a dragon?"

He shot her an annoyed look. "Figuratively. He's called the Dragon, and they revere him as a god. Adding scale spice to campfires is a tradition in the Kalesh army." He took a deep breath, pushed himself off the tree, and hurried on.

Though he gave the occasional wince, his face was focused, his steps quiet. Sable's footsteps next to him sounded terrifyingly loud. The smell of smoke grew stronger.

"How do you know about the Kalesh?" she whispered.

He held up his hand and stopped, sneaking up behind a wide bush. Sable hunched down and followed.

Atticus's wagon came into view. There was no sign of fire, and the smoke scent had faded slightly, but in front of the wagons a black-clad Kalesh warrior stood with a sword to Thulan's throat.

Sable sank down behind Andreese, grabbing his arm. "Sweet Amah," she breathed.

Atticus and Jae stood tensely beside the dwarf. The Kalesh man was dressed like the man yesterday. His black hood pulled up, black mask covering everything but his eyes. The only difference was his uniform had a thin, red band around his sleeve, like a mark of authority.

Along the near side of the wagons, another Kalesh warrior had Serene, Ryah, and a terrified Merilee backed up against the side of a horse, his sword held menacingly close to Merilee. Sable strained to see Ryah through the bushes. She looked frightened, but unharmed.

Serene fixed the man with a glare, her hands clenched into fists at her sides. She stretched her fingers toward him for a breath, then made a fist again.

The man pointed at Merilee's neck and spoke in a guttural voice.

Merilee clasped her hands over her silver necklaces. "They're all I have," she pleaded in a blubbering voice.

For once, Sable found the woman's reaction perfectly appropriate.

The Kalesh man stepped forward and yanked the chains, snapping them off Merilee's neck. She held on, gripping the necklaces tightly, until the man brought his sword up. With a sob, she let go. The man pointed his blade at her rings.

They were no more than twenty paces away. She gripped Andreese's sleeve and leaned close to his ear, her heart pounding. "Are there only two?"

He held up three fingers and pointed between the wagons, where a black arm was visible.

She twisted to look back into the woods. "Are there are more?"

Andreese shook his head.

"How do you know?"

"They're positioned for a three-man attack."

"Then why aren't they attacking?"

"Because they're talking to Jae," he whispered with a glare. "Be quiet."

Even in the sunlight, everything about the Kalesh men looked dark. She leaned against Andreese, and he grunted in pain.

"Sorry," she whispered, pulling back a bit, but not letting go of his sleeve.

At the front of the wagons, Jae held his hands up, showing he had no weapon, and said something in Kalesh.

The leader shook his head and gave a short answer.

Sable waited for Jae to translate, but he merely said something else in Kalesh. "Why aren't Jae and Serene doing anything?"

"They're trying to talk their way out."

Jae continued talking, and Sable strained to hear more, as though she could understand by sheer will. "I wish he'd translate."

"Jae told him we have nothing of value."

Sable turned to stare at Andreese. "You speak Kalesh?" she hissed.

"Shh." He glared at her.

Jae said something else, and the commander shifted his attention from Thulan to Jae. The Kalesh man on the far side of the wagons stepped into sight, focused on the conversation, as well.

The Kalesh leader asked an abrupt question, and Jae answered again.

"Andreese, if you don't start translating," Sable whispered, "as Amah is my witness, I will punch you in the ribs as hard as I can."

"Jae told him they'd be valuable prisoners," he whispered.

"Is he trying to get captured?"

"Better captured than killed." Andreese's voice was low and calm. "Sable?"

"What?"

"I need you to let go." He glanced down at his arm where her fingers dug into him.

She pulled her hand away. "Sorry."

Merilee, her face blotchy with tears, handed over the last of her rings. Ryah stood next to her, her chin lifted, but her hands shook at her side.

"Where's Purnicious?" Sable whispered.

Andreese shrugged.

"Where's Leonis?"

He pointed across the wagons into the treetops.

There, perched on a branch, sat Leonis, his bow drawn, pointed at the warrior threatening Thulan.

Andreese waved his hand and Leonis glanced over.

"He knows we're here?" Sable asked.

Andreese ignored her and pointed to Leonis, then the Kalesh warrior on the far side of the wagons. He then pointed to himself and the Kalesh man near Merilee.

Leonis shook his head and kept his bow pointed at the lead Kalesh.

Thulan will be fine. She's strong, Andreese mouthed with exaggerated intensity, pointing at the dwarf and flexing his arm.

Leonis glared at him, but swung his bow toward the Kalesh man on the far side.

Andreese picked up a rock the size of an apple and handed it to Sable. "When I signal, throw this past the leader so it lands behind him."

Sable gripped it tightly, pulling her attention back to the Kalesh leader. Her arm felt watery and breath came in shallow gasps.

"Sable," Andreese whispered.

She met his gaze.

"It's going to be all right. But I need you to throw the rock."

She shook her head, the motion feeling jerky. "What if I miss?"

"There's nothing to miss. All you have to do is hit anywhere in the woods behind the man. We just need him to be distracted for a moment." He set his hand on hers. "Take a deep breath. You can do this."

Sable drew one in and looked back at the Kalesh man. The fear squeezed tighter and her breath rushed right out again.

"No. Look at me." Andreese's voice was unruffled.

She met his eyes. "How are you so calm?" The words came out angrier than she'd meant them to.

"Because being scared won't help."

The words were warm with truth, and Sable focused on the feel of them.

"Take a deep breath," he said again, "and let it out slowly."

She did, and her heart slowed the slightest bit.

"Just keep breathing." His voice was steady and low. "We are not going to hide in the woods while our friends are threatened."

The warm words wrapped around her, and she latched onto them.

"No more cowering," she whispered.

A grim smile curled up the corner of Andreese's mouth. "No more cowering. The Kalesh have taken enough."

She clenched her jaw and looked back at the leader. The sight of his boots triggered an anger deep inside her. She breathed into it, letting her fury overshadow her fear.

She nodded again, stronger this time.

He squeezed her arm. "Wait until my signal."

Quietly, still hunched over his sore ribs, he crept through the trees toward the Kalesh man by Merilee.

Leonis waited in his tree, his bow trained on the man on the far side. The leader continued to talk to Jae, and Sable gripped the rock, taking deep breaths and focusing on how much she hated the Kalesh man's boots.

Andreese was half-way to his man. Sable shifted the rock in her hand, hefting it to get familiar with the weight.

A pop at her side made her jump.

Purnicious appeared, tucked up against the bushes, curled into a tiny ball, her eyes wide.

"Are you all right?" Sable whispered.

The little kobold nodded with quick, tiny motions. "We need to run," Purnicious whispered.

Sable shook her head, putting her attention back on Andreese. "Leonis is across the road with his bow, and Andreese is headed that way with a sword."

"But you have nothing," Purnicious whispered. "They'll kill you!" Her eyes were huge, the black pupils so wide they almost swallowed the purple.

"I have a rock," Sable said, holding it up with what she hoped was a reassuring smile. She set her hand on Purnicious's back. The kobold quivered with fear. "Stay hidden." Sable forced her voice to be more calm than she felt. "If the Kalesh come close, blink and get out of here."

Purnicious grabbed her arm. "What are you going to do?"

"Cause a distraction." She fixed Purn with a firm look. "Stay hidden."

"All you have is a rock." Her face looked so terrified that Sable paused.

"You're right." She picked up a thick stick from the ground. "Can you sharpen this?"

Purnicious set her finger on the stick and the end shrank until it held a sharp point.

"Thank you." Sable tried to give the creature a reassuring smile. "I'm done cowering."

Purnicious shrank back against the bush. "I'm not."

Andreese reached the tree nearest to his man, who still faced Merilee, Ryah, and Serene. Serene's eyes flickered back and forth from the man before her to where Jae talked to the other.

Andreese signaled to Leonis in the tree, then gave Sable a sharp nod.

She waited until the Kalesh leader glanced at Jae. "Isah protect us," she whispered, then hurled the rock. The stone slammed against a tree, then dropped to the ground with the sharp crackle of pine needles.

The Kalesh man whirled away from Thulan to face the noise. The dwarf dove backwards toward the wagon, scrambling onto the driver's bench for her hammer.

Jae lunged forward, grabbing the warrior's arm.

A muffled thud sounded from the far side of the wagons, and the Kalesh man on Leonis's side fell with an arrow in his chest.

Rushing out of the trees, Andreese's sword sliced through the air and into the Kalesh man's back. The warrior cried out once before Andreese swung again, his scream ending in a gurgle.

Andreese let out his own cry of pain and grabbed his ribs, sinking to his knees next to the dead man.

At the front of the wagons, the Kalesh leader slashed at Jae and spun. He raced along the wagons toward Andreese, shouting something guttural.

Ryah gripped Merilee's hand as they shrank back against the horse.

At the sight of the Kalesh man running toward Ryah, Sable gripped the stick tighter. "No more cowering," she whispered.

The Kalesh man ran past the bush, and Sable jumped out after him. Andreese shoved himself to his feet, and raised his sword. The Kalesh man paused just a breath to size him up.

In his moment of hesitation, Sable stepped up close behind him and pushed the sharpened stick against the man's neck. His hood was pulled up, but the fabric was thin, and she felt the tip jabbed into him. The Kalesh man froze.

Andreese kept his eyes fixed on the Kalesh man, unblinking.

The warrior shifted, and Sable pushed the tip harder. "Don't move."

The words came out terrified and thin, and she quailed at her mistake even as she saw Andreese wince. The Kalesh man wouldn't understand her words, but now he'd know they were said by a short, terrified woman.

The warrior blurred into action, spinning toward Sable. She jabbed the stick at his neck, but found only air. Leonis's bow twanged, and the warrior jolted, but his sword still drove toward her.

Sable dropped to the ground, her arm flying up in a futile effort to stop the falling blade.

With a loud *pop*, Purnicious flashed into existence between the warrior and Sable. The kobold lunged upward, grabbing the blade with her hand. In an instant, the blade shrank until it was no thicker than a pine needle. It broke off in Purn's hand with a tinny snap, and she tumbled to the ground, curling into a ball.

The Kalesh man froze, staring wide-eyed at his empty hilt. Andreese lunged up behind him, his sword raised.

"No!" Serene yelled, shoving Andreese away and slamming her hand onto the side of the Kalesh man's head. "*Dormio!*"

The warrior's body went limp and he toppled to the ground.

"Don't kill him!" Atticus ran up to them, holding out his hands.

Andreese stood with his sword raised, his breath coming in short, harsh gasps, glaring at the Kalesh man asleep on the ground. One of Leonis's arrows was lodged deep in the man's side.

"Andreese," Atticus said firmly. "Don't kill him."

Leonis came up from the far side, another arrow nocked in his bow.

Serene stepped in front of Andreese, who still had his sword raised. "We need to see what he knows, Andreese."

"We should kill him," he said between clenched teeth.

"I know," Serene said, her voice as hard as his. "But we need to talk to him first."

With visible effort, Andreese spun around and walked away, facing into the woods. His shoulders rose and fell with rough breaths.

"Tie him up," Atticus said, standing over the Kalesh man. "Serene, are there any more around?"

She shook her head.

Thulan came around the wagon, her hammer still in her hand. None too gently, Leonis tied the sleeping man's feet together, then tied his hands behind his back. Through it all, the man didn't wake. Leonis picked up the Kalesh sword and tossed it into the back of the wagon.

Thulan took the belts off the others too, along with their swords and scabbards. "They're carrying almost nothing. They must have a camp nearby."

"Andreese and I smelled smoke," Sable said.

"Are you sure there aren't more out there?" Ryah asked, looking into the forest with wide eyes.

Serene nodded, still kneeling next to the Kalesh man. "Positive."

Sable looked her sister over. "Are you all right?" Ryah nodded shakily.

The man Andreese had killed was lying near their feet, Merilee's jewelry still tangled in his limp hand. Sable knelt and uncurled his fingers, handing the necklaces and rings back to Merilee. The woman clasped them to her chest, bursting into tears.

"Let's sit down," Ryah said to Merilee, leading her toward the back of the wagon.

Purnicious still lay curled up in a ball on the ground.

Sable knelt next to her. "Purn?"

The kobold whimpered.

Serene stood and spun her eyes scanning the group. "Where's Jae?"

No one answered.

"Jae?" Serene ran toward the front of the wagons.

Purnicious moaned quietly. Sable set her hand on the kobold's shoulder. "Purnicious? Are you all right?"

Purn kept her eyes locked on the sleeping Kalesh man. She nodded quickly.

"You saved my life," Sable said.

Purnicious gave Sable the smallest smile. The kobold squeezed her hands to her chest, and a dribble of dark blue ran down her wrist.

Sable grabbed her hand. "Are you hurt?"

"Not badly," Purnicious said, opening her hand. Two gashes ran parallel across her palm where she'd grabbed the edges of the blade. Dark blue blood seeped out.

"Serene!" Sable called. "Purn needs—"

"Bandages!" Serene's voice sounded jagged and terrified. "Bandages!"

Ryah grabbed some fabric from inside the wagon.

Sable sprang up and ran toward Serene.

Jae lay on the road, a wide, dark circle of blood pooling under him.

CHAPTER THIRTY-EIGHT

SERENE HELD her hands to the side of Jae's neck, blood flowing quickly through her fingers.

"No," she whispered, the word rough. "No. No. No." With her eyes pressed shut, her face curled in concentration. Her eyes flew open, terrified, and she cast a wild look around. She shifted and slammed one hand down onto the grass next to her.

The grass around her hand withered. A circle of brown, twisted blades, stretched out almost faster than Sable could follow.

Serene's eyes closed, and she let out a whimper.

The blood from Jae's neck didn't slow.

Thulan took a step forward but stopped, helpless, clenching her hands on her hammer.

Jae's face was white, his eyes closed, his body still.

The patch of brown grass had stopped growing, and Sable stared at Serene's hand on the ground.

The grass doesn't have enough energy to do anything, Serene had said in the wagon. Sable spun around. An oak grew next to the road, a long branch hanging down over Leonis's head.

"Grab the branch!" Sable shouted, running toward Leonis. "Pull it down!"

Leonis frowned, but jumped and grabbed the branch, pulling it low enough for Sable to reach. She pulled it lower. The branch was still too high, until Thulan dropped her hammer and added her weight.

"Serene!" Sable bent the end of the limb toward her. "The branch!"

Serene's eyes flew open and she seized the end of the branch. Every leaf withered.

Serene let out a gasp of pain, but bowed her head over Jae, holding the branch with one hand and his neck with the other.

In a breath the entire branch was nothing but dried, curled leaves.

Searing pain shot into Sable's palms where she held the branch. Her arms grew cold to the elbows. With a cry, she let go. A moment later, Leonis cried out and yanked his own hands off.

Thulan held on longer, gripping the branch with both hands, her face creased in pain, and beginning to whiten.

"Let go, you miserably stubborn dwarf," Leonis said. "She'll kill you!"

"It'll spring up away from her," Thulan grunted.

The dwarf's face grew more pale. Sable looked around for a way to hold the branch without touching it. She grabbed Thulan's hammer from the ground and hooked the head of it over the branch. "Hold this!"

The dwarf released one hand and grabbed the hammer. Her eyes widened. When she pulled her other hand off, Sable caught a glimpse of a red, burned palm.

"Can you hold it?" Sable asked.

Thulan gripped the hammer with both hands and nodded.

The branch had withered completely. On the branch above it, the leaves began to curl. Then the one above that.

Serene's breath came in gasps, and a tendril of smoke rose from the wood where she gripped it.

Jae's blood started to slow between her fingers. There was so much blood on the ground, Sable didn't want to think about why it was slowing.

Finally, Serene unclenched her hand from the branch. The wood, dried and brittle, stayed bent. She dropped her head onto Jae's chest, still holding his neck.

"Bandage," she whispered.

Ryah knelt next to her. "Move your hand."

Serene looked up at her with a haunted, broken look. She peeled her fingers away, and the gash on Jae's neck widened. Sable drew back. It didn't look like it had healed at all.

Ryah pressed the cloth to Jae's neck, motioning for Merilee to bring her the waterskin. Merilee stood frozen, her face pale, eyes fixed on the blood. Sable yanked the waterskin out of her hand and knelt by her sister, pouring the water where Ryah indicated.

Only a trickle of blood flowed out of the wound now, and Ryah cleaned it before wrapping fabric around his neck. She placed her fingers on the side of Jae's neck, sitting there a moment.

"His heart is beating," she said. "Weakly, but it's beating."

Serene sank back, her arms limp, her hands palm up on her lap. They were red with blood, but both were also covered with huge, oozing blisters.

Ryah scrambled over to her with the water. "This is going to hurt."

Serene kept her eyes fixed on Jae's pale face and didn't answer. She flinched when the water ran across her palms, then sat silently while Ryah wrapped bandages around both hands.

"We need to get him to Stonehaven," Serene whispered. "There's a woman there who can help him."

"Can't you help him?" Ryah asked quietly.

Serene let out a shaky breath. "Not as much as he needs."

"How far is it?" Atticus asked.

She didn't look away from Jae's still form. "Not far. Just follow the road."

Atticus turned to Leonis and Thulan. "Set him up somewhere comfortable in the wagon."

"And the Kalesh man?" Leonis asked.

"Put him in the wagon, too," Atticus said. "We'll question him at Stonehaven."

"He's not going to last that long," Leonis said. "And if we try to move him with that arrow in his side, it'll kill him even faster."

Atticus looked down the wagons at the man. "Serene?" he asked gently. "Can you translate for me?"

She didn't answer.

Atticus blew out a long breath "We can't question him without Jae and Serene. So put him in the wagon. We just have to hope he makes it."

"Andreese speaks Kalesh," Sable said.

Atticus turned to look at Andreese, who leaned heavily against the side of the wagon. "You do?"

Andreese shot Sable a scowl. "We should leave him and let him die," he said harshly.

"He'll be dead soon enough," Leonis said.

Atticus fixed Andreese with a long look. "Will you translate for me?"

Andreese clenched his jaw but nodded. Gripping his side and taking small steps, he moved slowly back toward the Kalesh man.

Sable glanced at Ryah. Her sister sat with her hand pressed against Jae's bandages, adding extra pressure. "Do you need anything?"

Ryah shook her head. Serene still sat staring numbly at Jae, so Sable followed the others.

Atticus stood over the sleeping man, his arms crossed. "How do we wake him?"

Thulan gave the man's shoulder a nudge with her boot, but he didn't stir.

Andreese leaned down and gave the arrow a jiggle.

The man's eyes flew open and he let out a raw scream.

Atticus fixed Andreese with a hard look. "We are trying not to kill him."

"*You're* trying not to kill him." Andreese stood gingerly. "I'm waiting for my chance."

Leonis and Thulan took up positions on either side of the man, their weapons ready. Sable stayed behind Thulan and her hammer. Atticus knelt and pulled the man's mask off.

His face was long and narrow with a short black beard. He glared at the group with dark brown eyes.

"Why are you here?" Atticus asked.

In answer to Andreese's translation, the man clenched his jaw.

Atticus crossed his arms and waited. The man glared at Atticus for a long moment, then his mouth twisted and he began speaking.

"You will all die," Andreese translated the man's words. "Your people will be wiped away from the earth."

"Well, that's not friendly," Thulan muttered.

"We did kill two of his men," Leonis pointed out.

Thulan shrugged. "They started it."

"Why are you here, in the Nidel Woods?" Atticus asked the man, pointing to his dead companions. "Why are the three of you here, stopping travelers on the road? "

The man began chanting.

Andreese scowled. "Cleanse the land. Burn the filth. Raze the chafe… It's the same chant as the man yesterday."

"How far north have your people come?" Atticus asked. "How far from the plains?"

The man continued to chant, and Sable felt an anger growing in her at the guttural words. Andreese's hand tightened on the hilt of his sword and he shifted toward the man.

Atticus shot Andreese a warning look, before setting his hand on the warrior's leather breastplate. "What interest does the Kalesh Empire have in our lands when it's never been interested before?"

The warrior stopped chanting at the translation, then glanced around at the group, as though surprised at the question.

Andreese frowned at the man's answer. "He says we haven't been interesting before now."

Atticus considered the words. "What changed?"

The warrior gave a short answer.

Andreese gave Atticus a puzzled look. "We became valuable."

Atticus turned back to the warrior. "Because of what? Is there an army coming? Are you here scouting our land?"

The warrior's mouth curled at the question.

"He says, 'More will come. The land is no longer yours.'" Andreese frowned down at the man.

Atticus raised an eyebrow. "It still feels like ours. A few small bands of Kalesh may cause trouble on the Eastern Reaches, but the larger cities won't fall."

Andreese translated. The warrior laughed, the sound wet in his throat.

"Your cities have already fallen." Andreese translated. "What will your people do without your great city and your little lords."

"Little lords?" Atticus asked.

"He means the Northern Lords," Andreese said, not pulling his eyes off the Kalesh man. Andreese's sword hung loosely by his side, but his knuckles were white on the hilt and his shoulders rose with ragged breaths. He took a step toward the man. "*Pellotchett ketuus purtchotke.*"

Atticus glanced at Andreese. "What did you say?"

Andreese didn't look away from the Kalesh man.

"The Northern Lords still stand," Serene translated. She leaned heavily against the side of the wagon, her palms held out gingerly.

"*Pellotchett purtchotketus ke bellotchik set malla,*" the warrior answered, a grim smile spreading across his face.

"'The Northern Lords stand with collars on their necks.'" Serene glanced at Atticus. "He means they're slaves."

Andreese stepped forward, his voice low as he bit off words in the rough language.

"We will never be slaves," Serene translated Andreese's words, "to cowards who hide under the blanket of night and slaughter women and children."

The warrior's next words rolled out smugly.

"It does not matter how you slaughter cattle," Serene translated.

The Kalesh man let his head fall back and closed his eyes. He began the chant again.

Atticus leaned forward. "How many of you are here?" The man ignored him. "Is there an army coming?"

Serene leaned her head against the side of the wagon. "He's started the same death chant as the other. 'Remember my deeds, the blood spilled, the land cleansed.'"

Atticus sank back.

"We're not going to get anything else out of him," Serene said.

"Shame," Andreese murmured. Without another word, he stepped forward and plunged the Kalesh sword into the man's chest.

CHAPTER THIRTY-NINE

THE PLACE in the red wagon where they'd put Andreese yesterday was still empty, so they made as soft of a bed as they could with some curtains.

At Ryah's request, Purnicious created a mound of dirt over the bodies of the Kalesh, before the troupe started again toward Stonehaven. Serene sat next to Jae, but divided her attention between him and the forest around them, checking for more Kalesh.

"We should try to find their campsite," Andreese said, walking next to the others in between the two wagons.

"We stay together," Atticus said firmly. "Our priority is to get Jae to Stonehaven."

Merilee joined them, staying close to Ryah, watching the woods with wide eyes. She'd replaced her rings on her fingers, clutching her broken necklaces to her chest.

"You should have given him the jewelry right away," Ryah said gently. "I thought he was going to kill you for it."

Merilee shook her head, her face pale. "I can't give them up. They're all I have."

"Your father would give you more," Ryah said. "If you live in a castle, I'm sure he has more necklaces."

315

Merilee's expression sank. "No, he doesn't. My father has ruined us."

Sable and Ryah glanced at each other.

"He's invested everything my family owned and lost it. We still live in the castle, but we've had to sell everything in it. If I can earn enough as an actress, maybe I can save it." She looked at Ryah. "My father does not approve of me mixing with commoners, though."

Sable fought to keep an annoyed look off her face. Ryah did a better job of it.

"But when he sees how much money I can win," Merilee continued, "he'll change his mind." She straightened. "Someone has to do something."

Sable was saved from coming up with an answer by Andreese swearing loudly next to her.

"Walking is going to kill me." He hunched to the side, his feet shuffling and face twisted in pain.

"Attacking someone with a sword didn't help your ribs?" Sable asked, trying to keep her voice light. He scowled at her, but seeing her smile, he managed a very small, rueful smile of his own.

"Thank you for doing it anyway," she said to him. "You saved my sister, and the rest of us."

He gave a non-committal grunt.

"Is there anything I can do to help?" she asked.

He started to shake his head, but paused. "It would help if I could lean on you," he admitted reluctantly.

She ducked under his left arm. He put some of his weight on her shoulders and gave a sigh of relief. With their first step, though, she bumped her shoulder into him. He let out a hiss of pain.

"Sorry!"

They started forward, him grunting whenever she nudged against him. After the third grunt of pain, she bit back a laugh.

"It's not funny," he said through gritted teeth.

"I know. I'm sorry." She glanced up at him. "You really have trained as a fighter, haven't you?"

"Of course I have. Did you think I was lying about the military?"

"You sounded so strange I didn't know what to think."

Leonis, who'd been growing more irritable as the long, hungry day wore on, glanced up at the trees. "How much farther?"

"Not much," Serene answered.

Leonis frowned into the woods.

"There aren't any Kalesh nearby," she said.

Leonis grunted but didn't take his eyes off the trees.

As they walked, Sable glanced at the others. The bit of Jae's face she could see was terrifyingly pale, Andreese grimaced alongside her, and the others trudged in silence.

The day went on and on. When the sun was low in the sky, they rolled into a wide clearing. At the far side, a tall, plain, stone wall surrounded cluster of buildings, snugly grouped together.

"Finally," Andreese said through gritted teeth.

Several paths came out of the woods, meeting by the single gate. The wagons rolled to a stop, and Sable looked through at the little commune. The buildings were made of dark wood with neatly thatched roofs. Serene left Jae and walked to the gate. She lifted her bandaged hand and set her fingers, still bloody, on the gate for a moment, then stepped back and waited.

"Is there no way to knock?" Leonis asked, glancing around uncomfortably at the trees around them. "Do we have to stand out here all day?"

"I did knock," Serene answered coldly.

A stocky woman walked out of one of the larger buildings and strode toward the far side of the gate, peering through it. Her grey robe matched Serene's, except it wasn't splattered with Jae's blood.

"Diann!" Serene called.

"Serene?" the woman said, her voice harsh. "How dare you!"

Serene's eyebrows rose at the greeting.

"Take those wagons and whatever crowd you've brought with you," Diann yelled, "and leave. The gall of you coming here! You broke Merrick's heart, you traitors!"

"What are you talking about?" Serene stepped up to the gate. "Let us in! Jae is—"

"Every one of them gone!" Diann shouted over her. "Every book!"

Serene stared at her. "What?"

"Every book is gone!"

"Gone? Where?"

"What did you tell her?" Diann pointed a finger through the gate at Serene. "How could you?"

Serene stared at her, mouth open. "I have no idea what you're talking about."

"That High Prioress you and Jae cozied up to all winter sent her men to take the books. All of them!"

Serene stood in stunned silence. Then her face darkened, and she took a step closer. The woman's eyes widened slightly, but she didn't back away. "You let them?"

"Let them?" Diann's voice rose. "How were we supposed to stop thirty armed Sanctus guards? Merrick and I were the only ones here. Should we have fought them all? Killed them? Where's Jae?" She turned toward the wagons. "You have a lot to answer for!" she called.

"Where's Merrick?" Serene asked again harshly.

"He went with them. You don't think he'd trust the entire library to a bunch of illiterate guards, do you?"

Serene stared at her. "He's gone?"

"Yes." Diann crossed her arms and glared at Serene. "Gone."

"Let us in. Jae's hurt. Badly."

Diann glanced down at Serene's robe, as if just noticing the blood stains.

"Open the gate." Serene's voice rang sharp with command. She stepped closer. This time, Diann did step back. "It might have kept out thirty Sanctus guards, if you hadn't been stupid enough to open it for them, but you know it won't keep me out."

Diann glared at her, then slammed her hand onto something on the far side of the gate and closed her eyes. There was a clank and the metal shifted slightly before she pulled open the gate. "Get him into the common room."

Serene stalked through, heading for one of the larger buildings. "Thulan! Bring the wagon."

Diann frowned at the rest of them.

"Thank you," Atticus said, bowing to her from the wagon bench. "I'm Atticus."

318

"I know who you are," she said irritably. "Close the gate behind you." She turned and stalked off after Serene.

———

Diann sent everyone but Ryah and Serene away from the common room while they worked on Jae. Two men, not wearing grey robes and seemingly the only people in Stonehaven beside Diann, were shooed out with them.

The buildings of Stonehaven reminded Sable of the town with her parents on the Reaches. Each building had a homey, lived-in feel to it. It was built around a central courtyard, with chickens pecking about and two goats nibbling on grass near the wall. The common room with the kitchen was the largest structure. Several workshops stretched out along one side of the courtyard, and a small row of cabins lined the other.

"There are plenty of bunkhouses," the taller of the two men said, directing them toward the cabins. "Pick any you like and make your-selves at home."

Each bunkhouse had two or three rooms with nothing more than beds, desks, and a few shelves.

Andreese claimed the first one, where he collapsed onto the bed with a groan. In the next cabin, Sable found a room with two beds to share with Ryah.

Atticus came by not too long after, calling everyone to the common room. Sable cast a nervous look into the woods, before following the others into the well-lit room. Several long tables were lined up on the near side. At the other end, comfortable looking chairs clustered near an enormous fireplace. Jae had been moved to the room he and Serene shared, and according to Diann, he was weak, but sleeping.

A dinner of dense, spiced bread and yellow cheese waited. They ate with Diann and the two men who had helped them all find rooms. Diann introduced them as traveling scribes who occasionally visited Stonehaven, and while they didn't participate in the conversation, they listened closely.

When they were all seated, Serene joined them. "Tell us what happened to the books," she said, her voice still holding a dangerous tone.

"They came two days ago," Diann said. "Midmorning, four wagons appeared at the gate with thirty armed Sanctus guards. They told Merrick they were from the Dragon Priory, and of course, he let them in."

"He's too trusting," Serene said.

"Agreed," Diann answered. "Once they were in, they told him they were taking the books to the Dragon Priory where they would be safer than tucked in the woods in a bunch of huts that could burn to the ground at any moment."

Serene frowned. "Burn to the ground? Was that a threat?"

"Obviously," Diann said, "but Merrick refused to see it as such. He told them the books were fine, but when they pushed past him, he did nothing. I locked the library door, of course."

Serene frowned. "The library door doesn't have a lock."

Diann smiled grimly. "I may have heated the hinges until they melted." Her smile faded. "When Merrick realized what I'd done, he did that disapproving cluck he does..." Serene nodded with an annoyed expression, "and had the hinges working before I knew he was trying."

"He unmelted them?" Serene asked. "How?"

"I have no idea. Anyway, he let them open the door and carry out the books. It took hours, and they weren't nearly as gentle as they should have been, but Merrick merely stood by and watched. He saved two books from falling into the dirt, and directed the packing of the wagons.

"You could tell he was furious... Well, the guards didn't notice, but you would have. He covered the books with a blanket and an oil cloth. It wasn't one I'd seen before, so I don't know if he somehow whipped it up then and there."

"How would he possibly whip up an oilcloth?"

"I don't know." Diann shook her head. "You didn't see him. Remember how angry he was the time Tressian took the torch into the library and singed those scrolls above the door?"

Serene grimaced and nodded.

"This was so far beyond that." Diann grew quiet, then continued. "I've never been afraid of Merrick before. I was going to demand he stop them, but when he looked at me... Well, I couldn't say anything."

Diann sighed and looked at Serene. "You had no idea the prioress wanted the books?"

"Yes, she wanted them, but we told her she couldn't have them."

Diann gave her a flat look. "Seems you don't have the sway you thought you did at the priory."

"This makes no sense," Serene said. "The High Prioress has known for decades that we have a library here. Although she has been more interested than normal lately. But wanting the books and sending armed men to steal them are two different things." She sank back. "I can't believe Merrick isn't here."

"We were hoping to talk to him," Atticus said. "We've found some unsettling things on the Eastern Reaches. Towns burned by the Kalesh. And we encountered Kalesh soldiers dressed as raiders who claimed more were coming."

"Kalesh?" Diann stared at them. "The man who led the soldiers was Kalesh. I swear it. His accent was light, but it was there. And I saw a tattoo past the edge of his sleeve. If it wasn't Kalesh lettering, I'm blind."

"A Kalesh man directing priory soldiers?" Serene asked.

"He wasn't officially directing them," Diann said. "There was a captain who did all the talking and ordering, but the Kalesh man was in charge. He's the one who directed the guards inside the library. I told Merrick it was weird, but he didn't answer. Just left with them."

Serene's face was grim. "We need to go after the books."

"We will," Atticus said, "in two weeks."

"No." Serene shook her head. "That is entirely too long to wait."

"It'll take at least that long for Jae to be ready to travel," Diann said. "Even if his healing goes well."

"It'll go well." Serene growled.

Diann gave her a sympathetic look. "Only time will tell."

"Andreese needs to rest, as well," Atticus said. "And we have a play to learn."

Serene slammed her hand onto the table. "Forget the blasted play!

The Kalesh are invading, and the prioress is somehow working with them."

"We can't stay here!" Merilee declared. "Those Kalesh monsters are everywhere! We need to get as far away as we can, as fast as we can."

"Someone should be outside right now," Thulan agreed. "Is there anywhere better than a roof to keep watch from?"

"We don't need a watch. We're perfectly safe in here," Diann told her. "This place has protections of its own that will keep anyone out, in addition to wards that will let us know long before anyone gets near." She turned back to Serene. "And I agree with Atticus. There's no point in rushing off. The books are gone, and even if you caught up with them, what are you going to do against thirty guards?"

Serene flexed her bandaged hands. "I can think of a few things."

"And you know Merrick won't let you do any of them. The books are gone. Let Merrick get to Immusmala and talk to the prioress. He's far more likely to convince her to change her mind than you would be with all your threats."

"We're staying," Atticus said firmly. "We'll eat and get a good night's rest. Tomorrow morning, we start work on the play. If we hope to get the ear of anyone important in Immusmala, we need to win the tourney and earn the right to perform in front of them all."

"No one's going to care about our play if there's an army coming," Sable said.

Atticus shook his head. "No one knows an army is coming but us. Starting rumors among the common folk won't get us taken seriously. We need to get the attention of the priories, the Merchant Guild, and the Northern Lords. If we want any of them to listen to us, we need a platform to speak from. The tourney is the only way I can think of to get that platform."

The thought of armies and leaders felt horribly foreign. But the thought of the Kalesh in Immusmala, swarming down the streets, burning buildings while Talia ran...

Sable drew in a breath. "All right. I'll help with whatever you think will get us the attention of those who can fight back."

Atticus gave her an approving nod. "Tomorrow, we'll use the first and last scenes to have you and Merilee audition for the role of

Vivaine." He glanced around the table. Merilee fixed Sable with a cold look but said nothing. "If we all work at this, I think we can create something powerful." He glanced in the direction of the stables. "We have a lot of work to do on costumes and props."

"I can help with that," Purnicious piped up from next to Sable.

Atticus nodded his thanks, and everyone fell to eating, except Andreese, who sat slumped at the end of the table.

Serene glanced at him. "Diann, could you check his ribs? He bruised them a few days ago. I couldn't help much, but you may be able to. We'll need all the fighters we can get for our trip back."

Andreese looked up hopefully.

"Diann is the best healer I know," Serene told him.

The woman stood and walked around the table, setting her hands on his back. She closed her eyes, then nodded. "I can help."

He blew out a breath. "That is the best news I've ever had."

Sable kept finding herself straining to hear noises from outside. She finished eating and stepped outside, just to assure herself there weren't any. The tops of the trees around the commune were a brilliant green. She tried to absorb the peace of it all, drawing in a deep breath and looking up at the clear sky, but there was too much chaos inside her.

All she'd wanted was to get Talia, grab Ryah, and run away from Kiva. Even as she thought of it, the dream crumbled. If the Kalesh came, there would be nowhere safe to run.

Atticus was right. If they were to have any hope of fighting off a Kalesh army, they'd need the combined strength of the priories, the Merchant Guild, and the troops from the Northern Lords. They'd most likely need every farmer and every merchant in every town.

It would be impossible to unite all of them, though. Gaining the ear of the important people in Immusmala and the north was a start, but to stand against something as powerful as the Kalesh, they'd need to be unified.

Sable turned her face up to the sky. It was a rich blue, utterly unruffled by whatever tumult was happening with armies and invasions.

Who was possibly powerful to unite the entire land? The High Prioress?

A wave of exhaustion from the last few days settled over her, but she took a deep breath. She needed to run over Vivaine's lines again. There was no way they would win the tourney with Merilee as the first lady. There was a decent chance they wouldn't win it with Sable, either, but if that was the only way she could help, she'd give Atticus the best Vivaine he could imagine.

Serene came out the door behind her.

Sable dropped her gaze to the wall. "Since that wall is the only thing made of stone, I assume it's where Stonehaven got its name? Because I have to say, I expected a place with 'haven' in its name to feel...safer."

Serene gave a little huff. "Stonehaven is safer than anywhere I can think of."

The wall wasn't more than twice Sable's height and wasn't particularly thick. The rocks were uneven and rough. It looked more like an oversized sheep pen than a wall of protection. She imagined groups of Kalesh warriors gathering outside, and wrapped her arms around her body.

"It's stronger than it looks," said Serene. "And unscalable."

Sable let out a short laugh. "I could scale it easily."

The side of Serene's mouth curved up into the first smile Sable had seen since Jae had been hurt. "When we were younger, Jae, I, and some others used to play a game where we would try to get over the wall." She shrugged. "It's impossible. If you try to climb it, no matter how good the handholds are, you will slip off. If you set a ladder against the wall, it...won't work."

Sable raised an eyebrow. "How does a ladder not work?"

"Differently every time. It might shift to the side and fall while you're climbing. The bottom might slide out, no matter how deeply you set it in the ground. It might just snap in two when you're halfway up." She shook her head. "It doesn't matter what you try. You cannot get over the wall."

Sable looked at the unassuming barrier.

"It's the same if you try to shoot over it. The arrows all miss."

"They miss something this big?" Sable gestured around her.

Serene chuckled. "A wind will come up. The bow will twist funny.

You'll twist funny." She shook her head. "It doesn't matter what you do. You cannot get anything over the wall."

"How is that possible?"

"Merrick. He knows more about moving and storing energy than anyone I've ever heard of. He built Stonehaven over fifty years ago. In the early days, there was a colony of goblins that lived between here and the cliffs, and no matter what Merrick did, he couldn't keep them out of his garden. So he started to put wards on the wall.

"Merrick moves energy, but he happily calls it magic. He always says magic is like a story. It can be simple and to the point, or it can have layers that grow the story into something more than its individual pieces."

Serene gesture to the wall. "That is one of Merrick's stories. He began by making the stones hard to climb. Over the years, he wove in different ideas. In the process, they all started working together. Now, the entire wall works together to be impenetrable."

Sable stared at the wall. "We should hire him to protect Immusmala."

"If he had fifty years to do it, maybe he could."

Serene turned and faced a large, steeply roofed building. Sable followed her gaze.

"The library?" she asked.

Serene's mouth was set in a thin, angry line. "I don't think it's called a library if there are no books in it."

"There are none left at all?"

Serene glared at the building. "Let's go see."

She strode across the grass, Sable following. Her hands were newly bandaged, so she pushed open the tall, wooden door with her elbow. The interior was dim, Serene's footsteps echoing.

She set one finger on the wick of a candle next to the door, and it flamed to life. Serene let out a small grunt of pain and picked up the candle gently. The light illuminated a wide room with tables in the center, walls lined with shadowed, empty shelves.

Sable stood, stunned. There were dozens of shelves, taller than she was, set one next to the other the whole way around the room. Shorter shelves jutted out toward the tables. There was even a small, spiral staircase that rose to a walkway that circled the room, with more shelves.

The candle in Serene's hand trembled. Her back was to Sable, but the woman's whole body quivered. She turned slowly, her gaze raking the empty shelves.

"That ambassador," she hissed. "This was him. The books were his idea. He's the one who brought them up. It was the prioress who demanded we bring them to her, but the ambassador started it all."

"Why would he do that?" Sable asked, then the truth struck her. "He knows the Kalesh are here."

Serene turned toward her, the horrible truth on her face, too.

"They are going to burn Stonehaven down, aren't they?" Sable whispered.

The candle stilled in Serene's hand. "I'd love to see them try."

CHAPTER FORTY

SERENE LEFT THE LIBRARY, heading back to check on Jae, and Sable went to her room, running over Vivaine's lines. None of them were hard, but the pressure from her first night as Lady Argent was back. She couldn't lose the role to Merilee tomorrow.

It was more than just the money. The people of Immusmala would hate any portrayal of their beloved High Prioress by someone as bossy and domineering as Merilee.

But then, of course, there was the money.

She said the lines from the first and last scenes to herself twice, but the more she thought about the audition, the more stilted the words sounded. She finally fell back onto the soft bed with a groan. Ryah came in and dropped onto her own bed, reporting that Jae had woken enough to talk for a few minutes.

It had grown dark outside, and the exhaustion of the past two days caught up to Sable. Her eyes slid shut.

She ran through a wide valley, flames beginning to singe the ridges around her. Someone grabbed her arm.

She jerked awake to find the room pitch black, Thulan leaning over her.

"Quiet," whispered Thulan. "Ryah's asleep."

"What's wrong?" Sable demanded in a whisper, heart pounding. She strained to hear the sounds of an attack. The window was cracked, a light breeze blowing in, but there was no noise from outside.

Thulan motioned for her to follow and slipped out the door. Sable scrambled out of bed and pulled her boots on. She stepped out into the courtyard, her eyes straining to see in the darkness.

Sable grabbed Thulan's arm. "What's wrong?"

The dwarf held up her copy of the play. "Auditions are in the morning. Merilee's been practicing. You need to work on your lines."

Sable stared at her, blinking, then looked around the pitch-black courtyard. "What time is it?"

"Time for you to practice." Thulan started toward the common room where a dim light spilled through the windows. Sable looked after her for just a moment before hurrying to catch up.

"You woke me up in the middle of the night so we could rehearse? I already know the lines."

Thulan pushed open the door and walked in. A single candle sat on one of the long tables next to a crate.

"Sit," Thulan pointed at a bench and set the papers on the table. "If you want to win, you need to do more than say the right words. It shouldn't take long."

Sable sank down on the bench, not bothering to stifle a yawn. "Why are we doing this in the middle of the night?"

Thulan pulled a battered, short sword out of the crate. The silver paint on the wooden blade was chipping off, and worn leather wrapped around the handle. "We'll get a better sword before the play." She held it out.

It felt awkward in Sable's hand. "What do I do with this?"

Thulan turned back to the script. "Just hold it. Atticus will fix your motions later. You're not auditioning for your sword skills, but it'll help to have something in your hand." She began reading the final scene, Vivaine pleads with Balin to stop killing.

Sable closed her eyes and listened. Thulan read the words with rich, deep emotion, and Sable found herself desperately hoping Balin would listen.

"You should audition," Sable said when Thulan finished.

The dwarf flicked her fingers through her beard. "Because Prioress Vivaine is known for her nicely kept beard?"

Sable smiled. "I suppose shaving it is out of the question."

Thulan gave her a flat look. "That's not funny. Stand up and tell me the lines."

Sable repeated Vivaine's lines, but they felt stiff and awkward. Thulan gave her pointers of where to stand and suggested suitable gestures, but none of it felt natural.

"That'll have to do," Thulan said, unenthusiastically. "Atticus knows you can do Lady Argent. Maybe that will be enough."

"I hope so. I feel as awkward as I did during my very first play." Sable sank down onto a bench, setting the sword on the table. "You still haven't explained why we're doing this in the middle of the night."

"I'm not quite heartless enough to help you when Merilee might see us." Thulan dropped the sword back into the crate. "But if the Dragon Prioress sees Merilee attempting to portray her, she'll kill us without waiting to find out what the play is about."

"Then why is Atticus even letting her audition?"

"Because he's eternally hopeful that people will be better than they are. And Merilee brings with her a lot of wealthy nobles, which is exactly the sort of audience we need." She picked up the crate and started out of the common room. "Don't lose tomorrow."

Sable watched her go, then blew out the candle and headed back to bed. Ryah was still, and Sable fell into bed. She closed her eyes, Vivaine's lines circling in her head over an unsettling pool of nervous energy.

A sharp whisper woke her. Leonis's silhouette was outlined against the dim grey of the window. "Wake up, Sneaks," he whispered. "I can read you Vivaine's lines."

Ryah sat up and blinked at Leonis.

Sable gave her an apologetic look and moved closer to the window. "Thulan already did," she whispered.

Leonis made an annoyed sound. "She made them overly dramatic and feminine, didn't she?"

"She read them so well I wanted her to be Vivaine," Sable answered with a yawn. "And Vivaine is a woman, so feminine works."

"Do you remember them?"

"Yes."

"Say them to me."

"Leonis, I know the lines. Go away and let us sleep."

"You realize we only get paid if people like the show. No one's going to pay us if they have to sit through Merilee playing the High Prioress."

"Except she brings bigger, wealthier crowds," Sable pointed out, "so that's the chance for more money."

He paused, grimacing. "I really don't want to work with her anymore, and all of Balin's scenes are with her."

Ryah let out a little laugh.

Sable lay down and pulled the blanket back up to her neck. "Go to sleep, Leonis."

He sighed. "Just don't be stiff and awkward." He disappeared from the window.

Sable groaned. "I don't know if I should be flattered by everyone's willingness to help or insulted no one thinks I can do it on my own."

"I feel a little bad for Merilee," Ryah said sleepily.

"So do I," Sable answered. "But not bad enough to let her have the part."

It felt like only a moment later when a quiet pop sounded in the room, waking Sable again. Outside the window, the sky was greyish blue, so dawn must be close. Her eyes felt gritty, and she nestled deeper under the blanket.

"Mistress?" Purnicious whispered.

Sable cracked open one eye. "Good morning, Purnicious."

The kobold stood next to her bed, her black hair curling wild in all directions. She still wore the sage green dress she'd worn when Sable had first found her. All the tears and stains had disappeared, and the buttery yellow fabric that peeked out at the end of her sleeves was clean and soft. There was a good chance the kobold was better dressed than anyone else in the troupe.

"Where did you sleep?" Sable asked, lifting her head a bit. "You could have slept in here. I didn't even think…" She rubbed her face. "I keep forgetting about the mistress thing."

"Diann gave me my own room," Purnicious said with a nervous smile. "I slept wonderfully. I'm sorry to wake you so early in the morning, but the wastrel requests an audience."

Sable blinked at her. "Andreese?"

Purn cast a disapproving frown at the door. "He says he needs to speak with you. When I told him you were sleeping, he said it wasn't my place to decide whether you wanted to speak to him and he would start banging on the door if I didn't ask you." Her lips pursed in irritation. "Tell me you don't want to see him, so I can make him go away."

"By 'make him go away,'" Sable said, closing her eyes again, "I hope you mean shoo him away, not shrink him down to something tiny."

Purnicious was quiet for a moment. "I would try the shooing first."

Sable laughed. "Where is he?"

"Loitering outside like a vagabond."

"Tell him I'll be out shortly, and that it's stupid to be up this early."

"Yes, mistress." There was a little *pop* and the room fell silent again.

"I shared a room with three other girls at the abbey," Ryah mumbled sleepily from her bed, "and there was never this much activity. I had no idea you were this popular."

"Neither did I." Sable stood and pulled on her boots.

She stepped out into the dim, grey morning, still rubbing the sleep from her eyes, and found Andreese striding across the courtyard, swinging one of the Kalesh swords. He looked different, and she stared at him for a minute before she realized why. He wasn't hunched over.

She walked over to him. "You look better this morning."

He glanced at her, his gaze lingering on her head. "You don't."

She ran her hands over her hair. Her braid was loose and messy.

"You wake someone up before the sun, this is what you get." She gestured to his ribs. "Diann helped you?"

He smiled. "I love that woman." He swung the Kalesh sword with his right hand. "My ribs are tender, but I can finally move and breathe without horrible pain."

"Two useful things." Sable looked at the sword. "Why are you swinging that around?"

"It's for you." He held it out to her.

She drew back. "I don't know how to use it."

"I know. That's why I'm going to teach you."

"Why? So I can fight the Kalesh?"

"I'm not teaching you to fight," he said in an annoyed tone. "I'm teaching you how to hold the sword for your audition. Vivaine is supposed to know something about using a sword." He held it out to her again.

She took it, her fingers curling unwillingly around the leather-wrapped hilt. "Is this the sword that cut Jae?"

Andreese paused and looked at the blade. "I cleaned all four Kalesh swords that we picked up. I don't know which was which. But it doesn't matter. The man who wielded it is gone. That's just a piece of metal. And you're holding it like it's a bouquet of flowers."

"I'm holding the handle," Sable protested.

"You're holding it wrong. This is a sword. It needs freedom to move." He repositioned her fingers to a more slanting grip. "Don't grip it so hard. It's not trying to get away from you. Your hands are small, but the grip on this style isn't particularly large. With some practice, you'll be fine."

Andreese made another small adjustment to her hand, then taught her a simple swing.

"You know I don't have to swing this at anyone in the play," she said. "When I stab Balin at the end, it's almost an accident."

He frowned at her. "Vivaine is supposed to know something about swordwork."

"Yes, but she also knows about healing, and I don't need any of that to perform the play."

He sighed and crossed his arms. "In Immusmala, there will be several delegations from the Northern Lords who'll attend the plays. You have two different speeches where you are alone with nothing but that sword. If you stand there, holding it like a hammer and staring at it, they're going to be so annoyed they'll leave."

She studied him for a moment. He'd obviously bathed. There was no sign of blood in his hair or beard any longer. Now that he stood up straight, he was quite a bit taller than she was. Besides the exasperation of his last comment, his face was as pleasant as when he drank the wartroot tea, but with a less vacant look in his eyes.

"Why do you care if I get the part?" Sable asked.

He paused. "I don't know any of you well, but unless Merilee's acting is more pleasant than her normal demeanor, her version of the High Prioress is going to be awful."

"Maybe mine will be as bad."

He shook his head. "You're more..." He looked at her thoughtfully. "You're more likable." He gave her an apologetic smile. "Even if someone's not particularly pleasant to you. Just because they're in pain, of course."

She raised an eyebrow. "You obviously couldn't hear the things I was thinking about you." The sword felt heavy in her hand. "And that doesn't explain why you care about our play."

A glint of the anger she'd seen toward the Kalesh crept back into his expression. "It was the Kalesh who came to your town when you were younger, wasn't it?"

Her hand tightened on the hilt. "Apparently."

He clenched his jaw and looked into the distance. "No one realizes what they're really like. And Atticus is right. Using the Midsommer tourney as a way to get an influential audience is brilliant. If you don't win, it'll take weeks, maybe months, to travel to each of the Northern Lords we should talk to. And that doesn't include all the people in Immusmala that will need to be convinced that the Kalesh are coming." He shook his head. "If this play doesn't win, we can't warn people in time, and we'll be unprepared when the Kalesh come."

The truth of his words wrapped around her. She took a deep breath and held up the sword. "What am I supposed to do with this?"

"I'll teach you a few simple practice movements. They're easy to learn, and with a few tips, they'll look natural. You can swing it while you talk. That'll convince anyone in the crowd that you know enough about swords to play a woman who would."

Following his directions, she held the sword out and slashed downward.

He repositioned her arm. "Or they'll be convinced if it's a dark night with enough glittering distractions on the stage."

"Good to know your expectations are low."

He smiled. "Let's run through it again."

They did. Again and again. Sable's shoulder and fingers ached before the sun even cleared the trees. When her motions grew sloppy, Andreese took the sword.

"I'd rather not get wounded again just when I'm starting to feel better. At least you are holding it right. That'll have to be enough for the audition."

She shook out her hand and stretched her shoulder. "You've done this before, haven't you?"

"Been in a show?" He let out a sharp laugh. "No. I've never been one for plays."

"I meant you've trained people before."

He glanced at her, then back at the sword and nodded. "I used to train the new soldiers." Andreese was silent for a long moment before continuing. "I wanted to be a soldier my entire life. My uncle Trefor is a captain in Lord Runess' military units in the north. When I was eight, I spent the summer in the barracks, and from that point on, there was nothing I wanted to do more. The idea of being part of the defense that kept towns and cities safe sounded so heroic I couldn't wait to become a part of it."

He stopped. "My parents died when I was twelve, and my aunt in Ebenmoor took me in until I turned eighteen and could join Uncle Trefor's troops. His training put me ahead of the other new soldiers, and I was promoted quickly.

"But I began to notice that the heroic ideas I had of the military were far from reality. Lord Runess was merely trying to expand his holdings, like every other lord around us. The skirmishes we fought in, skirmishes good men died in, were nothing but attempts to grab land from our neighbors."

He blew out a breath. "Not only was there nothing heroic in any of it, there wasn't even anything honorable. When they won, the captains were rewarded with land and money. The entire system was corrupt... including my uncle."

The story had a sickening familiarity. "They sound like the gang bosses in Immusmala."

"That's exactly what they're like. Greedy children fighting over anything they think is valuable. I told my uncle how I felt, and he told me I needed to grow up and understand how the world worked. There was a Kalesh merchant who came through every once in a while, and my uncle, always curious about the Empire, had befriended him." Andreese kept his eye on his sword. "After I started voicing my frustration, he paid the merchant to take me to the Empire to be educated in a Kalesh school."

Sable stared at him. "You've been to the Kalesh Empire?"

He nodded. "They've taken dozens of lands, so plenty of foreigners are taught in their schools. I was so sick of the way things were with my uncle, I went gladly."

The unimaginable distance he must have traveled stunned her. "That's so far away."

He sighed. "I didn't even go very deep into the Empire. I was enrolled in a school in a small city at the western edge. They taught military strategy and history." He glanced at her. "The Empire is practically unstoppable, Sable. The only thing that's kept them from targeting this part of the world is that we're too small and too far away to be worth the effort."

"This explains how you speak Kalesh." She paused, her mind running back to the night her parents had faced the raiders. "Do you know many other people who do?"

Reese shook his head. "I've never known anyone who could before I met Serene and Jae. No one in this part of the world knows much about the Kalesh Empire. Not the important things, anyway."

She nodded. If the raiders had been from the Empire, then her parents had spoken Kalesh. The number of questions that fact raised was unsettling.

Reese gave the sword an irritated flick with his wrist. "The true Kalesh, the original people of the Empire, are the ruling class and rarely lower themselves to interact with those they think are beneath them. As far as they were concerned, I was a foreign barbarian. My time there was...unpleasant."

There was the taint of loneliness in his voice, though he kept his expression neutral.

"I wrote my uncle more than once asking him to send money so I could come home, but he told me to stay and learn more." Andreese let out a frustrated breath. "Finally, I got a job guarding a wealthy family and earned enough to pay my own way home. I returned to my uncle two years ago and tried to tell him the truth about the Empire, only to find that he had already hired two Kalesh advisors."

Sable frowned. "Did he listen to you?"

"No. I told him what they were like, what they did to countries around them. When I objected—strongly—to him hiring the Kalesh, he got so angry he kicked me out."

"So your uncle isn't going to be excited to hear what you have to say."

"No. But we need to make him listen. We need to make sure everyone listens, or we don't stand a chance." He looked toward the south. "My biggest worry is that if an invasion is coming, the Kalesh have already prepared us for it."

"How?"

"They'll weaken the economy, infiltrate governments, even embed themselves in the military. There is a story of a wealthy nation that had grown so reliant on the Kalesh that when the army appeared, the country surrendered on the spot."

"Why would anyone let them in?" Sable asked.

"Because they start with overtures that look peaceful. Who wouldn't want to build a relationship with the enormous Empire next door?"

Sable looked out the gate into the forest. "Are they doing that here?"

Andreese shrugged. "Did you see a lot of Kalesh in Immusmala?"

"Not where I lived, but the Kalesh don't care about Dockside." Sable thought of Lady Ingred's dress in Lord Renwen's office. "The wealthy do find Kalesh styles fashionable, though."

Andreese frowned. "Let's hope that's all it is."

CHAPTER FORTY-ONE

DIANN CALLED from the dining building that breakfast was ready.

"Thanks for your help this morning." Sable said to Andreese, glancing toward Merilee's sleeping quarters and feeling a fleeting pity for the woman no one wanted to win. The feeling was tempered by a surprising thought.

Sable wanted the role of first lady.

The more she thought about the lines, the importance of the show, and the threat of the Kalesh, the more she wanted to play Vivaine. To have the chance to do it right. So if by acting, she could convince people to listen... It wasn't fighting, but it was something.

No more cowering.

Andreese held the Kalesh sword out and she reached for it, but caught sight of Serene walking toward the common room. Sable dropped her hand. "I'll use the prop sword this morning. Until Jae gets better, Serene might not be able to see that one as just a piece of metal."

After breakfast, Atticus stood near the fireplace in the common room. "Merilee and Sable, I'd like to hear lines from the opening and closing of the play," he announced. "Leonis will play Balin, and anyone who would like to voice their opinion on the role of first lady may stay and watch." He smiled broadly. "I can't guarantee I will take your opinions into account, but you are free to voice them."

Serene moved down the bench until she sat next to Sable. "Have you found a way to relate to Vivaine the way you did with Argent?" she asked quietly.

Sable paused, a piece of bread half-raised to her mouth. "I don't know. There's something about how Vivaine can see that everything is wrong, but she's powerless to stop it. First with Balin leaving, then with him changing, then finally with being unable to stop him."

Serene nodded. "What are you powerless against?"

"Too many things to think about."

"If you don't think about them, they can't motivate you."

"All right," Sable said. "Most recently? I'm powerless against the Kalesh. Every time I think of them, I'm a child again, cowering in the cellar. Like how I was powerless to help Jae." She set the bread onto her plate. "When we start traveling again, I'll be useless if the Kalesh attack, and once we get back to Immusmala, all I'm doing is walking back into a world that is completely controlled by Kiva. A world I was willing to do anything to escape from."

The past few days had been so full of Kalesh, she hadn't even thought about how Talia was working for Lady Ingred. Maybe already discovered as a spy.

"Good," Serene said quietly. "That's the sort of fears you should feel as Vivaine." Her face was drawn, dark shadows under her eyes.

Sable hesitated . "Is Jae…?"

Serene's shoulders dropped. When she spoke, there was a worry in her voice Sable hadn't heard before. "He's weak. Our two-minute conversation exhausted him and he fell asleep in the middle of my explanation about how, heroically, I saved him."

"How ungrateful."

"Lady Merilee," Atticus said loudly, drawing everyone's attention.

"Would you start us off?" He bowed to her, and she stepped up to the fireplace.

Leonis joined her, and the two began. Merilee didn't bother to hold a sword, launching into the first handful of Vivaine's lines with a haughty gusto. The heartfelt conversation about the future with Balin was tainted by Merilee's accusing tone, and Leonis, in response, grew shorter in his replies.

They shifted to the final scene where Merilee strode toward the baledin, demanding he stop killing. Any nuance of Atticus's telling disappeared as Merilee attempted to verbally pound her points into Leonis. She checked the script before reading the final lines, her requests for Balin to stop sounding more like a command than a plea. And when Leonis fell, stabbed by an invisible sword, she stood over him triumphantly.

An awkward silence fell. Merilee looked over the room, frowning at the lack of applause.

Atticus stood. "Thank you, Lady Merilee. Sable? If you're ready."

Sable stood and brushed breadcrumbs off her shirt. Andreese pulled the prop sword out of a crate, and Sable walked over to take it. She held the hilt, feeling suddenly nervous.

He looked pointedly at her hand. "I hope you remember your lines better than you remember that."

Sable shifted the sword to grip it how he'd shown her.

He nodded and added in a whisper, "And I hope your version of Vivaine isn't quite so mean."

She turned to join Leonis. He took up a position near the fire, and she stood next to him, the tip of the sword trembling slightly. The weight of all the eyes on her chased away her first line.

The sword… She was supposed to say something about the sword.

The silence stretched until Thulan called, "It's beautiful."

Merilee let out a derisive snort, but Sable shot Thulan a grateful look. She turned back toward the fire, holding the flaking wooden sword toward it.

"It's beautiful," she began, imagining the sort of blade that would buy a young couple their own home. "The wood feels warm."

Leonis played Balin's part with a mixture of anticipation and

340

regret, and Sable felt the inevitability of his leaving grow. The power-lessness she had felt since her conversation with Serene flowed into the words. She tried to give Balin the space to follow his dream, but the weight of it all pulled at her.

They finished the first scene and began the final one. After the hope Sable had tried to stir in herself at the beginning, the idea of Balin as the tainted, hollow baledin took her breath away. What if, after every-thing, this was what Talia had become? What if she was never discov-ered? What if she loved spying on Ingred? What if all of this turned her into a dishonest, predatory person?

Sable pleaded with Balin to change, tried to get him to listen, but the more he refused, the more Sable's worry for Talia grew. When the sword pressed against Leonis's stomach, she sank to her knees beside him, horrified. Leonis grabbed the blade and cried out, and Sable could imagine his life being dragged away into the sword.

"Slow it down!" Sable cried. "You have to slow it down!"

Balin looked at her, his expression moving from stunned to an accusing betrayal.

"I didn't want to do it," he whispered. "You left me. I never wanted to do it."

There were no more words in the play, but his words caught at Sable. "I didn't—" she began, shaking her head, searching for some-thing to say.

Leonis cried out and collapsed onto the stage.

Sable pressed her eyes shut, telling herself Talia was fine.

The common room was silent for a moment before bursting into applause. Sable blinked up at them. Leonis sat up and grinned at her. She rubbed her face, trying to scrub away the last of the horror she'd felt.

Merilee sat at the far side of the table, her arms crossed, eyes shooting daggers at everyone clapping.

Sable moved back to her seat next to Serene.

"That was excellent," Serene said quietly.

Atticus stood and held his hand up for silence. "No matter how talented the actress," he began with a bow to both Sable and Merilee, "some are more suited to certain roles. I think Sable suits the role of Prioress Vivaine perfectly."

"What?" Merilee demanded. "She played the prioress as a sniveling, spineless woman who let Balin do whatever he wanted!"

Sable turned to stare at her. "Sniveling?"

"She played a woman who was emotionally connected to Balin and rightly troubled—" Thulan began.

"She played," Atticus broke in, "the version of Prioress Vivaine that I had envisioned. Lady Merilee, the role of Lavelle, the handmaiden, is also essential to the story and—"

"I am not playing the role of a handmaiden to a...a..." Merilee gestured at Sable with an outraged expression. "A commoner! Having a hand-me-down kobold doesn't make her special."

"Leave Purnicious out of this," Sable said.

"You do realize everyone here but you is a commoner?" Leonis said.

"Which is why I should be first lady." Merilee straightened. "Atticus, I insist."

"I'm sorry," he said mildly. "Sable will play first lady, and you can make the role of Lavelle memorable."

Merilee fixed Atticus with a haughty look. "I am not playing the handmaiden."

He looked at her for a long moment. "Then I have no role for you in this play."

Her mouth fell open and she flung a finger at Sable. "Ever since she came, you have acted like an old fool. If you leave this play in her hands, you will doom the entire troupe. She may have performed a passable Lady Argent, but she will bring such weakness to Prioress Vivaine's character that your reputation will never recover."

Sable straightened, and Ryah gave an indignant huff.

Atticus raised an eyebrow. "Sable plays the best Lady Argent I've ever worked with. And even if I am the oldest, most foolish leader of a troupe in all the known lands, I am still the leader. Sable has won the role of Vivaine fairly. If you would like the role of Lavelle, it is yours. If not, I'm afraid I don't have another female role."

"You also don't have another female," Merilee pointed out. "Are you going to have an invisible handmaiden?"

"Ryah could play the part," Thulan said.

Ryah turned to look a the dwarf with wide eyes.

"She," Thulan continued to Atticus, not giving Merilee the chance to argue, "would not even have to act. Everyone who's met Ryah knows she's kind, gentle, and brave enough to follow the woman she loved, even if she thought it dangerous."

Ryah shot Sable a shocked look.

Atticus turned a thoughtful look on Ryah. "You are very much like Lavelle."

Ryah, eyes still wide, sank down a little in her seat. "I've never acted."

"That won't deter Atticus," Merilee snorted.

"I think it's a fantastic idea," Leonis said. "She and Sneaks are close. It's perfect, natural. I vote for Ryah as handmaiden."

"As do I," Thulan said.

"I do, too." Sable smiled at her sister.

"I think it's a good idea," Serene said.

Merilee stood. "Atticus, you can't let these two useless women destroy the show."

"Alas," Atticus said, "you rejected the role, so we'll have to use whatever we can. Ryah, if you so wish, the part of Lavelle is yours."

Ryah glanced at Merilee, then back to Atticus. "I'll—I'll try."

He smiled broadly. "Excellent. Let's pull the table back to give ourselves more room, and get to work."

Merilee stared at him, aghast. "Atticus, you need me. I bring audiences to you that you won't find on your own."

"I agree," he answered. "Come with us and help us gain the attention we need."

"When you've thrown me out like a common wretch? You need me, Atticus."

He ran his fingers through his beard with a sigh. "It turns out I do not. If you are not interested in helping us further, please clear the room so we can begin our practice. You're welcome to travel back to Immusmala with us, of course, but we aren't heading back north toward your home. And I'm afraid I have no jobs left for you."

CHAPTER FORTY-TWO

LADY MERILEE STORMED out of the common room and Atticus, after a moments silence, set the practicing for the play into full swing. Much to Ryah's surprise, Thulan offered to work with her on the handmaiden's lines, and Leonis and Sable spent hours together rehearsing.

Early the next morning, before the sun had completely risen, Sable woke to hear Merilee's sharp voice outside, followed by a calm response from Atticus. Sable rolled out of bed enough to peak out the window and see Merilee climb up on a wagon with the two traveling scribes, and disappear out the gate.

The day was filled with more rehearsals. At dinner Jae was able to come sit with them. He was weak and terribly pale, leaning heavily on Serene's arm when he walked, but for the few minutes he was able to stay, he joined in the conversation cheerfully. As soon as he began looking tired, Serene escorted him back to bed.

Every morning, Andreese went out hunting. He'd bring back small game that Diann would serve for dinner. In the evenings, when Sable was exhausted, far more so than she felt she should be from a day of rehearsing, Andreese would find her and hand her the Kalesh sword he'd taken to wearing all the time.

He was set on her learning a combination of swings, which he called the first movement. When she pointed out that something called a movement should only involve a single action, not a series of thrusts and parries, he pointed out that she still looked ridiculous and this was as important as the rest of the rehearsal.

The third morning, Sable was crossing the courtyard when he walked through the gate, two wild turkeys slung over his shoulder. He pulled the gate closed and took a grey rock out of his pocket. When he touched it to the side of the gate, a low *clang* emanated from the metal.

"What's that?" Sable asked.

He shrugged. "Diann calls it a key. It unlocks and locks the gate."

She peered through the gate behind him. "Aren't you nervous you'll run into Kalesh in the woods? Or that they'll follow you back?"

He gave her an insulted look. "I'm hunting. If I'm quiet enough that the animals don't know I'm there, the Kalesh certainly aren't going to." He glanced out the gate. "Although I expected to see signs of them, I haven't."

"Did you find the campsite of the ones who attacked us?"

He shook his head. "I haven't gone that far south."

"Well, I'm glad you're back. It makes me nervous that you go out alone every day."

He raised an eyebrow. "What do you think I'm doing out there? Sauntering through the woods singing a little song, stumbling into Kalesh camps without knowing it?"

Sable smiled. "I hadn't imagined you singing. Until now." She glanced through the gate again. "Do you think Merilee made it away safely?"

He shrugged. "I followed the road they took and saw no sign of trouble."

"When did you do that?"

"The day she left." He frowned. "I would have gone with them as far as the edge of the forest if I'd known they were leaving."

Sable considered him for a moment. "You actually might be as noble as Merilee hoped you were."

Andreese shifted the turkeys on his shoulder. "I don't think that's the sort of nobility she was looking for."

It occurred to her that the only weapon she could see on him was the Kalesh sword. "How are you hunting without a bow?"

"Diann let me borrow a knife."

Sable raised her eyebrows. "You are getting close enough to kill things with a knife?"

"A thrown knife, yes." He headed toward the kitchen.

"If you're not rehearsing, we should work on the first movement again. You're still botching the third parry."

Sable groaned. The movement made her shoulder ache. "I'm afraid I can't do that, Andreese. I need to find Purnicious so we can discuss costumes."

"This evening then," he said over his shoulder. "And it's Reese. I haven't been called Andreese since I was a captain."

"That must be where you learned to be so bossy." He didn't answer. "I'm definitely going to be too tired to practice this evening."

"Not for something this important," he said, pushing open the kitchen door.

"It's not important, captain," she called after him, but the kitchen door swung closed.

She rotated her arm, her shoulder still aching from last night's work. Unfortunately, Atticus agreed with Andreese about the importance, so there probably wasn't any way out of it.

Sable found Purnicious near the wagons, fixing a tear in a curtain. The kobold had cheerfully fixed anything she found damaged, including tidying up the wood on Atticus's wagon. She'd restored any wood she'd found nicked or damaged, and had even carved the image of an actor, who looked remarkably like Atticus, onto a panel next to the back door.

"You always make everything better than it was before." Sable ran her hands over the carvings. "That's quite a gift."

Purnicious beamed at her. "There's always so much room for improvement." Her smile faded when she looked back at the black curtain in her hand. "Atticus made me promise to leave the curtains plain. Which is a shame. There's so much room here for bellishing."

"It would defeat the idea of black curtains if they distracted the audience from the play."

346

"I know." Purnicious sighed. She glanced into the courtyard, then flipped the seam over with a little grin. At the very bottom edge along the back ran a beautiful pattern of light green threads. "They'll be hidden under the hem when I'm done, but it makes me happier knowing it's there."

Sable grinned. "Me, too. Atticus hoped you could come discuss costumes with him."

"Finally!" Purnicious jumped down from the wagon. "I have so many ideas!"

Each day, Sable grew more and more comfortable with Vivaine's lines. Throughout the entire play, the woman struggled against things she couldn't change, wrestling with how responsible she was for the actions of Balin, and what part of the events were her own fault. Sable found herself relating to the woman far more deeply than she'd expected.

The first day they practiced in costume, Atticus pulled out Vivaine's plain, leather traveling vest to find gauzy fuchsia sleeves sewn on to it. "What is this?"

"I thought it needed some color." Purnicious sat on the middle of the long table, popping the last of a bowl of little green mushrooms into her mouth.

"No," Atticus said firmly. "No color. These are supposed to be neutral, practical traveling clothes. Take it off."

"But—," Purnicious started.

"Off!" Atticus tossed the vest to her. "And do it quickly. I want Sable dressed in that as soon as Leonis is ready."

The little kobold sighed and ran her fingers along the seam. The purple sleeves fell away.

The days began to pass quickly. Jae gradually grew stronger. Serene, who'd been terrifyingly intense when he'd first been hurt, grew less severe as he was able to join in their daily activities. When Sable arrived for lunch and found him sitting by himself in front of the fire, she sat next to him, giving voice to a question that had been circling her mind.

"Every time anyone brings up the Kalesh Ambassador," Sable said, "Serene gets angry. But you know him. Is he like the warriors? Is he…frightening?"

Jae shook his head. "He's a quiet man, but nice. He spent a good amount of time with the High Prioress over the winter. Serene and I spoke to him a few times to learn more about the Kalesh Empire." He frowned and gazed into the fire. "He talked to us easily, but in light of what we've seen, I realize he told us very little of substance. He talked about their music and stories, the way their emperor is revered and kept separate from the people. He talked about how the government is mostly run by the military and that they're experiencing a period of peace with their neighbors."

"Is there always a Kalesh Ambassador at the priories in Immusmala?"

"On and off. This one, Ambassador Tehl, arrived almost a year ago, saying that while Immusmala was far from Kalesh lands, they wanted to extend a hand of friendship."

"I wouldn't call what happened in Ebenmoor friendship."

Serene and Andreese came in to the room. Andreese took a chair near Sable, and Serene, after fussing a bit over Jae, sat close to him.

"Neither would I," Jae said. "Immusmala doesn't consider the Eastern Reaches much more than small, irrelevant towns, but I can't imagine the High Prioress would be unconcerned with the Kalesh destruction there. And if the Kalesh are a threat, Immusmala will be hard-pressed to protect itself."

"If we can talk to her," Sable asked, "will she listen?"

Jae paused. "I think so. She's a reasonable woman, and she cares deeply about the people."

"She cares deeply about her own power anyway," Serene said. "And hiring the Mira so she's surrounded with magical people."

"Who are the Mira?" Andreese asked.

"Women who have abilities similar to Serene and I," Jae said. "But they work for the priories."

"Vivaine hires them?" Sable asked.

"That's how the priories get the Mira and the Vena Sancta guards, which are their male counterparts," Jae said. "If anyone in the city develops a talent for magic, the priories offer them free room and board, free clothing, and free influence for life."

Sable frowned. "I thought the Mira were found by the goddess."

"That's what they want you to believe," Serene said. "But they're always found through the small, local abbeys, who insist the power is from the goddess and bring them into the Sanctuary."

"So… The Mira's miracles aren't from Amah?"

Serene shook her head. "It's just moving energy. There's nothing divine about it. You certainly don't have to serve their goddess to have this power."

Seeing Jae yawn, Serene stood. "Back to bed with you."

He nodded and rose. "The priories do a lot of good, but yes, they do scoop up people who have…special skills." With steps that were still slow and ginger, he headed back to his bed.

Sable watched them leave, more troubled than she'd expected by the idea that the Mira weren't really blessed by Amah.

Purnicious threw herself into fixing costumes. Her work was stunning, and Sable was constantly in awe of what the cheery little creature could do.

One morning, Sable awoke and started to pull on her boots, finding them edged with curling vines and leaves embroidered in black stitching. Another day, the white dress Ryah had worn for an abbess gown hung on a peg inside the door. The raw edges where Thulan had torn the ruffles off had been smoothed, and the dress had become simple and elegant, like a gown that might be worn by the High Prioress herself.

Ryah's role as Lavelle became more authentic every day. Her sweetness added a dimension even Atticus agreed improved the role. Instead of the determined servant, the handmaiden became a loyal, compassionate friend. And Sable needed no help at all to be terrified of the idea of Ryah being killed.

The other thing that made it even better was that if they actually won the tourney, Ryah would earn thirty silver. Adding that to what Sable would win, they'd have nearly a hundred silver between them.

For the first time, the idea of paying off Talia's debt felt possible.

When they'd been practicing for about a week, Ryah pulled her handmaiden's dress out of the costume crate and let out a gasp. Lacy frills had been added to each cuff and the bottom hem. A long line of white embroidery snaked along the edges of the ruffles with shapes that looked like leaping deer.

Catching sight of the dress, Atticus yelled, "Purnicious!"

The kobold popped into view.

"Put the dress back how it was," he ordered.

"But it's prettier this way," Purnicious objected. "It was so plain before."

"It's supposed to be plain. She's a handmaiden to a healer. She's one of the lowest-ranking women in the entire priory. It makes no sense for her dress to be more elaborate than anyone else's."

"I agree," Purnicious said enthusiastically. "Which is why I thought I could do a little work on Vivaine's, too. I thought a green sash—"

"No sash!" Atticus gave an exasperated sigh. "Purnicious, your work is amazing, but you need to leave the costumes simple. Please, stop adding color." He glanced at Ryah. "And ruffles."

Purnicious gave him a disapproving look and turned to Sable. "Do you want the sash?"

Sable bit back a smile. "I'm sure a green sash would be pretty, but Vivaine doesn't really seem like a bright sash sort of girl."

The kobold's shoulders dropped. She touched the frill on Ryah's sleeve, the lace disappearing. "Goodbye, lovelies," she sighed and shrank the rest of the cuffs out of sight.

When Sable met with Andreese that afternoon, she watched Purnicious head toward the wagons to work on more costumes. "Can you find more of those little green mushrooms we eat sometimes?"

"Yes. They grow all over the place." He looked at her curiously. "Do you like them?"

"Purnicious likes them."

"Purnicious could get her own at any time, just by blinking out to the woods." He frowned. "And she hates me. Why should I find her mushrooms?"

"She doesn't think badly of you since you fought the Kalesh, and since you helped me before the audition."

He raised an eyebrow. "I think she shrank the laces on my boots again this morning."

Sable bit back a smile. "That's sort of funny."

"It is not."

"Please, see if you can find some mushrooms," Sable said. "If you won't do it for her, pretend it's for me, or Ryah. Pick someone you like. But Purn's been working really hard, and I have nothing to give her as a thank you."

"If I'm the one who finds mushrooms, you still won't have anything."

"If you're getting them because I asked, then they're from me."

He sighed. "If I run across any, I'll pick them up. But no promises."

The next morning, though, she woke to a small cloth outside her door with a handful of green mushrooms in it.

"Purnicious," she called quietly into the courtyard. A moment later, the kobold popped into view.

"Good morning, mistress," she greeted her cheerfully.

"I got you a gift for all the hard work you've been doing. A thank you."

Purnicious peered at the bundle for a moment, a confused look on her face.

"Open it," Sable said.

The kobold stretched her blue, rootlike fingers toward the cloth and pulled it open. Her eyes lit up. "Green knobs!"

"You looked like you enjoyed them, so I asked Andreese to look for more for you."

Her hand froze. "For me?"

"Of course. I never see anyone else finishing off the bowl after breakfast."

Purn's eyes grew even wider than usual, and the purple glistened wetly. "You got them just for me?"

"Well, Andreese did, but I asked him to." She smiled, "so I'm counting it as my gift, not his."

The kobold took the cloth gently. "Thank you," she whispered.

Sable looked at the little kobold. Her green dress was so muted and mild. A question rose in Sable's mind that she couldn't believe she hadn't thought of before. "Purn, if you love color so much, why do you wear that dress?"

"Mistress Zephony gave it to m—" Purnicious stopped and looked up at Sable with nervous eyes. "I should wear something different for you! I didn't even think about it."

"You shouldn't wear anything for me. Come this way."

Sable crossed the courtyard to the wagons and pulled one of the costume crates open. "If you could dress yourself in anything, what would it be?"

Purnicious looked at the crate for a moment. "I would wear pants."

"Good. Make yourself your very favorite pair of pants, and a new shirt to go with it. Use these fabrics to make yourself clothes that you love."

A worried crease wrinkled the kobold's brow.

"It will make me happy to see you happy," Sable said, patting her on the head. "Once you're done, let me see what you've made."

Purnicious looked into the wagon. "Thank you, mistress," she breathed. She glanced down at the bundle of mushrooms in her hand. "Thank you for all of this. And thank the wastrel, too."

"Why don't you thank him yourself?" Sable asked. "And it might sound more sincere if you used his real name."

Purnicious gave her a wide smile. "But it wouldn't be as much fun."

CHAPTER FORTY-THREE

THULAN TOOK over the job of creating the sword for the play. She took one of the Kalesh blades to the small workshop behind the stables and, with Purnicious's help, filed the blade until it was a short sword. Wide and flat and considerably lighter.

Sable often found Ryah, who had very few scenes to rehearse, perched on a stool in the workshop chatting with Thulan or holding the sword still while the dwarf worked on it.

It was two days before Purnicious appeared wearing dark red pants, a sunflower-yellow tunic gathered around her waist with a tawny orange sash. The sash was edged with a delicate white lace.

"I love it!" Sable said, crouching down to feel the fabric.

Purnicious ducked her head and gave her a small smile. "It's been a very long time since I made something for myself."

"Well, I want you to be the best dressed kobold in the world," Sable said. "Please change or bellish or adjust your clothes any time you want."

Purnicious straightened and beamed at her. "Thank you!"

The first day Sable was able to use the prop sword, Andreese found her after breakfast to practice with it.

The blade was beautiful. Thulan had polished it until it gleamed. The edges were blunted, but the steel was so shiny it was hard to tell. Down the center of the blade ran two, thin grooves. Nestled inside them were two even thinner strands of fabric. A tiny flint was worked into the guard.

"Thulan will put oil in the grooves," Andreese said. "When you strike the flint, it should light flames all the way down the blade. But only one surface will light. That means we need to make sure you're only showing the lit side to the crowd, which rules out movement two, four, and five."

Sable swung the sword through movement two and realized the back of the sword would face the audience most of the time. "The others will work?"

Andreese nodded. "I know you've been using whatever movements you want during rehearsals, and they're looking good."

"They are?" Sable looked at him in surprise.

"At least for someone who's just starting."

"Ahh... I was feeling almost proud for a moment."

He studied her. "Which is your favorite movement?"

"Of the five almost identical ways to swing a sword?" He frowned at her, and she laughed. "I like three and five. They feel the least unnatural."

He nodded. "All right. We're going to concentrate on those two. You'll use three for the final fiery scene, so the correct side of the sword shows, and five for the other two."

Sable stretched out her shoulder that seemed eternally tired. "I can't say I'm disappointed to drop the others."

"Oh, you'll still do the others in practice," he said. "But we'll practice three and five more intensely."

She sighed. "Why?"

With a measured movement, he drew the Kalesh sword he always wore at his waist and faced off against her.

She took a step back and raised her hands. "All right. I'll practice all the movements. You don't have to threaten me."

"Movement one," he said, a note of command in his voice.

She raised the sword to the starting position of movement one, and Andreese swung his sword toward her. She instinctively jerked her sword into the next position, blocking him, then moved into the forward thrust without thinking. When the dull point of her sword poked into his chest, she yanked it back.

"Sorry!"

He glanced down and smiled. "For completing the movement? You did it right. A little twitchy, but right."

The hilt felt unfamiliar in her hand, as though something intrinsic to the blade had shifted. Instead of a prop, she suddenly held a weapon.

She switched it to her other hand and wiped her damp palm on her pants. A mix of wariness and tentative power swirled inside her. "That was terrifying, and you were moving slowly."

"Did you want me to attack faster?"

"I don't want you to attack at all. All this proves is that if someone attacks me at an embarrassingly slow pace, in the exact way I know to parry, I can thunk them in the chest."

"Which is exactly what a new soldier should be able to do."

"Andreese," she said, exasperated.

"Reese," he retorted.

She waved his words away. "I'm not a new soldier. I'm not any kind of soldier. Chances are, once this play is over, I will never touch another sword."

He sheathed his sword and crossed his arms. "Once this play is over, what are you going to do? Go back to Dockside?"

She raised an eyebrow.

"Ryah told me all about Immusmala and the gangs."

Sable felt a flare of irritation at how easily her sister shared things. "So?"

"So you don't want to learn to protect yourself because Dockside is so safe? Because there's no chance a Kalesh army will come and roll over every part of this land? Because you can't foresee a time you might need to protect yourself?"

"Yes, all those things are dangerous, but I'm not good enough with a sword for it to make a difference."

"And you won't be unless you decide to practice. A lot. But…" He ran his hand through his hair before meeting her gaze. "The Kalesh are coming, Sable, which means I have to go back to my uncle."

She paused. "I thought you were coming to Immusmala with us."

"I am. Only because I think the Northern Lords will be there. But then I have to go back. I have to be ready to fight with the best hope we have, and that's the troops in the north. But you…" The look he fixed her with was almost accusing. "When the Kalesh come, you are going to stand between them and your sisters, aren't you?"

"Of course I am."

"Not only that, I think you'll put yourself between the Kalesh and anyone who's in danger. And you'll do it whether you know how to defend yourself or not."

She straightened. "I'm not stupid. The Kalesh terrify me. I'll hide with everyone else."

"Really? Because back in the woods, you left a perfectly good hiding place to attack a Kalesh officer with nothing but a pointy stick."

She paused. "That might not have been the smartest thing I ever did." She gave him a self-conscious smile. "But it almost worked."

"It *did* work, until you spoke and he realized you were a tiny, terrified woman."

"Then what we should be working on is how to make me talk in a more threatening manner. And I'm not tiny."

He stepped closer to her, and she lifted her chin to look up at him, determined to not back away. Her head barely reached his shoulders. "I'm a pretty average height," he said. "Which means you're tiny. And yet you throw yourself into protecting other people without thinking."

He stepped back and fixed her with a piercing gaze. "The Kalesh are coming, Sable. People need to be able to protect themselves. So let me teach you what I can, and we can both hope it will be enough."

She looked down at the prop sword in her hand. "I thought we were just practicing for a play," she said, trying to put a grudging apology into the words.

"This has gone a bit beyond the play, don't you think?"

She gripped the handle, imagining swinging it at an enemy. "Should I be practicing with this? Or a real sword?"

His shoulders relaxed slightly. "We'll split practice from now on. The movements for the play you can do with that. For the others, you'll use one of the Kalesh blades."

She nodded and met his gaze. "Thank you, Reese."

He smiled slightly at the name, but it faded quickly. "I don't have enough time to teach you all you need." He looked at her earnestly. "Please try to learn what you can."

She nodded and lifted the prop sword to the opening position of movement three.

Andreese saw no signs of Kalesh in the woods, but when a fortnight had passed and Atticus declared it time to leave, the woods felt ominous again. The night before they left, Atticus assembled everyone in the common room.

Jae, walking in on his own, looked nearly back to normal, and Serene had stopped hovering enough to let him seat himself without assistance.

"I believe we're ready to perform the play," Atticus said, "and honestly, I wouldn't have imagined how well this troupe would fit the story." He turned to Sable with a smile. "It was excellent luck when you crept into the stage wing and hid in the shadows, Sable. I could not have picked a better Vivaine." He shifted his gaze to her sister. "And, Ryah... You've made Lavelle even better than I'd planned."

He looked over the group. "Tomorrow we will leave. We'll take the shortest route out of the woods in the hopes of avoiding any Kalesh. I'll feel safer once we get to open land. We'll have one night of camping in the woods and we should be out by noon the day after. If we move quickly, we can be back to coastal towns on the third day and perform our very first public show." He rolled forward onto his toes. "The good people of Cliften have no idea how honored they are to be the first to see the play that will win the summer tourney."

At the silence in the room, Atticus grinned. "I know you don't believe me. But just wait. By the time we reach Immusmala, the city will be talking about us."

"Or the prioress will be waiting with shackles," Leonis said quietly to Thulan.

The dwarf shrugged. "I don't know. I think dear Vivaine might be pleased with this one."

"Oh, she'll be pleased," Atticus said, sobering. "Now we just need to win the tourney and the chance to perform it one last time in front of the prioresses, the merchants, and the Northern Lords. Once we have their attention, we'll tell them about the Kalesh."

"Sure," Thulan said dryly. "Sounds simple."

They finished loading the wagons at dawn. Diann baked a heaping basket of biscuits and added two large crates of food for the road.

Purnicious had carved the wood along the back of the blue wagon with a forest scene, a path winding between tall tree trunks. The back of Atticus's wagon now featured a carved image of his face. Swirling letters that spelled out *The Duke's Figment of Wits Traveling Troupe* ran along the wagon's side.

When Atticus saw it, he stopped. Purnicious smiled nervously, but he chuckled and patted her head as he walked by.

Serene moved purposefully in and out of the buildings, with a growing pile of books she found tucked away in assorted places.

"What are you doing with those?" Diann demanded.

"I'm not leaving them here to be stolen." Serene wrapped the bundle in thick leather. "They're coming with me. There's a chance these are all that is left of the library."

"You are not taking them," Diann objected. "They'll be safe here."

Serene set the bundle inside a crate and packed them in a wagon. "We will keep these books safe, and bring the rest back here when we return with Merrick."

Diann frowned at her, but left the crate where it was.

Serene walked up to the stone wall by the gate and set her hand on it. Slowly, she began walking, gliding her hand over the surface, pausing to murmur to the stones. When she drew near, Sable stopped loading the wagons to listen. Serene spoke words she couldn't understand, but there was a richness to them. Not quite like when someone spoke the truth, but similar. As though the words themselves had some weight, some momentum. As though they were almost as solid as the wall.

"What is she doing?" Sable whispered to Jae.

"She's making sure none of the energy has worn away or grown brittle. The *vitalle* dissipates after a while. We don't usually store energy in stone for that reason, but for the wall, we make an exception."

Serene returned soon, having followed the wall all the way around Stonehaven.

Just as the sun started to rise, the wagons rolled through the gate. In the early sunlight, the forest was a brilliant green. Sable's fears of the Kalesh couldn't take hold in the fresh morning air. The whole world felt too alive to contain something so dark.

Jae and Serene rode with Atticus on the red wagon, leading them toward the path leading due west. The rest of the troupe fell in behind it with Thulan's wagon bringing up the rear.

"We should go southwest," Leonis called up to him.

"That road is too slow," Jae called back. "This one heads straight out of the forest, then meets up with a well-traveled road heading south. It'll be faster."

"Then hurry up about it," Leonis said, irritated. "I thought we were trying to get out of these woods quickly."

"Don't you like the forest?" Sable asked.

Leonis's gaze ran along the trees. "I do like the forest." His voice was tinged with something that almost sounded sad. "But some forests don't like me." He dropped his gaze to the wagon in front of them. "I'm going to make sure Jae remembers that we're in a hurry." He broke into a jog and disappeared around the wagon.

Aside from Leonis, the trip through the trees brightened everyone's spirits. The road was considerably smoother and wider than the trails they'd followed to get to Stonehaven, and they kept on a quick pace.

Near dinner time, the front wagon rolled out into a clearing.

Atticus pulled to a stop and Jae climbed down, calling for some help with unhitching the horses. Sable headed forward to help, and Andreese followed.

Leonis ran up from the back. "Get back on the wagons," he commanded, keeping his voice low. "We can't stop here. We'll be in a better place by nightfall." He grabbed Jae's arm. "Do not unhitch the horses. They can make it a little longer."

Serene started to climb down off the red wagon and paused, fixing Leonis with a glare. "What is it you're scared of?" she demanded. "Enough grumbling and brooding. Explain yourself."

Leonis spun, his eyes searching the trees. "You know what's in these woods, right?"

Sable glanced around, looking for black-clad warriors. She saw nothing.

"Yes," Serene answered. "But they never bother us. Merrick is on good terms with them."

Sable glanced at Reese. "Who?" she whispered.

Andreese was studying Leonis and didn't answer.

"They won't object to us having dinner in a clearing," Serene said.

"They'll object to me having dinner in the clearing," Leonis hissed, not looking away from the trees.

Reese leaned closer to Sable. "I just realized what Leonis looks like," he said quietly. "I can't believe I didn't see it before."

"Let's go," Leonis said, smacking the horse on the flank to get it moving.

"Too late," Thulan said from the cart behind them, looking at the edge of the forest.

Sable spun toward the trees.

It wasn't a Kalesh warrior who stood there, but a different sort of man—or maybe not a man. He was tall and thin, with long, straight hair that shone like copper. His tunic was light green, and his hand wrapped loosely around a staff. He fixed Leonis with a hostile look.

"You are not welcome here." His voice cut through the peace of the clearing.

A moment later, the weight of his words shoved against Sable.

They held the squeezing pressure of the truth, without the warmth. The truth of his words was almost solid.

"Leonis looks like an elf," Reese whispered.

CHAPTER FORTY-FOUR

"WE DIDN'T MEAN to bother you," Jae began, stepping forward to address the elf. "We just need to rest the horses—"

"I'm not here to see *him*," Leonis interrupted, fixing the elf with a stony expression. "We're just passing through."

The elf's face didn't soften. "You've caused him enough pain. It was understood that you would not come back."

The words pressed against Sable with so much force she took a half-step back and Reese looked at her curiously.

"Trust me," Leonis said, "this path was not my choice."

"And yet you chose it."

Leonis let out an annoyed breath. "Stop it, Victis. We're in a hurry. Our presence here has nothing to do with any elves. Just go back to your scheming. No one needs to know I'm here."

Victis's face was longer than a human face, smoother. There was a beauty to it, in a foreign way. Something struck her as familiar about him. She was sure she'd never seen him before, but he reminded her of someone. Sable glanced between him and Leonis.

"Leonis is an elf?" she whispered to Andreese. There was something similar about them, but compared to Victis, Leonis looked distinctly human.

"There's something elvish about him," Reese answered quietly.

"Did you really think the trees wouldn't tell us you were here?" Victis asked Leonis.

Something shifted in the forest along the edge of the clearing. A dozen more elves appeared, stretching out on either side of Victis. They were all stern except one. Dressed in a russet red tunic, an elf who looked younger than the rest of them watched Leonis with something like regret.

Leonis caught his gaze and held it, his shoulders relaxing slightly. He opened his mouth, but turned back to Victis before he spoke. "The longer you detain us, the longer it will take for me to leave."

"We're avoiding Kalesh warriors," Jae said, stepping forward and addressing Victis respectfully.

"And you thought we would protect you?" Victis demanded.

Jae stiffened. "No. This is the quickest way out—"

"No one has ever thought you'd protect anyone but yourselves," Leonis interrupted. "We need to get back to Immusmala and this is the way. These humans pass through here regularly."

"They do. Merrick is an old friend."

Every time Victis spoke, Sable braced herself. Compared to the warm, gentle pressure human truth created, this was like a physical shove. It wasn't that his words felt more truthful. They just felt more... solid. Like more than words. They didn't come from a single direction, they squeezed her from all sides, like being caught in an enormous grasp.

Victis considered the group. "You will move through the woods quickly."

Sable took a deep breath, trying to stretch herself wider. Trying to push against his words.

He turned his eyes on Leonis. "For Merrick's sake we will overlook your presence."

"For Merrick's?" Leonis demanded. "It's been ten years, Victis. You could overlook how everything ended for the sake of the rest of it."

"Ten years is only long in human lives," he said coldly, and the words slammed into her.

Sable flinched and Reese glanced at her. "Are you all right?" he whispered.

She shook her head. "His words are..."

"The Kalesh," Victis said, "have been passing through the woods in increasing numbers since the last new moon." He paused. "We have not seen them in these numbers for a decade."

Sable grimaced at the length of the speech.

Reese stepped closer. "Is he hurting you?" he asked in a whisper.

Sable shifted until she was partially shielded by his shoulder. "His words are strange and heavy."

Andreese paused. "I have no idea what that means."

"Are there any Kalesh near us now?" Jae asked.

"None that will reach you before you leave the woods."

Sable leaned against Reese's back. When Victis stopped talking, she took in a deep breath. Standing close to Reese helped a little. He felt more substantial than the words, and she pressed against him, leaving only her back exposed to the elf's voice.

"Not far ahead is a stream," the elf said. "You may camp on the far side of it. Tomorrow morning, you will leave the woods."

There was a rustling along the trees, and when Sable looked past Reese's shoulder, the other elves had disappeared. The elf in the russet shirt gave Leonis a barely perceptible nod. Leonis returned it before the elf faded back into the woods.

Victis took a step back, but Leonis stepped forward, holding up a hand to stop him. "Is he near?"

The elf's eyes narrowed. "He does not know of your presence. Nor will he."

Leonis held Victis's gaze for a moment, before asking quietly, "Is he well?"

Victis's gaze shifted to the first wagon, coming to rest on the front corner, where branches of Leonis's tree could be seen through the open window. His eyes tightened as he studied it, but when he looked back at Leonis, his voice was marginally softer. "He is an elf," he answered simply. His words had lost a great deal of the pressure.

Leonis looked as though he wanted to say more, but merely nodded.

"When you are gone," Victis said, "I will speak your name to him."

Leonis's eyes widened, but he tilted his head in a bow. "Thank you."

"Leave without tarrying," Victis said to Leonis, the pressure back in his voice. "And do not return."

Leonis gave him a small nod of agreement, and Victis disappeared into the woods. He didn't move out of view. He just...disappeared.

"Where did he go?" Sable whispered.

Andreese shook his head. "That was eerie."

Serene climbed down off the wagon where she'd stayed during the discussion and turned to Leonis, her arms crossed. "Care to explain all that?"

"No," he muttered. "But I will. Just not here. Victis was right. The stream isn't far."

They passed through the clearing and back into the trees before anyone spoke. Leonis led the way, his shoulders stiff.

"What happened back there?" Andreese asked Sable. "What does 'his words are strange and heavy' mean?"

Sable glanced at him. "It's hard to explain."

He studied her for a moment, obviously not satisfied with the answer. "Are you all right?"

She nodded and offered a smile that probably didn't look any more convincing than it felt, but was saved from having to explain more as Ryah and Purnicious hurried up beside them.

"I thought everyone knew Leonis was part-elf," Purnicious said quietly. "He looks like one."

"I've never seen an elf before," Ryah said. "That's why he has a magic tree, isn't it? It's an elven tree."

They discussed the topic in low voices until the wagon ahead of them splashed through a small stream and into a clearing. It wasn't quite dusk, and the group set up camp quickly, casting curious glances at Leonis, who ignored them all.

They settled around a fire, while Jae and Serene passed out food.

Leonis enlisted Thulan's help to pull his tree out of the wagon. Sable hadn't seen him move it since their last show, but he set it near the stream, and stayed near it, pinching off any leaves that were fading.

"You might as well tell them," Atticus finally said.

"They'll have guessed the important parts already," Thulan agreed, her voice unusually sympathetic.

Leonis blew out a long breath, but turned to look at the group. "My father is elven." He paused. "My mother was human."

When he didn't immediately continue, Jae said, "That's unusual."

Leonis's face was more drawn than Sable had ever seen it. He stayed next to his tree, rubbing a yellow leaf between his fingers. "My mother grew up along the edge of the Nidel Woods, not too far north of here. My father was a scout who patrolled that area. They met when my mother fell asleep in the forest and my father came across her. He'd never seen a human up close before, and curiosity got the better of him. She woke while he was standing above her and was suitably terrified.

"The elves have a tradition of not interacting with humans, so once my father calmed her down, they decided it would be better if they didn't mention what had happened to either elves or humans. But my mother was often in the woods hunting for mushrooms, and my father was curious enough about humans that they continued to meet."

Leonis looked down at the leaf in his hands. "As you can guess, they were eventually discovered, but by then, they were in love. Neither the elves nor my mother's family were pleased with the idea, but there are no laws against such a union, so the elven elders couldn't stop it."

Atticus's and Thulan's faces held more sympathy than interest, but all the other faces reflected the same fascination Sable felt.

"My father," Leonis continued, dropping the leaf to the ground and brushing off his hands, "is of the royal bloodline, although distant from the throne. He is, however, very well-loved by the queen, who granted my mother permission to live with the elves."

He sat down with the others. "They were wed in a ceremony attended by her family, and only two elves, and made their home on the edge of the forest. They were torn between the two worlds. When my father would visit the human world, he was treated with awe and often fear. When they went into the Nidel to the cities of the elves, my mother was treated like an outsider. They loved each other, but the burden of it began to wear on them both."

His face looked strained, older. Almost like it had back in Immusmala. Sable realized that what she'd often taken for weariness might be loneliness.

"My mother," Leonis continued, "aged as a human would, and my father did not. She had been twenty when they met, and when she was thirty-five, she became pregnant." Leonis stared into the fire. "Whether I gave them a sense of family, or I was too young to understand anything outside my own home, I remember both of them as happy."

The bittersweetness of the last words was wrapped in the warm feel of truth.

"It'd been generations since any half-elves were born, and I was watched with a morbid curiosity by everyone. When it became obvious I was starting to age more like a human than an elf, the elves lost interest in me. But out of respect for my father, I was still allowed entrance to the city."

"How old are you?" Ryah asked.

Leonis gave her a small smile. "Sixty-two."

Ryah's eyebrows shot up. "I thought you were only forty."

"For a human, I look young, but for an elf I look old enough to be an elder. There are two hundred year old elves who look younger than me."

"You should try to grow a beard," Thulan offered. "Almost everyone looks better with a beard."

"That's true," Reese said, scratching his own beard.

Leonis ignored them both and went back to his story. "I had a cousin, Cintis, who was almost like a brother, but beyond that, the elves were distant.

"Ten years ago, my parents traveled out of the woods, as they liked to do, and my mother was gravely injured. She died on the plains, and my father, heartbroken, returned alone." He clenched his jaw. "Something in him died that day. He was inconsolably lonely. He gave up his work with the elves, gave up leaving the house at all. He would only eat if I brought him food."

Leonis stared at the fire. "A few elves, Victis among them, claimed my mother and I had broken my father. That whatever was elven and good in him had been tainted. They wanted me out of the forest, and while I didn't want to leave my father, nothing I did helped him. One night, when I was trying to get him to eat, he told me that every time he saw me, he saw my mother."

He stopped talking for a moment. "And then he told me to leave. Said he couldn't bear to think about her anymore."

The truth in Leonis's words had grown steadily, and even though he kept his voice fairly even, there was a deep, aching hollowness in his face.

"So I left." His voice became firmer. "I traveled through the human towns north of here, quickly realizing it wasn't terribly obvious to them that I was half-elf. I'd been wandering for two years when I met Atticus, and I've been with him ever since. But Victis was right. I'm not welcome here, and I had been hoping to make it through without encountering any elves."

"Do you know any other half-elves?" Ryah asked.

"Humans and elves rarely meet, never mind spend enough time together to create children. The elders said that among certain elves, like the tree elves of the western forests, such a thing wouldn't even be possible. Those have become so close to the trees that they actually create new life in the ground, as though planting them. But while the Nidel elves are more closely connected to the world than humans, when they have children, it is much the same way as humans." He sighed. "But no, I don't know of any other half-elves."

"And honestly," a voice came from the trees behind Sable, "we don't really want any more mongrels running around the world."

CHAPTER FORTY-FIVE

LEONIS SNAPPED his gaze to the trees, a wide smile spreading across his face. The elf with the russet shirt leaned against a tree trunk.

"Maybe if there was another mongrel, Cintis, you'd have another friend."

The elf grinned. Sable braced for him to speak, but when he did, there was no pressure to his words. Just a light flutter through the air.

"Possibly." Cintis stepped toward the fire. "Of course, if you didn't exist, I'd never have befriended you, and lost all my elven friends." He was thin, like Leonis, but not quite as tall. His face was long, like the other elves had been, and his features delicate. "I might have made something of myself."

"Says the elf wearing a captain's knot." Leonis motioned to a strip of fabric tied around the elf's arm. "When did they make the mistake of promoting you?"

He shrugged. "They ran out of other eligible options."

Leonis crossed the clearing and grasped Cintis's forearm for a breath, before pulling the elf into a tight hug.

Cintis's thin eyebrows rose, but he returned the hug for a brief moment before pulling back and patting Leonis awkwardly on the back. "Stop being so human." He looked at Leonis's face. "When did you get so old? Last I knew, you were younger than I am."

"I still am. Which means you should at least look like you are allowed to be outside after dark." Leonis turned, grinning. "Everyone, meet Cintis, Captain of the Royal Guard and the closest thing to a brother I've ever had." He turned to the elf. "Will you join us for the evening?"

Cintis took in the group with a lively curiosity. "With all these humans, a dwarf, and a kobold? Gladly!" He paused. "There's more magic here than I expected. I could smell it from across the stream."

Leonis introduced Jae and Serene as Merrick's friends, and Cintis greeted them enthusiastically.

Thulan nodded politely to him, then stood and glanced up at the darkening sky. "I'll take first watch."

"There's no need," Cintis said. "You're within our borders."

"But the elves went away." Thulan glanced at Serene. "Didn't they?"

Serene squinted into the trees around them. "I think so. It's hard to say. The trees are more alive than normal. It's difficult to see past them."

Cintis nodded. "These trees are more aware than most."

Thulan shot a disconcerted look into the forest. "Sentient trees sound frightening."

Cintis laughed. "They cannot move or speak in a language you understand. They have no way to hurt you." He looked around the fire curiously. "Can you not tell they are more alive?"

"They're brighter," Ryah said. "More vivid."

"But if there are no elves nearby," Thulan said, "we should set up a watch."

"There are no elves," Cintis said, "except me and Leonis. But you are invited guests. We will ensure your safety."

Thulan raised an eyebrow. "I don't remember an invitation."

"Victis told us to camp here," Leonis reminded her.

"I'd call that more of a command," Sable said.

Leonis shrugged. "He still told us we could stay in the forest.

That's an invitation." He glanced at Cintis. "I about fell over when he did."

Cintis let out a light, fluttering laugh. "So did I. But he did, so nothing will harm you tonight."

"How can you be sure?" Andreese asked. "Especially if no elves are nearby."

"Because nothing comes through our woods without our knowledge. And if we don't want anyone to find you, no one will. The elves are not near, but they are aware. You are perfectly safe."

Thulan sized up the elf for a moment, then shrugged and settled back down.

"I've never even spoken to a dwarf before," Cintis said, peering at her. "And here Leonis gets to travel with one!"

"He doesn't realize how lucky he is," Thulan said.

Cintis shrugged. "He's slow. Where have you dwarves been? We haven't seen any since last winter."

Thulan looked sharply at him. "That long? We found the southern entrance blocked by a collapsed tunnel, but there are plenty of other entrances. They wouldn't just stop coming to the forest. What happened to their herds? Their orchards?"

"The herds have been wandering and the orchards are overgrown."

A worried crease formed between Thulan's brow. "How far north have you looked?"

"We haven't looked. We just noticed the herds and the orchards. Then realized we hadn't seen any dwarves since the snow melted."

Thulan frowned at him. "They have more herds and more orchards farther north, but I can't believe they'd just abandon these."

Cintis considered her for a moment. "Maybe I'll get someone to look into it."

Thulan raised a bushy eyebrow. "Because the elves care what happens to the dwarves?"

Cintis paused. "Not particularly. Unless whatever happened to them could affect us." He looked around the rest of the group. "Leonis, introduce me to the rest of your friends, then tell me what you've been doing for the past ten years."

Leonis made introductions, and unlike the conversation with Victis, everything was light and easy. Cintis's words were more like a breeze, a ripple in water, than any uncomfortable pressure.

Leonis, in a good mood for the first time all day, talked animatedly. Jae and Serene peppered Cintis with questions. Atticus watched everything with interest, probably storing up the conversation for future plays.

The clearing rang with laughter. Cintis shared stories from Leonis's youth, and Atticus or Thulan told stories of Leonis since he'd joined them. Cintis was endlessly curious about them all, questioning Ryah about life in an abbey and Andreese about the military. The elf found Sable's stories of the gangs in Immusmala almost unbelievable.

"If they are so corrupt, why are they not stopped?"

"Who's going to stop them?" Sable asked. "They have more strength than anyone in their territory, and the powerful people in the city don't care enough about places like Dockside to go through the effort of stopping them."

Cintis frowned. "They do not care about their own people?"

Sable laughed. "They care about their own people, but that doesn't include Dockside."

"There are people who would change things," Ryah said. "The abbess I lived with dreamed of breaking the hold the gangs had on the people, but what could she do? She fed the hungry when she could, cared for the sick, but she was only able to do those things because the gangs allowed her to."

Cintis turned to Sable. "Does your magic not help you? Without many humans having magic, it seems like it would give you an advantage."

Sable stared at him. "My what?"

"You have magic!" Purnicious squealed. "I thought you might!"

"I don't," Sable objected.

"Being able to feel when someone is speaking the truth sounds like magic to me," Serene said.

Cintis looked at her with interest. "You can feel the truth?"

"Yes... Well, sort of. It doesn't have to be the absolute truth. It just has to be something the person believes to be true."

His eyebrows rose. "What does truth feel like?"

"It's usually warm," Sable answered. "And it's not magic. At least not like Serene can do."

"That's what was happening when Victis was talking," Reese said. "You could feel his words. Was he being extra truthful?"

Cintis looked at her curiously. "I didn't know any but elves could do that."

Sable straightened. "You felt it, too?"

"All the elves can," Leonis said. "Victis is very persuasive when he orders people around."

"He has authority," Cintis agreed. "And his words carry weight."

"Literally?" Atticus asked.

"Of course," Cintis answered.

"When people really believe what they're saying," Sable explained, "I feel a warmth and a slight pressure. But with Victis, it was almost painfully strong. And there was no warmth."

"It doesn't feel painful to me," Leonis said. "Just persistent. Like a nudge to do what he asks."

"Judging from her reaction," Andreese said, glancing at her, "Sable felt more than a nudge."

"Have you felt anything else unusual?" Serene asked.

Sable paused. "This morning, when you were doing whatever you were doing to the wall, I could feel your words."

Serene studied her for a moment. "Those words funneled *vitalle* into the wards."

"They felt...rich. Substantial."

Jae considered her. "If what you're feeling is based more on whether the person believes what they're saying rather than that it being literal truth, maybe this works differently than you think. Maybe what you feel is the energy in the words."

Serene nodded. "Merrick says the way to infuse words with magic is to make them true." Her brow furrowed as she focused her attention on a dead leaf on the ground, touching it with her finger. "To light a flame, I say... Well, there are a lot of different things I could say. But if I use *incende*..." The word gave Sable the slightest push, "I make the word truly become what it means. I...fulfill it." Serene looked back at

Sable. "It feels like there's a similarity between infusing a word with the intention to make it real and someone telling the truth."

"I did feel some warmth by the first Kalesh man when Jae—" Sable paused and gave Jae an apologetic look. "When you used your magic. But I thought you just really meant whatever you told him in Kalesh."

Jae rubbed the back of his neck and shrugged. "I did really mean it."

Serene let out a short laugh. "He said, 'When you sow death, you reap death.'"

The group was quiet for a moment.

"Can't argue with that," Andreese said finally.

Sable turned back to Serene. "But if telling the truth is somehow similar to what you do, then everyone has the ability to do something magical."

"You don't have to convince me of that," Atticus said. "Anyone who's watched a good play or heard an enthralling story knows words are magic."

Serene gave Sable a probing look. "You and I need to talk about this more. There's a book I want to check that might shed some light on this."

"If we find the books," Jae said.

Serene's eyes went flat. "We will find the books and take them back. There is no way I'm leaving our library in Immusmala."

Sable let out a short laugh. "She's telling the truth."

Cintis considered Sable. "That's a very interesting skill."

Leonis grinned. "Sneaks is useful at the card table, as well."

Atticus frowned, as did the elf.

"Leonis," Cintis said to Sable, "is loose with his idea of how skills should be used."

"I am not," Leonis objected.

Cintis ignored him. "Be careful, Sable."

The elf's face was so serious, Sable shifted uncomfortably and smiled. "Is there some law as to how magic is to be used?"

"Only the same law everything else is under. That our own actions shape and change us, even the small ones." Cintis paused. "Especially the small ones."

For the first time, Sable felt a strong pressure in Cintis's words.

Sable glanced at Leonis, who had turned to frown into the fire. "I'll take that into consideration," she said quietly.

CHAPTER FORTY-SIX

"IN TWO NIGHTS," Atticus said, drawing everyone's attention, "we'll have our first performance. Now that it's dark, I think we should do a complete run-through." He glanced at Cintis. "Would you be interested in staying and being our first audience?"

Cintis's face lit up. "A show! I'd love to!"

Atticus marked off a stage on the ground, Thulan pulled out the props, and Leonis moved his tree into position.

"That's an elven tree, isn't it?" Ryah asked.

Cintis nodded. "Elves are strengthened by the energy that lives in trees, almost as much as we are by food. But the sede tree is remarkable. Sitting near a full-grown one is as refreshing as sitting in the middle of a grove of normal trees."

"Cintis gave this to me when I left," Leonis said. "It's too small to replace the energy I feel from a real forest, but it helps when I'm stuck in a treeless city for too long."

"It's the only sede tree that's left the Nidel Woods, as far as I know," Cintis said. "Of course, I only know of one elf who's left, too."

"I don't think I qualify as an elf." Leonis turned away and pulled the baledin's black cloak out of the wagon, shaking it out.

"What is that?" Atticus demanded, pointing at the cloak.

Leonis folded it quickly. "Nothing."

"I saw something." Atticus looked around the clearing. "Purnicious? Have you been bellishing the baledin's cloak?"

The little kobold's curly, black head leaned out of the back of the wagon, looking guilty.

"There's nothing to see," Leonis said. "Let's start."

"Show me the cloak," Atticus said with an icy tone.

Leonis paused. "I like it, Atticus. Don't make her take it out."

Atticus crossed his arms, and with a sigh, Leonis turned the cloak inside out. In the center of the black lining was an embroidered, flaming sword.

"That's amazing," Sable breathed, stepping closer. The neat, smooth stitches were all black, almost blending into the fabric. The sword wreathed in curling flames. "Purnicious! I love it!"

"You cannot embroider the baledin's robe!" Atticus flung the words at the kobold. "He is a dark, mysterious monster! He does not have intricate stitching on his shadowy cloak of death!"

"You won't be able to see it," Purnicious said quickly. "I used the exact same thread as in the cloak. It'll be invisible."

"I can clearly see it," Atticus snapped. "We can all see it."

"Only because you're holding it open!" Purn argued.

"She's right," Leonis broke in. "It's nearly invisible while someone's wearing it. No one in the audience will be able to see it."

"It can't stay there," Atticus said firmly.

"Just leave it for this practice," Leonis protested. "If you can still see it, she'll take it out. But, Atticus, look at it! Have you ever seen anything so magnificent?"

Atticus stepped closer to the cloak. "It is impressive, Purnicious," he said begrudgingly.

She gave him a grin. "I worked hard on it."

"It's stunning," Ryah said.

Leonis laid the cloak over the back of the wagon to wait until he needed it. "Can we begin now?"

After one last scowl, Atticus nodded. Sable and Leonis began the scene in Balin's forge.

The play went well. Cintis loved it, Jae stood and cheered, and even Serene and Andreese applauded enthusiastically. Atticus rattled off a list of things to work on, including everyone getting a good night's sleep, but in the end, he looked over the group with a pleased expression. "That was excellent. Let's go win a tourney."

When Sable rose early the next day, Leonis and Cintis were still in quiet conversation near the fire. Aside from looking tired, Leonis looked more peaceful than she'd ever seen him.

Thulan insisted Sable take the opportunity of the stream and get her hair washed again in preparation for the upcoming plays, and Serene and Ryah followed. The water was bitingly cold, and neither Sable nor the others opted for a full bath, but clean hair was refreshing.

"You've ruined me for having unwashed hair," she told Thulan as she rinsed out the last of the soap. The pine and lemon smelled as fresh as the elven woods.

"If you'd take more actual baths, you'd be almost presentable enough to take into dwarven society."

Cintis bade them goodbye, allowing Leonis to embrace him again before he left. "Regardless of what Victis says, come back sooner than ten years from now."

Leonis glanced into the trees. "I'll consider it."

"Victis won't stop you. It has been a century since an elf raised his hand against another," Cintis said. "What are you afraid of?"

Silence stretched between them for a moment. "My father doesn't want me here."

"He won't come find you in the human world," Cintis said, "not after he lost your mother there, but he'd like it if you came home."

Leonis kept his eyes on the forest. "Maybe someday."

Cintis started to turn toward the forest, then paused, a conflicted look on his face. "I know it must be hard for you, with the Kalesh back." He paused again. "I would travel with you if I could, but Victis would never approve it."

Leonis frowned at him. "The Kalesh?"

Cintis hesitated. "Because of your mother."

Leonis stared at him blankly. "What about my mother?"

His cousin glanced at the others, his face a mixture of confusion and wariness. "Your parents were attacked by a party of Kalesh as they slept. It's how your mother was wounded."

Leonis stared at his cousin, brows furrowed. "She was hurt in a fall."

Cintis shook his head. "She was attacked. I thought your father told you. I thought..." He looked helplessly at him. "I thought you knew."

"The Kalesh?" Leonis looked stunned.

A flicker of pity crossed Cintis's face. "That's why Victis sent elves to the plains. They found four scouting parties of Kalesh, and killed them all. As far as we could tell, they'd burned three towns on the coast and at least a dozen surrounding homesteads."

Ryah glanced over at Sable. "That's around the same time our town was attacked."

Sable's breath caught. "Elves!" She took a step toward Cintis, suddenly realizing who the elves reminded her of. "There were elves there the night my family was attacked! I didn't recognize them at the time, but they looked like you." She turned to Ryah. "They're the reason we're still alive."

Leonis watched the conversation, standing perfectly still. "I... No one told me. After my mother died, I spent the summer with my father at his home near the edge of the woods. He was so devastated I couldn't leave him. I didn't know elves were sent anywhere." He sank down onto a fallen log.

Cintis turned toward Atticus. "When we killed their scouts, ten years ago, no more came. But there are many more Kalesh on the plains now, all in small raiding parties, and they're entering the forest more boldly."

"Maybe the elves should chase them off again," Thulan said.

Cintis frowned. "I'm not sure that would work. They feel like they have more purpose than they did back then."

Atticus glanced at Jae and Serene. "We were worried that was the case."

"Be careful on your journey." Cintis glanced back into the forest. "The elves will protect you in the trees, but once you leave, hurry back to your cities."

The elf set a hand on Leonis's shoulder. "Come back to us soon. You have a place here, whether Victis thinks so or not."

Leonis nodded, but didn't answer. Cintis bowed to the rest of them and disappeared into the forest.

"Let's get moving," Thulan said, pausing to set her own hand on Leonis's shoulder before heading to the horses. "Lingering sounds like a bad idea."

The morning was clear and warm, and the road out of the forest was as well-maintained as it had been yesterday. They reached the edge of the trees long before lunch and found a wide road heading south toward the sea.

Leonis walked behind everyone, his head down. Atticus left him alone and had Thulan, Ryah, and Sable rehearse lines. When they paused for lunch, Andreese pulled Sable aside and drilled her on sword work. Purnicious put finishing touches on costumes and props, and the kobold's own clothes continued to shift, bit by bit. The pants grew longer, the tunic sprouted lace around the cuffs.

That night, they camped in a small grove of trees at the bottom of a hill. Far to the south, Sable thought she could see the grey-blue line of the sea. She felt a surprising longing to see it again after spending weeks inland.

Andreese had caught a pair of rabbits, which Ryah and Leonis roasted, while Sable relaxed against a wide tree trunk. The dark sky above was dotted with clouds, but a few stars had begun to peek through.

Reese sat down next to her, leaning back against the tree and letting out a yawn.

"Where'd you learn to hunt?" Sable asked him.

"When I was younger, my uncle used to take me to the forests along Scale Mountains for weeks at a time. He thought a bow and a knife were the best tools to hunt with, so that's all he let me use. If I didn't catch something, we didn't eat."

"Sounds hard."

"Not in those mountains. There was plenty of game. It's motivating to learn to aim well if your prey is very small and you're very hungry. I got good at rabbits pretty quickly."

"I've never even seen the Scale Mountains. The Tremmen Hills near Immusmala are the very southern end of them, I suppose, but they're not mountains." Sable looked west, as though she could see that far. "My life feels decidedly boring compared to yours."

"It is." A bit of a smile curled the edge of his mouth. "You're one of the most boring people I've ever met."

Sable rolled her eyes. "Then you've picked the right person to sit by as you fall asleep."

"I thought so."

Jae, who tired quickly and rode in the wagon most of the day, sat against a tree across the fire, taking requests for stories. While Thulan and Leonis argued over which he should tell, Reese yawned again.

"You do know we have plenty of food from Diann, right?" Sable asked. "You don't have to get up early every morning to hunt."

He kept his eyes closed. "It's not the hunting I get up for. It's the quiet. And the sunrise. Watching the sun come up is the best part of the day. After that, everything gets noisy and chaotic."

"Because the rest of us are awake?"

"Exactly." He tilted his head toward her and cracked open an eye. "You want to get up with me tomorrow?"

Sable raised an eyebrow. "Then it won't be quiet."

He made a grunt of agreement and closed his eyes again. "True, but you're boring enough that I'll probably forget you're there."

"Well," she said dryly, "as long as I won't disturb your peace."

His lips quirked as Jae began a heartbreaking tale about a small village and a band of trolls. Within minutes Reese was asleep.

It was still dark the next morning when someone touched Sable's shoulder. She swam up out of a dream of fire, smoke, and ravens to see the outline of Reese's head silhouetted against the deep blue sky.

"Shh," he whispered. "C'mon."

She stood, trying to rub the sleep out of her eyes, and followed him toward the trees. It was already warm, and a light breeze rustled the trees, masking any noise they made.

Reese reached the far edge of the copse and waited for her to catch up.

"What are we doing?" Sable whispered.

"Watching the sunrise," he answered, heading up the hillside.

Sable stared after him for a long moment, tempted to turn around and crawl back under her blanket. But the eastern horizon was a deep purple, and from the top of the hill, the sea might be visible. Rubbing her hands over her face to chase away the last of the sleepiness, she followed him up the hill.

Reese was sitting at the top, leaning against a downed tree trunk, looking off into the brightening east.

"If I talk loudly and often," Sable asked, dropping down next to him, "will this be the last time you wake me up this early?"

"If you do that, I'll start waking you only on rainy mornings so you'll be awake but have nothing interesting to see."

Sable looked south, hoping for a glimpse of the ocean from this high, but it was too dark to see. To the east, the flat plains stretched out to the horizon. The smoking remains of Ebenmoor felt closer than they had when they'd been in the forest. They hadn't spoken of the town since the day Reese had been found, but in the dimness of the morning, the topic felt more approachable.

"Do you miss your aunt?" she asked.

"I do. Besides my uncle in the north, she was the last family I had." He was quiet for a long moment. "I hope the end came quickly for her. For all of them."

Sable glanced at him. He watched the lightening sky with a sorrowful expression.

"My parents were both scribes," he continued quietly, "and we traveled widely. When I was ten, we were south of Ebenmoor in a small village. A sickness came through and both of them died."

Sable felt the familiar weight of those words. "I'm sorry," she said quietly.

He didn't take his eyes off the sky. "The prioress of the town took me in, although not happily. She was more excited about my parent's possessions, and when I told her I had a cousin in Ebenmoor, she set to finding someone to take me there as quickly as possible. It was three dwarves who she found."

"Dwarves? On the plains?"

"Traders from Turren travel in the eastern reaches, and across the northern lands as well, peddling stones and jewels for food and seeds and such. They were headed north, so she paid them to take me to Ebenmoor." He paused.

"She'd kept a portion of my parents' possessions as a fee for caring for me and burying them, then she paid the dwarves, and gave what was left—barely anything— to me. I walked with the dwarves all day. Near dusk we reached a crossroads. They told me Ebenmoor was a day's walk down the road, and left in a different direction, taking everything of mine with them."

"They just left you?" Sable said. "I understand why you don't like dwarves."

"I chased after them, telling them the prioress had paid them to take me to Ebenmoor. But they said she paid them to get me out of her hair. Which they'd done."

Sable shook her head. "And I understand why you don't like prioresses."

He sighed. "I did find my way to Ebenmoor. I spent the next years split between my aunt's home and visiting my uncle in the north, until I was old enough to join his troops. My uncle's world was exciting, but my aunt's felt like home."

They fell into silence again until the sky lightened to violet, then a pale yellow.

Sable pushed the toe of her boot against a small rock, half buried in the dirt. "My parents spoke Kalesh. I think."

Reese glanced at her. "How'd they learn it?"

She shrugged. "The night the Kalesh attacked, my parents spoke to them. I didn't understand the language, and until now I didn't know it was Kalesh. But they definitely spoke it. And the man who killed them acted like he knew who they were." The rock came loose from the dirt, and she pushed it around with her toe.

"Do you think your parents were Kalesh?" he asked.

"I have no idea. Do all Kalesh have dark hair and narrow faces like the warriors we saw? Because my parents looked nothing like that."

He shook his head. "They've conquered so many lands and inter-married with so many people, they can look like anything." He paused. "If your parents stood against them, maybe they were from some conquered group."

"Maybe." Sable pushed the rock back into the hole, and pressed it down. "It would be nice if they'd told us anything. I thought they'd lived on the Reaches their whole lives."

They sat in silence again. The sky was brightening, and the coming day seemed like it was rushing toward them, bringing with it the reminder that their first performance would be tonight. It felt pivotal. Like the first push against a stone high on a hill. Whatever direction this endeavor was heading, once the stone started rolling, it would be hard to change its course.

To Reese, though, the week probably didn't seem so daunting. "Are you excited to watch us perform the same show over and over?" Sable asked with a smile.

"The play isn't as bad as I'd expected."

"You're not going to think that once you've seen it a half-dozen times."

He snorted. "A half-dozen? There are parts I've seen a hundred times. I always catch the part where you and Balin argue and you leave."

"That's because we've practiced it a hundred times. Atticus thought we didn't do it justice."

Reese shook his fist in mock irritation. "This scene is pivotal. Pivotal!" he said in an excellent imitation of Atticus's voice. "Sable, your heart is breaking! Make ours break with it!"

Sable let out a tired laugh. "My problem with the heartbroken part is that Balin already chose his path. Vivaine doesn't know he's killing people, but she knows he did once and he doesn't regret it. I think her choice to leave is the right one for her and for Balin. Even if she's the one physically separating them, it began with Balin's actions. So Vivaine can feel sad, but this isn't unexpected."

"Ah," he said, "you're blaming the man for all the problems."

Sable laughed. "He is a murderer. If Vivaine is heartbroken, it's because he forced her to this place, not because she's separating them."

"So you think she did the right thing?"

Sable glanced at him. "Don't you?"

He shrugged. "I keep hoping it will end differently."

They were quiet for a few minutes. Birds had begun chirping, but the whole world felt drowsy and calm. The light spread and the view grew more vast.

"This is a good hill," Sable said. "Have you been here before?"

He looked around. "No. I've mostly traveled in the north. None of the Northern Lords come this far south, unless they're going to Immusmala."

"So you traveled with the troops?"

He nodded. "This is my first trip with an acting troupe. Which has turned out to be far more interesting than I ever would have expected."

"And by interesting, you mean enjoyable, right?"

He glanced over at her. "Aside from the occasional run-in with murderous Kalesh soldiers, yes."

"Despite the fact we have a dwarf?"

"Thulan changes everything I thought about dwarves," Reese admitted. "Although I'm still not sure she's typical."

"And is Ryah changing your ideas about the priories?"

"No. The more I get to know Ryah and see that she really is as sweet as she seems, the more I want to keep her away from everything related to the priories."

"They're not all bad, Reese."

He shook his head. "They wield too much power to be good. Serene agrees with me."

"That's because she's as cynical as you are. Ryah has been in an abbey most of her life. She knows what they're like."

"She's too nice." He frowned back down toward the camp. "I'm afraid someone will manipulate her into doing something."

Sable crossed her arms. "I won't let them."

He glanced at her with a dubious look. "I'm sure you'll try."

The sky to the east was a clear, bright golden color. Sable took a deep breath and plucked up a long blade of grass that had a fluffy head of seeds. "In light of the beauty of the moment, let's just agree to disagree."

Reese nodded slowly, studying her for a long moment.

Sable gave him an amused look, sliding the smooth grass through her fingers. "You're regretting inviting me this morning, aren't you?"

"No." He looked back at the sky. "I was thinking I should invite you more often."

The words sent a tense ripple through her stomach. Her fingers tightened on the blade, folding it over and sending the seeds rolling into her lap. He watched the bits of fluff scatter, a hint of a smile on his lips. Sable dropped the broken blade and wiped off her pants without looking at him. "It hasn't been horrible."

The land ahead of them was clear now, the hills rolling away with clumps of dark trees.

"Are you excited for tonight?" Reese asked, changing the subject.

Sable thought about it for a moment. "I am. And I'm also not. It feels like the peace of the past few weeks is about to end."

He nodded slowly. "It does."

"After this, it's just show after show, then we'll be in the city. Who knows how that will go."

"What are you going to do when this is all over?"

Sable looked down at her hands. "That all depends on whether I can free Talia."

"We will." He turned back to the sunrise. "We'll find her, and get her free."

Sable looked up. We? "I thought you'd be—"

Reese leaned forward, staring east with a sharp gaze. He swore and pointed across the quiet, empty looking plains near the coast. A wide smudge of darkness rose into the air. "Smoke."

CHAPTER FORTY-SEVEN

ANDREESE PUSHED HIMSELF UP, and Sable scrambled up next to him. The smoke was so far away it was almost on the horizon. Days off to the southeast.

Reese shielded his eyes and squinted toward the dark cloud. "That's really far south of Ebenmoor."

"The Kalesh are all over the Reaches." Sable said.

He let out a growl and they started down the hill.

Their news was met with grim expressions, and Atticus got them on the road as soon as possible.

He drilled them on lines all day, and pushed on by the thought of the Kalesh, everyone threw themselves into the practice. But by the time they rolled back into the small coastal town of Cliften, Sable was ready to perform the play just so the rehearsals would stop.

It had been just over a fortnight since they'd stopped in this town, but it felt like ages. The cluster of buildings was small, and enough other farmers from the surrounding areas were heading to Immusmala for the festival, that there were no rooms for the troupe to rent. So in addition to setting up the stage, they left space to set up camp between the wagons.

Jae, Serene, Atticus and Andreese went to spread the news about the Kalesh, while Sable and the others stayed to work on the stage.

A crowd gathered near them, and Leonis was greeted, as he always was, with friendly calls. Sable slid curtains on to long poles, waiting for him to disappear, as he always did, but instead he kept working on the stage while he carried on a conversation with the nearest townsfolk.

"You can't believe all these rumors," a burly man said to him.

"Saw Ebenmoor with my own eyes, Burrus," Leonis said, holding up one end of a long pole, while Thulan stood on a stool, attaching the other side to the back of the stage. "And we were attacked by three Kalesh men in the Nidel."

"They weren't Kalesh," Burrus scoffed. "What would the empire's soldiers be doing lurking in the Nidel Woods?"

Leonis turned to look at the man, lowering his end of the pole. "I was there. They were Kalesh."

"Leonis!" Thulan grunted as she tried to keep her end of the pole in place. Leonis pushed his side up again with an apologetic look.

"Tod says they're just normal raiders," Burrus continued.

"Tod?" Leonis turned again. "Tod can't tell a fish from a jackrabbit. You're really going to believe Tod over me?"

"Leonis!" Thulan called. She'd attached her end of the pole, and Leonis's movements were twisting her entire side.

"Sorry!" Leonis lifted his side again. "Go away, Burris. I have to work."

"No," Thulan said in exasperation. "Talk, just do it away from here. Ryah!" She called over her shoulder. "Come take Leonis's place. At least you can hold a pole still."

"But I'm helping," Leonis objected.

"You're better at talking then helping," Thulan grumbled. "Go convince these idiots that they're really in danger."

After a moment's hesitation, Leonis handed the pole to Ryah. "Take me to Tod," he said to Burrus, stepping off the stage.

"For years I've been on his case to help more," Thulan muttered. "What was I thinking?"

Sable helped Thulan and Ryah finish the stage. It was still the simpler, smaller version. One wide back curtain, and the six pallets of wood attached to each other to form the floor.

When it was done, Ryah donned the new white dress Purnicious had made for her.

"There is a mother with a new baby waiting for the abbess," Atticus announced as he walked past, looking at Ryah critically. "I'm sure she'll be glad you're dressed in something reasonable this time."

Ryah glanced down at the dress. "I'm glad I'm dressed in something reasonable." She headed off toward the crowd.

By sunset, whether from the dire news of the attack on Ebenmoor or interest in Atticus's play, the square of the small town was full of people.

As the troupe gathered behind the stage, Atticus turned to Sable with a curious expression. "Is Sable short for anything?"

"Issable. But no one calls me that."

"Issable." He smiled and nodded. "I like that. And the town you were from?"

She narrowed her eyes at him. "Pelrock."

He shook his head. "Pelrock is a dull name." Without saying more, he turned and climbed through the curtains onto the stage. His voice rolled out, greeting the crowd. He was met with cheers.

Serene came up beside Sable, looking after him. "He's a strange man."

"Agreed."

Serene turned to face Sable, a bright intensity to her face. "I've been thinking about the way you feel truth and realized something. I have never heard of a person who could sense *vitalle* but not control it."

The words were warm around Sable. "You think I can do magic?"

"I think you can control energy," Serene corrected her. "Of course, if it's true words can hold their own *vitalle*, then we can all control energy." She smiled. "But if you can feel it more than the average person, I think you can control it more than the average person, as well."

Sable considered the idea. "I don't think I can."

Serene drummed her fingers on her lips. "The first night you performed, when you realized Terrelus reminded you of Talia, what did you do differently when you returned to the stage?"

Sable shrugged. "I just imagined I was talking to Talia."

"When you feel the truth, do you feel it on your skin?"

Sable started to nod, then paused. "I don't know."

Serene leaned against the side of the wagon and looked at Sable thoughtfully. "I love Jae."

Sable let out a surprised laugh at the unexpected words, but she felt the warmth.

"I have since I was fifteen years old," Serene continued, and the warm sense remained. "I love everything about him. Even how ridiculously cheerful and friendly he is to everyone."

Sable raised her eyebrows. "That was...unexpectedly sweet."

"Not sweet." Serene wrinkled her nose in distaste. "True. Where did you feel it?"

"Not on my skin." Sable thought a minute. "It was...inside. Sort of. Or maybe not quite touching me. But I definitely didn't feel it on my skin."

Serene studied Sable. "There are times your acting is so real, I can't look away. I've watched Atticus, Leonis, and Thulan for years. They're all excellent and pull me into the story. But you... Sometimes when you speak, the words feel..." She let out an annoyed breath again. "They feel *real*. When I told you that about Jae, I meant it. Something inside me filled those words with meaning, because I wanted you to know how true they were.

"When you act, I feel that fullness coming from your words. They draw me in, and I want to believe them. If you can figure out how you do it, I think you'd be able to do it whenever you choose."

Sable looked out toward the audience, remembering how Lady Argent's lines had felt. "I know when that's happening," she said slowly. "I didn't know anyone else could tell."

"What are you doing at those times?"

"I forget I'm acting and start thinking of things that are true. When I do, the words get...richer."

Serene nodded. "When I move *vitalle*, I focus only on that. I don't pay attention to what's around me. All I think about is moving the energy from one place to another. It takes a strong desire." She let out a short laugh. "Maybe that's why Jae has never been good at it. He never strongly desires anything. He's just too pleased all the time."

"He strongly desired something when that Kalesh warrior stabbed you."

"He did." She thought for a moment. "And that was an unusual amount of power for him. Interesting."

Atticus's and Thulan's voices came from the stage, running through their introductory dialog, playing off each other with practiced ease, introducing the play that was about to start.

"I think you can do it," Serene said, her words warm with conviction. "If you just figure out how."

Atticus stepped through the curtain, rubbing his hands together. Thulan followed, while Leonis and a nervous Ryah gathered close. Atticus looked as though he was going to give some sort of rousing speech, but instead, he just grinned at them.

"Bells of truth," he said.

"Cries in the night," Sable answered with the rest of them.

For the first scene, Sable stepped out on stage holding the sword. Her lines were a bit rough at first, but she focused on Vivaine's longing for a simple life with Balin and the way that was being taken from her. When Balin started to follow darker paths, she held to the truth that he—and, by extension, Talia—just needed to be drawn back to the light.

Thinking of the conversation she had with Serene about the magic in words, she pushed that longing into her lines, infusing the words with the truth of it all, pressing them against Balin, against the world.

Leonis responded, his portrayal of Balin more genuine than anything she'd seen yet.

Moving through the soothing glow of Leonis's tree and the lights from the stage lanterns, the world outside lost in darkness, Sable fell into the story, into the ache Vivaine carried that grew stronger until the final scene.

When the play reached the climax and she stood before Balin in his black robe, facing what he'd become, the darkness in him broke her heart. He grabbed for her, and the sword flashed. She flipped the tiny

flint, and Thulan's oil burst into flames along the blade. Leonis fell to the stage. The fire was so brilliant that Sable yanked her hand back, dropping the blade onto his body, stunned for a moment, as Vivaine must have been, at what had just happened.

Ryah, dressed as the handmaiden, her face covered by a white priory veil, lay slain, as well.

The audience was silent as Sable sank to her knees and dropped her head into her hands, struck by how powerless Vivaine had been in the end. Her shoulders bowed under the weight of the tragedy.

Atticus stepped onto the stage and gave the narrator's final speech.

The audience burst into applause. Sable rose, picking up the sword, holding it in a way even Reese would be proud of. She turned to face the crowd, feeling oddly spent. She waited while Atticus introduced Thulan, Leonis, and Ryah, and they each stepped forward and bowed to the crowd.

Off to the side, she caught Serene's eye, the woman giving her a rare grin.

"And the first actress to ever do High Prioress Vivaine justice on stage," Atticus said dramatically, "I give you Issable of Shadowfall."

Sable stuttered in her step forward and looked at Atticus. Where was Shadowfall? He grinned broadly at her, and the audience cheered so loudly that she gave the sword a flourish, and bowed.

Sable climbed out of the wagon, wearing her own clothes again, finding Atticus standing there, holding out a few coins.

"What is this?" she asked.

"People pay when they've enjoyed the show."

Sable stared at the coins. Fifteen copper nummi. She opened her mouth, trying to thank him, but no words came out.

"I know it's not much," he said, "but the larger towns will bring in more. This is a good night in such a small town."

"For doing a play? It's...so much." Sable closed her fingers around the coins. "Thank you."

"You're welcome." He smiled. "Issable of Shadowfall."

She laughed. "Because you said you found me 'where the shadows fall at the side of my stage.'"

He grinned. "I knew you'd remember the words. Pelrock was too boring, and Dockside is too fishy."

"I am not from Dockside," she said firmly.

"I thought you might feel that way."

Sable picked up the sword and a cloth to clean off the oil.

"If the play goes this well every night," Atticus said, "there will be a lot of people trying to figure out where Shadowfall is. You were fantastic." He studied her seriously for a minute. "Perhaps better than Zephony would have been."

Sable gave him a little bow. "I doubt that, but I like Vivaine. She's relatable."

He nodded. "She is."

"She feels," Sable began, slowly wiping the oil off the sword, "like she was written by someone who knew her well. Maybe even admired her." She glance up at Atticus. "Admired her so much that he wrote her to be almost flawless."

A small smile turned up the corner of his mouth. "It's easy to admire someone when you're young."

She glanced at his white beard with a smirk. "And yet to still admire them when you're no longer young seems…significant."

Atticus crossed his arms. "What are you getting at, Issable?"

"My full name!" She laughed. "Am I in trouble, old man? Merely for pointing out that you're still in love with the Dragon Prioress?"

"I am not in love with her," he said, his voice low.

Sable grinned. "You forget I can tell when someone's lying."

He opened his mouth, then closed it again.

She laid out the cloth the sword was stored in and folded it over the blade. "I don't blame you, Atticus. I think half of Immusmala is in love with her, and they've only seen her from afar. She's…" Sable searched for the words. "She's one of the few people I've always admired. And I admire almost no one." She finished wrapping the sword. "But what troubles me, Atticus of Center Stage, is that something happened between you two, and she does not seem as enamored of you."

His expression was impossible to read.

"Is that going to cause us problems? Because winning that tourney may depend on what she thinks of us."

"It will not be a problem," he said firmly.

Sable waited for him to say more, but his words had the warmth of truth in them. Slowly, she nodded. "I hope not."

CHAPTER FORTY-EIGHT

WHEN SABLE WOKE the next morning, the sky was heavy with clouds, but she could tell it was long past sunrise. She had a momentary twinge of disappointment that Reese hadn't woken her. Not that there could have been much of a sunrise with this weather. Thulan puttered around the campfire, but a quick scan of their campsite showed no sign of Reese.

Her mood as muted as the weather, Sable moved closer to the fire. Leonis came around the wagons with Andreese, who carried a string of fish.

Thulan looked at Leonis suspiciously. "Where have you been?"

"Fishing," he answered, pointing at the fish.

Thulan crossed her arms. "You don't fish. You never do anything helpful."

"Well, he did today," Andreese said. "He knew exactly where the fish were. I am never going without him again."

Thulan raised one bushy eyebrow. "Fishing is a quiet activity. There's no way Leonis was quiet." She set a pan over the fire.

"If it leads to this many fish, I'll take the chatting." Andreese handed Thulan the line, then sat next to Sable.

"You're going to burn them if you get the pan too hot," Leonis said, leaning close to the pan.

"Go back to being unhelpful and give me space," Thulan answered, elbowing him out of her way.

"I'm not leaving you to ruin my fish." Leonis sat close to the dwarf. "I spent a lot of energy telling Andreese where to find them."

As the two of them continued to bicker, Sable leaned closer to Andreese and lowered her voice. "That is the first unsolicited work I've ever seen Leonis do. Last night he seemed to actually want to help with the stage, and now this. It's odd."

"He was very bossy about where the fish were and how I should catch them."

"That's what you get for picking him as your morning companion."

"I didn't. He was waiting for me when I woke up. Just sitting next to me. It was creepy. Told me there were fish in the stream and wanted me to catch them." He glanced at her, with the hint of a smile. "Are you envious I didn't pick you?"

She squinted up into the clouds. "I am a little disappointed."

He turned toward her. "Really?"

She nodded. "I'm hungry. Tomorrow, head out earlier so the fish are cooked by the time I get up."

The next few days went smoothly. The closer they drew to Immusmala, the more Sable contemplated the words and hopes of Vivaine. Until the very end, the prioress believed Balin hadn't really fallen as much as he had. Even during the final scene, she begged him to stop killing, to realize what he was doing and come back from the darkness.

As Sable pondered what she would say to Talia when she found her, Vivaine's words and hope kept coming to mind.

Every night, Andreese would wait around long enough to watch Sable hold the sword at the beginning before he'd wander off, showing up again at the end to make sure she stabbed Leonis well. He had endless corrections for her about her grip and swing.

The weather continued cloudy and cool, with no sunrises to be seen, but each day, Reese would find her as they walked and set her through another practice. The closer they drew to Immusmala, the more urgent his lessons felt.

As the movements became more familiar, an odd sense of confidence came with them. She was hardly at the point where she'd be able to defend herself, or attack anyone, but the sword had become comfortable in her hand, and the motions were almost habitual. Which felt both powerful and disquieting.

The road was well-traveled with farmers heading to Immusmala to sell their wares at the Midsommer Festival, and the troupe moved at an unhurried pace for the next few days, allowing news of their play to reach each town before they arrived.

Before each night's performance, they spread news about the Kalesh threat. In the small, isolated towns near the plains, at least some of the people took the threat seriously and began to gather their local, volunteer militia.

But by the time they reached Molas, the first town large enough to have a busy tavern, several shops, and a standing militia, the news was met with a careless indifference.

"There are always raids on the Eastern Reaches," the tavern keeper told Atticus. "None of it ever comes this far west."

"The Kalesh we met claim it will this time," Atticus said, his voice hardening.

"The Kalesh? Their merchants stick to the bigger towns, their wares too expensive for sensible folk to buy, but they're hardly threatening."

"It's not Kalesh merchants who are coming," Atticus argued.

Already annoyed by the nonchalant response, Sable didn't stay to hear the man's answer. She pushed her way out of the busy tavern and headed across the small square to where the wagons sat near the top of the sea cliffs.

From that height, she caught her first, distant glimpse of Immusmala, jutting out into the sea. The tavern keeper's dismissal sat heavily in the air. What if no one listened to them?

She looked at the distant city. It was a strange thought that over the past weeks, nothing had changed for Talia. The best Sable could hope for was that Talia was still working for Lady Ingred, and still firmly under Kiva's control.

Sable fingered the handful of silver coins Atticus had given her after the last show. It was five times more than the night before. Squeezing her hand around the coins, she looked at the lights of the city.

Maybe she'd actually earn enough to pay off Talia's debt. It was a stretch, but the little spark of hope in her clung tenuously to life.

Maybe Vivaine was the key that would finally get them all out of Dockside.

Of course, the closer the city came, the more a different fear surfaced.

It wouldn't take long for Kiva to find out that she was back in the city. And that Ryah was with her. He wouldn't expect them to be in an acting troupe, but standing on stage wasn't exactly subtle.

But if people in towns as small as Molas didn't believe the Kalesh were a threat, Atticus had his work cut out for him in the city. He'd need the biggest, most powerful platform he could get.

Sable turned her back on Immusmala. If Kiva found her, she'd deal with him. Until that happened, she had bigger things to focus on.

The next day, Sable walked with Reese behind the wagons under the pretense of practicing sword work, but really to avoid Atticus and his incessant drilling. Leonis joined them.

"I cannot practice those lines one more time," he grumbled. "The old man has never been this difficult."

Something had changed in Leonis since the night Cintis had joined them in the woods. Helping Reese fish had been just the beginning. He'd spent the evenings spreading the news of the Kalesh, he'd helped Thulan clean up after meals, until she sent him away for complicating things. He hadn't even looked for any card games in the towns they'd stopped in. But more than that, when he spoke, there was a somberness to his voice.

"Atticus is getting more uptight the closer we get to the city," Sable agreed.

"That's because he feels it, too." Leonis shook his head. "Even out here in the smaller towns, people are reluctant to believe what we have to say about the Kalesh."

They were silent again, the only sounds the creaking of the wagons and Atticus's voice calling out something dramatic up ahead.

Sable glanced at the two men beside her. As morbid as it sounded, the thought that all three of them had experienced the same sort of loss at the hands of the Kalesh felt oddly comforting.

Memories of her parents welled up in her, until she finally spoke.

"My parents were funny. My mother used to make up ridiculous stories to explain the simplest of things. Like how fairies had to tell each other tragic tales every night until they made enough tears to make the morning dew. Then my father would carve little fairies with dramatic, bawling faces and leave them all over for her." A handful of them had been perched on the kitchen table on that last, fiery night.

They walked in silence for a few minutes.

"My aunt made the best pork stew I've ever tasted," Andreese said eventually. "When it was cooking, the smell would draw people in Ebenmoor to the butcher shop for some. She used to have to make a vat of it."

The anger at the Kalesh that had been in Sable for as long as she could remember mixed roughly against her own grief and the sorrow of the men next to her.

"My mother was happy." Leonis looked into the trees, his face serious. "She kept my father happy. When she died, he stopped smiling. I've never once seen him smile without her."

Sable looked at him, a memory from that horrible night surfacing. "I saw elves once," she said quietly. "The night my parents died, they came out of the woods and killed the Kalesh attackers."

Leonis looked at her, his face a complicated blend of emotions.

"Maybe they were the ones sent to avenge your mother," she said.

"I'd never seen elves before. But they're the reason my sisters and I are alive." It felt complicated to be thankful for something that had only happened because Leonis's mother had been killed.

Sable frowned. "My mother used to sing songs in a language I didn't understand. She claimed it was elvish, but my father just laughed and said it was nonsense. But she also had an elvish bow."

Leonis frowned. "You think your mother knew elves?"

Sable shrugged. "Did you know of any humans named Stephan and Amelia?"

He shook his head.

Sable sighed. "The Kalesh have taken too much from too many. We have to make people listen."

They both nodded, but there was little hope in the action.

Folhaven was swollen with people.

Atticus guided the wagons into the main square on yet another drizzly afternoon. The streets, which had held only a spattering of people the last time they'd driven through, now teemed with crowds. Farmers brought crops to sell, merchants brought wares. Performers lined up along the roadsides, entertaining anyone who would watch. The festival wouldn't start in Immusmala until tomorrow night, but a preview of it spread across Folhaven, despite the gloomy weather.

A few people recognized Atticus as he passed, and little swirls of commotion began. He steered them toward The Listing Sails, a tavern on the far side where an enormous man began shooing people away, clearing a space for the wagons. Atticus thanked him, then disappeared inside.

The spot in front of the Millstone Inn where they'd set up their stage last time was filled with three high-end merchant carts selling Kalesh silks. The dragons were everywhere. They decorated scarves, skirts, shirtsleeves, handkerchiefs, dishes, small tapestries. The carts swarmed with people.

"Is it a bad sign that we've been replaced by people who admire the Kalesh?" Sable asked Leonis as he checked his tree.

He glanced across the square. "The Sails always saves us a spot before festivals," Leonis explained. "Setting up near the Millstone last time was Merilee's doing."

"Is it going to hurt us that she's not here?" Sable asked.

She expected an emphatic no, but Leonis paused and glanced at the people nearest them. The glimpse of his tree had garnered a little attention, and Leonis shifted it so it could be seen more easily. "Maybe. We'll have to work harder to gather a crowd." He looked at Sable. "But that's nothing we haven't done for years. And you're the right Vivaine for this play." He let out a chuckle. "Sometimes it's hard to refuse you in that last scene, Sneaks. Last night, Balin almost threw himself to his knees and begged for forgiveness."

"Sorry," Sable said with a grin. "I just feel those words very strongly."

"I can tell." He crossed his arms, and a shadow of concern crossed his features. "Whatever it is you're tapping into, you're not forcing me to believe you, but...you're doing something. I start to lose the truth of my own feelings because yours are so strong."

She shifted at the gravity in his voice. "Maybe it's because Balin's feelings are crazy, and Vivaine's are normal."

Leonis frowned. "No. Balin's feelings are rational, and I have no problem with their logic." He reached into the wagon and pulled out the prop sword. "At least until you try to convince me otherwise."

There was a solemnity to his voice that made her pause. "I'm supposed to be convincing you otherwise."

"Yes, but it's not meant to work. Whatever you're doing, just..." He paused. "Be careful. It's one thing to do it in the play, but if you start using this in real life..." He blew out a deep breath. "Now I sound like Cintis. Just be careful, all right?"

He handed her the sword

Though Serene had thought it possible Sable's words could affect someone else, the fact they actually did left her unsteady. The space between herself and Leonis suddenly felt tangible. As though it were waiting to be used instead of merely keeping them apart.

She gripped the hilt, and even though it was only a prop, she was struck by how savage of a thing a sword was. And how familiar it felt in her hand.

A disturbing ripple ran through her. Her ability to feel the truth was comfortably familiar as well. What if it also held a savage edge?

She looked back up at Leonis. "I'll be careful."

CHAPTER FORTY-NINE

A GROUP HAD GATHERED near the wagons. Leonis glanced at them, worry still shadowing his face. "Come on, Sneaks. Let's get the buzz started."

Sable followed him toward the crowd. "I have no idea what that means."

Leonis strode out from the wagons and up to the first people he saw. "Festival blessings on you all," he said extravagantly. "Have you come to see the Figment of Wits Traveling Troupe?"

A couple people shouted greetings, and a tall man in front nodded. "Heard you were doing a story about the Dragon Prioress. The one where her girl dies." His sounded skeptical.

"'Tis true," a man with shaggy hair and beard behind him called. "My cousin seen it in Molas. Says it was the best show he'd seen in years. If it's true, the prioress is a blasted hero, ain't no doubt."

"It is true." Leonis nodded to the fellow. "And I'd agree she's a blasted hero. We'll be performing one show tonight before we head into the Sanctuary tomorrow."

"Is that the girl who plays the prioress?" the shaggy man asked.

"It is," Leonis said, drawing Sable forward with a flourish. "Issable

403

of Shadowfall. Her performance has been called breathtaking and enamoring."

Sable stepped forward and bowed. "It has not," she whispered, but Leonis didn't answer. The crowd looked at her curiously, and she suddenly wished she'd spent a moment fixing her hair, or changing out of her wrinkled traveling clothes.

On top of feeling slightly disheveled, all the eyes on her so close to Immusmala made her feel vulnerable. The chances of someone she knew being all the way in Folhaven were slim, but she found herself warily searching for familiar faces.

"Well, my cousin was enamored," the shaggy man said to her with a laugh. "If you've a mind to settle down with a sheep farmer from Molas, young lady, I know one who'd poke his own eye out at the chance to speak to ya."

Sable opened her mouth, but could find nothing to say to such a statement.

"Tell your friends," Leonis called out, climbing onto the steps at the back of the wagon. "Here in Folhaven Square, before the crowds of Immusmala have the chance, you can see the true story of the prioress and the baledin! At dusk, at the Listing Sails, come hear the story that everyone is talking about! Come early and bring your friends!"

More faces around the square turned toward them. A few shouted greetings to Leonis, which he enthusiastically returned.

"Issable!" someone shouted from the crowd.

Sable tensed and she searched the crowd. A lanky youth caught her eye and gave her a wave.

"Issable!" he yelled again.

"Come up here and wave to your fans," Leonis said to her, offering his hand.

She tried to keep a smile on her face as he helped her up onto the steps. "Fans?" she asked faintly.

"Bow," he said quietly, smiling at the crowd. "Smile and wave. They're here to see you."

Sable gave a small bow to the crowd, and several people cheered loudly.

"How do they know who I am?" she asked under her breath.

"Because Atticus knows how to work a crowd, even before he's gotten to a town. Whatever welcome we get here in Folhaven, expect ten times as much in Immusmala." He glanced at her. "You should probably have Thulan fix your hair tomorrow. Maybe even wear something nice. At this point, they're expecting a glamorous actress."

Sable laughed faintly, and Leonis responded with an enthusiastic laugh of his own. "Good. Laugh. Look happy. Very good."

She gave the crowd a quick bow. "I need to go inside."

Leonis protested, but she climbed down and hurried inside the tavern, looking for Atticus. He was moving through the common room, talking, laughing, reminding everyone that the play would start when darkness fell.

"Issable!" He greeted her loudly.

She smiled stiffly at the cheers from the people in the room as she came up close to him.

"Kiva is going to find me if I keep getting so much attention," she said softly.

Atticus nodded slowly. "But if we don't get all the attention we can, we're less likely to win. And if we don't win..."

"I know. Nobody will pay enough attention to us to hear about the Kalesh." Sable ran her fingers through her hair. "I thought this would be worth the risk, but all it will take is one Vaya to recognize me and the entire troupe might be in danger." She paused. "They'll find Ryah."

Atticus frowned. "I thought Talia was the only one in danger from the gangs."

Sable blew out a long breath. "I may have made Kiva really angry before I left."

He crossed his arms. "How angry?" He studied her for a moment. "If Kiva discovers you, is he going to want to kill you? Or does he want something from you?"

Sable rubbed her face. "I don't know. There's something he wants me to steal for him, something I have a better chance of reaching than anyone else, so normally I'd say he wouldn't want me dead. But that was before I defied him and left. He might feel like he needs to make an example of me." She glanced toward the crowd. "I could wear some sort of disguise."

Atticus shook his head. "People are already recognizing you. Nothing is going to help our cause more than you being visible." He looked at her sternly. "But from this moment on, you don't go anywhere alone. If you need to be away from the rest of the troupe, take Andreese or Thulan."

Serene and Jae entered the common room and came toward them.

"Or Serene," Atticus added. "We have the show here tonight, then two nights in Immusmala. I'll have Andreese watch the crowd while you're on stage, and we'll be careful.

"You can stay inside until the show tonight," Atticus continued. "But starting tomorrow, on the way to Immusmala, we'll need you out in the open as much as possible. People are going to want to see you, but we'll do our best to keep you out of danger. You have no idea how valuable you are to our goals."

He gave her a rueful look. "I'm not a man who puts much stock in gods or goddesses, but when I think about how you came to be in the troupe now, at this specific time, for this role... It feels almost fated."

"It wasn't fate, or goddesses," Serene said, coming up beside them. "It was just two people recognizing a mutually beneficial arrangement."

Jae trailed after her. "You can suck the fun out of any story."

"Don't try to make it more exciting than it is," Serene said. "It was coincidence."

"If it were two regular people," Jae said, "I might agree. But it's Atticus and Sable."

Serene paused, and her exasperated look turned thoughtful. "You might be on to something. Not only are they irregular—"

"Irregular?" Sable asked, frowning.

"But their skills are similar," Serene continued, ignoring her. "Sable can sense the truth in people's words, and Atticus draws the truth out of people."

"People like us are drawn to each other," Jae said to Serene. "Maybe it was the same for these two."

"People like us seek each other out," Serene corrected him.

Jae shook his head. "Not always. The stories of how people are drawn to Merrick are astonishing."

Serene shrugged. "Every story is astonishing if you look closely enough."

"However it is that we met," Atticus interrupted, turning back to Sable, "I'm glad it happened. We will do all we can to keep you safe. And once this tourney is over, we'll help you get your sister."

Sable straightened. "You will?"

"Between Jae and Atticus," Serene said, "they know half the city."

There was truth in their words, but something much deeper and more fierce pressed in on her. She swallowed. "Thank you. It's been a very, very long time since I've had..." *Family* was the word she wanted to say, but an unexpected reluctance to claim something so personal closed her mouth.

Atticus set his hand on her shoulder. "You're part of the family, now." The warmth of truth from his words filled the air. "Welcome home, Sable." With a final squeeze, he walked into the crowd, calling out greetings.

Jae watched Atticus walk away, an envious expression on his face. "If I live to be a hundred, I'll never master the way he can say something so dramatic, yet pull it off so genuinely."

Sable laughed. Neither Jae nor Atticus would have any sway over Kiva, but merely the fact that she wasn't alone any longer made the situation in Immusmala feel more hopeful.

Andreese, Ryah, and Thulan sat at a table in the far corner of the common room playing a card game, and Sable went to sit with them. Jae, Serene, and Atticus stopped by to say they were going to spend the afternoon visiting the influential people in Folhaven.

"Ryah," Atticus said, "will you come with us? You look so much more genuine than the rest of us, people are more likely to believe this unexpected news of the Kalesh coming from you."

"I doubt that," she answered.

"Well, it's true." He rubbed his hands together. "This is just another performance, and you are the right actress for the part."

Ryah gave Sable a skeptical glance, but followed him out. They were gone for about an hour, and when they returned, Ryah flopped down next to Sable.

"The Kalesh silks are everywhere. And not just among the wealthy. Even the low-end shops have begun embroidering dragons onto their clothes. Half the people I saw today had some sort of dragon on them somewhere."

Andreese and Thulan frowned at the news.

"That doesn't bode well," Sable said.

Ryah sighed and leaned her head back against the wall. "No. Atticus, Jae, and Serene are all worried."

"Maybe Immusmala will be different," Sable said.

Ryah bit her lip. "Maybe."

News of their play, on the other hand, had been enthusiastically received. Wild speculation flew through the town as to whether the story was true, or merely a ploy by the priories to paint the High Prioress in a flattering light.

Atticus listened gleefully to two men debate just that as they walked by. "Nothing spreads news faster than people disagreeing," he said to the troupe, before sending them off to set up the stage.

They cleared a wide space near the wagons, and began the long process of setting up the full stage. After the smaller version they'd been using, this one felt enormous.

This performance was the best one yet. The lines now came easily enough that Sable barely had to think about them. She and Leonis had fallen into a rhythm, and the scenes about Vivaine and Balin's relationship came to life.

The crowd let out an audible gasp when she stabbed Balin, and when Sable stepped up to bow and Atticus called out, "Issable of Shadowfall," the cheers were deafening.

The next morning, a quiet knock at the door woke Sable. She blinked into the darkness for a moment before remembering she was in a room in the Listing Sails.

"Sable," Reese called quietly.

Sable tiptoed across the room, and cracked open the door. From the lantern hanging at the far end of the hall, she could just make him out.

"The clouds are gone," he whispered.

Sable glanced back at the window, seeing nothing but darkness. "How can you possibly tell?"

He smiled. "There are stars. Are you coming?"

"Is it cold?"

He held up a blanket. "Chilly."

She slipped her feet into her boots and followed him into the hall.

He glanced at her head. "I see the hair in utter disarray is normal for this early." She shot him a glare, and he laughed quietly. "After the noise and crowds of last night, I thought you could use some quiet."

"My room was quiet." She wrapped her arms around herself at the chilliness of the hall. "How are you going to find anywhere quieter in the middle of Folhaven?"

He shot a grin over his shoulder as he headed down the stairs. She followed him into the quiet common room. There was a little noise from the kitchen, but the tables were all empty. Andreese led her outside and ducked along the side of the building. The sky was lighter than it had seemed from inside, more of a rich blue than a black, and a slight breeze rippled through the quiet city. Near the back corner of the inn, Reese slung the blanket over his shoulder and started up a ladder fixed to the wall.

She followed him up onto the low-pitched roof. The wooden shingles were rough under her hands, and she followed him away from the edge to where he sat, facing the eastern horizon.

From this height, the roofs of Folhaven spread out below them. Most buildings away from the square were only a single story, and there was an unobstructed view to the east.

The wind blew across the roof. He moved closer and wrapped the blanket around them both. "Warm enough?"

She could feel the warmth of his shoulder against hers, and she drew her knees up, pulling the blanket around until it covered her legs. "It's perfect."

The shushing of the wind enveloped the few sounds of the city, and Sable closed her eyes, letting the calm of the moment seep into her.

He nudged her shoulder. "Don't go back to sleep."

"You can wake me when the sun rises."

"Won't be long now."

The clouds from the past few days had cleared, leaving only thin wisps of lighter grey against the stars. Slowly, almost imperceptibly, the clouds nearest the horizon took on a deep reddish glow.

They sat in silence as the light grew. Sable hadn't realized how little quiet there had been in the last couple of days. Her mind skipped from the play, to Talia, to the crowds that would come again today.

The blanket was snug against her back and legs. Reese sat next to her, perfectly relaxed, but Sable felt a tension in her own shoulders. His arm against hers was unexpectedly warm.

She couldn't remember the last time she'd been this close to anyone. When Talia and Ryah were little, they would climb into her bed if they were scared, but it had been purely so she could comfort them. Reese made no effort to talk. He just sat next to her and warmed her shoulder.

Something deep inside her loosened. The worry for Talia softened slightly, the busyness of the coming day receded. She closed her eyes again and breathed in the morning air and the slight scent of leather Reese always had. Her lungs stretched with the air, as though she hadn't breathed that deeply in months.

He glanced over at her with a small smile on his lips. "See? Nothing better than a sunrise."

She met his gaze.

It was more than the sunrise, but she nodded and refocused on the brightening horizon.

His presence, she realized, had become familiar. In the midst of all of the rehearsing, performing, and Kalesh worries, he was a pool of calm.

She couldn't remember the last time anyone had felt this comfortable. She watched the eastern sky, regretting that the sun would rise soon. From this point on, there'd be no more days of walking and practicing with a sword in a quiet spot while the horses rested.

She was acutely aware of his arm against hers. How solid it felt.

A question rose in her mind. The last time they'd watched the sun rise, he'd said, "We'll find her" when she talked about Talia. But finding her was hardly his problem, and there were bigger things going on in the world. Even though she didn't want to hear the answer to her question, she had to ask. "Are you leaving when we reach Immusmala?"

"I can't leave before the tourney," he said easily. "There's a chance you'll forget all your lines and embarrass yourself. That's not something I can risk missing."

She gave a small laugh.

"And we need to find your sister." His voice was so light he might as well have been talking about finding breakfast.

"That's not your problem, though."

He turned to look at her. "True. It's your problem, but if I can help, I will."

She let herself lean a little more against him. "Thank you." She turned back to the sunrise. "And after the tourney is over?"

He blew out a long breath. "I don't know. I have to do what I can to fight the Kalesh. And that means joining my uncle's troops. We need the Northern Lords, or we don't stand a chance."

"I know," she answered quietly. "I know that's what you have to do. I just..." She sighed. "The last few weeks have been good."

He nodded, but didn't say anything else, and they sat in silence while the edge of the sun finally slipped into view. A clatter from downstairs was met with a loud rebuke from someone in the kitchen. The creak of a wagon rolling through the square floated over the roof.

With a tiny *pop*, Purnicious appeared at Sable's side, her face apologetic. "I'm sorry to interrupt you, mistress, but Atticus is looking for you. He's adamant you find Thulan and get ready for the day." Her purple eyes flickered toward Reese, then back to Sable with a wince. "I'm sorry."

Sable sighed and nodded. "I'll be down shortly."

Purnicious disappeared, and Sable let out a long breath.

"When Atticus said he was going to win the world's attention with a play," Reese said, "I thought he was crazy. But he's done it." He leaned into Sable's shoulder. "You've done it. Your Vivaine is mesmerizing. Last night, I found myself actually liking a prioress."

Sable smiled at him. "Don't worry. When we reach Immusmala, you'll see the real Prioress Eugessa. She'll renew your lack of faith."

Sable unwrapped the blanket from her legs. "Are you coming down?"

"No one cares what I do this morning. I think I'll stay where it's quiet for a bit."

Sable tossed her end of the blanket at him. "Lucky."

She crawled to the edge of the roof and swung her feet onto the ladder. When she looked up, Reese watched her with an unreadable expression.

"Thank you for this." Sable gestured toward the sun. "I didn't know how much I needed it."

He nodded.

She paused. "And thank you for all the time you spent teaching me with the sword. I don't have a way to pay you back."

"Not having to watch you hold it like a bouquet of flowers is payment enough."

"I'm serious," she said. "I owe you."

Reese shook his head. "You gave me the chance to teach someone again. I haven't done that in a long time." A smile spread across his face. "It was fun."

Sable shook her head. "That doesn't feel like we're even."

He gave her a long look. "It does to me."

CHAPTER FIFTY

THULAN FIXED Sable's hair and painted her face with a light touch before they went down to the packed common room. People greeted her as Issable. She smiled and nodded until she reached Atticus standing at a small table where Jae and Serene ate.

"Can I get my food and eat it in the wagons?" she asked him quietly.

"Absolutely not." He gave her a wide smile. "This is exactly what we need. These people will reach Immusmala before us, and hopefully half our work will be done before we even set up our stage."

Sable sat down next to Serene and Jae. The quiet of the roof already seemed terribly distant.

The tavern keeper himself appeared with a plate of eggs and potatoes. "Not every day I get to serve the High Prioress!" he called out loudly, and several people cheered.

Sable thanked him and focused on her food, trying to block out the fact that people watched her from their own tables.

"What exactly am I supposed to be doing?" Sable asked Atticus quietly.

"That's the beautiful part. Just be yourself." He considered her for a moment. "If all goes well, there's going to be a lot of attention over the next few days. So here's a secret. If you play into it, it's more fun and less draining. This is just another audience, and they're looking for a story in getting to see you."

Sable's gaze caught on a woman watching her curiously. Sable almost turned away, but the woman looked so eager that Sable gave her a smile. The woman straightened and approached. Sable forced the smile to stay on her face.

"I watched your show last night. I've admired the High Prioress for my whole life," the woman said as she stopped next to her. "I never believed she'd done anything wrong."

"I believe this story is true," Sable said honestly. "And it's made me admire her more, too."

"We're headed to Immusmala today," the woman said, "and we'll be watching again tonight!"

Sable thanked her, and the woman disappeared into the crowd.

Jae watched her go, tapping his chin thoughtfully. "I think Atticus has a reasonable shot at winning the tourney."

Serene nodded. "More than I've ever seen him have in the past."

The road into Immusmala was crowded.

The traffic that had steadily grown on the roads for the past couple days had turned into a solid flow of people, wagons, and horses, all heading toward the huge city. Purnicious's carvings on the back of the wagons made the troupe easily recognizable.

Sable, now dressed in a dark blue dress that was too simple to be called fancy and too pretty to be traveling clothes, walked with Ryah, Jae, and Serene. Purnicious, who was always scarce when there were crowds, rode in the back of a wagon.

Atticus pulled over a few times. Supposedly to let the horses rest, but they'd traveled such a short distance, there was no need. While stopped, he stood on the front of the wagon, greeting the people who passed, talking loudly with any who wanted to discuss the play, announcing they'd be in the Sanctuary for the festival. And he insisted that Sable sit up on the driver's bench of the other wagon, in plain view.

People called out greetings to "Issable." Children looked at her with wide eyes. One younger man asked her if she'd consider breaking her vows to the priory and marrying him.

"Holy vows are for life," she answered with a rueful smile, and he shrugged, walking on.

Andreese climbed up and sat beside her, frowning at the man's back.

Sable glanced at him. "We're supposed to be friendly. What are you scowling about?"

"You're supposed to be friendly. I don't have to be." His frown deepened. "There's too much attention on you."

"You're not the only one who wants to do whatever they can to fight the Kalesh." At his disapproving face, she crossed her arms. "I can't head off to join the army. The only thing I can do is help Atticus get the attention of people who need to know what's happening."

"It still feels like too big of a risk." He was quiet for a moment. "Kiva's going to find you."

She turned on him, her irritation flaring. "What exactly do you think I should do? Hide? Aside from needing to help with this play, I need to earn a fortune to buy Talia's freedom. If I don't act, how can I do that? Because I'm tired of stealing from people, Reese, and actually excited that there might be an honest way for me to get money." His expression didn't soften and she glared at him. "So unless you have a useful idea, stop rehashing the things that could go wrong. Because I promise you, you can't think of anything I haven't already worried myself sick over."

He held her gaze for a moment. "Right. Sorry." He looked back at the crowd. "I'm just not comfortable dangling you out in front of everyone."

She took a breath to get hold of her anger. Even without touching him, he still felt solid beside her, and she admitted it was reassuring to have him there.

"I suppose having you scowling next to me isn't a bad idea," she said in a more modified voice.

He leaned back on the wagon with his arms crossed, watching the people passing. His Kalesh sword lay across his lap, and for the first time since they'd been attacked in the woods weeks ago, he looked dangerous.

When she didn't look away, he turned to look at her with a frown. "What?"

She grinned at him. "I've never had my own menacing bodyguard."

"This is my third time guarding someone," he said, not smiling back. "But the first time I've wished I had a little help."

They rolled into Immusmala in the early afternoon. The buildings grew steadily more impressive. Starting with wooden shops and growing to beautiful stone façades the higher they drove up the hill.

Walking alongside the wagons felt too exposed, and she climbed onto the seat by Thulan. They climbed up the long road to the top of the city, then traveled along the Spine, turning toward the Sanctuary. At the Veil Gate, Atticus pulled the wagons to the side, climbing down to talk to an older abbess, who fixed him with a displeased expression through her thin veil.

"I'm Atticus, and this is The Duke's Figment of Wits Traveling Troupe," he announced with a flamboyant gesture toward the wagons.

A few faces in the crowd turned toward them.

The woman's face soured even more. "The ones who dare to put on a show about our beloved High Prioress?"

The troupe gathered next to the wagon.

"Not a good start," Thulan muttered.

"It might be," Leonis said quietly. "If she's heard of what we're doing, so have a lot of other people."

Thulan glanced at the Sanctus guard standing inside the gate. "That's what I'm afraid of."

Atticus gave the abbess a short bow. "That is our troupe, but I think you'll find our play is not only true, but complimentary."

The woman's mouth tightened into a thin line. "Your play has revived ugly rumors about the High Prioress. But some guards saw you in Folhaven last night. Their positive report is the only reason I'm allowing you through the gate." She cast a disapproving look at the wagons. "You are cleared to perform tonight. Whether you earn the right to stay the second night depends on the content of your play. We neither condone nor support slanderous accusations against anyone, especially one as respected and beloved as the High Prioress."

"I understand," Atticus said. "And I have no doubt that once you see our play, indeed if the High Prioress herself were to see it, she would find it not only acceptable, but appealing."

"We'll be the judge of that," the woman said. "Which duke do you represent, by the way?"

Atticus gave her an amused smile. "No living duke. The name comes from the ancient story of Figment Hubert, the jester for Duke Kinssmon. The duke was betrayed by his brother in a deadly plot. The jester, through a series of stories, softened the brother's heart to the point where he sacrificed himself to save the duke."

"I didn't know that," Sable whispered to Thulan.

"It's not that great of a story," she answered under her breath, "but Atticus loves it."

The abbess looked unimpressed.

"It's a wonderful story," Atticus added, his smile edged with irritation.

She unrolled a long, thin scroll. "You may have spot fourteen."

Atticus's smile disappeared. "Fourteen?"

She frowned at him. "That is noted as sixteen spaces closer than you were for the Red Shield Festival."

"Yes, but that was because of a misunderstanding. We are usually put much closer to the priories."

"A misunderstanding with whom?" the abbess asked.

Atticus hesitated, then gave her a humorless smile. "Spot fourteen will be fine."

"May Amah bless your show," the abbess said without any enthusiasm and motioned them through the gate.

Atticus climbed back up onto his wagon.

"Fourteen isn't great," Leonis said quietly.

"Not great?" Thulan said, starting her horses after Atticus's wagon. "It's awful."

"What is spot fourteen?" Sable asked.

"Entertainers are assigned locations based on…" Leonis waved his hands toward the crowd.

"How much they grovel before the priories," Serene said.

"Figures," Andreese said dryly.

"It's based on their current popularity," Leonis said. "Although I'm sure popularity is judged by the priories, so there's some truth to Serene's idea, too. For the Red Shield Festival, we managed to get the very worst spot in the plaza. Number thirty."

"That's why you were so far away from the priories," Sable said. "What was the misunderstanding?"

"We never did get a good explanation from the old man about that," Thulan grumbled.

"At the mid-winter celebration," Leonis said, "we were in spot seven, which is normal for us. Puts us nice and close to the priories and the bulk of the crowds. But this summer, they put us at the end."

"Atticus was livid," Thulan said.

"It had to do with the priory," Serene said. "I didn't hear details, but I did hear the High Prioress use Atticus's name in hushed tones with her aide. Unpleasantly hushed tones."

"Excellent," Thulan said. "Just the sort of thing we need hanging over us as we try to pull off this play. The High Prioress herself already against us. At least in spot fourteen, it won't be quite as public a spectacle when they come to haul us away."

"In spot fourteen," Leonis said, "we're going to have to put some work into getting people to come to us."

"Will it make a difference to the judges?" Sable asked.

Leonis considered the question. "I don't know."

"How many judges are there?" Ryah asked.

"Ten. Five merchants and five abbesses. And there are three troupes performing, so each stage will have at least three judges. One lucky stage will have four."

"It's not lucky when they don't like your portrayal of a lovesick farm girl," Thulan pointed out.

"Those judges wouldn't have known good acting if it punched them in the face." Leonis waved off her words. "And our play this year is much better than that one was." He turned back to Ryah. "The judges rate the public shows they watch tonight and tomorrow. The highest rating wins the chance to perform in the Grand Stadia, with everyone important in attendance."

Atticus pulled his wagon into a space between an acrobatic act and merchant with a cart full of intricately woven blankets. They were along the Sanctuary wall at least eight spots from the end of the Priory of the Horn. Most of the crowd was closer to the priories.

"Care to explain whatever black mark we have against us?" Thulan asked Atticus as she pulled in the second wagon.

Atticus, still angry, shot a glare back at the small figure of the abbess back at the Veil Gate. "Who knows what she was thinking," he muttered.

"The woman at the gate?" Sable asked.

Atticus scowled up at her. "No." He opened the door of his wagon with a jerk. "Nothing we can change now. Let's get set up. Leonis, you're on crowd marshaling tonight."

Leonis looked as though he might object and demand more answers, but Atticus's face was so thunderous, he just shrugged and started toward the crowd.

"The story everyone's talking about," he called out as he walked. "Tonight, for the first time in Immusmala, the tale you won't want to miss…"

CHAPTER FIFTY-ONE

SETTING UP THE STAGE, Sable was torn between watching for Talia or Kiva and wanting to hide behind the curtains.

She'd expected everything to feel uncomfortable and different, but it was more unsettling that the city felt exactly the same as it always had. Of course, it wouldn't change in a month, but now that she'd been outside the walls, the world felt so vast. There were Kalesh and dwarves and elves. There were whole towns of people who didn't care at all about anything in Immusmala.

For a glorious time, Sable had almost stopped caring, as well. But now, back among the crushingly familiar buildings, it felt as though she'd never left.

The feeling of security she'd grown used to while traveling with the troupe thinned and turned brittle. As early as this morning, she'd felt like a different person than the woman who used to live here. But now that she was deep inside the city, all those differences peeled away in the salty air.

Atticus, Jae, and Serene all disappeared toward the priories and the heavier crowds. Leonis wandered the plaza, calling out about the show. Purnicious buried herself in the wagons, sorting through costumes, looking for anything to mend or bellish. Ryah and Thulan worked with Sable on the stage. The troupe already felt like it was spreading out away from her, and Sable's brittle feeling settled into what it really was—isolation.

Whatever camaraderie they'd had while they traveled ended with this play, and she was going to have to face Kiva alone. The longer she was in the plaza, the more desperate she felt to find Talia.

While Thulan and Ryah worked with Purnicious to fix the hem of the last curtain, Sable glanced up at the sun. They had at least an hour before they'd need to start getting dressed, and the streets of the city would be crowded enough that she should be able to move through them easily.

There was no sign of Atticus in the crowd. She felt a slight pang at how angry he'd be, but she slipped backstage anyway.

Reese leaned against one of the wagons with his arms crossed, giving her a flat look. He was dressed in grey pants and a blue tunic that looked almost like a soldier's uniform, his sword buckled around his waist.

Sable considered him for a moment, bracing herself for the coming argument. "I'm going to look for Talia," she said firmly.

"Good. You can also help me find out where my uncle is staying."

She paused at the unexpected answer.

"I'm surprised you waited this long. I was getting bored." He looked at her critically. "You are planning to put on some kind of disguise, aren't you?"

She scowled at him. "I'm not stupid enough to go into Dockside looking like myself."

He gestured to the wagon. "Then we should hurry before someone comes and disapproves."

Sable climbed into the wagon and opened the crate of wigs. She picked out a light brown one with curls that crowded in around her face, then started tying a linen cap over it when Ryah spoke from behind her.

"I want to go see Mother Perrin."

Andreese looked at Ryah, amused. "You two are more alike than people might think."

Sable ignored him and shook her head at Ryah. "That's not safe."

Ryah looked pointedly at Sable's wig. "You're really going to try that argument? Besides, I'll be safer in the Bend surrounded by Muddogs than here in the Sanctuary. Especially if you and Reese leave."

"That's a good point," Andreese said. Ryah shot him a grateful look. "We can take her." The Kalesh sword hung at his belt, a small knife sheathed next to it.

"The Bend isn't on the way," Sable objected.

Ryah crossed her arms. "I'm going with or without you."

"We don't have time to sit there while you chat."

"Then drop me off. I'll be back before dusk."

Sable let out a breath. "Only if you have a Muddog escort you back here."

Ryah's mouth dropped open. "They're not going to take the time to walk me back."

Sable raised an eyebrow. "If I tell Tomm you're in danger, he'll come himself."

Ryah shot her an annoyed look.

Sable pulled a green hat out of the crate and tossed it to her sister. They left the stage and made it out the Veil Gate without seeing any of the troupe. Drawing close to the alley where Talia had hidden with Pete and Boone, Sable peered sidelong into it, through the curly wig. Something moved along one of the buildings, and she jerked her head toward it. Her feet caught on the cobblestones and she stumbled forward.

Ryah drew in a sharp breath.

Reese grabbed Sable's arm, his hand perfectly steady. "I didn't think the walking was going to be the dangerous part of this trip."

The person in the alley moved into view, and it was just a boy carrying a package.

Sable straightened. "Sorry."

The Spine was crowded. People strode along the avenue loaded down with packages, stepping in and out of the different shops. The women wore fine dresses, the men bright tunics. They passed the largest shops and reached a stretch of busy inns.

"These are where the Northern Lords stay," Sable told Andreese.

He scanned the men leaning against the front of the buildings. "By the one with the colored glass windows, one of the men has Lord Runess's insignia." He looked away from the inn, his shoulders tense.

"What if your uncle won't listen to you?" Sable asked.

"There are other people I can talk to," Andreese said. "How much farther to the Bend?"

Sable led them a handful of streets farther until they reached the shop with the two stone turtles flanking the door. She turned onto the narrow street heading downhill toward the Bend. They walked a block before Ryah gave a small wave to a huge, heavily tattooed man leaning on the side of an abandoned yellow house.

He pushed himself off the wall. "You back, angel?"

"Angel?" Andreese asked under his breath from behind them.

Ryah smiled self-consciously. "I am back. At least for a day."

Sable pushed the curls from the wig out of her face. "Can you see her safely to the abbey?"

The Muddog gave Sable a dark look. Andreese crossed his arms and stepped up beside her.

Ryah set her hand on Andreese's arm. "This is Myren, Reese," she said, her voice calm. "He can take me the rest of the way. I'm perfectly safe. You two have better things to do."

"Ryah needs to be back in the Sanctuary before dusk," Sable said to Myren. "Tell Tomm she needs an escort so she arrives safely."

Myren's face turned dangerous at the note of command in Sable's voice, but Ryah stepped between them.

"I'll talk to Tomm," Ryah said to her sister. "Stop worrying. I'll see you in a bit." She turned to Myren. "Would you mind walking with me to the abbey?" He didn't answer, but when Ryah started down the street, he fell in next to her.

Sable let out a breath and glanced at Andreese. "Were you going to protect me from that giant man?" she asked with a smile.

"I thought about it. Until I realized how big he was." He turned back up the street. "Thank you for not picking a fight with him."

"You have a sword at your waist," Sable pointed out. "And the Muddog had nothing."

"He probably had enough friends close by that the sword wouldn't have made much difference."

They walked back up the narrow street and rejoined the wide avenue.

"You're not going to like this idea," she said, "but I've been sneaking in and out of Dockside for years. It'll be easier if I go by myself."

He kept his eyes on the large inns ahead. "That's not happening."

Sable frowned at him. "What if I sneak away while you're busy with your uncle?"

"Then I'll follow you, which will make us both more vulnerable. It'll be better if you just take me with you."

"That's totally unnecessary."

"Yet it's happening," he answered absently. They'd reached the inn where his uncle's men still stood outside. Reese studied it for a moment before moving toward the stairs.

"Let's get this over with. Then we can go tempt death in Dockside."

Sable followed him up the wide, stone steps, through the door, and into an entrance hall so ornate she stopped in her tracks. The stone walls were covered with bright tapestries in reds and yellows. Dark wood tables surrounded by plush chairs sat in the corners. In the open center, an enormous, thick rug covered the floor.

Without pausing, Andreese strode across the room toward a long desk manned by a black-clad, respectable looking steward. A dozen men in sharp military uniforms milled around, talking to elegantly dressed women, drinking from tall, thin, fragile looking glasses. Sable smoothed her hands down her dress and followed Andreese.

"I'm sorry, my lord," a steward was saying to Andreese. "No unexpected guests are permitted upstairs. If you'd care to leave your name, I will make sure Lord Runess is made aware of your desire to see him. Perhaps you could return tomorrow."

"I don't need to see Lord Runess. And I'm not leaving until I see the lord's commander, Trefor of Ravenwick. He is my uncle, and I promise you, he wants to hear what I have to say."

"No unexpected guests," the steward began again.

"Reese?" a voice called from behind them.

A broad-chested man strode across the room.

Andreese's face split into a grin. "Tylar! How'd you earn enough clout to be invited south?"

He shrugged. "When our captains disappear, they have to promote somebody."

Andreese embraced the man. "I'd have thought they'd find a better choice than you."

"Me, too." Tylar looked down at Sable with a smile and raised an eyebrow. "Have you settled down into domestic life?"

"No," Andreese answered quickly.

"Of course not," Tylar said easily. "She's too pretty for your mangy face."

"This is," Reese glanced at Sable, "Issable."

"Hello, Issable," Tylar said gallantly, taking her hand and kissing it.

Sable drew back in surprise, and Andreese fixed Tylar with a pointed look until he dropped her hand.

"If you get tired of Reese and his overly serious outlook on life," Tylar told her, "I'd be happy to escort you to the festival tonight."

"Tempting," she said, "but my evening is already spoken for."

"Is my uncle here?" Reese asked.

Tylar gave Sable a wide grin before turning back to Andreese. "He and Lord Runess are at the priory doing something fancy. Won't be back until after the festival tonight. Do you want me to tell him you're here?"

Andreese shook his head. "Let's not give him any time to stew. I need to talk to him, but it can wait until tomorrow." His gaze caught on something near the door and he froze, his hand twitching toward his sword. "Are those Kalesh soldiers?" he asked, his voice low.

Four men lounged at a table in the corner, each dressed in a black uniform with red dragons embroidered down the sleeve.

Tylar nodded. "A few have been hired. Good fighters."

Andreese's hands curled into fists. "How long have they been here?"

"Most of the summer. They keep a bit to themselves, but they're nice enough."

"Lord Runess employs them?"

"A dozen of them. Your uncle can introduce you. They're in charge of most of the training and drills, which only makes sense. They put our best fighters to shame." He elbowed Andreese. "They might even give you a run for your money."

Andreese nodded slowly. "We'll have to see one day." His voice was cold enough that Sable tensed, but Tylar only smiled.

"I'd have come south years ago if I'd known this city was so fun," Tylar said. "I've never seen so many merchants and shops. And it's only going to grow. Did you hear two more gold mines were found in the mountains last week? All the Northern Lords are looking for ways to claim land in the hills. I'm disappointed we're headed back north in a few days."

Sable stared at the man, an idea clicking into place. She set her hand on Andreese's arm. "We should be going."

He nodded. "Good to see you, Tylar." The warmth in his voice from before was gone.

"And you, Reese." Tylar clapped him on the shoulder. "I'm still holding out hope that you'll come back."

Andreese gave a non-committal grunt. "That's more up to my uncle than me." He headed for the door.

Once outside, he started up the Spine, his strides long enough that Sable had to hurry to keep up. His face was thunderous.

"My uncle's a fool for listening to the Kalesh. I warned him." He ran his hands through his hair. "This is worse than I thought."

"It is," Sable said. "But I just realized why the Empire is so interested in us all of a sudden." She pulled him to a stop. "We just found gold."

CHAPTER FIFTY-TWO

"THE FIRST GOLD was found in the mountains and rivers last fall," Sable told Reese, "and since then, they've started several mines. If those mountains are full of gold, that explains why the Kalesh Empire suddenly finds us so interesting."

Reese shook his head. "But that doesn't explain why they're burning towns in the east."

A woman ahead of them on the street wore a pale green shawl with a white dragon embroidered across it.

"What they're doing here," he continued, "sending merchants and ambassadors to Immusmala, is something they've done in the past. Even having soldiers help the Northern Lords train their troops builds relationships the Empire will exploit in the future. It would save them a lot of troops if Immusmala and the Northern Lords would just peacefully surrender whenever the Empire decides to actually threaten."

"If the Kalesh have done this before, why would your uncle accept help from them?" Sable asked. "Why would anyone for that matter?"

Reese clenched his jaw. "Because my uncle doesn't know. In the north, the Empire is just admired for its military prowess. They don't know that the Kalesh attacked the Eastern Reaches." He sighed. "They probably don't even care that anyone attacked the Reaches. My uncle sent me to the Kalesh partly to get rid of me, but partly to see if I could learn anything that would help him conquer his neighbors. When I came back and told him what the Kalesh were really like, he wouldn't listen. None of them would. They already had Kalesh advisors coming in peace and offering to share their knowledge."

The truth sat dully in Sable's gut. "They're not going to listen to Atticus, either."

Reese looked back toward the inn. "Now that I've actually seen the Kalesh attacking in the east, maybe my uncle will listen." His jaw tightened and he turned toward Sable, his face ragged. "The Kalesh killed his sister! He has to listen, right?"

Sable shook her head with a sinking feeling. "I don't know."

She paused at the top of a street leading down toward the ocean. People bustled along it. "This way."

"No," he said firmly. "We need to talk to Atticus."

She crossed her arms. "This is the reason I came out here, Reese. Atticus can wait a half hour. If you can't, go. I'll be back at the stage before dusk."

He glared at her, but flicked his hand in an irritated invitation for her to lead on. They walked in silence for a few blocks.

"Do you think Talia will be here?" he asked.

"No. She should have moved into Lady Ingred's home, but I have no idea where that is. She has a room in Dockside, though, and even if she's not there, maybe I can find a clue as to where Ingred lives." The roofs of the city spilled down ahead of them to the ocean. She let out a long breath. "But mostly, I don't know where else to start looking."

Everything about Dockside was sickeningly familiar. It wasn't long until the saltiness of the ocean smell was replaced with the stench of fish. Whether it was worse tonight than usual or whether she just wasn't used to it anymore, the smell was so thick she could almost taste it. The cobblestones beneath her feet grew rough and broken.

Next to her, Reese was silent, his nose wrinkled against the smell. The lower they walked, the more his eyes scanned the streets. There were plenty of people to watch. The taverns and gaming houses were already full. Lantern light and the smell of dredgeweed smoke poured out the doorways and windows. People milled around the front of small shops or loitered with friends.

She kept expecting to see Kiva's sharp, goblin face, finding herself tensing anytime she saw anyone vaguely his size.

"What's it like in the north?" Sable asked Reese to distract herself.

"Pretty," he answered. "Huge forests, lots of rivers. Peaceful. And none of the cities are remotely this big."

"Have you been to Colbreth Castle where Merilee is from?"

"I've never seen it, but I've heard of it. It's very small, but it sits on a cliff overlooking a wide river. Supposed to be very dramatic."

"Not surprising that's where Merilee grew up then." Sable shifted. The deeper they went into Dockside, the more it clung to her.

Reese glanced at her. "We're not all like the places we came from."

"I hope not."

A few blocks before the Nest, Sable turned into a smaller, quieter side street.

"How much farther?" Andreese asked. His hand rested on the hilt of his sword.

"Not far."

In two more blocks, Sable paused at the outlet to a wider street and glanced around the corner. She could see the side of the Nest, alight with candles. The street in front of it was busy. Sable searched the crowd, but saw no sign of Talia.

She linked her arm with Andreese's. "Act like we're out for a stroll," she said, pulling him forward into the street. His arm was tense —actually, his whole body was tense—but he walked with her across the street, and no one paid them any attention.

When they reached the end of the alley behind the Nest, Sable paused. "Do you see anyone in there?" she asked quietly.

He frowned. "That's where you want to go?"

She nodded.

"Of course it is." He sighed. "We'd better make sure it's empty." He looked down at her a little smile playing across his lips. "Don't get mad."

"Mad at wha—"

Andreese slipped his arm around her waist and, with a twirl, lifted her off her feet and spun her into the alley. She gasped and grabbed onto his arms as he set her down next to a wooden crate almost as tall as she was.

In the process, he crashed his foot into the edge of the crate. She flinched at the sharp crack that echoed off the alley walls.

"What was that?" she hissed. "Are you sure you don't want to ring a bell or call out an announcement that we're here?"

Reese stood close to her, his hands on her waist, his face close to hers. Compared to the stench of Dockside, he smelled refreshingly non-fishy. She gripped his arms, her heart pounding with shock and something more complicated.

"Shh." He wasn't looking at her. "I can't hear anyone coming if you keep talking." He watched over her head, looking down the alley.

"You did that on purpose?"

"If there are guards, they'll come investigate."

Beneath her fingers, his arms felt strong and for a breath she wanted to lean against him.

He glanced down at her and through the curls of her wig, a small smile crept across his face. "I think we're safe."

He didn't move, though, and Sable's heart thundered for a reason that had nothing to do with Dockside.

"Then why are we still waiting?" she whispered.

His smile turned to a grin. "Because Dockside smells terrible, but your hair smells good."

There was a warm intensity to his eyes, and his beard was a rich brown in the evening light. She wanted to lift her hand to touch his cheek.

"You can't smell my hair through the wig," she pointed out.

He leaned closer and breathed in. "Yes, I can."

His face was so close, for a moment she found it hard to breathe.

A handful of birds caught the sunlight in the sky above his head, and she noticed how dark the alley had become. She gently pushed him back.

"Smell my hair later. We need to hurry."

He stepped back, still smiling, and motioned for her to continue down the alley. She took a deep breath, instantly regretting it as the stench of fish filled her nose. Hurrying down the alley, she kept her eye on what should be Talia's room. But there was no candlelight in her window.

"Wait here," she told Reese. His eyes widened when she started to climb up the building, but he only turned and watched down the alley.

Sable climbed up the rough stones to Talia's window and peered over the edge. The evening light illuminated the room enough for Sable to see in.

The sight made her hands grip the windowsill until the edges dug into her palms.

It wasn't just that Talia wasn't there. The room was completely empty.

Sable's hands grew cold and damp. The bed was bare of linens, the desk empty. No shoes, clothing, or drawings were visible.

"Sable," Reese whispered from the ground. "We need to move."

She ignored him and tried the window. If she could get in, maybe there'd be some sort of clue as to where her sister was.

"Sable," Reese hissed. He had moved farther down to where another alley branched off. "Someone's coming."

Sable looked in the window one more time before starting down. Her hands were clammy, the stones slipping under her fingers. Voices from the nearby alley floated toward her.

When her feet reached the level of Reese's head, he whispered, "Jump!" He held his hands out. The voices were closer and she pushed herself off the wall and he caught her, quickly setting her onto the ground.

The voices became clearer, at least three men, and Reese pushed her up against the wall. "Pretend we were looking for somewhere private."

Sable's hands were shaking and she balled them up against his chest. "Talia's gone," she whispered.

He froze. "Gone?"

Sable pressed her eyes closed and shrugged. Where would Kiva have taken her?

"You there!" one of the men called. "What ya doing lurking behind the Nest?"

A new fear clenched around her. That man's voice sounded familiar. It was one of Kiva's Fangs. The tall, skinny one with the horrible teeth. Sable pressed her head against Reese's neck, burying her face in his beard.

"I know them," she whispered.

Reese's hand tightened on her arm. "Keep your head down." He turned around, keeping Sable behind him. "Just looking for a quiet place," he said, his voice casual.

Sable peered around Reese's arm, letting the curls from the wig hang in front of her face. She recognized all three of the men as Fangs. She didn't know their names, and normally, she guessed they wouldn't know hers. But if Kiva had made people search for her after she left, they might know it now.

The talker gave Andreese a thin smile, showing his teeth, black from dredgeweed. "I'm afraid we'll have to fine ya for being here. We Vayas don't like folk sneakin' in these parts."

"We don't have any money with us." Andreese shifted toward the way they'd come. "But we'll get out of your way. Festive night to you boys."

Black Teeth set himself in front of them, and the other two spread out to block the alley in either direction. "Yer not going anywhere until ya pay the fine." He leaned over to get a better look at Sable.

Reese moved in front of her.

The man's gaze dropped to Reese's side. "I think you can start by giving us that sword."

He shifted his weight and set his hand on the hilt. "I'm afraid I can't do that, friend." His voice was still easy. "I might need it."

"Yer not from here, are ya?" Black Teeth pulled a knife from his belt, and the two others did the same. "There's not enough room in th' alleys for good swordwork. If ya planned to fight us, ya shoulda brought a knife."

Sable stepped back until she felt the wall behind her, looking down so the wig covered her face. All three men held their knives with ease, and she had no doubt they knew how to use them.

"I'd rather not fight you, to be honest," Reese said. "It's a festival night. There are better things to be doing."

"Ya can go to the festival if you leave yer sword," the man said. "And the woman."

Reese let out a long breath. "That's definitely not gonna happen, boys." His voice was no longer light. "Trust me. The two of us aren't worth the fight." He glanced at the sky. "And at this point, we're in a hurry to be somewhere else. So if you're going to do something, get on with it."

The man to Reese's left feinted with his knife, but Reese didn't move. The man to his right lunged forward and Reese had his sword out before Sable's warning echoed in the alley. He barely shifted his weight, but his sword flicked smoothly and the man's knife skittered across the alley toward Sable's feet. He let out a yell and grabbed his wrist, backing away.

"Whoever told you alleys were too small for swordwork didn't know how to use a sword," Andreese said.

Black Teeth stared at him, his eyes narrowed. "We have a lot of friends within shouting distance."

Andreese gave an irritated sigh. "You'll get hurt before they get here. Which is unnecessary. I need to get my friend to an engagement tonight. I promise you, your knives are no threat to me, and if you don't let us pass, I'll be forced to prove it."

Black Teeth motioned to the other man, and the two lunged. Sable reached down and grabbed the knife at her feet, her hand shaking. But she needn't have bothered. With only a few strokes, Reese had cut the back of the hand of the man to the left, making him drop his knife, and held his sword to Black Teeth's throat. The third man hadn't even moved.

"Hand over your knife," Reese said.

The man tensed.

"Don't do anything stupid," Andreese said tiredly. "It's nice to see someone unwilling to give up, but there's an old saying, *Better to know when you've lost than when you've won.* Men make stupid mistakes when they don't realize they've lost." His sword didn't waver from the man's throat. "Your knife."

Black Teeth held it out, and Reese took it. "Please pick up the third one, Issable," he said without turning.

Sable stepped forward and picked it up. The handle was slick with its owner's blood.

Reese motioned for the three men to move aside, and they did, Black Teeth moving slowly while the sword was at his neck. "We're leaving," Reese said. "Go enjoy the festival."

Black Teeth glanced at Sable, and his eyes widened in recognition. He let out a short laugh. "Almost didn't recognize ya past all the curls. 'Twas stupid to come back, girl. Even with yer soldier friend."

Sable tensed, and Reese lifted the sword tip, raising Black Teeth's chin.

He grinned a blackened smile and spread his hands to the side. "Yer wrong, soldier boy. You have something very valuable." He paused. "Red, go tell the boss Sable's back."

The man with the cut hand turned wide eyes to Sable, then ran out of the alley. Reese tensed, but kept his sword where it was.

"I suggest ya two run," Black Teeth said. "Won't take long for the news to spread."

Reese didn't move. Black Teeth raised his hands and stepped back, motioning the remaining man out of their way.

"Let's go." Reese moved slowly past them, and Sable stayed behind him. When they'd gone a few steps, Black Teeth and the other man turned and ran the other way. Reese wiped his sword off on his sleeve and shoved it back into its sheath. "Get us out of here as fast as you can."

Sable ran down the alley. She slowed to cross the street at the end of it, then broke into a run again once they were in the next alley.

"Busy streets would be better," he said, running behind her.

"We'll hit one soon. Kiva will have a dozen guards stationed near the front of the Nest tonight. We need to get away from here quickly."

She led him into a winding series of alleys. "Do you need these?" She held out the bloody knives as they ran. Reese shook his head and she dropped them in a shadowed corner.

A few turns later, they reached a wider road that ran from the west end of Dockside up to the Spine. It was busy, and they melted into the crowd heading uphill.

Reese's right hand rested on his sword, glancing over his shoulder. "That didn't go particularly well."

"I noticed."

He glanced down at her. "Where do you think Talia is?"

Sable bit down on the fear that rose inside her. "I don't know. Even if she's living at Lady Ingred's, she should still have a room in the Nest. All Kiva's spies do."

"It doesn't make sense that he'd hurt her. From everything you've said, he's a businessman. Talia would work for him in a job she's well-suited for—"

"Well-suited?" Sable hissed. "She's not suited to be a spy."

"From his perspective, she is," Reese said. "You said she's pretty and likable. That sounds like what any wealthy woman would want in a servant."

"She's a lot more than just pretty and likable."

"I'm not saying he should use her, Sable," he said calmly. "I'm saying he'd want to. There's no reason he would hurt her. She's worth more to him healthy and on his side."

"I know." Sable clenched her hands. "But why is her room empty?"

Reese was silent for a moment before he shot her an apologetic look. "Now Kiva will know the name is Issable."

She blew out a long breath. "It was only a matter of time."

"From now on, you're at my side at all times," he said firmly. "No sneaking off. You want to buy a snack, get me. You get an idea where Talia would be, find me. Do not step one foot away from the stage unless I'm with you."

Sable scowled at him. "I'm not helpless."

"I didn't say you were. But not one step anywhere without me."

She glanced over her shoulder for the hundredth time. "Agreed."

Talia's empty room haunted her. To avoid the reasons swirling in her head as to why it was empty, she turned to Reese. "You are better than I expected with your sword. I've never actually seen you fight before. I was a little nervous when all three of them pulled out their knives."

"I was a soldier for twelve years," he protested. "What do you think I did for all that time?"

She shrugged. "I knew you could fight, but there were three of them."

"Three street thugs." He looked at her incredulously. "If I can't handle three boys who barely know which end of the knife to hold, I don't deserve to carry a sword in the first place."

"You weren't at all worried?"

"No." He shot a scowl at her. "I'm insulted that you were."

She laughed. "Well, I won't be in the future. Next time, I'll try to draw a bigger crowd of thugs so it's more of a challenge for you."

"An alley is too small for swords," he muttered, rolling his eyes. "What on earth do they think sword fighting looks like?"

The street they were on spilled out onto the Spine, and they moved quickly into the throng heading toward the Sanctuary.

Sable bumped into Reese's shoulder, a different sort of tension filling her at the memory of standing so close to him in the alley. "Every time things got tense back there, I noticed your answer was to pull me into a cozy corner."

"I'm not opposed to cozy corners." A smile creased the edges of his eyes. "And I didn't notice you disliking it, either."

She pressed her lips together, fighting against a smile. "Is that a strategy they taught you in the Kalesh school? Or did you learn it from your uncle?"

He grinned. "This was the first time I've ever used it. Before now, I've never been put in tense situations with beautiful women."

She raised an eyebrow. "You think I'm beautiful?"

He wrinkled his nose at her hair. "Well, you met Tylar. Most of my tense situations were with men like him, so by comparison..."

"Ah... So you're saying I'm more beautiful than Tylar."

"Definitely."

The sun was setting behind the hills to the west, and they hurried along the Spine. Dozens of lanterns were being lit along the road. The Midsommer Festival, celebrating Amah, was all about light. Whereas there had been monsters and darkness for the Red Shield Festival a month ago, this one was full of bright firelight.

They hurried through the Veil Gate to find three enormous bonfires already lit in the Sanctuary. The priories were lined with lanterns and torches, even along their roofs and up their spires. Torches lined the wall of the plaza, and dozens of braziers dotted the square. The crowd filed into the Sanctuary with them, swelling the number of people already there. Sable wove her way to Atticus's wagons, Reese close behind her, searching to see if Ryah was back yet.

She rounded the stage, almost running into a livid Atticus. "Where have you been?" he snapped. "Ryah was escorted back by a tattooed giant almost an hour ago! Where did you sneak off to, and why did it take so long? You should be dressed already!"

"We didn't sneak—" Sable started, but Atticus fixed her with such a furious look she stopped. There had been a definite air of sneaking. She'd never seen him so angry. "Sorry," she said quietly.

He turned to Andreese. "Did you find your uncle?"

"We found where he's staying, but he wasn't there," he answered.

Atticus stared at him for a moment. "Then what on earth have you been doing?"

Reese paused. "Sable wanted to see if her sister was in her room."

Atticus spun toward her. "You went into Dockside? Are you insane?"

"I was with her," Reese said. "We were fine."

Sable held her hands up, trying to placate Atticus. "I'm sorry. I didn't know it would take this long."

His mouth fell open in shock. "Is that *blood* on your hands?"

She turned her palms over to see red lines smeared across them from the Fang's knives. "It's not mine," she assured him, closing her hand.

"Sable!" Thulan yelled from the corner of the wagon. "Where have you been? You look terrible. Take off that stupid wig and get back here!"

"Coming!" Sable called and gave Atticus an apologetic smile before heading toward the dwarf.

Atticus turned toward Andreese, eyes narrowed. "Why does my first lady have blood on her hands?"

"You don't really want to hear that story. But there are things I need to tell you…"

Sable ducked around the wagon and pulled the wig off her head. "Sorry," she said to Thulan. "We got a little sidetracked."

The dwarf grinned behind her beard. "We have plenty of time. Just thought you could use an escape from Atticus. He's been on a tear since he got back."

"Where was he?"

Thulan took out her brush to begin the process of turning Sable into Vivaine. "He spent the day with the leaders of the Merchant Guild, trying to tell them about the Kalesh. He was not well received. The merchants have increased trade with the Kalesh recently, and there's a disturbing amount of Kalesh goods flooding the streets."

"We had a similar experience with the Northern Lords." Sable explained about the Kalesh and the learning about the gold mines.

Thulan nodded. "Gold is a good reason for them to come."

Atticus strode around the corner of the wagon, still looking unhappy, but when he stopped in front of Sable, there was something sympathetic in his face, as well. "I'm sorry about your sister. I promise, when this is done, we'll do everything we can to help you find her.

"But tonight, I need you to forget about her, forget about the Kalesh. We have a good-sized crowd." He stopped for a moment to listen to the crowd. "Better than I'd expected, actually. And we have four judges instead of the required three. Which is also good. At least people are intrigued."

He focused back on Sable. "Tonight, I need the best performance of your life." He smiled, tighter than usual, and set his hand on her shoulder. "I still cannot believe my luck in finding you. You are the right actress for this part."

The warm truth of his words squeezed around her like a blanket, and she nodded again.

Atticus glanced at Thulan. "Everything ready?"

"It will be," she answered, setting down the brush and dividing Sable's hair into the sections to braid. "If you'll leave me alone to do it."

Atticus smiled slightly and walked away, but before he was out of sight, his face had fallen into a scowl again.

"I thought he'd be his usual giddy self before this show," Sable said quietly.

Thulan's hands paused. "He was," she said quietly. "Until he disappeared earlier. When he came back, he was furious."

"About the Kalesh?"

Thulan braided her hair in silence for a moment. "Not unless he ran into some on his way toward the Dragon Priory," she said under her breath.

The truth sank into Sable. "He went to see Vivaine?"

Thulan paused. "I hope not," she said without much conviction. "Because wherever he went, it didn't go well."

CHAPTER FIFTY-THREE

WHEN SABLE WAS DRESSED, painted, and braided, Thulan moved on to
getting Ryah ready. Her time at the abbey had gone well, and she
seemed more relaxed than Sable had seen her in a long time.

Andreese stationed himself in the gap between the stage and the
wagons, deterring the few people who thought they might sneak a
peek behind the stage, and Sable stood next to him. Torchlight and
lantern light glowed from all parts of the Sanctuary, and the plaza
teemed with people. Plenty of faces were turned to the stage, laughing
and cheering as Leonis told a string of short, funny tales.

Near the front center of the stage, four people sat in chairs. The two
women wore priory white. One man was outfitted in the rich brocade
of a merchant, but the second merchant had a scarlet dragon embroidered on the front of his black tunic. The tunic itself almost shimmered
in the torchlight.

Serene strode up to Sable, her expression black. She glanced up
where Atticus stood on stage, talking to the audience.

"We have a problem," she said quietly. "There are rumors around
the city of attacks out on the towns in the Eastern Reaches."

Sable looked at her sharply. "That's good, isn't it?"

"It's not. The Kalesh Ambassador is telling everyone the attacks are by raiders the Kalesh have encountered before, and that they're well equipped and vicious."

Sable stared at her. "He has to know the truth."

"He knows," Andreese said, glaring out toward the priories. "Let me guess. He's using it to his advantage."

"The ambassador was so generous"—Serene's lips curled around the word—"that he offered to bring troops over to help drive the deadly raiders out before they reach any of the larger towns."

Reese let out a groan. "They did that to an island nation once. Staged pirate raids, then offered to bring soldiers in to help, and were welcomed in as heroes."

Sable stared at them. "The Kalesh are killing all those people on the Reaches in a ploy to get troops invited to the area?"

"Yes," Serene answered. "And it's working. Everyone believes there are raiders in the east so dangerous they're a threat to even the bigger towns. His offer of troops is being hailed as a noble, selfless gift."

"We can't let them bring in troops," Andreese said, his voice furious. "Once they have a standing army here and decide to take over, no one will be able to put up a fight."

Serene clenched her jaw. "Everyone is falling for it. The fact that Vivaine didn't immediately accept his offer has actually turned some against her."

"They're taking the ambassador's side against the High Prioress?" Sable asked. "Who would do that?"

"It's mostly merchants. They're worried that some of the larger towns, like Molas, could be in danger. They trade enough wool and crops in that area that they want it protected. Without, of course, sending any of their own guards to do the work."

Sable looked through the crowd, catching a glimpse of an embroidered dragon on the back of a woman's long, shimmering, silver shawl. "If everyone's convinced they're raiders, and that the Kalesh are only here to help, no one's going to believe us when we tell them otherwise."

Serene sank against the side of the stage. "Whatever speech Atticus has been working on for that, it'd better be the best he's ever written."

"Will anyone in the priory listen to you?" Sable asked.

Serene glared toward the lit spires. "They wouldn't let us through the door. Not even Jae could talk his way in."

"The prioress is still mad about your comments about the ambassador?"

"Either that or she doesn't want to face me about the library. We'll try again tomorrow." She wrinkled her nose in distaste. "I even sent an apology in the hopes that I can get in and check on the books."

"Maybe if she hasn't accepted the ambassador's offer, she'll listen to you about the Kalesh," Sable said.

"Maybe." Serene set her hand on Sable's shoulder. "You just channel all this frustration and sympathy for Vivaine into your words tonight and impress those judges. Getting the chance to tell the merchants and priories what's really happening on the Reaches might be a long shot, but it's the best chance we have of getting anyone to listen."

Atticus introduced the play, and when Sable finally stepped out onto the stage, the lanterns washed out anything more than the impression of a large crowd. Even though it had become habitual to channel her worry into the story, tonight she felt ragged by the worry for Talia and the new fears about the Kalesh. She felt utterly powerless to affect the outcome of either.

From the first moment Balin declared he would be leaving, her desperation rose. The gnawing fear of it all clawed to get out, so she took that desperation and pushed it into her words.

They flowed out of her like living things, filling the stage with their warmth. Wrapping around Leonis, spilling over the front of the stage toward the audience.

She wasn't pretending to be Vivaine any longer. She was part of the woman, pressing against the inevitable outcome, hoping it would be different this time.

Late in the play, when she learned how far Balin had fallen, the news nearly broke her heart. During the final scene, pleading with him to stop, the tears in her eyes were real.

As her words grew in truth, the audience was drawn in. At the end, the cheers and applause were thunderous.

Sable bowed with the others, spent from it all. The judges stood and applauded with the rest. She looked into the crowd, searching for Talia's face, but the mob past the bright lanterns was a faceless mass.

Atticus ushered them off the back of the stage, beaming. "That was magnificent, Sable." He gave her a deep bow. "Your best performance yet. Possibly the best I've ever seen. Your words..." He shook his head, then looked at Ryah. "Fantastic, as usual, my dear."

Ryah sat on a crate. "Is it enough to win?"

"It's a good start."

Purnicious popped into view next to Sable. "You were wonderful, mistress!" she said enthusiastically. "I snuck under the judges' chairs, and they loved it, too!"

Sable leaned back against the wagon behind her, feeling like she could fall asleep. "I have never been this exhausted."

"Well, rest for a minute," Leonis said, "then come out front with me to talk to the crowd."

"Not tonight," Atticus said. "I'll greet the judges, but the rest of you stay back here."

"Here?" Leonis asked, glancing around at the small space between the stage and the wall of the Sanctuary.

Atticus nodded. "Did you hear the buzz when we bowed? There's a mystery around us. How do we know the story? Where did Sable come from? Is the story true?" He grinned. "Nothing spreads news like mystery. None of you leave this area until the crowd has moved on."

"They already know me," Leonis pointed out.

"I don't want any of you answering questions about the play, or how we know it, or any information about Sable." He raised his hand to stop Leonis from arguing more. "Don't worry. There is some cinnamon bread and two bottles of leeswine in the back of my wagon."

Leonis perked up. "In that case, we're fine here." He went to the wagon, pulled out the wine and handed one to Sable. He settled on a crate with the other.

Atticus paused and looked at Ryah. "Except you, my dear. One of the abbesses wanted to meet you. Would you mind coming and talking to her?"

Ryah hesitated. "Why does she want to talk to me?"

"She thought your portrayal of a prioress's handmaiden was touching and genuine." Atticus smiled at her. "She's quite a fan."

Ryah rose, and with an uncertain glance at Sable, followed Atticus around the stage. Thulan pulled a wrapped loaf of bread out of the wagon.

A few minutes later, Andreese walked around the corner of the stage. "The crowd is breaking up."

Even in the darkness behind the stage, the light from the Sanctuary drowned out all but the brightest stars and the full moon. "Are they headed toward the priories?"

"Looks that way."

Sable glanced up at the moon, which was approaching the top of the sky. "Not long until midnight."

"No," Leonis said firmly. "Atticus said to stay here."

"What's at midnight?" Reese asked.

"The High Prioress comes out and gives her speech about light and goodness," Thulan said, handing a slice of bread to Sable. A spiral of dark cinnamon gave off a sugary smell.

Sable took a bite. The taste was so rich and sweet that she sat silently for a moment, chewing. She was so tired. All she wanted to do was crawl into the back of the wagon and sleep. But part of her needed to go listen.

"I want to see her," she said finally.

Thulan rolled her eyes, and Reese glanced at her. "Who?"

"Vivaine."

He snorted. "Are you going to call her that to her face?"

"No." Sable took another bite of the bread and chewed slowly. "I just want to see her." She glanced at Thulan. "We could go out if we didn't look like ourselves."

The dwarf sighed. "If I go to all that work, you should do something more interesting than watching an old woman pander to the crowd."

"I feel like I've been Vivaine more often than I've been myself the last few weeks," Sable said firmly. "I want to see her. I'm gonna need a different wig, though. That one might be recognized."

Thulan shrugged. "If you leave, there's more sweet bread for me."

"I know where the long, red wig is," Purnicious said, disappearing with a *pop*.

Sable paused. "Ryah would probably like to come, too."

"No," Reese said firmly. "I'm only taking one of you."

"She's still busy with Atticus anyway," Leonis said. "Knowing him, he'll milk this little interview for all he can."

It took less time than Sable had expected to be transformed. She'd changed into a plain grey dress. Thulan tucked her hair up into a bun, pinned the wig of red hair to her head, and used the paints to make her appear older.

"Put that long shawl over your shoulders, Sneaks," Leonis suggested. "It'll hide how boring that dress is."

Andreese looked at her critically. "I'm impressed, Thulan."

The dwarf gave a short bow, then sat back down and picked up her piece of bread.

"Maybe it's me that's impressive," Sable pointed out.

"No. It's definitely Thulan." Reese offered Sable his arm, but she shook her head.

"Kiva's Fangs know what you look like now, too," she pointed out.

"I'm not wearing a wig," Reese said flatly.

"With the right jacket and hat, you'll look like a moderately wealthy merchant." Leonis dug the items out. "The jacket might be a bit snug through the shoulders, but it should work at night."

Reese put them on and turned to Sable with an exasperated expression. "Good enough?"

"You look incredibly respectable and boring," she said, taking his arm.

"Great," he said dryly. "Let's go waste our time seeing a woman we don't really know be adored by the public."

Sable frowned at him. "We know a bit about her by now."

They walked around the side of the stage. Most of the crowd had left, but Atticus still stood next to the two male judges. He glanced up at them and his eyes narrowed. But he gave Sable a short, albeit disapproving, nod and turned back to the men.

"We only know what Atticus has told us about her." Reese headed toward the u-shaped courtyard inside the three Grand Priories. "And since he seems as besotted as the rest with her, I'm not sure we can take his view as truth."

"Atticus told us the truth about what happened," Sable said.

He glanced down at her. "Are you sure?"

She nodded. "Positive. You should trust him more. I've actually never heard him lie to anyone."

"All that means is he believes what he's saying," Reese said. "Not necessarily that it's true."

"You think he's been fooled about Vivaine?"

He was quiet for a moment. They'd reached the back of the crowd and he paused, but Sable stepped forward, pulling him with her.

"I just think a man in love with a woman might not see the complete truth about her." He glanced back over his shoulder toward where the stage had disappeared behind the crowd. "Have you considered that this entire play may merely be his attempt to woo her?"

Sable snorted. "Prioresses don't marry. The day Vivaine became a prioress, any hopes Atticus might have had of wooing died."

Reese made an unconvinced hum.

The steps of all three priories were still empty.

Sable glanced around the crowd. "This way."

She led him toward the Phoenix Priory, until she saw the familiar face of one of Kiva's men watching the crowd. Sable pulled Andreese to a stop and pulled the hair from the red wig closer around her face.

"This is the edge of the Vayas' territory," Sable said quietly.

Reese tensed. "First, why do they have territory here in the Sanctuary, and second, why would you bring us to it?"

"The gangs split the area in the Sanctuary so they're not stepping on each other's toes during the festivals. The pickpocketing is too lucrative to disrupt the truce." She nodded to their left. "That kid by the tree is the spotter for this area. The pickpockets will be busy tonight." She paused, catching sight of a well-dressed woman linking arms with an even better dressed man. "And Kiva's girls will be setting up their own marks."

"How?"

The spotter met the gaze of a woman with a wide green hat and rubbed his chin.

"See that woman in the green?" Sable asked. "She'll have that bag stolen soon."

Reese leaned to the side to see the woman better. "Why?"

"As a distraction."

In a few moments, a boy ran into the woman, yanked the bag from her arm, and ran into the crowd. The woman screamed, almost convincingly, and her gentleman ran after the boy, catching him quickly and rescuing the bag. During the commotion, another boy walked past the gentleman, his hand slipping into and out of the man's pocket almost faster than Sable could see.

Andreese snorted. "Not bad."

"They'll do it all night. The girls find eligible, wealthy men and bring them to this area. Everyone's looking for pickpockets, so they give them one to chase while they do the actual theft."

Reese glanced down at her. "Did you ever do that?"

"Pickpocket, yes. I never could pull off the pretty girl act."

He didn't answer, but his arm felt stiff.

Sable glanced up at him, feeling awkward. "I'm sure that sounds terrible to you, but at the time, I didn't have any other options."

He stopped and looked at her. "That doesn't sound terrible. What were you supposed to do? If I hadn't had my aunt in Ebenmoor, I'd have, well… I don't know what I'd have done. But stealing probably would have been the least of it." His expression was hard. "I'd like to have some words with the people who put you in that position, though."

"It's all right." She pulled on his arm to start him walking again, skirting the edge of the Vayas' territory. "Those days are behind me. I'm a famous actress now."

He turned his gaze back to the spotter. "You brought us over here because you think Talia might be in this area, didn't you?" He shook his head. "If the real reason we came out here was to lurk around the people we don't want to find you, we should have put together better disguises."

"Seeing Vivaine is the real reason," Sable assured him. "But if there's a chance to find Talia, too…"

He shook his head and let her draw him through the crowd.

"For the record, I think this is a mistake," he said, keeping his voice low.

"Noted." Sable shifted to see through the crowd.

Ahead, Sable's attention caught on a bit of auburn hair. Her fingertips dug into Reese's arm, and she shifted to see past the people blocking her. "There she is!" she whispered. "In the blue."

She dropped his arm and pushed past several people in her way. She could see more clearly now, and it was definitely Talia, looking not merely unharmed, but stunningly wealthy in a rich blue dress. Her hair was elaborately styled, the top pinned up, the rest hanging free down her back.

Sable pushed past the final group of people between them when the warm relief flooding her froze.

Looking perfectly at ease, Talia stood with her hand draped over the arm of Kiva himself.

CHAPTER FIFTY-FOUR

SABLE STARED at Talia's profile. It was her sister, without a doubt.

And the man next to her had his wild curls tamed just enough to pass for a wealthy merchant. He looked toward the priory, but the jagged point of his beard was familiar enough that Sable's stomach clenched.

"She's with Kiva," Sable whispered.

"Kiva?" Reese's voice was cold. His eyes fixed on the man with a chilling ferocity.

Sable stared at them. What were they doing together? Talia would have had to report to him plenty of times, but Kiva rarely wandered around arm in arm with his jays.

Reese's hands were curled into fists, and for a moment Sable thought he might head toward the gang boss. But instead, in a tightly controlled voice he said, "Let's get you away from him." He started to walk away, but she pulled him to a stop.

"I need to know she's all right."

He gave her an incredulous look. "She's cozied up to the gang boss, Sable. She's doing fine."

"That's hardly fine," she hissed.

"You know what I mean," he said quietly. "She's clearly not in danger."

Sable glared at her sister, wanting to argue, but he was right.

Kiva leaned closer to say something quietly to Talia. She smiled warmly at him. Kiva gave her a charming little bow and walked away.

Sable dropped Andreese's arm and started toward her sister.

"Don't," he hissed, grabbing for her.

She ducked away from him and hurried forward until she was right behind Talia. Kiva was nowhere to be seen.

Reese stepped up next to her. "This is not a good idea," he whispered.

Sable reached forward to touch Talia's shoulder, but her hand stopped. It was Talia, but she was so different. She was tall and beautiful and achingly young.

A wave of helplessness washed over her. Talia stood among everything Sable had tried so hard to keep her away from. The square around them, the very city itself closed in around them, and Sable suddenly felt foolish to ever have thought they could escape it.

Foolish to think they'd end up anywhere but here.

A long peal of bells rang through the night air, and the crowd quieted. Every face turned toward the Dragon Priory as the doors opened and the first of a line of white-robed, white-veiled abbesses walked out onto the raised rostrum.

"Talia," Sable said quietly.

Her sister glanced over her shoulder without any recognition.

Talia gave Sable a polite, distant smile. Her eyes flickered toward Reese, then back to Sable's face before they widened. She turned around sharply, her face shocked, and whispered. "Sable?" Her gaze flickered to the people around them who watched curiously, and she stepped next to Sable, facing forward again and linking their arms.

Reese moved behind the sisters.

"Where have you been?" Talia hissed. She glanced at Sable's face. "Where did you get that wig? And who did your face paint? It's..." She paused. "It's really well done." Her voice was half-annoyed, half-impressed.

"What are you doing with Kiva?" Sable demanded quietly.

"With Kiva?" Her face turned outraged. "I'm not with Kiva. He was getting my report."

"Well, you looked awfully comfortable with him."

Talia rolled her eyes. "You disappear for weeks, and when you come back, all you care about is Kiva?"

"No," Sable said, gripping Talia's arm tighter. "Sorry. I just... Are you all right?"

"Of course I am. You're the one who disappeared."

Up on the steps of the priory, one woman raised a lantern, calling out a blessing on the crowd.

Talia took in Sable's wig and face again. "Where have you been? And where's Ryah?"

The complexity of the answer to that question gave Sable a moment's pause. Instead, she said, "I went to your room in the Nest."

Talia's eyes widened, and she glanced around the crowd. "That was stupid. Do you want Kiva to find you? He was furious when you left." She turned back to study Sable's face. "He's been searching for you."

"We have to get you out of here," Sable said. "Can you be ready to leave in a few days?"

"Leave?" Talia's voice rose, and Sable shushed her, looking around. Talia clenched her jaw, lowering her voice. "I'm not leaving. Answer my questions. I am sick of feeling like I don't know what's going on. Where have you been? Where is Ryah? Why is Kiva so anxious to find you? No one is telling me anything, and I'm tired of being left in the dark."

"You can tell her everything," Reese said quietly from behind them, "but not here. We need to move before someone besides Talia recognizes you, Sable."

Talia turned to glare at him. "Who are you?"

He gave her a tight smile. "I'm Reese. Nice to meet you. I've heard a lot about you."

She gave him an incredulous look.

Three of the abbesses began a long, slow song, the bells rolling out a rich accompaniment.

"He's right," Sable said. "Meet me somewhere else."

JA ANDREWS

Talia kept her gaze on Reese for another breath, studying him. "Fine. Where? Our old rooms in Dockside?"

"Absolutely not," Reese said.

Sable shot him an annoyed look.

"I wasn't talking to you," Talia said, equally annoyed.

He let out a laugh. "I didn't see the resemblance at first, but when you're annoyed, you look just like Sable. She gives me that look all the time."

Talia's scowl deepened.

"Reese is right," Sable said. "I'm not going into Dockside again, and I'm definitely not bringing Ryah there."

"You know where she is?" Talia asked, gripping Sable's arm tighter.

"Yes, and she's anxious to see you. But not in Dockside." Sable glanced around the priory. Meeting anywhere in the Sanctuary would be too exposed. They needed somewhere safe from prying eyes.

Sable glanced in the direction Kiva had disappeared. An idea formed, and all the things that could go wrong immediately jumped to the front of her mind. She pushed them aside.

"You know the shop with the stone turtles?"

Talia frowned. "The one on the Spine?"

Sable nodded. "A block downhill from it is a deserted yellow house."

Her sister's frown deepened. "Why there?"

"Because it's the safest place I can think of. Meet me there tomorrow? At midday?"

Talia was still frowning, but she nodded.

"You'll come alone?" Sable asked. "No Pete and Boone this time?"

A flicker of regret crossed her face. "I'll come alone this time." Her words were warm with truth.

Sable opened her mouth to ask why she'd brought them last time, but Reese nudged her in the back.

"Kiva's heading this direction," he said quietly.

Talia's eyes widened as she turned to look. "Go." She started to push her away, but Sable held her arm for another moment. Her sister stood tall, a new air of independence wrapped around her.

452

"You look..." The words caught in Sable's throat. "I've missed you."

Talia's face softened for the first time, and the hint of a familiar smile curled her lips. "You, too."

Reese set his hand on Sable's back. "We need to move."

Sable nodded and walked away, glancing back a few times to see her sister looking toward the abbesses with a distracted frown.

When the song ended, the bells began again, this time with a joyful, wild abandon, and Sable found a space in the crowd far from the Vayas where she could see. Reese stopped behind her shoulder. His hand, which he kept on her back, was tense.

"Kiva is going to have her followed," he said quietly.

"You'll be there to protect us, right?" Sable glanced back and shot him a smile.

"If I'm your only protection against an entire gang, your plan is even worse than I thought."

"You don't have to come if you don't want to." The door of the priory opened, and Sable straightened to see better.

"Once you see the High Prioress," he asked quietly, "can we leave?"

"I want to hear what she has to say."

"No matter how much you like the version of her in the play, she's not going to be like that in real life."

Sable shushed him as the thin form of the Phoenix Prioress came out of the door, the blazing Phoenix resting on her outstretched arm. Glitters of red and orange trailed behind them as they walked. With a flick of her hand, the prioress sent the bird soaring up and over the crowd. The glowing feathers brightened as it arced through the air, like a breeze stoking the coals, and a long trail of sparks followed its flight.

Sable raised her face toward the bird as it flew near. The bits of fire trailing it sparked like embers of hope against the black of the night sky. They fell toward the crowd before dimming, but somehow, they left the feeling that where they landed, the darkness might be banished. That all the broken things in the world could really be made whole again.

Andreese gripped the shawl that hung down her back, his face turned up, some of the hardness from the day smoothed away, watching the Phoenix.

"That's Prioress Narine," Sable told him.

"I see why Ryah likes the phoenix priory," he said quietly.

The bird landed back on the prioress's arm, and they moved to the side. A darker shape moved out the door. Prioress Eugessa walked out, one hand on the black unicorn's neck, the other offering a lazy wave of blessing to the crowd. Her hair was a darker copper color than it had been at the last festival. The rings, bracelets, and necklaces she wore still glittered brightly.

"That," Sable said, "is Eugessa."

Reese glanced at the prioress, but fixed his gaze on the unicorn. "That's a dangerous looking animal."

The unicorn took its place across the rostrum from the phoenix, shifting and clacking its hooves on the stone, tossing its head. The lantern light etched lines along the muscles wrapping down its neck and across its shoulders.

Something glittered in the darkness of the priory, shifting closer to the front door. Shimmers of silver flashed down near the floor, and a slight glow appeared as the Dragon Prioress moved forward like a bit of starlight.

Sable leaned forward as the prioress stepped out. Even among the white robes and veils of the abbesses lining the rostrum, she glowed brightly. The torchlight caught in her robes, wrapping around her. Her head was bare of her normal veil, her long, white hair falling free and straight down her back. She smiled gently at the gathered crowd. Alongside her, the silver dragon moved smoothly forward. His head was high enough that she could rest one hand on its shimmering scales. The creature shifted and spread its wings for a moment, stretching them out behind her, while glints of torchlight skittered across them in ripples of fire and silver.

Prioress Vivaine stepped to the front of the rostrum, right at the top of the stairs, and raised her other hand in a blessing. For a moment, the Sanctuary seemed to lighten. The crowd hushed. Even Reese stood perfectly still.

A weight fell onto Sable's shoulders at the sight. Ryah had been right all those years ago. The prioress was a star from heaven. Sable's attempts to portray her on the stage felt humiliatingly barbaric. She shrank back a little against Reese.

"May the blessings of Amah fall on you," Prioress Vivaine began, her voice filling the plaza and soothing a little of Sable's discomfort. The warm press of truth rolled through the Sanctuary. Vivaine's words were always rich. "Tonight, at the beginning of the Festival of Light,"—She paused and gave the crowd a gentle smile—"may you see the way out of the darkness."

"That line is from Atticus's play," Reese said quietly.

"She says it every year on this night," Sable answered. "Atticus took the words from her."

He let out a small snort. "The man is good."

Sable glanced up at him in annoyance. "Or maybe what happened long ago still affects her."

Reese looked unconvinced, but he said nothing else.

The prioress continued with her annual blessing, calling for hope, peace, and light to come into the dark places of the world. Reminding them that Amah's great desire was to brighten the darkness that lived inside human hearts.

A new set of figures filed out from inside the priory, and Sable shifted to see them better. They weren't dressed in white, and murmurs rippled through the crowd.

"That's new," Sable said quietly.

Reese drew in a sharp breath. The men joining the prioresses were dressed in the dark, crisp uniforms of the Northern Lords. "Second from the right... That's Lord Runess."

The man was thin and balding, but stood tall and assured, his face stern as he looked over the crowd.

"The rest are the other lords."

"Why?" Sable asked. "This night is always about Amah's blessings. I've never seen anyone but prioresses involved."

Another man stepped out of the priory, and Reese stiffened, his hand grasping Sable's arm, almost painfully.

Dressed in a long, orange robe embroidered with a glittery yellow dragon, the ambassador from the Kalesh Empire stepped up next to the prioress.

"As Amah spreads light and love in our hearts," the High Prioress continued, "so she desires light and peace in the world."

The Kalesh Ambassador stood close to the prioress, and Reese breathed out a sound that was almost a growl.

The prioress motioned to the Northern Lords and the ambassador. "With our neighbors to the north and the east, we offer a renewal of our bonds of peace."

The warmth of the prioress's words surrounded Sable.

"So on this night, as we welcome the light of Amah, I have invited our dear friends to join us in the hopes that as the year rolls on, the bonds between us will continue to grow in depth and strength."

"She means it," Sable whispered to Reese.

The Kalesh Ambassador gave her a deep bow, and turned toward the crowd. He stepped forward and spread his hands, as though offering them a gift. "Good people of Immusmala," he began, "the Kalesh Empire is eager to increase the trade and connection between our lands."

"He means that, too," Sable said quietly.

"It is our deepest hope that strong bonds can be forged between us. That you will accept our assistance against the dangers that face you."

"Still true," Sable whispered. "Maybe he doesn't know about the Eastern Reaches. Maybe he really thinks there are raiders."

Reese shook his head. "He knows."

"I don't think so," Sable began, but the ambassador spoke again.

"May this summer mark the beginning of a connection between our people, bound together"—His voice suddenly sharpened—"by peace and mutual benefit."

The lie cut through the air like a knife, and Sable drew her shawl around her, trying to block out the coldness of the words. She stepped back into Reese.

"He's lying," she whispered. "He knows."

PART III

"The reason we should all pay attention to Sable's story isn't because it changed our world, we should pay attention because she came to learn the power of words, the power that each of us has to change the world around us."

-from *The History of Queensland*, by Keeper Will in the 402nd year of Queensland.

CHAPTER FIFTY-FIVE

SABLE AND ANDREESE strode behind the stage to where the troupe, Jae, and Serene, sat on a circle of crates, still enjoying the leeswine.

"The ambassador knows it's the Kalesh on the Eastern Reaches," Andreese said.

"And Vivaine is completely taken in by him," Sable added. "She even let him address the crowd, like he was her equal."

Atticus's expression darkened. "Tell us exactly what they said."

Sable repeated the words of both Prioress Vivaine and the ambassador.

"And you're sure he was lying?" Atticus asked.

Sable gave an annoyed look, then glanced around the group. "Where's Ryah?"

"We took her to the abbey to spend the night," Thulan said.

"Serene," Andreese said, "you were right. The ambassador stood far too close to the prioress to be just a political ally. Prioresses may not marry, but something is going on there."

Sable glanced at Atticus, but his face betrayed nothing at the news.

Serene sighed. "Then there's little chance we'll get back into the priory at all."

"You need to figure out a way to get back into Vivaine's good graces," Atticus told them. "Which means playing nice with the ambassador."

Serene shook her head. "We don't have a reason for them to let us in."

"Yes, we do," Jae said quietly.

Serene's eyes narrowed dangerously. "No. We don't."

"Serene brought more books," Jae explained to the group. "If we offered to bring them to the library in exchange for getting to work there and making sure the books are being cared for, I think Vivaine would let us in." He looked pointedly at Serene. "At which time you could apologize to the ambassador, and we could try to fix things."

Serene crossed her arms. "I'm not giving up the few books we have left."

"The crate we have is an eclectic collection, half of which are part of sets that she has the rest of. They're next to worthless, and you know it."

Serene's jaw clenched, but she didn't argue.

"We'll go in the morning," Jae told Atticus.

He nodded. "Good. As for the rest of us, we need to make sure we do our best performance tomorrow night." His beard split in a wide smile. "The judges tonight were very impressed. Lord Pollun said it was the best show he'd ever seen, and the highest one he'd ever rated."

He looked around the small group. "I think we can win tomorrow, if we do the same as we did tonight. And I don't need to tell you what's at stake. If we lose tomorrow, we lose any chance to speak to the Northern Lords, the Merchant Guild, and the prioresses together."

"Will it do any good?" Sable asked quietly.

"I don't know. We have the truth on our side." Atticus glanced at Sable. "And we know there's power in that."

He tried to put hope into his voice, but for once, his performance wasn't quite compelling.

The next morning, Serene stormed back to where Sable sat with Andreese, and picked up the small crate holding the last of their books. Jae trailed after her.

"What if they just take the books?" Sable asked. "And don't let you in?"

Serene looked grimly at the priory. "I'd like to see them try."

"Serene," Jae said mildly. "The point of this is to regain their trust."

"I am willing to bite my tongue with the ambassador, and to not attack Vivaine for stealing our books. But if they try to take these without letting us in?" Serene shook her head. "It will not go well for the priory."

"The whole priory?" Reese asked with a small smile.

"Yes," Serene answered and stalked away.

Jae looked after her with a worried expression. "There's a good chance this isn't going to go well." He glanced at the troupe. "Good luck tonight. If we get access to the books, we probably won't be back."

"And if Serene burns down the priory?" Andreese asked.

"Then I imagine we'll be in some sort of prison. Either way, we may miss the performance." Jae's shoulders slumped as he started after Serene.

"They're a strange couple," Reese said, watching them disappear around the stage.

Sable climbed into the wagon and knelt next to the crate of hats, looking for one that would hide her hair. "Do you want to try and talk to your uncle again?"

"Yes, but not until this afternoon. The man is always grumpy in the mornings."

"I thought soldiers loved mornings. Don't they get up early and march around before the sun is up?"

"Yes, but they're not all happy about it. We'll go there on our way back from meeting Talia." He grew quiet, but it felt like a pointed sort of quiet, so Sable glanced over to find him scowling at her. "This is a terrible idea, going to meet her in the city. It'd be better if you did it here."

Sable shook her head. "She was telling the truth. She'll come alone."

"That's what she told you last time."

"No. Last time, she didn't tell me anything. I asked her to promise to come, and she said she was too mad to promise me anything." She turned back to the crate. "She and Ryah deserve to see each other. Besides, if I'm going to convince her to leave the Vayas, I need to talk to her."

"What does Atticus think of this meeting?"

Sable pulled out a white cap. "Atticus was gone by the time I woke up this morning, so I guess he doesn't get a say." She glanced at Reese. "Do you really think I'd not go see my sister just because Atticus disapproved?"

"It's just exhausting coming along with you to dangerous places."

Sable sat back on her heels. "If Kiva hasn't figured out where I am yet, he will soon. So hanging out here all day isn't going to keep me safe, either. Besides, you're the one who said I could explain everything to her, just not in the middle of the festival."

"I'd hoped you'd put it off until after the show tonight."

Sable tied back her hair and tucked it under the white cap. She added a grey apron around her waist over the bland dress she wore. She didn't look exactly like a shop girl, at least not a reputable one, but she was unremarkable enough that no one should pay her much notice. She tossed a grey, worn vest at Reese. "Put this on over your shirt. You look too nice for where we're going."

He held up the vest with frown. "Isn't it a bit early? We have hours until midday."

"We need to pick up Ryah from the abbey." Sable smoothed the apron, as though that would smooth out the things that were likely to go wrong today. "We'll need a few of her Dogs, and I'd like to be at the yellow house early enough to be sure I arrive before Talia." She checked that her hair was hidden under the cap.

He slid his arms through the vest. "Sounds like we're in for a fascinating morning."

"You don't have to come."

"Yesterday proved that I do." He buckled on his sword belt and spread his arms. "Now, do I look disreputable enough to accompany you, m'lady?"

She smiled at him. "Your face still looks rather noble and lordly." He shot her an annoyed look. "That's better. When you frown, you look more intimidating."

"You make frowning so easy." He offered her his left arm. "Stay on this side of my lordly person so I have my sword arm free when you inevitably drag us into trouble."

She took it with a smile. "Agreed. Let's go get Ryah."

They found her in the fenced yard of the abbey with two other women, all three dressed in white robes. They sat on small stools showing several younger, dirtier girls how to sew together scraps of fabric.

Ryah hurried over to greet them, beaming. "It's so lovely to be back, Sable!"

Mother Perrin approached the fence slowly. Sable hadn't realized how bent her back was. Her head barely came to Sable's shoulder. Her face wrinkled up into a gentle smile. "Welcome back, Issable."

The words felt ill-fitting. Was she back? "Good morning, Holy Mother."

The abbess looked at Reese curiously. "You must be the young man from Ebenmoor."

He straightened at the words.

"Yes. This is Andreese." Ryah smiled. "It took most of the night to explain the whole trip to Mother Perrin."

"We need to go if we're going to meet Talia." Sable told Ryah. "We'll need the help of a few of your Dogs. And at least one high-ranking one. Preferably your friend Tomm. Can you work that out?"

Mother Perrin's smile faded.

"There shouldn't be any trouble," Sable told her quickly. "In fact, they'll be there to assure there isn't any."

"It's a dangerous game to pit the violent against each other," the abbess said quietly.

Sable paused. "I know. But I don't know another way to keep both Ryah and Talia safe."

The abbess considered Sable for a long moment, then raised a hand toward her. "Amah bless your plans, child." She dropped her hand to Ryah's arm. "And protect you all." Without another word, she hobbled over to the circle of women.

Ryah came through the gate. "Do we really need Tomm?"

Sable nodded. "Just to be safe."

Her sister's brow knit together, but she nodded and started around the block.

The Muddog's house was nicer on the inside than Sable expected. The exterior was peeling and dull like the rest of the Bend, but inside was a surprising number of colorful, expensive rugs. The furniture looking like it had been taken from one of the huge houses near the Spine. There were even a few tapestries on the walls.

Ryah was greeted with enthusiasm. Sable and Reese less so.

Reese stood behind the two sisters, his arms folded across his chest, his scowl in full force.

When Tomm entered the room, Reese tensed. The dark tattoos covering his bare scalp and sliding down his neck were more visible than they'd been the night Sable had taken Ryah away. He was still shirtless, covered with nothing but tattoos and the leather collar around his neck.

He wasn't as old as Sable had thought, probably younger than Andreese, but when he walked into the room, the respect he commanded was palpable.

He offered Ryah a smile, but when he turned his gaze to Andreese, his expression faded to something dangerous. Tomm carried no weapon, but Sable had to force herself to step forward and address him.

"Nice to see you again, Tomm," she said, giving him a strained smile. "We need your help."

He pulled his gaze from Reese and studied Sable. "Last time you needed my help, it was because you'd brought Vayas into the Bend."

Sable's smile soured to a grimace. "It's that same sort of problem."

Tomm's face hardened. "I did a little research since the last time. Now I know why the Vayas are so interested in you, Sable."

She drew in a breath at her name. "Kiva's going to keep looking for me, and Ryah, unless I can convince him to stop."

He shrugged. "Or I could offer you to Kiva in exchange for leaving Ryah alone."

Reese let out a low growl, and Tomm grinned at him. "I like a man who doesn't back down."

He crossed his arms and stepped closer to Sable. She forced herself not to back away.

"You have one minute to make me a better offer," he said.

"Tomm," Ryah said, stepping forward and setting one small hand on his muscled forearm. "We don't have a better offer. We just need your help."

He looked at Ryah for a long moment. She was so small standing next to him in her white dress. His face didn't soften, but he finally gave her a barely perceptible nod.

Ryah let out a relieved breath and smiled up at him.

Without any change of expression, he turned back to Sable. "What do you need?"

The sun had almost reached the midpoint of the sky.

Sable stood in the upstairs room of the abandoned yellow house, just inside the territory of the Muddogs. The entire second floor was one open room, three windows facing the street. A few old chairs and a rickety table stood along the back wall, a few stools scattered near the windows.

In the far corner, a staircase led downstairs to more bare rooms.

From the window, she looked up the street, watching where it connected with the Spine. The glass had broken out long ago, and the warmth of the summer day swirled into the room. Ryah and Reese each stood at their own window, Ryah at the center one with barely concealed excitement, and Reese at the far end with a nearly continuous stream of muttered disapproval.

He shifted his weight. "This is a terrible idea."

"It's going to be fine," Sable said to him for the hundredth time.

"It could be a bloodbath," he answered.

A woman with a white scarf over her hair paused at the top of the street before starting toward the yellow house. Sable's hands tightened on the windowsill.

Ryah drew in a breath. "That's her."

Sable pulled her eyes from Talia and kept her focus on the Spine.

When Talia had almost reached the house, Ryah leaned out the window and waved.

Talia's hand flew to her mouth. Sable wanted to keep watching the Spine, but Talia's eyes were wide with shock, and maybe a little fear. With a noise somewhere between a sob and a laugh, she rushed toward the door. Ryah ran across the room and downstairs. Sable stayed at the window, staring at the street where Talia had stood. The noise of the two sisters came muffled from below, twisting an old guilt in her gut.

For ten years, neither had known the other was alive. She leaned against the window frame, suddenly unable to take a deep breath. Talia had been right to be furious.

"Maybe Kiva didn't have her followed." Reese's voice cut through her regret.

Sable opened her eyes and looked back up the street. She clamped down on the swirl of emotions and forced her voice to be steady. "He knows I'm in the city. He'll at least have had her followed."

"At least?" he asked.

Two men appeared at the corner and paused. The taller of the two leaned casually against a building. It was Boone, Kiva's enormous bodyguard. The shorter stood with his arms crossed, looking pointedly down the street. He wore his usual vest, his hair curled out defiantly.

"Or, more likely," she said, "he'll come himself."

CHAPTER FIFTY-SIX

Tᴏᴍᴍ sᴛᴇᴘᴘᴇᴅ out from the shadow of a building and walked toward where Kiva waited in the Spine's neutral territory. The boss of the Vayas tensed, but didn't move. Tomm came within a few paces.

Ryah and Talia came up the stairs, and Sable took a deep breath before turning to face them. The wetness on their cheeks tore at her.

"I'm sorry," Sable whispered, stepping toward them. "To both of you."

The two sisters stood arm in arm near the top of the stairs. Instead of fury, Talia looked at Sable with a bemused look.

"You traveled with Atticus and his acting troupe?" Talia asked.

Sable paused at the unexpected question.

"And she's an amazing actress," Ryah added, grinning. "There's another performance tonight, and everyone thinks she'll win the tourney!"

"We might win," Sable corrected her. "Ryah has a role, too, as a handmaiden."

Talia laughed. At the sound, the tension coiled inside of Sable loosened.

"How far did you travel?" Talia asked.

"All the way to the Eastern Reaches," Ryah answered. "Then into the Nidel Woods and back again. With a very short trip into some dwarven tunnels. And we met some elves."

Talia's expression turned skeptical.

"It's true," Ryah said.

Sable wanted to cross the room to them, but she hesitated. She'd expected fury, not this.

Talia looked different. There was the fine quality of the grey summer dress, of course, and delicate braids wound through the top of her hair, leaving the rest to fall smoothly over her shoulders. Her fingernails were smooth and uniform, without a single speck of dirt.

But it was more than that. Talia stood differently. Straighter. Taller.

Sable had braced for her sister's anger, but this was almost worse.

She was unfamiliar.

The room that had seemed so small before now stretched out, leaving an enormous expanse of empty floor between them. Talia made no move to come closer, and Sable's feet stayed rooted to the floor.

The room was stiflingly hot. Sable's hair stuck to her neck.

Talia raised an eyebrow at Reese who still stood at the far window, his arms crossed, unhappiness clear on his face. "Hello, again. I forget your name."

He didn't relax, but he gave her a slight nod. "Reese."

"Reese." Talia said his name slowly, studying him. "You seem to be spending a lot of time with my sister."

Talia's tone was vaguely disapproving, and Sable straightened.

"Your sister keeps wanting to go dangerous places." Andreese glanced out the window.

Talia nodded. "She does that."

"Reese traveled with us—" Ryah began.

"I hardly think you're one to judge my companions," Sable said to Talia. "I don't traipse around with Kiva."

Talia frowned. "Neither do I."

"What happened to your room in the Nest?"

Talia crossed her arms. "It was too dangerous for me to visit Dockside. Lord Trelles is a suspicious man and had me followed. So Kiva set up a room near the Spine for me. It's above a shop of writing supplies, so no one will question why I'm there."

Sable digested the information. That was reasonable, and anything that kept Talia from Dockside was a good thing. "I'm glad you're not being tortured in some cell like I thought."

"Tortured for what? Information about you? I think it was pretty obvious to Kiva I didn't know where you were. I was as furious as he was that you'd disappeared."

"You were furious?" Sable demanded. "You told him where to find me!" She flung her hand toward Ryah. "You told him where Ryah would be."

Talia shook her head. "I didn't," she said. "He already knew. I don't know how, but he knew I was meeting you. Pete and Boone showed up in my room a few hours after you left and said they were coming with me." Her gaze faltered. "They said Kiva wanted to apologize to you after some argument you had, that you and Ryah might be in danger from the Muddogs, and that he had an offer he thought would change your mind about leaving." She gave a regretful shrug. "I believed them."

Sable bit back her response.

"I know it was stupid," Talia continued quietly. "They were just guessing that I was going to meet you, but I fell for it. Kiva was so angry when we didn't find you. He kept saying you betrayed him by leaving."

She stepped forward. "Sable, he's still furious. You can't go anywhere near him. You shouldn't even be in the city. The way he talks…" She glanced at Andreese. "You should get more bodyguards, because I think he wants to kill you."

Sable drew in a breath. "Has he threatened you?"

Talia shook her head. "He's been…" Her expression grew apologetic. "He's been good to me." She shifted forward. "Sable, I know you think I shouldn't be a jay, but I'm good at it. Lady Ingred suspects nothing, and I'm privy to so much that happens in their home. I hear her father's business meetings, I have access to the family's schedule."

She paused, glancing at Ryah, then back at Sable. "I can make a difference here. I can do things that could really help."

Her enthusiasm left a cold lump in Sable's stomach. "Help who?"

"The poor," Talia said, as though the answer were obvious. "Everything the merchants do keeps them wealthy and the lower districts poor. They take advantage of cheap labor and play the workers against each other." Her face lit as she stepped forward, dropping Ryah's arm. "With the information I have access to, there's a chance we can change that. We can rally to get fair wages—the wages they'd pay a middle-class worker."

Sable searched for something to say.

When she didn't speak, Ryah stepped forward. "That sounds like a good thing." It was hard to tell whether she was trying to encourage Talia or placate Sable.

"I'm doing something important," Talia said. There was something pleading in the declaration.

"You're spying for Kiva." Sable wanted to grab her shoulders, but she settled for curling her hands into fists. "He is never going to do things to help the poor get more influence."

"It's the reason he got me this job." Talia said, her face earnest.

"So you could help the poor?" Sable ran her hand through her hair, trying to keep her voice even. "You are the poor, Talia. Lady Ingred's secretary must be paid a good wage. Where does that money go? Into your pocket to pay you for your hard work and compensate for the danger you're in?"

Talia pressed her lips together.

"Sable," Ryah broke in.

Sable ignored her. "It goes to Kiva, doesn't it? Like everything else. The only person Kiva wants to see have any influence is himself. Not you. Not anyone else from Dockside. Certainly not the poor he controls."

"You're wrong about him," Talia said, crossing her arms. "Did you know he was orphaned when he was young? He came to Immusmala with his parents, but they were both sick. They were taken in by a small abbey near the river, but both died. He's been on his own since he was younger than any of us were."

Sable shook her head. "That doesn't make him like us."

"The prioress who cared for his parents took everything from him and turned him out onto the streets." Talia's face was ablaze with indignation. "She took their clothes, their horse. Apparently she even took a ring his mother had given him on her deathbed."

"That still doesn't mean he's like—" Sable stopped, frowning. "What ring?"

Talia shrugged. "I don't know. A ring. The point is, he's clawed his way up to where he is by knowing more about his enemies than they know about him. And the merchants are our enemies, whether you see it or not. I'm more than happy to work with Kiva to spy on them."

Sable stared at her. An abbess stole his mother's ring?

"They're done talking," Andreese interrupted from the window.

She pushed the thoughts of the ring from her mind and turned back toward the street. "You're not working with Kiva, Talia. You're working for him."

Tomm, Kiva, and Boone walked toward the house.

Talia moved to a window and one hand flew to her mouth. "How did he find me?"

"He's probably had you followed since I left," Sable said. "And definitely since he knew I was back."

"But—" She turned frightened eyes to Sable. "You should leave!"

"He won't do anything to me here." Sable looked down to the street, seeing at least three Muddogs watching the house. "I hope."

When she looked back at Kiva, he was staring up at her, his face calm, but his eyes seething. The expression shot an old, familiar dagger of fear into her, but she forced herself to hold his gaze.

"You knew he'd come?" Talia asked.

"I was hoping. Better he find me here than somewhere else."

"He's going to kill me for sneaking over here," Talia said faintly.

"You're his loyal jay," Sable said, trying to keep the fury out of her voice. "He'll get over it."

"I'd like to point out, again," Reese said, moving over and putting his back to the corner, "that I don't like this."

"Noted," Sable said, shooting him an irritated look. "Again."

"I don't, either," Talia agreed. She took Ryah's arm and pulled her away from Sable, moving back to the wall between Andreese and the stairs.

Seeing both sisters back away, made her side of the room feel even more isolated. But it was better if they stayed back. She glanced outside to see Kiva enter the house, then turned to face the stairs.

Kiva and Boone slowly came up the stairs, escorted by Tomm and four Muddogs. The Dogs spread themselves out along the back wall and at the top of the stairs. Boone took the far corner across from Andreese. Kiva stopped in the center of the room, facing Sable.

Sable felt a drip of sweat run down her back. Kiva kept his face calm, but she could see beads of sweat on his temples. The air sat stagnant, trapped there by the palpable animosity in the room.

"Using the Dogs to broker a meeting?" Kiva said. "I'm not sure if I'm angry or impressed."

"They're not here for me," Sable said, keeping her voice even, focusing on the fact that the Muddogs had control of the room and had told Ryah they'd protect all three sisters while the meeting lasted. No Dogs were close enough to Sable to protect her from Kiva, but Tomm leaned against the wall close to Ryah, much to Talia's discomfort.

Kiva must have consented to their terms for them to have let him come this far into their territory. He'd have agreed to no violence, and they would have guaranteed his safety, at least for this short time.

Sable straightened. For once, Kiva wasn't in control.

Of course, neither was Sable. But it was better than any alternative she could think of. "It's Ryah the Muddogs are protecting."

Kiva raised an eyebrow and turned to consider Ryah. "I can see why. Such a lovely, innocent face." He tilted his head to the side. "A girl who wants to be a prioress enough to be in the Choosing, yet also consorts with a gang. Your whole family is interesting, Sable."

Ryah shifted uncomfortably under his gaze.

Kiva turned back to her. "All of this was unnecessary. You could have just come to me. You and I have too much of a history for me to hold a month of poor choices against you." His voice was even, but the cold lie cut through Sable.

"I'm so sorry I doubted your honor," she said flatly. "I'm done with the Vayas and wanted to make that clear while we're on neutral ground. After my last job for you, I owe you nothing. I want your word that you'll leave me alone."

Beneath the curls of his beard, she thought she saw his jaw clench.

"Ryah," Sable continued, "is also not yours. These Muddogs are fond of her."

Kiva glanced back at Tomm.

The man nodded. "Ryah and the abbey she lives at are under our protection."

After a moment's hesitation, Kiva inclined his head in acknowledgment. Sable let out a small breath of relief.

"If she comes into my territory," Kiva said to Tomm, "I cannot guarantee her safety."

"If she's foolish enough to go into Dockside, she's outside our protection," Tomm agreed.

With wide eyes, Ryah looked between the two, her hand gripping Talia's arm.

Kiva nodded. "Talia, though, is under contract with me," he said, still addressing Tomm.

Talia shrank a little at the words.

Tomm shrugged. "We're not here to interfere in your business."

Sable stepped forward. "Talia is done with you, too. I have fifty silver." Out of the corner of her eye, she saw Andreese tense at the words. Everybody in the room turned toward her with interest, and she paused. Maybe that hadn't been the best thing to announce in this situation. She forced her focus back to Kiva and lowered her voice. "It's yours right now. After tonight, I'll have the rest of what she owes you."

"And how much is that?"

"A month ago, her debt was one hundred and fourteen. I'll assume you've inflated it as you always do. So, in addition to this fifty, I'll pay you one hundred tomorrow."

Kiva crossed his arms. "So the reports about you are true." His gaze measured her. "How'd you manage to get into an acting troupe?"

"It's been a strange couple of weeks."

"That it has." His gaze pierced her so deeply that she wanted to shift, but forced herself to stay still. Something predatory that had hung back in his gaze moved forward. The smile he gave her was chilling.

"If you've heard the rumors," she said, "then you know my winnings from tonight will be enough to pay you."

"If you win," he said. "But a bigger issue than that is that one hundred and fourteen silver was her old debt. Talia has proven to be invaluable, and I've spent hours training her on the things she needs to know to impress her employer. We've also had to procure new rooms in order to keep her safe. In light of all those things, I'm afraid her debt has increased significantly."

Sable's fists clenched. "How much."

"I'll have to check the ledger," he said. "But offhand, I'd guess it's near five hundred silver."

Sable stared at him. Five hundred?

He was relaxed, but his eyes bored into her with sharp greed and something uglier. He started toward Sable, and she tensed.

Reese's wrist flicked.

A knife stabbed into the floor in front of Kiva's foot. He jerked to a stop with the first sign of nerves she'd seen.

A Muddog pulled a knife out of his own belt and took a step toward Andreese, who slid his sword an inch out of his scabbard.

"Kiva is here under a flag of truce," Tomm said, his voice grim.

"Not with me," Reese answered. "That's close enough to Sable."

Kiva glanced toward Andreese, sizing him up. Reese met his gaze, his face hard. Kiva huffed out a short laugh. "Never thought I'd see you with your own guard, Sable." He shrugged. "Of course, I never thought I'd see you as a famous actress."

He turned back to her, and Sable forced herself to hold his gaze. With a lazy smile, he stepped up until the toe of his boot pressed against the knife. She saw Reese bristle, and she resisted the urge to shove Kiva back.

"I know what you will win," he said quietly enough for only her to hear, "and it has nothing to do with silver."

The words caught her off guard.

"The winner," he whispered, "is invited inside the priories."

Despite his easy posture, she saw anger simmering under the surface.

Sable stared at him. It always came back to this. "Was the ring really your mother's?" she asked, keeping her voice low.

His eyes flinched. He stared at her in silence for so long she thought he wouldn't answer. "Prioress Eugessa told me my parents' bodies were burned," he finally said, his voice so low Sable had to lean closer to hear, "along with all their possessions, to keep sickness from spreading in the city." The quiet words pressed on her like an ocean swell. "She left me with nothing, claiming I was blessed to have survived. And then, at the meeting with her the day of the Red Shield Festival, she had my mother's ring on her hand." He leaned forward until she could feel his breath on her face. "I want it back."

The truth was warm and close around them, but what he asked for was impossible.

"I can't."

A dangerous light flashed in his eyes.

"There's more at stake here than your obsession, Kiva," she whispered. "If we win, I can't do anything that would damage our relationship with the priories. I'm not stealing from one of them. What you want is more impossible now than it was before."

His face twisted into something terrible. "I asked for a horseshoe," he hissed, "and you brought me a horse." Worse than his anger, there was something desperate and unhinged in his voice. "This is no more impossible than that."

Sable wanted to back away from the frenzied look in his eyes. "This is a thousand times more impossible."

Kiva's face stayed hard, but he shrugged. "Then we have nothing to discuss. If you want your sister free, that is the price."

He stepped back. "Talia," he ordered loudly, not bothering to look away from Sable, "say goodbye to your sisters. If they come near you again, their lives—and yours—are forfeit."

Ryah clung to her sister with wide eyes while Talia looked warily at Kiva.

Disregarding all the Muddogs in the room, he turned and walked to the top of the stairs, then glanced back at Sable. "You're right. Your contract with me is finished. You're free to move about the city as you wish. But if you step foot in Dockside without what I want, I'll slit your throat myself."

CHAPTER FIFTY-SEVEN

TALIA GAVE RYAH A TEARFUL GOODBYE. Sable almost crossed the room to hug her, but Talia's expression stopped her.

"All of this is your fault, Sable," Talia said coldly. "If you'd have kept things as they were, and let us bring Ryah home, we could all be together."

Sable stared at her. "Together as slaves!"

Talia looked at her with a mixture of anger and pity. "Ryah and I might have thought it worth the price. If you'd bothered to ask us." She gave Ryah one last hug, then followed Kiva down the stairs.

Ryah watched her go, her face pale. She moved to the window next to Sable, watching Talia head up the street behind Kiva, dwarfed by the giant Boone.

"I'm sorry," Sable whispered to her.

Ryah leaned her head on Sable's shoulder. "I wouldn't want to be under Kiva's thumb."

"I think it's time you left, too," Tomm said to Sable. "And if you ever expect the Dogs to do your dirty work again, Kiva will be the least of your worries."

Sable glanced at the tattooed men standing around the room. She walked up to Tomm, ignoring Andreese's tight-lipped scowl. The heavy pouch of fifty silver sat useless in her pocket. She pulled it out and held it out to Tomm.

His eyes narrowed dangerously. "You think we're for hire? Like your own personal guards?"

All the Muddogs in the room shifted, and Andreese took a step closer to her.

Sable met Tomm's gaze. "Think of it as a thank you for keeping Ryah safe all these years."

He studied her for a long moment, then took the pouch.

Sable gave him a weak smile. "And maybe payment for an escort to bring her to the Sanctuary before dusk tonight?"

His hand clenched around the pouch. "Ryah will be safe because she's our angel. Not because of you."

Sable glanced at the Muddogs still lining the room. "That's good enough for me. Thank you."

After getting a quick hug from Ryah, Sable led Andreese down the stairs and back up onto the Spine.

Reese kept one hand on the hilt of his sword. "Do you trust Kiva to leave you alone?"

She glanced behind them. "At least until he sees whether we win the tourney." She told him about the ring Eugessa wore, and Kiva's history with it.

"Is it valuable?"

Sable shook her head. "I saw it up close. It's a silver butterfly with sapphires on the wings. At least I think they're sapphires. They were blue, but cloudy enough they couldn't be worth much." She paused. "He was telling the truth, though. It was his mother's."

"Do you think she really stole it?"

The spires of the priories came into view over the wall of the Sanctuary. "When I saw the ring, Eugessa told me she got it from some poor, dying souls who gifted her their worldly possessions."

Reese raised an eyebrow. "If they were Kiva's parents, it seems unlikely that they wouldn't give their earthly possessions to their son."

"Agreed."

"Was the prioress telling the truth about how she got it?"

"I don't know. There was an element of truth to them, but Eugessa's words are always…off somehow." Sable shook her head. "I don't know how to explain her. It's like she both believes it and knows it's a lie at the same time. Like maybe she's worked hard to convince herself it's the truth, even though she knows it isn't."

"Are you going to get the ring for him?"

Sable glanced back over her shoulder. "I wasn't kidding about it being impossible. I'd have to break into the Priory of the Horn, at night when she's not wearing it, find the ring, then sneak back out. I've pulled a few heists in my day, but never in a building I had no access to, no idea of the layout, and was filled with Sanctus guards."

"What did Kiva mean about the horse?"

"That stupid horse…" She shook her head. "Kiva wanted me to steal a silver horseshoe once, but it had way too much sentimental value to the merchant who owned it." She told him about stealing the silver horse stamp instead. "Kiva bought things on the credit of that stamp for a full month before the merchant started receiving the bills and changed his seal."

Andreese raised an eyebrow. "I see why Kiva liked you working for him."

"He likes anyone who makes him money or brings him information."

"Then the fact that right now Talia's doing both should keep her safe."

The Veil Gate came into view. It looked smaller and more mundane than it had a month ago.

They walked into the plaza in silence.

Above the Priory of the Horn, the spires stabbed up into a clear blue sky. Around the thin-windowed building the Sanctus guards stood, as they always did, keeping the crowd away.

There was no way Sable could get that blasted ring.

Aside from the difficulties of the theft itself, Eugessa wore it for sentimental reasons.

And stealing something sentimental was always messy.

Sable stared at the spires of the priory, wanting to break them off.

The truth was, despite the impossibility, she was going to have to steal it.

Because Kiva also wanted the ring for sentimental reasons, too.

And not getting it for him would be a lot worse than "messy."

Reese left Sable with Leonis and Thulan before heading out to try to talk to his uncle again. It was too early to begin getting ready for the night's performance, and Atticus was nowhere to be found, so the three sat around snacking on some nuts Thulan had bought.

Leonis perched on the edge of the thick pot holding his tree, a bottle of leeswine in his hand. His face was drawn.

"You hate the city, don't you?" Sable asked him from her seat on the edge of a large crate.

"The first day is never bad." He took a drink. "But there is nothing living here at all. Nothing. The entire thing is stone and dead wood."

"Stones are alive," Thulan said around a mouthful of nuts.

Leonis didn't bother to respond.

"Would a full-blooded elf hate it even more?" Sable asked.

"No full elf is stupid enough to come to the city," he muttered.

Sable glanced at the two of them, surprised at how familiar they'd become. "What do you think is going to happen after the tourney?"

Leonis and Thulan exchanged glances.

"I mean, if we're not headed to imminent war, is Atticus going to go north?" she asked. "Because my sisters are both here."

"If he's going north," Thulan said, "I'll be with him for a while. But I need to go to the other entrance of Torren and see what's happened with the dwarves. There's no reason for them to have deserted the southern door."

Sable stopped with a nut halfway to her mouth. "You're leaving the troupe?"

Thulan shrugged. "Maybe not forever. But I need to know what's happened. I had promised Atticus I'd stay long enough to do the tourney, but once it's done…"

Sable looked at Leonis, who didn't look nearly outraged enough for this announcement.

"You're just going to let her go?" she asked him.

"Actually, I thought I'd travel with her as far as the Nidel."

"I'm not staying with the elves," Thulan said, exasperated. "I half-tolerate you because you're only half-elf. I'm not spending any time at all with the full-blooded, pretentious ones."

"Even if they can get you north quickly?"

"For the hundredth time, they aren't going to help me!" Thulan said. "It's bad enough I'm a dwarf. I get the feeling knowing you makes things even worse."

Sable dropped her hand with the uneaten nut back into her lap. "You're both leaving? You can't. What about the Kalesh? And the troupe?"

"I've talked to Andreese," Leonis said. "If the Kalesh attack, I want to fight. He said he can use me in the north. I'll join his uncle's troops, but I need to tell my father first." He swirled the leeswine slowly in the bottle. "I never knew it was the Kalesh who killed my mother. Now that they're back, I need to fight."

Sable sank back on her crate. "I can't believe the troupe is going to split up."

"Did you think you were the only one with an old life that needed some cleaning up?" Thulan asked.

Sable rolled the nut between her fingers. "Yes," she said ruefully, "I guess I did."

"We don't expect you to leave Immusmala with us," Thulan said. "And without you, Ryah won't come." She sighed. "The Kalesh invasion changes everything."

"Does Atticus know?" Sable asked.

"Of course he does." Leonis took a long drink. "It's useless to try to keep secrets from that man."

Sable popped the nut into her mouth. "The first day out of the city, when I'd just met you, you two argued, by way of poor Terrelus, about what were compelling reasons to leave home."

"I never argue with Leonis," Thulan said. "I tell the truth, and he refuses to see it."

Sable smiled. "If it matters, I understand why both of you left your homes, and I think the reasons were good." She pressed the truth she felt into the next words. "It takes a lot of courage to consider going back."

They were quiet for a moment.

"That's kind of you to say, Sneaks," Leonis finally said.

"It was kind of her to say your reason was good," Thulan answered. "I always knew mine was."

Leonis ignored her. "What will you do?" he asked Sable.

"Get Talia free, then take her and Ryah and go somewhere we'll all be free together. And, I suppose, try to avoid the Kalesh."

They were silent as they ate their nuts. Over the top of one of the wagons, Sable could see spires of the priories. "If we win the tourney, do we get a tour of all the priories? Or just the Dragon?"

The dwarf shrugged.

Sable chewed thoughtfully. If they got a tour of the Priory of the Horn, finding that ring might almost be feasible.

From the back of one of the wagons, Purnicious hummed a lilting tune as she rummaged happily through the costumes, fixing any problems she found.

Sable straightened. Purnicious!

She almost tripped as she pushed herself off the crate and rushed to the back of the wagon. "Purn!" Sable lowered her voice and leaned into the wagon. "Could you blink into the Priory of the Horn and help me find something?"

Purnicious glared in the direction of the priories and shook her head. "No. I don't like those buildings."

"Why not?"

"They're dark. I can't see through the walls at all. In fact, I can't even see what's on the other side of the columns in front of them." She frowned and shook her head again. "There's some magic there, and I don't like it."

Sable's shoulders sank, and she let out a deflating breath.

"Why?" Purnicious asked, wiping the frown off her face and turning back to the rip in Leonis's costume.

"There's an object in there that was supposedly stolen."

The little kobold's purple eyes flickered toward the priories again and a crease formed between her brows. "Something about them is…" She met Sable's gaze and shrugged. "Mean."

"If we win the tourney, we are supposed to get a tour of the priories. Do you think it will hurt us to go into them?"

She shook her head. "Humans seem to go in and out of them fine."

"That's true." Sable sank against the side of the wagon.

Purnicious set down the cloak. "What is it you need from inside the priory?" She looked at Sable expectantly, her violet eyes wide. Her hair hung over her shoulders in two unruly ponytails tied with bright yellow ribbons. Her vest was edged with a new line of scarlet embroidery.

Sable paused before answering. But something in Purn's expression reminded Sable of how Talia used to look. Something about the way Purnicious trusted her.

"Kiva says one of the prioresses stole his mother's ring."

Purn raised a black eyebrow. "From what you have told me, Kiva's stolen enough from other people that he can hardly complain."

Sable laughed. "That is an excellent point, Purn."

"And that doesn't seem like the sort of thing you'd want to help him with."

"I don't. But he insists it's the only way to buy Talia's freedom."

Purnicious gave Sable a curious look. "Would you like me to check on her?"

Sable straightened. "On Talia? Could you do that?"

"Of course." She folded the cloak and set it aside.

"I don't know where she is."

Purnicious cocked her head again, as though looking for a joke. "She's your sister."

Sable nodded, unsure of what that meant.

"I've been able to sense her since we got into the city." Purnicious closed her eyes. "Ryah is currently walking along that wide avenue on her way here. And Talia is in a large home not far off that road." She looked at Sable with a proud smile. "They're not far from each other, although I doubt they know it."

"You…" Sable stared at her, eyes wide. "Purnicious, that's amazing! I'd love it if you checked on Talia. But don't be seen. I don't know how she would react if she saw you."

Purnicious grinned. "They'll never know I was there."

With a little *pop* she disappeared.

Sable stared into the empty wagon. "I wonder if that will ever get less unsettling."

A few minutes later, Ryah walked behind the stage, waving to a tattooed Muddog who immediately headed back out of the Sanctuary. Sable told her about Purnicious as they carried the costume crates closer to the stage.

With a little *pop*, Purnicious appeared again.

"How's Talia?" Sable asked, squatting down next to the kobold.

Purnicious frowned at her, and Sable grabbed her shoulder. "Is she all right?"

"Talia is fine," the kobold assured her. "She's lovely, and looked happy and busy. The woman she works for, though..." She shook her head. "She is not a nice lady. And her father, the rich man, is even worse. That house feels...angry."

Sable blew out a breath, trying to dispel the fear. It was nothing she didn't already know. "Could you check on her sometimes?"

Purnicious nodded. "I'll keep my eye on her."

Sable squeezed Purn's hand, and the kobold winced. Sable frowned and turned her hand over, finding an ugly purplish-red mark across her palm. "What happened?"

Purnicious smiled sheepishly. "I also tried to get into the priory for you. I thought maybe if I was close, I could see what was inside and maybe get in." She shrugged. "But the walls were still dark, and when I set my hand on it, it burned me. It's shielded somehow. I'm sorry, mistress. I don't think I could even walk through the door."

"Oh, Purn," Sable said. "I'm sorry."

The kobold shrugged. "It'll heal. Plus, I get to bellish a pretty bandage. I think I'll make it light green."

Atticus was nowhere to be seen, but the sun was starting to drop in the west, so the troupe began preparations for the show. When Atticus did appear, he offered them a smile, but his shoulders were tense. He looked at them all and nodded, almost to himself.

"Just do what you did last night." He paused, then muttered, "We'll be fine."

The words were directed more at himself than them. Without saying anything else, he climbed into the wagon and began rummaging for his own costume.

Thulan watched him for a moment, frowning.

"I thought he'd be...excited," Sable said quietly.

A crash came from the wagon, and the sound of Atticus swearing.

Thulan raised an eyebrow. "So did I."

CHAPTER FIFTY-EIGHT

ATTICUS'S MOOD had not improved by dusk, but he was hiding it better.

"We have four judges again," Thulan said, coming off the stage from where she'd been entertaining early arrivals.

Atticus looked up sharply. "We do?"

"Unless someone else has snuck into the judges' seats."

Atticus straightened. "I've never heard of one troupe getting extra judges on both nights. How's the audience?"

"Already bigger than last night."

For the first time all day, Atticus smiled a real smile. "Maybe we'll win this thing after all." He headed onto the stage. Sable heard him call a greeting to the crowd, who responded with cheers.

Sable finished getting dressed as Vivaine just when Atticus called out his introductory lines explaining the play.

When she stepped onto the stage, she didn't immediately fall into Vivaine's role. The spires of the Priory of the Horn loomed distractingly over the side of the stage.

She found herself glancing into the crowd, looking for Kiva, or Boone, or Talia.

Partway through her first scene with Balin, Leonis stepped closer than usual. "Focus!" he hissed into her ear, then stepped back and continued his lines.

Sable dragged her attention back to him. *Right. Focus.*

Balin was explaining that he'd be training for two years, and her next lines would be Vivaine longing for things to be different. That ache and Vivaine's helplessness bled into her.

"Two years?" Vivaine's hollow shock at the number was a perfect match to Sable's shock at Talia's new debt. A number too big to face, too massive to overcome. She filled her next lines with that longing, that deep, gnawing ache of wanting things to be different.

And the play came alive.

Balin asked her to come with him, but she couldn't. When he went to leave, she embraced him, clinging to him the way she'd wanted to cling to Talia.

The play finished and Atticus strode out on stage, his earlier despondency replaced by a towering confidence. He delivered his final speech, and the audience burst into cheers. Sable bowed with Ryah, Thulan, and Leonis to thunderous applause. The judges were hard to make out past the lanterns, but she could tell they stood with everyone else.

"Now we head to the priories and wait for the judging," Atticus said quietly. "They should have the winner by midnight. Stay in costume."

They climbed down and moved with the crowd toward the three huge priories. Sable caught sight of Andreese moving toward them.

"How was the meeting with your uncle?" Sable asked.

Reese grinned. "Great."

"Really? Nothing has been going great."

"This one did. Thanks to you."

She frowned. "Me?"

"My uncle is a very big fan of the theater. He wasn't interested in hearing from me until I mentioned that I knew The Figment of Wit's Traveling Troupe and could get him a seat near the front." He smiled.

"He loved it. Mostly, he loved you. He wants me to come by tomorrow morning and talk to him again, as long as I promise to introduce him to you as soon as I can."

"At least someone in your family has good taste," Sable said, smiling. "Too bad he didn't pass his love of theater on to you."

"I liked it tonight. Maybe even loved it."

Sable raised an eyebrow. "High praise from a man who's 'never been one for plays'."

"Everyone loved it. You were... How did you do that?"

"Give you good taste? I have no idea."

He shook his head. "When you spoke..." He raked his fingers through his hair, quiet for a long moment as they moved with the crowd closer to the priories. "It's been a long time since I thought about my uncle and the military," he finally said. "I've thought about how angry I am, but I haven't thought about what I lost." His gaze traveled to the top of the lit spires. "Tonight, while you spoke, all I could think about, was that when I walked away from him, I gave up every dream I ever had."

His face was pensive. "And it wasn't just me. I swear, everyone around me felt the same thing—that longing for something they want but can't have." He looked down at her. "Before my uncle left tonight, he hugged me. I don't think he's hugged me since I was a kid. And he made me promise I'd come see him tomorrow. He said, 'I've pretended for too long that I don't miss you every day.'"

"He did?"

A smile curled up the edge of his lips. "I told you, people like me."

Sable laughed. "One person does anyway."

Reese leaned closer and lowered his voice. "On a less happy note, the Kalesh were everywhere. There is a whole unit of them, thirty-six men total, housed with my uncle's men. And he has two Kalesh captains as advisors. Worse, he listens to them. He introduced me, and I got to spend most of the time listening to him gush about how much they were teaching him about military strategy and weapon design."

"Did they seem...underhanded?"

He let out a humorless laugh. "When I brought up the raiders in the east, one of them laughed and the other tensed. I don't have your skills, but I know when people are hiding something, and those two definitely were."

"Are the Kalesh worming their way into all the Northern Lords' troops?"

"From what I can see, yes."

Sable walked next to him silently. They reached the back of the crowd and followed Atticus, who weaved his way toward the front where other performers and artists were gathered. "If we don't win this, whatever chance Atticus has of convincing people of the truth will disappear."

"You'll win," Reese said. "I caught parts of the other shows. They were nothing compared to you."

She glanced up at him. "That's a lot of play watching for a man who doesn't like them."

"Maybe you're changing my mind about that, too." He stretched to see above the crowd. "Isn't it going to be awkward for the High Prioress to present an award to you for doing a great play about herself?"

"The High Prioress doesn't present the awards. The Prioress of the Horn does. Each priory has a specialty of sorts, and the Horn is supposed to recognize blessings of Amah. Of course, according to Prioress Eugessa, the goddess's blessings are shown mostly financially, so the wealthy are the ones closest to the divine."

"And the poor people, like Ryah's abbess?"

"Clearly not pleasing Amah, or she'd be more successful. But she claims winning the tourney is a sign that Amah is pleased, so she awards the winners herself."

"What do the other priories specialize in?"

"The Priory of the Dragon is about holiness, being set apart for the goddess, and the Priory of the Phoenix is about life, rebirth, and redemption."

"I like the Phoenix best," he said.

"So do I."

Andreese stopped at the bottom of the stairs to the Priory of the Horn, before the line of Sanctus guards. A pair of Mira, the hems of their robes glittering silver, walked along the edge of the stage, waving their hands at a line of torches to light them.

"Did they just light those with their fingers?" Reese asked quietly.

Sable nodded. "They're Mira. The prioresses say they're blessed by the goddess. Serene says they're just people like her. Of course, that doesn't really make them any less impressive."

Three younger abbesses came to the far side of the platform, singing a hymn to Amah and Isah, their voices floating above the people. Atticus motioned for them to come, and started up the stage to the rostrum. The guards stepped aside to let him through.

"See you when you've won," Reese said quietly. "Don't let the evil prioresses get you."

Sable shot him a smile and followed Ryah up the stairs. They joined the other artists and performers waiting. Sable took her place next to Ryah and Thulan, Atticus and Leonis standing behind them. The crowd was fenced in on three sides by the priories, a thousand faces lit by the bright torchlight of the plaza. It felt vulnerable to stand in front of a crowd that she could see so well. Her gaze roamed constantly, looking for Kiva or Talia.

She found neither. What she did see were several shawls and tunics decorated with embroidered dragons.

The Grand Prioresses stepped out of the door of the Priory of the Horn, followed by their armed Vena Sanctus guards, and the crowd quieted. Prioress Narine, holding her Phoenix on her arm, stopped near the back, as did Prioress Vivaine, her dragon curling around her feet. Prioress Eugessa strode to the front of the rostrum, her black unicorn at her side.

She wore her white prioress robe, her hair framing her head in thick, copper curls, her eyelids painted with the glittering, green paint.

"The blessings of Amah," she began, holding her arms up to the sky, "are poured out so generously on those who please her. She blesses her beloved with skills to make beautiful art, song, and stories. While many try to please the goddess with their attempts to create beauty, only those blessed by Amah herself succeed.

"Each year, it is our job," Eugessa said, gesturing to the other prioresses before pressing her hand to her own chest, "to seek out those who have pleased the goddess and reward them."

Thulan let out a soft snort. Sable glanced over at the dwarf, but she watched the prioress with an expression of polite interest.

"Too bad for the folks who aren't artistic," Leonis whispered from behind them.

"No hope of them pleasing the goddess," Thulan agreed dryly, keeping the respectful expression on her face.

"Amah blesses for many reasons," Ryah said quietly. "And she is pleased by all those who are kind and good. Even dwarves who act surly and half-elves who mock her."

"If you all don't stop talking," Atticus whispered, managing to make it sound threatening, "I will feed you to Vivaine's dragon."

From the handful of artisans, Eugessa announced the winner—the jeweler who'd had the gold bracelet at the Red Shield Festival. Today, the same woman held a chain with a gold pendant shaped like a leaf.

"May Amah always be pleased with my work," the jeweler said, offering the gold necklace to the prioress with a curtsey.

A young abbess stepped up and presented the artist with a small copper trophy shaped like a burning candle, then a small pouch that clinked when it fell into her hands.

"Unless there's a good amount of silver in that pouch, that woman was just paid a copper trophy for a gold necklace," Leonis said quietly.

"I'm serious about the dragon," Atticus hissed.

The winning singer, a broad-chested man, stepped forward and was awarded with his own copper trophy and bag of coins.

Eugessa turned to the three acting troupes at the side of the stage. "This year, the plays were excellent. However, one stood out above the others." Her words were warm and rich, and she turned her orange-lipped smile on Atticus. "Not only was it a work of great skill,"—The words remained warm—"but we were blessed with a story about our own dearly loved High Prioress."

The coldness of the final words drove into Sable like an icy blade and she stiffened. Ryah glanced over, but Sable tried to keep her face composed. Prioress Vivaine stood at the back of the rostrum looking pleased.

"The winner of the stage tourney is The Duke's Figment of Wits Traveling Troupe!" Eugessa held her hand out toward them.

Atticus stepped forward, smiling broadly and bowing to the prioress, then the crowd. The Sanctuary broke into loud cheers, and Sable stepped forward with the others, acknowledging the applause with bows. She smiled automatically, bowing like it was the end of a performance.

"Thank you. This is a great honor," Atticus said, his voice rolling over the Sanctuary. His words were truthful, but not quite as warm as Sable would have expected.

Eugessa raised her hand for silence. "I have been assured by the High Prioress herself,"—She waved a hand at Vivaine, who inclined her head in acknowledgment—"that the tale is indeed true."

A ripple went through the crowd. Atticus made an especially deep bow to the High Prioress. "It is an honor to share this truth with the world." Those words were richer.

The High Prioress made no reaction beyond her normal, serene smile.

Prioress Eugessa handed the candle trophy to Atticus, then held out a pouch of coins. Three hundred silver. The uselessness of even that much money made it nearly impossible for Sable to keep smiling.

Eugessa set the pouch in Atticus's hand with a hollow clank.

The smallest finger of Eugessa's hand glittered blue, and Sable's eyes locked onto the butterfly ring.

CHAPTER FIFTY-NINE

EUGESSA LOOKED down the line of actors. Her gaze lingered curiously on Ryah for a moment, and Sable wondered if she recognized her from the Choosing. But when the prioress walked closer, it was Sable she stopped in front of.

The butterfly ring was so close, Sable clasped her hands together in an effort not to reach for it.

"Here we have our Prioress Vivaine," Eugessa said, her voice rich. "For your portrayal of our beloved Holy Mother, for capturing her kindness and her wisdom"—Whether she believed that was indiscernible—"and for making us love the High Prioress even more dearly than we had"—The words sharpened into a lie so cold Sable flinched —"we thank you." With a smile that didn't reach her eyes, Eugessa continued. "I look forward to seeing how Amah blesses you in the future, Issable of Shadowfall." As if the warmth in those final words wasn't disturbing enough, the Prioress of the Horn grew brighter. Sable blinked, trying not to recoil from how disturbing that truth was.

Sable managed a stiff bow to the prioress, and the crowd erupted in cheers again.

Eugessa turned back to the Sanctuary. "Tomorrow morning, the winners will be honored with a tour of the priories. At midday, Felis will grace us with a concert in the Grand Stadia. And at dusk, Atticus and his troupe will perform their play one more time, for the High Prioress herself."

The crowd applauded, and Atticus led them off the rostrum. They gathered at the bottom of the stairs, the crowd breaking up around them as the prioresses turned to go back inside. Atticus gripped the trophy and the pouch tightly, his smile fixed stiffly on his face, and no one spoke for a moment.

"I've always imagined winning the tourney would be more... cheerful," Leonis said.

"As did I," Atticus said quietly.

"Did you see all the Kalesh clothing in the crowd?" Thulan asked. "It wasn't just the wealthy merchants wearing it."

Atticus's gaze scanned the crowd with a troubled look. "I think we may find that winning the tourney was the easy part of our plan."

Andreese pushed through the crowd to stand at Sable's shoulder. "The Kalesh Ambassador was at the far end of the stairs, Atticus. He did not look pleased when you won."

Atticus frowned. "We just performed a play that made Vivaine look fantastic. He shouldn't dislike us."

"He knows Serene and Jae traveled with us," Andreese pointed out.

The frown deepened on Atticus's face. He looked around, but there was no sign of the ambassador. "That's troubling." He was silent for a moment. "If he already dislikes us, let's hope the rumors of his influence in the priories are overstated."

"That's seeming less likely by the moment," Thulan said.

Atticus glanced back up to the now empty rostrum and nodded. "Tomorrow can't come soon enough."

The next morning, Sable added both her and Ryah's winnings, ninety-five silver, to her pouch, but it sat in her hand like a lump. Between all the payments from the shows, it held one hundred thirty silver.

When had a treasure this big become too little?

The world felt strange this morning. The tourney was over. They'd won. But despite having worked toward that goal for weeks, it felt empty. They'd earned the chance to stand on stage before all of the powerful people in Immusmala and the northern lands. Atticus had worked on his speech for weeks, but the sheer amount of influence the Kalesh enjoyed in the city made it less likely anyone was going to believe anything Atticus had to say.

"Time to go," he said, rapping on the outside of the wagon.

Sable pushed back the thoughts. It was time to see what the inside of the Priory of the Horn looked like.

Ryah's face popped into view with a wide smile. "Atticus says we may get to talk to the prioresses themselves!" She disappeared around the side of the wagon.

The idea of coming face to face with Vivaine made Sable pause until Ryah called for her to hurry.

One of the Sanctus guards escorted Atticus, Thulan, Leonis, Ryah, and Sable across the Sanctuary and up to the front doors of the Phoenix Priory.

Climbing the stone steps almost felt surreal. Thinking of Purnicious's burned palm, Sable closed her hands into fists as the guard led them through the tall doors, but she felt nothing unusual. Aside from awe.

The door opened to a long hall with stone floors and rooms on either side. The hall was open to a high ceiling. Elaborate, two-story stone columns rose around the outskirts, the stonework resembled twisting trails of flames.

Thulan gave an astonished hum and stepped closer to the nearest column, examining the carvings.

Sable turned in place. The room was soaring and weightless. It reminded her of the phoenix in flight, trailing sparks and drawing everything up toward itself.

"The priories were made with the help of dwarven masons," a thin voice said from a doorway behind Sable. "I've always thought the stonework looked so much like fire it could ignite at the slightest encouragement."

Prioress Narine, the Grand Prioress of the Phoenix, stood in an archway leading to a long hallway. The Sanctus who had escorted them stood stiffly at attention.

There was a moment of stunned silence before Atticus stepped forward and bowed. "We're honored to meet you, Holy Mother."

"And I you, Atticus," she said, an amused smile on her face. "I'm looking forward to your play tonight."

Thulan stepped forward and gave her a bow, as well. "How old is this building? I had no idea the dwarves built anything in Immusmala."

"Well over one hundred years old. Long ago, a Dragon Prioress raised an army to help the dwarves fight off attackers from the north. In gratitude, King Tolldoth III sent workmen to the city to build the prioress a church. They say the grand mason fell in love with her, and as a gift, he built two more." She gave them a speculative smile. "Whether that part is true, I don't know, but Dragon Prioresses do have an enchanting way about them."

"Possibly not to a dwarf," Thulan said, her eyes running over the scrollwork in the arch above Prioress Narine's head. "But this work is magnificent."

"Come," the prioress said, heading into the wide entry hall. "I'll show you my favorite carving."

Thulan started after her immediately, and Leonis followed, looking amused. Atticus exchanged stunned looks with Ryah and Sable.

"The prioress herself is giving us a tour?" Sable asked quietly.

"I suppose we shouldn't waste the opportunity," Atticus said, ushering them forward.

Prioress Narine glanced back at Ryah as they walked. "You are the young lady from the Choosing."

Ryah blushed at the words.

"I'm sure that day wasn't what you'd hoped," Nadine continued, a grandmotherly sort of warmth in her voice. "I myself was also not selected during a Choosing."

"You weren't chosen?" Ryah asked, stunned.

"I was devastated," the old woman said. "I worked my way into this priory the way most do—by many years of serving in other places." She looked up, her gaze trailing along the intricate stonework.

"But now I can see it was a blessing from Amah that I was allowed to stay in my small abbey longer." She gave Ryah an earnest look. "Our paths sometimes don't turn the way we want, but nonetheless, they are our paths and are bound to lead us where Amah intends for us to go."

Nearly hidden behind a huge column, at the edge of a carving of a vast oak, the roots of the tree grew suddenly unfinished. Tucked behind the column was the carved form of a sleeping dwarf, resting against the unfinished root, his chisel and hammer still in his hand.

"That's Master Tenrul!" Thulan exclaimed. "There is a similar sleeping dwarf hidden along the back of the throne of the high dwarf in Torren." She stared at the wall in wonder. "You were honored indeed if Tenrul worked on the priories. And there are bound to be more carvings like this around."

"I've lived here for twenty-three years," the prioress said, "and I'm still discovering little bits of humor carved into the walls."

She turned and called to a white-veiled prioress walking by. "Abbess Nalla, these are the winners of the Midsommer tourney. Could you show them the work hall, then escort them to the Dragon Priory?"

At her nod, she turned back to the troupe. "It was lovely meeting you all, and I'm looking forward to tonight with a great deal of plea-sure." She gave them a smile and walked away down the hall.

Abbess Nalla smiled warmly at them through her thin veil, and started down a long hallway. "Upstairs is reserved for living quarters, but this is the main working hall."

Sable glanced up to the high ceiling and the railings. "Where does the phoenix live?"

"Upstairs in the Grand Prioress's suite," Nalla answered.

Sable followed the others down the hall, glancing in the rooms they passed. All were decorated with beautiful stonework, and veiled abbesses sat in many of them, copying scrolls or sewing.

Atticus looked curiously into each. "I had a friend who visited this priory once, before Prioress Narine was here. He said the main hall was covered with beautiful tapestries. Did the prioress move them?"

"You could say that." Nalla pushed open a door that led outside.

"She said no one could eat tapestries, so she auctioned them off to the Merchant Guild." She let out a resigned sigh. "She made a fortune, and this is what she spent it on."

They stepped out into a wide garden that filled the space between the Priory of the Phoenix and the Priory of the Dragon. A few well-manicured bushes led into it, but past those were rows and rows of vegetables. Sable had never seen such a large garden.

"It produces a lot of food, but..." Nalla glanced back to the priory. "I do sometimes miss the tapestries."

They wound their way through the garden until they reached a door at the front corner of the Dragon Priory. One of the Sanctus guards let them in, and Sable stepped into the priory expecting... something. But aside from a slightly minty scent, the building felt almost normal.

A long corridor ran along the front of the priory. Mottled light from stained-glass windows facing the plaza filled the stone hallway. They traveled halfway down the building until they reached the wide front doors and the enormous entrance hall just inside it. Like the Phoenix Priory, this one was open to the floors above, but instead of being merely stone, this hall was filled with color. Besides the brightly colored stained glass, large tapestries decorated the walls and banners hung from the railings. White-gowned abbesses moved in and out of hallways and doors.

Atticus stopped at the side of the room, his eyes following three women not dressed in white. Each wore a long robe in a different color, but they all had white, twisting dragons embroidered on the skirt. One of the women spoke quietly in Kalesh.

Abbess Nalla spoke quietly with a stern looking abbess. "Abbess Wennia will escort you around the Dragon Priory," she said. "It was nice to meet you all, and I'm looking forward to the show tonight."

Atticus thanked her, and she headed back toward the Phoenix Priory. Abbess Wennia gave them a tight nod, her look of disapproval clear even through her thin veil. "Welcome to the Priory of the Dragon. If you'll follow me, and not touch anything, I'd be honored to show you some of our priory."

She didn't sound particularly honored, and the nearest guards scanned the group. One of them focused on Atticus. Atticus gave the man a friendly smile and followed Wennia into the wide hall.

Sable's gaze shifted from white-robed figure to white-robed figure, suddenly nervous to come face to face with Vivaine.

Wennia led them through the entry hall and down a long corridor, where she showed them several rooms filled with tables and abbesses writing on scrolls. At the end of the hall, the abbess stopped at a tall, arched door. Reddish light spilled out into the hall.

"This is the chapel where the High Prioress comes to pray." She looked at them sharply. "Only a prioress may step inside."

Sable moved up to the door next to Ryah and Thulan.

"It's beautiful," Ryah breathed.

The stonework in the room was more simple, but the far wall of the small chapel held an enormous stained-glass window. The lower portion of the window was filled with vines and flowers creeping up the trunks of two enormous trees growing at the sides. Their branches touched at the top, framing a blazing red sunset.

The room was filled with a half-dozen wooden benches, all facing the window.

"This chapel is lit by Amah herself," Wennia said.

Sable stared at the glass for a long moment. There was something off about the room. Something she couldn't quite define.

She moved to the side so the others could see, placing her hand on the doorframe. The sharp edge of a stone flower jabbed into her palm. An intricate swirl of flowers climbed up the wall. She leaned into the room, trying to follow it up. The inquisitive, stone face of a tiny mouse peered at her from under a flower petal.

"Thulan, did you see—"

"Do not enter the chapel," Wennia snapped, and Sable yanked her head back. Wennia waved them back down the hall. "The rest of the priory is given to living quarters, so I'll escort you to the front doors. I'm sure you have much to do today to prepare for tonight."

"Does the priory have a library?" Atticus asked.

"The library is not on the tour," she said. "If you'll follow me, I'll see you out."

Sable glanced at the others. "We haven't toured the Priory of the Horn yet."

Wennia turned an unconcerned look on her. "I do not offer tours of priories that are not my own."

"But they told us we would get to see all three." Sable forced herself to smile at the abbess. "I've always dreamed of seeing that one."

Thulan raised an eyebrow, and Ryah looked at her curiously.

"I was told nothing about that," Wennia said stiffly. "And touring the Priory of the Horn after seeing the Dragon Priory would be a disappointment. You are, however, free to go to the Horn and request a tour."

She started back down the way they'd come. Atticus studied Sable for a moment before turning to follow.

Ryah came up next to her. "You've always dreamed of it? I think there are rules about lying to an abbess." She frowned. "Does this have to do with whatever you and Kiva were whispering about?"

"The less you know about it, the better," Sable said, starting down the hall. "But I might be able to help Talia if I can get inside the Horn."

Ryah gave her a calculating look and opened her mouth, but a soft voice floated out of a partially open door ahead of them. Atticus jerked to a stop in front of them.

The door swung wider, and the High Prioress herself stepped into the hall.

Sable shrank back slightly. The prioress was tall. Taller than Sable had expected. Nearly as tall as Atticus. She wore a plain white robe that fell to the floor, her hair braided over one shoulder in a shockingly mundane style.

"The entire set needs to be copied," she said over her shoulder. "The sooner, the better." She turned and paused at the sight of the group in the hall.

Ryah grabbed Sable's hand.

"Holy Mother," Wennia said with a deep curtsey, "I'm sorry to have disturbed you. I was just leading these people out."

Prioress Vivaine's gaze stopped on Atticus, who stood so stiffly he might have been carved from stone like the rest of the building. The prioress stared at him for a heartbeat before a smile spread across her face.

"Atticus," she said, stepping forward and reaching out a hand. He took it, his motion stilted, and bowed deeply. "It's been a long time, my old friend." Her words were nothing but a common greeting.

Atticus twitched, but when he straightened, he had a wide smile on his face. "Too long, Holy Mother." His words, unlike hers, were warm.

A glitter of silver flashed behind Vivaine. Her dragon slipped up beside her, his scales catching the sunlight and sending glints of white and gold skittering down his body.

Atticus looked at the creature warily, but Vivaine merely smiled. "This must be your famous troupe." Her expression was warm, and the light from the room behind her brightened the hall. "I haven't seen the play myself, merely heard of it from others, but I understand I am indebted to you all for a flattering portrayal of my younger self."

Sable stood stiffly beside Ryah, who gripped her hand tightly.

"It was time the world learned the true story," Atticus said.

She gave him a slight nod, then turned to smile down at Thulan. "It's been a long time since we've had a dwarf visit the priory," she said kindly. "I'm sure you are able to appreciate the stonework even more than the rest of us."

Thulan nodded, pulling her eyes away from the dragon. "I haven't seen anything like it outside of the throne room in Torren."

"That must be a magnificent place." A hint of regret came into her smile. "When I was young, I always wanted to see the dwarves. I'm afraid I'm a bit old to travel that far now."

She turned to Leonis with a curious expression. "You, sir, have an elvish sort of look."

Leonis straightened at the remark. "My father is elvish."

"I knew some elves in my youth." The wistfulness was back in her voice. "Pellis was a particular friend." She glanced at Atticus. "But I suppose many people know that now."

"I know Pellis! That's who helped you with Balin's sword?" Leonis turned to Atticus, frowning. "You called him Peldin in the play."

Atticus gave a self-conscious smile. "I knew it started with a P."

Vivaine's gaze caught on Ryah, and her eyes widened. "Oh, child!" She stepped forward, and Ryah froze. "You're the dear girl from the Choosing."

The dragon slid forward with her, his unblinking gaze fixed on Ryah.

"M-my name is Ryah, Holy Mother," she said, giving the High Prioress an awkward bow, her eyes locked on the dragon.

"There has been much talk in the priories of how close you came to being selected." Vivaine's grey eyes took in the dragon's focus on Ryah. "I foresee good things in your future, child."

A timid smile grew on Ryah's face, and she bowed her head.

The dragon turned its face toward Sable, shifting forward another half-step. A chill ran up Sable's neck as the emotionless, slitted eyes fixed on her.

"And who are you, my dear?" Vivaine asked quietly. "My dragon isn't usually so intrigued by people."

"This is Issable," Atticus said. "The woman portraying you in the play."

Vivaine let out a long laugh that echoed through the hall. "Maybe he recognizes that." She kept her eyes on Sable for another moment, her gaze warm, but curious. She set her hand on the dragon's head and he relaxed, dropping his gaze.

Atticus stepped closer to Vivaine. "Perhaps we could have a moment of your time, High Prioress, to discuss some urgent matters that have nothing to do with the play? I've been anxious to speak with you."

"The High Prioress is a busy woman," Wennia said brusquely. "I apologize again, Holy Mother, for the interruption."

Vivaine considered Atticus for a moment. Her eyes were a solemn grey. "I have a little time. Please, come into my study."

She turned and pushed open the door to reveal a room with two large desks covered with papers, another table against the far wall was equally full. The dragon moved smoothly into the room, heading for a large patch of sunlight on the floor.

Atticus stopped short in the doorway.

Sable came up behind him and froze.

The Kalesh Ambassador, wearing a long, orange robe with a flaming red dragon embroidered up the side, leaned over a desk, studying a map.

The man looked up at them, letting the parchment roll closed. He walked toward the High Prioress with a warm smile. He was nearly as old as Atticus, but instead of curly hair, his was cropped close, his beard trimmed neatly. He stopped so close to Vivaine's shoulder they were almost touching, and looked at the group curiously.

"May I introduce Ambassador Tehl from the Kalesh Empire," Vivaine said, setting her hand on the man's arm. "Our loyal ally, and a dear friend."

CHAPTER SIXTY

"AH, THE NOTORIOUS ACTING TROUPE." The Kalesh Ambassador
tempered the words with a friendly smile that Atticus did not return.
His faint accent lent a crisp feel to the words. Leonis and Thulan fixed
the man with cold looks, and Ryah gripped Sable's hand even more
tightly.

"Ambassador Tehl," Vivaine said, "graciously agreed to help me
write a treaty between Immusmala and the Empire that we are hopeful
will bring years of peace and prosperity to our land."

The warmth of her words filled the room.

"Has he?" Atticus asked, his voice tightly controlled. "How
generous of him."

"Anything to help the High Prioress," the ambassador said, his
voice not particularly truthful. "There is much to be gained from our
two lands working together." The warmth of those final words made
Sable shift.

There was no resemblance between him and the Kalesh warriors
they'd met in the woods. His face was neither long nor sharp. His grey
beard was trimmed neatly around his chin, and his eyebrows, the only
hair that remained dark, were set in curious arches over clear, probing
dark eyes.

"What was it you needed to tell me, Atticus?" Vivaine asked. "The ambassador and I have a good deal of work still to do, and since we have entertainment planned for this evening,"—She smiled warmly at the troupe again— "we'll be cutting our work short today already."

Atticus pulled his gaze away from her hand on the ambassador's orange sleeve. "Would it be possible for us to talk privately?"

Vivaine frowned slightly. "You can talk freely in front of the ambassador."

Atticus glanced back and forth between the two of them, then cleared his throat. "As you may know, since the Red Shield Festival, we've traveled onto the Eastern Reaches."

She nodded. "When Jae and Serene left with you, I know that was what they had planned."

At their names, Atticus glanced out into the hall. "Are they here? I had hoped to speak to them, too, but I haven't seen them since yesterday."

"I believe they're busy in the library," she said.

"What was it you wanted to tell the High Prioress?" Ambassador Tehl said. "I'm afraid we don't have much time."

Sable glanced at Vivaine to see how she would respond to the man stepping in, but she merely fixed Atticus with an expectant look.

Atticus focused on the man, his face hardening. "On the Eastern Reaches, we discovered a town burned to the ground."

"Dear Amah," Vivaine said, bringing her other hand to her heart. "Were many hurt?"

"Nearly every soul was killed," Atticus said, still watching the ambassador.

"How tragic," the High Prioress breathed. "A dispute between towns?"

"Not according to the single survivor."

The ambassador nodded somberly. "I've heard the news. Raiders torturing the Reaches."

The silver dragon shifted on the floor.

Atticus shook his head. "The man who survived the attack says it was Kalesh warriors who burned the town in the dark of night, slaughtering everyone there."

"Kalesh?" Vivaine asked. "Why would the Kalesh destroy small towns in the Eastern Reaches?"

"That is the exact question we asked two different Kalesh warriors we encountered in the Nidel Woods," Atticus said.

The Kalesh Ambassador did nothing more than raise an eyebrow.

"Both of them," Atticus continued, "claimed a force of Kalesh was coming to wipe out our land."

Vivaine let out a short, rippling laugh. "Tehl, do you have any knowledge of an approaching army you haven't told me about?"

The ambassador grinned and shook his head. "If an army were coming, I wouldn't be working such long hours on dull paperwork."

Sable studied the man. His words had a turbulent feel that made it too complex for her to gauge the truth of them.

"Perhaps someone is trying to give our Kalesh neighbors a bad name," Vivaine said lightly, her hand still resting on the ambassador's arm. "Although why they would want to, I don't know. We're on the verge of a historical alliance with them. The work we're doing here will benefit Immusmala and all the lands around us more than you can imagine."

Sable felt the truth wrap around her, and her stomach sank at the prioress's faith in the man.

The ambassador's face remained pleasantly calm. "Perhaps they are envious of something," he offered. "Perhaps someone is displeased with how close the Empire and Immusmala are growing. A subset of the merchants perhaps, worried that trade will be affected." He gave Atticus a bland smile. "Or an old ally who finds themselves becoming less relevant than they once were."

"I doubt any old allies are threatened by a huge, faceless Empire that can hardly find Immusmala valuable in light of all the lands it already possesses," Atticus answered easily.

The pressure of the words between the two men was enough to make Sable lean back.

"Ambassador Tehl looks like he has a face to me," Vivaine said, reaching up to touch the ambassador's cheek.

Atticus's gaze dropped to her hand, and even Ryah stiffened at the gesture. Vivaine set her hand back to the ambassador's arm.

"Why is it that the Empire is taking such an interest in Immusmala right now?" Atticus asked, his voice losing any semblance of pleasantness.

"The great Empire is always looking for new allies," the ambassador said.

"It seems to me that most of your allies have been brought in at the edge of a sword."

Vivaine narrowed her eyes at Atticus's tone.

"In the past," the ambassador said, "we did rely on military force. But in these modern times, we are working toward more peaceful partnerships with our neighbors."

"If they become valuable enough?"

"Atticus," the prioress said sharply. "I did not invite you in here to insult my guest."

The dragon's head rose at Vivaine's tone, but the ambassador laughed.

"It's all right. I believe your old friend doesn't trust me, Vivaine."

Atticus flinched at her name.

"I hope time will prove that I come in friendship," Ambassador Tehl said, still smiling, "not as an enemy."

"As do I," Atticus said, without a hint of humor.

"I believe we're done, Wennia," the High Prioress said. She glanced at the troupe, her gaze lingering on Sable. "I look forward to seeing the play tonight." Even though her voice was relaxed, something about her gaze held Sable's eyes. "I've never sat through an entire tale told about me, and I'm interested to see how you perform it."

The truth of the words pushed against Sable and she managed a slight bow, suddenly believing Vivaine had honestly thought the best of Balin, even after all the horrible things he had done.

"We're honored to perform for you," Atticus said with a bow.

Vivaine raised one hand, and a thin beam of light from one of the windows landed on her sleeve, spreading a slight glow of white. "May Amah bless your day and your words tonight."

The prioress lowered her arm, and the light faded. Vivaine and Tehl turned and started back toward their desks.

"This way, please." Wennia's tone was a command, not an invitation. "You've taken enough of the Holy Mother's time."

Atticus strode out of the room after her, and the others followed. As they approached the front door of the priory, Sable hurried up next to Abbess Wennia. She focused for a moment on the need to get into Eugessa's priory before she spoke.

"We were supposed to see all three priories this morning," Sable said, trying to infuse the words with longing.

Wennia gave her an annoyed look.

"We really don't need to," Leonis said.

Sable forged ahead, thinking of Kiva's feral look when he spoke of the ring. "We were told just this morning that we could. I'd hate to put you out further, Holy Sister, but if you could just take us as far as the door and introduce us, they would certainly help us if asked by someone as respected as you." She tried to infuse those words with truth, but they felt a little hollow. "Getting to see that priory, as well, would mean more to me than you could ever know." Those words felt rich as they left her mouth.

"Yes," Ryah answered. "It would mean so much."

Thulan frowned at Ryah, and Leonis let out a sigh. Atticus fixed Sable with a questioning look.

Wennia's face softened slightly. "I suppose I could walk you to the priory." She turned down the hall that ran along the front of the priory, heading toward the Priory of the Horn.

"Thank you," Sable said sincerely. "May Amah bless you richly for this." The words rolled out rich with relief, and Abbess Wennia straightened slightly.

"Thank you, child." She glanced at the others over her shoulder. "Come along. I don't have all day."

Outdoors, in a much more formal garden separating the Dragon Priory from the Priory of the Horn, Abbess Wennia found a younger abbess to hand them off to, and in moments, Sable found herself stepping into the Priory of the Horn under the watchful eye of four Sanctus guards.

The only word for the interior was gaudy. The tapestries were flecked with silver threads. Small tables in every nook held vases bursting with flowers or small sculptures. Richly colored rugs covered the floor.

Sanctus guards stood at nearly every corner, watching them closely.

The layout of this priory was similar to the other two. One hallway along the front, a vast gallery in the center, open to the floors above, several hallways leading off of it. Abbess Leanne was the most talkative guide yet, gushing about the artwork and the tapestries. She showed them three rooms with large fireplaces and shelves of silver trinkets.

Sable walked next to Leanne, feigning interest in every detail. "Where does the prioress herself live? I can only imagine how amazing her rooms must be."

"They are amazing," Leanne said. "I've never been inside them, but I've peeked in the door, and…" She gave a sigh. "Stunning."

Just like the Dragon Priory, the Priory of the Horn was bustling with people. It was mostly filled with white-veiled abbesses, but there were some colorful Kalesh robes, as well.

Leanne glanced back at the group with a smile. "Come this way." She led them down a long corridor near the back of the priory. The doors were tall and ornate, the rugs on the floor thick enough that each step felt like walking on cushions.

"There are so many treasures," Sable said, trying to keep her voice awed instead of disgusted as they passed another table with a silver sculpture of Amah.

"The prioress has been so blessed," Leanne said. "The people love her so much they shower her with gifts."

Sable gave a hum that she hoped sounded like agreement.

"The next door is the prioress's apartment," Leanne said quietly as she led the way down the hall. She didn't stop, but slowed enough that Sable could glance inside. Instead of a bedroom, she looked into an enormous sitting room containing a half-dozen couches and tables. Silver plates of food sat on almost every surface. She could just see a wide bed through a far door. An abbess, carrying a heap of white robes, came from somewhere to the right.

There were two tall windows on the far wall, covered with wrought-iron bars shaped to look like vines.

"Isn't it glorious?" Leanne asked, leading them farther down the hall.

"It's big," Sable said, glancing behind her.

"Enormous," Leanne agreed. "She has a sleeping room, a closet, a dining area, that big sitting room, and a closet large enough to walk into just for jewelry."

"That's...overwhelming," Sable said honestly.

"The last room I can show you," Leanne said, leading them back toward the front of the priory, "is the music room. Do any of you play instruments?"

Sable fell back and let the others comment on the large room filled with more instruments than she had ever heard of. Whatever hope she had of being able to reach that butterfly ring dwindled away. Not only was every entrance and every hall guarded by Sanctus guards, Eugessa's rooms were as big as a house. Even if Sable could do the impossible and sneak in while Eugessa slept, it could take hours to find one small ring.

By the time they were done with the tour, it was past noon, the Grand Stadia was emptying from the concert by the winning singer. Atticus, who'd barely spoken since they'd seen the High Prioress, stalked toward the wagons. When they reached their stage, he ordered them to take it apart just enough to move it to the Grand Stadia, then stormed to the front of his wagon and pulled out the papers where he'd written his speech for after the play tonight. With a scowl, he flipped through it.

Thulan and Leonis shared a look, then began working, giving Ryah and Sable directions on which parts to disassemble and which parts to leave.

Purnicious popped into view at Sable's side. "I'm so glad you're back, mistress!" She grabbed Sable's hand. "I couldn't feel you once you'd gone into the priories." She glanced at the others, then lowered her voice. "Were you able to find the ring you were looking for?"

Sable shook her head. "I'd need to turn invisible and pop through walls to have any hope of getting that."

Purnicious made an annoyed huff. "I wish I could do it for you."

"I don't really want you stealing for me."

"Is it stealing if we're returning it to the person it belongs to?" she asked.

Sable sighed. "I don't know."

Purnicious patted her hand. "I checked on Talia, and she's fine." She frowned. "But I don't like that house."

Sable studied the little kobold. "That's the second time you've said that. Why?"

Purnicious scrunched up her face. "I don't know. I can't quite decide why. Lord Trelles is cruel and horrible."

"Is he cruel to Talia?" Sable asked sharply.

"No... Talia is never anywhere near him. Of course, Lady Ingred is cruel and horrible, too. Again, not to Talia. She seems to like Talia. But they have a lot of decorations around the house with dragons on them."

"That's not too surprising," Sable said. "The wealthy in Immusmala are obsessed with the Kalesh right now, and Lady Ingred is among the wealthiest."

The kobold nodded. "And Lord Trelles just got word that they found another gold mine. This one might be bigger than his last."

"Purnicious!" Leonis called from the other side of the wagons. "The curtain ripped!"

Purnicious leaned forward. "We should get Talia out of there. I don't know why, but I don't like that house."

"I couldn't agree more," Sable said.

"Has anyone seen Purn?" Leonis called, and Purnicious gave Sable's hand another pat before popping out of sight.

They had most of the stage broken down and loaded into the wagons when Andreese stormed up. "We are too late!"

Sable looked up from where she and Thulan knelt next to the last curtain post. Reese's face was livid.

"Atticus!" he called. "We're too late!"

Atticus climbed out of the wagon, scowling. "What are you yelling about, boy?"

"The Kalesh haven't just infiltrated the Northern Lords. They *control* them, in all but name."

"That's impossible," Sable said, coming up next to him. "Why would they let that happen?"

"I just visited my uncle," Reese said, his voice furious. "The man is completely controlled by two Kalesh *advisors*. They call themselves captains, but the Kalesh men call them *pellot*, which means lord or, in a military setting, a really high-ranking officer. Much higher than a captain."

"So?" Atticus said. "It makes sense military advisors would be high-ranking."

"Not this high." Reese shook his head. "Plus, the regular soldiers are *tellt*. That's no regular soldier ranking. That's more like captain. I'd say every Kalesh warrior here is incredibly well-trained and high-ranking. Even the ones who are masquerading as regular soldiers."

"The Northern Lords must know that," Atticus said. "You can't be the only one who speaks Kalesh."

Reese let out an annoyed breath. "I don't know anyone else who does. Before I went there, the Northern Lords just had the vague idea that the Kalesh were a strong, distant Empire." He shook his head. "Every northern soldier I talked to reports to a Kalesh officer."

"Maybe it's just your uncle's troops that are so deeply under their control," Atticus said.

"I checked with three other lords, by far the most powerful in the north. All of them are the same. The Kalesh are in charge in all but name."

"Did you tell your uncle about Ebenmoor?" Sable asked.

"Yes, although I had to do it while one of his 'advisors', Nellek, was in the room with us, because he just couldn't bear to send the man away long enough to hear how his own sister was murdered by the cowards in her sleep!"

"What did he do?" Atticus asked.

"He had the gall to ask Nellek if it was possible!" Reese jabbed his finger at his own chest. "I was there! But that doesn't matter because Nellek says the Kalesh have no reason to be on the Eastern Reaches."

"Do you think he was lying?" Sable asked.

"Yes. The look on his face when I mentioned where Ebenmoor was…" He let out a growl. "He knew."

Atticus sank back against the side of the wagon. "I never expected this. The High Prioress is entirely too close to the Kalesh Ambassador, too. I—"

"Oh," Reese interrupted, holding up his hand. "That's another thing. Do you know what the solders call the ambassador? Not *styrek*, which means ambassador, but *trestet*, which is the highest ranking general in their military." He flung a hand toward the priories. "There's a *trestet* embedded in with the most powerful woman in Immusmala, and at least one *pellot* controlling each Northern Lord!"

He looked at Atticus and shook his head, taking a deep breath to calm himself. "This isn't a case of the Kalesh coming into a city and trying to gain favors. This is a precise military maneuver, and the Kalesh are already in control."

The torchlight didn't stain the High Prioress's robes to a ruddy hew...Instead, she almost glowed with a pure, white light, as though the moon, long lost behind clouds, had draped its light over her.

CHAPTER SIXTY-ONE

SABLE STARED AT ANDREESE, shaking her head as though she could negate his words.

"You can do your play tonight," Reese said, "but nobody is going to listen to anything you say against the Kalesh." He glanced around at them. "I think it's dangerous for you to try. The Kalesh here are elite soldiers."

Atticus shook his head. "We have to try."

"What we should do," Reese said, "is kill the ambassador."

"What?" Ryah exclaimed, her face aghast. "No!"

"There's a snake in the city, and that man is the head." Andreese leaned back against the blue wagon. "The only way to cripple them is to chop it off."

"What are you proposing?" Thulan asked. "That we walk into the Dragon Priory and kill him while he's standing inappropriately close to the High Prioress?"

"No. We can't actually kill him right now," Reese said. "At this point, he's so well thought of, he'd be seen as a martyr. Wars have been lost or won by the timing of an assassination. The moment of attack shapes everything."

"We're not going to kill him!" Ryah exclaimed.

"I agree. I think it would be a mistake." Leonis nodded.

"Yes," Reese answered, "but it may be a bigger mistake not to. There is a well-designed operation going on in this city, as well as throughout all the large cities of the north. Chipping away at the edges of it by, say, separating Nellek and my uncle won't change anything. The ambassador is the key."

"I'm inclined to agree about the head and the snake," Atticus said. "But first, we need to expose the ambassador and separate him from the priories." He glanced at the troupe. "Which has always been our plan. We need tonight to be so compelling that everyone will listen."

Reese shook his head. "It's not going to work. My uncle wouldn't even believe we'd captured and spoken to Kalesh warriors." He threw his hands into the air. "He just refused to believe it."

They were silent again.

"We have to say something," Ryah said. "All those poor people in Ebenmoor, and who knows how many other towns. The books the Kalesh stole from Stonehaven. We can't pretend we don't know."

"Purnicious heard that another gold mine was found," Sable said. "If there's half as much gold in those mountains as the merchants hope there is, the Kalesh are here to stay."

"And if their economic and political attempts don't work," Atticus said, "they'll be familiar with the Eastern Reaches, so they could send troops."

"Atticus," Sable said, "I hope your speech tonight is compelling enough that everybody listens."

"If there's one thing you know how to do, old man," Leonis said, "it's how to make a crowd listen, even if they didn't intend to."

Atticus stared at the ground for a moment, then nodded. "Get the last of this loaded. We need to start setting up in the theater." He turned and climbed back into the wagon.

Entering the Grand Stadia with the troupe was utterly different than walking in with the crowd during the Choosing. Instead of entering through the doors that faced the Sanctuary, the wagons rolled around the side, past two Sanctus guards, to a small alley between the back of the theater and the tall wall that surrounded the Sanctuary. They parked their wagons near a wide door and began carrying in the curtains, costumes, and props.

Carrying an awkwardly long curtain pole, Sable followed a young woman dressed in priory white through a series of hallways until she pushed open a door and Sable stepped out onto the stage itself.

The smooth stone platform filled an area ten times larger than Atticus's stage. An enormous awning stretched out above her, but the rest of the Stadia was drenched in sunlight. Sable stepped forward numbly. Row after row of benches rose in a wide arc around the stage. The first few rows looked normal, but by the time Sable's eyes reached the last row, it was so high and so small it looked unreal.

Sanctus guards, still and somber, stood at the entrances.

"Well," Thulan said, stopping next to her, "that's...big."

Atticus strode across the stage, nodding to himself. He climbed down the stairs at the front of the stage and up a dozen rows before turning to look at them, raising his voice. "We're going to have to modify the curtains a bit. Is Purnicious nearby?"

Sable worried for a moment that the kobold wouldn't be able to come into the theater, but she popped into view next to Atticus. The nearest Sanctus guard flinched at the appearance of the little creature, watching her with narrowed eyes. Atticus pointed at the stage, giving her directions.

Leonis and Ryah stepped onto the stage, pausing before setting down their own loads. Ryah glanced over to where she'd stood for the Choosing before turning and moving quickly off stage.

"Lots more to bring," Leonis said, heading back to the wagons, and Thulan followed.

Sable stood alone on the stage for another moment. She tried to imagine walking across the vast stage, delivering Vivaine's lines while the prioress sat in one of the balcony seats along the side.

Every bit of truth she'd ever tried to infuse into the lines suddenly felt thin and shallow. The prioress was a real person, a different person than herself, and the audacity of thinking she knew what the woman was feeling made Sable want to slink off stage.

A low whistle of astonishment made her flinch. Andreese stepped up next to her, carrying an armful of curtain poles. "They have nothing like this in the north."

He caught sight of Sable's face, frowning. "Are you all right?"

She shook her head. "I can't perform here," she said quietly.

He looked around. "Why not?"

"She's going to be here." Sable pointed at the balcony where Prioress Eugessa and Narine had sat during the Choosing. "She'll be right there. I can't pretend to be her when she's right there."

Andreese paused, then set down the pile of poles. "Then everyone who expects to see a play about her is going to be pretty disappointed."

Sable scowled. "You know what I mean. The only way I've been able to play her is by putting what she felt in terms of my own life. But... I don't know if that's anything like what she really felt. How am I going to focus on what I think when she'll be staring at me the whole time?"

"She'll be a lot harder to see past the lights." Reese studied her for a moment. "Your High Prioress isn't some mysterious creature, Sable. She's a person. Like you. No matter how much this city idolizes her, she's still human. Human enough to be tricked by a foreign ambassador, and if what Leonis and Thulan say is true, human enough to have fallen in love with him."

"I know she's human—"

He held up his hand to stop her objection. "The reason everyone likes your portrayal of her is that you make her human. But not in the way I would, which would point out all her flaws.

"For instance, I would point out that she picked a spoiled merchant's daughter over Ryah at the Choosing. Now, even though almost every abbess I've ever met is completely useless, anyone who's been near Ryah for half a minute knows she'd be different. Ryah would make the best abbess the world has ever seen."

The idea brought a small smile to Sable's lips. "That's true."

"But you have managed to bring out the fact that Vivaine is human in the best possible way. When you speak, we know what the prioress is feeling, but that's because we recognize it in ourselves." He leaned forward. "The only way you can play her is by putting her story in terms of your own life. It's what drives this entire tale."

Sable shook her head. The balcony where the prioresses would sit was so close to the stage, she could almost picture Vivaine sitting there, watching.

"Nothing's changed," Reese continued, taking her hand.

She turned to look at him, focusing on the familiarity of his face.

"Nothing's changed in your life," he repeated. "Talia is still in the same situation she was before, and there's still no way you're getting to that butterfly ring. The Kalesh are still taking over everything, and they're further along in that goal than we'd expected." His hand tightened on hers. "Everything you've felt during this story is still the same. Your Balin is still the same. Don't worry about the audience or the size of the stage. People need to hear what you have to say. They need to feel it the way I did last night. The way my uncle did." He let out a short laugh. "If you can make my stoic uncle feel something, you can do anything."

She gripped his fingers. "I haven't felt this terrified since the first night I performed."

"It's nothing you haven't done dozens of times before." He smiled. "And my uncle commented that it was nice to see an actress who knew how to hold a sword."

She gave him a faint smile. "Next, you'll have to teach me how to throw a knife right in front of someone's feet." She narrowed her eyes. "Or did you mean to hit Kiva and missed."

"I wanted to hit Kiva. But I decided that might not go well for you."

"Me? The Muddogs would have killed you for breaking their treaty with Kiva."

"There were only five of them."

"Plus Kiva and Boone."

"Five, seven…What's the difference?" He grinned at her. "It would have been more satisfying to hit him than the floor."

"Since both of my sisters were in the room, I'm glad you restrained yourself."

His smile turned grim. "No promises next time I see him, though.

I'm not a fan of men who rule through tyranny and fear." He glanced up at the balcony where the prioresses would sit. "Or women, for that matter."

"Please don't throw a knife at the High Prioress!" Sable said. "She's hardly a tyrant."

He squinted at the box. "I think she's more of a tyrant than people can see. But I promise I won't throw a knife at her. There's something decidedly cowardly about killing an unarmed woman."

"She's not unarmed," Sable pointed out. "She has a dragon."

"Good point." He furrowed his brows. "I really don't know how to fight a dragon. Most of the stories I've heard make it sound difficult."

Sable smiled at him and squeezed his hand again. "Thank you. I feel…better."

He looked out over the empty seats again, making an irritated noise. "I'm going to try to get back into my uncle's good graces so I can sit with him during the play. Hopefully, during Atticus's final speech about the Kalesh, I can get a sense of what the Northern Lords think. Of course, sitting with him will mean sitting with the Kalesh. But I imagine that will be educational, as well." He glanced at her. "Maybe today would have gone better if I'd have taken you with me."

Thulan dropped a pile of poles onto the stage with a clatter. "Don't worry. The rest of us will carry all this. Wouldn't want to interrupt you two with something as trivial as preparations for the most important performance of our lives."

"Sable and Andreese!" Atticus yelled from halfway up the auditorium, where he sat writing. "Stop wasting time and help!"

"He knows I don't work for him, right?" Reese asked.

"But I do." Sable pulled her hand away. "And I'm conscripting you to help."

Ryah carried in a huge pile of curtains, and Leonis followed her with more.

"I already helped," Reese said. "I banished your pre-performance jitters."

"That's not enough. What's the point of having burly soldier friends if they don't help carry heavy things?" Sable headed off the stage after Thulan.

"To throw knives at your enemies." He followed her. "And defend you from thugs in alleys."

"I'm headed to an alley right now. You can save me from curtain poles."

Organizing the stage, costumes, and props took a good portion of the afternoon. When things were settled, Atticus ran through a couple scenes on the stage, mostly for Sable's and Ryah's sake. Moving across such a big surface felt different than the small stage they usually performed on.

Reese found his way up to the balcony where the prioresses would sit and leaned against the railing, smiling smugly at Sable the entire time until she forced herself not to look in his direction.

When they had satisfied Atticus that they knew how to use the larger stage, he dismissed everyone, except Sable. Most of them went backstage. Leonis, looking wan, leaned against the table that held his tree, closing his eyes.

"I rewrote the speech for tonight," Atticus said to Sable. He held up three papers covered with his thin, smooth script.

"Is it going to work?"

Atticus gave her a slight smile. "Possibly. Shall I read it to you?"

"Sure," Sable said. "Should we call the others back?"

"They're not the ones who need to hear it."

Sable frowned at him. "They'd want—" She stopped short, the truth hitting her like a wall. "You want me to give the speech?" She stared at him incredulously. "No one's going to listen to me! You're the one people will listen to."

"I can write a compelling speech," Atticus said. "I can even give a compelling speech. At least I thought I could, until I met you."

"I'm not doing this." Sable crossed her arms. "You're crazy if you think this is a good idea."

"It's the best idea I've had since offering you a job."

"It is," Leonis called from his tree.

Atticus nodded. "You're the one who can say these words and make people feel them."

She took a step backward, still shaking her head. "I have no idea what to say."

He lifted the pages with a smile. "That's why I wrote it out for you. Now listen to them, and listen well, because we don't have a lot of time." He cleared his throat and looked down at the speech.

"Atticus, wait," Sable set her hand on his arm, her heart pounding. "You can't expect me to do this. There's too much riding on it."

He met her gaze. "You are the only hope we have of getting anyone to listen." The truth of his words filled the stage, adding a warmth and richness that it had been missing. "You are the one who can convince them we're telling the truth. You're the one who can get them to see the horror of Ebenmoor, the hatred those warriors had in the woods." He paused, but the truth stayed close around her. "Even the dark terror from your own town long ago."

She started to object, but he kept speaking. "The only thing that will get through the complacency and admiration they have for the Kalesh is a true, moving, personal story. And you have that. People need to know the truth. We cannot sit by and let them stay ignorant."

His words were rich and pressed in on her from all sides, tempering her own fears.

"I know," she whispered.

"It has to be you, Sable."

She let out a rough breath, thinking of the Kalesh warriors surrounding their wagons in the woods, of the wounded man following Purnicious. Of the pounding of black boots past the cellar door.

No more cowering.

Sable nodded.

Atticus let out his own breath of relief. "Are you listening?"

She nodded again.

He cleared his throat and began to read.

CHAPTER SIXTY-TWO

WHEN DUSK SHADOWED the Grand Stadia, Atticus shooed the troupe backstage.

The initial set was in place and Sable was dressed for the opening scene, waiting for Thulan to be done fixing her hair. Ryah adjusted her handmaiden's dress in front of the largest, clearest mirror Sable had ever seen.

Her nerves about performing had been eclipsed by nerves about giving the speech at the end of the show. Atticus's speech was excellent.

At no time did it accuse the Kalesh in Immusmala of plotting anything sinister, but it would certainly raise doubts. Written as a biography of herself, it was Sable's explanation of how she came to be here tonight, acting on the most coveted stage in the world. The ending was a plea to help those on the outskirts. Those who did not live under the protection of the priories and the Merchant Guild. A plea to the Kalesh Ambassador to investigate the horrors and prove his good faith by helping the poor souls on the Eastern Reaches.

There were enough mentions of infiltration to put ideas in anyone's mind, and hints that the new gold mines would look like quite a prize to any foreign power.

If those two ideas didn't get the attention of the Northern Lords and the Merchant Guild, Sable didn't know what would.

"I found someone who knows you," Andreese's voice came from behind her.

Sable tried to turn to see, but Thulan grunted and held her hair tightly.

Ryah did turn, and her face lit up. "Talia!"

Sable jerked her head again, but Thulan's grip on her hair was too tight.

"Wait," Thulan commanded in a gruff voice. She slid a hairpin into Sable's hair. "Okay. Carefully. Don't mess up what I've done," she threatened.

Sable turned to see Talia standing in the doorway, hugging Ryah.

"What are you doing here?" Ryah asked.

"I was brought along to accompany Lady Ingred," Talia answered over Ryah's shoulder, glancing curiously at the dwarf.

"This is Thulan," Sable introduced. "She's been doing my hair and face."

Talia hid her surprise at the "she" well, and gave Thulan a smile. "Sable's face paint is fantastic. But don't you hate how her hair is always a mess?"

"It's like a rodent's nest," Thulan agreed.

"You're accompanying Lady Ingred?" Ryah asked. "That sounds prestigious."

"It's not, really." Talia was dressed in a stunning yellow dress, her hair pinned up in elaborate braids. Her face paint was subtle and clean, but didn't completely mask the tightness around her eyes.

"You look rich," Ryah said, touching the sleeve of Talia's gown.

"That's the point. I'm supposed to blend in. Ingred says this is the perfect place for me to figure out who's who among the wealthy." She sighed and held up a green piece of fabric. "And do things like find a way to mend a ripped scarf, even though we're in the middle of the Grand Stadia."

"You came to the right place. We can take care of that." Sable started toward her, but paused. Talia stood stiffly by the door with Andreese next to her, almost as stiff. He looked furious. Sable gave him a questioning look, and he gave her back the slightest shake of his head.

"Actually," Sable said, turning her attention back to Talia, "a ripped scarf is perfect, because I really want you to meet someone." She glanced around. "Purnicious?"

The kobold popped into view next to Sable. "Yes, mistress?"

Talia let out a little shriek and pressed her hand to her mouth.

"You'll get used to that." Sable smiled at her sister. "Talia, this is Purnicious."

Talia dropped her hand and stared at the little blue creature, taking in her wild, black curls and her long ears.

"She's Sable's kobold," Ryah said helpfully.

"It's very nice to finally meet you, Talia," Purnicious said with a curtsey. "Do you need help with that scarf?"

Talia looked at Sable. "She's yours?"

"I am bound to her," Purnicious said over the objection Sable was about to make. "Because she saved my life. Which means I'm bound to her whole family, including you. Although I'm bound first to Mistress Sable." She beamed up at Talia. "Your dress is lovely."

Talia gave her a bemused smile. "Thank you."

"The scarf?" Sable asked.

Talia handed it to Purnicious, who shook out the fabric. An embroidered, white dragon curled along the edge, and the kobold frowned at it. "I don't fix Kalesh things."

"But it's for Talia," Sable pointed out.

"She'll never find anyone who can fix it as well as you," Ryah agreed, "and it'll please Lady Ingred."

Purnicious sighed. "For you, Miss Talia, I will fix this rip. But there's a loose thread in the dragon's tail, and that, I will not fix. It's bound to unravel eventually, and the scarf will be the better for it."

"Of course. Just the tear," Talia said. "I'm terribly grateful to you." She glanced around the room, taking in the frowns at the dragon. "What's wrong with the Kalesh? Two of them come to the house nearly every day, and I'm almost positive Lord Trelles is buying his gold mining property with loans from them."

"This just gets better all the time," Thulan grumbled, tossing a hairpin back into her box.

"The Kalesh seem nice," Talia said. "And helpful."

Sable shook her head. "They're not."

Ryah grabbed Talia's hand. "It was them—back home. With the black boots." She looked at Talia with wide eyes. "Back *home.*"

Talia stared at her. "You're saying the Kalesh killed our parents?"

"We ran into warriors exactly like them on the Eastern Reaches near the ruins of another burned town." Sable nodded toward Andreese. "He was the only survivor."

Talia turned wide eyes to him. "And you're sure they were Kalesh?"

"They claimed to be from the Kalesh Empire." Reese shrugged. "While speaking Kalesh."

"How far away was this?" Talia asked, glancing behind her, as though warriors might rush through the door.

"On the Eastern Reaches." Ryah set a reassuring hand on Talia's arm.

"But it's all connected," Sable said. "The Kalesh there, and the ones here."

Talia's fear turned to skepticism. "The Kalesh all the way out on the Reaches may be dangerous, but the ones here aren't burning homes."

Sable felt a ripple of irritation. She opened her mouth to argue, but Ryah spoke first.

"Is Lady Ingred going to worry if you're gone too long?"

Talia gave a short laugh. "Not as long as I'm with a big, strong soldier like Andreese."

Sable raised an eyebrow and glanced at Andreese. "A what?"

"Lady Ingred's words, not mine," Talia said, holding up her hands. "Andreese found us while Lady Ingred was bemoaning her ripped scarf. He claimed to know a seamstress right here in the theater, and Ingred found the gesture very heroic."

"Oh yes," Sable said dryly. "All the great heroes mend scarves."

Reese nodded. "She was extremely grateful. Told me twice how much she hoped to see me again." He looked thoughtfully at Sable, smiling for the first time. "You forgot to mention how striking Lady Ingred is."

"Striking?" Sable frowned at him. "She's wealthy, not striking. A lot of simple minds confuse the two."

"You sound a little envious," Talia said.

Reese grinned at her. "She does, doesn't she?"

Sable crossed her arms. "I'm not envious."

Thulan snorted from behind Sable, but didn't say anything.

"I don't need your special skill to know that's a lie," Talia said, and Ryah let out a laugh.

Sable shot them both annoyed looks. "Purnicious, don't fix that scarf."

"Too late," she said, handing it to Talia, almost shyly.

Talia held it up, searching for the mended section. There was only the slightest line where the rend had been. Barely more than a wrinkle.

"Amah's shiny bum! That's amazing!" She turned to Purnicious. "How did you do that?"

Purnicious burst out in peals of laughter.

"Amah's shiny what?" Ryah asked, grinning.

Talia clapped her hand over her mouth. "I'm sorry, Ryah! I didn't mean—Lady Ingred says it all the time. It just slipped out!"

Ryah laughed. "I haven't heard that one before."

"Do abbesses know a lot of ways to swear by Amah?" Thulan asked grinning.

Ryah nodded. "My favorite is 'by Amah's stumpy knuckles.'"

Talia laughed and put an arm around Ryah's shoulders. "We need to find a way to see each other. Often."

"We can send messages through Purn," Ryah said.

Talia glanced down at the kobold. "I'd like that." She glanced behind her again, and the worried look returned. "I should go."

Sable took a step toward her. "Does Ingred suspect anything about you?"

Talia shook her head, a little too quickly. "I don't think so. But yesterday, one of the stable grooms disappeared. The rumor was that Lord Trelles thought he was spying for one of his rivals in the

Merchant Guild." She ran her fingers over the scarf. "No one knows what happened to him."

"Talia," Sable said, "you need to get out of there."

Her sister gave a humorless laugh. "So I could spend my life hiding from Kiva and Lord Trelles, both?"

"Talia—" Sable began.

"I'm fine," her sister said firmly. "Or I will be if I get back there with this scarf."

Before Sable could stop herself, she crossed the room and threw her arms around Talia. Her sister squeezed her back tightly.

"Andreese says you're amazing on stage," Talia said quietly into her hair. She pulled back and for a moment, she looked scared and young again, but she forced out a weak smile. "The whole world is finally falling over at your beauty, and I didn't get to do your paint."

"I'm sorry," Sable said. "About everything. I can earn a lot here. When I can pay Kiva off, he'll have to let you go."

Talia didn't bother to smile at the idea. "It's already nearly five hundred silver. He makes it more every day." She glanced down at her hands. "You were right. Once you're under Kiva, there's no way out." She met Sable's gaze again. "You'll never catch up. We both know that." She stepped back and straightened her shoulders. "And I'm not sure I want you to."

The scared look faded from Talia's face.

"I'm doing good things there, Sable. I have access to all sorts of information on the Merchant Guild. Ingred trusts me and gives me free rein of the house. I've heard her father's meetings. If the Kalesh are really a problem, I can tell you what they're up to. I can tell Kiva." The look she gave Sable pleaded with her to listen. "Everything the Merchant Guild does keeps places like Dockside poor. I can help Kiva end that."

"Kiva has no interest in helping Dockside. Not unless it benefits him."

"You always think you know better." Talia stepped back, her face angry. "You aren't there. You don't see how things are. Kiva can cripple the Merchant Guild if he just has the right information. I'm going to help him."

"Talia," Sable started, reaching for her hand. "Kiva is only interested in what's good for himself."

"You don't know everything, Sable," she answered coldly. "I'm staying where I am." She turned to Ryah and pulled her into a hug. "I'll see you soon, Ryah. We'll find a way."

Ryah hugged her tightly. "Soon."

Talia stepped back and headed for the door. "Good luck, all of you."

Sable followed her to the doorway. "Be careful, Talia."

Her sister strode down the hallway, not looking back.

Reese stood next to Sable, both of them watching her disappear.

"If even Talia doesn't believe us about the Kalesh," Sable said, "do we have any hope?"

"We do if you're giving the speech." He looked down at her for a long moment. "It's the right choice, but…be careful."

She set her hand on his arm. "It's a good speech."

"I hope so, because everyone's going to think it's yours."

Sable expected him to follow Talia. Instead his anger softened slightly as he leaned closer and took a deep breath. "I suppose it's still not the right time to point out your hair smells good." A rueful smile crinkled the edge of his eyes.

A whole different sort of tension poured into her, and an actual smile crept onto her face. His arm felt warm under her hand. "Maybe not quite yet." He held her gaze, and for a moment she forgot about speeches.

Thulan muttered something behind her, and Reese stepped back, a smile curling the edge of his mouth. "That's a shame," he said quietly.

Sable smiled up at him. "Aren't you supposed to be with your uncle?"

His eyes went flat, and the muscles in his arm tightened.

"What's wrong?"

"My uncle refused to speak to me." His hand curled into a fist. "The only people he brought with him tonight were Kalesh."

She gave him a blank look.

"Every year, it's an honor for officers to be chosen to join him at the theater. And he chose four Kalesh men." He glared down the hall, as though he could see the gathering crowd. "When he saw me outside, he sent a Kalesh officer to tell me to stay away. Said if I couldn't be polite to his men, I wasn't welcome." He turned back, his eyes blazing. "His men? He called the Kalesh his men."

"Reese…" she started.

"You don't understand," he said. "By calling them his men, he's making a pledge to them. The Northern Lords care for their men, watch over them. Their code says they will do everything in their power to protect 'their men.'" His eyes were furious. "He has pledged his loyalty to them—the monsters who murdered his sister! And if he has, so have the others."

He ran his hands through his hair. "The Kalesh control the northern troops, the Merchant Guild, the priories. Whatever we thought to stop here has already happened. Our speech is too little, too late."

The hall filled with rich truth, and everything about him brightened at the fervor in his words. Strands of reddish brown stood out in his beard, and honey-colored highlights laced through the brown of his eyes.

She shook her head. "We still have to try."

He clenched his jaw and grabbed her shoulder, his face desperate. "I don't want you to give the speech. I know you're the best choice, but it's too dangerous."

She shoved his hand off, her hopelessness and anger boiling over. "You're not the only one who wants to stop the Kalesh. But words are the only weapon I have. If there's any chance of convincing people of the truth, I'm going to try. Even if it's dangerous."

He pulled his arm away from her. "And if you fail?"

"Then I guess you get that fight you've been looking for."

CHAPTER SIXTY-THREE

Reese left and Sable went back to her chair. Thulan started on her hair again without comment. Leonis strode into the room, dressed as Balin. "Atticus is looking for you, Ryah. He's at the back of the stage."

Ryah smoothed her costume in the mirror, her face worried.

"You have nothing to worry about," Thulan told her. "Just do what you always do."

Ryah gave her a quick smile and ducked out of the room.

From the corner of her eye, Sable could see Leonis rummaging through one of the crates. He glanced at Thulan. "Did you tell her yet?"

"I've been busy fixing her hair," Thulan answered, detangling a hairpin and smoothing out a lock of hair. "Twice."

"I blame Reese," Sable muttered.

"So do I," the dwarf grunted.

Leonis glanced at Thulan. "You insisted you be the one to—"

"Kiva keeps raising Talia's debt, doesn't he?" Thulan interrupted.

Sable sighed. "Yes. It's enormous now."

"We figured. Would three hundred and fifty silver help?" Thulan asked.

Sable froze. "What?"

Leonis leaned into her view and smiled. "Would it?"

"Yes, but—"

"Good," Thulan said sternly. "Keep your head still."

Sable looked at Leonis questioningly.

"Thulan has no life," he explained, "and nothing to do with her winnings from the tourney, or from what she's hoarded over the last several years. She wants to give it to you and Ryah to help Talia pay her debt."

"Thulan!" Sable exclaimed, turning. The dwarf tightened her fingers, but Sable batted at them until Thulan let go. "We can't take that!"

Thulan took a hairpin out from between her teeth and met Sable's look with a shrug. "Consider it payment." She rolled the hairpin between her fingers. "It's been a long time since I remembered what family felt like. Ryah helped me remember that. But I know she'd never take the money." She met Sable's gaze. "You will. Because it's for Talia."

Sable jumped up and threw her arms around the dwarf. Thulan stiffened, before patting her awkwardly on the back. "If you cry and ruin your face paint, I'm not fixing it."

"Sixty-five of the silver is mine," Leonis said. "I'm not as miserly as Thulan, so I've spent most of my earnings, but you two are welcome to whatever I have. I certainly can't think of a better use for it."

Sable turned and hugged Leonis, as well. "Thank you. I know you have plenty you'd like to do with your winnings."

Leonis shrugged. "Seeing Cintis reminded me of some things I'd forgotten." He patted her back more comfortably than Thulan. "Now, sit back down so Thulan can repair the damage you just did to your hair. Again."

Sable sank into the chair. "I don't know what to say." Her eyes felt wet, and she blinked to keep the tears from messing up her face paint.

Leonis handed her a small handkerchief.

"Just convince that sister of yours that getting away from Kiva is a good idea," Thulan said. "Then get her and Ryah somewhere safe."

Sable gently dabbed at her eyes. All three of them together, going...

anywhere. "Talia could come with us to the Nidel Woods and Torren. She'll explode with happiness at the idea."

"Another human," Thulan sighed, pulling her fingers through Sable's hair, more gently this time. "I just keep collecting more humans."

"You're destroying any reputation dwarves have for grumpiness," Serene said from behind them. "People are going to start thinking dwarves are sweet little things."

"Serene!" Sable tried to turn her head again.

"No," Thulan said forcefully. "You will sit here, perfectly still, until I'm done. Leonis, push Serene out and lock that door."

"Ignore Thulan," Leonis said, "and come in. We've missed you."

Serene came over in front of Sable, dark shadows under her eyes.

"How are you?" Sable asked.

Serene leaned against the table covered in brushes and face paint. "Exhausted. We've been trying to catalog the books, but they were dumped into a room with no order whatsoever. It's been nearly impossible to sort it all out."

"Is Merrick there?"

Serene scowled. "We haven't seen him. He's quarantined with some sickness the Kalesh claim would be harmful to the rest of us, so he's only treated by their healers."

"That's not suspicious or anything," Thulan muttered, tugging on Sable's hair.

"Is he really there?" Sable asked.

Serene nodded. "I haven't seen him, but I can feel him in the room they say he's in. He's weak, though. The Kalesh are in charge of the library, but they're letting Jae and I work in it, as long as we help them organize and catalog it all." She crossed her arms. "I'm positive some books are missing, though. Jae thinks we just haven't found them yet, but I can't find any of the books I wanted on moving energy, including the one I wanted to look in for you, Sable. I also can't find two books that have detailed maps of the Northern Lords' cities and the coastal area near Immusmala."

"Does anyone have any good news at all?" Thulan asked.

Serene glanced out the door, then lowered her voice. "Did any of you know Atticus was at the priory before the tour this morning?"

Leonis stopped rummaging and turned toward her.

"Twice," Serene said. "He was refused entry both times."

Thulan's hands stopped. "Why?"

Serene shrugged. "The only reason I know about it is because the guards told me I wasn't to let him in. Not that they've let me anywhere near the doors. Until tonight, Jae and I have been kept in the library or the small room next to it they've given us to sleep in. They even bring us meals there. They're very polite, but if we try to leave, they come up with an urgent thing they need us to help with."

"That might explain why Atticus has been in such a bad mood since we've arrived," Sable said.

"It's the first reason I've heard that makes sense," Thulan agreed, starting to braid again. "Assuming we ignore the fact his going to the priory doesn't make sense in the first place."

"Atticus is known there," Serene said. "He always has been. Jae and I assumed it's because he's relatively famous and is always in the Midsommer tourney. But we're realizing it's not just the regular abbesses who know who he is. It's the guards. They all know what he looks like and seemed to assume that he'd try to come again."

"And he's obviously still in love with Vivaine," Sable said. "Maybe the two of them are in more contact than we know about."

Leonis crossed his arms and looked at Thulan. "If he did something to vex the Holy Mother last spring—like that day he was inexplicably cranky leaving the city after the spring shows—that would explain our terrible location during the Red Shield Festival."

Thulan's hands stilled in Sable's hair again. "And his sudden urge to write a play singing her praises."

Sable's shoulders sank. "This is all an elaborate love letter to the High Prioress?"

The room was quiet for a long moment.

"No matter what it started as," Serene said, "it's a play people are fascinated to hear, and if you all play it well tonight, they all might just listen to the other things we have to say." She shook her head. "Including Vivaine."

"Any other bad news we should know about?" Thulan asked, tucking a hairpin into Sable's hair.

Serene frowned. "There's some schism between Eugessa and Vivaine."

"Everything nice Eugessa said about Vivaine at the ceremony last night was a lie," Sable agreed.

"That's not too surprising." Serene nodded. "Eugessa has never been thrilled that Vivaine outranks her, but it's escalated lately. Apparently, the ambassador was the only Kalesh allowed into the priories at first, until Eugessa invited dozens of wealthy Kalesh merchants into hers. So Vivaine brought more into the Dragon Priory, and now there's this unspoken contest of where the Kalesh spend more of their time. It's strange." She shook her head. "And each of the prioresses brought Mira with them tonight. Not in their balcony, but almost like additional guards."

Thulan frowned. "Are they a danger to us?"

Serene shrugged. "A few of them are adept at manipulating fire. That's mostly what I've seen them do. I'm not sure what other skills they have. I've heard some of them can read thoughts, or something along those lines. Since I'm not sure that's even possible, I doubt it's true. The priories don't really know how to train the Mira. They just teach them silly tricks for dramatic affect when they're near the prioresses. If we could train them for a bit..." She shook her head and turned to Sable. "By the way, Merilee is here. And sitting very close to the front."

Sable groaned. "That's what I need. Her glaring at me the entire performance."

"I didn't want you to be surprised. Judging from the look she gave me, there will definitely be a lot of glaring."

"Amah's shiny bum," Thulan said. "I'm glad we don't have to pin our hopes on her tonight."

Serene snorted at the phrase and nodded. "Me, too."

She looked toward the door. "I'd better get back." She stood and set a hand on Sable's shoulder, giving her a tight smile. "Just think, if things were going well, you wouldn't have that horrible dread in your stomach to draw from."

"Finding dread won't be a problem tonight," Sable answered.

"They're going to be enthralled by you." The truth of Serene's words nudged against Sable. "Just like they always are."

Serene left, and Leonis sighed. "I'm glad you're here, Sneaks. But I'm starting to doubt even you will be enough for this."

Thulan finished Sable's hair, and she stood, moving to the large mirror. A stranger looked back at her, dressed in the clothes of a young Vivaine, the front of her hair pulled back into a twisted braid, the rest of it tumbling down her back.

She smoothed the front of her dress, focusing on the opening scene. Serene was right. There was plenty of dread to fuel her words.

Atticus hurried into the room, Ryah close behind.

"We're out of time. Let me see you all." He didn't look exactly happy, but there was a fierce energy about him. "The Stadia is full of the exact people we need."

"Andreese came by," Sable began.

"I talked to him." Atticus frowned. "It's obvious the Kalesh are much more entrenched here than we had expected, but the play will win them to our side, and Sable's speech at the end will open their eyes. Even a sliver of doubt in the city will be a blow to the Kalesh."

"Why have you been trying to get into the Dragon Priory?" Thulan asked bluntly.

Atticus looked at the dwarf, then glanced around at the rest of them. "For the past ten years," he said frankly, "I've brought Vivaine reports on the places we've traveled."

The room was silent for a moment.

"You spy for her?" Leonis asked, slowly.

CHAPTER SIXTY-FOUR

"I PREFER to think of it as reporting the activities of the world," Atticus answered. "Our troupe has a unique view. We mingle with common people, but we're invited into the homes of the nobility, too." He shrugged. "It's information Vivaine's found useful."

"Then what happened last spring?" Leonis asked.

Atticus hesitated before answering. "When I went to make my report last spring, I found her with the Kalesh Ambassador at dinner. I was used to giving her my reports in private, but she insisted he be present." Atticus's jaw clenched for a moment. "He was more attentive to her than I was comfortable with, and I may have spoken out of turn. Vivaine informed me that my services were no longer needed and sent me out."

"Which is why we were punished during the Red Shield Festival by getting the worst possible location for our stage," Thulan said.

Atticus nodded. "She's refused to see me ever since. Until the tour, I hadn't been able to see her, no matter how hard I tried."

"You didn't think this was something we should know?" Leonis asked.

Atticus shrugged. "Vivaine is only one part of this whole thing. There are many more people who need to hear what we have to say.

And this play was the thing that was going to make them curious enough to listen."

His words were greeted with a skeptical silence, but he smiled. "What matters at this moment is that you all look perfect, and it's time to begin."

He looked at them all in turn. "Bells of truth."

There was only a breath, before they all replied, "Cries in the night."

Despite everything, when Sable stepped onto the stage, the desperation she needed to tap into was right at the surface. Candles had been lit across the front of the stage, set in front of beautifully polished mirrors that reflected the light back at her, illuminating the platform. If Merilee was in the first few rows, she was indistinguishable in the darkness. If Vivaine herself sat in the nearest balcony, Sable couldn't tell.

She entered, holding the sword Balin had made, and moved it slowly through the movement Reese had taught her, the motion familiar enough now that it required no thought.

Leonis stood near a painted forge. The stage felt empty and wide, the night air cool after the closeness of the room backstage.

She poured the uneasiness she felt about the future into her words, and the stage soon felt as it should—wrapped in words, longing, and hope.

The longer she was out there, the more the edges of the Stadia became visible. The balcony with the prioresses sat on the left, closest to the stage, and the white of the prioresses' robes was the first thing Sable could make out. It took longer to see the orange robe of the Kalesh Ambassador sitting at Vivaine's left.

The audience responded perfectly, and the story gained momentum as Balin stole the life from his first victim to heal himself.

Sable was deep in the middle of the tale before she caught sight of Talia sitting behind Lady Ingred in a balcony behind and above the prioresses. Her attention was fixed on Sable.

In the final scene, when Sable stood with Ryah, facing the cloaked baledin, her voice almost choked on the pleas for him to stop. She pictured the Kalesh standing there, reaching for Ryah, and her words tore out of her.

"Balin, stop!"

But Leonis reached forward and grabbed Ryah's arm. Her sister crumpled to the stage, and Sable gripped the sword.

"Please," she pleaded.

Her own knees buckled as she swung the sword at Leonis's arm, striking the flint with her thumb.

Flames raced down the blade, and the sword crashed into Leonis, who twisted and enclosed the end in his cloak. Sable cried out for him to stop drawing in the power, but Leonis toppled to the stage, too, the sword flaming brightly against him.

Sable shielded her eyes from the light of the sword, and Leonis let out a feral scream. She drew back, away from him and Ryah's still form.

With a final cry, Leonis collapsed and the sword went out.

There was utter silence in the crowd for a moment, before loud, rolling applause washed over the stage. Sable stayed still, breathing heavily, waiting for Atticus to come make his final speech. The applause continued until he finally stepped on stage and raised his hands for silence.

Sable tuned out his words, realizing that as soon as he was done, she would start the speech he'd written. She sat on the stage, next to Ryah, running over them in her mind.

Atticus finished his lines to the thunderous applause of the crowd, and Sable and the others stood to bow. When the applause had gone on long enough, Atticus motioned Sable forward, and the others left the stage.

Sable caught a glimpse of Reese, standing just off stage, watching her with a ragged expression.

"Amah has blessed us this summer to work with Issable," Atticus started, setting his hand on Sable's shoulder.

The crowd cheered again, and she gave them a slight bow. Standing close to the front of the stage, she could make out some faces, and her attention caught on one unhappy expression three rows back. Merilee glared at her with such venom that Sable almost flinched.

Looking for someone more supportive, Sable glanced up to see Talia beaming at her. Even Lady Ingred looked thrilled.

In the prioresses balcony, the ambassador watched the stage with polite interest. His expression was matched almost perfectly by the High Prioress, whose face was calm, except for her eyes, which studied Atticus sharply.

Atticus was talking again, and Sable pulled her attention back to him.

"—as a treat to those of you gracious enough to come to our show, I've asked Issable to speak to you of the unusual path she has trodden to come to this place."

An interested murmur rippled through the crowd and Atticus stepped back. Sable drew in a breath to banish the nerves and began.

"During the Red Shield Festival, I would have never imagined that I would have the privilege to be standing here today, or have been able to spend the last weeks trying my best to tell the story of our beloved High Prioress."

She turned toward the prioresses' balcony and bowed. Vivaine returned it with a gracious nod.

Sable dropped her gaze to the lanterns at the front of the stage, trying to block out the pressure of all the eyes on her, bringing to mind the first real line of the speech.

"A month ago, I lived here, in Immusmala, convinced that the city streets around me were dangerous." She looked away from the bright lights and back out over the now dim faces of the crowd. "Like so many of us who live here, the city felt like the entire world. I gave no thought to anything outside of it. I didn't even think about much outside my own little corner of the city." The truth of the next line washed over her with a heavy dose of guilt. "And I, of all people, shouldn't have forgotten that there are many more horrors in the world.

"Ten years ago, my town was attacked in the dark of night." Letting the darkness of the auditorium remind her of that horrible night, she continued. "My parents hid my sisters and me in the cellar, where we watched through the cracks as our whole world burned to the ground."

She talked briefly about meeting Atticus and traveling east. When she reached the burned ruins of Ebenmoor, the audience hung on her words. She paced slowly toward Vivaine's balcony, and when she turned slightly, she caught a glimpse of Reese still standing in the shadows at the side of the stage, his hate-filled gaze fixed on the ambassador.

It had been weeks since she'd thought about what Reese had lost that night. What Purnicious had lost. The senselessness of it filled her words as she told of finding the warrior in the forest, of his claims of destruction.

The more she mentioned the Kalesh, the more murmurs rippled through the audience. She let her eyes adjust, seeing the people she spoke to, looking at their faces. She met Merilee's gaze. The woman had stopped glaring, and her face had taken on a bit of the terror from the Nidel Woods.

Sable could see it in the faces in the crowd. They believed her.

Sable was aware of the prioresses' and ambassador's gazes, but she didn't look toward them. "Stepping back into this city," she said, finally, "I can't help but notice how much Kalesh influence has entered Immusmala and the cities to the north."

She paused, working up the courage to finish the speech.

Turning resolutely, she faced the High Prioress and the Kalesh Ambassador. "Some Kalesh have threatened a great destruction to our people. Ambassador Tehl, if you are a friend of Immusmala, we beg you to investigate the murders on the Eastern Reaches and explain to us how your Empire can commit such atrocities against innocent people."

The auditorium was silent. Sable felt every gaze turn toward the balcony where the ambassador sat.

The High Prioress set a hand on the ambassador's arm and began to rise. But the ambassador said something quietly, and she sat back down.

The ambassador rose and stepped to the front of the balcony, facing Sable. She forced herself to look up at him, trying to keep her expression neutral, relying on only her words to force him to talk. He looked at her for a long moment before turning to face the audience.

"I applaud the courage it took for Issable to share this with us," he said in a loud, unruffled voice.

Out of the corner of her eye, Sable saw Reese straighten, but she kept her focus on the ambassador.

He turned back to face her. "The horrors you experienced in your travels, and in your own town, are truly tragic. The good people of the Eastern Reaches deserve as much safety and peace as the rest of us."

She felt nothing in those words.

His face took on a fatherly sort of sympathy. "But I'm afraid whoever blamed them on the Kalesh was lying to you. The Empire has no plans to invade any of these lands."

The lie was so sharp she flinched.

The ambassador turned back toward the crowd. "We bring nothing but peace and the hope of mutual prosperity."

The lies cut into her chest.

Turning back toward the stage, Ambassador Tehl stretched out his hand. "I vow, dear child,"—His voice held the soothing tone of a grandfather to a hysterical girl—"to look into these crimes and bring whoever is responsible to justice."

There was a muttering of approval in the crowd, and Sable felt the fury inside her start to rise.

He smiled gently down at her. "We cannot allow some cowardly band of men to harm the good folk of the Reaches or sully the good name of the Kalesh Emp—"

A flicker of motion flashed from Reese's shadow.

The ambassador's body jerked backwards. His face twisted in shock and pain.

Reese shrank back into the darkness.

Ambassador Tehl toppled back into his chair, a knife sunk to its hilt in his chest.

The High Prioress screamed, and chaos exploded.

CHAPTER SIXTY-FIVE

THE AMBASSADOR'S body lay lifeless on his seat. The High Prioress's scream was joined by Eugessa's and shouts of horror from the crowd.

Sable turned to stare at Reese, standing in the shadows just off stage. He met her gaze, his face bleak.

"Get her!" the High Prioress shrieked.

Sable yanked her attention back to the balcony.

Vivaine pointed at Sable, her face twisted into a furious mask. "Stop her! She killed the ambassador!"

A hand grabbed Sable's arm, but she yanked away.

"Come," Atticus hissed. "Now."

This time when he grabbed her arm and pulled, she stumbled after him.

"It was Reese," she whispered, clutching Atticus's arm as he pulled her toward the back of the stage. "It was Reese."

"Shhh!" Atticus face was pale.

"Stop her!" cried Vivaine.

Sable glanced over her shoulder. Sanctus guards and Mira shoved their way through the panicked crowd toward the stage.

Atticus pulled Sable to the room they'd prepared in backstage.

Ryah, once again dressed in her own clothes, clung to Thulan's arm, her face terrified. Leonis's and Thulan's expressions were grave.

"Sable," Thulan said, pulling her arm out of Ryah's grasp, "you need to get out of here. Now."

Sable stared at the dwarf. "Me? It was Reese. Did you see him?"

Leonis hissed for her to be quiet and hurried to the door, looking down the hallway. "Get her out of here, Thulan."

"Sable!" Ryah said, stepping forward. "What happened? Is the ambassador dead?"

"I think—" Sable's words were cut short as Thulan shoved Ryah's abbess costume into her hands.

"Come!" Thulan grabbed Sable's hand and pulled her toward the door. Ryah started to follow, but the dwarf shot her a hard look. "Stay with Atticus, Ryah."

"Take her out the back," Atticus said to Thulan. "We'll leave by the side door. Meet at the pub with the nets."

The dwarf nodded and propelled Sable out the door and toward the back of the Grand Stadia.

Footsteps pounded down the hallway from the direction of the stage, and Thulan broke into a run.

"Where are we going?" Sable raced along beside her, ducking around turns. "Why is Vivaine blaming me? It was Ree—"

Thulan hissed for her to be quiet. "Unless you want him to hang, shut your mouth." She slowed to a stop and pushed the door to the alley open a crack, peering out. "When you get around the corner, change into the dress and the veil. Maybe you'll look enough like an abbess to pass for one in the dark. Go. Get to the plaza and blend in with the crowd."

Sable gabbed Thulan's arm, her heart pounding. "What about you? And Ryah?"

"Atticus will make sure she's safe. The rest of us will split up."

Sable stepped out into the warm closeness of the dark alley. The tall city wall loomed up in front of her, shouts echoing off it, muffled and chaotic. The wagons partially blocked one end of the alley, but Thulan pointed the other way, toward the Priory of the Phoenix.

"There's a tavern on the north side of the city near a huge fountain. The outside is decorated with fishing nets. Meet us there. Go!"

Thulan gave her a small push, and Sable started running. Over her shoulder, she saw the dwarf run in the other direction, disappearing past the wagons. Sable clutched the abbess costume to her chest.

She reached the corner of the huge theater and peered around into another long alley between the Grand Stadia and the fenced edge of the Priory of the Phoenix. Half way down the theater, a crowd of people spilled out a small door and hurried toward the plaza.

Behind her, men shouted, and she caught a glimpse of something moving just past the wagons. Icy fear for Thulan stabbed into her as she ducked around the corner.

The end of the alley where Sable stood was in deep shadows. She yanked off the clothes she'd worn for the final act of the play and pulled on the abbess's dress. Cries and shouting came from both behind the theater and out near the plaza, but none came close. She tucked the little comb on the veil into her hair, then tossed her other costume over the fence into the bushes of the Phoenix Priory. Taking a bracing breath, she hurried toward the plaza. No one took any notice of another veiled abbess as she melted in with the frantic people pushing their way away from the theater. In the darkness, her veil should act like a mask, hiding her face, but she still kept her head down.

Agitated bits of conversation bombarded her.

"—killed him!"

"—tried to assassinate the High Prioress—"

"Did the troupe plan it?" a man beside her asked.

"They must have!" the woman next to him said in shock. "And after the prioresses honored them!"

Sable stumbled along with them, feeling numb.

Reese had killed the ambassador.

The thought chased everything else from her mind.

Yes, he'd been angry, but killing the ambassador?

A new thought pierced through the numbness. It was the ambassador he'd meant to hit, right? Not the High Prioress?

She shook off the thought. Of course it was the ambassador.

Beyond the fact that it was never the prioress he'd wanted to kill, Reese had proven he could hit his target with a knife.

Sable spilled into the plaza with the rest of the crowd surging away from the theater. She reached a tree set on a small mound of earth, and climbed up next to the trunk, searching the crowd for any sign of the troupe.

A knot of Sanctus guards and Vena Sanctus with their glowing halberds, left the Stadia. The guards pushed through the crowd, escorting the Grand Prioresses to safety. The Phoenix Prioress passed not far from Sable's tree, looking pale and shaken. Vivaine was escorted to the Dragon Priory. Eugessa's copper hair could just be seen inside her ring of guards as they ushered her all the way into the Priory of the Horn.

There was a small *pop*, and Purnicious appeared beside her. "Mistress! Are you hurt?"

"Purn!" Sable knelt down and gave her a hug. "I'm fine. Where's Ryah? Is she safe?"

Purnicious closed her eyes, then pointed to the far side of the Grand Stadia. Sanctus guards surrounded Atticus's two wagons as they moved slowly through the crowd. "In there."

Sable gripped the kobold's shoulder. "They arrested her? And the others?"

"Let me get a better look." Purnicious popped out of view, and Sable was left holding nothing but air. She craned her neck over the crowd to see the wagons. Each was driven by a Sanctus guard, and there was no sign of any of the troupe.

Purnicious popped back into view and grabbed Sable's leg. "The whole troupe is inside the wagons. They're not bound, but there are lots of guards. And two Mira." She looked up with wide eyes. "One of them looked right at me!"

"Were you visible?" Sable asked.

She shook her head so fast her curls swung wildly. "She saw me anyway."

"Is Ryah all right?"

"No one is hurt." She glanced up at Sable. "But Ryah looks scared."

Sable swallowed down the rising panic. "Do you know where Talia is?"

Purnicious closed her eyes again. "Walking out of the plaza." The kobold disappeared for a moment, then came back. "With Lady Ingred. She looks shaken, but unhurt."

"Have you seen Reese?"

Purn shook her head. "Was he the one who…"

Sable nodded. "He said it's what needed to happen. I didn't think he'd really do it, though."

She scanned the plaza again. There was no point in going to the tavern Thulan had told her about. The troupe, along with all the money, was trapped in the wagons, moving slowly through the crowd.

Sable had nothing.

No money. No friends. No butterfly ring. All she had was one small kobold and a useless ability to play the High Prioress on stage.

She straightened.

The money was likely lost, but maybe there was a way to get the butterfly ring, and free the troupe.

The riskiness of the plan made her pause. Getting the ring would be dangerous enough, and if she could convince the guards the troupe wasn't guilty, she'd likely be headed for the noose herself.

She pushed down the nerves that rose.

No more cowering.

"Can you make me look like a real abbess?" she asked Purn.

Purn raised her eyebrows. "So you'll blend in? Very smart, mistress." She looked at the dress critically. "The shape is wrong. I can try to fix it, though." She knelt, running her hands along the edges of the dress, making it more robe-like.

Sable looked at the Priory of the Horn, and gripped her hands together to keep them from shaking.

Purnicious looked up at Sable's veil. "I can't make that as long as an abbess's veil, not quickly anyway, but…" She motioned Sable to lean down, then ran her hand along the edges, leaving them jagged. "That makes it look torn. People will think it ripped in the chaos."

Sable stood back, smoothing the dress with damp hands. "How do I look?"

"Like an abbess." Purnicious smiled, but her nose wrinkled. "Unless someone looks closely."

"Thank you." Sable knelt next to her. "Please keep your eye on both Talia and Ryah."

Purnicious frowned at her. "Where are you going?"

"Into the Priory of the Horn."

Her eyes widened. "You don't look that much like an abbess!"

"I will never have a chance like this again, Purn. And that ring is the thing that will free Talia."

Purnicious shook her head frantically, but Sable continued.

"I'll be fine. I'm an actress, remember?" She gave her as confident a smile as she could muster. "I need you to watch out for Ryah and Talia. Help them if they need it."

"I can't sense you when you're in those buildings!" Purnicious's eyes were wide with fear.

"I should be out before dawn," Sable assured her. "Just keep your eye on my sisters. And…" She glanced back toward the Stadia. "See if you can find Andreese. He has a lot of explaining to do."

"Don't go in the priory," Purnicious pleaded. "You'll be caught."

"Maybe," Sable said, "but I have to try, Purn."

"But even if you find the ring and get Talia free, Ryah isn't."

"True…unless someone confesses to the assassination and convinces everyone the troupe wasn't involved."

"But they'll hang Andreese for it! And what if I can't find him?"

"I know." Sable patted the kobold's shoulder. "Someone needs to confess to it."

Her eyes widened further. "You can't, mistress! They'll hang you!"

Sable forced herself to nod. "Better me than Ryah."

Purnicious shook her head wildly, but Sable squeezed her shoulder, hoping the kobold couldn't feel her hand trembling. "Keep an eye on my sisters. I'll call for you when I'm back out."

Before Purnicious could convince her otherwise, Sable started toward the Priory of the Horn.

CHAPTER SIXTY-SIX

THERE WAS enough chaos in the plaza that when Sable fell in behind a clump of abbesses, no one paid her much attention. Eugessa's Vena Sanctus strode back out of the priory, starting across the plaza toward Atticus's wagons. Sable crowded close to the abbesses when they neared the Priory of the Horn, and the guards waved them in quickly.

Sable stepped through the door, her hands trembling. The large entry hall was lit with torches along every wall, casting flickering shadows and an orange glow over everything. The abbesses huddled together, talking in shocked whispers. The Kalesh, their own colored robes muted behind Sable's veil, strode through the room with furious faces. The braver of the abbesses offered quiet sympathy and apologies, but the Kalesh brushed past them.

Sable walked through the entry hall and toward Eugessa's chambers, her mind racing for a reason to enter them. A slim, veiled abbess stepped out of a room carrying a pile of towels, and Sable almost crashed into her. Apologizing, she ducked through the open door.

Shelves of linens lined the walls. Sable walked to the back wall and found a shadowed nook at the end of the shelves big enough for Sable to hide in. A plan began to take shape, and she grabbed a small pile of the thickest towels she could find. They were softer and more plush than anything Sable had ever felt.

She put on the air of a busy abbess and stepped back out of the linen room, turning down the hall toward Eugessa's chambers. The prioress would still be wearing her jewelry, but if Sable could just get in and get a view of the room, she could hide in the linen room until late tonight and find the ring then.

The Grand Prioress's rooms were abuzz with activity. Abbesses hurried in and out, and no one batted an eye when Sable stepped in. She gripped her hands together under the towels to keep them from shaking. Eugessa's voice came from a room off to the right, complaining about something being too cold. Sable walked closer, until she could see Eugessa standing next to an enormous tub in the center of an expansive washroom.

"It might as well be frozen," Eugessa snapped at a woman next to her. "Get more hot water now. I have blood on my hand!" She raised her arm, her fingers outstretched as though covered with something repulsive. "Blood!"

The abbesses scurried out of the way for another woman carrying a large, steaming pot. She was followed by two more. Sable stepped to the side, trying to stay out of the way.

"—appalling display of barbarism," Eugessa continued. She unclasped a necklace and dropped it into a tray sitting on a long table next to the tub. Focusing her attention on an older woman standing attentively at her side, she continued in a furious voice. "I've never been so humiliated to be part of this city. An assassination! Right in the Sanctuary! What sort of monster kills a good man like that? And the Kalesh…" She blew out an irate breath. "We'll need to do something before the Kalesh leave completely!"

The woman nodded as Eugessa pulled off her other necklaces, then started on her rings.

Sable stared at the prioress's fingers. Her breath came quickly, fluttering the edge of her veil.

"Don't stare," an abbess next to Sable hissed in her ear. "Get those towels to the table."

Sable yanked her gaze from the Grand Prioress and forced herself to walk to the far side of the tub. Towels, cloths, soaps, and oils filled this end of the table, with the tray of jewelry on the other end. She set the towels on the edge, then spent a moment shifting things around, hoping it looked like she was making room for the stack. Out of the corner of her eye, she saw Eugessa pull off her last ring and drop it into the dish before dipping her fingers into the tub again.

"Finally," the prioress said, holding out her hand with an irritated motion. An abbess offered her a towel, which Eugessa used on her fingers, then dropped onto the floor. She snapped her fingers at the nearest abbess, who hurried over to help her out of her white gown.

Sable kept her head down, sliding the bath salts over to make room for the towels, lingering until Eugessa stepped into the tub, turning her back to the dish of jewelry.

Giving the stack of towels one last nudge, Sable stepped over to the towel Eugessa had dropped, and picked it up off the floor.

She was only steps from the jewelry. The older abbess and Eugessa discussed plans for a brunch with the Kalesh in the morning, while the other abbesses gathered things and began to leave the room, or at least back away to the walls.

Sable caught a glimpse of the cloudy blue stones in the butterfly ring. Holding her breath, she stepped to the table, set the dirty towel partially over the dish, then squatted down to the floor, as though cleaning something up. When she stood, she looped her finger through the ring, and picked up the towel.

Her heart pounded so loudly, she felt sure everyone must be able to hear it, She wrapped the towel around her hand, clenching it and feeling the ring press into her finger.

She started toward the door when Eugessa's voice cut through the room.

"You there. What are you doing?"

Sable froze, the two women near the door looking straight at her. Slowly, she turned. Eugessa reclined in the tub, only her head above the steaming water, staring directly at Sable.

Sable opened her mouth to talk, praying that between the steam and the veil her face wasn't recognizable.

"Just cleaning up some water." She tried to infuse the words with some sort of richness, but they came out thin and untrue. She gripped the towel tighter.

"How dare you?" Eugessa's voice was full of disgust. Her face curled into a contemptuous sneer.

Every muscle in Sable's body was tensed to run. She glanced at the windows, but they had wrought-iron vines fixed across them. There was only one door out of the room, and two abbesses stood near it, but if she ran...

She took a small step backwards toward the door, gripping the ring in her fist.

"You"—Eugessa pointed at her with a bare hand—"look like you rolled in the dirt. And your veil is torn! Get out of my room until you are presentable."

Sable's mouth dropped open, and for a moment, she just stared.

"Get out!" Eugessa commanded. She turned back to the older abbess. "Tilly, how could you let someone so horrible in where I'm bathing?"

Sable spun and rushed out of the room, almost knocking over a heavyset abbess in the way. Ignoring the woman's protests, Sable ran into the hallway, turning a corner as quickly as she could. Several people looked at her curiously and she forced herself to slow to a walk.

She pulled her hand out from the towel enough to see the butterfly ring, before stuffing it back in the towel.

She turned down another hall, heading back toward the front entrance, straining for any sound of alarm coming from the prioress's room, but she heard nothing. Ahead of her, the hallway opened into the torchlit entry hall, and she slowed even more. Her breath came in quick gasps, fluttering her veil. She forced her breathing to slow. She walked out into the entry hall, trying to look purposeful. There were still abbesses milling around. She didn't see any Kalesh.

She turned toward the front and jerked to a stop. At the open door stood six Sanctus guards.

"—still missing," one was saying. "The High Prioress wants the priories locked down. She may be a danger to the Grand Prioresses."

One of the guards started to push the huge door closed, while another studied Sable. She forced herself to give him a polite nod, then continued straight across the hall into another passageway, her mind racing.

She needed to loop back to the linen room and hide. If she pulled a few things in front of her, she could wait until morning, then find a way out.

She kicked herself for not coming to the priory sooner. She'd had something resembling an abbess gown for weeks now, and if she'd slipped into the priory yesterday, maybe no one would have recognized her face. Today, if she was forced to lift her veil, it was over.

The hall ended at another that ran along the side of the priory. Windows opened up into the darkness of the manicured garden between the Priory of the Horn and the Priory of the Dragon. Sable ran to the closest, finding the same wrought-iron vines protecting the outside of it. She'd never fit through those small gaps.

She almost turned back toward the linen room, when a door near the front corner of the priory, leading outside, caught her eye. Voices came from somewhere off to the left, and she hurried toward the door. She dropped the towel behind a large potted plant. The voices grew louder. Male voices, which meant either Kalesh or Sanctus guards.

Sable slipped outside, letting the door close quietly behind her.

A few torches made islands of light along the manicured walkways between the Priory of the Horn and the Dragon Priory. The high wall that enclosed the entire Sanctuary loomed up on the far side of the garden. Next to Sable, a tall hedge curved away, connecting to the front corner of the Dragon Priory.

Through that hedge was her escape. On the other side of it lay the Sanctuary plaza. If she could rejoin the crowd without being noticed, maybe she could make her way out of the Sanctuary and deliver the ring to Kiva.

She followed the hedge, until she found a gap and squeezed through, only to come up against a stone wall. It was short enough that she could just reach the top. She scrambled up and peered over.

The plaza was flooded with torchlight.

Sanctus guards and city constables stood lined up, cordoning off the area close to the three priories. The crowd had all been pushed back. More guards stood on the steps of the rostrums, and others circulated through the crowd.

Between Sable and the line of guards was a wide, empty stretch of flagstones. If she climbed over this wall, a hundred eyes would see her.

She dropped back down behind the hedge and dropped her head against the wall.

There was nowhere to go, but she couldn't stay here. It must be long past midnight. In a few hours, the sun would rise and this garden would be flooded with light. She looked into the darkness between the hedge and the wall. Maybe she could hide here and wait for…

What? The guards thought the prioresses were in danger. They weren't just going to give up protecting them because the sun rose. And tonight was the last night of the festival. Which meant tomorrow at midday, the plaza would be cleared and the Veil Gate closed to the public again.

She sank back against the wall. Across the garden was the taller Sanctuary wall. It was easily six times taller than Sable, with a smooth enough surface that she'd be hard-pressed to climb it. Even if she could, the only thing on the other side were cliffs overlooking the sea. There might be a thin path on the other side of the wall, but the thought of a misstep on her way down made her shudder.

She saw a torch appear along the base of the Sanctuary wall, moving slowly. Of course they'd be patrolling out here. It was only a matter of time until they came close enough to see her.

Sable slipped out of the hedge. Back into the priory was the only option. She needed to find a good hiding place, and soon.

The ring glinted on her hand. It wouldn't matter that she was wearing a veil if someone recognized Eugessa's ring on her finger. She bent down and tucked it into the top of her sock. Stepping out onto the curved path along the hedge, she heard men's voices from the direction of the Priory of the Horn. She caught a glimmer of torchlight through the branches.

Turning, she ran toward the Priory of the Dragon. The side door they'd exited from this morning, which felt more like weeks ago, sat at the end of the path, and she hurried inside, pulling it shut behind her.

Sable stood at the end of the long hall that ran across the front of the priory. The torchlight of the plaza shone through the stained-glass windows with stunningly bright colors, the light jarring after the dark garden. She could see Sanctus guards down the hall near the main entrance, and Sable slipped into a corridor running toward the back of the building. Every window she came across was covered with more wrought-iron vines.

Maybe if she could get all the way over to the Priory of the Phoenix, she could find an escape. It was closer to the Grand Stadia, but they might not expect her to head back that direction. And Prioress Narine seemed less likely to fill her priory with guards than either of the other two.

The first two halls heading in the right direction were dead ends. The next was long and, thankfully, empty. She turned down it. It was slightly brighter than the others, but hopefully her veil and dress would hide her if she ran into anyone.

She was halfway down the hall before she realized where she was.

The open door to her right was the High Prioress's chapel.

The doors to Vivaine's office were just ahead, cracked open. Her eyes widened and she stuttered to a stop. This would be a very bad place to be caught.

The thought had barely crossed her mind when male voices and footsteps echoed in the hallway.

Sable ducked inside the chapel.

The voices rang through the hall over the sound of enough footsteps that there must be a dozen men coming.

Sable slid around the open chapel door, tucking herself into the shadows between it and the wall. She pressed back until the stone carving on the wall dug into her back. The footsteps paused near the chapel, then continued.

She waited for them to fade before leaning around the door to look into the room. The huge stained-glass window was dark and the room shadowed, except for the bit of torchlight spilling in from the hall.

She flipped her veil away from her face, but it was so dark, she could barely make out the benches filling the center of the room. The disquieting sense that something was off about this room still niggled at the back of her neck. Something out of place she couldn't quite put her finger on.

Whatever it was, at least the chapel was empty. Sable looked along the walls for any other doors, any means of escape. What she needed was a way out that wasn't being guarded. Once outside again, she'd tackle the problem of how to get away from the priories, then how to get out of the Sanctuary so she could deliver this stupid ring to Kiva.

The dark, stained-glass window felt almost brooding.

Sable straightened.

A window with no bars.

To get out, she'd have to break one of the beautiful, larger panes. The idea made her cringe, but maybe she could at least see through it and find out what was on the other side. She started forward, only reaching the closest column on the wall before she realized what was off about the room.

She was deep inside the priory. Why would there be a window here?

But it had glowed with sunlight earlier.

Was there a hidden courtyard beyond it?

Maybe some hidden escape?

She stepped forward.

"Mistress?" a little voice whispered.

Sable spun around. A tousled mass of black curls hurried toward her from the hall.

"Purnicious!" Sable knelt and pulled the kobold into a hug, feeling the little creature trembling against her. "How did you get in here? I thought... Wait. First what's on the other side of that window?"

Purnicious cowered lower, her eyes wide with fear and her mouth pinched into a thin, frightened line.

"Nothing," a sharp voice cut in.

Sable snapped her attention to the doorway.

"But I imagine that might make you like it more." The High Prioress Vivaine stood there, her face furious. "That window is a fake, a ruse." Her gaze cut into Sable. "Everything about it is a lie."

Sable drew back from the woman, pulling Purnicious with her, until her back pressed against the rough surface of the column.

Vivaine stood straight, her hands curled into fists, her body quivering with rage. The prioress's white robe caught the ruddy light from the torches in the hall until it glowed like coal.

Purnicious crowded against Sable.

Vivaine slowly stepped into the room.

"You have doomed us." The prioress's words were laced with hatred, and the weight of the truth in them pressed Sable back against the stone. "You have doomed us all."

CHAPTER SIXTY-SEVEN

SABLE FROZE at the ferocity of Vivaine's words.

The High Prioress's face was twisted in fury.

Purnicious clung to Sable's leg, her body shaking. "I'm sorry, mistress," she whispered. "I'm sorry!"

She set her hand on Purn's curly hair and pushed the little kobold behind her. "I didn't do anything. We had to tell you the Kalesh were coming. They're killing whole towns in the east, they've gained control of the merchants, and even here—"

"I know everything the Kalesh are doing," Vivaine's voice cracked through the room. She stepped farther into the chapel. At the edges of the dim torchlight, her gown darkened to a seething red. "Ebenmoor was the fourth town—by far the largest—and they've destroyed two homesteads along the western front of the Nidel Woods. Their troops walk freely in the north. They have swarmed our city for over a year, and they crawl through the hills looking for gold." The truth in her voice filled the room like a dense fog. "They are everywhere and taking over everything I have ever loved."

Sable stared at her. "You knew?"

"Did you really think a stupid, desperate little thing like you would know more than me? You? A thief? From Dockside?"

559

Sable flinched.

"Yes, I know who you are, Sable. I know everything about you. I know who your sisters are, where they are, who Talia really works for." She stepped closer, and her voice dropped to a low growl. "And I know what you have hidden in your sock."

Cold fear wrapped around Sable. She stared at Vivaine's face, searching for the benevolent, serene woman who blessed the crowds, but there was no sign of her. This woman's eyes were dark chips of grey ice, holding only fury and disgust.

Sable could hear no noises from the hall. The High Prioress was tall, but terribly thin. She'd be no obstacle. Sable could push past the old woman and run for an exit—

"Eugessa stole that ring like the mewling coward she is." Vivaine stalked forward again until she stood along the back of the nearest bench. "I would like to take every bit of ill-gotten treasure in her priory and bury her with it. But you..." Her voice curled harshly around the word. "You don't deserve to have any of it. You are too small, too insignificant of a player in this game to have such an important piece."

Sable tried to wrap her mind around what she was hearing. The ring pressed against her ankle, but she ignored it, asking the bigger question. "If you knew what the Kalesh were doing, why were you so close with the ambassador?"

"Ambassador Tehl? The man you murdered?"

"I didn't—"

Something shifted in the hall. A glitter of light flashed into the chapel before the head of the silver dragon eased into the room. Sable sucked in a breath. The dragon fixed her with an emotionless gaze from grey, slitted eyes. The reddish torchlight from the hall skittered across his scales.

Purnicious buried her face in the back of Sable's robe. Sable spared the kobold a glance. "Get out of here," she whispered. Purn gripped her tightly and didn't move.

The dragon moved forward until its head was next to Vivaine's hip. She set her hand on the ridge above his eyes, trailing her fingertips along his scales.

"You didn't throw the knife," Vivaine said quietly. "But I know who did. And I know he did it for you."

The words pulled Sable's eyes from the dragon back to Vivaine's face. "He did not!"

The words were out before she realized they were a mistake.

A grim smile twisted up the edge of Vivaine's mouth. "So you know he did it."

Sable shook her head, the glittering scales of the dragon drawing her gaze again. With every tiny movement, shattered splinters of light danced along the length of his body and flickered over his wings.

"I didn't want that to happen," Sable whispered. "All I wanted was to tell everyone the truth. To tell someone who could stand up to the Kalesh and stop them."

"Because you know so much better than us." The prioress's voice was hard with disdain.

"We thought you didn't know!" Sable pushed away from the column. The dragon let out a low hiss, and she stopped, but weeks of worry and anger seeped together and lit, flaring into something too powerful to hold back. "Why would I think you had any idea what was happening when you were cozying up to the ambassador like a giddy schoolgirl?"

Vivaine's eyes flashed. "Because he was the only way to save this city. The only thing that would keep the Kalesh army from marching across Immusmala was the treaty we were going to sign on the next new moon. At our wedding."

Sable blinked at her, speechless for a moment. "You can't marry. You're a prioress. Even if you were in love with the man, marrying him is impossible. You'd lose your position in the priories."

"I am not a prioress." The words cut through the room, low and dangerous. "I am the High Prioress of the Dragon Priory. I have run this city for forty-three years. I know every corner of it. I know all your petty gang bosses, all the conniving merchants who think they're in control. I know every Kalesh who's set foot in this city. I control the people. I am the one who keeps them safe from greed, crime, and foreign enemies." She drew herself up. "If I decide to wed, the city will accept that decision with open arms and celebrations. Because they trust me. But you…" Her hands curled back into fists. "You destroyed everything. The man who could save us from the Kalesh is dead, with your knife in his chest."

"Serene was right," Sable threw at her. "You were in love with the ambassador."

Vivaine's mouth tightened in condescension. "You are intimately acquainted with the story of the only man I ever loved."

Sable paused. "Balin?"

Vivaine's face did not soften. "I was young and foolish."

The dozens of times in the play Balin had lain dead at her feet, the sword protruding out of his black robe, suddenly felt horribly, searingly intimate. Right here in front of her was the woman who had finally stopped the baledin. Her sword hadn't folded harmlessly into an actor's robe. It had driven deep into the flesh of a living man.

"You really killed him." Sable's words came out somewhere between shock and admiration.

"Had I known then…" Vivaine shook her head. "I cut Balin off from all his chances to do more good. He could have helped many at the price of so few."

Sable stared at her for a moment. "What?"

"I should have let him live. Helped him. So much good could have been done by a man of his power, and together, we could have minimized the expense."

Purnicious gripped Sable's leg tightly. "You are a bad woman," she said. "Bad."

Sable tried to grasp what Vivaine was saying. "You'd have let him continue killing people?"

"The sword you so beautifully showed us in the play would have helped. But even if it hadn't, I should have let him live. When I was young, I was foolish enough to believe that good things come at no price. But it is impossible to have powerful good without some pain preceding it. The best we can do is limit the harm we do, while doing the most good we can." Vivaine nodded slowly. "It is possible that had I married the ambassador, the priories would be changed, even weakened. But the city would be saved, so breaking my vows would be a small price to pay."

Vivaine turned to face the dark window, her fury tinged with resignation. "But none of that matters now. You killed him, and we cannot stand against what the Kalesh will send our way."

Sable took a step forward, her fists clenched. "I didn't kill him."

A growl vibrated the dragon's chest, and Sable felt it in the stone under her feet. Purnicious squeaked in fear.

"Not with your own hand." The prioress turned and gestured through the open door. "Look."

Sable leaned forward to see into the dimly lit hallway, unwilling to step any closer to the dragon. For a moment, she saw nothing, then the hallway shifted, as though she'd stepped into it. The view turned to show the length of it, running toward the center of the priory.

Sable grabbed the back of the nearest bench, but the room wasn't moving. Just the view out the door. She gripped the wood. "What are you doing?"

"Showing you what you need to see."

The picture of the hallway moved faster, as though they were racing down it. The view turned to the left, doors and stonework flying past. The hall ended at a door guarded by two Sanctus guards. The picture slid through a thin crack under the door and down some dimly lit stairs.

Sable pressed back against the bench, almost unable to look away. "What am I seeing?"

Vivaine didn't answer.

"You have magic," Sable breathed. "What are you doing?"

"Directing the light." Vivaine's voice was cold, her face drawn in concentration. "This distance is not easy. Watch."

The view curled down the stairs and out into a low tunnel.

In a moment of clarity, the inexplicable brightness that always surrounded the High Prioress made sense. "You bring the light around yourself, don't you?" Sable turned to look at her, the feeling of betrayal surprisingly strong. "Everyone thinks it's Amah's blessing, but it's just you."

Vivaine gave her the briefest withering glance before returning her focus to the hall.

The view slowed as it approached a door. Sable's breath felt heavy, as though she were approaching something terrifying. She leaned back farther, away from the barred window cut into what was obviously a cell door.

They slid through, and Sable's breath caught.

In the corner of a small, shadowed cell lay Reese.

"Oh no," Purn whispered.

His face was bloodied, his clothes torn. His hands and feet were bound by rough ropes, and he leaned limply into the corner, his eyes closed. The fingers of his hands sat at awkward angles. At least three of them clearly broken.

The view drew closer, and she could see his chest rising in shallow breaths.

"Reese?" she said.

The image of him didn't move.

The blood on the side of his face was dried and dark, just like it had been at Ebenmoor. "Is that real?" she gasped.

Vivaine nodded.

"How?"

"He gave himself up. Confessed to everything."

Sable stepped forward, reaching her hand out toward him.

"He's not within your reach." Vivaine's voice was tinged with regret.

Another question shouldered its way into Sable's mind. She pulled her eyes away from Reese to focus on the High Prioress. "Why do you have a dungeon?"

"For assassins and traitors. That man murdered the ambassador in cold blood."

Sable's anger resurfaced. "Oh, I think there was enough blood on the ambassador's hands that some of it was still warm."

Vivaine dropped a chilling look to Sable's face. "It wasn't Tehl's blood I was referring to."

"It's the only blood that matters here."

Vivaine turned away and studied Reese's still form. "Andreese of Ravenwick. It appeared he had a promising career in the north at one point, before throwing it all away because of his prejudice against the Kalesh."

"If by 'throwing it all away' you mean trying to save us all, I agree."

"Andreese claimed he worked alone and only used the troupe to get close to the ambassador."

"If he confessed, why does he look like he's been tortured?"

"We had to be sure he was telling the truth." Vivaine glanced at Sable. "He didn't just use the troupe, though, did he? There's a bit more to his relationship with you than that."

Sable ignored the question and kept her eyes fixed on Reese. "What are you going to do to him?"

"His sentence has already been announced. He'll hang at dawn."

The words slammed into Sable even before she felt the weight of their truth. Purnicious let out a gasp.

Sable turned to Vivaine. "You can't! He thought he was saving the city, saving the north. He said we were already in a war and the quickest way to cripple the Kalesh was to cut off the head of the snake."

"I don't care what his reasoning was. He killed the man—the only man—who could have helped us. His knife doomed us all."

Sable crossed her arms. "I thought you blamed me for that."

"Oh, I do, dear. Your Andreese did it purely for you."

Sable gave her an incredulous look. "Then why did he do it while I was arguing with the ambassador? He'd know it would look like I was responsible. You called for my arrest immediately."

Vivaine gave her a withering look. "You had just set yourself up as the ambassador's enemy. Andreese knew if he waited until after the show, any act against the ambassador would be attributed to you. The only time he could throw the knife and be assured no one would actually be able to blame you was if he did it before you left the stage, while a thousand witnesses could prove you didn't throw it."

Sable looked back at Reese. *The moment of attack shapes everything.* He'd waited long enough to know the ambassador was going to try to sway the crowd, then struck before Sable was out of everyone's view.

Sable shook her head against the idea he'd been pushed to do it then because she'd chosen to speak out. "No."

"You can't be so stupid and blind that you don't see it. Not a woman with your skill."

Sable turned back to Reese. What she'd taken for shadow on his shirt glistened when he breathed, and she realized it was blood. Her hands clenched at her side. "What does my acting have to do with anything?"

"Oh, it's not your acting skills that make you valuable. Although I will say you performed a very flattering portrayal of me, for which I thank you. The people loved it."

Sable shot her a glare. "Had I known what you were really like, I would have portrayed you differently. As it is, I made you far too much like Ryah."

Vivaine cocked her head to the side. "Yes, Ryah is a sweet, idealistic sort of thing, isn't she?"

Sable flinched at the familiar way Vivaine said her sister's name. She took a step closer to the High Prioress, ignoring the dragon. "In a way you can't possibly understand."

Vivaine let out a short laugh. "That's more like it. I was worried you were too scared and mousy to be of use. I should have known the way to get your hackles up was through your sisters."

She looked down at the dragon, running her fingers along his head and down his neck. "I've had plans for Ryah ever since the choosing. Do you know Argyros almost picked her? Can you imagine? Him selecting Ryah over Lord of Wrenwith's daughter? What could some insignificant girl from the Bend offer the Dragon Priory?" Vivaine put her hand under the dragon's chin and lifted his head, looking at him curiously. "Yet for her to have something that almost convinced Argyros to pick her, against my will... That was impressive."

Vivaine scratched the dragon's chin, and he stretched his head up toward her. With a fond smile, she turned back to the hall and flicked her hand toward the image of Reese. The scene drew back out of his cell door and down the hall. It turned and slid through a different window, and Sable drew in a sharp breath.

Huddled on the floor in another cell were Atticus, Thulan, Leonis, and Ryah.

CHAPTER SIXTY-EIGHT

UNLIKE ANDREESE, none of the troupe looked injured. Leonis looked more wan than she'd ever seen him, and Atticus held his head in his hands. Thulan glared at the door, her arm wrapped around Ryah's shoulders, who sat curled into a ball, her knees pulled up to her chest.

Argyros focused on the image.

Purnicious let out a small whimper.

"They did nothing!" Sable stepped forward. "You know they did nothing!"

"I do," Vivaine agreed. "But the people demanded action, and I could hardly let the troupe walk free. Even if anyone believed they were innocent of the actual murder, they're quite guilty of inciting hatred toward the Kalesh."

"What are you going to do to them?" Sable demanded.

Vivaine's gaze settled on Atticus. "I haven't decided yet."

"You know they aren't responsible for the assassination."

"Do I?" The High Prioress cocked her head to the side. "If there is one thing Atticus knows, it's how to put on a show. The timing of that knife... I would wager Atticus coached your knife-throwing admirer as to when would be the proper moment."

"He did not. His entire goal has been to get us to the platform where we could share what we knew in order to head off violence."

Vivaine kept her eyes focused on the old man. "You really think Andreese could time something so perfectly? Your speech, the ambassador's answer, the knife... There's a dramatic feel to it that has Atticus's fingerprints all over it."

Sable opened her mouth to object. Except she'd seen Atticus's plays for years, and now she'd acted under his direction. The build-up of tension, the apparent failure, the sudden victory...

It was exactly Atticus's style.

"Atticus has always been useful to me." The prioress studied the old man with a rueful sort of frustration. Her words had so much truth they filled the room like warm honey, and the light around her face grew sharper. "If the young man had planned anything ahead of time, Atticus would have known. He can get a secret out of anyone."

In the cell, Ryah's shoulders rose with a quiver, and Thulan tightened her arm around the girl's shoulders, deepening her glare at the door.

"Is that why you pushed him away when you were seducing the ambassador?" Sable asked. "Because you knew he'd find out the truth of what you had planned?"

"There was no need to seduce anyone. The ambassador was half in love with me from the beginning. By the end, the only price he'd accept for our freedom was my hand. A price I would have gladly paid. But Atticus would have never sat by and held his tongue."

Vivaine watched the old man in the cell. Beyond a few deep sighs, he hadn't moved, his face still buried in his hands. Sable watched the prioress. Her initial fury had faded to a simmer, and Sable realized the woman was still assessing her position, still mulling over her next step.

"As angry as I am with him, he's still useful. The play was a stroke of genius. I should have had him perform it years ago."

She smoothed her hands down the front of her robe. "One thing you'll learn, if you ever gain the strength to take off the naïve glasses you see the world through, is that what we want is rarely the best thing."

She turned to Sable and fixed her with cold, hard eyes. "Do you know how many months it took me to finalize the treaty with such tiny concessions? Can you imagine it? The land safe, and the only person suffering is me?" She clenched her jaw. "For ruining that, I want to kill your assassin, kill your troupe, and most of all"—The truth coalesced around her, the features in her face brightening in sharp detail. Strands of silver in her hair caught the dim light—"kill you in a public, grand display that will begin our renegotiations with the Kalesh."

Sable took a half step back before stopping herself.

Argyros shifted forward, and Vivaine set her hand on the scales of his neck. "But Atticus has given me a harder choice."

The High Prioress's intense gaze locked on Sable. "I never really cared about Atticus." Vivaine bit off each word.

The thinness of the lie cut into Sable so deeply that she flinched.

Vivaine's eyes widened. "He was right. You can tell when someone lies."

A hollow fear cracked open in Sable's gut, her gaze twitched to the curls of the old man's head. He'd told Vivaine?

The betrayal snapped something deep inside her. Leonis and Thulan sat there beside him. And Ryah. Had he betrayed their trust, too?

"Don't blame him." Vivaine's voice was lighter, but she watched Sable with a deep, possessive sort of intensity. "It was Argyros who first told me there was something unusual about you. You stood out there in my hallway with your sister, and he was drawn to both of you." She paused. "Can Ryah sense the truth, as well?"

Sable shook her head. "She's just kind—truly kind. The way a prioress should be. Maybe Argyros thought it was time someone like her entered the priories."

Vivaine laughed. "I don't think that's the only thing unique about her, although I'd grant you that true kindness is rare. Regardless, when Atticus came back, as I knew he would, I pressed him for answers." She shrugged. "He's used to telling me secrets."

"The only secrets he doesn't seem able to learn are yours." Sable's words came out harsh.

She turned thoughtful eyes on Atticus. "He knew a younger, more innocent me. He just never believed I would change." Her face softened a moment. "And you, of all people, know I only tell the truth. Lies are too hard to keep track of. Telling the truth, selectively depending on your audience, is always a better path."

Sable glared at her. "I vouched for you."

"It's not my fault you didn't listen to what I said. I never claimed the Kalesh were faultless, just that we were working on a plan that would be mutually beneficial."

She considered Sable for a long moment. "It never bothered me that Atticus doesn't know me anymore." She didn't bother to hide the sharpness of the lie. "He's too idealistic to understand who I am now. But he has complicated things, because I would be foolish to kill someone with your talents."

"So you'll play the role of the gracious, merciful prioress," she said dryly, "and set us all free?"

Vivaine raised an eyebrow. "I am gracious and merciful as often as possible, but no, you can't go free." She tapped her fingers on Argyros's head. "To make up for what you've done, you'll work for me. I need your skill when I reopen negotiations with the Kalesh."

Sable crossed her arms. "I will never work for you."

"Of course you will, because the only way to mitigate their sentence,"—She gestured at the image of the cell—"is a pardon by the High Prioress."

Sable stared at the woman, wondering how she'd ever missed the calculating look in her eyes. "What do you want?"

"Prioress Narine is ill. She grows weaker, little by little."

The Prioress of the Phoenix hadn't seemed ill, but the truth of Vivaine's words killed any objection Sable could raise.

"She will soon need constant care. And you will provide it."

Sable waited for a reason that would make any sense of that command, but Vivaine merely waited.

"I'm not a healer," Sable finally said.

"Narine is beyond the healers' help." The High Prioress's voice was tinged with sorrow. "They will make her comfortable, but I'm afraid that is all that can be done."

"She looks healthy."

Vivaine's face took on a look of disdain. "Tell me. Is it your vast experience as an actress or a thief that makes you such an expert on health?"

Sable studied the prioress. "Why me?"

"Because as weak as Narine is, she'll need her aide at her side whenever she attends a meeting with the Kalesh. And I will make sure the dear prioress is in attendance at every one of them."

Sable shook her head slowly. "And you want me to tell you when the Kalesh are lying."

"I want you to tell me when anyone is lying."

"What makes you think I'll tell you the truth?"

"I would hope that your word, in exchange for your sister's and your friends' lives, would be enough. But it's not necessary. I will know."

"How?"

"Why don't you ask your little kobold?"

Purnicious was still huddled behind Sable's legs. Sable turned to her. "Purn?"

The kobold pulled her face away from Sable's robe and whispered, "Her Mira can read your mind, mistress. They read mine. They knew where you were as soon as I did." She let out a sniffle. "I'm so sorry, mistress! When I went to check on Ryah, they caught me! The Mira did something, and I couldn't blink! She brought me in here." Purnicious shuddered. "In this building, I can't do anything! I can't blink, can't turn invisible. The world refuses to move for me!" She pressed her face back into Sable's robe, little sobs shaking her shoulders.

"It's my fault, Purn," Sable said gently, setting her hand on the kobold's head. "I was the one foolish enough to come in here and send you somewhere dangerous."

"Nothing magical enters the priories without our knowledge," Vivaine said. "My Mira will be able to read your mind as easily as this little creature's. Whether you sense lies or truth, I'll know without you saying a word."

"If your Mira can read minds, what do you need me for?"

Vivaine studied Sable. "Her powers have limitations. They can only read one person at a time and she needs to be physically touching them to do so. The more duplicitous the person's thoughts, the harder they are to decipher. You, on the other hand, can read an entire group of people at once, can't you?"

Sable tried to funnel all her fury into the glare she gave the prioress.

"But more than that," Vivaine said softly, a glint of greed flashing in her eyes that reminded Sable of Kiva, "my Mira can't influence other people's thoughts."

Sable's stomach sank. Atticus had even told her that?

"I didn't believe it," the High Prioress continued, "until the play tonight." A faint hunger laced her eyes. "And not only during the play, but your speech at the end. You had everyone believing you. People who adored the Kalesh started doubting them—just from your words."

Sable's breath came faster. The chained feeling she'd always had with Kiva tightened around her again. Her eyes flickered to the troupe, still huddled in the cell. "If I help you, you'll free the others?"

"No, mistress!" Purnicious turned horrified purple eyes up at her. "You can't help this woman!"

"Tomorrow," Vivaine said, ignoring the kobold, "in a desperate attempt to prove your loyalty, you will publicly beg me to join the priory, to serve in whatever way I see fit. Atticus, Leonis, and Thulan will be released. It will be announced that they knew nothing of the assassination attempt. They've garnered quite a bit of fame, and I'd hate to have their reputation tarnished when they've done so much to help me."

"What about Ryah?"

Vivaine looked at the girl huddled on the floor. "I think I'd like to keep a closer eye on that girl, and she does seem well-suited to a priory."

Something between hope and dread flickered inside Sable.

"Eugessa is always looking for pretty young handmaidens. And as Ryah proved to us in the play, it's a role she fits well."

"Not Eugessa," Sable said flatly.

"Oh, dear girl," Vivaine said softly, "this is not your decision."

Sable clenched her hands into fists at her side. "And Andreese?"

"He has confessed to throwing the knife."

"Please." Sable tried to step forward, but Purnicious gripped her leg too tightly. "You can't hang him. He was only trying to save the land, like you."

Vivaine's expression remained unmoved, but she trailed her fingers through the air, the image in the hall shifting back to Andreese's cell. He'd sank lower, the dark stain on the front of his shirt more visible.

"Please," Sable said again, unable to look away from the hair matted on the side of his head. The blood had dripped into his beard, and her fingers reached toward him again. "I'll help you. I'll tell you every time anyone is lying to you. Or when they're telling the truth. Or whether they care about what they're saying. I will help you read every single person you interact with." She tore her eyes away from Reese and fixed them on the High Prioress. "But if you hang him, I will do everything in my power to thwart every single thing you ever try."

"At the expense of our land?"

Sable clenched her jaw, and the corner of Vivaine's mouth curled up in triumph.

"No. Even if I hang him, you won't throw away the whole world just to spite me. But I admit, it will be easier if I have your willing cooperation."

She considered Sable for a long moment. "If you want the gracious, merciful High Prioress to pardon Andreese, then at dawn tomorrow, in front of the gallows, you will pledge yourself to me."

A breath escaped Sable, at the thought, but she nodded.

"Then I will spare his life and merely banish him from the city."

Sable glared at the prioress, but nodded again.

"And from that moment, you will faithfully serve me to the very best of your ability. Because make no mistake. I will know where Andreese of Ravenwick is at all times. I will know where Atticus, Leonis, Thulan, and Ryah are. I will know where Talia is."

The truth pressed against Sable.

Vivaine stepped forward, and Argyros slid closer with a dry, rasping hiss over the stone floor until Sable could feel the dragon's warm breath on her hand.

Vivaine's voice dropped low, the press of the truth almost unbearably strong. "From this moment, you are mine."

CHAPTER SIXTY-NINE

VIVAINE FLICKED her fingers toward the hallway, and the image of the cell wavered. Sable lurched toward it, but Ryah disappeared from view and she was left staring into the empty hall outside the chapel.

The prioress looked at Sable calculatingly. "Before we stand in front of a crowd in the morning, let's see how good you are at keeping your word. Come."

As she started out of the chapel, Argyros fixed Sable with his emotionless gaze. She followed the prioress, Purnicious staying as close as possible. The dragon fell in behind them, his scales slithering across the floor.

Vivaine strode down the hallway. "It's time for a small test to see how fully you will support me."

"I already told you I would."

They turned down the long hall from Vivaine's image, and Sable saw the guarded door at the far end. She swallowed. They were going to the dungeon.

"You will remain at my side," Vivaine commanded quietly as they walked, "and help me as you promised. We have agreed what will happen to the others. You will support me unquestioningly in the upcoming conversation, or I will lock you in your own cell, hang

Andreese when the sun rises, and let the rest of the troupe rot in the dungeon for their part."

Sable clenched her jaw. "And when I help you, and you release the others, what happens to Purnicious?"

Vivaine glanced back at the kobold. "It would be cruel to keep her in the priories. Her magic doesn't work here. It would only cause her discomfort."

"Your care for her overwhelms me," Sable said dryly. "If she could find me, she has some power here."

"Her connection to her mistress is more instinctual than magical." Vivaine frowned down at Purnicious. "It's a shame. I have a million uses for a kobold, if she could work here." She turned forward again. "She's no danger to us, so she is free to leave with the troupe."

Purn grabbed Sable's hand. "Mistress, I can't leave you!"

"Go with Atticus." Sable squeezed the knobby blue fingers. "Ryah will be in a priory, too, so you won't be able to reach her, but Atticus will help you. You can keep your eye on Talia, maybe. Or Leonis is heading back to the Nidel Woods. You could go back home."

Purnicious's purple eyes filled with tears, and she clung to Sable's hand. The two guards straightened at the sight of the High Prioress.

"Please escort us to the prisoners," Vivaine said, her voice back to its gentle tone.

Sable shot her a scowl, but the High Prioress ignored her. The guards opened the door. One led the way down while the other waited, giving Argyros plenty of room before following.

They reached the narrow stone passage at the bottom of the stairs. Sable gripped Purn's hand tighter. At the far end was the door to Reese's cell.

"Can I see him?" Sable asked quietly.

Vivaine didn't bother to answer but stopped at a closer cell. The guard opened the door.

Vivaine stepped in, and Sable followed, her entire body feeling too coiled to move properly.

Ryah glanced up, her eyes widening. "Sable!" She started to scramble to her feet.

"Stay back," the guard commanded, pulling out his sword.

Ryah froze, and sank back down by Thulan, her eyes fixed on Sable. "Are you all right?"

Sable nodded, searching her sister for any sign of injury. She looked unhurt. They all did.

Atticus had straightened and watched Vivaine with a look too complicated for Sable to untangle. Leonis's head rested wearily against the wall. His skin was pale, and his arms hung limply. Sable bit her lip to keep from speaking to him. What had they done with his tree? Thulan merely glared at the prioress with such a menacing look that Sable was surprised the guards didn't restrain her.

Vivaine stepped toward the group, giving them a gentle smile. "We have been able to determine that you were not complicit in the assassination. I apologize for the unpleasant night you've had, but we had to be sure." She stepped to the side, gesturing to the door. "Atticus, you and your troupe are free to leave. The guards will escort you out. But I do ask that you gather your things and leave the city today. This event has caused a great deal of turmoil, and we must restore order."

"Even Sable?" Ryah asked.

Vivaine turned a benevolent smile to Sable, and she had to force herself not to glare at the woman. "I meant that Atticus, Leonis, and Thulan were free to leave." Enough people glared at her that she raised her hand, as though she were going to dispense blessings. "The man who committed the assassination, Andreese of Ravenwick, was seen with your troupe a great deal before the horrible event. We need to assure the people that you were not involved, so Sable and I have had a conversation, and I believe we've found a solution."

Vivaine turned to Ryah. "There are some openings in the Grand Priories," she said kindly. "I believe if you were to join us here, it would be a show of good faith to the people that there is no ill-will between us."

Ryah's mouth dropped open. She sat speechless for a moment. "Thank you, Holy Mother."

"Sable and I have discussed our options. Our dear Prioress Narine of the Phoenix Priory is ill, and getting weaker. I need an aide to care for her."

Ryah sat forward.

"Sable," Vivaine said, smiling sweetly at Sable, "has generously offered to fill the role."

Ryah blinked and turned a stunned face to Sable.

Outrage pushed its way up Sable's throat. Unable to force her face into a smile, she fixed her eyes firmly on the floor.

"For you, my dear," Vivaine continued, turning back to Ryah, "Sable chose the honored role as handmaiden to Prioress Eugessa."

Out of the corner of her eye, Sable saw Ryah sink back against the wall. "Sable?" she asked quietly.

Vivaine turned a pleased, expectant look on Sable.

Sable drew in a deep breath. She couldn't muster a smile when she finally met Ryah's eyes, but she focused on how desperately she wanted her sister to walk out of this cell, and her next words came out reasonably steady. "The High Prioress and I discussed it, and I support her fully. This is the best plan. For everyone."

Thulan fixed her with a flat gaze. Atticus's eyes shifted between Sable and Vivaine.

Leonis let out a humorless laugh, his head still resting against the wall. "If you'd delivered all your lines that poorly, Sneaks, Atticus never would have let you perform that first show."

Vivaine stiffened so slightly Sable thought she might have imagined it. Sable met Leonis's gaze and felt a weight roll off her at his words. She offered him a small smile.

He returned it weakly. "You'd better work on your delivery for whatever the Holy Mother wants you for in the future."

"The guards will escort you to your wagons." Vivaine's eyes were slightly narrowed, but her voice was still serene. "And bring Ryah to the Priory of the Horn." She began to step out of the room, but paused. "The assassin has confessed. He will hang at dawn."

Ryah gasped and grabbed Thulan's hand.

"Because you knew the misguided young man, Atticus, if you wish to stay in the plaza until the unpleasant deed is accomplished, I will allow it. But then you will remove yourselves directly. We are anxious to return calm to the Sanctuary."

Sable knelt down next to Purnicious. "Go to Atticus." The kobold nodded tearfully and walked across the cell to collapse into Atticus's lap. Sable watched her for a moment before daring to meet Ryah's eyes.

Her sister stared at her, heartbroken. Sable opened her mouth to say something, but Vivaine called to her from the hall. The prioress's voice was gentle, but Sable heard the threat in it. She closed her mouth and followed.

The only sign of the coming dawn was a slight brightening of the sky. Sable stood dully inside the open entrance of the Dragon Priory, her eyes fixed on the black shape of the gallows at the foot of the stairs outside.

Sanctus guards surrounded her. At least a dozen were stationed in the entryway, more on the rostrum outside. Despite the early hour, the plaza was filled with people. The thrum of conversation hovered somewhere between disquiet and excitement.

Sable was dressed in her dirty, torn dress from last night, but her veil had been taken by a disapproving abbess. Unhurried footsteps approached from behind and the guards shifted.

Vivaine came up to Sable and leaned close to her, setting her hand on Sable's head as though in blessing.

"You remember your lines?" Vivaine asked softly.

Sable shot her a venomous glare.

The prioress looked amused. "Atticus said you were good at memorizing." Her smile faded. "If you don't sell your sincerity to the crowd, your Reese will hang."

Sable forced herself to stay still until the prioress removed her hand. Then she turned back to the gallows, trying desperately to get a handle on the anger raging inside her.

A scuffing noise behind her made her turn.

Two Sanctus guards escorted Andreese into the entry hall. Ropes bound his feet, leaving him only enough room to shuffle. They'd cleaned his hair and beard. The gash on his face was still red and vicious, but they'd given him a new shirt. The only parts of him still bloody were his bound hands.

His eyes were fixed straight ahead, unseeing, his shoulders back, face set in a mutinous scowl.

Sable took a step toward him, but the guard next to her clamped his hand around her arm.

Reese looked over at the motion and his mouth dropped open. He lurched toward her, yanking his arms away from his guards, almost falling before they wrestled him back.

"She's not involved!" he spat toward the High Prioress. "You know she's not involved!"

"Reese." Sable pulled against the guard still holding her. "I couldn't let them hang you!"

He stared at her for a moment. His shoulders sank and the furious look on his face bled out, leaving him looking exhausted. "You were supposed to run," he whispered, his tone crushed. "Atticus said he'd help you run."

CHAPTER SEVENTY

SABLE'S BLOOD turned to ice at the words. "He knew?"

Reese just looked at her, his expression defeated. "What did you do?"

Sable opened her mouth, but couldn't bring herself to do anything but repeat, "I couldn't let them hang you."

"Both of you trying so hard to save the other," Vivaine said softly. "It's very sweet."

"Don't do anything she asks, Sable!" He pulled against the guards again. "You can't trust her! You know you can't!"

Vivaine gave a tired sigh and looked at a Mira standing along the wall with her hands clasped before her, tucked away in her sleeves. The woman stepped forward, pulling her hands out. She touched Andreese on the temple.

His eyes glazed and his shoulders slumped. He shook his head to shake it off, but the unfocused look stayed in his eyes. He let out an inarticulate growl.

"Take him outside," Vivaine said. "And make sure he stays quiet. The people have seen enough ugliness. They shouldn't be exposed to more lies."

His guards pushed him forward, followed by the Mira. As Reese shuffled past, he met Sable's eyes with a dull look.

"Reese." She took a small step after him, but the guard held her arm in a steel grip.

Vivaine stepped up next to Sable, watching Reese shuffle out the door. "Poor soul," she murmured, her voice sorrowful.

Sable flinched at the coldness of the lie, but the abbesses around them looked at Vivaine with sympathy and adoration.

The High Prioress looked out the door, a tragic expression on her face, while the guards pushed Andreese toward the gallows. The noise of the crowd outside swelled when they saw him.

The sky began to lighten, but the gallows lay in the shadow of the Dragon Priory.

Vivaine let out a deep sigh and glanced at Sable. "Let us go bear the heavy burdens we must."

"I only wish I had your strength," Sable said quietly, keeping her voice low. "You make these dark deeds look so…natural."

The High Prioress spared her an unreadable look. "I am merely here to do Amah's work." Down by her side, her fingers stretched slightly, and the entryway lightened. The thin morning light wrapped around her, and the white of her robe glowed softly.

Sable bowed her head toward the prioress as submissively as she could, hiding her face while she tried to wipe the disgust off it. Still looking down, she forced her voice to be filled with admiration. "Her blessing on you is clear for us all to see."

The abbesses around her murmured in agreement.

Vivaine didn't answer, but walked placidly through the door. The guard released Sable's arm and pushed her forward. Sable shot him a dark look, and followed Vivaine onto the rostrum, trying desperately to keep the fury inside her off her face.

Reese stood on the platform of the gallows, almost as high as the rostrum itself. He looked up toward them, but his gaze was unfocused.

At the sight of the High Prioress, the crowd quieted. Prioress Eugessa stood off to the right, her black unicorn next to her, both fixing Andreese with a look of stoic judgment. Prioress Narine held her phoenix on her outstretched arm, but the bird trembled slightly, and the prioress watched Andreese with sympathy and sorrow.

Sable followed Vivaine to the center of the rostrum. The High Prioress raised her hand and quieted the crowd. "At the breaking of this day," she began with a heavy voice, "we should be mourning the loss of a dear friend of our city. But instead, we are here, carrying out the unhappy role of justice." She turned a tragic face toward the gallows for a moment before gesturing to the side of the crowd.

"Through the night, we have determined that Atticus and The Figment of Wits Traveling Troupe had no knowledge of the horrible crime that was committed. We at the priories are grateful to Atticus for the stories he tells, and offer him our blessing as he leaves this city and continues his travels."

A ripple of murmurs ran through the crowd, and people craned to see where she pointed. From up on the rostrum, Sable saw Leonis's head a few rows from the front, the white curls of Atticus next to him. If Thulan or Ryah were there, they were hidden behind taller people.

A thin, hunched abbess in the front row caught Sable's eye. It was Mother Perrin. Sable looked desperately around the woman for Ryah, but saw no sign of her. The small, wrinkled woman watched Sable with a sorrowful expression.

The words the abbess had said the night Sable had come to take Ryah echoed in her mind.

"May Isah protect you and keep you. May he give you strength to do the things that must be done, to care for those you can, and to choose the paths that are best, even when they seem too hard."

The knot of fury and fear in Sable's stomach didn't relax. If this was what strength from the gods felt like, they were more useless than she'd thought.

"I have personally spent time with Issable of Shadowfall." Vivaine graced Sable with a gentle smile, and she braced herself for the line that would signal her own speech. "I can assure you that despite the fact the violent crime was committed during her speech, she is nothing but loyal to Amah."

Sable stepped forward and dropped to her knees, bowing her head

583

next to the High Prioress. Out of the corner of her eye, she saw Reese twist against the guards holding his arms.

"Holy Mother," Sable began, funneling the desperation and horror of the moment into her voice, "we are appalled that this man would use our play in such a terrible way."

Reese stilled.

"While we had our concerns about the Kalesh,"—She forced the next words out—"the good ambassador had already begun to assure us we were mistaken." She closed her eyes, unwilling to see what effect the words had on Reese. The agony of having to say the next line was true enough that her eyes filled with tears. "May Amah forgive me, but I had hints of the violence in the killer. I should have seen this coming."

She drew in a breath, and her shoulders shuddered with her fury. Hoping it looked like sorrow, she finished the speech.

"If you will forgive me, Holy Mother, I will commit my life to the service of the priories as penance for any wrongdoing I have done. Thank you for your mercy to our troupe." She squeezed her eyes shut and clenched her hands together in her lap. "And for the swift justice you've brought to the good ambassador's murderer."

The crowd broke out in a rumble of noise.

The prioress's gentle fingers lifted her chin. "Stand, my child."

Sable stood, her hands still clenched, her body shaking with the effort to control her anger. She kept her head bowed, but couldn't stop herself from looking toward Reese.

He stood utterly still on the platform, his face pale.

Sable dropped her gaze to the ground.

"That was very moving," Vivaine murmured.

The High Prioress raised her hand for silence. "Andreese of Ravenwick acted alone to carry out this terrible act." Her voice was a perfect blend of sorrow and firmness. "And as dear Issable has said, justice must be carried out swiftly." She looked tenderly toward the gallows, her grey eyes wet. "However, I believe that despite his violence, Andreese was doing what he thought was right. Sadly, he is a misled young man, but Amah tells us always to err on the side of mercy."

Sable's eyes found Andreese again. He watched her with a disbelieving look, shaking his head slightly. She forced herself to meet his gaze as Vivaine finished.

"Instead of death, Amah has lightened your sentence to banishment. You will be escorted from the city of Immusmala immediately. If you are found here again, the penalty will be death."

The crowd shifted and muttered. Andreese's gaze didn't waver from Sable's.

She bit her lip, and the tears that had filled her eyes during her speech trickled down her cheeks.

Vivaine raised her hand in blessing toward Andreese, then waved it toward the crowd, before solemnly turning to re-enter the priory.

Sable stood for a breath, Reese's gaze biting into her. His shoulders lost the last of the resistance they'd had. The firm hand of a Sanctus guard pushed on her back, and Sable turned away and walked into the priory, leaving the brightening morning behind.

Inside, Vivaine stood by the nearest window, and Sable joined her. The panes of colored glass were light yellow at the bottom, and looking through them was like looking through a veil. On the gallows, the guards roughly shoved Andreese toward the stairs. His head sank forward, and he went without a fight. Sable watched until they climbed down and disappeared into the crowd.

Across the plaza, the morning sunlight had reached the top of the Veil Wall, shining brightly on the light stones.

Sable gripped the edge of the thin table in front of the window. A small, silver dish sat smugly on it holding porren seeds, which trickled their minty smell into the priory. It smelled clean and fresh, but the building around her felt exactly how the towering walls of Dockside always had. Pinning her in and crushing any hope of escape.

A guard swung shut the front door of the priory and the hall dimmed, except for the brightness of Vivaine's robe beside her.

"I know you think you just lost everything you ever wanted," the High Prioress said quietly. "But you did what needed to be done. Someday you'll thank me."

Sable turned to look at her, incredulous.

Vivaine kept her eyes pointed out the window. "When I left Balin, it felt like I lost everything. But in reality, it wasn't me who left. It began with Balin changing, and he pushed things to the point where I had to leave."

A sick sense of familiarity rolled over Sable at the words. It was exactly what she'd thought of Vivaine in the story, exactly what she'd told Reese. That it hadn't really been Vivaine's fault.

"You're in the same situation," she continued. "Andreese has forced your hand. It seems as though you're betraying him, but in reality, he betrayed you already, by putting you in this position."

Sable stared at her. "You're the one putting me in this position."

Vivaine gave a derisive snort, and straightened her shoulders, brushing off her hands, as though wiping off something unpleasant. "The guards will take you to Prioress Narine. There will be a meeting this evening with the highest ranking Kalesh in the city. They are enraged, and we must start working immediately to fix this." She turned to face Sable. "You will accompany Narine. And I expect you to keep your word." She offered Sable a smile that didn't reach her grey eyes. "Remember, Amah can see everything."

The truth of those words filled the hall.

"It's so convenient that her servant can, as well," Sable murmured.

Vivaine gave her a faint smile. "The blessings of Amah are wonderful."

The High Prioress started to turn, but paused and held out her hand. "Eugessa's ring."

Sable's hand clenched on the table. Near the front doors, the six Sanctus guards stood attentively. More guarded the door at the far end of the hall. There was no way out.

The place in the crowd where Leonis had stood was now a tangle of strangers' faces. The gallows were empty. The people of the city slowly moved away from the priory, leaving the plaza empty of all but white-robed prioresses and Sanctus guards.

The sick feeling in her stomach turned from despair to fury. Vivaine had taken them all and scattered them. They had worked so hard to get this woman's attention, and it was all for naught. Talia was trapped with Lady Ingred. Ryah was confined to serving Eugessa. The rest of the troupe had been sent out of the city. And Andreese... She looked into the crowd, but the windows blurred it too much for her to find the guards leading him away.

The anger seeping into her was familiar. It was the same she'd felt toward Kiva, and toward the Kalesh men who'd destroyed so much.

Vivaine still stood, waiting, her hand outstretched, grey eyes like chips of granite.

Sable drew in a deep breath. Not to banish the rage, but to feed it. Slowly, she reached down and pulled the silver butterfly ring out of her sock. In the morning light, the silver gave off weak glints, and the stones looked cloudy and dull.

Sable rubbed her finger across the butterfly. All the hope that had sat in this ring was gone, leaving it cheap and ugly.

She considered the prioress for a moment.

Everything had gone wrong, yet here she stood, face to face with the most powerful woman in Immusmala.

Sable glanced down at Vivaine's waiting hand, then turned and dropped the ring onto the silver tray with the porren seeds.

Vivaine's face hardened at the weak clink. One of her eyebrows rose. "Your word that you will do as we agreed?"

"I've already given it."

Stepping closer, Sable lowered her voice and pushed all the truth she could into her next words.

"I am not your pawn, Vivaine." The words wrapped around them and the prioress's eyes widened slightly. Sable pitched her voice even lower, fueling her words with everything inside her. "I can do all the things Atticus told you. And if the—" She glanced around the priory "—*goddess* has seen fit to put me here, in her Grand Priories, spending every day among her most blessed servants, and surrounded by all her power and influence…"

The prioress's jaw twitched.

Sable gave a small shrug. "Then Amah must want me to use it."

Viviane studied Sable for a moment, a bleak smile turning up the edge of her mouth. "I look forward to working with you, Issable."

Sable returned the look. "As do I, Holy Mother."

THE END

FROM THE AUTHOR

Thank you for reading *Dragon's Reach!*

I know, we didn't leave Sable and company in a great place.

Are you angry? You look a little angry.

Well, I have two ways for you to funnel that anger...er...let's call it passion:

OPTION #1) PREORDER BOOK 2!

Book 2 in Sable's story, *Raven's Ruin,* is out!

Find Raven's Ruin at
www.amazon.com/dp/B088NH1QPC

(Book 3, *Phoenix Rising* will be following hot on its heels, and will finish the trilogy.)

OPTION #2) LEAVE A REVIEW!

A review is worth more to an author than the a butterfly ring would have been to Sable around chapter 7.

And chapter 13.

And, well, the rest of the book.

If you enjoyed *Dragon's Reach* and have the time to leave a review, you can do so on Amazon.

THE UNEXPECTED OPTION #3) READ THE KEEPER CHRONICLES!

Sable's story is leading us toward the creation of the country of Queensland, and the very first Keepers.

What's a Keeper? I'm glad you asked. I wrote a whole trilogy to tell you. It's called **The Keeper Chronicles**, and while it takes place hundreds of years after dear Sable's adventures, it can be read at any time.

Find the Keeper Chronicles on Amazon!

You can always find a list of all my books on my website at jaandrews.com.

Happy Reading!

Janice

Raven's Ruin - Keeper Origins Book 2
Coming Soon

Book 2 of The Keeper Origins continues to follow Sable in her attempt to save the land from the invading empire.

To be notified when new books are published, you can sign up for JA Andrews' newsletter on her website, jaandrews.com.

ACKNOWLEDGMENTS

Thank you to all you readers who picked up my books, bothered to read them, then took a moment to leave a review. Getting to write stories that people enjoy is a dream I never thought I'd get to live.

Thank you to Cheryl Schuetze, Barbara Kloss, and Karyne Norton for your invaluable critiques of the early, long, rambling version of Dragon's Reach. This story would be nonsense without you.

Thanks to newsletter readers Brook Bend and Adrian Spence for coming up with the name for Stonehaven.

And most of all, thank you to my husband. You're the first one who believed I could write a book, and the one who's still thought so, no matter how many clenchings and thicknesses were tangled up in the story. For this book in particular, your comments and critique made it indescribably better. I love you.

ABOUT THE AUTHOR

JA Andrews lives deep in the Rocky Mountains of Montana with her husband and three children.

She is eternally grateful to CS Lewis for showing her the luminous world of Narnia.

She wishes Jane Austen had lived 200 years later so they could be pen pals.

She is furious at JK Rowling for introducing her to house elves, then not providing her a way to actually employ one.

And she is constantly jealous of her future-self who, she is sure, has everything figured out.

For more information:
www.jaandrews.com
jaandrews@jaandrews.com

facebook.com/JAAndrewsAuthor
twitter.com/JAAndrewsWriter
instagram.com/jaandrewsbooks

CPSIA information can be obtained
at www.ICGtesting.com
Printed in the USA
LVHW111530190922
728745LV00024B/603/J